Forever in Your Embrace

KATHLEEN E. WOODIWISS

Forever in Your Embrace

AVON BOOKS ◆ NEW YORK

FOREVER IN YOUR EMBRACE is an original publication of Avon Books. This work has never before appeared in book form. This work is a novel. Any similarity to actual persons or events is purely coincidental.

AVON BOOKS
A division of
The Hearst Corporation
1350 Avenue of the Americas
New York, New York 10019

First Avon Books Trade Printing: October 1992

AVON TRADEMARK REG. U.S. PAT. OFF. AND IN OTHER COUNTRIES, MARCA REGISTRADA, HECHO EN U.S.A.

Printed in the U.S.A.

OPM 10 9 8 7 6 5 4 3 2 1

To
My Three-Year-Old Granddaughter,
Amber Erin
Who Makes Everyone in the Family Feel Special

*A Special Thanks
to
Carolyn Reidy
For Allowing Me Enough Space to Write from the Heart*

Chapter 1

Russia, somewhere east of Moscow
August 8, 1620

THE LOWERING SUN SHIMMERED THROUGH THE DUSTY
haze that loomed in languid stillness above the treetops,
suffusing the tiny particles of sand with vibrant shades
of crimson until the very air seemed aflame. It was an
ominous portent, for the reddish aura gave no promise of
rain or respite to a parched and thirsty land. The excessive heat of summer and a lengthy drought had scorched
the plains and barren steppes, wilting the endless sea of
grass down to its densely matted roots, but here in the
mixed wooded region of Russia, bordered on the north
and east by the Volga River and on the south by the Oka,
the thick forest appeared relatively unscathed by the
lack of rain, though the company of travelers who sped
through the vast wilderness still suffered the same.

In her full score years of life, the Countess Synnovea
Zenkovna had seen a wide variety of faces her homeland
could present. They were as unique as the changing sea-
sons. The long, brutal winters were a test of endurance
for even the heartiest, but with the advent of spring, the
thawing ice and snow could create deceptively treacherous bogs, which in times past had proven formidable
enough to dissuade hordes of marauding Tatars and

other invading armies. Summer was a temperamental vixen. Warm, lulling breezes and the gentle patter of rain could placate the soul, but when the season was unmercifully imbued with dry, scorching temperatures, it served vengeance on those foolish enough to travel beneath its broiling sun, a fact which had not been overlooked by the Countess Synnovea prior to her departure from home. She was presently and unequivocally convinced that the greatest hazard to herself and her small entourage of attendants was the voluminous clouds of choking dust stirred aloft by the whirling wheels of her huge, black coach and the thudding hooves of the horses, making it difficult, if not totally impossible, for any of them to savor a fresh breath of air. From every aspect, the conditions were intolerable for a lengthy trek through Russia, especially one which had been embarked upon with equal amounts of urgency and reluctance.

If not for Tsar Mikhail Feodorovich Romanov urging her to come to Moscow ere the week was out and a full dozen of his mounted guards sent under the direction of Captain Nikolai Nekrasov to serve as her escort, Synnovea would never have even considered venturing upon such an arduous journey until the heat had adequately diminished. Indeed, had some less exalted personage given the command, she would have begged leave to remain at home in Nizhniy Novgorod to properly mourn the death of her father.

Synnovea stifled a moan of despair ere it passed her lips, for she knew full well that it was a waste of energies for a mere countess to belabor her lack of options when the Tsar of all the Russias had given a command. To be told that upon her arrival she would become the ward of his cousin, the Princess Anna Taraslovna, had brought the brumes of gloom upon her already grieving spirit, and she had been unable to muster anything more than a dismayed acquiescence to his summons. Immediate compliance was the only prudent choice for any proper subject. She was, after all, the late Count Aleksandr

Zenkov's daughter and now, much to her chagrin, the recipient of His Imperial Highness's concern.

The tsar had not elaborated on his purpose for assigning her a guardian, and his rationale was not to be questioned. Considering the many honors which had been heaped upon her sire in recent years, his performance as an outstanding emissary might have warranted this attention from the tsar, but even with both her parents now dead, Synnovea found it difficult to think of herself as a helpless waif or even a young woman in need of protection, for she had passed an age when most maidens marry.

Neither a youngling nor a pauper, yet treated like one, Synnovea mused ruefully, then cringed inwardly as she was reminded of a more viable cause for Tsar Mikhail's dictate. Her elongated state of spinsterhood had perhaps contributed greatly to his decision, especially if he thought the matter had somehow been neglected by her father, who had nourished the hope that she would someday discover a love the likes of which he had shared with her mother, Eleanora. Though he had refrained from pressuring her into an arrangement of marriage and seemingly had dragged his feet while procuring a spouse for her, Aleksandr Zenkov had seen to her welfare quite well otherwise, securing lands and wealth in her name, while gaining assurances from the tsar that upon his death nothing would be stripped from her. He had seen her tutored with as much care as any nobleman might require for his son and, after the death of her mother some five years back, had enlisted her assistance in the realm of diplomatic affairs and foreign dignitaries, which ultimately had involved her in his extensive travels abroad. Having had an English mother, Synnovea could speak that language as fluently as she could Russian, and with a good grasp of French as well, she had been able to pen letters to officials in all three. Count Zenkov had trusted her with the sole responsibility of that task.

Resting an arm on the padded sash of the small side window, Synnovea clasped a dampened handkerchief to her brow as she sought to suppress a sudden dizziness and a threatening nausea. The conveyance had become a writhing instrument of torture, unyielding in its wild gyrations as the wheels rumbled and jounced over the deeply rutted road. To some degree, the tinkling and jangling of the horses' necklets and harness bells had mellowed the din of the drumming hooves. Nevertheless, a dull throbbing ache had settled insidiously in her temples, prompting her to squeeze her eyes tightly shut against the painfully bright rays of the lowering sun until the coach passed into the mottled shade provided by a stand of tall trees. Even when she dared to open her eyes again, Synnovea saw everything through a spotted red haze that came close to matching the ruby-red interior.

"You are distressed, Countess?" Ivan Voronsky inquired with a condescending smirk.

Synnovea blinked several times before she could focus her gaze on the man who, through no design of her own, had become her traveling companion and temporary protector, of sorts. For all of her instruction and abilities, she found it immensely disconcerting that she would soon be placed under the tutelage of strangers and, toward that end, was being escorted to her destination by an individual whom she strongly suspected was a Polish sympathizer and a leftover fanatic of Sigismund's Jesuits. The dour-faced, black-garbed, self-proclaimed scholar and cleric had established his darkly austere presence in the opposite seat, from whence, with a pompous perusal, he had continually subjected her and her aging Irish maidservant to a rudely critical inspection. He wore his high-minded piety like some accolade of well-deserved honor, and when he looked down his long, thin, pointed nose at her, Synnovea had the distinct impression that he had already judged her and found her wanting. Were he to assume a like amount of authority and power as the Spanish Inquisitors, Synnovea was sure she would have found herself locked away in a damp dungeon in some hellish place, where she'd be forced to pay penance for heresy because she had not given him unquestioning reverence or paid him homage above mortal men. Her perceptions had been progressively abetted by his overbearing attitude and comments he had made during their enforced proximity, perhaps spoken to glean an accurate accounting of just where her loyalties were rooted. It was nothing Synnovea could exactly lay a finger to, but his manner provoked her suspicions just the same.

"I am hot! And I'm dirty!" Synnovea complained with an exasperated sigh. "I'm sick of this unrelenting pace that has left me so tired and bruised I can't even remember what it's like to feel otherwise unencumbered! At every station along the way, we've had to exchange horses because of their exhaustion. Prithee, sir, tell me why I should *not* be distressed when we haven't been allowed a like amount of time to rest in the whole of these three days?"

On the seat beside her, Ali McCabe shifted restlessly, offering mute testimony to her own discomfort. The Irish maid looked far older and much more frail than her three score two years normally indicated, for the journey had exacted a heavy toll from the elder, nearly depleting her heretofore invincible stamina.

Sniffing arrogantly, Ivan Voronsky started to voice a reply, but paused as he spied a small bug that had attached itself to his dark sleeve. The cleric seemed amazed by its impertinence to be there, and making much of his repugnance, he plucked it free and cast it out the window with a contemptuous flick of his short, stubby fingers. Finally he deigned to lend his consideration to Synnovea and imperiously gave answer. "My dear Countess, it was the expressed wish of the Princess Anna that I hasten back lest the whole of her plans be set awry. Out of respect for her bidding and the behest of His Majesty, we have no other choice but to obey."

Annoyed by the man's spartan logic, Synnovea flicked her fingers across her own sleeve and promptly wrinkled her fine, elegantly straight nose as a small cloud of dust billowed up from the dark green and black striped silk. She had acquired the fashionable traveling gown in France at the cost of no small sum and could only conclude that by now it had been sufficiently soiled to alter its continued usefulness, if she should, by some stroke of good fortune, find Anna Taraslovna more tolerant of her foreign fashions than the cleric appeared to be.

Lifting her gaze, Synnovea could not mistake the import of Ivan's derisively jutting brow as he witnessed her piqued frown. Her ire was again provoked, and of a sudden she was sure that she could endure the dust and discomforts of the road better than Ivan's abrasive presence in her coach. "Perhaps, sir, you would care to enlighten us by explaining your reason for insisting that we travel in broad daylight. We might have escaped the worst of this heat and perhaps some of the dust had you allowed us to journey by night as Captain Nekrasov suggested."

"The night belongs to the devil, Countess, and the tender soul should be wary of treading where demons are wont to trod."

Synnovea rolled her eyes upward, pleading for heavenly support to allow her patience to endure. The fact that they had already suffered through many hellish torments undoubtedly had not even entered into the cleric's consideration. "I suppose you have naught to complain of, sir, since you have addressed yourself to issuing the directives which have set us to this pattern of flight."

Ivan paused briefly to ponder her thinly veiled barb and offered a more plausible excuse than he had heretofore condescended to lend. "Rumors were being bandied about in Moscow of a band of renegades roaming through the territory. Such miscreants are wont to pounce on the unsuspecting beneath the stealth of darkness, and I thought it prudent for us to journey during the daylight hours to escape the possibility of being waylaid."

"A wise decision 'twould seem," Synnovea rejoined dryly, "if by some miracle we manage to endure the heat."

Ivan seemed as impervious to her jibe as he appeared to be to the harsh conditions. "If you are uncomfortable, Countess, might I be allowed to say that your extravagance is fully at fault. A simple *sarafan* might have better served your needs, while modestly adhering to the customs of a Russian maid."

Synnovea realized that Ivan's unbridled faultfinding chafed as much now as it had at the onset of their journey, when he had been sharply critical of her European mode of dress. The conventional *sarafan* would have disguised her form better with its loose lines that flared slightly in an otherwise straight descent from shoulder to floor, but with the layers customarily worn beneath and over the costly gowns, it seemed extremely doubtful the garment could have offered any measure of relief from the heat. Obviously, the closely fitting gowns she wore disturbed the cleric, for in no uncertain terms he had let it be known that he loathed the tight bodices which were stiffly bolstered by stomachers. But then, he had no more liking for the full skirts that were often expanded to great widths by hooped farthingales or the lavishly expensive lace-edged ruffs and cuffs and the high, stiff collars the late Queen Elizabeth of England had, by her example, encouraged women to wear. Synnovea's own penchant for the stylish fashions had evidently scandalized the cleric's strict concept of appropriate apparel. Had she matched his own stoic black garb, she might have fallen into better favor with him.

"I suppose you're right," Synnovea replied, repressing the urge to argue with the opinionated man. "But after sailing so many times abroad, I've become accustomed to the styles of the French and English courts and have ceased to think anyone might find offense in them."

"There you err, Countess," Ivan Voronsky quickly asserted. "Indeed, had I not the discipline and mind of a saint, I would detach myself posthaste from the duties to which the Princess Anna has set me and seek another means of travel. Truly, I have never seen a Russian-born maid so partial to wearing those vulgar foreign trappings."

"Oh, sirrr . . . " Ali's voice trembled with barely restrained ire as she dared to intrude. "I can understand that ye've no ken o' what's accept'ble 'cross the seas, seein's as how perhaps ye've never ventured beyond these here climes. I'll be tellin' ye true, sir, 'tis a whole different world over there, ter be sure. Why, I've no doubt ye'd be amazed at the license some high-born ladies take ter walk an' talk right out in the open wit' men who be neither their priest nor their kin. Queen Elizabeth was one. Nary a soul in England expected her ter be locked away in a tsarina's *terem*, nor even wanted her to be secluded in a castle from the rest o' the world, wit' only women an' a few holy men attendin' her. Why, ter be sure, sir! Can ye imagine all those fine, high-rankin' lords flockin' around the late queen, an' nary a Brit thinkin' it a sin?"

Synnovea's mouth twitched with barely suppressed humor as the tiny maid made light of the cleric's narrow-minded views, but when Ivan rose to the woman's bait with outraged contempt, Synnovea quickly lost all feelings of amusement.

"Disgusting behavior! Indeed, I have to wonder why I'm here at all after the many visits your mistress has made there. I fear my protection has come much too late."

Ali McCabe drew her tiny frame up sharply as if she had been stung. Having closely attended the countess from her infancy, she took umbrage at the man's insinuation. "As if me own sweet lamb's not the innocent she's always been!" The aging servant twitched on the seat as she grew steadily more irate. "Whether it be here or there, sir, I can assure ye no man has laid a wayward hand ter me mistress."

"That remains to be seen, does it not?" Ivan challenged. "After all, you have only her word."

Synnovea was aghast at the man's suggestive slander, and though she opened her mouth to make a heated protest, she quickly resolved to let the stodgy little cleric think what he wanted to, since it seemed he would do so anyway.

Ali did not show as much discretion. "Seein's as how ye're ridin' in the countess's coach, as well as eatin' the meals an' stayin' in the rooms she be payin' for, sir, ye might consider treatin' her wit' the proper respect due a lady, just ter show ye're grateful."

Ivan fixed the tenacious little maid with a piercing glare, haughtily conveying his disapproval. "You've been ill-tutored in the treatment of saints, old woman, else you'd know that charity is expected, particularly from those who can afford it. 'Tis apparent you've not been in this country long enough to understand our customs."

The maid cast a slanted glare toward the man, yearning to liberally pierce his self-inflated pride as she recalled the day the cleric had presented himself at the countess's stoop. Straightaway, as if fearful of the idea of expending a few coins of his own, he had let it be known that he was without coin or possession beyond the clothes on his back and those few he carried within his black valise. Thereafter, he had dumped the burden of his subsistence upon her mistress, as if he had every right to claim her benevolence. Only the day before, Ali had seen him try without success to dissuade the countess from giving a generous purse to a young mother who, after the sudden collapse and death of her husband, had been left stranded with her infant daughter at a coach station. His attempt to halt the countess's largess had been onerous enough, to Ali's way of thinking, but when he had dared suggest the contribution be given to him instead, so he might carry the gift to the mother church (or so he had said), she had felt the spurs of indignation dig deeply into the flanks of her Irish temper. His solicitations had convinced her that he was far less concerned with the needs of the poor than with his own wealth and status.

"Yer pardon, Yer Eminence." The address was somewhat exaggerated as Ali yielded to her unmeasured distrust of the man. His previously announced claims of exalted importance and elevated genius had seemed more like hot-winded boasts to her, while his abrasive disposition had given evidence of an underlying contempt for anything he considered frivolous or trivial, which seemed to encompass everything that was not immediately important to him. " 'Tis a simple fact that I've not laid me poor eyes on a real saint o' the church in some years now, though there's a few who'd be havin' folks believe they are. Wolves in sheep's clothin', in other words. But that's neither here nor there, seein's as how ye're so fine and saintly yerself."

The veins in Ivan's temples became darkly distended beneath his thin, pale skin. His small, beady eyes fixed on the servant, as if by dent of will he could concoct some incantation that would make the woman vanish before their very eyes. He failed abjectly, even in his attempt to frighten her, for Ali McCabe was of much stouter heart and backbone than any servant he had heretofore been acquainted with. The fact that she had come from England with Count Zenkov's bride some twenty-odd years ago and been treated with the deference of a favored servant had instilled within her an unwavering loyalty and a firm confidence in those she served.

"You dare question my authority? I am of the church!"

"Of the church?" Ali repeated in a curious tone. " 'Ere be many far an' wide, sir. Which be the one what sanctioned ye?"

Ivan sneered in the face of her probing inquiry. "You wouldn't know the order, old woman. It was founded a great distance from here."

Ali had almost been expecting such an answer, for this was not the first time Ivan Voronsky had skirted around any discussion dealing with his affiliations and ordination. His evasive answers only piqued her curiosity the more. "An' the direction, sir? Which would it be? Up or down?"

For a moment, Ivan seemed about to explode, then his tone became insulting. "Were I to hold out any hope that you would have the knowledge and understanding of the province from whence I come, woman, I might deem an answer worth my breath, but I see no reason to discuss such matters with an old dullard of a servant."

Ali snorted angrily and twitched so much in outraged indignation she nearly lost her seat. Synnovea dropped a gently restraining hand upon the elder's arm and lifted her gaze to the pinch-faced man. She reserved little hope of establishing any kind of peace between her two companions, for they glared at each other as if they contemplated a duel to the death, but on the outside hope that she could halt another serious explosion of tempers, she managed a look of plaintive appeal as she addressed the man. " 'Tis understandable that we quarrel among ourselves when the discomforts of this journey have sorely tested our good humor, but I pray you both take ease of this bickering. 'Twill only extend the ordeal."

Had Ivan been of a softer or more kindly bent, he might have given pause to Synnovea's plea, for her expression was indeed most winsome. He might have even admired the translucent radiance of the large, thickly fringed green eyes which slanted provocatively upward beneath winged brows. They were a curious blend of shades, variegated shards of jade flaring out from the dark pupils, changing to a deeper hue of ebon-brown near the outer rims. He might have also appreciated the creamy fair skin now glowing with a moist, reddish sheen at her cheeks or at least savored the fragile beauty of the stunning features, perhaps even taking note of the delicate nose, the softly curving lips, or the long graceful line of her throat. And most assuredly, had he been one of ardent heart or been cast from the same mold as other men, he would have been held much in awe by her sterling beauty. Ivan Voronsky, however, was not like other men. His greatest love was for himself, and he was more of a mind to think that feminine pulchritude was a finely devised tool of a darker realm, used primarily to divert extraordinary men like himself from a more exalted path.

"You err if you think the Princess Anna won't hear of this, Countess. You've allowed your hireling to insult me, and I shall be most specific in telling her this tale."

Synnovea made her own conjectures as to Ivan's origins as his hissing whisper seemed to fill the confines of the coach. Despite the warmth of the day, she felt a shiver go up her spine as his penetrating glower bore into her. Refusing to be intimidated, she responded to his threat with a chilling sincerity to her tone. "Tell her what you will, sir. And should I be of such a mind, I might caution His Majesty about those who still hold out hopes of a Polish pretender or another false Dmitry gracing the throne. I'm sure the Patriarch Filaret Nikitich would find your sympathies misplaced, considering his recent release from a Polish prison."

Ivan's small, dark eyes shot sparks as he recognized the threat in her words. "Misplaced sympathies? Why, I've never heard of anything so preposterous! However did you manage to invent such an absurd idea?"

"Was I mistaken?" Surprised by the trembling disquiet within her, Synnovea feigned an aplomb she was momentarily bereft of. "Forgive me, sir, but with all your talk about the possibility of a direct descendant of Tsar Ivan Vasilievich being alive, I could not help but recall two previous occasions when the Poles tried to place a man upon the throne by claiming he was Tsar Ivan's own son come back to life again. How many times must Dmitry be revived to carry on the tsardom after his father killed him in a fit of temper?"

Ivan loathed being challenged by a woman, particularly one who had acquired just enough knowledge and awareness of the events of the world to be dangerous. It was even more irritating to be forced to assuage her suspicions. "You do me a grave disservice, Countess. What I spoke of were no more than conjectures derived from reports I had heard some months ago. I hold the tsar in the highest esteem, Countess. Indeed, I would not be here if the Princess Anna did not trust me implicitly." He inclined his head briefly as he gave her his pledge. "Despite your doubts, Countess, I shall prove myself a worthy escort, certainly one of higher merit than His Majesty's guards, who are, after all, no more than common men incapable of entertaining any emotion beyond their own selfish lusts."

"And what of you, sir?" Synnovea inquired with a touch of skepticism as she thought of the gallant Captain Nekrasov, who had been praised throughout his career for unswerving valor and his gentlemanly manners. "Have you vaulted well beyond that moat which poses a hindrance to mortal man and founded your feet firmly upon the lofty elements of sainthood? Forgive me, sir, but I seem to remember as a child being cautioned by a kindly priest not to think of myself as some magisterial gift to mankind, but with humbleness of mind consider my frail form to be temporal and, with a fervent zeal, look toward a higher source for the wisdom and perfection I am lacking."

"What have we here? A learned scholar, by some chance?" Ivan laughed, seemingly with humor, but there was a hint of malice behind his words. He was a man who had set himself to the supreme task of influencing the misguided, yet he found it difficult to remain civil to anyone who failed to recognize his potential importance and questioned his greatness. "Imagine such wisdom ascribed to so fair a form. Egads! What is to become of those ancient clerics who, for their enlightenment, adhere to the weighty tomes of bygone eras?"

Synnovea was sure the man was ridiculing her for voicing a logic that was, in his mind, worthless. He had his own scheme for the universe, and far be it for any such as she to try and dissuade him from his purpose. Still, she could not resist a comment. "When a person has a fault deeply rooted within his reasoning, though he may study the works of a thousand ancient scribes, he is no wiser than before if he zealously nurtures that fault."

"Your logic astounds me, Countess."

Daring to meet his smilingly cynical stare, Synnovea decided that any discussion with Ivan Voronsky was a useless endeavor. It seemed advisable to retreat into silence and endure the hardships of the journey without drawing further comment from him.

The four-in-hand swept past a thick stand of lofty firs growing close upon the road, leaving the widely spreading boughs swaying in its wake as the sweating, foam-flecked steeds strained to pull the weighty coach up yet another incline. The animals were nearly exhausted from the harsh extremes and the persistent pace, yet the driver's whip continued to flick out with a fiery urgency to encourage them to expend whatever energies they had left in a quest to reach the next station before nightfall. The escort of soldiers, with their faces and tunics noticeably darkened by the grime of the road, valiantly kept pace with the conveyance, though even those well-seasoned stalwarts were beginning to show signs of sheer exhaustion. With at least another grueling day of travel remaining before they reached Moscow, Synnovea was certain there was not one among them who did not anticipate a night's lodging in the village up ahead, as did she. They had all endured the strain long enough to be thoroughly anxious to have the journey at an end. The seemingly endless trek, the miserable conditions, the countless hours spent in the saddle or the spine-jarring jolts and wild lurching of the carriage had all coalesced into a most diabolical torment, one which seemed particularly bent on stripping the last shred of pluck from everyone.

With a grimace, Synnovea braced back against the red velvet cushions and sought to keep herself firmly in place as the team raced around a sharp bend. Heavy fir branches snapped back hard against the sides of the coach, momentarily startling the occupants, then above the clamor of loudly crashing branches and thundering hooves, a more deafening, terrifying sound intruded, wrenching frightened gasps from the three and bringing them upright in their seats.

"We're being attacked!" Ivan exclaimed in sudden panic.

Synnovea's heart went cold with dread in the awesome commotion that followed. It seemed like a frozen moment in time wherein a quickening volley was fired. Another musket exploded on the heels of the second, and the sound reverberated in diminishing waves through the forest. Another report cracked loudly from the area of the footman's perch at the rear of the coach, then a fifth discharge pierced hearts with burgeoning fear as a shriek of pain was wrenched from the servant. As the man's echoing screams receded, the driver brought the team to a sudden, jolting halt. A heartbeat later the door was snatched open, and the three in the coach found themselves gaping at the unwavering bore of a huge flintlock pistol.

Chapter 2

*"O*UT!" THE THUNDERING TONES OF THE COMMAND wrenched a start from the three as a giant of a man leaned through the door, fortifying the ominously huge flintlock. The slanting gray eyes of the brigand flicked from one to the other of them until his gaze came to rest upon Synnovea, then his mouth widened into a leering grin that was half-masked by a long, drooping mustache.

"Eh now, what a pretty pigeon we caught."

Synnovea elevated her chin a notch, more to keep it from trembling than to attempt any display of bravado, for she was absolutely terrified of what the presence of this miscreant meant to all of them. The man's appearance was so fierce and wild-looking, it was difficult to determine just exactly what his origin might have entailed or to what country he gave allegiance. His head was bald except for a thatch of tan hair which was bound near the scalp with a thin leather cord and was left to hang free over one ear. A faded sky-blue military coat, which had previously graced a Polish officer of wide girth, now hung open to better accommodate the massive chest. Perhaps for the same purpose, the sleeves had been stripped away, leaving the bulging arms bare and unrestricted. A dingy yellow sash was wrapped about his waist, and boldly stripped, wide-legged pantaloons had been stuffed into the slouched tops of a pair of boots that were frivolously adorned with silver buckles.

With more spirit than she had imagined herself capable of, Synnovea demanded, "What do you want from us?"

"Treasures," the rogue answered with a chortle. Lifting his powerful shoulders with a casual movement, he briefly enlarged upon his reply. "One kind or another. It make no difference."

Ivan craned his neck from his dour little collar and warily eyed the weapon that threatened them. He anxiously considered his prospects for survival and came immediately to the determination that if he informed this brash intruder of his importance, the fellow would be reluctant to do him ill. As he hastened to advise the burly fellow, he conveniently avoided any mention of the church, deciding the occasion warranted a closer association with people of influential power.

Clearing his throat, Ivan claimed a more dignified posture than he had been able to project since their forced halt. "I urge you, sir! Take heed to yourself that you do not set awry the disposition of the tsar by doing harm to those he favors." He clasped a stubby-fingered hand to his narrow chest as he introduced himself. "I am Ivan Voronsky, and I've come from His Majesty's cousin for the purpose of escorting the Countess Zenkovna to Moscow. . . . " He swept a hand to indicate Synnovea, but the hulking giant's grin had not wavered. Ivan's apprehensions intensified as he realized he had failed to impress the man. So great was his panic, he screeched the next words out in a desperate rush. *"By order of the tsar!"*

The brawny man who blocked the doorway began to guffaw in deepening mirth until his wide shoulders fairly shook, utterly shattering Ivan's expectations. When the bandit sobered enough to speak, he reached out and poked a long, thick finger into the darkly garbed chest of the other, making that one wince in pain. "What you mean, you come as escort? You too skinny to fight Petrov. You make a jest, eh? You grow some, maybe then you fight."

Ivan's pinched features quivered with ill-suppressed emotions. A blend of fear, fury, and humiliation rendered him nearly incapable of speech and action, yet when the pistol beckoned, he was persuaded anon to obey. Sporadic chuckles still shook Petrov's heavy shoulders and thick-thewed arms as he stepped aside to allow the thin man enough space to alight.

Ivan stumbled to the ground in hasty compliance and then froze in awe, having suddenly gained an unrestricted view of the large host of raiders that surrounded them. No matter what direction he turned, he faced a heavy bulwark of mounted men dressed in all manner of array. Each bore an assortment of weapons, either clutched in hand, tucked in sashes, or crisscrossed over their chests. At the rear of the coach, the footman held a bloodsplotched handkerchief over his ear as he cautiously eyed the invaders. On the ground below him, his still-smoking musket lay in the dust near the rear wheel, and from the scrawny back of a mottled gray steed, another armed rogue covetously admired the red livery as he watched for any further signs of resistance from the servant. A similar threat was carried home to Captain Nekrasov and his men by the score or more highwaymen who held loaded muskets on them. It was widely presumed by the captives that any attempt to oppose the gang would be tantamount to soliciting complete annihilation.

Ivan Voronsky promptly decided that even such a gifted and learned man as himself would not be looked upon with favor or respect by these fierce barbarians. As Petrov stepped near again, he gulped in freshening apprehension and began to quake, for he was certain the huge, towering oaf meant to commit violent mayhem on his person. Petrov only smirked in amusement and sauntered casually past him as he returned to the door of the conveyance. Reaching to the far side of the seat which had been vacated by the cleric, he swept up the black valise Ivan had guarded so zealously during the journey and, with a boisterous laugh, dumped its contents into the dust at his feet.

Seeing his possessions plummet to the ground, Ivan was snatched to an abrupt awareness of just what he was about to lose to the thief. With a cry of alarm, he bolted forward, sweeping his arms out in an anxious quest to gather his belongings before his leather pouch was discovered, but he was brushed roughly aside by Petrov, whose well-practiced ear had detected a familiar sound. Plucking the purse from the tangled mound, the ruffian chortled in glee and, tossing it into the air, was promptly rewarded by a weighty clink of coins.

"Give me that!" Ivan cried, jostling the larger man in his attempt to retrieve the purse. After the failure of his first appeal, he was moved to resort to his traditional form of persuasion. "It belongs to the church!" he frantically attested. "I was only carrying tithes to the Moscow church! You must not steal from the church!"

"Aha! The little crow now flap his wings like the big hawk, eh!" Petrov glanced toward the two women who watched in dismay from the doorway of the coach, and grinned at Synnovea. "Little man protect his gold more than you, pretty lady."

In search of more wealth, the brigand squatted on his haunches and tore apart the dark vestments that lay in the dust, reducing them to little more than tattered shreds. His hunt proved unsuccessful and, with a vengeance, he whirled upon Ivan, eliciting a frightened yelp from the smaller man as he snatched him up by the front of the black frock and leaned his bronzed face near the pale, bony visage. Ivan twitched like a little bird caught in a trap as he gaped up into what had become, at very close range, a cyclopean eye.

"You tell Petrov where you hide more gold, eh?" the thief cajoled in conniving contempt. "Maybe then, little bird, he won't squash you."

Though Synnovea had been granted little sympathy from Ivan during their flight from Nizhniy Novgorod and had felt more than slightly repulsed by the sight of his hoarded wealth, she could not allow him to be abused without offering some defense. "Let him go!" she enjoined from the coach. "The satchel is all that belongs to him. Everything else you see is mine! Now let him go, I say!"

Petrov complied, and Ivan sagged to his knees in enormous relief as the brigand stepped over him. Now lending the countess his full attention, Petrov displayed a wide-toothed grin as he magnanimously presented a thick-fingered hand to her. Accepting his assistance, Synnovea stepped down to the ground as courageously as her trembling limbs would allow and then nearly retreated as the band of thieves loudly gave vent to a cacophony of wild hoots and exaggerated roars of approval. Their response only heightened her trepidations, for a score or more immediately swung down from their steeds and shouldered each other aside as they sought to closely view the uncommon beauty of this high-born *boyarina*. Their assaulting eyes left no curve untouched, no piece of garment intact, until she felt completely naked beneath their ogling stares.

Synnovea tightened her jaw to keep her teeth from chattering as a violent trembling beset her. She was afraid of displaying the full extent of her alarm lest they torment her the more, but everywhere her flitting gaze darted, it was met with lecherous leers of anticipation.

Ali McCabe was no idealistic fool to hold out any hope that any of these lawless brutes would honor the gallant creed of a high-born lord while they held so precious and beauteous a captive within their grasp. Scrambling down from the coach, the tiny woman snatched up a short, sturdy stick from the ground and hastened to place herself squarely between her charge and those who tried to reach out and test the pliant curves. Though it could well mean her own death, the maid was adamant about defending her mistress till the last breath was drawn.

"I'll warn the lot o' ye vile vermin!" she railed in frail, screeching tones. "The first beastie ter lay hand ter the Countess Synnovea will deal wit' me. An' though ye may well best me, I swear ter do ye ill afore I die!"

Her threat was met with loud guffaws of amusement, and the marauders, ignoring her threat, continued to reach out their grubby hands. Ali was as cantankerous as an old Tatar warrior and swung the cudgel with mean intent, cracking a goodly share of knuckles and noggins that came within close proximity of her mistress. Tempers flared beneath the vicious swat of her bat, and now with teeth bared in angry snarls, the outlaw band began to crowd her, intending to show the tiny woman just how easily they could trample her beneath their heels.

From a vantage point outside the confines of the fray, Captain Nekrasov had been closely observing the events and could now perceive that he had been virtually forgotten. The altercation gave him the opportunity he had been searching for to make a move in the ladies' defense, and most intent upon action, he rose to the occasion, leaning forward in his saddle as he raised an arm to clobber a nearby raider. In the next split second, the deafening roar of an exploding pistol cracked through the air, heralding a shot that tore with blinding, splintering pain through his arm. He screamed at the sudden agony of it and clasped a hand to his reddening sleeve, then glanced around with a start of surprise as he found the threatening muzzles of at least five flintlocks staring up at him. That same number of men had bolted forward to halt his interference, and by the fixed snarls on their faces, they were ready and more than willing to use the weapons.

A dastardly scamp squinted up at the captain and waggled a musket toward the officer's chest. "Yu'll die, Kapitan!" he warned portentously. "Yu move one eyeball, an' it'll be death fo' yu." He snapped his grimy fingers as he demonstrated how quickly they could dispense with him. "Just like that!"

The captain lifted his gaze from the man as the thieves began to shuffle back, hurriedly opening a path to allow another giant, this one flaxen-haired and clean-shaven, to leisurely rein his black stallion through their midst. The newcomer held a smoking flintlock in his right hand, and as he shoved the weapon into his sash, he grinned at Nikolai Nekrasov. "Your efforts to defend the ladies against so many, Captain, give me cause to think you either daft or extremely foolhardy. So have a care for your own life, and mayhap you will live out the day."

This one's leadership was clearly evidenced by the dispatch with which the bandits gave way before him as he maneuvered his steed to a place where he could more easily observe and assess the proceedings. From the viewpoint of the captives, it seemed rather farfetched to imagine the obeisance of his followers had been earned by some paltry deed, which gave rise to the dreadful suspicion that this one was even more dangerous than his followers.

The thieves eyed their commander in a cautious plumbing of his mood and, seeing nothing more disquieting than a contemplative smile, they laughed with boisterous merriment, accepting his silence as consent. As the thickening rabble eagerly returned their attention to the countess, they gave no heed to Ali, who was unmercifully buffeted about and squeezed in a crushing vise that virtually rendered her incapable of further movement.

Synnovea twisted away from this one and that, horrified by her predicament and immensely appalled by the filthy fingers that reached out to seize her. As if of one body and mind, the men moved forward, taking a step as she retreated the same. All around her, Synnovea saw eyes gleaming in avid lust and though she strained away from their pawing hands, the rending of cloth attested to their eagerness to unmask whatever delights remained hidden from view. Her hat was knocked askew, and a puffed sleeve was torn from its mooring at her shoulder.

The stiffly pleated ruff was no less exempt from their greedy divestment than the insert of silk ruching that trimmed the stomacher. In mounting fear Synnovea sought to turn aside from their clawing fingers as they snatched at her bodice, wrenching it partially open and bringing into view the long ivory column of her throat and the fullness that swelled above a lace-trimmed chemise. One glimpse of the creamy flesh seemed to incense the men even more as they reached out almost in frenzied haste to rip away whatever else they could grasp.

"Rutting louts!" the pale-haired leader bellowed without warning, startling the brigands, who stumbled back in sudden awe. Their passions cooled rapidly beneath the icy gaze that swept them. "What do you think you're doing? Would you maul her to death ere we leave this place? Is that how you would treat such a rare prize? Hell and damnation! She may be worth a pretty coin to us alive! Now loose her and stand aside, the lot of you! Henceforth, I will claim this wench for my own!"

Daring any to defy him, the lord-of-thieves urged his steed forward through the quickly opening ranks. The two women struggled to subdue their astonishment and dread as the ruffian approached them, for they saw in him the same kind of menacing threat his men had conveyed, only in singular number. His frightening demeanor lent no assurances that his claim would be any better.

Bracing a muscular arm across the elaborate horn of his saddle, the outlaw rogue subjected Synnovea to a meticulous scrutiny that slowly ranged over the slender length of her. From his elevated seat, he was afforded a most enticing view of a deep crevice plunging downward between pale breasts, and though Synnovea sought to preserve both her dignity and modesty by holding herself slightly aloof from his inspection as she clasped the torn bodice over her bosom, the man was definitely intrigued by what he saw. His leisured grin conveyed only a small measure of his admiration as he made his apologies.

"Forgive my delay in coming to your aid, Countess. My men are wont to seek diversions where they can find them and demand recompense where they have hitherto found injustice."

"Injustice, do ye say now!" Ali squawked, outraged by his statement. "As if we were not within our proper rights ter defend ourselves ag'in murdering rabble!"

The man ignored the disdain of the tiny maid as he directed his reply to her mistress. "What you see around you are men whose only possessions were stolen by those who reduced them to serfs or prisoners for purposes beyond the simple kin of the innocent. We have no love for rich *boyars* who wield their power as if they were born of the devil's own. Believe me, Countess, had we been of such a mind, we could have added to your misery by killing your men. Your footman and the captain of your guard were foolish to challenge us, so be glad they're alive and my aim true, for I might have taken exception to their attempt to wound or kill us." The rogue casually swept a hand toward the escort of guards who were being ordered to dismount. "Anyone who intends to do us ill is in peril of his life."

Synnovea lifted her chin imperiously, realizing it had sagged a small degree as she endured a moment of monumental dread. Though the man had spoken with a well-tutored tongue, she was nevertheless riveted by the disquieting thought that here indeed was a fierce barbarian the likes of which had once ridden with Genghis Khan and his army of Mongols, except that his sky-blue eyes and flaxen hair were products of a different breed. His face was deeply bronzed by the sun, and his firm, square jaw neatly devoid of whiskers. His hair was clipped so close to his head it seemed more like a scruffy skullcap. To be sure, he was as handsome as his demeanor was terrifying.

Struggling to subdue the tremor in her voice, Synnovea inquired, "And what is it that you and your fellows intend?"

With unmeasured confidence the man smiled down at her. "To share a portion of your wealth . . ." His eyes slowly caressed her again in avid appreciation of what he beheld as he added, "And perhaps, for a time, the richness of your company." He threw back his head and laughed uproariously as if struck by his own humor, then sobered and clapped his arm across his wide chest in a crisp salute. "Permit me to introduce myself, Countess. I am Ladislaus, misbegotten son of a Polish prince and a Cossack wench, and these"—he swept his arm in a wide arc to encompass his roughly garbed compatriots—"are my royal courtiers. They serve me well, do they not?"

The outlaw band chortled at his wit, but his declaration elicited another contemptuous sneer from Ali. "A bastard barbarian!" she jeered. "An' a thief, ter boot!"

Ladislaus was amused by the brashness of the gnat-sized woman. Chuckling softly, he nudged his stallion forward a pair of steps, deliberately separating the maid from her mistress. "Aye! That I am, woman. My father sought to pay his due by seeing me taught a gentleman's manners and language, but he felt no inclination to gift me with his name or his title. Thus, I am what I am."

Ali glowered up at him with eyes that fairly snapped with indignation and, lifting her makeshift weapon, swung it toward the stallion, but in swift reaction Ladislaus kicked the piece from her hands, spinning the elder about. Staggering away several steps, Ali struggled to regain her balance as the man threw a leg over the horn of the saddle and slid to the ground, but before he could take a step, the maid was there in front of him again, launching another attack upon him with her cudgel. The muscular arm swept out almost gently to knock the club away, but Ali caught the limb and clung to it with a tenacity of one who is often led by a swiftly riled temper. As testy as an outraged bee who has been swished away by the tail of a horse, she sank her small teeth into the dark skin. A low growl issued forth from the thick throat as Ladislaus jerked free. In the very next instant, his fist shot forward until the hard knuckles struck smartly against the small, wrinkled chin. It was no contest. Ali's eyes rolled back, and she slowly slithered to the ground as a senseless void overtook her.

"Yooouuu *monster!*" Synnovea railed in swiftly swelling tones. Infuriated by his treatment of her maid, she flew at him and raised her slender arms in a vengeful pummeling of his chest and head until Ladislaus sent her stumbling away with a chuckle and an upflung arm. As she staggered to a halt, Synnovea gave vent to a whole string of disparaging appellations. "You cowardly, simple-pated buffoon! You scoundrel! You churlish lummox!" She paused long enough to catch her breath and continued in a somewhat lower, but equally caustic, sneer. "Is this proud feat your best? What say you, knave? Have you no like courage in face of one your size?! Or does the dainty form appease your valor better?"

Ladislaus stepped to block her passage as she tried to stalk past him to reach her maid, but when she lifted her gaze to his, he was suddenly convinced that he stared into the most enraged green eyes he had ever had the occasion to view. The fire-spitting orbs fairly seared him in her hot displeasure.

"You have no need to fret, my lady," he consoled pleasantly. "Your servant will live through this with naught else but an aching head to boast of."

"Should I, then, be grateful for your gentle care of us?" Synnovea challenged snidely. It infuriated her that she and all who were with her were completely vulnerable to the frivolous whims of these black-hearted plunderers and there was absolutely nothing she could do to thwart this offense, other than verbally chide him. "You have abused the captain of my guard! My footman! And now my own loyal maid! You have halted my coach on this lonely road to do your evil upon us while you give your foul consent to your murderous band of cutthroats for whatever mayhem they might construe. Would you, Lord Beast, have me fall to my knees before you in humble apology for daring to travel where your murderous band lurks? HA!" She tossed her head and scoffed at the very idea. "Were I armed, sir, you would be breathing your last! That is how well I sympathize with your reasoning or value your care of us! I have no doubt that your father, whoever he may be, fervently regrets what he did spawn during a night's whimsy."

Bracing his large fists against his waist, Ladislaus laughed in hearty amusement at her threats and logic. "I'm sure the old rascal has had much cause to repent, my lady, for I give him no more homage than he's given me. 'Twas only his pride of siring a man-child after begetting a whole brood of daughters that led him to see me tutored at all. He even tried to take me into his home after his wife died, but my sisters could not abide the idea of having their father's bastard whelp under the same roof with them, and they chided him for bringing such shame upon the family."

"A shame which I'm sure you've delightfully extended by becoming a thieving rogue," Synnovea retorted. "So now, 'twould seem you make an earnest effort to extend your revenge upon him by entrapping others in your devious exploits."

"You truly delight me with your imagination, my lady," Ladislaus assured her as his eyes danced with mirth. "You are not only beautiful, but witty as well." He laughed and made much of the conclusions she had drawn. "To say that I revel in revenge when I have such extraordinary opportunities to seize treasures as rare as you would lend far too much weight to my vindictiveness. My lady, I'm truly of a kinder heart than that!"

Synnovea clenched her fists in the folds of her skirts and vowed not to reveal the full extent of her dread of this man as she gritted out a retort. "Fiendish knave! You chortle like a mindless idiot and make brave noises only after you've seized the weapons from our hands. With nigh to three score men at your side, I noticed that you made your appearance well after the danger had passed, like some weasel afraid of being seen."

"I keep my wits when these other rogues lose theirs." Ladislaus made the excuse with a jovial grin, unaffected by her criticism. "I keep watch until all things are made secure."

"You are naught but a nameless coward who lurks in obscurity while your pack of wolves strips away the wealth of honest men," she argued with venomous derision.

"Think what you will, Countess," Ladislaus responded with a confident grin. " 'Twill change naught." He gave the maiden another long perusal, admiring her fair looks and soft womanliness as his eyes dipped again into the tempting valley between her breasts. He reached out a hand and lightly rubbed his knuckles against a hotly flushed cheek. "Fate has surely smiled upon me this eventide, my lady, to bring such a delightful *boyarina* within my keeping. I am indeed honored by your presence."

Synnovea fought a sudden impulse to retreat before his smoldering gaze. She flung off his hand, rejecting his compliment, and glared back into the sun-bronzed visage with all the heat and defiance she could engage. She held her stance without wavering, though in all of her travels here and abroad she had never seen a man so tall or with shoulders quite so broad or powerful. Above hide breeches, which closely hugged his narrow hips, he wore a red sash and a leather jerkin which hung open to reveal a heavily muscled chest. His arms were bare and bulging with rippling sinews, providing visual evidence of a strength that could easily immobilize her.

"Well, I am *not* pleased to be here!" Synnovea replied with haughty vigor and was promptly frustrated by his unfaltering smile.

"You can rest assured, Countess, that I shall enjoy this night with you as I have no other." His voice carried a deep huskiness that portrayed his heightening infatuation.

Synnovea was determined to serve quick death to the notion that he would expect her ravishment to be as enjoyable as some tender interlude exchanged between them. "If you think I'll be a willing student, Lord Beast, then let me advise you otherwise."

"I won't mind your struggles, Countess, let me assure you." Ladislaus lifted his shoulders briefly to display his lack of concern. "In truth, I have in years gone past grown tired of women who follow about my heels and squabble over me. I have become more appreciative of those who are more aloof. I'm sure your reluctance will prove immensely stimulating." White teeth gleamed in sharp contrast against his dark skin as he grinned back at her. He was well aware of her loathing distaste and even more aware of the fact that this was no common camp follower who stood before him, but a *boyarina* of good breeding. She had the regal look of the high-born with her fine, delicate features and lofty bearing. Should he dare make a judgment, he would even guess that she could, with naught but an eloquently condescending stare, threaten the ardor of a less courageous man. He had seen proof of a fiery spirit, and it had done much to erase his first impression that this was a thoroughly cold and haughty wench. Not even remotely so, he reaffirmed in his mind as a growing warmth thawed his ice-blue eyes.

The high-crowned hat had given her a jaunty appearance, although it now sat ridiculously askew atop her head. Its black hue lent a richness to the green lining of the brim, which was turned back on the side and fastened to the crown with an emerald-studded clasp. He could only guess at the length of her hair, for the silken black tresses had been woven into an intricately braided knot at her nape. Wayward wisps, disturbed by her recent mauling, flared outward from her temples, as if set on end by the raging of her temper.

Ladislaus grinned broadly as he swept the hat from her head. Plucking the jeweled brooch from its nest, he held it up in a dimming shaft of light where he could examine it better, then with a backward glance, tossed it over his shoulder to his second-in-command. Petrov caught it within his cupped hands and whooped in glee as he rubbed the piece fondly against his own coat.

" 'Tis yours, my friend, for spying out this lady's coach," Ladislaus declared.

Petrov's grin broadened beneath the massive mustache as he called back, "What say you, Ladislaus? This be a bauble well worthy of your attention."

Chuckling softly, the lord-of-thieves slipped an arm around Synnovea's waist and, ignoring her outraged gasp, snatched her close against his side. "As you can see, Petrov, I have in my possession a far more enticing piece than that simple brooch, one that will warm me on a long winter's night."

"And Alyona?" Petrov queried with a sharply jutting brow. "What you think she do?"

Ladislaus shrugged casually. "She'll have to learn to share me."

"Let me go!" Synnovea cried, straining against the solidly muscled chest as his embrace tightened. The muscular arm held her captive with an ease that maddened her, and in sharp disdain, she turned her face aside as he bent his head near. "Please! I implore you! Let me go!"

Chortling softly, Ladislaus nuzzled her ear. "Not until I've pleasured myself with you, Countess . . . and maybe not even then."

He swept his arm downward around her voluminous skirts and, lifting her with an easy strength, dropped her casually over his shoulder, nearly jolting the breath from her. He paused to glance curiously over his shoulder as a sudden scuffling shuffle ensued around the captain. This time Nikolai had kicked his horse forward in an attempt to come to the aid of the maiden, but the steed was swiftly caught and firmly held by several ruffians who reached up to drag the struggling officer from his saddle.

"Come now, Captain," Ladislaus mocked with chiding scorn. "You can't expect to keep her for yourself! You're only a servant of the tsar!"

Chuckling, he jostled Synnovea more securely onto his shoulder and whacked her fondly across the buttocks. The highly enraged countess shrieked in protest as she beat her fists against his broad back and demanded her release. "Let me go, you vile wretch!"

Unconcerned with her struggles, Ladislaus strode back to his stallion and there, facing his men, barked a series of brusque orders as they gaped at him. "Why do you gawk at me like fools? Get to work, the lot of you! Strip these men and the lady's coach! Take whatever you can lay hand to! Then ride back to camp and await me there! The men I sent into Moscow will soon be returning with our new compatriots. Tell the women to prepare a feast for them, for no doubt they've nearly starved shackled on the city streets and will want to rejoice in their newfound freedom. I'll join the feasting after I've sported with this wench a while." A slow grin twisted his lips. "If she proves a worthy piece, the tsar may have to find himself another doxie."

A short distance away, Ivan Voronsky justified his own lack of participation in the lady's defense as he witnessed the proceedings. To be used to appease the lusts of this barbarian was obviously what the countess deserved for having worn such wanton fashions. If she had attired herself in the proper apparel of a *boyarina* and given credence to his warnings, she might have avoided being accosted. Why should he draw the attention of the thieves away from her and court disaster because of her foolishness? But then, the flaxen-haired rogue seemed quite smitten with her, and who was to say she would have been safe wearing the rough canvas of a ship's sails?

Synnovea was lifted to the back of the thief's horse, and
once settled, she made a quick assessment of her chances
for escape. It seemed the time for resistance was ripe,
for the possibilities would be greatly diminished once
Ladislaus mounted behind her.

The reins had been left dangling across the stallion's
neck and a short, many-tongued lash hung from the
saddle horn, close to her hand. Synnovea did not dare
waste the opportunity. In a desperate bid for freedom,
she seized the bridle in one hand, the whip in the other,
and brought the latter down hard across her captor's
arm, slashing at him furiously, again and again until
he reached up to snatch it from her grasp. Eluding his
long fingers, she leaned back and braced a slippered foot
against the hardened chest, then shoved with all of her
strength.

Ladislaus stumbled back in keen surprise at the force-
fulness of the lady's thrust. He was a man well seasoned
in contests of brawn, for he had oft been met by the enemy
in combat, but he had marked this winsome maid far
too delicate of frame and limb for such a determined
onslaught. Still, she was no serious match for a man who
could be called a man.

Ladislaus quickly recovered his balance and, with a
backhand swipe, knocked the whip aside, leaving the
slender arm bruised and throbbing and, for a moment,
completely useless as it dropped limply into her lap.
Clenching her teeth against the throbbing pain, Synnovea
jerked on the reins with her other hand, but the long
fingers were immediately there, wrenching the lines
from her. In roweling dread of what the next moments
would bear, she kicked at him again, knowing she had
not the stamina to oppose him for long. Yet as long as
her strength endured she was stubbornly committed to
that cause. Her attempt to drive him off, however, was
proven far too feeble, for the stalwart ruffian stood resolute against her efforts. In the next breadth of a moment
Synnovea became aware of just how frail her efforts were

against such boldness and brawn as Ladislaus thrust a broad hand beneath her skirts and seized her knee. Synnovea gasped in outraged modesty and tried to shove him away, but his grip only tightened until she could feel his fingers digging cruelly into her flesh. The pressure intensified to an excruciating degree until she was forced to yield, and yield she did, ceasing her struggles at once, even though her eyes still smoldered with unsuppressed hostility.

Having won the skirmish, if not yet the war of wills, Ladislaus loosened his hold and admiringly stroked his hand upward along her naked thigh. Synnovea's shocked gasp and reaction were hardly subdued. With a low, rising shriek of rage, she hauled back an arm and delivered a blow to his cheek with enough force to make the brigand's ears ring.

"Take your filthy hands off me, you vulgar viper!" Her eyes fairly flashed with fire. "The tsar will have your head for this!"

Ladislaus glared up at her as he withdrew his hand from her skirts and wiped the back of his knuckles across a reddened cheek. He had guessed rightly when he had judged this lady to be of no timid, docile bent. On the contrary, she was proving to be completely intractable in every sense of the word.

"Before that day arrives, my lady," he rumbled, "your precious tsar will have to first find men worthy enough to catch me. And though there are rumors in the wind that he's hired cavaliers from abroad to instruct his soldiers on the art of war, they shall not defeat me. There is none in his army I have not already bested. Look you yonder if you doubt my words." He illustrated his statement by indicating the guards who were being crowded together, then he reached out and, clasping both her wrists, held her fast as his eyes bore into hers. "If you are foolish enough to hope that some brave champion will save you"—he gave a quick jerk of his chin toward Captain Nekrasov, who had been trussed up tightly, and then, just as curtly, indicated the outraged Ivan Voronsky, who was presently being ordered to shed his clothes—"then consider the wayward path of your reasoning. None will come to your rescue, at least none that I can see."

Synnovea curled her fingers as she tried to lift a hand to claw his face. "Nevertheless, Lord Beast," she ground out, "you will pay for this offense. You will be caught, tried and hanged. And I'll be there to see it! I promise you that!"

Ladislaus only laughed at her pitiful attempt. "On the contrary, Countess, you will be the one taken and used. You are my prisoner, as long as I choose to keep—"

His last words were silenced by a deafening roar of exploding pistols as a sudden din filled the forest glade. Ladislaus's head snapped around with a jerk, just as three of his men crumpled to the ground. He seemed momentarily aghast as he watched a fourth fall forward in the saddle and slowly slide to earth, there to lie in grotesque oblivion with eyes wide and staring sightless toward the darkening sky.

The narrow pass echoed with another loud volley that blended with the clatter of hooves as a large detachment of mounted soldiers charged into view. Leading the attack, a dust-covered, helmeted officer raced forward, brandishing a sword high above his head as the startled miscreants stumbled over each other in their haste to flee. The raiders had no time to recover their wits before the soldiers were upon them. The officer's steed surged far beyond those that followed, encouraging the thieves to close ranks around this enemy who had dared to come into their midst. With a savage eagerness, they swarmed about him, intending to drag this foolish mortal from his saddle and be done with him, but like an avenging warrior, the man filled the air with screams of dying men as he swept and slashed his blade right and left. One after another fell beneath the wicked, deadly stroke of his sword until fear struck the hearts of the brigands.

The man seemed impervious to his enemies' weapons until, at the outer limits of the fray, a huge, barrel-chested

Goliath took up a lance and sailed it toward the officer. It crashed against that one's helmet and sent it flying. The cavalier reeled unsteadily in the saddle, eliciting a cheer from the highwaymen, and then slowly slumped forward to brace himself with an arm across the neck of his stallion. He shook his head as if trying to clear his muddled senses, and the bandits took heart, convinced the officer had been seriously impaired. They were just as certain that he would soon feel the full wrath of their revenge.

Perhaps none awaited that event with as much relish as Ladislaus, who watched with deepening satisfaction as his men made ready to dispense with this antagonist. Synnovea could only groan in roweling despair as the band of rogues gave vent to a triumphant blast of deafening bellows, already celebrating their anticipated victory. They surged forward en masse to finish their prey, and it was no more than half a moment later when they realized their mistake. Though stunned, the officer was not unaware of the danger around him and reacted with a combination of well-versed skill and intuitive instinct. Spinning his horse in a tight circle to keep the felons at bay, he swung the heavy sword in a broad, undulating sweep, nearly beheading a few who had dared the most. When finally the officer fought clear of his daze, the reddened blade flashed again with more clever aim, flailing its victims and leaving them to fall lifeless to the ground.

Synnovea saw the man's searching gaze reach beyond the melee surrounding him to ferret her out. In that moment, he seemed much more than a man to her, though the wringing wet hair was matted close to his head and his dirt-smudged face was hardly more than an indistinct blur in the rapidly dwindling twilight. His breast of armor was tarnished, well dented, and now liberally smeared with blood. Still, if she had ever formed a vision of a knight in resplendent trappings, he was all that and more to her in the brief passing of that instant.

Seeing now that his enemy was capable of giving chase, Ladislaus wasted no further moment. With a shouted command for his cohorts to depart, he swung up behind his captive, slamming his hard body against her back. He cared not a speck for the lady's discomfort while he concerned himself with their safety. Jerking the reins, he whirled the steed about and kicked his softly booted heels against the gleaming flanks to send the animal racing away in full retreat.

Synnovea was relieved the arm that encircled her waist was strong and capable. Otherwise, she might have found herself dashed upon the ground, for the stallion fairly flew along the trail. He was of mixed Friesian descendancy, strong, long of limb, and swift of pace. He could easily outdistance the shorter-legged breeds common to Russia. Yet when Ladislaus yanked the animal around to survey the path behind him, Synnovea saw that the officer had given chase and was actually gaining on them. The brigand was greatly astounded. He cursed savagely as he spun the stallion about again and kicked him into a frightening race through the trees. The solid trunks were merely swiftly passing shadows in the darkening copse, and though Synnovea held her breath in paralyzed apprehension of that moment when disaster would halt them, in the back corner of her mind she was amazed at the agility of the steed. Without a doubt, the stallion was quick and nimble-footed, and the man who rode him of equal merit. Still, the pair who gave chase followed like baying hounds led eagerly onward by the scent of their prey.

Synnovea cringed as branches snatched at them in avid greed, cruelly yanking at the bound tresses and opening long rents in her sleeves. She raised an arm to shield her face from the spiny, brittle claws that slashed at her and raised reddened weals across her arms. Silently she prayed the punishing ride would come safely and swiftly to an end, yet when she glimpsed an opening up ahead, her fear intensified into a concern that they would actually escape. In panic she glanced over her shoulder, but she could not see past her captor's bulk and could hear nothing beyond the fury of their own passing, the stallion's pounding hooves, and the harsh breathing of the man who held her.

They broke into the clearing, and Ladislaus once again swung his mount about to apprise himself of the whereabouts of the officer. Heretofore no steed had equaled the pace of his own beast, and after the wild plunge through the trackless forest Ladislaus expected to find himself far ahead of the other. It was indeed a shock to see how short a distance actually remained between them and the one who gave chase.

It was no more than the pause of a heartbeat before the ominous shape of the dark chestnut stallion and its rider charged out of the trees nearly on top of them. Synnovea gulped back a startled scream, certain the forceful advance would kill them all. She glimpsed piercing steel-blue eyes beneath sharply scowling brows, and with a sickening dread she awaited the collision, feeling much akin to a helpless sparrow about to be broken by the swift assault of this hunting hawk.

Ladislaus jerked his arm free and fumbled for his knife, but immediately the other man was upon them. The officer launched himself from his steed and slammed into the man behind her, sweeping Ladislaus from his seat and, by some strange miracle, leaving her still mounted. That fact alone gave Synnovea cause to wonder at the prowess of the soldier, but in the very next instant she grimaced as she heard the two men thud against the ground. It seemed but a second later that she heard hard-clenched fists meeting solid flesh and the rustling of dried leaves as the pair wrestled beneath the stallion. Glancing down, she caught the flash of Ladislaus's dagger as it was lifted high, but another hand shot upward and caught the sturdy wrist to hold it from its mark.

The now skittish stallion pranced nervously as the two men grappled beneath him and stirred up small clouds of dust that rose all around them. Faced with the imminent threat of the animal panicking and running away with her, Synnovea sought to forestall such an experience and cautiously reached down to search for the dangling reins as she slowly stroked the stallion's neck and whispered soft, cajoling words in an effort to calm him.

Of a sudden Ladislaus's head jerked backward from the force of a well-delivered blow and thumped into the underbelly of the stallion. In the next instant Synnovea found herself fighting to keep her seat as the steed, shrieking in fright, reared up on its hind legs. Twisting her hands in the flying mane, she clung to it with desperation, fully aware of the danger of being swept along on the back of a crazed horse. The front hooves struck earth briefly, hardly enough time for Synnovea to settle herself before the horse took a gigantic leap forward. Her heart matched the vaulting stride, and she was nearly launched from the saddle before the animal settled into a terrifyingly reckless, zigzagging flight that took them once again through the trees. Though her pulse kept pace with frantic skips and bounds, Synnovea tried not to yield to the utter foolishness of panic. She knew that it was necessary to gain control over the stallion lest she find herself the victim of her own unbridled hysteria, but it was hard to barricade herself against the cold prickling fear that assailed her.

Leaning close over the animal's neck, Synnovea flowed with his movements in a concerted effort to allay his alarm. She spoke in a forcefully subdued, tightly restrained voice as she tried again to capture a flying rein, but the threat of falling inhibited her reach, and she was forced again and again to retreat to the security of the flying mane. Then, as she stretched a hand out in that same anxious quest, a low branch flipped the rein upward, projecting it within close range. Anxiously Synnovea swooped her hand around to catch it and, in sobbing relief, clutched the leather strap in her trembling grasp. Good fortune was with her, for hardly a moment later she managed to capture the other rein in a similar fashion.

Success rallied Synnovea's spirits. Grasping the reins securely, she claimed a small measure of control over the beast, at least enough to turn him onto the path that led back toward the area where the carriage had been halted. Even so, the stallion was reluctant to slow his stride, and though she could see the dark shadow of the conveyance through the deepening gloom, Synnovea could not establish enough restraint on the headstrong animal to lend her any hope that she would be able to halt him once they reached it.

Nikolai Nekrasov was sitting near the coach, having submitted himself to the well-practiced care of the sergeant who was, at present, bandaging his arm. When the sound of thundering hoofbeats drew the captain's attention to the lane, he looked up to see Synnovea approaching at an alarming speed. Jumping up, he shouted for his men to make ready to halt the horse, and together they raced forward to form a barrier of sorts across the road where they awaited the charging animal with arms spread wide. The stallion, however, had a mind of his own. A short distance from the human trap, he came to a stiff-legged, jolting halt, then reared and clawed the air with his hooves. It seemed his intent to continue his flight as he came down, for his eyes flicked about in search of an avenue of escape. This time, Synnovea was fortunate enough to have someone near enough to come to her aid. The captain snatched her from the saddle as the sergeant seized the bridle and held on tightly as the stallion danced sideways in wild-eyed alarm. The sergeant's soothing words and reassuring pats quieted the animal's fears, and finally it acquiesced to the gentle hand.

Synnovea leaned in trembling relief against Captain Nekrasov, feeling as if all the strength had been drained from her limbs. She savored his comforting arm around her, hardly realizing the full extent of Nikolai's appreciation as his eyes dipped briefly into the torn bodice. He gradually released his constricted breath until he claimed control of his racing senses. The faint brush of his lips against her hair seemed accidental as he continued to lend her support, and Synnovea gave him no further heed as she quickly responded to Ali's weak, plaintive plea to come near.

"Me lamb," the servant mewled as the driver stopped bathing her brow long enough to brace her up in a reclining position. "Let me look at ye."

Submitting herself to the other's inspection, Synnovea made her own assessments as to the maid's condition as she searched the aging features in the deepening dusk. A large, blackening bruise now marred the tiny, wrinkled chin, and even in the meager light, her pallor was quickly noted.

Ali struggled to sit up as she tried to see her mistress better, but the exertion proved too much, and she collapsed back into the supporting arms of the coachman. Seeing the tattered condition of the younger woman, Ali wept and moaned in worried misery, thinking the worst. "Oh, me lamb! Me lamb! What did 'at foul beastie do ter ye?"

"Truly, Ali! I'm all right," Synnovea reassured as she sank to her knees beside the elder. "The tsar's officer came to my rescue, and no great disaster has befallen me. I've suffered only a few minor scratches, 'tis all."

Ali softly sobbed out a prayer of thanksgiving. "Thank the blessed heavens, ye're safe."

"Lift her inside the coach, Stenka," Synnovea quietly bade the gray-haired driver and attended the man closely as he and the footman complied. "Gently now, she's had the worst of the fray."

"Jozef an' I vill take care of her, mistress. Have no fear," Stenka gently replied and then coaxed, "Rest yurself now. Yu've had a bad fright."

Synnovea noticed a bandage had been wrapped about Jozef's head, and in concern, she laid a delaying hand upon his sleeve. "Your wound? Is it serious?"

Jozef shook his head and grinned. "No, my lady, but there's a hole in my ear big enough to put a cork through."

"Some lady vill find that convenient," Stenka responded with humor. "She vill lead him 'bout by the ear 'stead of the nose."

Synnovea patted the footman's arm in a conciliatory manner and managed a teasing smile. "You'd best be wary, Jozef. In Moscow there are plenty of pretty maids who'll take advantage and lead you astray."

"I'll eagerly watch for them, my lady," Jozef promised her.

Satisfied that Ali was in capable hands, Synnovea lent her attention to the situation around her. Nikolai's men had suffered only minor wounds and were hurriedly repacking the carriage. The detachment of soldiers which had come to their rescue had given chase to the miscreants, and no member of either force had remained behind. A short distance from the coach, the ground was littered with the dead, and from what she could determine in the swiftly gathering darkness, the highwaymen were the only ones who had suffered loss, no doubt because they had been completely surprised by the soldier's attack.

Aware of the need to be gone from the place before any of the raiders returned to reclaim their plunder, Synnovea faced Captain Nekrasov. "We must leave quickly ere we're pounced on again."

In full agreement Nikolai faced his men and gave the order. "Finish packing up whatever is left and let us be off. We must make haste to take the countess to a place of safety."

Synnovea glanced about in some confusion, realizing she had not seen the cleric since her return. "But where is Ivan? What has happened to him?"

Captain Nekrasov chuckled and raised his able arm to point toward a shadowed area beyond several tall trees standing in the distance. Frowning in confusion, Synnovea stared through the darkness until a vague, pale blur became distinguishable as the half-shrouded form of a small, naked man. "They stole away his clothes, Countess, and every piece of spare garment we had with us to boot. We have nothing to share with him."

Synnovea debated the alternatives, but was most reluctant to offer anything from her own trunks. Ivan had been so averse to the European gowns, she had serious doubts that he would consider accepting the frivolous finery, even out of desperation. Ruefully she suggested, " 'Twould seem he has no other choice but to search for clothing among the fallen."

"I've already assigned that task to one of my men," Nikolai informed her, inclining his head toward the carelessly strewn bodies. "Though the selection may not meet with Ivan's approval, 'tis all there is."

Synnovea silently demurred the idea of undressing the dead and quickly excused herself. "I will wait in the coach with Ali."

Though night soon overtook them, Synnovea and her small party of attendants were quickly on the road again. The pace was more cautious now as the moon cast ominous shadows far ahead of them and each bend in the road was carefully approached. Still, the air was cooler and far better tolerated than the oppressive heat of the day.

Once again, Synnovea had to endure the presence of Ivan Voronsky, but this time he was not so prone to argue after being thoroughly humiliated. When he talked at all, he was prone to mumble angry insinuations against Captain Nekrasov and his men, for he was certain that they had been moved out of spite to find the most outrageously obnoxious garments available. He was greatly disturbed by their contributions and not the least bit grateful for the outlandishly large breeches and leather doublet, both of which reeked of old sweat and garlic, a combination which made it imperative for the diligent application of scented handkerchiefs to the noses of the two other occupants of the coach.

Synnovea refrained from making any excuse to placate Ivan's complaints, preferring instead to keep the kerchief in place and not test the fumes that wafted from the clothes. She was just as appreciative of the darkness that hid whatever gory stains bedecked the garments, for she desired complete oblivion to the kind of death wound the garments' previous owner had suffered.

They were well on their way again before it dawned on Synnovea that she had made no attempt to send one of Captain Nekrasov's men out in search of the officer who had rushed to her rescue. The thought of the man lying wounded or dead in the forest made her own lack of response seem shamefully devoid of compassion, and she chided herself for seeking her own security while forgetting the safety and comfort of one who had endangered his life to save her. She had acted with no more valor than Ivan had when, without so much as a protest or a lifting of a finger, he had stood aside and allowed her to be mauled by those lawless rogues. She felt less than proud of herself, nor could she believe she would find quick relief from the dejected mood into which she had suddenly descended.

Chapter 3

THE HUGE, GOLDEN MOON NESTLED LIKE A NEWBORN babe within the cradling arms of the towering pines, firs, and larches until, by slow degrees, the lustrous orb was weaned from its earthly breast and was sent soaring upward in a wide arc across the night sky. The myriad twinkling stars were humbled by the brilliance of the larger sphere, and more so those which hovered near, for in some shame they hid their meager glow behind its radiant aura. Far below its orbit, the lunar rays condescendingly marked the path that wandered through the small village and set aflicker the rustling leaves of the oaks and birches that lined the road, turning them into scintillating flashes of light as a soft breeze stirred the branches to life.

The soldiers and conveyance traversed the deeply rutted thoroughfare, passing rows of gray, wooden cottages adorned with painted carvings and fretworked gables that turned inward upon the lane. Small sheds gathered like ragged skirts around the rear of the houses and were joined together with board fences to form an outer wall of sorts to provide a windbreak against the chill winds that savaged the village in the dead of winter.

An assortment of faces, both young and old, pressed close to windows and doors as the stately carriage rumbled past with its compliment of tattered guards. Even by moonlight the grandeur of the coach could be swiftly discerned, as was noted, in sharp contrast, the miserable appearance of its escort. It was apparent to all who watched that the soldiers and their equipment had been sorely abused. Filthy, torn, bruised, and bloody, the small company of men generated a wide range of speculations as to the cause.

No one was more aware of their appearance than Captain Nekrasov, that officer who had always been nattily garbed and a model of proper etiquette. At his sharp command, his detachment rode into town with the practiced cadence that lent a semblance of dignity otherwise lacking in the procession. The entourage passed a single-domed wooden church in stoic silence, yet when Stenka halted the carriage before a sizeable inn and a bathhouse was espied nearby, sighs of relief were heard from the grime-coated guards as they swung down from their mounts.

Captain Nekrasov entered the inn to make the necessary arrangements for the comfort of his charge. His bandaged arm and bloody tunic drew many a pondering stare, yet one did not halt an officer of the tsar singlemindedly intent on his duties. Unwilling to extend the innkeeper's confusion by the appearance of two torn and disheveled women, Synnovea was content to wait in the privacy of her coach, lending whatever assistance she could to Ali, who had taken on a pallor that sharply accentuated the purplish black swelling on her tiny chin.

Ivan Voronsky quietly departed the carriage and hied himself off to the church to seek out more appropriate garb to wear the next day. As he skittered off, keeping to the darker shadows, he held his hat on with an upraised arm that shielded his face against recognition, remote though the possibility was. His abrupt departure, however, allowed Synnovea the opportunity to breathe normally again, and for that she was immensely grateful.

The innkeeper was proud of his new bathhouse, and as he directed his male guests around the facilities, he boasted heartily of its clever features. The guided tour

allowed Synnovea the solitude she needed to help Ali
to their room. By now, the servant's head was throbbing
so painfully that even the slightest movement made her
weak and queazy. It was Synnovea who carefully tended
and undressed the elder, as the loyal Ali had done numerous times for her. After taking a light supper and a basin
bath, the maid climbed upon the narrow cot and fell into
an exhausted slumber.

Synnovea desired more than a token washing and was
of a mind to settle for nothing less than a thorough cleans-
ing and a soothing soak for her own sorely abused body.
She realized, however, that the men had much the same
notion in mind after depositing their gear upstairs. In
passing her door, they made as much noise as a stam-
peding herd of young colts as they jostled and elbowed
each other aside in a lighthearted quest to be the first to
reach the bathhouse. Listening to their cavorting descent,
Synnovea could not find it in her to begrudge them this
respite and resigned herself to await that moment when
they would be finished with their ablutions. The delay
was not so objectionable when she knew she would have
more leisure time to herself if she made last claim on the
facility.

Occupying her time by selecting garments for the following day's journey, Synnovea laid out a plainer gown
to wear, one that would more properly guard against the
intrusion of Ivan's scorn. It was a small concession, but
it would serve much more for her own ease of mind and
comfort than it would satisfy any of his strictures.

She untangled the long braids and painstakingly
brushed out the snarls, leaves, and debris that had
become ensnared in her hair, then she left it to fall unbound to her hips. She doffed her torn gown and stripped away her petticoats. As she undressed, the officer
whom she had abandoned came to mind, and again the
uncertainty of his situation made her remorseful over her
own lack of caring concern. He had been heroic against
so many, and though that rough barbarian, Ladislaus,

had been intent upon killing him with his knife, she whispered a belated plea that he had been brought safely through the confrontation.

Gathering a voluminous robe around her slender body, Synnovea sat down to wait. Leaning her head back against the chair, she tried to form a mental image of the officer, but she was unable to draw together any definite detail of his features, at least none that completely satisfied her. She had been permitted hardly more than a brief glimpse, and then only under frightening circumstances and insufficient light. The face was a void in her memory, perhaps never to be recognized again. She could only remember her own blended feelings of awe when, at every turn of the hand, he had been there, hovering like a sharp-eyed relentless hawk, until finally he had pulled down his prey.

Synnovea sighed and turned her thoughts elsewhere. By the morrow evening she would be in Moscow, where she would have to present herself at the Taraslov manse. She had no idea how she would be received or how well she would be able to adjust to their life-style and their authoritative rule over her own life. Her qualms were not so easily placated when her impressions were based on one actual meeting and many conflicting rumors that had dealt not only with the Princess Anna, but Prince Aleksei as well. Time would see the consequences of this arrangement which the tsar had forced upon her, and for her own peace of mind, she hoped her fears would be gently put aside by a mutual respect that would grow between the Taraslovs and herself.

Synnovea's attention perked as the soldiers, much subdued by their baths, began to drift back in varying numbers. As they moved slowly past her door, she was wont to wonder what trick her mind was playing on her, for there seemed to be three times as many who came back compared to those who had left, but when their prolonged return made her impatient to have them safely abed and the bathhouse to herself, she could not rely on the accuracy of her judgment. She tried calming her restive mood by being practical. After all, when their muted, cheerless voices bespoke of their exhaustion, she could surmise with a full measure of confidence that she would soon be basking in the privacy she desired in the bathhouse.

Much to her disappointment, however, her lavation was set aside for a second time when Ivan, in passing the soldiers on the stairs, commanded a way to be made for him. He answered their exaggerated reactions to his foul-smelling clothing by announcing he was on his way to the bathhouse, where he intended to wash away any residue of filth that might remain from their putrid offerings. Synnovea considered the possible reasons for his delay, hoping to bridle her freshening irritation with the man. Then the realization dawned that Ivan Voronsky would never have lowered himself to associate in such a casual manner with the guards. From the remarks he had made, he considered them nothing more than crude, common men who were far removed from his self-exalted person-age. Had he been able to dictate the order of priority in the first place, Synnovea was sure he would have demanded time to finish his bath before allowing anyone else to enter, but she was just as certain the soldiers would have laughed him to scorn for attempting to steal a march on them.

The inn finally grew still and hushed after Ivan's return to the small, private cubicle he had elected to take, and Synnovea deemed that it was now her time to enjoy the solace of a bath. She quickly snatched up a clean night-gown and the small satchel she had packed with toilet-ries and made her way downstairs. Outside the inn, a cool breeze rustled through the firs which rose like a tower-ing, protective fortress beyond the bathhouse, bringing to her nostrils the fresh, pungent fragrance of their swaying boughs. The burble of a tumbling brook melded with the soothing night sounds. High above the treetops, the bril-liant moon shone down from its lofty realm and held back the darkness with a wondrous glow that clearly defined the pathway to the low-roofed structure.

The door creaked in the hushed stillness as Synnovea pushed it slowly open and stepped within. At the far end of the room a fire flickered in a large hearth, illumining the dark chamber with a shifting amber glow. From a rafter, a dim lantern hung and shared its wan light, lending an eerie life to the mists that drifted upward from the stygian surface of the pool. The rising vapors twined aimlessly through the massive beams, as if probing for a way of escape. In their failure, they merged into a thickening, swelling haze that shrouded the interior.

Cold water, shunted through tin flumes from the stream outside, gurgled as it ran into a huge vat. Like some craven iron beast, the enormous kettle squatted on spindly legs over a hearth of its own. Steaming water trickled cheerily over its funneled lip into the main bathing pool where, on the opposite side, the overflow was channeled through a shaft that returned the waters to the rivulet outside. On this warm summer's night, the fire had been allowed to dwindle, and beneath the swollen belly of the kettle, a large bed of coals gave off a dull red glow that lent its own blush of color to the curling vapors and the tenebrous gloom of the deeply shadowed room.

Synnovea's deep, translucent eyes reflected the meager light as her gaze followed the swirling mists upward to the rafters high above. The bulwark of heavy beams had been built to withstand the long winters and had been made of such sturdy construction it was conceivable that for a multitude of years to come, the sturdy bathhouse would welcome weary travelers to its steamy embrace.

Synnovea paused for a long moment at the portal to carefully peruse the interior, lest she find herself in error about being alone. Nothing stirred within the darkly shaded, shrouded depths except the shifting flames that cast dancing shadows into the mists. The only sounds came from the crackling fire and the trickle of water running into the pool. In the spacious hearth, smaller kettles of water hung over a fire which was kept burning, and upon a nearby table, pitchers and basins were readily available for an advanced scrubbing with soap. Wooden tubs had also been provided for those who chose a more languid or thorough soak in a warmer bath.

On a bench near the pool, a man's robe had been left, and Synnovea made a mental note to inform Captain Nekrasov on the morningtide that the garment was there in the event that he or one of his men had left it.

Synnovea dropped her satchel onto a nearby stool, too tired and sore to think of anything beyond a bath and a long, soothing soak in the pool. She prepared the former herself until the wooden tub was brimming with steaming liquid. From a small vial she had brought, she dribbled scented oils over the surface, then carefully laid out a bar of perfumed soap and a large towel. She ran slender fingers through her long, black tresses to remove any snarls that might have escaped the earlier brushing, then gathering the long, silken length and coiling it like a heavy rope, she formed a large knot on top of her head and secured it with an ornate comb. Soft, curling tendrils plummeted downward against her brow and neck as the topknot loosened a bit, but for the most part the dark mass was held ensnared.

Slowly Synnovea freed the ties that held the robe secure and let it slip from her shoulders. The cloth drifted downward, unveiling her naked body in a dazzling rush, until she caught the garment with a swirling motion of her arm and flung it away. As it settled in a billowing cloud on a nearby bench, Synnovea paused in sudden uncertainty and tipped her head, wondering at the soft, breathless sighing sound the silk had made, much like the slow expelling of a deep breath.

Nothing more came but the melding murmurs of fire and water, and she shrugged away her doubt and bent to the task at hand. Her nerves had been tested beyond acceptable limits for her to give much credence to the lurid shades of her own imagination.

Lifting a foot to rest it on the rim of the wooden tub, Synnovea inspected the dark spots above her knee where that crude highwayman had left bruised imprints of his fingers. She formed a vision of that lord-of-thieves trussed up like a goose awaiting his judgment and fondly savored the notion. Then her brow furrowed at an intruding thought, and she released her breath slowly as she repeated a silent petition for the safety of the officer.

Another bruise at her waist caught her eye, and cupping a breast within her palm, she pressed the fullness upward to examine the bluish mark more carefully. She vividly recalled having suffered much pain and trauma during Ladislaus's flight through the woods, and for that, too, she hoped she had been avenged. His brawny arm had clasped her so tightly she had feared her ribs would crack.

Oh, she dearly hoped the officer had delivered to that brute a punishment well worthy of his crimes. The pompous brigand had boasted that none of the tsar's soldiers could touch him. She was exceedingly glad that he had been much in error.

Synnovea smiled ruefully to herself as she stepped into the half barrel, and with a long, pleasurable sigh, lowered herself into the scented bath. A delightful interlude passed as she allowed the steaming water to relax her and ease her aching muscles. After a time she began to wash, lathering the soap up well over her entire body until her face, shoulders, and bosom were covered with a whitish foam. Lifting first one sleek limb and then the other, she worked the suds up thickly along their length.

Freeing her topknot, Synnovea lathered her hair, then tossed the fragrant bar to the bench. Leaning her head over the edge of the tub, she arched her back as she lifted a bucket above her head and rinsed the soap from the strands, letting the water flow through the long tresses and splash to the floor. She squeezed the excess from her hair, then left it unbound as she raised a dripping sponge and dribbled its contents over her shoulders. The runnels ran down over her bosom, cascading in eager channels through the white frosting until the rounded orbs glistened cleanly in the rosy firelight.

Long moments passed while Synnovea savored the luxury of the bath, then realizing the hour was growing late, she braced her hands on the rim of the tub and, with an energetic heave, pushed herself to her feet, momentarily setting her breasts abounce. An odd sound, much like a watery gulp, came from the direction of the pool, and she paused in sudden trepidation as her gaze carefully probed the swirling vapors close above the water. A movement near the steps caught her eye, and she jerked her head around with a gasp, only to laugh in relief as she spied the frog that squatted there.

"You intrude, my little friend," Synnovea laughingly scolded and tossed the contents of a bucket his way, sending him leaping away.

Reassured once again, she finished rinsing herself, using the contents of the brimming pitcher she had left nearby for that purpose. From it, she poured warm water down her body until the lather had been washed back into the tub. By now, the heat of the room was enough to draw a fine mist of sweat from her pores, and she left the tub for the cooler waters of the pool.

Descending the stone steps at its edge, Synnovea sighed with pleasure as she sank into its dark depths. She thought the innkeeper clever to incorporate a pool of such depth inside a bathhouse, when it was most often the routine that bathers, after steaming up in heavy humidity, scampered outside to cool themselves in a nearby stream, river, or even banks of snow, whatever the weather and location allowed. She knew for a fact that even in the coldest of months some would dare the chill for such an experience. Her English mother, however, had instilled within her father the need for a private bath, and through the years Synnovea had clung to that custom. Whenever the occasion warranted her to make use of a public facility, Ali made the necessary arrangements and paid out coins to secure her solitude, while Jozef and Stenka stood guard. Under the circumstances, Synnovea had not wanted to disturb any of them tonight, nor had she felt a need to do so, for Captain Nekrasov kept himself and his men well in line.

Leisurely Synnovea stroked through the water, letting the thickening haze envelope her as she swam toward the far side of the pool. Her long hair flowed on the surface behind her, like an opening fan of ebon hue, while the ends became lost in the shadows that closed in behind her.

Of a sudden Synnovea gasped and recoiled in astonishment and dread as her hand made contact with something human. A wide, furry chest! Then as she sank downward, her thigh brushed the loins of a man, and in panic she struggled to propel herself away from the offending nakedness, but she was so stunned and intent on haste, she nearly drowned herself in the process. Lurching backward with as much grace as a floundering cow, she plunged below the surface of the water and promptly came up choking and gasping for air. Strong hands reached out to lift her by the arms, but she fought them off, certain she was in impending danger of being ravished.

Having successfully escaped the helping hands, Synnovea began to sink below the surface again, this time closer against the man. Their wet bodies slid together as her head went under, but she hardly noticed, for in sudden trepidation she realized she was taking in more water than even a competent fish should. This time when the man clamped an arm about her waist and drew her up, she flung both arms about his shoulders and gasped for breath between strangling, wrenching coughs. So great was her panic, she scarcely realized her breasts were squeezed tightly against the stalwart

chest or that somewhere below the surface of the water,
her thighs rested intimately against his loins. The fleshly
heat he displayed did not impact her awareness until
much later, when she was far less anxious about drawing
a normal breath.

Her alarm ebbed to some degree when she managed
to clear the water from her nose and throat and then
sucked in enough air to fill her lungs. Carefully she
inhaled, drawing in deep drafts, and realized the man
was watching her with an amused but dubious frown. A
touch of indignation pricked her that he should find some
humor in her predicament, and she drew back to consider
him with a haughty stare, completely disregarding the
fact that she was stark naked in his arms. Water dribbled
down from the long, tangled mass of sopping tendrils,
leaving her vision somewhat impaired by the droplets
trickling through the wetly spiked lashes. The vapors lent
a strange bewitchment to the moment, yet the distortion
she saw was not from her own hindered sight or confused
perception. Indeed, a seer was needed to say whether or
nay the man was even human. Synnovea decided she
lacked such magical discernment as she closely perused a
badly lacerated visage. A large, protruding bump grossly
elaborated the curve of his brow where the skin had been
split open. The swelling extended down into his eye,
nearly closing it. A second lump bulged his upper lip,
and above this protrusion another bruise darkened his
cheek. Providing some small evidence that his face was
not totally misshapen, his jaw appeared carefully hewn of
granite, while his nose was shaped with a noble, aquiline
leanness, though in truth Synnovea was somewhat dubious of her conclusions since she was reluctant to stare too
long for fear he would think her rude. The short, wet
strands of his hair shaded his eyes, but she thought they
were almost a subtle steel-gray rimmed with a deeper
jewel-blue. Even in the shadowed room, softer lights
twinkled within the shining depths as a lopsided smile
lifted the smaller corner of his lips.

"Forgive me, Countess, I didn't mean to frighten you. Nor was it my intent to cause you harm or embarrassment. Indeed, my lady, I never in my wildest yearnings ever imagined my bath would be interrupted by such a high degree of womanly beauty. I was rather dazzled by the sight and reluctant to see it end."

Synnovea scarcely noted that he had spoken to her in English, but in a heated rush, replied in kind. "You would spy upon me without making me aware of your presence? Simple truth, sir! Why are you here? Am I to assume you've come for evil purposes?"

"Banish the thought, my lady. I came here when my duties permitted it. Several of my men needed attention, and by the time I dressed their wounds, everyone else had left the bathhouse. I was certain I would be alone and was much amazed when you joined me. I fear I was momentarily confounded and struck dumb by your entrance, and then it became clear to me. Though I could see you, you could not see me." He lifted wide, sleekly bulging shoulders in a casual shrug as he offered the excuse. "I fear it proved too great a temptation for a soldier in need of feminine companionship."

"Indeed, sir!" Synnovea fairly flung the words at him. "I can well understand why you are in want! Have you no ken that a gentleman would have informed me of his presence at the very beginning?"

An amused grin twitched at the edges of his bruised lips as his eyes glowed through the shadowed gloom. "Alas, Countess, I do not claim to be a saint. I greatly enjoyed the interlude and the perfection you displayed and, for the life of me, could not bring myself to interrupt. Were I any less a gentleman, I'd surely take advantage of this most provocative embrace. . . . " He settled her a bit closer as she, in some irritation, tried to push herself free again. Her thighs brushed hard against him, snatching his breath and flicking a fiery brand across the fibers of his senses until he dared not move for fear of losing complete control of his hard-won poise. With some difficulty, he drew rein on his quaking passions and continued in a warm, mellow voice, stilling her struggles as his words struck home. "Still, since I have already saved you from one ravishment this evening, 'twould seem I am bound by honor to carry you to safety again."

"Saved me? You mean . . . " Synnovea's lips pursed in a silent Oh! as she realized just who the man was.

"You left ere we were properly introduced, my lady," he reproved, distracted by the slick, wet feel of her soft breasts against his chest. He doubted that there had ever been a moment in his life when he had been assaulted by such exquisite torture or when the need to maintain a ruse of imperturbable calm had been so crucial to his aspirations. He was certain she would have immediately flown his embrace had he foolishly revealed the extent of his infatuation with her womanly form. "And though you are a delicious sight to behold, my lady, and even more delectable to enfold, I must admonish you for your bad manners. . . . "

"This is no time to discuss bad manners, mine or yours! Let me go!" Synnovea struggled briefly in the circle of his arms and was surprised when he spread his arms wide, leaving her hanging about his neck by the strength of her own grasp. She reddened profusely beneath his deepening grin and, with a stifled groan, dove away from him. Swimming back to the edge of the pool, she glanced quickly over her shoulder as he followed more leisurely. In urgent haste, she managed to ascend the steps and, in a flying dash across the room, swept up her robe and swiftly donned it.

Thus armored, Synnovea faced him as he climbed those same stone stairs. She did not want to be surprised should he attempt to approach her, but as she watched him in dire dread of what the next moments would bring, she was struck by a sense of amazement. Though obviously far from handsome, he was exceptionally well formed otherwise. He was as tall as Ladislaus, but not nearly as thick or bulky. He had a hard-muscled look

about him, and recalling the agility and easy strength
he had displayed battling the miscreants, she could only
guess at the discipline he practiced keeping himself in
good fighting form. His ribs were tautly fleshed, his chest
firmly muscled beneath a matting of crisp hair. His waist
was lean and hips narrow. . . .

A gasp escaped Synnovea as his loins came fully into
view, and she whirled with burning cheeks, shocked
to the depths of her virginal innocence. Though well
traveled, she had nevertheless been carefully sheltered
during the full span of her life, and even with a score
of years behind her, this was her first glimpse of a
completely naked man. And to her utter astonishment
he did not appear the least bit chagrined by the boldness
he exhibited.

Synnovea heard his soft, chuckling laughter coming
near, and she whirled in apprehension, wondering wildly
if she would have to fight him off, but he only sought the
robe which had been left across the bench. Careful to keep
her glance brief and well elevated, she glowered at him,
then jerked around again, sorely incensed that he had
watched her bathe and had made no effort to alert her
to his presence.

"You can turn around now," he informed her with
mirth liberally pervading his voice.

"Good!" Synnovea replied in exasperation, annoyed
that he should find so much humor in what had been to
her a most embarrassing and dreadful experience. "Then
I can leave!" Casting a glare at him for good measure,
she began to gather up her possessions. "The very idea!
Spying upon me like some sneak-thief! You are the most
despicable knave I've met in some time!"

"Not since this afternoon, at least," he responded with
an indolent shrug. "Or did you appreciate that thief's
company more than mine?"

"That highwayman? Ha! Ladislaus has much to learn
from you about boorish manners!" Her curiosity got the
better of her, and Synnovea canted her head slightly to

give him a sidelong stare. "What happened to the brigand anyway?"

The man emphasized his displeasure with an angry snort. "The cowardly wretch fled when you raced off! On *my* horse! A most worthy steed. Believe me, I haven't a ken which vexes me more, losing that rogue or that horse! Had I not tried to help you when the stallion reared, I might have been able to capture the man. But were you grateful? Oh, nay, my lady! You gave no slightest heed to my welfare. If not for my men searching the woods for me, I'd still be out there somewhere! I am here, Countess, with no special thanks to you!"

Synnovea raised a dainty chin, pricked both by his admonishing tone and her own conscience. "You seem dreadfully put out by your loss."

"And well I should be! I'll not likely find another steed half as gifted in the field as that one!"

"On the morrow I will tell Captain Nekrasov to leave you the stallion that belonged to Ladislaus," she stated in stilted aloofness. "Perhaps that will placate you."

The man scoffed. "Hardly! It cost me a goodly sum to have my own stallions shipped here from England. . . . "

"From England?" she repeated in surprise, then realized what she had overlooked before. His subtly clipped speech clearly betrayed his place of origin. "Is that where you're from?"

"Aye!"

"But you led a Russian troop . . . " Synnovea began, then recalled Ladislaus's comment about foreign cavaliers being hired to teach their fighting skills to the tsar's troops. "You're an officer in His Majesty's service?"

Though he wore nothing more dashing than a long robe, the man gave her a debonair bow, a gesture which might have been accompanied by the clicking of heels had he worn something more substantial. "Colonel Sir Tyrone Bosworth Rycroft at your service, Countess. Knighted in England and now Commander of the Third Regiment of the Tsar's Imperial Hussars. And you are . . . "

"This is hardly the place for introductions, Colonel," Synnovea replied hurriedly, deciding it was better not to provide him with a name. She could just imagine him spreading this lurid tale of their meeting among his troops and friends.

A slanted grin lifted a corner of the swollen lips. "And you are the Countess Synnovea Altynai Zenkovna, en route to Moscow where you will be under the tutelage of Princess Taraslovna, the tsar's cousin."

Synnovea closed her mouth, realizing it had sagged open in surprise. Breathlessly she concluded, "You know a great deal about me, sir."

"I desired to know," Tyrone commented with an air of confidence that shattered her own. "When we arrived at the inn this evening and I found that you had also taken shelter here for the night, I made inquiries among your escort. Captain Nekrasov refused to discuss you, but the good sergeant proved a bit more generous with the facts. I was much relieved to learn that you are not married, especially to that pompous little upstart who serves as your companion." He arched a brow, pointedly awaiting some declaration as to her relationship to the man. "He was just leaving the bathhouse when I came in, and from his demeanor, I would imagine that he thinks much of himself or his station in life."

Though she vehemently desired to deny any close association with Ivan, Synnovea refused to appease the colonel's curiosity. It was best to dissuade the man from gaining further knowledge of her, lest he should become bothersome or prove an embarrassment.

Gathering her satchel, Synnovea moved toward the door but found her progress thwarted by the colonel. He stepped before her, and his uneven lips eased into a gentle smile. "Will you allow me to see you again?"

"It is impossible, Colonel," she declined coolly. "I shall continue on to Moscow on the morn."

"But so will I," Tyrone assured her softly. "I led my men on exercises in the field. We are scheduled to return to Moscow by the morrow's evening."

"Princess Anna will hardly approve."

"You are not . . . betrothed?" Tyrone held his breath in anticipation of her answer. He could not fully explain even to himself why he should suddenly forget the ache of his shattered life and once again allow a woman to strike sparks in his mind.

"Nay, Colonel Rycroft, of course not."

"Then with your permission, Countess, I would like to pay court to you." Tyrone was crushingly aware of his own impatient rush to settle the matter, and despite being a score, ten and four years of age, he was aware that he was acting much like an eager young whelp ensnared in a frenzied, rutting heat over a wench. But then, it had been some time since he had made love to a woman, and even his young wife, that fair and beauteous Angelina, had never looked as fine, either with or without her clothes.

"Your proposal overwhelms me, Colonel." Synnovea was more than a little astounded, yet she was thankful for the shadows that hid the rush of color to her cheeks as she recalled the feel of his warm, well-defined body against her own in the pool. His petition, of course, was out of the question, but for caution's sake she deemed it more fitting and wise to soften her rejection. "I shall have to think about it for a time."

"I shall await your pleasure. Until then, my lady, I bid you adieu." Colonel Rycroft swept her another courtly bow and then straightened as she moved past him. Watching her hurry across the room, he admired the gentle swaying motion of her hips beneath the silk robe and was vividly reminded of that moment in the pool when his hand had brushed her buttocks and she had nestled closely against his loins. His long-starved passions had not yet cooled, and he knew he would have to endure a long restless night, tormented by his desires and a relentless onslaught of decidedly lascivious imaginings.

The portal opened with the same creaking sound that had announced her entrance and closed again to leave him staring at its oaken planks. His eyes could not penetrate the dense wood, and as he listened to her hastening footsteps, another vision came to mind, one that was dark and dismally devoid of warmth. It was a painful apparition from his memory of the graveside where he had muttered his last ragged and bitter farewell to his dead wife.

Colonel Sir Tyrone Rycroft turned abruptly with a muttered curse. What fool's folly had set him on this path of heated lust? How could he dare to entertain the hope that he could trust another woman when he had not yet gathered the tattered shreds of his emotions and resumed a life unhampered by haunting memories? The scars he had thrust down deep into his mind burst forth in renewed agony.

The dawning sun had not yet touched the land with its warming glow when Synnovea roused her companions and bade them to hurry. At Captain Nekrasov's bemused inquiries, she laid the cause of her haste to a desire to have the journey well behind her. She did not dare reveal the fact that she was afraid she had attracted the attention of an unwanted suitor and that it was expedient that she leave ere he rose and sought out an answer from her.

"Leave the stallion for Colonel Rycroft," she bade the captain as he escorted her to her coach. " 'Tis the least I can do to repay him."

Ali was still extremely sensitive to movement and had to be carried to the coach by Stenka. With the gentle urgings of her mistress, she leaned back against the pillows Synnovea had tucked within the corner of the seat and once again allowed sleep to overtake her.

Synnovea braced herself in the opposite corner and closed her eyes, refusing to be drawn into a conversation with Ivan. She had bade Stenka to waste no moment on this, their last day of travel, and if it so pleased him, to take an unfrequented path that, although somewhat more challenging, would get them to Moscow faster.

Soon they were on the road again, and Synnovea breathed a sigh of relief, well assured that she had seen the last of that English rake. She only hoped he was enough of a gentleman to refrain from gossip, though he had failed that standard already. It was disconcerting enough that her own vivid memory should recount again and again the happenings in the bathhouse without the tale being spread abroad to every eager ear in Moscow.

It was a half hour later when the Commander of the Third Regiment of the Tsar's Imperial Hussars rose from his cot, wincingly stretched his stiff, aching muscles and staggered naked across the tiny cubicle that had sufficed as a room. Nudging the foot of his second-in-command in passing, he muttered an order and left that yawning one to fulfill it as he searched out a candle to light.

Another half-turn of the hour saw the first hint of the sky lightening to a dull blue. Colonel Rycroft tucked the battered helm beneath his arm and descended the stairs to make a morning inspection of his men who waited outside. As he passed through the open door, his eyes flitted to the right of the porch where he had last seen the coach. Alas, there was nothing there but the black stallion tethered to a post. A muttered curse escaped his lips as he frowningly scanned the road, already aware that he would find no evidence of the countess's presence.

She's flown! The thought gnawed at him and sorely tested his mood, yet from somewhere in the deepest depths of his memory there came an image of a pair of eyes to haunt him, sometimes jade, sometimes deep ebon. More disturbing to his constitution was the vision of her sleek, ripe form entirely vulnerable to his gaze.

Tyrone ground out another expletive beneath his breath. He should have known he'd frighten her off with his confounded anxious fervor! He had moved on her like a hound after a bitch in heat, and he couldn't blame her much for having flitted off in a frantic rush.

Tyrone let his breath out in short drafts as he sought to curb his annoyance. His men awaited him, and after he had driven them with an iron fist the whole week, they deserved better from him today, especially since they had put the outlaw band to rout. What did the girl matter anyway? He could buy the services of another easily enough. Indeed, he seemed ever pressed to reject the advances of those brazen trollops who followed the soldiers' camps or traversed the area in Moscow reserved for foreigners in search of a companion for an hour or a whole night.

Still, the idea of accepting the leavings of nearly every man in the tsar's army left him totally uninspired. He was after more than a sordid, feverish fondling of a passing harlot. Despite the fact that he was reluctant to be ensnared in marriage again, he wanted to ease his passion with a woman whom he could exchange a mutual affinity with and perhaps even cherish. What he truly desired was a mistress who would be content to stay with him and not be inclined to test the strength of her persuasions on another swain.

"The Countess Zenkovna left you a horse, Colonel," Captain Grigori Tverskoy announced, jerking his thumb over his shoulder to indicate the steed. "Will it not serve you as well as your own?"

"I fear the brigand got the better of the trade," Tyrone remarked ruefully. "But he hasn't yet seen the last of me."

"Will you go after him again?"

"When it is convenient," Tyrone assured the younger man. "I have more pressing affairs to attend in Moscow ere I give him my full attention."

"We can report to the division that we have slain ten and three of that brigand's followers, though I would rather carry the details of our fight to the tsar himself." A laconic smile traced the captain's lips. "General Vanderhout delights himself overmuch in your many conquests, Colonel, but it is his reputation that grows apace."

"The Dutchman is anxious about his future here," Tyrone mused aloud. " 'Tis the best pay he's yet received, and he does not want to lose it ere his contract runs out. Thus he makes his efforts look good."

"At your expense, Colonel."

Tyrone reached out a hand to clasp the other's shoulder. "A general is always responsible for whatever happens in his division, whether good or bad. Vanderhout's command of foreign officers is under the close attention of the tsar, and their exploits reflect on him." The colonel shrugged and then winced as his lip cracked with his effort to smile. " 'Tis this side of it, Grigori! For us to protest his practice of claiming fame where he has not earned it would make us seem small and petty. Ergo, *tovarish*, we must take the general's conduct in stride. We have no other choice."

The Russian sighed with disappointment. "The general's ineptitude wears on me, Colonel. In making a comparison, you have much more to offer. He takes the ideas you freely supply and incorporates them as his own, and from what I've been able to discern, it almost seems as if you subtly but deliberately advise him, just to keep him from making any costly mistakes."

Tyrone mused in silence for a moment before he gave Grigori an answer. "I've had more experience in the field, 'tis all, my friend, but I'm sure General Vanderhout would not be where he is now without some ability."

Grigori grunted in dubious derision. "I wonder."

Chapter 4

T HE MARKETPLACE OF KITAIGOROD STILL BUSTLED WITH
lively activity even though the afternoon was rapidly
dwindling and twilight would soon be approaching.
Stenka maneuvered the coach along a narrow street,
passing vaulted alleyways where a labyrinth of gal-
leries existed. The bazaars displayed a collection of
wares in organized rows for the benefit of patrons.
Flax, hemp, icons, silks, earrings, and melons had
their own particular *ryady* from which each was sold,
along with a wide variety of other articles, ranging all
the way from vegetables and fish to amber, pearls,
and furs.

The small detachment of ragshag soldiers followed as
the coach wended its way near the heart of Moscow,
but the small troop was largely ignored as merchants
loudly hawked their wares and bands of *skomorokhi* put
on their masked mimes, musicals, and puppet shows.
Prisoners with their feet in stocks pleaded for bread
and nourishment which the city did not supply, while
blind and crippled beggars diligently shook their cups
as they blended their chants for alms into a strange
cacophony of sounds, amid which could be heard the
low grunts and rumblings of bears that performed clever tricks for their handlers. Here, rich *boyars* in their
sumptuous *kaftans* and high-peaked or rounded hats
rubbed shoulders with poorly or prosperously dressed

peasants, whatever the size of an individual's purse allowed.

A visitor could not ignore the abundance of churches, chapels, public baths, and taverns in the area, all of which were frequently used by the populace, especially the latter two. It was no secret that Russians relished their long, steamy baths and strong, stout libations.

The large conveyance continued to progress over the heavily timbered road while Stenka cried "Padi! Padi!" to urge meandering crowds to make way for them or "Beregis! Beregis!" to warn others to take care. Swift, elegant little open *drozhki* skirted around them with incredible ease, while the summer sledges moved at a slower pace, forcing Stenka to haul the team toward the side of the road as the smaller vehicles approached from the opposite direction. In wintertime the *troikas* would have halted the progress of a larger conveyance altogether as the brisk sleighs raced with three horses abreast down the lane.

Synnovea had visited Moscow on numerous occasions and though no less sensitive to the beauty and excitement of the city, she could not disregard the fact that only a few moments remained of the freedom she had long savored under her father's protection. For most of the day she had been unmercifully haunted by bold reveries of her encounter with Colonel Rycroft in the bathhouse. Although she might have elected a more handsome gallant to take the place of the colonel if she had been able to dictate events to her liking, she could not disallow the fact that it had been an undeniably titillating experience, nor could she deny that even with his misshapen features, there had been something incredibly interesting about the man, at least enough to make her blush whenever she remembered his all too manly form. Every time her flushed cheeks darkened to a profuse shade, she found good cause to be thankful for the sweltering heat. What lurid details she had disregarded in a time of panic, she now dwelt on and sometimes savored like any mind-less, dream-bound chit with a penchant for salacious preoccupations. The recurring, often graphic recollec-tion of the moment when her unclad bosom had been pressed tightly against his chest and her loins had all but embraced the naked fullness of his was so provocative in recall, she found her nerves ajangle with a concern that her companions might somehow detect her wanton musings. For once, she was glad that Ivan thought only of Ivan and Ali hid her aching head beneath the folds of a cool, wet cloth.

Her monkish companion had deposited his narrow form in the back seat of the carriage early that morning, and now the rays of the lowering sun thrust their way into the carriage windows upon Ivan. The man all but preened in the rosy aura, as if he imagined it some well-deserved halo or, more farfetched, held aspirations of presenting a sublime visage to his audience, like some colorfully plumed cock. So great was his vanity, he failed to realize how vividly the brightness highlighted the deep, ugly pockmarks that liberally scarred his bony cheeks. Apparently he had also dismissed the fact that he was garbed in the only robe the priests of the village church had been able to spare, which closely resembled a tattered rag, leaving him looking far more shabby than stately.

His disposition, however, had taken a definite turn for the better since their arrival in Moscow. If Synnovea had considered herself a fair judge of people's moods, she might have been tempted to make such an assumption from the smug smile the man wore. He seemed almost anxious to reach the Taraslov manse, as if delivering her to the custody of her new guardians was some great feat upon which he could feed his insatiable desire for recognition.

The coach left the narrow passageway and entered the open area of Krasnaya Ploscha, which the English were wont to translate to Red or Beautiful Square when giving directions. The great, red-brick wall of the Kremlin rose up like a vast, many-turreted crown above the city, encircling among other structures several multidomed cathedrals, the bell tower of Ivan the Great, the Palace of Facets and the nearby Terem palace where the next tsarina would someday be housed. The white facades and golden domes that adorned many of the buildings gleamed like a sultan's treasure beneath the brilliance of the late afternoon sun, while other bejeweled edifices, courtyards, and gardens clustered close about them, well protected behind the enveloping wall.

The Frolovskaia Tower was heralded as the main approach to this mighty fortress, and near it, another bauble of architectural brilliance glimmered, this one the Pokrovsky Sobor or, as it was more frequently called of late, the Cathedral of St. Basil. The exotic grandeur of this creation had already bedazzled many a viewer with its many towers and bulging, uniquely shaped domes and spires that glistened like the multihued scales of a fish. Legend had oft repeated the tale that after the cathedral's completion, Tsar Ivan Vasilievich, known beyond the borders of Russia as The Terrible, had ordered the eyes of the architect gouged out to prevent the man from designing another edifice of similar design somewhere else in the world, but the story was refuted by many who argued that after Vasilievich's death, the architect, Postnik Yarolev, had returned in full possession of his eyesight to add another chapel in which to house the tomb of the holy man, Basil the Blessed, who had vehemently denounced Ivan's cruelties and by whose name the cathedral later came to be called.

Stenka clucked to the horses as they crossed the open promenade in front of St. Basil's and the squat platform of the Lobnoe Mesto, or the Place of the Brow, from whence the patriarchs bestowed their blessings on the people or, beside it, rebels and felons were beheaded or tortured for their crimes. Stenka soon turned the team away from the Kremlin into another lane, along which rich and powerful *boyars* lived in large wooden mansions. Synnovea came to alert attention when she recognized some of the houses, among them the stately residence of the Countess Natasha Andreyevna. The woman had once been her mother's dearest companion and was the only confidant Synnovea could trust for help and counsel, should things go awry with the Taraslovs.

A few short moments later Stenka reined the four-in-hand off the main street into a circular drive and drew the animals to a halt before an impressive mansion. Synnovea took a deep breath, bracing herself for the meeting to come. The event she had dreaded had finally arrived, and there could be no more delay.

Captain Nekrasov hurried to dismount and hastily dusted himself off as he came around to the side of the carriage facing the house. Opening the door, he smiled upward as he presented his able arm to the one he had come to cherish. Synnovea calmed her trepidations, gathered her poise, and responded in kind as she placed a slender hand upon his sleeve. After assisting her to the ground, Nikolai waited in patient manner as she adjusted and smoothed her skirts, then with an inquiring look, received her nod and faced the tall doorway.

Synnovea heaved a tremulous sigh and moved beside him up the stone path, dismayed by the idea that she would be placing herself shortly under the authority of strangers. As she neared the structure, a flash of light from the second story caught her eye, and peering upward, she paused as she saw the Princess Anna framed in a window located above the front portal. A yellowish glow of candles burning somewhere behind the woman silhouetted her form, and even in the loose *sarafan* she wore, Anna looked *khudaya*, a word used to mean both thin and bad, or more appropriately, painfully thin. Of course, when most Russian men admired

fleshier women, the word had oft been used to describe
any slender form, including a maid as shapely as
Synnovea.

With a tentative smile, Synnovea lifted a hand in a
gesture of greeting, but much to her dismay, the princess
gave no sign of welcome or any hint of salutation that
might have helped to lighten the fretful mood of her
guest. Like a silent wraith, the woman retreated from
view, allowing the draperies to fall in place beyond the
panes.

Dropping her gaze, Synnovea struggled a moment,
tormented with feelings of loneliness and estrangement.
Any comfort she might have derived from a warm greeting was now replaced with a morbid sense of gloom.
She didn't want to be here, away from her home, away
from all the things her father had cherished and carefully
nurtured.

Sensing that everything was not as it should be with the
maid, Nikolai spoke in a tone of concern. "Will all be well
with you here, Countess?" he asked, still not daring to display his growing affection for her. He had no idea what
he might do if circumstances went amiss for her, but he
felt strongly committed to offering his assistance just the
same. "If there ever should come a need . . . "

Synnovea did not allow him to finish, but gently laid a
hand upon his arm in an effort to reassure him . . . and
perhaps even herself. "The Princess Anna is very kind,
I'm sure." Synnovea hoped she sounded more convinc-
ing than she felt. "Right now we are hardly more than
strangers, and she's probably as anxious as I am about
this meeting."

The captain was not so easily persuaded, but to upset
the maid by lingering on the subject was far removed
from his understanding of lending comfort. Yet he felt
a dire need to state his offer more clearly and did so
in careful tones, lest he betray the full measure of his
heart. "I shall consider it an honor if you will allow me
to serve you in whatever manner you should desire or

require, my lady. I will be receiving a promotion next month and shall be in the service of the tsar henceforth as an officer of the castle guard. Should you find that you have need of me, you can send your maid to summon me to your side." Almost emphatically, he declared, "And I will come, my lady, or I will send no one less than His Majesty, Mikhail Romanov himself, to give you my excuse."

Synnovea was overwhelmed by his chivalrous, if somewhat unrealistic, offer. She glanced up at him, braving a smile, but her eyes glistened with a start of tears. "You're very gallant and kind, Captain Nekrasov, and I'm honored by your pledge."

"It has been a privilege escorting you here, my lady," Nikolai assured her warmly, meaning more than he actually conveyed.

With a strengthening resolve to persevere through the forthcoming meeting with Anna, Synnovea murmured encouragingly, "My name is Synnovea. I would deem the familiarity appropriate for a friend."

"Synnovea," the captain breathed above a whisper as he gently squeezed the slender hand that rested on his arm. "And my lady, if you would honor me in like measure. My name is Nikolai."

"Nikolai?" A halting nod came in response to her query, and with a soft, calming sigh, Synnovea allowed herself to be led to the portal by the courtly gentleman.

At the massive door the captain lightly rapped his knuckles against the wooden plank to announce their presence, and a moment later a steward garbed in a plain white *kaftan* swung open the portal. Nikolai faced the man and, with the undaunted manner of one well acquainted with giving orders, instructed the man, "You may inform the Princess Taraslovna that the Countess Zenkovna has arrived."

The servant eyed the captain's bandaged arm briefly before he stepped aside and, with a sweep of his hand, bade them enter. Synnovea was ushered in on the arm of her escort as the steward announced, "The Princess is awaiting you, Countess."

The hall seemed almost bright in comparison to the deepening dusk outside, for it was lit with a score or more candles burning in candelabrums. Synnovea was invited to sit while she awaited the mistress of the house, and after being reassured of her comfort, Nikolai hastened off to direct his men in the unloading of her baggage.

Ivan was slightly miffed at being left behind since he considered his presence of unique importance to the princess and had found no adequate show of respect in being ignored by the captain while that one hastened to attend the countess. He descended the steps of the carriage by himself, and then toddled hurriedly up the walk in borrowed sandals. He sniffed in annoyed arrogance as he passed the captain, causing that one to glance back in bemusement at the rapidly departing form.

"What ails the cleric?" Nikolai asked as he joined his men.

The sergeant voiced a likely conjecture. "I do believe, sir, that he took offense because you gave careful consideration to the Countess Zenkovna without extending a like amount of respect to him."

"I wasn't aware that he was deserving of any," Nikolai replied with dubious amusement. "I've seen no clear evidence of his importance or greatness. Indeed, he's probably an embarrassment to his order, whatever that may be."

The sergeant chortled in agreement. "Perhaps he is at that, sir. If you ask me, he's naught but a weed sprung up from a wayward seed. He's bound to mean trouble for some unwary soul one of these days. I pray it not be the young countess, though I sense the man will at least try."

"For her sake, Sergeant, I hope you are wrong."

Upon entering the hall, Ivan pompously cast a glance about for the steward, but finding the man gone, he bestowed a chilling glare upon Synnovea for the attention she had received. "Captain Nekrasov seems to be quite taken with you, Countess. I'm sure your pride is greatly bolstered by your triumph in acquiring yet another conquest."

"Yet another?" Synnovea repeated cautiously. "Who was the first?"

"I doubt that you've limited yourself to a mere two or three, so you need not play the innocent for my sake. The way that beast, Ladislaus, looked at you, it's a miracle you're even here."

Synnovea almost breathed a sigh of relief. For some reason she had been thinking of Colonel Rycroft and was half afraid the cleric had meant him. "I'm sure that Ladislaus saw me as nothing more than a fleeting diversion. By now, he has probably found another coach to attack or some woman to entertain him. I sincerely regret the fact that he was not captured."

" 'Twas that Englishman's fault, no doubt." Ivan made the conjecture aloud, winning Synnovea's regard.

"Englishman?"

"The one who rode after you and Ladislaus," the cleric explained. "Obviously the man was no match for the thief. Indeed, I was quite astounded by the man's appearance when I saw him at the bathhouse last night. Ladislaus clearly won the fray."

Synnovea opened her mouth to correct him, but as Ivan waited for her to speak she realized how foolish she would be to court Ivan's curiosity. If she pretended not to even know the colonel, it would no doubt be to her benefit.

A moment later the Princess Anna Taraslovna made an appearance at the head of the stairs, presenting a vision of shimmering gold as she paused on the landing to peruse her guests. A gold-veined veil covered her pale hair and was held in place by a pearl-encrusted *kokoshniki*. The elegant headdress copied the adornment of the golden stitched brocaded satin *sarafan* and was worn with an exalted pride, as if it were some bejeweled diadem of a noble queen.

Anna greeted her guests with a brief smile before descending the stairs with willowy grace. She was of an age about two score and bore herself with a dignified, yet pragmatic confidence that brooked no interference or refusal. She was as tall as Synnovea, and her good looks, though somewhat worn and chafed with the passing of years, were marked with a lean, squarish jaw and aristocratic features. Small, telltale wrinkles between her brows and around her lips bespoke of the weight of frowns that more oft rested there. The lightest trace of a dewlap trembled at her throat, which was otherwise long and elegant. Her eyes of silver-gray were bright and alert behind dark lashes and finely plucked brows, thin-drawn as if by a single sweep of a quill. Her gaze never rested anywhere for very long, but when met amain with a hawkish stare, it flitted away like a bird hastily taking to flight. Long years ago Anna had learned that it was an effective way of diverting another's attempt to question her, for if pressed, she could then pretend she had not even heard. She had become most clever in its use, deftly keeping other lords and ladies from challenging her authority.

"My dear Countess," Anna murmured cordially, extending her arms in cordial greeting as she swept across the hall to welcome her guests. "It's so good to see you again."

Synnovea sank gracefully into a deep curtsy, acknowledging the status of the other, though in Russia there was certainly no dearth of princely *boyars* and their ladies, even after Tsar Ivan the Terrible had indiscriminately laid waste to so many during his reign of terror. "Thank you, Princess. 'Tis indeed a relief to have the journey behind me."

"I trust everything went well and that Ivan proved to be of great comfort and assistance to you. I was sure he would be."

Synnovea managed a fleeting smile in answer to the princess's inquiring perusal. "We were delayed for a short time yesterday by thieves, but I shall leave Ivan Voronsky to relate the details of the attack. He was offended nigh as deeply as Captain Nekrasov was wounded."

In obvious bemusement Anna looked to Ivan for an explanation, but after making a brief assessment of his ragged appearance, she was quick to suggest, "You will, no doubt, want to refresh yourself before we talk."

Her attention was drawn to the front portal as some of the soldiers carried in Synnovea's larger chests on their backs while others toted smaller ones on their shoulders. Briefly eyeing the wealth of trunks, Anna made only a modicum of effort to subdue a slight frown of annoyance as she faced the steward who had returned with a tray of wine. "Boris, be good enough to show these . . . ah . . . gentlemen . . . upstairs to the countess's chambers. You may also escort the good Voronsky to the quarters I've reserved for him. There are clean garments he can use in the blue chest."

The servant nodded and, with a sweeping gesture of his hand, directed the men to follow him. Trailing through the door behind them all, the sergeant entered the hall with another huge chest resting on his shoulder. As he passed, he set a dusty valise at Ivan's feet, then climbed the stairs behind the others.

"Oh, but I see you've brought clothes with you . . . " Anna hurried to say as she recognized the satchel, but when Ivan slowly shook his head, she stared at him, greatly perplexed.

"On the contrary, Your Highness, I've been stripped of every possession I had taken with me, even the clothes from my back. Indeed, I am much relieved to have escaped with my life." Ivan laid a hand limply into the palm of the other and, raising a brow, leaned forward slightly to lend dramatic emphasis to his words.

" 'Twas most terribly threatening, Princess, of that I can assure you, but as you can see, I have accomplished your bidding and escorted the countess here to you, despite the great loss I've suffered."

"Anything you have been deprived of, good Voronsky, will certainly be replaced posthaste, but you must tell me of this event," Anna implored. "Come to my chambers when you have properly attended your needs. I would hear of this disaster soon lest I be overwhelmed by curiosity and worry."

"I will hasten to assuage your concerns even now, my lady. Though I suffered unduly, I am alive and here to speak of my hardships," Ivan valiantly avouched and, with a brief dip of his head, took his leave.

Left alone with Synnovea, Anna casually contemplated her attire as the green eyes lifted briefly to follow the ascent of the soldiers. Though modest and plain, the gown was unmistakably foreign, which only served to remind Anna that she would have to endure the presence of one who had been nurtured and instructed in her youth by a mother who had come from a different country and culture. Remembering the edict of her cousin, she could only bemoan her despair in the inner sanctum of her mind. Oh, why did Mikhail have to send this creature, of all people, to live with us? 'Tis apparent she does not regard herself as a Russian *boyarina*!

Forcing a smile that was at best stiff, Anna swept a hand toward the great chamber located to the left of the entrance hall. "Would you care for some refreshments before dinner, my dear? Boris has brought us chilled glasses of Malieno to savor on this warm day. Elisaveta, my cook, keeps the flasks stored near the ice that's hauled into the cellar in the wintertime. I find it quite refreshing myself."

Synnovea settled into the chair Anna indicated and, accepting the libation, sipped slowly of the dark red wine as the princess took another goblet for herself.

"Let me first express remorse for your father's untimely death, my dear. I understand he took a fever and died quite suddenly."

"Yes, we were not expecting it." Synnovea fought back a rush of tears as she reflected on her recent loss. "He seemed so hale and hearty before coming down ill. We were truly surprised by the suddenness of his death."

"We?" Anna latched onto the word with keen attention, perceiving it held great significance. She would have done anything to find an alternative to what the tsar had enforced upon her. "Did you have other relatives with you at the time? 'Twas my understanding you have no kinsmen here in Russia with whom you might have gone to live, other than myself, of course, but we are nothing more than strangers. Perhaps your aunt was visiting from England, and you've been thinking about going back with her."

Synnovea stared back at the woman, realizing Anna felt as entrapped by the tsar's decree as she did, and was obviously anxious to be rid of her. Mikhail might have imagined he was showing great compassion toward them both, Anna as a childless wife, and she as a young woman without parents, but he had apparently failed to understand that as two entirely different individuals, never having cherished each other before and totally bereft of the bonding of blood ties, a definite likelihood existed of them becoming rivals caged in the same house together, one of them forced to extend her hospitality, while the other was compelled to accept it. Synnovea could only wonder if there would soon come a day when one of them would have enough daring to approach the tsar with a plea to be released from this arrangement.

"Did you have someone visiting you at the time of your father's death?" Anna queried again with some exasperation. She found it extremely annoying to be kept waiting for an answer.

Synnovea replied with care, remembering the princess's displeasure when her father had taken Natasha with them to a gathering of rich *boyars* and their ladies a few months before his death. Anna's aversion to Natasha had been evident from the first, which allowed Synnovea little comfort as she made her answer now. "The Countess Andreyevna was visiting us at the time, Princess. She's a good friend of the family."

"Oh!" Anna drew herself up in cool reticence, unable to feel anything but animosity whenever the name of that particular countess was mentioned. Her hatred of the woman stemmed back to a time before her marriage to Aleksei. At the last social where they had briefly met and again crossed swords, Anna vividly recalled needling Natasha about being the mistress of Aleksandr Zenkov, but the dark-eyed countess had scoffed in amusement at the idea and had dismissed her insinuations as farfetched fantasies. Natasha had then scolded her for believing such wildly distorted illusions, as if she were nothing more than a child bereft of the ability to discern truth from fiction. "I was not aware you were a personal friend of the Countess Andreyevna, Synnovea. Indeed, I would have thought you'd resent the woman, what with her stealing your father's affections away from your mother and trying to take her place in your life."

Synnovea's face grew flushed as she was warmed with the fiery heat of indignation. She would have spoken out in swift defense of Natasha, but she could not subdue the trembling outrage she felt and feared she would immediately convey her highly agitated state if she dared to even speak. Briefly lowering her eyes to the goblet she clutched, she forced herself to stare into the dark liquid until she could regain some confidence of her ability to answer calmly. After a moment she managed to meet the woman's probing stare with cool poise. "I believe you misunderstand the relationship my father enjoyed with Natasha. 'Twas not one esteemed by lovers, but a friendship based on mutual respect. Natasha was once my mother's most cherished friend before she became ours. And as far as I know, my father and Natasha were never lovers and never discussed plans to marry each other. They were simply good friends, that is all."

If the girl could defend such an immoral woman, Anna disdainfully mused, then it was obvious she was in dire need of schooling on the proper decorums of society.

Natasha! Anna's brain nearly screamed the woman's name out in bitter hostility. A widow after three husbands and with a whole host of other men chasing after her, eager to be the fourth! The very idea of that woman being so casual with men! Inviting them to her socials as if they were longtime friends . . . or lovers! There is only one name she can be called. Harlot!

"As far as you know," Anna goaded with a tight smile that barely disguised the malice which churned within her.

"As far as I know," Synnovea responded with stilted coolness as she again lowered her gaze to the wine. It was a ploy to hide her emotions, for it was not wise to let the princess read the resentment she was presently attempting to overcome. It would likely set the pair of them at odds within the first few moments of their meeting.

"How long did you say your mother has been dead?" Synnovea replied in a strained whisper. "Five years."

"Speak up, Synnovea!" Anna snapped, ignoring how trite and petulant it might have seemed for one of her standing to act in such an undignified manner, but she had never asked for this girl to come here! She most certainly did not want her here! "I can barely hear what you're saying. And I don't like to be kept waiting for a reply either. You're not backward, or at least you don't appear to be. Therefore, I insist you pay heed to what is being said and be more prompt with your response. Is that too much to ask?"

"As you wish." The reply came readily enough and in clear tones, though Synnovea fought to suppress her own quickening irritations. The princess had grown highly agitated with her, as if thoroughly resenting her defense of Natasha, and now seemed to be venting her spite. Synnovea realized the folly of being drawn into a quarrel with the woman so soon after her arrival, and yet to demur in Natasha's behalf would surely have set Anna totally awry.

"That's better." Anna set her goblet aside and rose to her feet as Boris followed the soldiers down the stairs. As Synnovea set her glass down and followed her example, Anna made haste to dismiss her. "I'm sure you'll want to refresh yourself before the dinner hour. Boris can show you to your chambers."

Knowing there was still an arrangement to be made, Synnovea dared to delay the woman. "I pray a moment more of your time, Princess, if you please."

Anna faced her again with brows sharply heightened over cool, gray eyes. She seemed totally amazed by the younger woman's temerity to demand even a moment of her time. "Yes? What is it?"

"I brought servants with me to attend my needs while I'm here, and I need to arrange a place where they may stay. If you have room here to house them, that will serve my purposes well. My coach and horses should be stabled also, if there is space."

The thin lips twisted in rampant displeasure. "You've taken much upon yourself if you think to keep them here, Synnovea. There's little enough room for your maid in your chambers, without expecting us to house your coachmen and equipage as well. You would be prudent to send them back to Nizhniy Novgorod. We just don't have the space to accommodate them here. Besides, 'tis highly unlikely you'll be needing them while you remain with us."

Synnovea's answer came quickly, just as the woman had bade her to respond, and with a great deal more cordiality than she was presently feeling. "Then if you might allow my coachmen to rest here for the night, I shall make other provisions on the morrow. I should not like to be without my carriage while I'm here and thereby impose an inconvenience upon you when I have a need for their use."

Synnovea fervently desired to live in peace with her new guardians, certainly until that time she could disentangle herself from their protection and become her own mistress, but if it meant being imprisoned within the confines of their home and permitted to venture out only at their whim, she knew she would not be able to endure such restrictions for long. She was not a child, and she did not believe it was Tsar Mikhail's intent for his cousin to treat her like one.

"And just where do you think you'll keep them?" Anna asked caustically.

Though Synnovea perceived beforehand that her suggestion would prick the woman to the core, it was a far more acceptable alternative she was about to present than what Anna had in mind for her. "I'm sure if there's no room for my coachmen and carriage here, the Countess Natasha will permit me to use her stables while I'm here. She lives down the street, only a short distance away."

"I know where she lives!" Anna railed, offended by the girl's efforts to instruct her. Her irritation was sharpened even more by her inability to think of a plausible excuse by which she could fortify an outright denial of the girl's petition. Reluctant though she was to placate her charge in any way, she realized she would have to grant the request, for she knew the folly of testing her cousin's sense of fairness or trying to silence the wagging tongues of gossips. Some people had an uncanny way of delving into clandestine motives and subjecting them to the full light of discovery. Indeed, she would be greatly pained if she had to answer to Tsar Mikhail because of this obtrusive little creature he had sent to live with them.

Finding absolutely no joy in compliance, Anna disguised her retreat as submission to another's authority, though it was rare indeed she acceded to anyone but His Majesty's dictates. Even then, she had a strong aversion to accepting her cousin's will over her own, a fact which she kept carefully to herself. Still, by maintaining a position of stoic reluctance now, she hoped to discourage future confrontations. Aleksei didn't care one whit about the arrangement, but by laying the burden of the decision temporarily on his shoulders, she could grant the girl's request on the morrow and demand proper remunerations be made to compensate for the added expense of housing servants and stabling horses.

"Prince Aleksei will be here for dinner," she finally informed the girl. "He can make the final decision himself whether or not to allow your coachmen to use our facilities while you're here." Having said that, Anna excused herself with a curt nod and stalked off, throwing back over her shoulder, "Boris will see you to your chambers."

Synnovea heaved a long, slow sigh of relief, feeling as if she had just won a horrendous battle, but only by the skin of her teeth. She was beginning to suspect the Princess Anna was going to be even more difficult than she had first surmised. If these last few moments were any indication, she would certainly have cause to worry what the ensuing days and months would bring.

Returning outside, Synnovea gave instructions to her coachmen and left them to find their own way to the stables as she said farewell to Captain Nekrasov and his men. "Thank you for your care and kindly considerations, Nikolai. I hope we shall meet again in the future."

Gallantly Nikolai bestowed a kiss upon her fingers. "Adieu, my fair lady, but I pray not for long."

Synnovea swallowed against a restricting tightness in her throat as he looked at her for the first time with visible longing. She could not respond, for she had no way of knowing what the morrow would bring. "Take care, Nikolai . . . *druga*, my friend."

"I am honored by your friendship, Synnovea. Perhaps we shall meet again . . . and soon. It would give me great pleasure to see you . . . now and then."

Lightly touching two fingers to her lips, Synnovea reached out and pressed those same against his lean cheek. "Even if we are destined never to cross paths again, Nikolai, remember that I shall value you as a man worthy of my trust. His Majesty did me great service by sending you to accompany me here. I am truly indebted."

Synnovea stepped away before Nikolai could make further comment and waved to the soldiers, who grinned back at her and responded in kind. Turning from them, she helped Ali inside and supported the maid with an arm wrapped securely about her thin waist as they made their ascent up the stairs to the suite of rooms Boris led them to. As the steward withdrew, Synnovea heard Captain Nekrasov call out an order to his men and went to the front window, where she leaned against the frame and watched them swing astride their mounts. A moment later, a rattle of hooves marked their departure down the road.

With a pensive sigh Synnovea faced the chambers wherein she would be housed while under the wardship of the Princess Anna and her husband, Prince Aleksei. A trio of candelabrums gave light to the rooms, and even within their radiance, she could find no fault in the accommodations given her. A tiny cubicle just off the bedchamber was furnished with a narrow bed and the basic essentials to meet Ali's needs. The main bedchamber was spacious and comfortably furnished with a velvet chaise, several large chests adorned with silver closures, a pair of dainty chairs set at a small table for private dining, and a great canopied bed draped with red velvet and golden hangings of heavy silk. The accommodations were fit for royalty, but at the moment Synnovea felt much like an impoverished pauper within their opulence.

Insisting upon Ali's complete recovery, Synnovea led the maidservant into the narrow cubicle and bade her to rest until the other servants were called to eat.

Blowing out the tapers in the small compartment, Synnovea pushed open a narrow window to catch the cooling evening breezes and then withdrew to her own bedchamber, closing the door quietly behind her. There, Synnovea doffed her clothes and poured water into a basin to wash away the sticky grime of the day's passage. When the bath was concluded, she wrapped a long robe about her naked body, snuffed out the candles, and then collapsed in pure exhaustion upon the chaise. She felt both physically and mentally drained. Anna's formidable moods had exacted a heavy toll both on her energies and peace of mind. She needed solace and rest from the ordeal of their meeting, yet as she reclined on the pillows, sleep seemed as elusive as the legendary firebird Tsar Ivan had searched for in a Russian fable. Her mind wandered far afield, lingering momentarily on the servants she had left behind to tend her home and the myriad questions they had presented about her expected return, which had been beyond her ability to answer. In the event that she should soon marry and go to live in her husband's home, she would have to decide whether to dismiss the staff and dispense with the house, or to keep them for the purpose of providing her and her husband with seasonal escapes.

In greater detail Synnovea mulled over the fears and trepidations she had battled after receiving the tsar's message. Her apprehensions had not been based so much on the realization that Anna was his cousin and touted to be his favorite. Some close to the monarch had dared speculate that it was the princess herself who had made such a claim, since her kinship to Tsar Mikhail was considered distant, at best. After all, Anna had only recently moved to Moscow from the small province wherein she had grown up, and Tsar Mikhail had been sequestered for most of his life in a monastery where his mother had found a safe haven from the dark plots, schemes, and intrigue of ambitious *boyars*. It seemed a simple fact that whatever their bond, Anna and Tsar Mikhail had not

been able to share any measure of time together in the
years past, lending doubts to their deep regard for one
another.

Still, it was not the relationship of the two which worried Synnovea, but rather Anna's frequent displays of
animosity, which had been evident at their first meeting, when she had treated Natasha like some kind of
vile vermin. Now, with Anna's most recent insinuations
about Natasha roiling in retrospect through her memory, Synnovea was hard-pressed to think kindly of the
princess.

Stuffing the pillows beneath her head as she curled on
her side to face the door, Synnovea continued with her
pensive musings. Natasha had socialized with affluent
boyars for many years, but Anna had obviously failed
to recognize her as a person of any import. In light
of the princess's close association with Ivan Voronsky,
Synnovea was wont to wonder if the cleric had instigated
Anna's rebuff of the Countess Natasha. Earlier in the year
Natasha had reproved the man for his gauche manners
in insulting one of her guests and had kindly advised
him to be more considerate in the future. Having clearly
discerned his overt contempt for anyone who was not
immediately appreciative of his every thought and deed,
Synnovea could well imagine the scope of his complaints
to those who would lend a sympathetic ear, which quali-
fied Anna exactly.

As for Prince Aleksei, Synnovea had heard it discreetly
whispered that he had a roaming eye, which purportedly
was prone to wander to maidens much younger than
his wife. For years the blame of a barren womb had
been laid upon Anna, but of late, gossips were more
inclined to surmise the judgment against the princess
had been unfair since it was widely suspected that Prince
Aleksei had scattered his seed among a whole battery
of virgins whose reputations had never been publicly
compromised by evidence of his adulterous propensities.
Synnovea had found such hearsay greatly disturbing, for

she had no idea what she would have to face once she became ensconced in the Taraslov home. It was one thing to vie with Princess Anna, but quite another to be raped by an amorous lecher.

For a time, it seemed impossible for Synnovea to calm her rambling thoughts, but finally she was able to sleep and give rest to her troubled mind. It was only a brief respite, however, for it seemed to Synnovea as if she had barely fallen asleep before she was again being awakened. But by what? Her mind roamed in a detached search for the cause of her disturbance. She could not remember hearing a sound. It seemed almost as if she had sensed something, something she could not quite lay a finger to.

From beneath the weight of sluggish lids, the jade-green eyes wandered in a drowsy inspection of the dark red ceiling, which seemed to loom close above her. A brighter shaft of light stretched across her heavenly vista, making it seem strange and foreign. It reached to the wall to her right, which was decorated with thin, ornate flourishes that gleamed golden in the soft beacon. Languidly Synnovea lifted a hand to test the bright ray and thought it strange that only the tips of her fingers caught the glow, and they, in turn, were cast in similar form against the wall.

Synnovea's brows gathered as she grew more perplexed. Where the light cast a shadow upon her hand and the wall behind it, the two shapes coalesced into a strangely familiar configuration, much like the head and shoulders of a man.

The shadow moved, and Synnovea gasped in sudden astonishment, realizing the shade was no figment of her imagination. Coming upright on the chaise, she swung around toward the door and, to her surprise, saw that the portal had been pushed open while she slumbered. A tall manly form was silhouetted against the light that streamed in from the hallway, but as she watched, the intruder stepped casually beyond the doorway to the left and, with muffled tread, disappeared from sight.

Synnovea understood clearly what the man had been staring at when she glanced down at her exposed limbs. Feeling her cheeks burn with an indignant blush, she snatched the silken robe tightly about her, covering her bare limbs and unbound breasts against the chance of further perusals as she jumped up and ran barefoot to the door.

She braced against the frame as she cautiously leaned through the opening and peered up and down the hall. No evidence remained of anyone having been there, not even the quickly shuffling footsteps to verify another's dispatch in fleeing the corridor. Heavy sconces hung in pairs here and there on the walls that buttressed the hallway, and their squat tapers provided enough light to dispel any shadows. Across the passageway to her left, a door stood ajar, opening onto a room that was as dark as the night outside.

The man had to be hiding there, Synnovea concluded with a shiver of fear, for she had given him no time to flee downstairs. If he waited there for her to either follow or return to her room, it seemed prudent to forestall the possibility of their confrontation by locking her door and bracing a chair against its sturdy plank, just for good measure. Thus, Synnovea secured her safety and, for the benefit of dissuading anyone within close proximity from testing the latch, slid the bar home quite noisily.

Synnovea had no real doubt as to the identity of the lecher, though it chilled her heart considerably to think that, in a matter of a few hours since her arrival, she had not only been confronted by a rather formidable Princess Anna but, while she slept, had been rudely ogled by a most notorious debaucher of women. Prince Aleksei Taraslov!

Chapter 5

SECURE BEHIND THE BOLTED DOOR OF HER CHAMBERS, Synnovea carefully prepared herself for her first evening inside the Taraslov manse. As much as she considered prostrating herself before Tsar Mikhail and begging him to release her from this prison he had inadvertently created for her, it would not be wise to do so. She would only expose herself to harsh criticisms. If not from him, then surely from Princess Anna and Prince Aleksei, who would not look with compassion on her complaints. They would resent any airing of grievances that would make them seem less than worthy of the tsar's trust, and who could predict what they would do or say to save face? They could twist her petitions to their liking, possibly causing severe judgments to be leveled against her. Very simply, she might be maligned as an ungrateful chit, completely intractable and hopelessly self-willed. It was therefore crucial that she hold her peace and endure whatever hardships might arise until that moment she gained her freedom.

Her situation was not unlike being on a field of battle, Synnovea decided in gloomy retrospect, for there existed no place of quiet rest where she could savor a sense of serenity or security. Perhaps a soothsayer possessed the ability to predict what lay in store for her while she was under the guardianship of the Taraslovs, but her perception was limited to the present moment. She only knew

that while she remained in their house, she would have
to be wary of both Anna and Aleksei. Letting down her
defenses would be sheer folly. She could not trust either
of them, even for the briefest moment. To survive intact,
she would have to exercise sharp cunning as her armor
of defense and bolster her flanks with care, prudence,
and great patience, all the while praying fervently such
precautions would be enough. Perhaps then, she would
somehow prevail and remain unscathed until that day
when she would be released from their custody.

Firm in her newly formed resolve, Synnovea clothed
herself in the traditional garments of a Russian maiden,
hoping in this way to guard against Aleksei's rudely
prying eyes and perhaps even avoid Anna's disfavor.
If the princess's preferences could be judged by Ivan's
biased convictions, Synnovea mused, then she was better
off by far wearing the customary attire of her homeland.

Over a ribbon-trimmed underskirt and a shirtwaist
fashioned with full, billowy sleeves, she donned a
sarafan of rich ruby satin elaborately embroidered with
threads of silk that matched the rich sapphire hue of
the blouse. Upon this stitchery, an ornate overlay of
gilded threads had been sewn to enrich the artistry
of the piece, copying the pattern of the tiny, gilded
flowers that embellished the blouse. Low-heeled slippers of blue were bedecked with the same needlework
and were further adorned with a wedge of gold around
the sole. Her long, lustrous black hair was intertwined
with sapphire ribbon and woven into a single braid,
as was the Russian custom for an unwed maid. Upon
her head, she settled a rounded *kokoshniki* formed in
the shape of a crescent, upon which tiny jewels and
beads of blue and red shimmered amid the elaborate
needlework. Lastly she fastened on earrings of finely
worked gold filigree set with delicate clusters of tiny
rubies.

When the last bow was tied and the last clasp fastened,
Synnovea assessed the results in a long, silvered looking

glass, a luxury she had enjoyed at her own home and was very grateful to have here. In judging herself ready to join the three downstairs, she did not consider the possibility that she might have dismissed her comeliness far too lightly and casually disregarded the enhancement of her beauty by the rich clothes. It had been far from her intent to achieve such a stunning radiance that she would provoke entirely diverse reactions among her companions, yet upon entering the great hall, Synnovea realized her blunder and chided herself for not having had the foresight to wear something akin to the dark, hooded cape of a hermit monk ere she deigned to join the three.

The sly, seductive narrowing of Aleksei's eyes and the ebullient smile that curved his generous lips readily evoked an impression in Synnovea's mind of a snake pursuing a bird, clearly for the purpose of devouring it. A glance toward Anna caught the woman just as a sharp frown of jealousy was being forced beneath a stiffly fixed smile of greeting. No words parted the grimacing lips, but the prince proved himself more vocal.

"My dear Countess Synnovea," Aleksei murmured warmly as he stepped forward to take her hand and to cradle its slender length between both of his. Garbed in a red silk *kaftan* bedecked with golden embroidery, he looked like some bronze-skinned sheik from the deserts of Arabia. His warm brown eyes glowed with provocative fervor as they held her gaze in a commanding vise. Beneath a carefully groomed mustache, his red lips widened into a sultry smile. "I had nigh forgotten how lovely you are, my dear. You look as enchanting as the elegant swan who favors us with her beauty."

A barrage of accusations tempted Synnovea's tongue, and though her eyes chilled briefly to indicate her displeasure with his unabashed invasion of her privacy, she wisely held her silence. She was not above purloining some subtle revenge, however. Utilizing the same skill she had employed with foreign dignitaries who had forgotten themselves and become too brash or obtrusive, Synnovea gracefully extricated her hand from his, forbidding him the opportunity to kiss the long, pale fingers as she opened a bejeweled fan between them. Cleverly she denied his compliments as well, aware that Anna was regarding them with cold, hard enmity frozen in her eyes. Being the main recipient of that chilling glower, Synnovea could well understand in that moment what it felt like to be hated intensely by another woman.

"I am humbled that you bestow such words of charity upon me, Prince Aleksei." She feigned a doleful look of regret. "Though sweet succor to my ears, I fear your kindness is exceeded only by your pity for me."

Her gentle scolding brought a smile of amiable humor to Aleksei's sensuous lips. If he recognized the vexation in her distant manner, it served but to whet his appetite even more. He was intrigued by her spirit, for he had oft derived ecstatic pleasures from conquests made on the most reluctant virgins and from their subsequent compliance to his every whim. Because of the accessibility of her tremendous beauty, this particular maid promised to be exceptionally sweet provender upon which, with frequent tenure, his ravenous passions could indulge. Her grace and charm would no doubt lend great satisfaction to the tryst, at least more than any he had recently savored.

Aleksei met Synnovea's aloof stare, while his own smoldering gaze promised a most affectionate and fervent seduction. He was confident of achieving his goal. What woman could long resist his amorous attentions and hawkish good looks? His black hair, streaked with gray at the temples, and his warm, swarthy complexion enhanced his handsome features and accentuated his appeal, even with a total of two score three years behind him. As he leaned toward Synnovea, his husky whisper conveyed an unfaltering boldness as he inquired, "Are you really so innocent of your marvelous beauty and its effect on men, Synnovea?"

"Good sir, you would turn a girl's head with your kindness!" Synnovea admonished, recognizing the challenge in his gaze. It seemed he only waited for her to take up the gauntlet before he launched an attack.

"Kindness?" He laughed warmly. "Oh, nay! 'Tis infatuation, pure and simple."

Feeling threatened by his temerity, Synnovea lifted the fan higher to flick it before her hotly burning cheeks. She could understand more fully why his reputation had preceded him. He applied his beguiling enticements with the crafty art of a true philanderer and boldly advanced his exploits with unmitigated verve and unswerving alacrity. He seemed not the least bit inhibited by his wife's presence, but was brazenly forward, showing little regard for her feelings, while he forced their guest to strike down his bombastic overtures and parry his comments in such a way as to deflect the sharp blade of Anna's resentment.

Synnovea rose to the challenge of accomplishing such a feat, for she was just as determined not to fall victim to his lascivious gambits, nor would she allow him to entertain for even a moment the idea that she would become just another willing diversion for him. Circumventing his pranks, she answered adroitly, deliberately drawing Anna into the contest. "No need to extend your mercy to the extreme, my lord. Though I can well see the high degree of beauty I must be judged by, I am quite resolved to endure the shortcomings of this poor flask you see before you, knowing 'tis far beyond my capability to hold a candle to Anna, who would shame the very sun with her radiance."

Aleksei drew back to stare with a jaundiced eye at his glowering wife and managed a brief twitch of a smile. "Why, of course," he replied with a dearth of enthusiasm, then allowed himself to be more magnanimous. "I suppose 'tis like the gem that is too close at hand."

"Sometimes," Anna interjected in glacial tones, barely moving her tensed lips, "the rare jewel is overlooked when a more colorful, yet far less worthy bauble attracts the eye."

Ivan came from the windows where he had been all but obscured by the shadows and gave Synnovea a lengthy perusal that was by no means intended as a compliment. "Why, Countess, I'm greatly heartened by the fact that you've regarded the garments of your homeland suitable to wear. I thought you were averse to them."

"On the contrary," Synnovea answered carefully, cognizant of his penchant for degrading those who, in his mind, held no special place of import. "I simply had no desire to see such treasures ruined by the journey."

"Surely, you had less extravagant attire to wear while traveling," Ivan argued, revelling in the power afforded him by the disfavor Anna had already demonstrated toward the girl. It seemed a simple feat to extract his revenge at every turn of the hand and still remain a saint in the eyes of the princess.

Aleksei interceded in Synnovea's behalf, well aware of the hostility she had fallen prey to. He disregarded as irrelevant the fact that his wayward predilections were primarily to blame for his wife's animosity. For the most part he ignored Anna's temper tantrums and only visited her bed when no other distractions were conveniently at hand. Like most women, she found it hard to resist his lustful bent, but her penchant for nagging usually drove him off in hot pursuit of unexplored territories.

"Synnovea is fortunate to be so well traveled. I'm sure if she wore such a costume in England she would fall prey to a variety of envious and equally critical stares. As she has already clearly demonstrated, she has become well versed in both cultures and is just as comfortable in our *sarafans* as in those horribly stiff English ruffs." He turned to Synnovea as he continued. "I do applaud your diversity, my dear. You are clearly young enough to be pliable to a variety of changes."

Anna gritted her teeth in a badly feigned smile as her husband lifted a purposefully dull gaze to her glare. It maddened her no small degree to see his dark brow raise challengingly. If he did not escape the manse, as was his habit to do at late hours, she promised herself to take him to task for flaunting the youth of their ward so blatantly in her face.

Boris entered the room to announce that a *zakuski* had been laid out in honor of the guests and then promptly withdrew as Anna faced Ivan and Synnovea. "I'm sure by now you are both famished and no doubt thoroughly exhausted from your recent encounter with those horrible thieves." She ignored Aleksei's start of surprise and continued with her carefully delivered ruse of concern. She was anxious to air her displeasure with her husband in the privacy of her chambers and made the necessary excuses for a speedy withdrawal. "I shall endeavor to remember your great weariness and not delay you overlong with my chattering."

Having presented to them the opportunity for an early retirement, Anna led the way into the dining hall, but not without directing a warning glower over her shoulder as Aleksei fell in behind Synnovea. There, he could content his nefarious urges with a closely attentive eye upon the younger woman's gracefully swaying hips.

They stood around a small side table to partake of the *zakuski* of caviar, ham, sardines, the lean pork sausage called *balyk*, and other delectable selections often served before the main meal. In making his way to the table, Aleksei deliberately passed near the girl to savor the soft, elusive fragrance of English violets that drifted from her before halting near his wife. Boris laid out an intricately woven bread basket filled with slices of freshly baked *khlebny* and poured a lemon-flavored vodka for the men and a milder wild black cherry *chereunikyna* for the ladies.

Pausing briefly to accept a piece of bread heaped with a generous portion of caviar from his wife, Aleksei stood back with his libation and availed himself of the opportunity to question their new charge. "What is this about thieves, Synnovea? Am I to believe you were accosted by renegades on your journey?"

Synnovea opened her mouth to reply, but Anna hastened to interrupt with her own version. "A ghastly tale of murder and mayhem." The princess shook her head almost sorrowfully as a long, dismal sigh slipped from her. "Poor Ivan was fortunate to escape with his life. And dear Synnovea, why 'tis absolutely inappropriate to say what that horrible thieving wretch claimed from her after he seized her and rode off into the forest. . . . "

Synnovea gaped at the woman, feeling thoroughly victimized by the suggestive statement. The coy smile that rested on Anna's lips was benign, though the hard, flint-gray eyes glinted piercingly, openly displaying the malice she intended with her insinuations. Her motives seemed simple enough to her young guest. Beyond a mere ploy to embarrass and cause her undue shame, Synnovea was sure the other woman's goal was to forestall any attempt her husband might make to engorge his insatiable lusts upon yet another virgin. Though she cared not a whit about satisfying Aleksei's prurient aspirations, Synnovea certainly had no desire to see her name deliberately sullied by the maliciousness of another.

Aleksei looked between the two women, clearly taken aback by his wife's revelation. "What is this? Dear child, have you been offended by those ruffians?"

"I fear the tale has been much enlivened by hearsay, my lord," Synnovea replied with a dexterity she hardly felt capable of, at least at the moment. She tossed a covert glower toward Ivan, where she laid the blame for the spawning of this latest infraction, and explained with care, "There is no need for alarm. I was saved from ravishment by the timely appearance of a commander of His Majesty's Hussars. Were Colonel Rycroft here, I'm sure he would attest to my claims, which he will no doubt set down in a report to the tsar."

Aleksei leaned back in his chair, obviously more at ease now. Though a self-proclaimed gallant, he had always prided himself in the care he had taken to avoid those grim maladies associated with indiscriminately lewd activities. His own father had suffered many ills and woes stemming from the disease until finally, amid excruciating agony and frenzied hallucinations, the man had ended his own life. Even to this day, Aleksei was haunted by the memory of that wild-eyed, slavering being slicing his own throat. Nearly overwhelmed as a young man by the horror of that ghastly sight, he had vowed with a solemn oath that he would never let himself fall prey to that kind of dark, pernicious scourge. It was exceedingly more comforting and gratifying to mount the tender, pristine thighs of a virgin and, for a time, expend his lusts upon her until he would eventually grow bored enough to seek other diversions.

"And this colonel?" Aleksei directed his attention to the dark-haired beauty. "He was perhaps the one who escorted you here?"

"Captain Nekrasov was appointed that task by His Imperial Highness," Synnovea informed him. "The one who actually came to my aid is an Englishman in service to the tsar. He was on practice maneuvers in the area with his men when he happened upon my halted carriage and put the thieves to rout."

"An Englishman!" Anna exclaimed, aghast at the idea that a foreigner could claim such rank in Russia. "What is my cousin thinking of to incorporate an Englishman in his troops?! Or is this more of his father's doings? Patriarch Filaret will have us all killed in our beds by bringing foreign mercenaries into the city!"

"My dear, how can you speak of the good patriarch like that?" Aleksei mocked.

"Ivan can tell you! Filaret has assumed the powers of the tsar through his son. His ambitions have asserted themselves beyond the duties of patriarch. Indeed! He would sit on the throne in place of his son if not for the fact that Boris Godunov forced him to become a monk to save his own tsardom."

Aleksei scowled darkly at the cleric who conveniently addressed his attention to the food. "Such talk is dangerous, Anna, and you know as well as I do that His Majesty has no real interest in ruling Russia without his father's counsel. His negotiation for peace with Poland was not only to gain an armistice, but to obtain the release of Filaret as well. True, the treaty cost us a number of Russian towns and cities, yet it gained us a far more valuable asset, I think. Patriarch Filaret Nikitich has the wisdom to make the right decision for our country. If he has brought foreigners here to secure our peace and train our troops, I can find no fault against the man for wanting to strengthen our capabilities and defense. They need to be!"

"What are you saying, Aleksei? This Colonel Rycroft is an Englishman!" Anna seemed amazed that her husband could lightly accept such a notion.

Synnovea rallied to the colonel's defense, not entirely sure why she should feel so offended in his behalf. "That rogue, Ladislaus, made light of the abilities of the tsar's men until Colonel Rycroft confronted his pack of wolves, and then the thief had to lament the loss of those brought down by the colonel's sword. I, for one, am most appreciative of the Englishman and his skill, for I would not be here enjoying the safety of your house if not for him."

Anna mentally sneered at her statement and rejoined in genteel aloofness. "Of course, my dear, you would be grateful for such a one. After all, your mother was English, but other *boyarinas* would be more discriminating than to value the presence of a foreigner." Her mouth curved in a sagacious smile as she made the conjecture, "I suppose you found the colonel attractive."

"Not particularly," Synnovea replied stiffly, somewhat miffed that Anna could suggest that her feelings of appreciation could be inspired by the handsomeness of a man. "In truth, Captain Nekrasov was much more pleasing in appearance, though not quite as daring with a sword. I valued the captain's attendance, but he was given no opportunity to save me."

"Such a fortuitous occasion might be construed as divine providence, unless by chance there was a weightier hand guiding events," Anna needled. "It was fortunate indeed that this Englishman was near enough to come to your aid." She smiled cunningly as she added, "And as you declare, just in the nick of time. Perhaps he was only waiting there to advance your appreciation of his exploits."

Synnovea countered with uncompromising fervor. "In light of the danger the man was in, I can find no evidence to support any insinuation that would suggest he had somehow arranged the attack for his own gain. 'Tis simply inconceivable. He nearly laid down the highest price a man can possibly pay for my rescue. I, for one, am overwhelmingly grateful for having escaped those brigands unscathed and equally relieved that Colonel Rycroft came through it alive."

Anna bestowed her regard upon Ivan, who was cramming a caviar-stuffed pancake into his mouth with such greed, one was wont to wonder if he intended to embark upon a long fast within the next several days. "Was that the way you perceived it, good Voronsky?"

The beady eyes flicked upward in surprise and momentarily fastened on the princess, then realizing an answer was expected, he worked his lean jaw vigorously to dispense with the large mass in his mouth. Swallowing hard, Ivan washed it all down with an ample swig of vodka, then shot a glance toward Synnovea to find himself the object of her curiosity. Wiping the back of his hand across his mouth, he cleared his throat and spoke for once in agreement with her, knowing she could name him a liar if he dared dispute her words. " 'Tis much as the Countess Synnovea has said." He noticed a spark of irritation in the silver eyes and hastened to mollify the princess. "However, 'tis not possible for any of us to discern what was in the heart of the Englishman. He was rather brutal in his assault on the thieves."

"What?" Synnovea was incredulous. "Sir! Are you suggesting that Colonel Rycroft should have treated them like errant children and slapped their wrists or perhaps waited to launch his attack until they had actually killed one of us? From the rumors I've heard, thieving bands like Ladislaus's very rarely show compassion for their victims. They seize and slay, whether or nay a man be noble or common born. I say we are lucky to have escaped alive! And as to that, I'm sure you have cause to remember Petrov threatening you with dire consequences unless you gave him more coin to appease his greed."

Ivan validated her claim, seeing his chance to derive a greater measure of concern from his benefactress. "And quite violently so. The giant oaf would have thought nothing about taking my life."

Aleksei considered the cleric with a slyly malevolent smile. "I see no scars from your encounter, Ivan. Positively, you seem in right good health and of superior appetite. I daresay, we shall be enjoying your company for many a meal yet."

A deep red blush stained Ivan's pockmarked face as he felt the other man's gibe. The prince was immensely fond of casting aspersions indiscriminately upon his poor frame, perhaps because they both knew from whom he could garner protection. Being favored by Anna certainly had its reward. Her presence guaranteed him impunity from physical aggression, which gave him a wide measure of prideful arrogance. He was not above flaunting his position over the prince or even needling him about it now and then. Actually, the idea seemed quite appealing, and a superior smile touched his thin lips as Ivan yielded to the temptation. "As it seems now, Prince, you will undoubtedly be seeing more of me."

"Oh?" Aleksei's dark brows jutted sharply upward as he awaited the man's explanation.

"The princess has wisely prescribed a daily tutoring of your new charge."

"What?" The single word came unbidden from Synnovea's lips, and she turned to stare aghast at the princess, appalled by Ivan's announcement. "You don't mean to say that you've engaged this . . . this . . ."

"Countess Synnovea!" Anna snapped sharply, halting the flow of words that threatened to rush forth from the astonished woman. "Remember your place!"

Synnovea drew herself up in rigid silence, daring no further utterance while she bristled with outrage. This was not a situation she could passively endure for very long, and her mind ranged far afield, searching for some avenue of escape, for it was clear in her mind that she would not be able to cope with Ivan on a diurnal basis. Their journey to Moscow had assured her of that!

Anna studied the younger woman with cool reserve. " 'Tis well that you've been sent to me for instruction, Synnovea," she remarked condescendingly. "You've obviously been much coddled by your father and have been allowed to nurture some rather unpleasant tendencies. That will cease, of course. I will not tolerate boorish manners . . . or an argumentive disposition. If you are wise, my dear, you will quickly learn to curb those inclinations. Do you understand?"

It was apparent to Synnovea that any protestations she might be tempted to make would be promptly considered of a quarrelsome nature. Being thus warned against speaking her mind, she could think of naught to say in her own defense, though inwardly she continued to stew.

The pleased smirk that Ivan wore gave evidence of his own satisfaction as he witnessed what was, in his mind, a well-deserved subjugation of the countess. He was just as eager to heap burning coals of fire upon the back of the hapless victim. "You may trust that my directions will be most thorough, Princess. I will address myself with great diligence to polishing her manners."

Aleksei seemed immensely pained by such a prospect. "Surely this is some kind of jest, Anna. Synnovea has no need of more tutoring. From what I've heard she's been well enlightened by some of the very best mentors in this country and abroad, even as much as I have been. You can't possibly mean to prolong this arduous climb to erudition."

"The girl needs instruction in the rigors of life and conventional decorums." Anna voiced her opinion obstinately, daring any to challenge her decision.

"Damned nuisance, if you ask me!" her husband retorted. Slamming down his glass, he turned with a harsh frown and, without making excuse or explanation, stalked to the pair of doors leading into the hall and threw them open.

"Where are you going?" Anna demanded, sensing that she was about to be denied his company for yet another evening.

"Out!" Prince Aleksei halted within the hall and, bracing his arms akimbo, bellowed for the steward. "Boris!"

A patter of rushing footsteps was heard in the waiting hush that followed his summons, and the white-haired servant breathlessly made an appearance. "Here I am, sir."

Facing the man, Aleksei continued in the same thundering tones. "Hie yourself out to the stable and tell Orlov to ready my *drozhki* with my fastest horses. I'll be going out this evening."

"Immediately, sir?"

"Would I urge you to such haste if I had the patience to wait for our guests to dine?" Aleksei questioned sharply. "Of course I mean immediately!"

"As you wish, sir."

Synnovea lifted her gaze to find Anna staring rigidly toward the place where, only a moment before, her husband had stood. The typically pale cheeks were now imbued with a vibrant shade of red. Otherwise, except for a small tick in her left eye, she appeared to have taken on the rigidity of stone.

Even Ivan dared no further comment, and the meal was soon entered and stoically endured. Synnovea was completely distraught over the idea of Ivan becoming her tutor, and though she would have savored each course under normal circumstances, the roasted grouse with its cranberry sauce seemed as tasteless to her as the flaky pastry stuffed with steamed asparagus and dressed with a light cheese sauce. Ivan was profuse with his compliments to Elisaveta, the cook, and devoured every morsel with equal gusto, amazing Synnovea, who watched in some awe as he ate. His slight frame seemed inadequate to handle the amount he consumed, and she wondered how it was possible for him to accomplish such a feat.

When the meal came thankfully to an end, the two guests retreated to their respective chambers. The Princess Anna was left to make her own way to the rooms which she shared far too infrequently with Aleksei. Even their arguments were more tolerable than the loneliness that greeted her and the wild imaginings of her mind that placed her husband in the arms of another woman.

The night proved as wearisome for Synnovea as the journey she had just endured. She found nothing within the stuffy shadows of her bedchamber to assuage her apprehensions, for she could only foresee doom in the days and weeks ahead. If there was one thing Ivan seemed accomplished at, it was provoking her temper, and how in the world would she be able to sustain a quiet, gentle manner under such arduous conditions? She would be defeated ere she even began!

Synnovea tossed restlessly upon her bed, unable to sleep while her mind raged on in a state of turmoil. It was only when her thoughts drifted unbidden to

Colonel Rycroft that she was strangely lulled into a peaceful slumber as her musings drifted back to that moment when he had held her close to his sleek, wet body.

Chapter 6

THE HEAT OF THE NIGHT WAS OPPRESSIVE, HOLDING THE land in a stagnant vise until the morning sun lifted its burning face above the horizon and unleashed its sweltering heat far beyond the vales and hillocks that surrounded the city. Even at an early hour, the dusty roads seemed to shimmer in undulating waves beneath the full light of the heavenly fireball, and those that could, took shelter where they found it, whether in grand manses or beneath the lackluster trees that struggled for survival.

Oblivious to the insidious warmth that was creeping through the house, Ali rose from her tiny cot, much refreshed after a long, restful night's sleep. She busied herself in the narrow room, bathing, dressing, and unpacking her belongings until, finally, sounds of movement came from the larger chamber. With a quick knock and a cheery smile, she bustled into the room, then halted abruptly, seeing her mistress sitting up in bed with an elbow braced upon a knee, staring listlessly out the window. The solemn countenance of the young woman hinted of a troubled spirit, and Ali laid a consoling hand upon the slender arm, thinking she knew the reason for the countess's dismay. "Ah, lamb, be ye mournin' again for yer pa?"

Though Synnovea forced a smile to reassure the elder, the sparkle of tears in her eyes readily betrayed her pensive mood, and with a wistful sigh she replied, "If I'd been wise, Ali, I would have eagerly sought marriage while Papa was still alive, then I wouldn't be here now, contending with the dictates of these strangers."

The maid sensed something was truly amiss. She had not been with her mistress all these many years without learning to perceive her moods. "Me lamb, have the Taraslovs been unkind ter ye?"

Synnovea dared not reveal the extent of her concerns. The maid was too loyal to keep still for a lecher spying on her and would not abide such debauchery as what the prince had in mind. Nor, for that matter, would Ali take kindly to the idea of the princess engaging Ivan as her tutor. Still, that single fact could not be hidden with a veil of secrecy like the others, for it was about to become part of her daily routine.

"I was in error, Ali, when I thought we would soon be parted from Ivan," she carefully stated. She saw the woman's brows raise sharply in suspicion and, with a small shrug, explained, "He is to instruct me while I'm here. Anna has declared it so."

"Ye don't say!" The diminutive woman set her fists firmly on her narrow hips and snorted in contempt. "An' what would the little weasel be teachin' ye? How ter hide from yer left hand what yer right one be doin'? Aaarrgghh!" She shook her head in acute disgust. "I've had a bad feelin' in me bones 'bout him. Beneath those dark robes, he's lackin' a charitable heart, 'at he is!"

"Nevertheless, Ali, we must endure his presence in silence, lest we provoke the princess. I fear she dotes upon the man." A darkly winged brow raised in question as Synnovea met the tiny woman's gaze. "Do you understand?"

"Aye, that I do, me lovely. Still, if the Princess Anna is imposin' his teachin' on ye, what must she be thinkin' herself? He's not so hard ter see through, if'n a body be carin' ter take a good look. Makes me wonder if'n she has all her wits about her."

"I suppose we'll understand in time what Anna sees in him. Until then, give her no cause to take us to task, and I will try my best to keep my wits about me and refrain from telling Ivan what I think of him." The corners of Synnovea's lips lifted puckishly as an idea came to her. "Though I might be able to plead a few days' rest ere my studies begin."

A mischievous gleam brightened her eyes as she again raised a meaningful brow to the servant who, catching her intent, responded with a little, gleeful cackle and a sprightly jig. "Ter be sure, me lovely! Ye're deservin' as much, comin' all the way from Nizhniy Novgorod in such a dither. An' bein' attacked by thieves, ter boot! Why, 'tis a wonder ye've endured this long without faintin' away."

And so the two plotted to confound the schemes of the Princess Anna, at least for the day. When well assured that the household was up and moving about and tending to Anna's needs, Synnovea sent down the excuse by way of the Irish maid, conveying the message that she was temporarily indisposed with a headache and would be unable to address her attention to Ivan's instructions. It was not entirely a lie Synnovea concocted, for every time she thought of being forced to study Ivan's views, her head began to ache, and knowing full well that it would cause her great travail to persevere through his daily counsel, she decided she needed some time to herself to bolster her spirits. Most of all she feared the reins by which she held her temper closely in check would be tested far beyond reason, and she knew if she became entangled in a direct dispute with the man, Anna would be tempted to respond unkindly. It was better by far to make excuses for the moment and let the other woman question the validity of her plea than to court absolute disaster outright.

Feigning a doleful sympathy, Ali carried Synnovea's regrets to the princess, giving the explanation that the journey had proven too strenuous for her mistress and that it might take a day or two for Synnovea to fully recuperate. Anna had to accept the excuse or confront her charge openly and accuse Synnovea of falsehood, and though she was tempted to march straight to the younger woman's chambers and question her, just to establish her authority, she thought better of it and decided to bide her time for at least the day, then she would see what the girl's manner would be. Anna smirked to herself in satisfaction. It would indeed be a miracle if the countess was able to tolerate her chambers the whole day long.

Ensconced upstairs, Synnovea was not made cognizant of how narrowly she escaped the Princess Anna's interrogation, but by mid-afternoon she began to question her own rationale for avoiding Ivan's lectures at such great discomfort to herself. Whether someone with a vicious bent planned it deliberately or the location of her rooms had never been given serious consideration, she became totally convinced that there was no place in the whole manse hotter than her chambers at that particular time of the day. After the day-star reached its zenith, her rooms, situated on the west side of the house where they would naturally catch all the heat of the afternoon, became a sweltering oven. In winter the chambers might prove comfortable, but they were extremely unbearable under the cruel, flaming tongues of the summer sun.

In debating her alternatives, Synnovea realized there were none she cared to take. She could not easily seek escape from her chambers without drawing some inquiry or challenge from Anna, and she refused to give the woman that satisfaction. Thus, to better cope with the heat, she lounged about in a thin shift that soon became a transparent film over her perspiring skin. Ali pushed the windows wide to allow the warm, sultry breezes to flow through the rooms, but the scorching heat was unrelenting while the sun still hovered high in the sky. Seeking a way to combat the discomfort her mistress was suffering, Ali went down to the kitchen and persuaded Elisaveta to let her fetch ice from the supply that had been stored in the cellar the winter before. She brought back a large chunk to the upper rooms and, after breaking it apart in smaller pieces and securing them in a linen towel, gave the compress over into the welcoming hands of her mistress, who was anxious for any relief. Heaving a long sigh of pleasure, Synnovea rubbed the cooling towel over her bare skin, leaving refreshing wet trails when the ice began to soak through the cloth.

No longer able to bear the stuffy, breathless warmth of the room, Synnovea perched on a windowsill where a small tree shaded it from the sun and afforded her privacy from the road. She settled herself cross-legged upon the ledge and lazily stroked the damp cloth along her arms as she observed the comings and goings of passersby urgently intent upon completing their jaunts and finding shade. Too annoyed by their own discomfort to concern themselves with her obscure presence, those who ventured forth soon retreated from sight, leaving the thoroughfare virtually empty.

Leaning her head back against the frame, Synnovea laid the ice-laden towel around her neck and closed her eyes as she allowed her thoughts to roam homeward. Losing herself in comforting daydreams, she could almost smell the breezes that wafted from the rivers near Nizhniy Novgorod. She even fancied that she heard the rattle of hooves as she recalled the numerous times her father had ridden up the lane toward their home and she would run out to greet him. Even the familiar creak of his leather saddle as he dismounted in front of their house seemed stirringly detailed in her memory. Still, her recollections were somewhat flawed, for it came to her that she had missed hearing the soft tinkling of tiny bells that had always heralded his approach on horseback, for it was the custom of Russian gentlemen to bedeck their mounts with silver bells, necklets and wealthy trappings, allowing their approach to be heard from some distance away.

The muted click of booted heels on a stone walk brought Synnovea's reverie to an abrupt end. It was clearly not the stride she had come to recognize as her father's. Realizing she had allowed herself to become lost in fantasy, she opened her eyes abruptly and, tilting her head to one side, peered past the branches to get a better view of the thoroughfare. For the present moment the street was still devoid of travelers, but when she shifted her gaze downward toward the pathway leading to the front portal of the Taraslov manse, she saw striding there a tall man groomed in a leather doublet and brown, thigh-length boots pulled up high over narrow fitting, fawn-colored breeches. His shirt was flawlessly white with a wide, pointed collar that was open to allow for the heat of the day. The wide-brimmed hat he wore prevented her a clear view of the man's face, but he had the proud bearing and crisp, purposeful stride of a military officer, though that possibility puzzled her. She could not imagine Nikolai Nekrasov or anyone of similar reserve wearing such bold, European garb, not that the appearance of this particular fellow wasn't pleasing. On the contrary, he was quite dashingly outfitted in the mode of a cavalryman who disdained the wide-legged pantaloons of the common foot soldier. Still, his breeches would have been considered shamelessly snug when compared to the long *kaftans*, which reached almost to the ankles of the men who wore them. This man's manner of dress was more reminiscent of a cavalier in England than in Russia. . . .

Synnovea smothered a small gasp of dismay as she suddenly realized just who the man was. Most anxious to assure herself of his identity, she leaned down cautiously to peer through the lower branches of the tree and almost gasped when her worst suspicions were confirmed. There, tethered to the hitching post near the entrance to the drive, was an animal Synnovea was sure had become forever forged on her memory. Her wild ride through the forest on the back of the headstrong stallion had left such an impression, she would be leery of approaching another steed for some time to come. Once the pride of Ladislaus, the tall, black horse now glistened from the care and attention of his most recent owner.

Worrisome doubts cast the darkest veil of suspicion upon Colonel Rycroft's reasons for coming. The thought intruded, What if he meant to cause her shame? Would he seek revenge because she had left him without granting him permission to court her? If his intentions were for evil, would he tell all to Princess Anna?

Or was she being too skeptical of his motives and not giving him a chance to prove himself a gentleman? After all, he had been in a position to take her by force and had held himself in restraint.

The brief pummeling of anxiety eased to a more tolerable level as Synnovea made an effort to control her panic. Deliberately turning aside her doubts, she acknowledged that the colonel's presence offered a welcomed distraction from the punishing heat and certainly a most promising diversion from the boredom of her confinement. When she had been all but wallowing in the tedium and despair of her predicament, it seemed rather silly to fly into a state of hysteria or burrow down in a hole like a fearful mole just because the colonel had been bold enough to come to the Taraslov manse.

Though proper decorum made demands that any pleasure in his presence be promptly squelched and that she regard him with stilted aloofness, Synnovea leaned back with a sigh of relief, savoring her freedom to enjoy a few delights in the secrecy of her mind. It was rather stimulating to assess the colonel at her leisure. Having admired the memory of him in the altogether, she now let her gaze glide over him with meticulous care, hardly aware that her eyes gradually took on a warming glow.

It was truly a pity that the man was not more handsome, Synnovea lamented, when he was so marvelously well proportioned otherwise. The long, muscular thighs accepted the sleek, glovelike fit of the boots with ease, but then, having gained firsthand knowledge of the flawlessness of their length, she was not surprised. The snug breeches seemed eager to flaunt the detail of his narrow hips and tautly muscled buttocks, yet beneath the cloth, the manly bulges were now more confined and subdued, though perhaps no less arresting to an innocent maid who blushingly recalled the moment he had stepped from the pool.

An abashed giggle escaped Synnovea as she became aware of the source of her curiosity, but she quickly squelched her amusement when she remembered that Ali might be near. Grimacing gingerly, she cast a cautious glance around to see where the maid had taken herself, and, to her great relief, discovered the woman had left the chambers and had not been witness to her strange behavior.

Anxious to hear what Colonel Rycroft would say to Boris as the front door was pulled open, Synnovea leaned outward as much as she safely dared. She was most curious to know what matter had brought him to the Taraslov manse and dearly hoped he would not disappoint her by proving himself a cad.

"*Dohbriy dyen,*" he greeted, tucking his hat beneath his arm. "*Pazhahlasta.*" After the polite plea, he carefully pronounced the syllables, "Goh-voh-reet-yeh lee vwee poh-ahn-*glee*-skee?"

Synnovea cringed at his effort, and immediately there followed a long pause through which he waited. It was obvious to her that Boris, who spoke no English, had gone to fetch his mistress, who could.

"May I be of assistance to you, sir?" Anna inquired upon her arrival at the front portal.

Captain Rycroft swept his hat in a gracious bow and addressed her. "The Princess Taraslovna, I presume?"

"I am she. What is it that you want?"

"A favor, if you would be so kind," Tyrone responded, then with a soft chuckle, offered an apology. "I've not been in your country for very long, and my Russian is very poor. I fear I must have confused your butler.

Forgive me for the intrusion, but I am Colonel Rycroft, Commander of the Third Regiment of His Majesty's Imperial Hussars. I was fortunate enough to be of service to the Countess Zenkovna on her journey to Moscow, and I wonder if I might be permitted to speak with her for a few moments."

"I'm afraid that will be quite impossible, Colonel," Anna replied stiffly. "You see, the Countess Zenkovna is not feeling well enough to receive visitors today. She has retired to her chambers, and only her maid is allowed to see her."

"Then perhaps I might be permitted to return tomorrow," Tyrone suggested.

"Have you a reason to bother her?" Anna's tone had taken on a definite staleness.

"One of my men found a brooch that we believe belongs to her. I would like to question her about it, if I may."

Anna stretched forth a slender white hand to receive the mentioned item. "If you wish me to give the brooch to her, Colonel, I shall see that it is taken up to her straightaway."

Tyrone handed over the piece, then as the princess made to close the door, he stepped nearer, placing a booted toe upon the threshold to prevent her from shutting the portal. Anna gaped down at the formidable wedge and then looked up at him in surprise, wondering if she should scream.

Tyrone smiled pleasantly and clarified his position. "If you don't mind, Princess Taraslovna, I shall await an answer. You see, if the brooch doesn't belong to the Countess Zenkovna, it should be given back to the man who found it."

"If you insist," Anna replied icily.

"I must," he answered simply.

"Then wait here," she snapped back. "I shall fetch her maid for you. I'm sure the woman will be able to recognize the piece if it truly belongs to her mistress." Anna lowered her gaze pointedly to his foot and then raised a meaningful brow as she warned, "Boris will attend the door while I'm gone."

With a casual nod to the woman, Tyrone stepped back several paces. As he awaited her return, he clamped his hat on his head again and, strolling away from the door, leisurely moved toward the tree, that very same one which hid the upper windows of Synnovea's bedchamber.

Smothering a gasp, Synnovea pressed back against the window frame and held her breath as Tyrone paused in the outer boundaries of the shade. She chanced no movement, lest he discover her, and her heart soared in a frantic flight as she anticipated what might happen if he should glance up. Her thin chemise was far from adequate as a covering, and though she dared not risk a brief glance downward for fear of attracting his attention, she felt the delicate batiste clinging cloyingly to her wet skin. Yet as she stared down at him in roweling apprehension of detection, it was almost as if some sharp instinct warned the man that he was being watched. Abruptly he raised his head, and Synnovea gasped as she found herself caught. Frozen by the shock of her discovery, she could only gape at him, while Tyrone, in so brief a moment, savored every facet of her beauty, from the slender bare arms, the dark hair piled casually high upon her head, soft tendrils curling wetly against her throat, to the thin, gossamer web that clung like a hazy film over her delicately hued breasts. The slow grin that came to his lopsided lips gave evidence that he had not missed the smallest detail of her display. Her appearance satiated his sharply honed curiosity and completely gratified his reason for coming. In truth, this vision of incomparable beauty assured Tyrone Rycroft once and for all that he had not imagined her.

Synnovea leapt from her perch with a muffled groan of despair and flung herself far from the window where she stood panting for breath. Her cheeks flamed more from the scorching heat of his perusal than the sultriness of the room, and now her heart kept time with her racing mind. What must he think of her? What tales would he spread abroad of her brazen exhibition? Had she not given him enough to stare at in the bathhouse without completely embarrassing herself a second time? Oh, if he would just go away! Back to England where he belonged! Without further humiliating her!

The front door creaked as it was pulled fully open, and Tyrone snatched his mind free of its entanglement and turned abruptly from the window, sweeping off his hat as he concentrated on cooling his hot blood. Whatever else came of the day, his brief glimpse of the countess had been well worth the long, sun-blistering ride from his quarters.

Ali stepped out into the light and squinted up at the tall man in some curiosity, considering his badly bruised visage a long moment before she cautiously asked, "Ye be the one what saved me mistress?"

" 'Tis my honor to claim that fame," Tyrone replied amiably and winced as he tried to grin at the old woman.

Peering down at the emerald brooch now nestled in the palm of her hand, Ali tapped it lightly with a gnarled forefinger. "This be the Countess Synnovea's, all right. What be yer reward for findin' it?"

"The reward is not mine to claim. The piece was found on the ground by one of my men. If your mistress so desires, she may lay the favor to him, but I would not have you trouble her now for a reply. I shall return on the morrow. Perhaps by then I might be allowed the privilege of addressing the countess personally."

"I see no need for you to trouble yourself," Anna interjected crisply from the doorway. "We shall have the reward sent to your regiment."

" 'Tis no trouble at all," Tyrone assured her in good spirits. "I would take great comfort in seeing the countess again . . . to assure myself of her good health, of course."

He met the chilling gaze of the princess and deliberately ignored what it implied, having adroitly claimed an excuse to return.

Tyrone glanced down to see the sparkling blue eyes of the Irish maid resting on him with smiling approval and realized he had gained an ally. Despite the discomfort he embraced whenever he stretched his bruised and slightly swollen lip, he gave the tiny servant his best attempt, displaying gleaming white teeth behind a crooked smile.

"Would ye be needin' yer hurts tended?" Ali offered with alacrity, then looked around in disappointment as Anna impatiently cleared her throat.

"I'm sure there are physicians to whom he can go," the princess stated, not even bothering to hide her annoyance with the pair.

"I fear an occasion for such attention is limited to the reluctance of your benefactress," Tyrone responded with another painful grin. "I must be on my way, but if you will, you may carry my solicitations for a quick recovery to your mistress. I hope she will be feeling better on the morrow when I return."

"Oh, she will be," Ali assured him. "I'll see to it!"

Tyrone swept the women a brief bow and, settling his hat on his head, chuckled softly as he retreated down the walk to where his mount waited. Even if he had not won the consideration of the countess, at least he had gained the support of someone very close to her, who might prove most effective in persuading the younger woman to think kindly of him.

Chapter 7

Synnovea wasted no time in making her way downstairs to the dining hall the next morning. After being assiduously provided with evidence that the afternoon heat could turn her rooms into a place of horrendous torture, she gave up all pretense of being indisposed for another day, having come to the firm decision that she was not particularly fond of being roasted alive. Her slender feet flashed in a dazzling blur beneath her skirts as she descended the stairs with a lighthearted ambience and a newfound tolerance for Ivan Voronsky. She doubted that even the cleric's stodgy instructions could be as punishing as the sweltering discomfort she had been forced to contend with in the solitude of her own chambers.

Ivan had entered the dining hall only a few moments earlier, and when Synnovea swept in with a cheery smile and a morning greeting, he reacted as if he had devised his strategy well in advance of her appearance. He nearly stumbled over himself skittering around to bar her possible departure from the room, no doubt fearing she would be tempted to escape like an errant child once she was confronted.

"This morning, Countess, we shall address ourselves to the value of humility and self-denial," he announced as he followed her along the sideboard and heaped a pewter plate with honey cakes, sautéed potatoes, and petite sausages simmered in sour cream.

Synnovea raised a brow in wonder, growing somewhat doubtful after all of her ability to suffer through Ivan's long-winded dissertations, especially when the subject was one he evidently knew nothing about. She heaved a mental sigh of resignation, however, arguing with herself that it was far better to be bored than to be broiled.

Slanting a skeptical glance toward his overflowing plate, Synnovea could not resist a query. "Self-denial in what respect?"

"Well, in manner of dress to begin with," Ivan replied, sniffing arrogantly. He looked very dour and supercilious in his dark vestment, as he no doubt considered commensurate to the seriousness of his duties. But then, Synnovea mused, he probably would convey the same demeanor if he wore nothing at all, not that she was at all interested in having her suspicions confirmed.

Wondering what he had found in her manner of dress to fault her for this time, Synnovea lifted her plate aside and looked down at herself. For her morning apparel she had selected a *sarafan* of turquoise silk embroidered with bouquets of pink flowers. Ribbons of pink and turquoise were entwined in her lone maiden's braid and were fashioned in a diadem delicately embellished with clusters of tiny silk flowers. In view of the fact that she was clad in the traditional fashion of her homeland and was sufficiently covered from neck to toe to wrist, Synnovea could not fully understand his objection.

"Is there something wrong with what I'm wearing?" she inquired, her curiosity piqued. "Is this not the proper attire of a Russian *boyarina*?"

"A bit too colorful to be considered demure." Ivan expressed his opinion prudishly. "Somewhat reminiscent of a peacock, if you have ever had the occasion to see one. No modest maiden should strut about like some pretty hen in her finery."

Synnovea played the innocent, disinclined to accept his assessments with the same appreciation Anna might have imparted, though she doubted the cleric would have been willing to offer any criticisms to the princess. One did not wisely bite the hand that nourished it. "I thought peacocks were male birds."

"That is strictly beside the point!" Ivan snapped in an indignant huff. "And as a young maid and now a scholar of mine, you should learn to show proper respect to your savants and be humble of both spirit and mode. After all, the tsar is looking for a bride, and who is to say what maid he will finally select."

Synnovea promptly rejected the notion. "With all due respect to His Majesty, I do not wish to become subject to the intrigue and jealousies associated with that particular position. I am quite content living my life outside the confines and stricture of a *terem* and avoiding the worry of what potion might be added to my food. His Majesty has suffered much in trying to find a bride, but not so much as his intended might have had to endure."

"What do you mean?" Ivan watched her narrowly, trying to plumb her logic.

Casually Synnovea settled herself at the table. "Maria Khlopova was once Tsar Mikhail's prospective bride, and look what happened to her."

Ivan joined her at the table, placing his well-laden plate before him as he took a seat. In his opinion his student needed to be shown an example of what might befall a woman full of wiles and deceit. "That was nearly five years ago, but if you're able to recall the circumstances, Maria was undone because she sought to conceal her illness from Tsar Mikhail so she might become his tsarina. If not for her untimely collapse into violent and convulsive frothing right there in front of His Majesty and his guests, she might have accomplished her deception. Sending the Khlopovs to Siberia was hardly punishment enough for the trickery they planned."

Synnovea stared at the man, rather amazed at his lack of knowledge. Apparently some of the more recent occurrences at court had escaped his attention. "Oh, but didn't you hear? Shortly after his return from Poland, the Patriarch Filaret uncovered a plot by the Saltykovs to discredit Maria Khlopova and her family," she informed him. "It seems that several members of the Saltykov family doused Maria's food with an emetic, then they bribed several physicians to spread the lie that she had an incurable illness. Patriarch Filaret told his son of their deeds, and that is why His Majesty has recently banished the Saltykovs from his court and confiscated some of their lands." Synnovea casually shrugged as she added, "Although it's done poor Maria little good now."

Ivan was somewhat confused and carefully voiced a statement of fact. "But the Saltykovs are relatives of Tsar Mikhail's mother. Marfa would never abide such an edict against her kin, even from her son. You must be mistaken, Countess."

Synnovea allowed him the benefit of a kindly smile. "And that is exactly why Marfa now staunchly refuses to give her consent to her son's marriage to Maria Khlopova. She was positively in an uproar over his treatment of her kin." Briefly Synnovea addressed her attention to her plate before coyly lifting her gaze to the dumbfounded man. Though wisdom pleaded caution, the opportunity to subtly suggest that her knowledge equaled or surpassed his was far too tempting to resist. It would only be a gentle gibe anyway. "Do you suppose you've had enough instruction for the day? I do so wish to visit the Countess Andreyevna this morning ere it gets too warm. Mayhap we could continue our discussion on the morrow."

Ivan's pockmarked cheeks reddened and flexed with rage as he lowered his dark eyes to his food. He resented being mocked and made to appear the ignorant simpleton, especially by the Countess Synnovea, whose sire had been rich enough to hire the very best sages and master tutors to instruct his daughter, while he, on the other hand, had found it necessary to grovel and abase himself with menial tasks in order to acquire every bit of

knowledge he could, all in an effort to crush those revil-
ing jeers that still haunted him from his youth. After the
death of his mother, he had attached himself to the *starets*
and the priests of the church merely for the purpose of
learning the written word and delving into their weighty
tomes and ancient archives. He had shared their paltry
meals and tattered robes only to enrich his mind. Now,
having obtained a patroness of wealthy standing, he was
not about to be generous to those who had known only
a life of ease. He would not let this fine-feathered bird
flit about as she pleased after making sport of him. She
would have to learn to be wary of his importance and
mastery . . . or else.

"On the contrary, Countess, you may *not* be excused
today or any other day unless it is *my* recommendation."

Ivan turned away from her as if in stern rebuke, but it
was only to protect himself from the curiosity of those
innocent green eyes. He was experiencing an abomin-
able, assailing weakness which he strove to hide and
which he utterly detested, a nervously twitching eyelid
that could not be controlled and a tremor in his hands
which was violent enough to cause liquid to spill from
over the edge of any glass he could be holding. In the
dark, innermost recesses of his mind, a dismal memory
formed of his mother standing over him, shouting insults
at him when he was but a boy, and though he had tried
countless times throughout his lifetime to scour that
apparition from his brain, he was still tormented by the
affliction it caused.

The spasm passed as quickly as it had come upon him,
and Ivan was again able to compose himself. Drawing a
deep, steadying breath, he faced the maiden, who had
congenially addressed her attention to the meal, as if
undisturbed by his denial. He found her lack of concern
hardly gratifying. Indeed, it gnawed at his own content.
He preferred to taste the succor of revenge and devised a
plan to make her pay twofold.

Ivan's thin lips stretched stiffly in a contemptuous

sneer. "It has come to my attention, Countess, that there are duties in the kitchen to which you can devote your energies instead of wasting your time associating with such questionable creatures as the Countess Andreyevna. She is hardly the sort of woman a young maid should attach herself to."

Somewhat startled by Ivan's response, Synnovea leaned back in her chair and frowned at him, knowing full well where he had gained his information. It seemed there were no secrets kept between Ivan and the princess. "What say you, sir? Are you cognizant of the woman you slur? The Countess Andreyevna is a woman of sterling character."

"Hardly!" Ivan scoffed. "I've heard of those receptions she gives. Rich *boyars* and high-ranking officers. Her reasons are obvious. A widow after three husbands, she is only searching for one rich enough to keep her wallowing in luxuries from now until she dies."

Synnovea recognized the depth of his spitefulness and her own foolishness in taunting him. His slander clearly conveyed the animosity he felt toward Natasha, and yet she could see no just cause for him to malign the woman except to provoke her to wrath. Synnovea found it nearly impossible to maintain her reticence beneath such slurs, but she would be falling right into his hands by losing her temper if that was truly his intent. The best way to deal with a man of his ilk was to deftly turn his jibes aside and pretend they had no effect. "The kitchen, you say? Well, of course. But what would you have me do there that I should consider part of my studies?"

Ivan assumed a haughty air. "Apparently, Countess, you need to learn the humbleness of a servant ere you are proclaimed fit for the institute of marriage with any Russian gentleman. The Princess Anna gave me leave to instruct you as I see fit, and 'tis my first order of the day to teach you about the ignoble concept of servitude and the hardships of serfs and peasants." His small eyes flicked over her wealthy garb, losing none of their dullness. "I'm sure you'll want to change into something less ostentatious while you're working in the kitchen."

Synnovea rose from her chair and removed her plate from the table, steeling herself against any show of emotion that Ivan might construe as resentment or injury. She would not allow him the privilege of seeing her disturbed, whether by his aspersions against a loved one or by his edict. The latter was of no consequence. What the cleric evidently did not know about her was that she had not only served as mistress of her father's house after the death of her mother, but she had often worked alongside the servants when close attention to detail and directions were needed, especially in preparing the house for guests or cooking special dishes for visitors and her father. She had taken a personal delight in helping the gardeners plant and tend the flowers and vegetables and seeing their labors manifested into food for the table and large, riotously colored blossoms. If Ivan thought he had gained some advantage by ordering her to work, then he had once again displayed his ignorance.

"If you will excuse me," Synnovea begged graciously, "I must return to my chambers to prepare myself, as you suggest."

Ivan stared at her askance, somewhat suspicious of her obliging mien. "If you think to barricade yourself in your chambers again today, Countess, I beg you reconsider. I'm sure the Princess Anna will not tolerate you dawdling when I've assigned you specific duties."

"Why, I wouldn't dream of it, sir!" Synnovea tossed a chiding chuckle over her shoulder as she crossed to the door. "Really, Ivan," she used the familiarity to exemplify her own lack of veneration for him, "there's no need to fret yourself. I'm only taking your advice."

Ivan was left alone to contemplate her reaction, which he again found most disconcerting. He had expected an argument, at the very least the furious diatribes of a thoroughly enraged female. Instead, she had seemed almost delighted with his directive. Much bemused, he made a mental note to keep track of the countess throughout the day, just to make sure she addressed herself to her chores and did not escape behind his back. He was not of a bent to trust women, especially one so prone to make light of him.

Returning to her chambers to doff the rich gown and don in its stead the peasant garb which she wore during those times she lent herself to household duties, Synnovea found herself confronted by Ali, whose suspicions were sparked by her abrupt return to change clothes. Though she carefully explained that her assignment now included a short stint in the kitchen, she had to discourage the woman from flying downstairs in a fomenting frenzy to confront the cleric.

"What?! He takes it 'pon himself ter order ye 'bout as if ye were some common drudge!" Ali was simply livid. "A pox on the man!"

"I'll be doing nothing more than what I did at home," Synnovea reasoned as she tried to calm the maid, who, despite her bantam size, was given to exhibitions of temper and temerity befitting a mother bear whose cub had just been set upon. " 'Twill not hurt me in the least, I assure you."

"Aye, me dearie, but 'twas yerself what decided the chores ye'd be doin' an' not 'nother body givin' ye commands like some high an' mighty lord, which 'tis plain he thinks himself ter be." Ali flounced in a high dander about the chambers as she vowed with great passion, "He'll rue the day he set his mind ter doin' ye ill."

"Ali McCabe! You'll not let either Ivan or the Princess Anna have the satisfaction of seeing us put out by the man's peevish bent! We'll abide by Ivan's dictate graciously, do you understand?" Receiving no response, Synnovea stamped her foot in a demand to be answered by the cantankerous little woman. "Ali! Do you understand?"

Petulantly the maid folded her skinny arms across her flat chest and pouted, not in total agreement with her mistress. "He's a wily, beggarly little scamp, that he is."

Though Synnovea had some difficulty maintaining a disapproving frown when the temptation to laugh was far greater, she raised a warning finger in front of the woman's nose. "I want you to promise me, Ali, that you'll do all you can to keep the peace while we're here."

Ali glared at the threatening digit and assumed her best martyred demeanor. Briefly she cast her eyes heavenward as if appealing to the saints and sucked air through her teeth to indicate her distress. Finally with a wry shake of her head, she relented. "Aye, I'll be doin' it, only 'cause ye told me ter, but 'twill not sit well wit' me, ye know that!"

A soft chuckle escaped Synnovea as she laid a comforting arm about the narrow shoulders and copied the woman's brogue. "I know that, Ali me dearest, but 'twill be better this way. We'll not be givin' Ivan or the Princess Anna reason ter complain. Mayhap by a wee bit o' kindness, we'll be turnin' aside their anger an' resentment."

"Hmph! That'll be the day, for sure! Aye! Though the priests assured me such miracles have a way o' happenin', I still have me doubts believin' ye can gather wool searchin' through a wolf's lair."

"Help me finish dressing," Synnovea cajoled through her lighthearted laughter, "then you can put away my clothes while I go downstairs and confront the cook." She chuckled again as she paused to consider the wisdom of Ivan's decree. "Poor Elisaveta, she may be in for a bit of a shock. With me in her kitchen, she might well burn the food."

" 'Twouldn't hurt none if 'n she did," Ali rejoined tartly. "The way that crow, Ivan Voronsky, has been fillin' his craw, it'll serve him right ter have ter choke down burnt vittles for a while."

As predicted, Elisaveta, the sad-eyed cook, gawked in open astonishment when Synnovea entered her domain dressed not entirely like a servant, but not quite like a noble lady either. Had Ivan glimpsed her apparel,

Synnovea might have put even his morose convictions on servitude to rout, for the lace-trimmed white blouse, along with the bodice of forest green, and her wide, white apron decorated with variegated rows of trim and worn over a full skirt lavishly embroidered with a colorful profusion of flowers, combined to create a most fetching costume. Layers of lacy petticoats gave the skirt volume, but beneath the ankle-length hem could be spied slender, slippered feet and darkly stockinged ankles that were about as trim and shapely as a man could hope to view. A large, lace-edged kerchief covered her dark head, and the single braid was left to hang unadorned to her hips.

"Countess!" Elisaveta cried in slack-jawed astoundment. "What be you doin' here?"

"Why, I've come to help, Elisaveta," Synnovea announced cheerily. "Is there something I can do?"

"*Nyet! Nyet, spaséeba!*" the plump woman squawked and waved her hands wildly above her head, as if sorely beset by worry. She had never heard of anything so preposterous! "The princess will never allow such a thing to happen! You are a guest!"

Synnovea did not intend to drive a wedge between servant and mistress. Indeed, she abhorred the idea of telling the cook that she had been ordered to work, but a little honest flattery could bring about the same objective. "Oh, but, Elisaveta, I'd like very much to learn how to create those wonderful dishes you're so gifted at making, so I might instruct my own servants when I return home to Nizhniy Novgorod." Giving the woman a pleading look, she coaxed sweetly, "Will you not teach me?"

The cook waggled her graying head as a tentative smile touched her lips and finally deepened into a grin that dimpled her round cheeks. Tucking her massive arms under the folds of her apron, Elisaveta snuggled them up close beneath her large bosom as she revelled in the compliments. "I can show you what I know, Countess."

"Then I will surely learn all there is to know about

cooking," Synnovea smilingly surmised. "What will you teach me first?"

"Well, this be what I'm doin' now," Elisaveta announced as she waddled over to a long wooden table where she had been cleaning and heaping up separate mounds of carrots, onions, truffles, and wild mushrooms. "When I finish choppin' these, I'll be making *pirozhki*. The master likes the little stuffed patties very much."

Synnovea glanced up at the woman in sudden worry. "Do you expect Prince Aleksei to return soon?"

"Oh, he's usually not gone more'n a day or two, at the most. Knowin' him, I figure he'll be comin' home either tonight or in the morn'n." Elisaveta sighed heavily. "If'n it weren't for Prince Aleksei, there'd be no need for me to cook. The mistress eats no more'n a sparrow when the master's here and almost nothin' at all when he's gone. It's a pity to see all this food go to waste."

"Surely there are enough servants in the house to take care of what is not eaten." Synnovea made the conjecture as she perused the various boiling pots and large bowl of dough that waited to be rolled out.

The gray head moved sorrowfully with a negative answer. "The mistress won't allow the servants to eat what's been prepared for her and those what sit at her table. 'Twould spoil their taste for simple food, she says. There're so many others who could benefit, if only . . ."

The jade-green eyes chased upward to the glum-faced woman as a lengthy pause was followed by a long sniffle. Aware of Synnovea's inquiring gaze, Elisaveta hastily brushed a hand across her cheek where a tear trickled slowly downward. Steeling her square jaw, the cook blinked away the brimming wetness with fierce determination.

Synnovea felt her own heart wrenched by the sadness of so much good food going to waste when, without extra cost to the Taraslovs, a goodly number could be helped.

Sharing a moment of the woman's misery, she laid a gentle hand upon the stout arm. "Do you know of someone in particular who is in need, Elisaveta?"

The chin trembled despite the cook's efforts to keep it firm, and almost reluctantly she nodded. "It's me sister, Countess. Her husband died this past winter, and she's poor in health, with a young daughter o' three at her side. She cannot work to make ends meet, and they're wastin' away to nothin', the two o' 'em. An' here I be, in this fine house, fixin' all this fancy food, but I can't take anything to her or even leave to help her."

"Well!" Synnovea settled her hands on her waist as she firmly decided the course of action she would take. If this was the state of affairs in the Taraslov manse, she would not sit quietly by and do nothing! "I've a maid I can send to buy food and whatever else is needed, and a coachman to take her to your sister. Though I may not be allowed to leave myself without special permission," Synnovea gave a small shrug as Elisaveta looked at her in surprise, "they will not trouble themselves too long on the absence of my maid."

"Ye mean ye can't leave here without me mistress givin' the say?" the cook questioned in surprise.

" 'Tis only for my protection," Synnovea assured her with a smile and a gentle pat.

"Humph!" Elisaveta drew her own conclusions as she cast a glare toward the kitchen door, intending it for the woman who roamed well beyond it. She had once been employed by the family who had given birth to the Princess Anna and had formed several opinions of a daughter who would send her own aging parents to live in a monastery because she desired to live alone with her husband in the house she had grown up in. Even when the princess had made the move to Moscow, she had not allowed her parents to return home, lest they disturb the order of the house.

By late afternoon Synnovea had finished her chores in the kitchen and, after dutifully asking approval from

Ivan, went behind the house and found a place to rest in the dappled shade of a tree growing near the entrance to the Taraslov garden. There she relaxed while awaiting the return of Ali and Stenka, who had left some time earlier on their mission of goodwill. Elisaveta came often to the door to peer out in silent question, but Synnovea could only shake her head in answer, having viewed nothing more than a few small carriages and a handful of mounted riders on the thoroughfare in front of the manse. These she dismissed as readily as they appeared and returned her attention to the verses she had found in the weighty tome which Ivan had given her.

Dusk had tainted the sky with gloom before Synnovea finally espied the coach coming down the lane. Elisaveta was busy laying out the evening meal and chafed with frustration because she could not leave her duties when the countess rushed through the kitchen to announce that Ali and Stenka were returning at long last. Hardly pausing, Synnovea passed through the dining hall and was hurrying across the vestibule when Anna strode from the front portal with a harsh frown on her face.

"You should have discouraged that man from coming here when you first met him!" the princess rebuked, incensed that she had been called once again to the door to answer the inquiries of that arrogant Englishman. The man apparently lacked the sense to know when he was not welcome or was too pigheaded to accept the fact. "Colonel Rycroft was intent upon seeing you again and had the audacity to tell me he would return on the morrow, as if another visit will do him any good!"

Synnovea's eyes chased to the door as she remembered Colonel Rycroft saying he would be coming today. She had been so anxious about learning the condition of Elisaveta's sister and niece that she had forgotten. "Is Colonel Rycroft here?"

"He was here a moment ago! But he's gone now," Anna informed her caustically. She flung up a hand in the same manner she had used to banish him from her stoop. "I told him you didn't want to be disturbed, and certainly not by him, ever again! I gave him some coins as a reward to carry back to his man when he tried again to use that as an excuse for his return, though I have grave doubts that he'll be giving it away to someone else. A simple trick for gain, if you ask me."

Synnovea sought to curb her irritation, resenting the fact that the woman had taken it upon herself to dismiss one of her callers without first informing her of his presence. Even if Colonel Rycroft was an Englishman bent on courting her, she would have preferred sending him away herself. "You say Colonel Rycroft will be returning on the morrow?"

"If he dares to ignore what I said, he may, but it will do him little good," Anna declared emphatically. "I will not let you see him!"

"I can find no harm in showing the man a few common courtesies," Synnovea replied frostily, ignoring the fact that she might have been less than friendly to him herself. She had not forgiven him for his intrusion into her bath, but she reserved the right to berate him for those offenses herself. Outwardly, she was wont to show a different disposition. "After all, the man accomplished my rescue and was most daring in the performance of his duty."

"That hardly gives him the right to be accepted in this house, as if he were some Russian-born *boyar*," the princess retorted. "You will honor my wishes, Countess, or wish that you had."

"And so I shall," Synnovea assured her with a brief, tight smile. The subject of Colonel Rycroft's return was hardly worth getting into a fracas over, though she resented the woman laying down laws with dire threats to insure that her requests would be carried out to the letter.

Striking a dignified pose, Anna reclaimed her haughty demeanor as she informed her charge, "I shall expect to be paid back promptly for the monies I gave to the man in your behalf . . . which brings me to another matter of great importance. You have monies enough to compensate for your own existence here, as well as the servants you have brought. I think it only fair you pay accordingly, therefore I will attach to your debt the rents I feel are owing to me and write you out a notice of your weekly obligation. You will be expected to pay such funds at the beginning of each week."

"If you so desire," Synnovea replied, wondering if the decision to charge her rents sprang from a sense of greed or a growing resentment of her presence in the manse.

"I'm glad you're so agreeable, Countess."

Declining comment to the converse, Synnovea begged excusal. "If I may, Princess, I shall go now and dress for dinner."

Rigidly Anna inclined her head, granting permission, and watched as the younger woman crossed the hall, but when Synnovea passed the stairs and continued toward the back of the house, she hurriedly followed several steps.

"Where are you going?" she questioned angrily and stated the obvious. "Your chambers are upstairs!"

Synnovea never paused in her stride, but tossed an answer over her shoulder as she gained the doorway. "I'm going to fetch Ali to help me dress. She's out in the stable with Stenka!"

Anna shot a worried glance toward the front door as Synnovea departed through the rear. She had no way of accurately accounting for the passage of time that had elapsed since she had sent the colonel on his way, but she was not about to take any chances that he might still be dawdling outside.

With her lips tightly set in a fretting grimace, Anna raced to the front portal and snatched it open, more than primed to chastise the man for his delay. Finding no one to vent her rage upon, she casually sauntered out on the stoop and glanced up and down the street in both directions. The horse was gone from the tethering post and the thoroughfare was empty, save for a lone carriage wending its way past their house. Breathing a sigh of relief, Anna closed the door again, well assured the Englishman had left as she had commanded him. With immense satisfaction she moved to the stairs and climbed them, confident that she had successfully crushed the colonel's aspirations for winning the attentions of a rich Russian countess.

Leaving the house, Synnovea dashed along the narrow pathway to the stables and was in the process of rounding a hedge when she caught sight of the familiar black stallion tied to a hitching rail near the rear gate. She stumbled to a halt on the stone steps as her eyes flew in a frantic search for the indomitable colonel. He was standing near the coach with a leather helm tucked beneath one arm, while his other hand rested casually on the hilt of a sword that hung from his side. He seemed quite amiable as he conversed with Ali, whose eager giggles were mingled with sly looks and animated flourishes of her translucently pale hands. Synnovea had taken casual note of the man's height before, but now, when he stood before Ali, she could see that he was tall enough to dwarf the tiny woman by at least two hands or more. The gray head barely reached to the middle of his chest.

On this occasion he was garbed more in the mode of a working soldier than he had been the previous day. Somewhat rough and worn, but equally slender leather boots were pulled high over narrow breeches of tanned hide, while a thick leather cuirass covered his chest. Even in the dwindling light of the sun, a full-sleeved blouse worn beneath the breastplate appeared startlingly white against the deeply bronzed visage. Dark bruises were still visible around his eye and cheek, but the large lumps that had once distended his brow and lip had dwindled in size, lending him a more human appearance. His hair had been recently clipped close to his nape and was now smoothly combed, allowing the sun-bleached streaks to show amid the tawny brown.

Ali glanced around and, finding her mistress standing a short distance away, beckoned eagerly to her. "Mistress! Here be the man what saved ye from the highwaymen!"

Immediately Colonel Rycroft turned to search Synnovea out, and his eyes, though unfathomable in the closing darkness, seemed to glide over her from head to toe in a lingering appreciation of everything they touched. Synnovea had no way of discerning the workings of his mind or where his imagination wandered, and perhaps that was just as well for her own peace of mind, for Tyrone Rycroft was quickly coming to the decision that he admired her almost as much garbed in clothes as he did when she wore nothing at all. But then, a memory of her exit from the wooden tub nearly snatched his breath as it flashed again through his mind.

Synnovea found it difficult to speak to her tenacious suitor when he made no effort to hide his avid interest in her. She felt the heat of a blush suffuse her cheeks as he smilingly devoured every detail of her, from the shapely ankles and slender feet that brought her gracefully forward to the wisps of hair that had escaped the kerchief to curl softly against her face.

"Countess Synnovea, I am greatly favored by your appearance and your apparent good health." He swept into a courtly bow, and then upon straightening, set aside his helmet and closed the distance between them, giving her a grin that she was just beginning to suspect was naturally lopsided. His eyes glowed with such warmth beyond the dark lashes, she was positive that no smile she had ever received from a man had ever turned so quickly into a leer. "I feared I would be forced to leave here again, bereft of the solace of your companionship, perhaps once and forever more. To be sure, the merest glimpse of you nourishes my mind and heart."

The burning heat in her cheeks could not be lightly arrested when he plied her with such words of ardor, yet the sudden suspicion that he had perhaps practiced them on many another maid sufficiently accomplished the cooling. Synnovea was set to discourage him in his amorous ambitions, whatever they were, for she could only imagine what his continued visitations would do to her reputation should he persist.

"The Princess Anna just now advised me of your visit," Synnovea stated cautiously, knowing full well that he would take encouragement from the merest politeness and construe it as an indication of her willingness to receive him. "I regret that you've had to come all this way from your camp to fetch the reward, Colonel. I could have sent Stenka to carry it to you."

Tyrone thrust a pair of fingers into a small purse that he wore at his waist and plucked a pouch of coins from it. Taking her hand, he turned it over and laid the soft leather bag within her palm, then closed her fingers around it, for a moment holding her hand within the warmth of his. "I shall gladly pay the man myself as evidence of my delight in your company," he avouched with a boldness that was warmly persuasive and as supple as silk. "I only used the reward as an excuse to see you again. Had I chosen, I could have sent my man to fetch it."

Synnovea pulled her hand away, fearing he would detect her leaping pulse and mistake it for something more than it was. When his mere presence set her on edge, how could she not feel a restive disquiet at his touch?

One glance at Ali told her that the petite woman was secretly applauding this man as a challenger for her heart. She disliked disillusioning the maid, but the colonel was definitely not in her plans, either in the near or distant future. Even if she had thought him handsome, which did not seem so farfetched now as it had in the bathhouse, he was still a roaming adventurer who apparently called no country his home, not even England.

"I cannot allow you to pay for the return of my brooch, Colonel." Synnovea sought to return the purse and was frustrated by his refusal to accept it. "I fear you can ill afford the loss of the coins."

"The cost is of little consequence to me, my lady," Tyrone assured her chivalrously. "The prize I seek is worth far more."

"But your sacrifice is pointless, Colonel. The Princess Anna would prefer you didn't return at all." Synnovea chose her words in all truthfulness, though she knew she used the other woman's command to achieve what she had no real desire to accomplish herself. His dismissal was what he plainly deserved and a deed that needed to be done. She should have suffered no qualms discouraging him, and yet she could not address herself to the task. "I'm under her guardianship and must respect her wishes. You must also."

Raising a querying brow, Tyrone stared into the green orbs until they fell in nervous confusion before his direct gaze. After a long pause, he released a pensive sigh as he contemplated her downcast eyes and blushing cheeks. Briefly peering askance at Ali, he saw indications of the servant's disappointment in the small, troubled frown she wore and in the worry that clouded her eyes. Had he been of such a mind, he might have offered some hope to rally the woman's spirits right then and there, for he knew well enough that when he wanted something badly enough, he was naturally disinclined to accept a simple no for an answer until absolutely certain there remained no slightest hope for him. After their meeting in the bathhouse, he had come to the realization that the Countess Synnovea Zenkovna was a woman whom he could not easily forget. When he was not at all sure her answer had arisen from her own desires, he was wont to consider the rejection as only a small hindrance to his principal goal, and that was simply to win the maid for himself.

"Perhaps the Princess Anna will come to change her mind about me in time. I can only hope that she may," Tyrone rejoined. Knowing full well that he could panic the girl again with the declaration he was about to make, he kept his voice smooth and pliant, though the fires of his aspirations were kindled anew by the nearness of her.

"But I must confess, Countess, I'm more concerned with your desires and wishes than I am with the feelings of others. You offer the brightest hope for companionship I've seen here, and I'm most reluctant to ignore the fact that you exist, merely because I've been ordered not to return. The very sight of you kindles my imagination, and I find myself hopelessly enamored." He paused a moment to allow her time to digest his words, then continued with a lazy shrug. " 'Tis a fact I've learned in my life that when great toil and effort have gone into winning a prize, it is esteemed much more than if it had been easily gained. Countess"—he managed a twisted grin—"I can only avouch that I've not yet begun the battle for the honor of your company."

Synnovea was aghast at his unswerving persistence and unmitigated gall. If she had given him special leave to court her as he pleased, he could not have appeared more brazen or confident of himself. "Colonel, I beg you consider the authority under which I now reside." She made a heroic effort to persuade him despite her doubt that anything would move him from his position. "I'm not free to do as I will. I must adhere to the wishes of those who now decide matters for me."

"Would it help if I petitioned the tsar for his favor?" Tyrone queried with a hint of humor shining in his eyes. He closely attended her reaction. If she were truly cold and haughty, then he would have his answer soon.

The lovely mouth dropped open in utter amazement, and Synnovea stared at him, aghast that he could suggest such a thing. The initial shock of his question eased only slightly as she hurried to deny the possibility. "Indeed no, sir! Gracious, no! I mean, the whole of Moscow would be aflutter with the news! You must not! I forbid it!"

Ali coughed behind her hand as she fought a private battle not to cackle in glee. She had been an eager witness to the colonel's courtship and had found it hard to contain herself from giving encouragement to her mistress. She was absolutely ecstatic with his determination to fight for what he wanted. Surely, this was no feebleminded, weak-willed swain who could be tossed about with every conflicting wind, she thought with riotous pleasure. This man knew his own mind and zealously sought what he desired to have! And with a name like Tyrone, he had to have a fair amount of Irish blood in him somewhere! It would account for his unfaltering fortitude, to be sure!

"No need to worry, my lady," Tyrone assured Synnovea with a grin. Her response had not cooled his ardor in the least. "I'll win his favor first, then make my petition."

Synnovea clapped a hand over her mouth in horrified dread that this man would actually take his suit all the way to the throne. Surely, he was jesting! Surely, she had nothing to fear! Surely, he would not!

"I must return to duty," Tyrone informed her. "I've a late drill and, on the morrow, a full day on the training field. Even if the Princess Anna hadn't warned me away, I doubt that I would have been able to break away long enough to see you, at least for a while, but never fear," he added with a promise, "you'll be seeing me again."

Tyrone gave her a brief bow and then, retrieving his hard leather helm and snugging it on his head, strode back to the stallion. Swinging up in the saddle, he turned the steed about to face the two women and casually touched his fingers to his brow in a salute of farewell. Synnovea stared after him as he rode from sight, thoroughly amazed by the man's persistence.

"He's a bold man," Ali commented with a smile twitching at the corners of her wrinkled lips. In the silence that followed, she cast a brief glance toward her mistress and smugly folded her arms across her chest. "Ye know, he reminds me o' yer pa when he came courtin' yer ma! He wouldn't take no for an answer either until he finally persuaded yer ma's kin ter give her ter him in marriage. But then, me dearest Eleanora, God rest her soul, she thought the sun an' moon rose an' set just for Count Zenkov!"

"Well, I don't think the sun and moon rise and set just for Colonel Rycroft! But I can well imagine that he would try and tell them what to do!" Synnovea fumed, drawing a gleeful cackle from the woman.

"What can ye expect, me dearie?" Ali tossed her head in delight. "He's a commander of His Majesty's Hussars! An' an Irishman ter boot, I'll wager!"

Synnovea released her breath in an exasperated huff and fixed the scrawny woman with a pointed stare. "And you, Ali McCabe! You're supposed to be on my side! Not his! The way you were eyeing him, a body would think you were measuring him up for an appointment as my husband!"

"Now, now, me lamb, there's no reason ter be gettin' yerself in such a snit," Ali cajoled. "I just like the man, that's all."

Another vexed sigh, this one definitely related to a snort, accompanied a glower of genuine distrust. "I know you well enough, Ali McCabe, to have no doubts that you will be discovered as an accomplice to the colonel should he persist in this foolhardy endeavor. You are not to be trusted around the likes of such a man!"

"Can I help it if'n I've got a fine eye for pickin' a prime man?"

Synnovea settled her hands on her slender waist and groaned in mute frustration. The occurrence was rare indeed when she could outargue Ali McCabe, and she gave up trying. "I don't suppose you remember what I sent you out for."

Ali took insult at any insinuation that she might be growing addled and forgetting her duties. "Ye know I do, an' a poor sight I saw!" Her temper settled as her mood changed to one of compassion. "Elisaveta was not far wrong. Her sister is in a bad way. I cooked an' did for her an' Sophia, the little girl, an' then gave a few coins an' a promise o' more ter a neighbor woman so she'd look after 'em 'til I could come back. With a little care, they'll be fine, but Danika'll be needin' ter find work ter support herself an' her child once she's up an' about."

"I doubt if the Princess Anna will allow her to come here to work, not with a child alongside," Synnovea mused aloud. "Do you have any ideas?"

Ali shook her head sadly. "None, mistress, but surely 'ere be somethin' we can do."

Considering her limited options, Synnovea spread her arms wide in frustration and then let them drop limply to her sides. She could think of no better plan than sending the pair to her home in Nizhniy Novgorod, but she knew the long journey could not be easily endured by a woman in a weakened state. It seemed an eternity before another idea was finally born and Synnovea's face began to brighten with hope. "Perhaps the Countess Natasha would be willing to hire her on."

"Are ye thinkin' the Princess Anna will be lettin' ye leave here ter visit the Countess Natasha?" Ali doubted the possibility of such an occurrence. "Ye know she has no likin' for the countess."

"I shall make a point of asking Anna to let me go to church," Synnovea said resolutely. "Surely she cannot say me nay, and I'll be able to speak with Natasha about the matter then."

"An' once she finds out ye've talked with the countess, 'tis in me mind she won't be lettin' ye go back."

"She can't be as forbidding as all that," Synnovea replied, but her words lacked conviction.

Ali responded with a genuine snort of derision. "The princess won't take kindly ter ye seein' the countess behind her back."

The slender shoulders moved in an indistinct shrug. "We can only wait and see what happens. 'Tis unlikely that Anna will be letting me go out soon anyway, but perhaps later she might." Taking Ali's arm, she bade the woman, "Now come along. Elisaveta is waiting to hear about her sister. And I must get dressed for dinner before Princess Anna comes out in search of us!"

A short time later, Synnovea, gowned in the turquoise *sarafan* she had worn that morning, joined Ivan and the Princess Anna in the great hall. Shortly thereafter the woman presented a bill, but it was not until Synnovea had returned to her room that she noticed Anna's accounting for the reward did not match the sum Tyrone had given her in the pouch. Either he had taken some of the coins out or the princess had greatly enlarged the figure she had supposedly given him. Since there had been no need for the colonel to return the purse, that only left her to wonder about the greed of the princess who had more than enough wealth of her own.

In the morning Synnovea returned to the dining hall to find Ivan already filling his plate. He seemed rather smug with his performance as disciplinarian and closely watched for further infractions that he might pounce on. Synnovea was almost relieved when the front door was thrown open and Aleksei came striding into the room, looking as formidable as the burly Petrov. He was unshaven, and his red eyes bespoke many hours quenched with copious libations and riotous living.

"You there!" he bellowed at Ivan, giving the smaller man a violent start. The plate slipped from the bony hands and crashed to the floor, where it gyrated in undulating circles, flinging food helter-skelter. Aleksei seemed almost mesmerized by the twirling dish until the motion ceased, then he raised his glowering dark eyes and fixed them on Ivan. "You seem brave enough when my wife is present," he taunted contemptuously. "Why do you quake with fear now, little toad?"

Ivan swallowed convulsively and tried to ignore the vindictive prodding of the other man, but when he spoke, his voice cracked with trepidation. Little evidence remained of the brashness he had displayed in the presence of his benefactress. "The Princess Anna has not yet awakened, Your Highness. Do you wish me to fetch her for you?"

"When I want my wife, I'll fetch her myself!" the prince bellowed, setting the cleric back on his heels. It was only when he glanced toward the disquieted Synnovea that Aleksei made an earnest attempt to control his temper. Though his nostrils still flared with anger, he released his breath in low, irritated snorts until finally he was able to speak to the other man in a reasonable tone. "I've just been informed by a messenger that Anna's father has fallen ill in the monastery. Her mother would like her to come ere long. It is in my mind that Anna will deem you a worthy escort. Therefore, were I you, I would make preparations for the trip."

Ivan seemed stunned by the prospect of another long, difficult journey ahead of him, especially when they could be attacked again. "But I just returned from . . . "

"I'm sure if I know my wife, you'll have a few days to make ready," Aleksei stated with lanquid indifference. Having thoroughly detached himself from any smallest concern for the other man's discomforts, he raised his head in silent eloquence and stared at some distant point until Ivan quietly left the room.

" 'Twould appear you will be spared Voronsky's instructions in the near future, Countess, at least for a time." Aleksei took up a plate and began selecting tidbits from the platters Elisaveta had laid out upon the sideboard. He cast a glance askance to note Synnovea's reaction and caught the worried frown that marked her brow. "Do I detect a hint of sadness in your sweet visage?" He smiled slyly, knowing well what troubled her spirit. "Or a concern that the two of us will be ensconced here entirely alone? Except for the servants, we shall have the house completely to ourselves."

Synnovea faced him unflinchingly. "On the contrary, Prince Aleksei. I'm sure your wife will now approve of me staying with the Countess Andreyevna in her absence. 'Twould be unseemly for you and I to remain here together without a proper chaperon. You know how tongues are wont to wag, and I would not see your sterling character besmirched by my presence here."

Aleksei threw his head back and laughed heartily at the absurdity of her suggestion. "You are a woman of clever wit, Synnovea. I find myself much refreshed by your presence." His warm brown eyes gleamed as he stroked a knuckle beneath the edge of his mustache. "I shall enjoy getting to know you better."

"When we are properly attended by others, of course," Synnovea agreed with only the slightest trace of a challenging smile.

Settling briefly into a pert curtsy, she left him to dine alone and made her way upstairs to her chambers. She was not at all anxious to be within close proximity to the man when Anna gave vent to her tirade.

Chapter 8

A<small>N EARLY MORNING BREEZE WAFTED OVER THE CITY AS</small>
Tsar Mikhail Feodorovich Romanov leisurely strolled
along the walk which stretched atop the Kremlin's high
wall. His dark eyes closely followed the drilling of a
mounted regiment as they rode down below in the
vast, open area of Red Square. The horsemanship of
the commander of the elite cavalry unit easily claimed
his attention, for he had seen very few riders with a talent
to equal his, except for perhaps the Cossacks who could
easily mesmerize the casual observer with their daring
equestrian skills. Though General Vanderhout, in speaking to several Russian generals, had boasted of his own
successful accomplishments in devising the tactics which
supposedly had directed a detachment from his foreign-
led division in a foray against a large band of thieves,
Mikhail had been much enlightened when he had bade
the newly promoted Major Nekrasov to report on the
Countess Zenkovna's journey to Moscow and had heard
a tale of highwaymen, led by a bastard of Polish and Cossack descent, attacking the young *boyarina*'s entourage
and then being put to rout, without prior design, by a
certain English colonel and the Russian Hussars he had
trained, part of the same regiment which, unbeknown to
them, performed for him now.

The crisp performance and pulsing cadence of the
mounted Hussars struck Mikhail's heart with zealous

fervor as he watched from his elevated position. The helmeted heads turned in unison at the sharp count of their commander, and beneath the gilded rays of the morning sun, their swords flashed in dazzling brilliance as the men lifted the weapons high and then snapped them blunt-side against their shoulders. It was a presentation he had not previously witnessed, but an exercise he was just now beginning to realize he greatly enjoyed. He would have to make a point of meeting this Englishman in the near future, for the officer obviously had a flair for organizing flamboyant exhibitions in an open field, as well as effectively proving his military prowess in actual combat.

Mikhail cocked his head thoughtfully and peered askance at his officer of the guard, who stood just beyond the Field Marshall. "Major Nekrasov?"

At the summons, the officer promptly approached and, with a briskly executed salute, paid a soldier's obeisance to his sovereign. "Yours to command, Great Tsar of all the Russias."

Mikhail clasped his hands behind him as he perused the neatly uniformed officer. "Major Nekrasov, do you speak English?"

Nikolai was somewhat surprised by the question, but answered without hesitation. "Yes, Your Exalted Worship."

"Good! Then will you kindly inform the commander of the regiment whom we are now viewing that I would like the opportunity to address him within the next several days. He may make a request for an audience in the petitioner's box and will be informed some time thereafter of my reply. Do you have any questions?"

"None, Your Excellency."

"The man is a foreigner," Mikhail stated. "Instruct him on the diplomacy of the Court so he will not embarrass himself or cause me to see him punished."

"Yes, Your Excellency."

"That is all."

Nikolai clasped an arm across his breast and went down on a knee before the tsar, who with a brief, casual gesture granted him dismissal. With great dispatch the major took his leave and, several moments later, having descended to the ground level through the closest tower, hailed the commander of the Hussars as he hastened across the field toward the tightly maneuvering riders.

"Colonel Rycroft!" he called again, but after failing to gain a response a second time, he hurried across another lengthy space before trying again to be heard above the noise of clattering hooves and the sharply barked commands. "Colonel Rycroft!"

Finally the summons penetrated the din, and Tyrone turned his mount to face the one who approached. Recognizing the major, he gave a nod to Captain Tverskoy, temporarily yielding the drilling of the cavalry unit to his second-in-command. Pushing back the leather helm, Tyrone wiped a knuckle across a sweating brow as he awaited the rapidly advancing officer.

"Colonel Rycroft!" Nikolai cried again with great excitement as he halted beside the Englishman. "His Majesty the Tsar would like to see you!" He raised his arm and, half turning, pointed toward the high wall, directing the colonel's gaze upward to the men who stood there. "He has been watching you for some time now!"

Tyrone raised a hand to shield his eyes from the sun and squinted up at the small cluster of high-ranking officials that had gathered there. "What do you suppose he wants with me?"

"You've impressed him!" Nikolai answered in amazement, almost in awe of anyone who could perform such a feat. "You are to arrange an audience with him in the next several days!"

Tyrone dragged the reins loosely through his fingers and, gathering them close, rested his hand upon the pommel of the saddle as he cocked a brow at the major. The tsar's recognition was what he had been striving to achieve, but he was rather astonished at how quickly he had gained his objective. "And how should I go about accomplishing that?"

"I am to personally instruct you on what is expected, Colonel. If you are free this evening, we can meet at my quarters. The sooner you respond, the better you will show respect for His Majesty."

"Of course," Tyrone agreed, giving up his plans to ride out to the Taraslov house later on in the evening. In the last pair of weeks he had drilled his men with such dedicated diligence he had given himself no time for appeasing a strengthening desire to seek Synnovea out. He had thought if he could persuade Ali to arrange a meeting this very afternoon, he could perhaps salve his yearning to talk with the girl and plead his cause once again. Of late, the dark-haired beauty seemed to occupy his mind with singular persistence. Even in the dead of night, he would wake from a fitful sleep with her face before him, a sense of her naked softness lingering hauntingly against his skin. The difficulty was in banishing those lewdly provocative imaginings from his mind, and though he would pace the length and breadth of his bedchamber in an effort to set his thoughts on something less disturbing, he would be left painfully tormented by his growing hunger for her. This meeting with Major Nekrasov was more important than his planned visit only because an audience with the tsar could be most effective in gaining him what he really wanted. It was what he had been aspiring to obtain. Without a doubt, Tsar Mikhail could open any door in Russia that had been abruptly slammed in his face.

A pair of weeks had fled since Synnovea's arrival at the Taraslov manse, and in that time she had been forced to endure Ivan's phlegmatic instructions, Anna's terse diatribes, and Aleksei's zealous pursuits, albeit the latter well out of earshot and eyesight of his wife. Synnovea was beginning to feel as jittery as a small sparrow beneath the sharp eye of a black crow. It seemed in every shadowed area she passed there lurked a danger of being surprised by the prince and, even more disturbing, the possibility of being fondled in a direct or feigned manner as he confronted her in the halls, the chambers, or on the stairs. It was maddening, to say the least, to find herself the prey in this game of chase, but Aleksei seemed intent on taking advantage of every opportunity that presented itself while Anna devoted most of her time and attention to aiding Ivan Voronsky in his ambitious climb to fame.

As for the Princess Anna, she had postponed her visit to her father's bedside, deeming the planning of a reception honoring Ivan more important. The two had become almost inseparable and, while Aleksei roamed elsewhere, would ride off together in the princess's carriage to visit *boyars* of great power and wealth in an effort to abet whatever kindred spirits they could and, if the atmosphere was right, carefully encourage any adverse sentiments that might exist against the Patriarch Filaret Nikitich.

Early Wednesday morning, Prince Aleksei informed his wife that he would be attending business affairs in a neighboring city and did not expect to be back until late the following day. His announcement left Anna feeling confident about leaving her charge alone in the manse while she and Ivan went out. It never entered her mind that she was being duped.

Shortly after the pair made their departure in the afternoon, Synnovea sent Ali off with Stenka to attend the needs of Elisaveta's sister, Danika, and her daughter. Both were making good progress after nearly starving; the mother was looking forward to the possibility of finding work in the Countess Andreyevna's house.

In the absence of Ali, Synnovea settled herself down at a small table in the Taraslov gardens to search through the works of Pliny the Elder that supposedly dealt with the natural history of man, in hopes of gaining a more vivid understanding of some outlandish claims Ivan had made, which she had considered too farfetched to even give credence to and, after some research, deemed just as ridiculous as before.

It was shortly after the tolling of bells at the three-o'clock hour when a somewhat surprised Boris opened the door for Prince Aleksei. Regaining his wits, the servant hastened to address the master of the house.

"We weren't expecting you to return until the morrow, my lord."

"A change of plans, Boris." Aleksei glanced casually about. "Is my wife here?"

"No, my lord. The Princess Anna left more than an hour ago with—"

"The good Ivan Voronsky, I suppose." Aleksei allowed a little irritation to show for the benefit of the servant, who hurried to allay any explosions of husbandly jealousy.

"They went to visit Prince Vladimir Dimitrievich at his home, my lord. I'm sure the Princess Anna would be delighted if you joined them there, sir."

"What? And suffer through another lecture of that old *boyar*'s prospects for producing other progeny in his dwindling years?" Aleksei laughed with a negative shake of his head as the steward hid an amused snigger behind a gloved hand. "I think not, Boris. At his advanced age, Prince Vladimir should be thinking of dividing up his wealth to the sons he already has rather than thinking of begetting new ones."

Leaving the hall, Aleksei made his way leisurely through the house and finally out to the gardens, where he found Synnovea sitting with her chin propped in her hands. Intent upon her studies, she did not notice him until he had drawn near.

"My dear Synnovea. . . ."

The softly coiffed head snapped up in surprise, and as Synnovea met the prince's smiling gaze, his name escaped her lips in an astonished rush. "Prince Aleksei!"

For a moment Aleksei stared into the most startled green eyes he was sure he had ever beheld, then a deep chuckle escaped him as he plumbed the depth of her sudden disquiet. She was about as skittish as a young hare which had just been cornered by a wily fox.

"Prince Aleksei!" Synnovea repeated with more vigor as she quickly rose to her feet. "We weren't expecting you to return until the morrow. My goodness, won't Anna be surprised!" Her breathless tone readily conveyed her nervous distrust. "She should be back any moment now, I'm sure. . . . "

Synnovea's words dwindled to a wary silence as his dark eyes gleamed back at her in dubious amusement. "Come now, my dear Synnovea," he gently reproached. "We both know Anna is wont to dally overlong whenever she accompanies Ivan on one of his jaunts to fame. She has ambitions not unlike his, you know."

Almost in mesmerized distraction, his gaze dipped to where the square décolletage taunted him with a bolder view of her creamy-skinned bosom than he had hitherto been afforded. A crisp, lace-trimmed ruff adorned the slender column of her throat and was coyly fastened with a dainty lavender ribbon that matched the flowery lawn of her gown. Below it, the close-fitting bodice accentuated the slenderness of her waist, while the precarious neckline left him almost panting in suspense. He licked his lips in anticipation of that moment when the delicious fullness might exceed the limits of its restrictive covering and appease his hungering gaze with a more revealing view.

The light summer gown of European design had obviously been donned well after Anna's departure and perhaps had been intended for coolness rather than for display, but he was certainly not one to complain about her gown, for it allowed him to savor the sweet, pleasurable delights of her beauty. Though he recognized the fact that he was not as well traveled as their charge, he was persuaded to think the girl could enchant men all over the world with her stirring beauty.

"May I join you?" he inquired, momentarily presenting his best manners.

"O-of course," Synnovea replied, wondering how she could reply otherwise. Indeed, had she taken the initiative to tell him nay, he probably would have seized her outright.

Aleksei sought to close the space between them, and in swift reaction, Synnovea stepped around the table to pour herself a chilled glass of watered wine. Managing a tremulous smile beneath his warming regard, she gulped a sip before she remembered her manners. Most reluctantly she swept a hand to indicate the pitcher of wine and a small plate of cakes which Elisaveta had brought out to her. "Would you care for some refreshments?"

Aleksei smiled at her guise of gracious hostess, well acquainted with the ploys of a timid maid. Her actions were merely a ruse to place a barrier between them, as if by some miracle the tiny table would offer her protection against the encroachment of a passionate suitor.

"Perhaps a glass of watered wine," he murmured, dragging off his headdress. Laying the cap aside, he braced both hands on the table and leaned forward to take note of what she had been reading. "Pliny the Elder?" Peering at her with some skepticism, he flicked a hand toward the pages of the tome. "What weighty matter has Ivan now been expounding that you must consume your free time reading Pliny the Elder?"

Synnovea's chin raised a notch as she remembered Ivan's jeering condescension when he had learned that her knowledge of the man's writings was most limited. "Ivan said that Pliny the Elder was a genius who had spent most of his waking hours either reading, penning notes, or studying the works of others and that any fairly astute student should closely attend his writings, as if," she stressed the last pair of words to indicate her annoyance with her tutor, "they had come down with the laws of heaven."

Aleksei's mouth twitched with humor as he perceived that her pride had been badly mauled. "And what think you now after you've explored some of Pliny's works? Is he as wise as Ivan purports?"

The softly coiffured head was tossed high with scorn. "What?! Mouthless men who subsist upon the mere fragrance of flowers? Umbrella-footed men who shade themselves from the sun with such strangely gross extremities? 'Tis absolutely absurd to believe Pliny was unquestioned as a prodigy, even in Roman times."

"Of course, that was only a sampling of Pliny's most imaginary works," Aleksei remarked as a grin broadened his sultry red lips, "but such observations make one question his credence as a scholar." He straightened and eyed her with close attention. "So now what do you think of Ivan's logic? Do you embrace or reject it?"

Synnovea shrugged cautiously, not knowing what he might reveal to Anna if she dared to foolishly divulge her aversion to the man. " 'Tis merely my own thought, of course, but it seems that in some matters Ivan is not entirely correct or as brilliant a scholar as some would have."

"My wife would not agree with you," the prince remarked with casual candor as he accepted the goblet Synnovea offered him. "But then, my dear, I'm more inclined to endorse your views. The man has been a thorn in my flesh ever since he attached himself to my wife. He seems to have the ability to sway her reasoning to correlate with his. 'Tis indeed a rare gift he has, for it's more than I've been able to do in a full score years of marriage."

Aleksei lifted his head and gazed out over the carefully tended garden. He was not a man who gave himself over to the enjoyment of such simple pleasures, but with Synnovea close at hand he felt himself almost relaxing in the peaceful tranquility that surrounded them. Perhaps if he had wed a woman who had been able to content herself with his wealth and princely possessions instead of being driven with an insatiable ambition to have the best of everything, he might have been content as well and devoted more of his attention to nurturing a love for her. There were times now when he felt almost driven to flaunt his many conquests before Anna, as if he sought revenge on her for the disquiet churning within him.

"Will you walk with me through the garden, Synnovea?" he asked, continuing around the table. Halting close beside her, he took her arm and swept his other hand toward the flower-bordered paths in an invitation for her to join him. " 'Tis been more than a season of years since I've taken time to admire such riotous blooms."

Synnovea warily accepted and moved along the path beside him. "Elisaveta will be expecting me in the kitchen in a few moments," she stated, allowing for a timely escape should he become amorous. "I promised I would help her make bread, so I mustn't be away long."

"A simple walk through the garden won't require too much of your time, Synnovea," Aleksei assured her. "I must leave again shortly, anyway. I left some important documents behind when I left this morning, and I had to come back and fetch them. I thought everyone had gone, and then I noticed you were out here." He raised his head again and slowly inhaled the sweet, heady fragrance that wafted from several large blossoms growing nearby. "I had almost forgotten such pleasures exist."

Glancing over her shoulder, Synnovea noticed they were no longer within sight of the house, for the draping limbs of a tree now obscured the trail behind them. "Perhaps we should go back now."

"Not yet, Synnovea." His hand slipped downward to clasp hers, and when she recoiled in nervous trepidation and tried to pull away, he laughed and raised his free hand to indicate the path ahead. "Did you ever see the dovecote? It's just up ahead."

Hearing a soft cooing sound beyond them, Synnovea conceded for the moment and let him draw her with him. He released her hand as they approached a tall, white circular coop where a dozen or more pigeons calmly roosted or flew back and forth from their nests. The fluttering of wings warned of an approaching bird, and Synnovea turned to observe the flight of a dove until it settled with a last, brief flap of wings to a slender perch jutting out from an empty cubby.

"This could be dangerous," Aleksei observed drolly as another bird flew directly overhead. "Let's get away before we find your pretty gown spotted." Seizing her hand again, he pulled her along behind him down a path that turned sharply away from the cote. Though Synnovea sought to disentangle her fingers, knowing they roamed farther away from the manse, Aleksei held fast and bade over his shoulder, "Don't be afraid, Synnovea. Come! I've something else to show you."

He brought her in sight of a small hut nestled against a high wooden fence which served as a barrier around the estate. Dragging her with him onto the wooden planks of the porch, he pushed open the door and would have ventured inside, but Synnovea balked at the idea of being hauled into the dark cottage against her will. Stiffening her limbs much like a stubborn young calf, she braced her feet wide and refused to be drawn another step forward.

"No, Aleksei!" she cried. "This is not right! Please! Let me go! I must go back to the house!"

Aleksei chortled in high glee as he stepped back to her. His eyes glowed brightly as they plunged deeply into the troubled green pools. "Come inside, Synnovea," he coaxed, inclining his head ever so slightly toward the open door. "Let me make of you the woman you deserve to be. No one will know we've spent this time together." His red lips parted in a compelling smile. "The servants are loyal to me, and none of them will tell Anna that I've been here today, so we need make no excuse to her." With a brief nod, he indicated the door again. "No one comes here. The old woodcutter that lives here in the wintertime has gone away now. He won't be back until fall. We'll have the cabin completely to ourselves. You need not be embarrassed or afraid."

"No!" Synnovea shook her head in a passionate denial. "This thing you intend will never be, Aleksei! 'Tis not right!"

"Right? Wrong?" He tossed his head from side to side. "Who can argue that this is wrong when we are meant for each other, Synnovea?"

"*I can!*" she declared hotly.

His shoulders lifted in a languid shrug. "I will take you as I will, Synnovea. 'Tis of little consequence if you struggle. In time you will come to enjoy my caresses."

Aleksei tried to slip an arm around her waist to pull her close, but Synnovea snatched away and glared back at him with eyes flashing with a feral glint. "If you force me against my will, Aleksei," she warned in a low, ragged tone, "then I swear you will reap my revenge. I'll go to Anna myself and tell her of your evil deed. I'll *not* be one of your trollops to be seized and taken at your whim! Even if I have no choice but to go to Tsar Mikhail himself, I'll see that you pay for any offense you commit against me!"

An abortive laugh came from Aleksei as he stared back at her. Still clasping her wrist, he stood before her with feet widespread and smirked with unmitigated confidence. "Think you that you can threaten me and dance away to your delight, my girl?! Nay, let it never be said. Your words will spill on deaf ears, for I will make of them a lie and pledge my troth that you speak falsely. Anna will hear no slander from you. So you see, my dear, how shallow your threats really are? Truly, Synnovea, there's no use fighting me. I'll have you when and where I please." His eyes caressed the tempting fullness above her gown, and his voice deepened. "Even today, my sweetling."

Smiling benignly, he slipped his fingers quickly into the hollow between her breasts and caught hold of her gown. Synnovea gasped in outrage, but before she could react or snatch away, he jerked his hand downward with a vicious swipe, ripping the stomacher free from the bodice.

"*No!*" Synnovea stumbled back in surprise and gaped at the man as if he had lost his wits.

"You've become the very essence of my desire, Synnovea. This thing between us was meant to be."

The dark eyes lowered, and his breath dragged harshly inward as he stared. Synnovea's gaze dropped, following his, and she saw to her dismay that the delicate chemise offered her no worthy comfort above her stays, but wantonly exposed her bosom as its fullness strained tightly against the thin batiste.

Aleksei stretched out a hand toward her again, and with an infuriated gasp Synnovea leapt away in an urgent attempt to flee. It did her little good, for he caught a hand in her hair and, hauling her backward, lifted her up into his arms. Shouldering the door aside, he pushed his way into the cottage, kicked the panel closed behind him, and crossed to where a narrow cot occupied a corner of the room. It was covered with several wolf's pelts, which seemed to completely enfold Synnovea as he dropped her upon the bed. Aleksei watched her intently as he snatched open his *kaftan*, and though Synnovea's eyes flew about the cabin in a frenzied search for an avenue of escape, he seemed totally confident of what the next moments would bear. He tossed the outer garment aside, leaving a thin shirt and close-fitting leggings to cover his long frame. As he moved a step to her left, Synnovea glimpsed an open space between him and the small bedside table standing near the head of the cot. Hoping to quickly scurry through, she scrambled to her knees, but he was faster and shoved her back down upon the pelts. Holding her thus, he jerked the cot away from the wall and settled astride the narrow bed, stilling her wild thrashing beneath his greater weight. In an impatient endeavor to pull her skirts up to her waist, he lifted himself slightly to tug them out from between them.

Synnovea's tenacity was hardly subdued. Bracing herself on her elbows, she tried quickly to wiggle out from under him, but almost immediately Aleksei settled his weight upon her again, preventing her escape. Gritting her teeth in frustration, Synnovea glanced toward the table and, spying a small honing stone which had been left there, reached out to seize it within her grasp. Aleksei's attention was diverted by a coveted view of a bare thigh and his eagerness to uncover more. He never saw the small fist tightly embracing the rock as it curved upward in a wide arc. Forcing every bit of her determination and strength behind the blow, Synnovea caught him squarely against the side of his nose, setting it abruptly askew.

"AAAaaooohhhHHH!"

The pained yowl seemed to shake the hut right down to its very foundation as Aleksei reeled backward from the blow, clasping his hands to his face. A vivid array of colors bedazzled him for a moment as an unbearable agony blinded him to everything else. Several large droplets of blood splattered downward onto his white shirt, and as his sight cleared and he spread his hands, he gaped down in slack-jawed awe at the red splotches, as if in disbelief. It seemed almost beyond credence that his blood could be spilled by such a winsomely slender maid, but the anguish was too intense for him to doubt the fact. With a surging groan, he swept his hand beneath his nose, trying to wipe away the dribbling redness, but he was bleeding too profusely now to stem the flow. The slightest touch sent sharp, splintering shards of excruciating pain shooting into his brow, from there expanding and seeming to reach to the very ends of his nerves. He found the anguish too great to bear, and losing all desire to fulfil his lustful cravings, he lifted himself from the bed and stumbled in a pained stupor to the washstand, where he snatched a towel and pressed it tightly to his nose.

Synnovea did not pause. Amid a wild flurry of flying skirts, she leapt from the bed and raced out the door. No one witnessed her frantic entry into the manse a moment later, but it was not until she had locked the door of her bedchamber behind her that she felt safe from Prince Aleksei and whatever revenge he might seek. There, oblivious to the heat, she waited with bated breath until at long last she heard his carriage leave. His stallion trailed behind at the end of a tether, lending her some hope that he wouldn't be back for several days. When the conveyance finally disappeared from sight, she heaved a deep sigh of relief, immensely glad she had survived his attack without suffering undue loss.

Chapter 9

IT WAS THE THIRD SUNDAY AFTER SYNNOVEA'S ARRIVAL when cooling breezes finally brought welcome respite from the hot, sweltering days of summer. Scudding gray clouds chased across the early morning sky and gave some hope to hearts yearning for rain. It would only be a few weeks now before the weather would begin to cool, and the intense heat would be but a memory.

Aleksei had returned a pair of days earlier, giving the lame excuse that he had broken his nose after a fall from his stallion. For the sake of his handsome profile, he had endured the anguish of his nose being righted by a physician and was wont to liberally indulge in strong intoxicants to ease the pain. A dark purplish swelling around his nose and beneath his eyes still tarnished his handsome visage, and by now it could be determined that a definite lump would remain to mar the manly sleekness of it and to remind him by whose hand he had acquired the wound. For the present moment he was reluctant to challenge Synnovea's stilted reserve. He was no longer doubtful of her ability to do him ill, at least for the present, and he feared another such blow would see him completely undone, for he was loath to endure the same torture all over again. The idea was enough to make him extremely leery of approaching the girl until his nose was completely healed.

On this particular Sunday, he had announced that he would remain at home, for his vanity prevented him from pursuing other light of loves until the break was completely mended. Anna had made arrangements to go with Ivan to a private chapel belonging to the immensely wealthy *boyar* Prince Vladimir Dimitrievich. Since neither Ivan nor Anna wanted the ancient, a widower with a heart for marriage, to be distracted from their discourse by the presence of a comely young maid, the possibility of Synnovea accompanying them to the *chasovnyas* was considered out of the question, but while her husband remained abed, Anna did not trust the girl to stay behind either. Thus, she was left with little choice but to allow Synnovea to arrange her own sabbatical, as long as it was well away from the Taraslov manse and the invalid, Prince Aleksei.

Whatever Anna's reasons for letting her go, Synnovea was elated to have been granted freedom for the day. Even Anna's severe threats and dire warnings to return by late afternoon could not squelch her enthusiasm. So great was her feeling of freedom, Synnovea almost raced to meet the conveyance when Stenka pulled it around in front of the manse. She was more than eager to enjoy the world outside of her rigidly enforced confinement.

Synnovea had carefully outfitted herself in a *sarafan* of ice-blue satin liberally adorned with heavy white lace and seed pearls. A similarly embellished *kokoshniki* had been settled upon her head, and a blue ribbon, sewn with the same dainty pearls, had been woven through the single dark braid. A cloak of matching design was taken into the carriage, but Synnovea chose to leave the garment behind as she prepared to alight, for it was still too warm to wear it and the sun had begun to peek intermittently through the clouds, lending her a good measure of confidence that the weather was about to clear.

Stenka halted the coach a short distance from a church located on Red Square, close to where the Countess

Natasha Andreyevna had paused outside her own carriage. The woman, recognizing the coachman and the conveyance he drove, hurried to greet her young friend as Jozef swung open the door. Espying her, Synnovea descended the steps in a lighthearted rush as Natasha laughed in glee and threw her arms wide in invitation. In a thrice of steps the young countess was enfolded within the elder's embrace.

"I should scold you for not coming to see me!" Natasha fussed and drew back amid a profusion of tears. "Have you forgotten that I'm not welcomed at the Taraslovs'?"

"Oh, Natasha, you know I haven't forgotten," Synnovea replied as her own gaze blurred, "but Anna hasn't allowed me to venture from the house until today." She laid a consoling hand upon the slender arm of the other. "However, I suspect there may be a change coming soon."

"It sounds as if Anna has isolated you in your own personal *terem*, as if you were some grand tsarina." Natasha made the conjecture ruefully as she searched the beautiful green eyes for an answer. "It must be extremely difficult for you to live under such restrictions when you were nurtured with the same freedom as women all over England and France. Your mother laid a good foundation for you by instructing Aleksandr in the genteel deportment of an English gentleman, and for a Russian, your father was astoundingly receptive to her persuasions, but then, Eleanora had a most endearing way about her. But you say there is some hope that circumstances will soon be altered?"

"There is that possibility." Synnovea gave a small nod, then lifted a hand to caution the elder. "Mind you, there's been no indication as yet that Anna will actually be going, nor should I even say she will allow me to leave while she visits her ailing father, but I rather suspect she'll not feel too safe leaving me alone with Aleksei."

"Well, I can hardly blame her there," Natasha responded wryly and raised her brows briefly to silently lend emphasis to her insinuations. "The man's a rake, of the first merit." She patted the slender hand of the younger. "Take warning, my child."

Synnovea's own brows flicked upward as she agreed with the woman. "Oh, I've learned to be wary. Indeed, I fear to leave my rooms while that greedy crow waits to pick my bones."

"Do you have any idea when Anna might leave?"

"If she goes at all, it won't be until some time after next Saturday. That's when she intends to honor Ivan Voronsky with a grand celebration."

"Ivan Voronsky?" Natasha spoke the name incredulously and then looked at the younger woman with increasing sympathy. "Oh, my dear Synnovea, I do pity your situation. I only wish His Majesty had seen fit to send you into my care. I'm sure he had no idea we were such close friends, especially if he gave any heed to Anna's gossip and was convinced that I was only interested in your father. He probably thought he was doing you a favor by sending you to Anna. After all, Anna is his kin, and under normal circumstances, it would be deemed an honor to be the ward of the tsar's cousin. Tsar Mikhail greatly admired your father, and now that Aleksandr has been taken from us, I know His Majesty wants to be assured of your welfare, so don't judge him too harshly, my dear."

"I shan't, of course. He's already proven the depth of his concern. But tell me, Natasha, if Anna leaves Moscow to visit her father, will you allow me to stay with you?"

"Oh, my child, need you ask?" Natasha chuckled gayly. "Of course, you may! Indeed! I'll not hear of you staying with anyone else!"

The bells in the belfry began to clang above their heads, and as the last grew silent, a lilting hymn drifted from the church. The two women turned their attention to the sweet, melodious voices that seemed to beckon as they walked arm in arm into the magnificently embellished interior. A rosy aura, softly cast from the mica windows,

surrounded them as they stood together in the section set
aside for women and children. There, they murmured
prayers and sang songs, listened to the oration of the
priest and the angelic hymns of young boys dressed
in white vestments. It was a restful, peaceful time, like
many others they had previously shared in that same
church, except that now they knew there would only
be the two of them after the services. The memory of
Aleksandr Zenkov remained sweet to each, and they
clasped hands in understanding silence when their
thoughts turned to him and their eyes misted with tears.

It was some three hours later when they emerged
from the church to find that the clouds were now
looming dark and impenetrable above the city. A fresh
splattering of droplets brought with them sweet respite
and a refreshing essence, but Synnovea stood under the
portico in mute dismay, reluctant to see another gown
ruined. She contemplated the seemingly endless breach
that lay between her and the coach, a space that had
become quickly filled with a large mass of people, many
flowing from other churches located nearby, and a maze
of conveyances caught in a crowded, congested tangle.
It would be some time before Natasha's coachman or
Stenka could maneuver their carriages around in front
of the church to pick them up.

"Stenka is closer," Synnovea announced. "He can pick
both of us up and take you back to your house."

"Until the path clears enough for him to get through,"
Natasha observed as she assessed the situation, "we'll
either have to run for it or stay here. From the way the
sky looks, I rather doubt we'll be able to avoid a storm in
any eventuality." She lifted her own cloak in an invitation
to shelter them both. "Shall we try to reach your coach
before the rain starts in earnest?"

Accepting the offer, Synnovea huddled with the woman beneath the costly tent and matched her hastening
strides as they left the portico. It seemed the rain only
awaited their departure from shelter, for they had

barely ventured forth when a sudden, heavy downpour was unleashed upon them. As the crowd rapidly
dispersed ahead of them, Synnovea caught sight of
Jozef scampering down from the rear of her carriage
to open the door for them, while Stenka leaned down
from the driver's seat and directed another man, who
had halted beside the coach, toward the place where
she was. The man, garbed in a long cloak and wide-
brimmed hat, twisted around to look where the servant
had pointed, and Synnovea came to an abrupt halt as she
recognized the undauntable Colonel Rycroft. He found
her immediately through the maze of people and came
running toward her.

Synnovea had no opportunity to retreat or even a
chance to react, for without warning a force from behind caught her solidly against the back and sent her
sprawling forward to her hands and knees. The culprit,
a huge simple-minded lummox who had panicked when
he had found himself separated from those who led him,
glanced down briefly as he plowed past her. Even then,
he almost stepped on her in his frenzy to find a familiar
face. Close behind him, a group of strapping youths raced
for their mounts, nearly treading on the heels of the oaf.
With the heavy rains coming down in blinding sheets
all around them, they remained heedless of her presence
until they were directly upon her. By then, it was too
late for an orderly evasion. Trying to avoid stepping or
falling on her, they leapt over, around, and finally upon
as one fell short of his goal and came down upon her
foot, wrenching a cry of pain from her lips. Synnovea
was presented no latitude to get to her feet while she
faced the imminent threat of being trampled. She could
do naught but huddle in dread of that moment while the
deluge of rain cascaded upon her to thoroughly saturate
her clothes.

Frantically aware of her young friend's predicament,
Natasha pushed against those who came dangerously
close, but her strength was far too flimsy against such

stalwart forms. "Begone with you!" she railed at them from beneath her cloak. "Can't you see where you're going?"

In the next moment a dark shape loomed over them, discouraging the progress of the men and causing Natasha to stumble back in some awe. A long cloak formed a protective screen around Synnovea as she was lifted to her feet by the strongly competent hands of Colonel Rycroft. Vaguely she was aware of him sheltering her with his own body as she took a limping step forward, but before she could take another, he bent and swept her up in his arms. They were iron-thewed and completely capable, the very essence of every fantasy a maid might hold dear, and although Synnovea was not one to be so easily won, the circumstances were such that she gave Tyrone no resistance, but clasped her own arms about his neck with nearly the same intensity she had used when she had been faced with the threat of drowning. His hat offered some protection from the pelting bombardment of rain, and she gave no consideration to the proper decorum of an unwed maid as she leaned her brow against his cheek. In response, Tyrone lifted a shoulder to cradle her more securely and ran with long, sprinting strides to her carriage, bearing her weight as easily as he would a young child.

Utterly flabbergasted by the boldness of the chivalrous man, Natasha Andreyevna gaped after them for one short, astounded moment before she, too, hastened toward the coach, albeit at a much slower, more ladylike pace. Her cloak did her little good now that it was completely soaked, and her slippers were so full of water it was hard for her to keep them on, which only hindered her progress.

"Are you all right?" Tyrone questioned solicitously as he lifted Synnovea into the coach.

"Yes, Colonel Rycroft, of course. Thank you." Synnovea was embarrassed by her soggy appearance and most reluctant to meet his gaze.

As she pulled away from him, Tyrone watched her wince and brace herself cautiously on the edge of the seat. Curiously he reached out to push the hem of her soaked gown away from her ankle and saw where a large black bruise now swelled the side of the slender foot. "You're hurt!"

"Truly, 'tis nothing!" Synnovea gasped. Blushing at his forwardness, she quickly dragged her foot away from his grasp and hauled her sopping wet form to the far corner of the seat. Once again she avoided his gaze as she struggled to cool her flaming cheeks. " 'Tis naught but a bruise, I assure you, Colonel Rycroft. 'Twill heal quickly."

Tyrone could not fully understand why she should be so abashed by his inspection when he had seen and held far more of her than a shapely ankle, but since Jozef waited beside him at the door, he was persuaded to hold his silence rather than remind the girl of that earlier event.

"A cold compress might help," Tyrone suggested, having dressed many a wound in his years as an officer, not to mention a few of his own as well. "Stay off the foot if you can."

" 'Twould seem I'm indebted to you once again, Colonel." In some confusion Synnovea blinked the droplets from her lashes as she finally yielded her gaze to his unwavering regard. She wanted to pluck the *sarafan* away from her breasts as she felt water trickling down the valley between them, but was afraid to move, lest he notice the way the cloth clung to her. His eyes delved into hers instead, as if he probed her inner thoughts. Not knowing what he searched or waited for, Synnovea felt obliged to offer, "May we take you somewhere, Colonel?"

"There's no need," Tyrone declined, still distracted by his musings. "My horse is near."

Nevertheless he made no effort to leave but continued to stare at her in some bemusement. He could not help but wonder how many more faces of her character waited to be glimpsed and treasured, like a collection of precious pearls on a strand. First, he had viewed the outraged countess clutched in the arms of her captor, then the wanton seductress taking her bath and later perched in the window. He had seen her as the winsome sprite in peasant garb and now the vulnerable young girl in need of a champion to defend her. Though she seemed hesitant and abashed by this most recent occurrence, Tyrone was crushingly sensitive to the strongly protective instincts that had surged within him when he had seen her fall. His reaction was far more complex than he could rationally explain, for not so long ago he had been absolutely sure that all those softer, more vulnerable emotions a man could feel for a woman had been destroyed by betrayal and deceit. Though he greatly desired to claim the young Countess Synnovea as his mistress, he was not at all sure he wanted his heart entangled in a chase he had heretofore considered merely a rutting fever.

Tyrone mentally detached himself from his pensive mood and chuckled as he glanced down at his soaked garb. "I fear, my lady, that neither of us is in any condition to be of much comfort to the other, at least not in a way that is proper." Had he not been so certain that she would turn him down flat, he would have invited her to go back to his quarters with him even now. There he would have explored the advantages of lending her comfort, tending her ankle, and providing her with dry clothing, but to make such a suggestion would be allowing his base instincts to rule where caution was vital. Resisting the urge lest he find all of his hopes completely dashed before his very eyes, Tyrone touched the dripping brim of his hat as he met the troubled green eyes. With a hint of a smile he warmly promised, "Another time, Synnovea."

He turned abruptly and sidestepped Natasha just as the woman reached the carriage. Clamping his hat firmly upon his head, he hunched his shoulders against the rain and swung onto the back of the black stallion, then rode off through the downpour with only a brief, backward glance.

Natasha felt definitely akin to a drowned rat as she climbed into the carriage to sit beside the younger woman, but she was far more interested in the gallant deeds of the stranger than her own ponderously weighty, soaked condition. When she noticed Synnovea's sudden, nervous preoccupation with her ankle, however, she curbed her curiosity and abstained from delving into the subject, sensing the girl's reluctance to discuss the incident. Although she had every intention of finding out who the man was eventually, for the present moment at least she would respect the privacy of her young friend.

"My dear Synnovea, I'll be most upset if you haven't made plans to come home with me for a visit this afternoon," she stated. "You left some clothes there the last time you visited with your father, and since you don't have to be back until much later, I'd take great delight in chatting with you for as long as you dare. Can you not manage to lend a small measure of your time with an old friend?"

"I can, but only for a little while," Synnovea assured. "Otherwise, Anna will be upset with me. I certainly don't wish to return to the Taraslovs' until she is there to keep Aleksei well within the proper bounds of protocol."

"Then it's settled." Natasha gave a nod to the soggy footman. "We can be off now, Jozef, if you're disposed to leaving this deluge."

Chuckling to himself, the man twitched in his sodden garb and closed the door. He climbed to his perch and settled his hat upon his head, assuming a dignified pose as Stenka clucked to the team of horses.

Synnovea tugged the bedraggled headdress from her head and heaved a sigh in wistful detachment. "He always catches me at my worst."

The softly whispered complaint reached Natasha's ears in spite of the noisy pelting of droplets on the carriage roof. Though she tried not to appear overly eager or unnaturally inquisitive, her curiosity was kindled to a roaring flame by the girl's statement. She could not silence an inquiry. "Who, dear?"

Realizing she had been caught thinking aloud, Synnovea tossed Natasha a glance askance and lifted her shoulders in an evasive shrug. "No one, Natasha. No one at all."

"Oh," the elder muttered glumly as she slumped back against the seat in roweling disappointment. She knew the girl would never break her silence when it was a matter she held dear, and obviously the topic of the stranger was a subject Synnovea preferred to keep concealed, which made Natasha wonder all the more. If the maid's reactions were any kind of an indication, then she was inclined to think that the man, whoever he was, had made quite an impression on her.

Natasha sighed forlornly as she needled, "I suppose I must remain ignorant of the identity of the gallant gentleman who carried you to the coach, for 'tis clear you have no intention of confiding in a friend."

In restive unease Synnovea dismissed the matter. " 'Twas no one of any import, Natasha. Really!"

The elder countess responded with a sublime smile. "Nevertheless, I can see that you've been thoroughly distracted by the man."

A deep blush stained Synnovea's cheeks, and to hide it she began to pluck at her skirt and fuss about her clothes. "Ruined! Absolutely ruined! And it was one of my favorite gowns!"

"You did look exquisite in it," Natasha reflected. "But then, my dear, you look simply exquisite in anything you wear. Of course, that's why you attracted the man in the first place. He seems quite taken with you."

Synnovea desperately scoured her thoughts in search of another subject upon which they could comfortably discourse, and she almost relaxed as she recalled the reason she had wanted to see her friend in the first place. "Oh, dear Natasha, forgive me for being so bold, but Anna's cook has a sister, who though ailing now, will be needing work when she improves. Might you have a need she can fill?"

Natasha wasted no moment in asking, "Can she possibly cook?"

An ambiguous shrug accompanied Synnovea's reply. "I fear I know very little about Danika, other than the fact that she's in need, but I can surely ask Elisaveta what her experiences have been."

"If she can cook, send her around when she's well," Natasha suggested. "My old cook died since you last visited with me, and I've a great need to find a replacement ere I lose my wits trying to teach the scullery maid how to boil water. You know with all the guests I have, the meals can be something of a disaster without a proper cook on hand."

"The woman has a child at her side," Synnovea cautioned her friend. "A daughter of three."

Natasha smiled at the thought. " 'Twould be good to hear the laughter of a young child around the house. There are some days when I get very lonely in that huge place, despite all the company I have. The house needs a little sparkle to brighten its dark mood. And if you are kept from my side, dear Synnovea, then I must find another little girl to cherish." This time Natasha did not feign the long, wistful sigh that hinted of a nostalgic mood. "I wish I would have been able to have children of my own. I outlived three husbands, and none of them could give me a child, as much as I wanted one."

The slender hand of the younger countess came to rest with genuine affection upon the elder's, and a gentle smile curved the winsome lips as Synnovea assured her, "Natasha, I shall always think of you as the woman I've loved nearly as dearly as my own mother."

Bright tears blurred the dark eyes as Natasha looked upon the other with great fondness. "And you, my dear beautiful Synnovea, are the daughter I never had, but wanted so very desperately."

* * *

Several days elapsed after Synnovea's initial meeting with Natasha before she was again allowed to venture beyond the Taraslov manse. Her ankle had caused her no more than a single day's discomfort, and then she was back on her feet again. The house was being prepared for Ivan's reception, and it was in this endeavor that Anna sent Synnovea out to make purchases of food in the marketplace of Kitaigorod. She was given strict orders on what to buy, where to get it, and how much to pay for it. Anything above that cost would have to come out of her own pocket. Anna took pains to stress that fact and advise Synnovea to be prudent, lest she pay the cost herself. In addition, she was warned not to dawdle or, Anna promised, there would be dire recompenses to pay.

Stenka halted the coach on Red Square near the markets of Kitaigorod, and Synnovea went the rest of the way on foot with Ali and Jozef to fetch the requested items. She had worn her peasant attire, not wanting to give vendors the impression that she had wealth, for she knew they would be more inclined to settle for less if her affluence was doubted.

Synnovea marked the time when she began, taking Anna's threat seriously, and shopped efficiently, accepting the advice and wisdom Ali and Jozef offered. Each time the basket was filled to its brim, the footman rushed back to the carriage to empty it, while the two women continued browsing through the *ryady* for the best vegetables and fowl. Amid the squawking and honking of outraged hens and geese, Synnovea and Ali finally returned to the coach with Jozef, just as a company of mounted soldiers in complete and resplendent regalia approached. Synnovea's heart thumped in quickening excitement as she recognized Colonel Rycroft riding at the fore of the troop on a different steed than she had ever seen him with. This one was a dark, livered chestnut, as beautiful as the one she had first espied him on, which prompted her to wonder if this was another he had paid to have shipped from England. She would have paused to stare in stirring admiration except that Ali, intent upon catching the man's eye, did a sprightly scamper around the coach to wave her arm and shout his name as he rode near.

"Colonel Rycroft! Yoohoo! Colonel Rycroft!"

"Ali! Stop that!" Synnovea gasped, abashed at the undignified conduct of her servant.

Ali promptly obeyed, but realized to her great delight that she had already gained the officer's attention. An amused grin twitched at Tyrone's lips as he honored the servant with a casual salute, then his eyes searched beyond her for the one whose face now filled many of his waking moments and all of his lusting dreams. Shaded by a polished helm, his blue eyes glinted with a light of their own as he located, amid several crates of ducks and chickens, the profusely blushing and thoroughly mortified countess, who at that precise moment eminently wished for a large crevice to open in the earth beneath her feet and completely swallow her up. The hole failed to appear, and Synnovea was forced to stand where she was and submit to the colonel's swiftly probing inspection as he rode past. Stiltedly she responded with a nod as he inclined his head in greeting, for it was absolutely impossible for her to ignore the fact that the wayward grin was decidedly more pronounced and that people close around her had turned to stare. Had it not been for the loud honking and cackling of the fowl, she might have heard a kindred sound from the ladies whose heads came together like melons rolling into a steeply sloped ravine.

Unbeknown to Synnovea, at the outer rim of the commotion stood the serenely smiling Countess Natasha Andreyevna, who digested the event with great relish and, with equal enthusiasm, the comments of her princely companion, who, as an administrator of the tsar's courts, was knowledgeable about the current happenings within the palace.

Synnovea moaned in misery when she realized they had attracted the curiosity of nearly everyone around them. "Ali McCabe! You have made me rue the day my mother hired you!"

Stenka and Jozef choked back their laughter and deliberately devoted themselves to loading the purchases into the carriage, while the Irish woman wiped away a giggle with the back of her hand. Feigning innocence and confusion, Ali met the accusing stare of her mistress. "What did I do?"

"Everything worthy of damnation!" Synnovea groaned and lifted a hand in plaintive appeal. "Oh, for a plain and simple servant who knows when to keep her *silence!*"

Lowering a sinister glare upon the woman, Synnovea addressed her with a chiding finger once more in evidence. "You, Ali McCabe, have caused me tremendous distress this day! Do you not ken that I've been trying to avoid the attentions of Colonel Rycroft? And what do you do but hail him from afar, like some tavern wench, at the top of your lungs! And to the glee of every long-winded gossip within range of hearing! Have you no ken what you've done to me? 'Tis sure to get back to Anna's ears ere we arrive home!"

"Hummmph!" Ali folded her arms in a petulant pout. "As if me own dear self never swaddled yer backside from the day ye were born! As if I've no wits in me poor noggin ter know what ye be needin'! Ye bemoan me manners when it's yerself ye needs be lookin' ter! Tyrone is a right foin gen'leman, even if I have ter say so meself! An' if ye had eyes in yer foin head, ye'd be thinkin' so, too!"

"Tyrone, is it? An' who be lendin' ye permission ter be usin' his Christian name?" Synnovea mimicked. "Are ye so in league with the man that ye're now his copemate? Tyrone, indeed!"

" 'Tis a right foin Irish name, i'tis!" Ali argued. "A proud name, ter be sure!"

"Colonel Rycroft is an Englishman!" Synnovea stated steadfastly. "Knighted on English soil! He is *not* an Irishman!"

"Oh, 'tis the good Sir Tyrone, is it? Well, I'll wager me skirts his mother was a proper colleen ter win a man's heart." Ali grinned back at her mistress, who threw up her hands in sudden disgust.

"I've neither the patience nor the time to argue with a woman of your temerity, Ali McCabe," Synnovea fussed. "I must get back ere the Princess Anna sends out a search party to bring us back."

"Aren't ye the least bit curious 'bout where the colonel's takin' his men decked out in all that finery?" Ali asked, hoping to incite some interest. "Couldn't we follow a bit ter see?"

"Never!" Synnovea served quick death to the notion. She was not about to allow the indomitable colonel the privilege of thinking she was after him. Why, the very idea of lending him encouragement made her quake. He had already proven himself persistent. She could only wonder how assertive he could prove to be with only a little encouragement.

Chapter 10

Prince Vladimir Dimitrievich was a barrel-chested, white-haired, mustached *boyar* with a total of seventy years to his claim. He had been married and widowed twice and, in those unions, had sired a total of seven sons. It was well known that he was keeping a discerning eye out for a third possibility upon which to spawn a new crop, and though many a father was willing to present his daughter as a potential bride in hopes of somehow gaining access to the old man's wealth, Prince Vladimir was as cautious and discriminating as an ancient dowager afraid of losing her titles and assets to some unscrupulous rake. Despite his white hair, Vladimir was as virile as a good many men half his age and decidedly more adamant about proving himself capable of exercising his manly functions. He was evidently proud of his unfaltering prowess and, when met with encouragement, waxed gleefully ribald and openly suggestive on the subject of his abilities, especially when a young, winsome maid caught his eye and he gave himself over to his boastful tendencies.

Vladimir's offspring were all strapping young men with a penchant for excessive carousing and heavy brawling. Their tempers were short, even with each other, and from the simplest source, they could usually glean some excuse for competing against other hearties. Indeed, in contests of brawn they derived no greater pleasure than to defeat a whole army of foes, friends, and family alike. To say that they were an unruly rabble might have been putting it mildly. Still, they were a likable lot in many ways. It only took a person of sharp perception to figure out what those qualities were.

Anna Taraslovna knew she was tempting fate by requesting the presence of Prince Vladimir Dimitrievich and his seven sons at the reception honoring Ivan Voronsky. The unruly family was aggressive enough to reduce the whole affair to a mere shambles if they were provoked, but she could think of no viable way to separate kith from kin or, more pertinently, father from sons. Indeed, she would likely deem it an enormous miracle if the pugnacious family managed to get through the entire evening without resorting to fisticuffs, which in the main comprised her greatest worry. The only reason she even considered inviting them was out of regard for Ivan and his desire to replace the priest whom Vladimir had hired for his private chapel and then dismissed a pair of months later. Ivan had shrewdly lent a sympathetic ear to the old man's complaints about the narrow-mindedness of the monk who had had the gall to chide him for his intemperate propensities, not the least of which was his fondness for vodka. In light of Vladimir's vast wealth, Ivan was totally dedicated to the idea of Anna inviting the whole family, lest the old man be offended by the exclusion of his sons.

As much as she worried about the hazards of inviting the rambunctious clan, Anna was even more concerned about the risk of allowing her ward to attend. Many who were well acquainted with the young countess would have considered her an unlikely source for trouble, but Anna was most contemptuous of such logic. Not only could Synnovea's beauty attract the ardent attentions of Aleksei, but the unwavering admiration of the ancient Vladimir Dimitrievich as well.

Extremely reluctant to allow the girl any leeway in either area, Anna made a point of seeking Synnovea

out in her chambers before the guests arrived to prescribe the proper decorum that would be required of
her throughout the entire evening. Had Anna been able
to keep her ward from the festivities without arousing
the curiosity of the guests, who either knew Synnovea
personally or were aware of her through a former association with her father, she would have done so without
hesitation.

It was only after Anna actually saw her charge dressed
in her finery, however, that many of her apprehensions
congealed into a cold lump of dread in her chest. Arrayed
in winter white, Synnovea looked as dazzling as any
fabled snow queen, lending the greatest weight to Anna's
fears. Having intruded into the younger woman's chambers without knocking, Anna was momentarily taken
aback by the sight that greeted her, then, striking down
her own awe of the other's stunning good looks, stalked
across the room to confront Synnovea at close range. "If
I see you cavorting like some mindless little twit among
my guests or hear one whisper of complaint about your
actions, I swear you will not be allowed to leave this
house until you have been adequately punished for every
offense. Do I make myself clear? Though you may have
enjoyed your freedom under Count Zenkov's lax authority, I shall expect you to conduct yourself with acceptable
humility and be as demure and reserved as any proper
Russian maid should be."

Synnovea responded with a stiffly fixed smile, hardly
cherishing the woman's threats. "Indeed, Princess. You
have taken special pains to make me cognizant of your
wishes."

A spark of anger ignited the gray eyes. "Do I detect a
hint of sarcasm in your tone?"

Synnovea had taken exception to the fact that the woman continually tried to intimidate her. "My mode of conduct is normally rather reserved, Anna, so it seems rather
pointless for you to advise me on the proper etiquette of a
lady. After all, I have managed to attend such functions

before without causing others to suffer undue embarrassment."

"We're not talking about your comportment at the courts of the French and English, but here in *my* house!" Anna flung back. "I will not tolerate such unrestrained behavior while you are with my guests!"

"If you're so afraid of me humiliating you, Anna, why don't you just lock the door and be done with it!" Synnovea struggled with a quickly fermenting resentment of her own as the princess glared back at her. "I really am quite content to stay here in my chambers if it will help ease your concerns."

Anna straightened her thin form imperiously. "Unfortunately there was a need to invite several acquaintances of yours who have gained recognition as attendants to the tsar. Therefore, your presence would be missed." Anna sniffed in imposing arrogance as she continued. "I understand you are a close friend of Princess Zelda Pavlovna. She will be here, though her husband could not separate himself from the duties assigned to him by the Field Marshall. She will be attending tonight's social with her parents. I'm sure you know them better than I do."

At the heartening prospect of being able, at long last, to converse with her friends, Synnovea relaxed and graciously conceded to the woman's directives. After all, it was not her conduct which was really at the crux of their discord, but the princess's overbearing tendencies. "Be at ease, Anna. I shall lend considerable attention to complying with your desires."

"Good! I'm glad to see you've decided to be reasonable for a change."

Synnovea bit her lip and, by a strong effort of will, refrained from retorting to the woman's suggestion that it was she who was being difficult. Indeed, any argument to the contrary might have gotten them into an altercation that would have likely ruined the whole evening.

In the silent space of time that followed, Anna drew in a long breath before releasing a tedious sigh and revealing a concession she had disdained making. "Against my better judgment, I've been gracious enough to extend an invitation to the Countess Natasha, and she has responded affirmatively." Anna ignored her ward's sudden smile of delight and deliberately avoided any mention of her reasons, which centered mainly on the idea that Natasha would be able to occupy the major portion of Synnovea's time and thereby reduce the threat of the girl associating in areas which were most delicate in nature.

Whirling abruptly, Anna swept across the room and paused at the door to look back at Synnovea. The rich, pearl-encrusted *sarafan* and *kokoshniki* were beautiful beyond anything Anna could remember ever seeing, and though she had expended the contents of an enormous purse on her own gold-and-yellow creation, Anna was struck with the realization of her failure to even closely rival the younger woman's stunning appearance. In light of Synnovea's beauty, Anna mused dolefully, there was now a possibility that all of the precautions she had taken would be sundered before her very eyes, and she would see her rival unwittingly become a victor in this struggle for ultimate supremacy.

"You needn't hurry down, Synnovea. The guests are just beginning to arrive, and it will be some moments yet before they are all here. Natasha said she won't be coming until later anyway."

Anna made her departure before any further comment could be made and hurried downstairs to assure herself that all was in readiness. She almost dreaded the moment when Natasha would approach her and wondered if she would be able to set aside her pride long enough to offer some semblance of a gracious greeting to the woman. It would be difficult at best.

Synnovea stayed in her chambers for another hour at least, having clearly comprehended the fact that it was Anna's desire. Still, she was anxious to visit with her friends. Beyond this evening, she had no idea what she

would be doing. If Anna continued to procrastinate on
leaving to see her father, there was no telling when she
would be able to go and stay with Natasha. For all the
concern Anna had thus far demonstrated for her father,
the man could die and be buried in the grave before she
would consent to rearranging any of her social outings
and engagements with Ivan.

Leaving her chambers behind her, Synnovea moved
down the hall toward the stairs and was about to make
her descent to the hall below when she was taken suddenly aback by the rapid advance of Aleksei, who bounded
up the steps. The suspicion was firm in her mind that he
had been waiting within close proximity and had made
his ascent only after hearing her door close and her footfalls in the corridor. She had no recourse but to wait until
he reached the landing. With unswerving confidence, he
paused before her as his gaze leisurely climbed from the
bejeweled toes of her satin slippers to the pearl-adorned
crest of her *kokoshniki*. His red lips parted in a slow, sensual smile that brazenly hinted of his prurient bent, while
his dark eyes smoldered with warming lust.

"I've been meaning to talk with you, Synnovea," he
murmured, gently testing his still-tender nose with a
knuckle, as if the sight of her gave him cause to remember
the injury. "Though other men might have been offended
by your determination to preserve your virtue, my dear,
I must take into consideration that your nature is perhaps
different from most women and, being in the situation
you are in, you have serious concerns. Suppose we were
to be found out and you were subjected to the contempt
of your friends and the hatred of Anna. Terrifying prospects, I must agree. Still, the pain of discovery seems
far more remote than the consequences you will most
definitely suffer if you continue to deny me. . . . "

Synnovea was resolved to hear none of his threats. She
had already heard enough intimidations from Anna to set
her on the sharp edge of her temper. In angry reticence,
she sought to step past him, but his arm quickly slipped

about her waist to halt her flight. For a surprised moment, she stared up into his silently taunting smile, then with a horrendous jerk that nearly snapped her head from her shoulders, he sent her reeling dizzily to the far wall, where she crashed with a jarring jolt. Momentarily stunned by the force of her collision, Synnovea staggered unsteadily, holding a hand to her head to halt her convulsing world. Aleksei followed and, with that same confident smirk twisting his red lips, caught her almost gently by the throat, only to shove her back hard against the wall.

"You needn't hurry away, my lovely white swan," he mocked and lowered his face toward hers until she could feel his hot breath searing her. "You won't be missed downstairs for several moments yet, my dear. You see, Anna is totally absorbed with introducing Ivan to her guests, which leaves us freedom to enjoy ourselves."

Synnovea clawed at the long, thin fingers as they gradually tightened around the jeweled band of her collar, restricting the flow of blood to her head and seriously hampering her ability to breathe. In rising panic she began to twist and writhe as the encroaching pressure against her throat began to darken her world. As if from a great distance away, she heard his soft, ridiculing laughter.

"You see, Synnovea? I've reserved this little demonstration just to show you that it is futile to continue your struggle against me. You cannot hope to stop me from taking what I want. I would prefer your willing response, but until you submit, I'll be forced to continue to instruct you on the follies of resisting me."

Of a sudden Aleksei loosened his grip and stepped back, allowing Synnovea to collapse in weak-kneed relief against the wall. Desperately sucking air into her lungs, she laid a trembling hand upon her bruised throat and lifted her eyes to the man as he braced a hand on the wall above her head and leaned over her. He stood so close, the full scope of her vision was limited to his face and the vivid blue silk *kaftan* he wore.

"I would have been gentle with you in the woodcutter's cottage, Synnovea, but now I've grown impatient and yearn to settle the matter quickly." Lifting her upright, he caught her wrists and forced them against the wall on either side of her as he slowly perused her face. "You glow with the radiance of a silver moon, Synnovea, but you remain as aloof as a virgin queen . . . a snowmaiden who has seized my heart. That is what they call you, isn't it? I've heard them say, The Countess Synnovea Altynai Zenkovna, the snow queen! The icemaiden! Are you as cold as they say, Synnovea? Or will you melt in my arms and become the firebird I've roamed this whole earth to find?"

"I warn you, Aleksei!" she choked raggedly through her constricted throat. She paused and closed her eyes for a moment as a dizzying faintness assailed her, then she gritted her teeth with a fierce determination. Reclaiming some portion of her diminished strength, she challenged the veracity of his threats. "You will have to kill me right here and now if you persist with your foul deeds! With what little breath you've deigned to leave me, I'll scream and bring this whole house down upon your head. I swear I will!"

"Oh, Synnovea, when will you learn? You have no recourse but to give me what I demand." As if he found it needful again to demonstrate his greater strength, Aleksei slipped his hand behind her neck and clasped her cruelly by the nape, forcing her to rise to the very tips of her toes until his dark eyes, from very close range, pierced the searching green. "If you still think me incapable of redress, my dear, then lend a careful ear. If you continue to deny me, I vow that I will see you betrothed to the first doddering ancient who is old enough to vindicate me. Perhaps thus bound in wedlock, you'll be willng to welcome the manly thrusts of a more competent suitor." He lent emphasis to his words by slamming her

back forcefully against the wall and crushing her with his
weight. Even though Synnovea winced anew at the pain
he inflicted, she would hear none of his threats.

"Get away from me!" she choked as her hands came up
to feebly push against his broad, unyielding chest. "Just
leave me alone and let me be!"

"I'll leave you alone!" he snarled, throwing off her
hands and snatching her to him. His mouth came down
to seize hers with unbridled greed as he forced her lips
to yield to the insulting intrusion of his tongue. His arms
clasped her close, crushing her in a cruel vise as his broad
hand moved behind her back to clasp her buttock.

Synnovea struggled against him, totally repulsed by
the man and his embrace. Her brain screamed with his
audacious affront, and now filled with a silently seething
rage, she reached back an arm to grasp the heavy sconce
she knew was hanging on the wall just above her head. In
the flickering descent of sputtering candles, she brought
the weighty piece down with a vengeance, smashing it
against his thick skull.

Aleksei staggered back in a stunned daze and clutched
a hand to his brow as a reddish aura pulsed in front of
his eyes. Synnovea gave the lecher no further chance to
check her flight, but tore free and flung herself down the
stairs, nearly stumbling in her haste to flee until she came
in sight of Boris, who paused in the lower foyer and, half
turning, stared up at her in surprise at her undignified
flight.

Though her whole being trembled from the assault
made upon her person, Synnovea steeled herself against
such an overt display of panic. Deliberately slowing her
breath, she feigned an ambience of serenity, despite the
quaking tremors that still beset her, and continued down
the stairs at a slower pace, though her heart raced wildly
with a fear that she would hear Aleksei's footfalls on the
steps behind her.

Gaining the lower level, she hurried to the kitchen
on the pretext of overseeing some last-minute details.

She knew she needed a place of refuge where she could be far removed from the curious stares of Anna and her guests and reasonably safe from the revenge of Prince Aleksei. There, with her back turned to Elisaveta, she brushed nervously at the unrelenting tears that welled within her eyes, repeatedly sniffing and blowing her nose into a handkerchief the woman supplied. The cook wisely dared no questions as she pressed a glass of wine into the young countess's shaking grasp, and gratefully Synnovea sipped the Malieno, desperately needing its soothing qualities to quell the violent shivering that shook her to the very depth of her being.

It was a long time before the trembling disquiet finally ebbed and Synnovea made an effort to repair her appearance. She found that feat much easier by far than mending the damage done by the strangling vise Aleksei had held on her throat, for she now suffered from a rasping hoarseness in her speech and a burning rawness in her throat.

Much later than she had supposed, Synnovea made her entrance into the great hall, where Ivan, bedecked in a black silk *kaftan*, seemed to preen in the admiration heaped upon him by Anna and some of her acquaintances, who were not above indulging the tsar's cousin with ingratiating adoration, whatever the particular bent of her penchants. Others, who were more reserved and somewhat reticent about offering the man praise, watched from a respectful distance.

Synnovea paused near the entrance to the great chamber and from the outermost perimeter formed by the circle of guests, she cast her gaze about in search of Princess Zelda until she espied the woman standing with her parents near the far end of the room. By the stilted formality of the three as they listened to Ivan, it was obvious to Synnovea they were not greatly enchanted by what they were hearing. As she also gave heed, Synnovea realized the reasons for their distress, for Prince Bazhenov had served as one of the envoys for the star in the negotiations between Russia and the country Ivan currently spoke out against.

"I tell you, my friends, this country is at an impasse. We have lost our access to the Baltic by way of treaty with Sweden, and even now they are usurping our trade in Novgorod and other important cities. They have most mysteriously been granted fishing rights on White Lake, and I swear we will soon be outnumbered by the Lutheran extremists here in our own country. If we do not soon resist them, they'll be fathering your grandchildren! Mark my words!"

A confused rumble of voices could be heard from some of the guests, but none dared voice any disapproval of the authority which had allowed the Swedes to infiltrate their country so insidiously. Prince Bazhenov was one who spoke out in valiant defense of it.

"With Sweden's aid, Tsar Mikhail has brought us the first peace we've known with Poland after many years of conflict. What would you suggest we do now?" he queried suspiciously. "Take up arms against Sweden?"

Ivan was cautious about answering, having perceived the loyalty the old prince felt for the tsar. "Above all, we must be careful *never* to alienate anyone against the tsardom, for there beats the heart of our very lifeblood." He paused briefly for effect as he pressed the tips of his fingers together in a contemplative pose. "Perhaps if we sought the advice of another accomplished strategist who is knowledgeable about such affairs, we can gain some insight as to the diplomacy and tactics we should employ against the Swedes."

"Besides the Patriarch Filaret, you mean?" Prince Bazhenov jeered.

Ivan spread his hands in sublime innocence. "Are not two heads better than one?"

The elder harrumphed loudly, displaying his displeasure over the discussion. Begging Princess Anna's pardon a moment later, he excused himself and his family from the reception with the plea that he had to attend an early morning inspection with the tsar and needed his rest.

Trailing behind her parents as they prepared for their departure, the Princess Zelda glanced around in search of Synnovea and smiled in sudden pleasure when that one finally emerged from the press of people.

"I thought we would have time to talk," Zelda whispered regretfully in her friend's ear as they hugged each other. "My husband has been telling me things I was sure you would want to hear, but as you can see, we must leave. Papa is nearly beside himself. Whoever this Ivan Voronsky is, he has not endeared himself to Papa!"

"I'll see you as soon as I'm able," Synnovea promised in a softly rasping murmur. "We can talk then. 'Tis not safe now."

"Take care," Zelda bade as she brushed her lips against the other's cheek.

Watching from the doorway, Synnovea waited until Prince Bazhenov had handed his family into their carriage and the conveyance had pulled away before she retreated into the house, allowing Boris to close the door behind her. She paused at the entrance of the great hall, listening to Ivan's voice drone on incessantly, but found his views immensely disconcerting. Leisurely she withdrew to the dining room, where she soon gained the attention of several *boyars* who gathered close around her. They numbered seven in all and closely resembled each other in height, brawn, and visage, with three of them having light brown hair and the youngest four black. Even the quickly widening grins that spread across their faces hinted of their kinship.

"Enchanting!" one of them sighed. He grinned at Synnovea, then with a mock swoon he fell back into the arms of one of his companions, heaving an exaggerated sigh.

"Captivating! Completely dazzling to the eye!" another one avowed exuberantly, closely eyeing her.

"Permit me to introduce myself, *Boyarina*," the tallest one bade. "I am Prince Feodor Vladimirovich, eldest son of Prince Vladimir Dimitrievich, and these"—he swept a hand about to indicate his cohorts—"are my brothers, second-born Igor, then Petr, Stefan, Vasilii, Nikita, and Sergei, the youngest."

As he introduced them, each man stepped forward with a broad grin and clicked his heels in a gallant bow. Then Feodor placed himself in front of them, apparently as spokesman for his brothers, who crowded close around him. Together they awaited her response as the eldest inquired, "And your name, *Boyarina*?"

Smiling graciously, Synnovea sank into a deep curtsy before them as she strained to keep the rasp in her voice softly subdued. "I am the Countess Synnovea Altynai Zenkovna, recently arrived from Nizhniy Novgorod."

"Do you have any sisters?" Sergei asked eagerly and then complained, "There are so many of us, but only one of you."

For the first time that evening, Synnovea was able to smile with a lighthearted amusement as her tensions began to ease. She accompanied her reply with a coy shrug. "I fear not, Prince Sergei. As fate would have it, I was an only child."

"And your husband?" He cocked a dark brow wonderingly as he asked with bated breath. "Where is he?"

Soft, husky laughter preceded her answer. "Your pardon, most gracious prince, but I have none."

"A pity!" he lamented with a chortle. Smoothing his *kaftan* in a confident manner, Prince Sergei swaggered around his siblings and came before her to present himself once again. "Permit me, Countess, to express a deep appreciation for your beauty. In all my score of years on this earth, I have never seen a maid so wondrously fair. You would do me the greatest honor if you would allow me to court you. . . . "

Immediately he was shoved aside by the dark-eyed Stefan, who bestowed a warm smile on her as he stepped into the place formerly occupied by his brother. "Sergei's but a boy, Countess! A youth of no experience, but I've a

score and ten years to my claim, and though 'tis also true
that I've seen none to equal your radiance, I think you
will agree that I am better-looking than Sergei."

"Ha!" the hulking Igor scoffed and swung his arm
in a backward motion to send Stefan stumbling away.
Stroking his handsome beard, Igor settled in a bold stance
before her as his blue eyes twinkled back at her. "None
of my brothers can equal my experience . . . " With a
challenging brow raised, he glanced from side to side at
his siblings as he boasted, "Or my good looks."

Hearty guffaws accompanied his statement, attesting
to the skepticism of his brothers, who then commenced to
argue among themselves. Amid all the squabbling, there
was also an excessive amount of rough jostling and painful nudging.

"Not so! I am the best-looking!"

"Come now! Would you have the countess believe such
lies when I am here for her to see?"

" 'Tis a shame you've not taken a good look at yourself
lately. I'll warrant I've seen better faces on the hind end
of a bear!"

Synnovea was about to giggle, but sobered instantly
as the offended one doubled his fist and bashed the
nose of the one who insulted him. The brothers quickly
braced themselves to settling the matter by force until
a loud "Harrumph!" came from directly behind them.
The sound had an effect on the men that Synnovea
found amazing. It cooled their tempers as abruptly and
efficiently as a large pail of icy water. They quickly
stumbled back to open a path for an elderly man who
ambled forward with a rolling gait, as if he had spent his
lifetime on the deck of a ship. Not even Colonel Rycroft
or Ladislaus matched this one's height, for the man had
to be at least a half head taller than either of those two
men. Synnovea had some difficulty hiding her awe as the
white-haired man approached her. A huge hand came to
rest on Sergei's shoulder as the ancient halted beside the
youngest of the brood.

"What is this bickering about now?" he rumbled in a deep voice, closely perusing the young woman.

"The Countess Zenkovna has no sisters, Papa," the youth answered. "We were trying to decide which one of us will court her."

"Indeed?" The elder had already formed an acute interest in the comely maid and was much encouraged by the comment of his son. Though a bit slender for his taste, she was pleasantly rounded in all the right places and had the height to easily accommodate his enormous frame. In anticipation of such an event, he swept a forefinger beneath his heavy mustache, flicking up the ends, and bestowed upon her his most ardent smile, displaying a full set of white teeth. "If you will allow me to introduce myself, Countess. I am Prince Vladimir Dimitrievich, and these, as I'm sure you've recently ascertained, are my sons. Have they introduced themselves?"

"Most capably, my lord prince," she responded, dipping again into a curtsy. Glancing past his arm, she saw the Princess Anna forging a channel through those guests who had meandered to the doorway to watch the antics of the princely brood.

"What is going on here?" the princess demanded, trying to sound gracious, but failing. Whatever disturbance was transpiring, she marked Synnovea as the source of the trouble. A sidelong glare from her gray eyes clearly conveyed that fact to the younger woman, who immediately wondered what punishment Anna would try to lay upon her.

"My sons and I were making the acquaintance of this fair maid," Vladimir explained. "Might I ask why we were not informed of the Countess Zenkovna's presence sooner?"

Princess Anna opened her mouth to explain, but halted in a sudden quandary. After several confused starts, she finally managed a feeble excuse. "I wasn't aware you wanted to meet her."

"Nonsense! Any man would be interested to meet a woman with her looks! At least she won't bore me weary!"

His comment carried the full weight of his rejection of Ivan, as well as a firm rebuff for Anna's attempts to sway his considerations in favor of the cleric. Though he might be deemed an ancient by the standards of some, he had not yet lost his wits.

Feeling temporarily defeated, Anna made a brave attempt to smile and quietly murmured to Synnovea. "I believe I just saw the Countess Natasha's carriage coming up the lane in front of the house. Would you care to go and greet her, my dear?"

"Yes, of course," Synnovea eagerly responded and again sank in gracious obeisance before the elderly prince. "If you will excuse me, Prince Vladimir, my friend has arrived and I am most anxious to see her."

The old man inclined his head slightly, giving his permission, and Synnovea slipped through the guests, bestowing nods of greeting to friends and acquaintances as she went. When she entered the main hall, Synnovea caught sight of Prince Aleksei coming down the stairs. Though there was no immediate evidence of his wound, he moved very carefully down the steps, as if he feared his head would tumble from its perch. In response to her hesitant glance, his dark eyes bore into her with an unspoken promise, assuring her that this affair between them would not be finished until he had his revenge or his way with her.

"Synnovea, my dear child!" Natasha cried from the doorway, claiming her attention. "Come here, and let me look at you!"

Leaving Aleksei to glower after her, Synnovea faced the woman and eagerly extended her hands in greeting as she hurried to her. "Natasha, you look absolutely ravishing!"

The elder laughed and sashayed around in a circle to allow the younger woman to view her. Synnovea did so with approval. Natasha's black and silver-trimmed *sarafan* had been well chosen to lend emphasis to her soft, darkly lashed ebon eyes and to compliment her porcelain skin. When left undraped, the dark hair, having become liberally streaked with gray in recent years, seemed almost touched with a hoary frost, but now the mass was covered by a delicate silver veil that flowed around her shoulders and cascaded down her back in shimmering translucent folds. A *kokoshniki* adorned with finely wrought silver filigree affixed with precious stones crowned her head.

It came to Synnovea as she admired Natasha's beauty that whatever enmity Anna bore the woman, it must have been conceived from a simple seed of jealousy. It was evident that the pale-haired good looks of the princess had declined far more rapidly than Natasha's, though Anna was younger by three years.

"This has been a wonderfully delightful week," Natasha avouched with a warm chuckle. "I've been fortunate to hear the most interesting tidbits of gossip which I think you'll be anxious to hear."

"If it's about Prince Aleksei, I'm not sure I want to," Synnovea muttered laconically. "I'm beginning to detest the man!"

"Oh, I wouldn't bore you with that kind of rubbish, my dear," the older countess promised. "What I've been hearing is much more exciting!"

Synnovea looped her arm through the elder's and led her to the great room, where they sat together on a padded bench in a quiet corner. "Princess Zelda wanted to share something with me too, but she had to leave ere she could tell me. Now here you are, Natasha, seeming enormously thrilled with your news. Perhaps you should give me some hint of its import. Has Tsar Mikhail chosen a wife perchance?"

"Oh no, my dear." Natasha smiled in anticipation, but paused a moment as Boris came to offer them a small variety of libations from a large silver tray. Thanking the man as she accepted a goblet of fruited wine, Natasha waited until he had passed on to the other guests before she leaned close to Synnovea and confided, "I was sure you would be eager to learn that there's been a lot of talk about a certain Englishman. . . . "

Synnovea's soft, lovely mouth parted in surprise, and almost warily she asked, "Might that Englishman be Colonel Rycroft, by chance?"

Natasha hid her amusement as she sipped from her glass. Almost innocently she inquired, "Isn't he the same one who rescued you from that Polish renegade . . . Oh, what was his name?"

"Ladislaus?" A delicately winged brow arched in sharp suspicion as Synnovea questioned the woman. "Where did you hear about Ladislaus? I don't remember ever mentioning anything about his attack on my carriage."

The silver veil shimmered in the candlelight as Natasha wagged her head and affected a demeanor of disappointment. "To think I was the last one you told! I am simply crushed!" She heaved a feigned sigh of regret. "I'm beginning to wonder if you even care about me."

"I only spoke of that brigand when I had to!" Synnovea offered in her own defense.

"Oh, I've been hearing some rumors about him, too," Natasha commented. "It seems he's been seen a time or two in Moscow since that event, but has managed to elude the tsar's soldiers. There's some horrendous rumbling of gossip about him wanting to repay the colonel for the losses that he and his men suffered by his hand."

"I'm sure the colonel would welcome a confrontation if it would mean the return of his horse the brigand stole," Synnovea remarked. "But I rather doubt their encounter would be a contest of arms the fainthearted could easily watch."

"At the present time I don't think the colonel is concerning himself too much with Ladislaus, my dear," Natasha dared to speculate. "I think he has other things of greater import on his mind."

Synnovea peered at Natasha obliquely, now most curious to hear what she had to say. "Just what rumors *did* you hear about Colonel Rycroft?"

"Why, my dear, I'm utterly amazed that you haven't heard all about it yourself. Colonel Rycroft has been making petitions to the tsar to court you!"

Synnovea stared aghast at her friend, feeling the heat of a blush creeping into her cheeks. "He didn't actually dare?!"

"Oh, but he did! Most persuasively, too, from what I hear!" Natasha assured her. "He explained very carefully about having had the opportunity to meet you when he saved you from the band of thieves, and then he asked if there were any Russian laws that would restrict him from paying court to a certain young *boyarina*."

"I am ruined!" Synnovea moaned in abject misery.

"On the contrary, my dear. Mikhail told the colonel that he would seriously consider his petition after reviewing more of the facts. But of course, since then, there's been no assurance given to indicate that His Majesty will grant the colonel his request. It seems that Major Nikolai Nekrasov also entreated the tsar for the same favor shortly after Colonel Rycroft made his plea. If I would dare venture a guess, I'd say Nikolai heard of the Englishman's petition and decided to establish his own claim."

"How dare they drag my name before the tsar without first asking me!" Synnovea fidgeted upon the bench in petulant indignation. Didn't she have something to say in the matter?

Natasha contemplated her young friend with a brow raised in dubious wonder. "Have you become so predisposed to the customs of other countries, Synnovea, that you've forgotten how such affairs are handled here? You should know that asking a maid first for permission just isn't the way an arrangement of courtship is accomplished here in Russia. I'm sure if either of the two men had been confident of Prince Aleksei granting them approval, they would have gone to him, but Anna made it apparent, especially to Colonel Rycroft, that he was not welcome in this house, so he went to a higher authority." Her brows raised briefly in a tiny shrug as she added, "The tsar himself, no less."

"I've given Colonel Rycroft no encouragement!" Synnovea protested.

Natasha noticed that she offered no similar statement in the case of the major, which could be construed in two different ways. Either she had encouraged Nikolai and cared not to reveal that fact or she had never thought of him with any serious consideration. Colonel Rycroft was undeniably a man among men and could make a young woman forget other suitors. Still, Natasha desired to know which of the two the girl favored. "And did you encourage Major Nekrasov?"

Synnovea gasped, scandalized at the very idea. Why, she had never given encouragement to any man! "Are you mad? Of course not!"

Natasha chuckled as she was given an answer. "A man like Colonel Rycroft needs no encouragement, does he? He will simply seek out what he desires to have. And 'tis most apparent that he desires to have you, my dear."

"I don't even know the man!" Synnovea insisted.

"Now what is this that you say, child? Was he not the one who saved you from Ladislaus? Was he not the one who carried you to your coach only a few days ago?" Natasha's lips curved into a gratified smile as her friend's cheeks brightly glowed with color.

"Yes, of course."

"Then the two of you have obviously met," the elder pointed out.

"Only briefly!" Synnovea emphasized her words, as if she struggled to make herself understood. "Never formally!"

The older countess nodded slowly in sublime serenity. "Apparently it was enough to spark the colonel's interest."

"I intend to discourage the man!" the younger declared emphatically.

"What a shame." Natasha's feigned dejection was accompanied by a soft, wistful sigh. "I must admit I'm among the ladies who are simply agog over the colonel. Indeed, there hasn't been this much excitement over a man since the first false Dmitry tried to claim the tsardom a good twenty years ago and his remains were blown out of a cannon. I tell you, Synnovea, Colonel Rycroft excites me!" Almost dreamily she drummed her slender fingers lightly upon her friend's arm. "Have you seen the way he sits the back of a horse, my dear?" She already knew the answer, but hurried on with her boasting. "Ramrod straight he rides, yet with fluid movements that make him seem an integral part of the horse. Can you imagine such a man in your bed?"

"Certainly not!"

Natasha ignored the breathless denial the younger woman made. Though Synnovea disputed the possibility that such a thought had ever entered her mind, Natasha knew better. She could tell by the progressing tide of color creeping upward to the other's temples. She chuckled with humor at the girl who hid her blushing face momentarily behind her hand before she suddenly giggled. "So you *have* noticed him?"

The pearl-encrusted headdress dipped forward ever so slightly in acknowledgment. "Briefly."

"Oh, Synnovea," Natasha sighed. "Were I a score years younger, I would certainly see that such a man would be adequately distracted by my attentions."

Affectionately Synnovea clasped the woman's fingers within her own. "Dear Natasha, I do not understand your infatuation with the man, but I genuinely admire your enthusiasm. If ever I should relent and admit the colonel into my presence, I shall make haste to introduce him to you."

"No need for that!" Natasha chortled. "That event has already taken place. Prince Zherkof introduced us after the colonel put on an exhibition in the Kremlin the other day. It was magnificent, my dear! You should have seen it! I was completely bedazzled by the horsemanship of the colonel and his troop. I think the tsar was pleased, too! At least, he appeared to be!"

"When was this?" Synnovea queried carefully, wondering if she had also seen him on that day, the very same that Ali had made her rue.

Natasha's lips twitched faintly as she fought a small battle with her composure. "Well, I'm not exactly sure, my dear, but it also seems that I saw you in the vicinity of Red Square that day, too. Did you go to Kitaigorod to shop for something, perhaps? And were you perchance wearing your peasant attire?"

Synnovea's pride was buffeted by the thought that the woman may have witnessed the event that had won the curious regard of everyone around them. "I was there, but I didn't see you."

"Oh, it doesn't matter, really," Natasha assured her, noting her distress. "What does matter is the fact that I've had the opportunity to invite the colonel to my home next week, along with some of his officers, Prince Zherkof, and a few of my most intimate friends. And of course, my dear, you are invited as well. I do most earnestly plead that you persuade Anna to allow you to attend. I've heard rumors that she's finally decided to go see her father, which might allow you the freedom you want. Your presence at the affair would no doubt encourage a windfall of handsome men."

Synnovea regarded the elder with a dubious smile. "Is it *my* company you seek or that of the men?"

"Both!" Natasha answered with unabashed vigor and laid her hand again upon the younger woman's arm as she smilingly coaxed, "And this time, dear sweet child, please don't be so formidable and aloof. I'm sure if I hear the name the icemaiden bestowed upon you one more time, I shall give up trying to find you a proper husband. I told your father, 'Aleksandr,' I said, 'that girl should marry ere she's too old to have babies!' And he said to me, 'Natasha, stop your nagging! I'm waiting for her to fall in love!' Bah!" The woman threw up her hands in a gesture of frustration and leaned close to Synnovea to share a bit of advice. "The way you fall in love, my dear, is to make babies with a man like Colonel Rycroft. I'll wager you wouldn't be so cool and distant with him sharing your bed."

Synnovea gasped at the suggestion. "Natasha! You are absolutely scandalous!"

Natasha heaved a wistful sigh. "That was what my last husband said, and we were married the longest of the three." Then her eyes gleamed in warm remembrance as she confided, "But then, Count Emelian Stefanovich Andreyev"—her tongue rolled the name off with loving ease—"never, to my knowledge, ever looked seriously at another woman all the time we were married."

Synnovea had often sensed that Natasha had loved her last husband more than the other two, and her heart warmed with the thought of the love and excitement the couple had shared. "Should I ever marry, Natasha, I'll come to you for advice. I'm sure you hold all the secrets for keeping a husband happy and content."

The Countess Natasha chuckled at the notion. "I can probably tell you a thing or two." She paused briefly to further contemplate the matter, and then nodded with more conviction. "In fact, I can probably tell you a great deal about holding a husband's attention. And should you marry a man of whom I approve, I will try to be most diligent in that instruction."

Synnovea became distrustful. "And, of course, you would direct me concerning your choice?"

"Naturally, my dear." The corners of Natasha's lips twitched upward in a sly smile. "I should like to begin the formalities by inviting Colonel Rycroft to talk with you when he comes." She held up a hand to halt the flow of words as Synnovea opened her mouth to protest. "Is it so much to ask? After all, Colonel Rycroft did save you from being kidnapped and violated by that rogue thief." An eyebrow lifted meaningfully as she asked, "Can you not be gracious to the man, seeing as how he saved you from so dire a fate?"

Synnovea expelled a long sigh of exasperation. She was becoming extremely weary of the reminder. "You will nag me until I agree, and so I shall, but 'twill not be to my liking. I warn you of that!"

Natasha folded her hands in genteel contentment. "We shall wait and see how adamantly you disdain the man, my dear."

"Though you may have a bent toward matchmaking and are a true *svakhi* at heart, Natasha, 'twill do you no good to plan. The Princess Anna will never allow the colonel to court me. She simply detests foreigners."

Natasha lifted her head and smiled pleasantly. "As I've told you, my dear, the man has attracted the attention of the tsar. 'Tis rumored that His Majesty has been so intrigued and entertained by the mock battles and forays and all the drills the colonel and his men put on, that every weekday morning he goes out and stands on the wall of the Kremlin to watch them. In view of that, my dear, do you think Tsar Mikhail will be so ill-disposed toward the colonel that he will long deny him his heart's desire? My dear Synnovea, I would not put odds on Anna's power to persuade Tsar Mikhail otherwise, if he happens to grant the colonel's request."

"You truly are infatuated with this man, aren't you?" Synnovea made the conjecture in some wonder.

Smiling, Natasha pondered the other's supposition for the briefest of moments before changing it slightly. "Taken with the man would be a better description of my feelings, my dear. 'Tis my opinion that men like Colonel Rycroft are a rare breed."

Chapter 11

A FIERCE STORM SWEPT OVER THE CITY IN THE WEE morning hours, whipping the trees into a violent frenzy and setting shutters to flapping noisily along the darkened thoroughfare. Deep sighs of relief were slowly expelled in the peaceful lull that followed, for it seemed, for a while at least, that the tempest had finally passed beyond them, yet in the space of a few short hours the hushed stillness was again shattered by another vicious assault that slashed the city of Moscow and the area around it with savage winds and pelting rains.

The changing conditions seemed but a mild portent of what was to happen in Synnovea's life after her tumultuous encounter with Aleksei, for she had barely been able to relax in the serenity that had at last settled over the city before her own tranquility was again rudely disrupted, this time by the Princess Anna. It was not enough that the woman stood outside the locked door of her bedchamber, insistently rapping on the portal and demanding entrance in authoritarian tones. Such simple deeds were most effective in forewarning the two occupants of the seriousness of her mood, but when the door was opened and Anna swept into the room, the event seemed somewhat akin to the blowing in of another violent squall. No dreaded harbinger of doom could have derived as much satisfaction from the delivery of a dire omen as Anna did when she proclaimed her edict.

"Aleksei asked me to ponder his suggestion, and now that you've managed to lure Prince Vladimir Dimitrievich away from more serious considerations, I can only agree with my husband. Actually, it was Prince Vladimir who approached Aleksei about the matter last night. It seems the lecherous old *boyar* was quite taken with you, as were his sons."

"But I only spoke with them briefly. . . . " Synnovea insisted, wary of what the woman was about to reveal.

"Nevertheless," Anna continued, imperiously touching a lacy handkerchief to a thin nostril, "with the situation now facing us, we have no other choice but to arrange a marriage for you. Our guests were simply abuzz with rumors of Colonel Rycroft's effrontery." Her tone became incredulous. "Why, the very idea of that lowborn knave asking the tsar for permission to court you! 'Tis simply outrageous! Believe me, my dear, when this matter is finally put to rest, you can be certain of one thing. The colonel's ambitions will not be allowed to come to fruition. I'll see to that! This very morning I've taken the initiative to send a missive to Prince Vladimir, confirming our approval of your marriage to him. Although the old *boyar* will want to keep this matter private until all is secure, such a contract will forestall any interference from the Englishman or anyone else who seeks to win you, including Major Nekrasov."

Thoroughly stunned and shaken by the announcement, Synnovea stared back at the woman, feeling as if she had just been slapped across the face. Distantly she was aware of Ali standing near the door of her narrow room with a bony hand clutched to her throat, looking positively horror-struck. The servant's dismay was nothing more than a reflection of her own spiraling apprehensions, Synnovea mused dismally, and though Ali had no clear understanding of what had brought about this betrothal, the suspicion was strong in Synnovea's mind that her fate had been decided not this morning by Anna, but last night when she had vehemently rejected

Aleksei's overtures and threats. She was sure it was his trap that was presently closing around her, as he had warned her it would. He had vowed she would have to yield herself to him or pay the consequences, and now it seemed she would be paying for the rest of her life. She would be wed to an ancient who, though perhaps not yet doddering or daft, was far removed from her cherished dream of a young, handsome suitor.

"Prince Vladimir is anxious to have you as his bride, and we've indulged his impetuous haste by giving him consent to arrange for the nuptials during my absence. Ivan and I depart on the morrow to visit my father, and since Ivan has commitments which he must attend to in Moscow ere the month is fully out, I've made provisions for our return a fortnight hence. You can be married the following week. . . . "

"So soon?" Synnovea was astounded by the dispatch with which Anna had set her plans into motion.

"I see no reason why we have to suffer through a long delay before the wedding." Anna arched a pale brow inquisitively as she settled a dull-eyed stare on her ward. "Do you?"

Synnovea could think of a variety of plausible excuses. "Given a few more days, I might be able to prepare for the occasion better. I could have a new gown made, and there needs be handkerchiefs sewn as gifts for the *boyarinas* who will serve as attendants. . . . "

Anna's response was crisp. "Prince Vladimir is far too old to endure a lengthy wait, Synnovea. You'll have to be satisfied with the time you've been granted."

Resisting the tears that threatened, Synnovea turned away in troubled reticence. It seemed everything had been laid out for her, and she would have no choice but to follow the direction they had chosen for her. She would not even be permitted enough time to enjoy the usual celebrations and festivities associated with a betrothal or a forthcoming marriage.

Anna went to the front windows and gazed out on the tree-lined thoroughfare as the street began to stir to life with briskly passing coaches and *boyars* riding steeds still fresh and frisky with the early morning chill. Despite the seemingly disastrous failure of the prior evening, she had still been hopeful of Ivan's abilities to recoup the ground he had lost to her ward even after she had retired to her bedchambers for the night. Her heart had even soared with pleasure when Aleksei came to her and demonstrated once again his overpowering persuasiveness in the area of passionate pursuits, but when in the glowing aftermath of her bliss, she had lain in his arms and listened to him relate the old prince's proposals and the deceitful little ploys of their ward, it had seemed in that moment as if her whole world had suddenly turned topsy-turvy.

"Natasha came to me last night and begged me to consider the possibility of letting you visit with her during my absence," Anna said stoically over her shoulder. "I was certain you would agree and have given my consent. I'm sure Natasha will be delighted to help you prepare for your wedding."

"There's not enough time to consider even a few frivolities," Synnovea rejoined with a noticeable lack of humor, "much less see anything actually accomplished."

On the surface Anna seemed to ignore her charge's sarcasm, but she took out her spite in a way which had already proven tremendously gratifying. By dictating the events of the younger woman's life, she had clearly established her power and authority over her rival. "Aleksei and I have been gracious enough to accept Prince Vladimir's invitation to discuss the final preparations for the wedding this evening, and we've taken it upon ourselves to assure him that you will be coming with us."

"How kind of you."

Anna smiled in smug pleasure as she detected a break in the other's voice. "You might be relieved to know that

Ivan is busy preparing for our early morning departure and will have no time for your lessons today. I must advise you that he's extremely annoyed with you. He is convinced you deliberately set out to thwart his plans to become Vladimir's priestly mentor. Therefore, I would suggest you avail yourself of every opportunity to make amends ere we meet with your venerable betrothed tonight. 'Twill perhaps make the evening more congenial since Ivan has asked to accompany us. It may be his last chance to direct the old prince's attention toward a more constructive cause rather than fulfilling his base desires with you."

"I wish him good fortune," Synnovea responded with morose sincerity. " 'Twould be of great comfort to me if he manages to turn Vladimir's head with his aspirations. I would not be averse to the idea at all."

Anna quickly assumed a guise of astonishment. "Why, Synnovea! You don't seem at all pleased by your betrothal. Can it truly be that you're upset by—"

Synnovea was well aware of the woman's gloating satisfaction and made bold to interrupt. "You said I would be allowed to visit with Natasha while you're gone. When may I expect to leave?"

Anna shrugged casually, relishing her ward's distress. "You may pack up whatever you'll be needing now, then you can leave early in the morning if you're of such a mind. That is, if you really desire to stay with her. . . . "

"Of course, I do." Synnovea stared at her, perplexed, wondering what rude and tedious insinuation the woman was alluding to now. "Why shouldn't I?"

Anna could not contain a disdaining sneer. If not for the fact that Aleksei had complained about the girl making advances upon his person, she might have allowed Ivan more time to convince Vladimir of the merits of his proposals before acquiescing to the marriage. But when her husband had revealed the invitations he had already discouraged, she had been spurred by a rage to exact every measure of revenge she could upon the young countess.

"Oh, what with me being gone and Aleksei conveniently here all alone, I thought perhaps you might want to . . . "

"Forgive me, Anna." Synnovea stressed the apology, making only a meager attempt to disguise the barb she intended, "but I wouldn't dream of compromising your husband's reputation by staying here during your absence."

"No, of course not." The gray eyes grew ice-cold with malevolence. Though Anna was convinced otherwise, she was reluctant to accuse Synnovea directly. The girl would only deny it, which would instigate further slurs and arguments. Such an undignified fray would not lend anything to her posture of elevated power, through which she intended to reap a greater measure of revenge.

Even through her trauma, Synnovea recognized the fact that Anna wanted her out of the house. Despite her pretense of magnanimously indulging Natasha because of some kindly dispensation on her part, she could not even imagine the woman tolerating any other arrangement during her absence. Knowing full well what threat would exist if she remained within close proximity to Aleksei, Synnovea felt more than a bit outraged by Anna's suggestion that she was eager to stay alone with him in the same manse. Indeed, had Anna given her a choice in the matter, she would have gladly left before the hour was out.

Anna smirked in barely constrained glee as she needled her charge further. "Just think of it, Synnovea, in a thrice of weeks you'll be Vladimir's bride. It should please you considerably to know that you'll be the mistress of your own house and the wife of such a wealthy *boyar*. In light of the fact that he's so taken with you, I'm sure you'll be able to wheedle from him whatever your heart may aspire to have." The thin lips lifted briefly in a contemptuous smile. "Although, I must say, I've seen no hesitancy on your part to quell your penchant for satisfying your own whims. Your self-indulgence is readily apparent in the abundance of costly gowns and jewels you own. Still, as Vladimir's wife, you'll be far richer than you are now. That reality should lend you some measure of comfort when you have to endure his awkward attempts in bed. Though 'tis rumored Vladimir is still fully capable of servicing a maid, I'm sure it won't be the greatest experience for you, at least not like it would be if you were wed to a much younger man, especially someone as accomplished with women as Colonel Rycroft appears to be."

A dark, winged brow lifted with a skeptical quirk as Synnovea watched Anna stroll leisurely across the room toward her. "I was not aware that you knew Colonel Rycroft well enough to be able to offer any opinion on his experience with women."

"Oh, I hear things here and there." Anna waved a hand through the air with an attitude of casual indifference. "He seems to be the subject of every *boyarina* who has ever seen him. The fact that he lives in the German district with all the other outcasts who come to our country increases his opportunity to gratify his manly appetites. Or did you think you were the only bird that English hawk desires to sink his talons in? 'Tis widely rumored among those who know that there's at least a half dozen strumpets for every foreigner who is housed there. To even suggest the colonel would deny himself of their availability while vying for your hand seems rather farfetched, don't you think?"

"Your conjecture is only that," Synnovea rejoined with a flippant aloofness she was not necessarily feeling. She was not entirely certain why she should be so offended by the woman's suggestion. "You can't possibly know what the colonel does in his private life unless you spy on him."

"Humph!" Anna tossed her head at the girl's challenging disbelief. "Fool you be if you think Colonel Rycroft hasn't tasted his share of trollops. He'll scatter his seed all over the countryside before he leaves here, mark my words, but if you're so ignorant of men that you can't believe he'll take another woman into his bed, then I have better things to do with my time than to argue with you over the depth of his coarseness."

Anna stalked to the portal and, laying a hand upon the knob there, turned to contemplate her ward. After hearing the allegations made by Aleksei, she had felt an enormous desire to gouge out those green eyes and viciously claw the creamy-skinned visage until the only kind of perusals a man would be apt to give her would be a pitying kind. Still, in view of Synnovea's unmistakable distress, she had reason to feel ecstatic with what she had actually achieved.

The thin lips twitched briefly in a triumphant smile, and with an almost imperceptible dip of her head, Anna swept from the room like a swiftly departing gale, confident that her decree had been effective in shattering her ward's aspirations for attracting a husband with both youth and vitality.

The squeak of hinges sounded much akin to a death knell in the gloomy silence that abruptly descended over the chambers. Now having no encouraging expectations for her future, Synnovea slumped upon the bed like one whose breath had been knocked from her. Indeed, she would have felt no different had her life been declared condemned. She stared in utter despair at nothing in particular, disturbed by the injustice of what was being done to her. It was a weight too burdensome to bear in mute tranquility, and as a harsh sob welled up within her, she flung herself upon the bed, crying out in painful anguish against the grievance. Listlessly she pummeled a fist against the bedclothes as she wept and bemoaned the day she had ever entered the Taraslov manse.

"Oh, me lamb! Me lamb! Do not weep yer heart out so!" Ali pleaded pityingly as she came to give her mistress comfort, but Synnovea shook her head passionately, refusing to be consoled, for there was no solace that could assuage her misery. There seemed no hope for her future, either for the morrow or for all the days and years to come.

"Pack up everything," she choked through her tears. "If I fall under heaven's mercy, I'll not be coming back here *ever* again!"

"Can ye not stop this thing they're doin' ter ye?" Ali asked in worry. "Can ye not go ter Tsar Mikhail an' beg for his mercy? Or escape ter England an' stay wit' yer widowed aunt?"

"I can go to no one," Synnovea answered bleakly. "Least of all to England. If I sought passage on a ship, I would never be allowed to return. The contract has been signed, Ali, and as of this morning, I'm the promised bride of Prince Vladimir Dimitrievich."

Anna's elaborate script acknowledging Vladimir as her betrothed had sealed her fate, and not even Aleksei could now undo what he had set into motion. Only Tsar Mikhail or Prince Vladimir could break the pact, His Majesty by whatever reason he might ordain, or the old man by giving evidence of her unworthiness. The likelihood of such an occurrence seemed very remote if Vladimir had asked for her hand so soon after their meeting. He had no doubt been apprised of enough of her breeding and background to be thoroughly convinced of her merits as a potential bride and would not be swayed from his goal. With zealous revenge Aleksei would have given his personal attention to informing the old *boyar* of all the details.

Synnovea's thoughts raced in an anxious frenzy to find some avenue of escape from her predicament. A half dozen options came to mind, but such notions as insulting Vladimir or telling him how vehemently she disdained the idea of becoming his wife were rejected as quickly as they were entertained. Even if it meant giving up her freedom, she would not cause the man such ominous hurt to gain her own end. Such an act might lead him to the grave, and she refused to have his death on her conscience. Nay, if ever he declined to speak the vows with her, he would have to be the one to find fault with her.

Closing her eyes, Synnovea rested her cheek against the counterpane, letting the tensions ease from her body as she forced her thoughts to roam elsewhere. She made no effort to redirect her musings away from those provocative imaginings Colonel Rycroft had instigated in the bathhouse with his casual disregard for his own manly nudity and her naïveté. It seemed rather useless to torment herself with such wanton fantasies now when she would never enjoy the bliss of their fulfillment. Yet as the young wife of an ancient *boyar*, such memories might be all she would ever have. Her brief encounter with the Englishman might well have to suffice as a conciliation for everything she would be missing in her marriage, for she would never be able to enjoy the excitement and delight of being joined in marriage to a man of noteworthy frame. Such reverie was perhaps far more than some women were gifted with in a lifetime, but Synnovea was inclined to wonder if her brief view of such a magnificent specimen might have spoiled her for the mundane and ordinary and made her less than tolerant of what she was about to receive.

Despite the contradiction of her dreams and longings, a plaintive sigh escaped Synnovea as she resigned herself to making the best of the situation, for she could discern no possible remedy for what had been declared. At least Prince Vladimir was not totally repugnant, as some men might have been, and she was not destined to become bored while his seven sons resided with them. On the contrary, in light of the brothers' bent for mischief, there existed an enormous probability that she would be motivated at times to beg for a little privacy and peace.

Steeling her jaw against the continuing disquiet that threatened to dissolve her fragile forbearance, Synnovea wiped away her tears and left the bed. She lent her full attention to helping Ali pack up their belongings, taking some small comfort in the possibility that she would never have to darken the Taraslov stoop ever again.

After the last of her trunks had been loaded and delivered to Natasha's residence in preparation of her early morning departure, Synnovea made a point of seeking Ivan out in his chambers and returning the books he had loaned her. It was obvious from his arrogance that he had given up all hope of elevating her to a higher level of intelligence or finding any redeemable qualities within her character.

"I hope you will be happy now, Countess."

A long, weary sigh slipped from Synnovea as she met his repugnant glare. She felt utterly drained, as if all of her energies had been completely depleted by Anna's decree. She could not even find enough fortitude to deflect Ivan's gibes. "I will try to be."

"How can you not be," he derided, "with all that wealth at your disposal?"

"Happiness doesn't necessarily depend on a person's wealth, Ivan," she stated dully. "A man could acquire all the riches in the world and still be utterly miserable. Possessions are a poor substitute for loving friends and family."

Ivan scoffed at the idea of such platitudes. "What has a family ever meant to me? I despised my mother. My father? Well, 'twas told me that he was killed shortly before my birth, but I was given my mother's name like any misbegotten offspring. I never saw any evidence that he ever existed, and if he did, I'd have been much fonder of his memory had he left me some inheritance to see me nourished and clothed until I was able to fend for myself."

"I'm sorry, Ivan," Synnovea murmured in genuine empathy, beginning to understand why the man was so tormented. "It must have been very hard for you growing up."

" 'Twas hard," he admitted with a self-exalted smirk. "But I overcame it all to make something of myself. I'm here by no one's help but my own."

"Are you not lonely at times?"

"Lonely for what?" he asked sharply, as if taken aback by her question.

"People? Friends? Someone perhaps like Anna who appreciates what you are, what you do. . . . "

"No one appreciates what I am and what I accomplish more than I do myself."

His answer was so curt, Synnovea saw no reason to continue with the discussion, for it was apparent Ivan had long ago rejected the notion that friends and a loving family were important to one's well-being. She found it difficult to imagine such a solitary existence even being worth living.

The time came for Synnovea to prepare herself for their visit to the vast estates of Prince Vladimir. She spent a leisurely hour doing so, not caring how she might anger Anna by her delay in coming down. When she finally presented herself in the lower hall ten minutes past the hour designated for their departure, the princess was not the least bit inclined to hide her impatience.

"Well! You certainly kept us waiting!" Anna scolded. "But then, you awful girl, I'm certain 'twas your intent!"

Synnovea held herself distantly detached from the three though she could hardly disregard Anna's heated glower and Ivan's pugnacious scowl boring through her. It was Aleksei's prurient perusal rudely appraising her womanly curves that thoroughly outraged her. Even after wreaking his vengeance upon her, he was unable to keep his eyes from sliding down her iridescent green silk *sarafan*, as if he still considered her a potential mistress. With stilted decorum Synnovea faced Anna and asked, "You did want me to look my best for Prince Vladimir, did you not?"

The princess could hardly deny her charge's success

in accomplishing that deed. The delicate artistry of the gilded stitchery which liberally adorned the stiff collar, the lower sleeves, and hem of the *sarafan* the girl wore and the matching bejewled *kokoshniki* that crowned her dark head could only have been created by a gifted artisan. The black hair, lustrous fair skin, and green eyes, combined with a sleek but curvaceous figure, complimented the garment far beyond the abilities of most women. Still, Anna was not above soliciting some criticism from the two men, who seemed for once of kindred spirit, at least in their desire to seize some measure of redress from the girl.

"What do you think, Aleksei?" Anna faced her husband with a questioning brow raised. "Was the wait worth the results?"

The swarthy prince managed a tolerant smile for his wife, knowing what she wanted to hear. Although Synnovea's beauty was nearly without equal, he was convinced that she had to be taught a serious lesson to bring her to heel. He was determined to see her comply with the marriage to Vladimir and equally resolved to take his pleasure of her when the time was ripe. To serve Anna's end now, no matter how trite her disparagements seemed, would lend her confidence for an early morning departure, for he was not at all willing to see his plans for enforcing his will upon their ward thwarted by his wife's presence in the manse. "In view of Synnovea's accomplishments, my dear, perhaps we should consider delaying our departure a bit longer."

"We've endured too much as it is," Ivan complained tersely. "I beg you, let us be off."

Aleksei bowed stiffly for his wife's benefit. "At your pleasure, my dear."

Anna moved past Synnovea to accept Ivan's arm, and as they led the way through the front portal, Aleksei took up his usual position at the rear where he could freely peruse the nether curves of Synnovea's back. After Ivan and Anna climbed into the carriage, he pressed close behind her in a guise of impatience to be away, just to nurture a prurient fetish. Though the silently smoldering glare Synnovea cast over her shoulder failed to faze him, her small heel bearing down painfully on the toe of his boot immediately convinced him of the need to retreat a respectable distance.

When they reached the Dimitrievich mansion, the ancient prince eagerly expounded on the merits of Synnovea's beauty. He was exuberant in his praise and made haste to welcome her into his lavish mansion, taking her hand and gracing it with a fervent kiss before leading her into the great hall where his sons stood arrayed in their rich *kaftans* and their most gracious manners. Ivan and the Taraslovs were left to follow in the wake of the newly betrothed couple and had to settle for places of less prominence when Vladimir ceremoniously escorted Synnovea to a cushioned chair which sat next to his own.

Ivan was clearly disturbed by the arrangement. Before he had been arbitrarily demoted by the girl, he had tasted the rare sweetmeat of success when he had risen briefly to a powerful position as Prince Vladimir's guest of honor. Now his attempts to draw the old man into conversation were only randomly given heed to, while in sharp contrast the old *boyar* doted on every word that issued forth from the smiling lips of his betrothed.

Synnovea deliberately dismissed Ivan's glowers as she laughed and chatted with her future husband and his sons. For a short time Anna and Aleksei retired with the elder to discuss the nuptials, but when they returned, Ivan's outrage reached its zenith when Vladimir presented Synnovea with an emerald necklace, earrings to match, and a betrothal ring that was large enough to stagger the wits of the cleric.

"I'll dress you in robes of gold, my dearest Synnovea," Vladimir generously promised, "and precious jewels of every color!"

"Tut, tut, Prince Vladimir," Anna chided through a stiff smile. "You're bound to overindulge the girl with such extravagant gifts. I would seriously advise you to pamper her less and keep her more submissive if you wish a well-ordered marriage."

Her comments caused Aleksei to lower his libation and stare at his wife in amazement, but Anna ignored the implication of his stare. It did not matter to her if he silently challenged her own compliance to his husbandly authority. What vexed her was the idea of such treasures being wasted on one she absolutely abhorred. When Ivan had been so close to winning the old man's participation in his affairs, Anna found no pleasure in acceding anything to the girl who would undoubtedly squander the costly gifts. She could only think of how such wealth might have helped Ivan to gather the *boyars* to his cause. Indeed, what she and Ivan found even more astounding was the countess's pleading request that the jewelry be kept in Vladimir's care for safekeeping.

"Just until the day I come here to live," Synnovea sweetly urged, "for I could not easily bear such a great loss if they were mistakenly mislaid." She kept her gaze directed demurely downward, for fear of meeting Ivan's darkly glowering stare. Though his profession embodied all the honorable attributes one should possess in dedicated service to a higher order, she was not necessarily willing to trust the cleric, especially after Petrov's discovery of his carefully hoarded wealth. She was beginning to suspect that he was one of those who used their robes as a sham to bilk whatever fortunes could be easily gained from others apt to accept all clergymen as humble and honorable men. Ali had put it bluntly enough when she had described Ivan, and Synnovea could only agree. A wolf in sheep's clothing, was he!

Vladimir gladly deferred to Synnovea's wishes when she laid a hand gently upon his arm and looked beseechingly into his eyes. After bestowing an ardent kiss upon her slender fingers, he gathered up the treasures and gave them over to Igor, who took them away and restored them to a place of security.

"My own mother was beautiful," Sergei stated as he presented Synnovea with a glass of Visnoua, a libation that reminded her of the red wine she had, on a few occasions, sampled in France. "But I think my father has outdone himself this time in selecting you as his future bride."

"You are kind beyond measure," Synnovea responded, struggling with a gracious smile as she sipped from the silver goblet.

Feodor came to her as the youngest of the brood stepped away. With a sweeping bow, he delivered a large bouquet of flowers to her. "Like these cherished blooms, my lady, you grace us with your beauty and perfume."

Feeling at odds with herself because she could not summon anything more than a hollow display of pleasure, Synnovea gathered his gift into her arms and lowered her face into the blossoms to savor their sweet essence. With a trembling sigh, she lifted her head again and managed a smile for him. "You do me great honor, Prince Feodor, to compare my unworthy looks to such glorious marvels of nature."

Her eyes grew misty with tears as he took her hand and bestowed a light kiss upon her fingers. It was the anguish of feeling totally undeserving of their esteem that made Synnovea want to escape through the nearest door. She was painfully aware that in comparison to her own despicable behavior and foreboding, their gifts of words and tender treasures came forth with sterling sincerity.

As the eldest moved back, Stefan stepped forward to lay a garland of green around her neck. "Your company is cherished far above rubies and gold, Synnovea. Be assured that as a whole, the sons of Prince Vladimir Dimitrievich are enamored with your charm."

Synnovea smiled through a new misting of guilty tears. Almost against her will, she had been charmed by their

gallant display of manners, but their praise did little to
ease the weighty burden of regret that lay upon her chest.
"Forsooth, kind sirs! You woo me with such sweet tidings
and eloquent speech, my tongue staggers lamely in search
of equally rich prose."

Vladimir reached out again to gather her slender fingers and bring them to his lips. "In truth, Synnovea,
were your tongue forever silenced, we would still be
enamored by your sweet presence in this, our boorish
surroundings. We are but churlish clods in need of your
gentle, transforming touch."

Despite her rich enjoyment of their company and their
gallant attempts to show her how much her presence
pleased them, Synnovea could not evoke any feelings of
joy with which to kindly reciprocate their compliments.
Even though she managed to subdue her panic through
Vladimir's impetuously impassioned kiss, which he lowered with great gusto upon her lips as they took their
leave, she remained incredibly distraught by the irrevo-
cable marriage arrangements. Had Vladimir begged her
to be his daughter, she would have gladly yielded him
that honor, though she had loved her own sire deeply,
but to think of the old prince as her husband and to
consider everything which that particular position would
entail, she was no less desirous to be liberated from her
betrothal to him than she was to be gone far away from
the Dimitrievich manse.

Even while Synnovea lay abed that night, the tears continued to spill unheeded upon her pillow as she stared up
at the canopy above her head. Though her lips grimaced
in silent misery, her mind whimpered beneath the cruel
whip of her despair. Wearily she begged for some sweet
spirit from heaven to lend rest to her frazzled brain and
somehow impart to her a way she could be honorably set
free without wounding the old man overmuch. It was a
troubling dilemma in which she found herself, for despite
their reputation, she savored the friendship of Prince
Vladimir and his family of sons, though regretfully not

enough to arouse any eagerness in her breast to be bound by an oath of wedlock to Vladimir, and certainly not until that unmeasured time when widowhood finally came to release her. She did not covet the elder's death, nor did she want to yearn for such a fate for him in a marriage in which she would find no solace for her dreams of love and contentment.

Chapter 12

⤳ ⤶

THE FIRST MORNING RAYS OF THE SUN HAD JUST
stretched out across the land when Ali came to her
mistress's bedside to awaken her. A short time later
Synnovea left the chambers and made her descent.
While Anna had remained upstairs to take care of some
last-minute details which affected her own departure,
Prince Aleksei had taken up a waiting stance just outside
the front portal and was there when Synnovea stepped
from the doorway. He halted her with a hand on her
arm, then frowned wincingly at the dawning sun that
shimmered brilliantly in the sky, seeming rather pained
by the presence of that particular sphere.

To see Aleksei suffering after a long night of copious
imbibing that had begun at Vladimir's manse was small
propitiation for the resentment Synnovea was presently
feeling toward the man. She was tempted to give him
a fair piece of her mind, but she resisted the urge and
grudgingly allowed him a moment of her time, assured
that no further acts of aggression would be made upon
her person while they stood in clear sight of Ali, Jozef,
and Stenka.

"Allowing you to leave here was Anna's idea, not
mine," Aleksei informed her sullenly.

"I recognized your intent to keep me in your lecherous
lair the day you announced Anna would be leaving,"
Synnovea acknowledged with careful reserve. It was

only for the sake of her servants that she even made the attempt to feign a cordial mood. "Still, I'm much bemused how you might have hoped otherwise. Anna is no fool, you know. That's why she's so anxious to see me married off to Vladimir. She wants me out of the house and well away from you." A slight forward movement of her slender shoulder prefaced her next comment. "Of course, she has just cause."

"Anna has even more reason to hate you now than she did before," Aleksei taunted. "After I told her how you accosted me, she was most eager to see you wed."

A lovely brow slanted upward in surprise. "Well, I see you're not above telling farfetched lies, Aleksei, but your little ploy to discredit me will have no bearing on my actions, so be warned."

"You be warned, my girl." He slashed the words through clenched teeth as he struggled a moment to maintain his aplomb. "I have no intention of letting you escape what has now been decreed. Though Natasha has a nasty habit of trying to confound proprieties to meet her own tastes—"

Once again Synnovea raised a challenging brow as she interrupted. "And what of you, sir? Have you not done the same?"

Aleksei ignored her intrusion and continued in a cynical tone. "I'm sure Natasha will try to undermine your betrothal by inviting to her home those very same men who can tarnish your reputation. . . . "

Synnovea stared at him in amazement, never having considered the ruination of her honor as a means by which she could avoid marriage with Vladimir. Such a ploy would be a stiff price to pay for her freedom, a price she was not at all sure she was willing to yield. Still, it might be worth contemplating if she found herself truly desperate. "I can see how you might be worried about my reputation, considering the fact that Vladimir would be most reluctant to attach himself to a maid whose virtue has been besmirched," she answered disparagingly. "But for the life of me, Aleksei, I cannot imagine that you'll be content to see me married off without trying to extract some further penance from me, which leaves me to wonder how you intend to plan a tryst to claim me as your conquered victim. 'Tis been widely rumored that you have a preference for virgins, but then, so does my betrothed. Are you willing to allow Vladimir first taste of the unblemished fruit before you seek retribution?"

"If need be, I'll make an exception in your case," Aleksei promised with a hint of a sneer.

"So good of you," Synnovea derided crisply. She glanced away as she sought to regain control of her flaring temper, and then turned on him again with renewed vigor, wanting to shatter that cocksure arrogance. "If it falls within my power to frustrate your purposes, Aleksei, let me be the first to assure you that I will use every wile within my capability to see your plans thwarted and your ambitions put to naught, even if I have to take Colonel Rycroft into my bed to see the deed done."

The dark eyes flared with rage as his hissing words lashed out at her. "Think you that such a thing can happen while I yet breathe, maid? You do err in conjuring such fantasies of deception for yourself, my lovely, for I'll not let another man have you!"

"Not even Prince Vladimir?" she questioned jeeringly.

"By him, I will reap vengeance upon you for the injury you've done me! 'Twill not be long after you've survived a few of his straining attempts that you'll be begging me to satisfy you. Nay, you'll not escape marriage to Vladimir, for I'll hire men to watch you and any house you're in until the very moment the vows are spoken! There will be no help for you, my beauty. None will come to your rescue, not even your precious Englishman."

"That remains to be seen, doesn't it?" Synnovea managed an ungracious smile as her lashes hovered low over a glare. Reaching out, she tapped her fingers lightly upon his arm, as if casually instructing a naughty student.

"Were I you, Aleksei, I would avoid any mention of this matte to your wife before her departure, for I intend to protect myself henceforth from your malevolent bent. If need be, I'll take my complaints to Tsar Mikhail himself and let him deal with both of you as you justly deserve. I swear I will!"

With a last, irritated rap of her fingers on his arm, Synnovea turned from him and, a moment later, climbed into the carriage that would take her away from the Taraslov manse in what she dearly hoped would be her final departure.

It was a short, brief excursion down the thoroughfare to the larger Andreyevna mansion, but for Synnovea the passage of time seemed even more concise as her thoughts began to roam in an ever widening range of possibilities. She could not lightly dismiss from mind the idea that Aleksei had unwittingly presented her. The most important question she had to find an answer for was whether she preferred to keep her honor unblemished in a miserable marriage, or if she was willing to sacrifice her reputation to gain the freedom to choose her own way of life and perhaps even a husband. The second option, although tempting, could bring damaging slurs against her that she might never recover from. Society was wont to judge a fallen woman harshly, and it could mean being ostracized by her peers. Still, if she could somehow manage to bewilder the gossips and preserve the secrecy of her actions or, for that matter, even feign her debauchment (if such a feat were indeed possible), then her ploy might yield her everything she desired for her own happiness.

When the carriage pulled into the drive, Natasha hurried out to welcome her with cheery greetings and a jubilant smile, and for Synnovea the morning seemed suddenly brighter. Not only was she to be ensconced in the home of a close friend, but now, thanks to Aleksei, she had a small glimmer of an idea to cling to. With time being so limited, she would have to decide quickly if such a sacrifice would be worth it all once everything was said and done.

Despite the clarity of her choices, however, Synnovea realized that finding an acceptable answer to the riddle which confronted her was far more involved and complicated than she could rightly do justice to in the mere space of a few days. It was not until she ventured out with Natasha and Ali to a small, rough-hewn chapel located beyond the outskirts of the city that she actually became cognizant of just how closely Aleksei watched her comings and goings.

The three of them had set out to lend their services to a kindly monk who devoted himself to great acts of charity. Whether old, blind, wretched, decrepit, or lame, those in need were never turned away from the little church where the kindly Friar Philip dedicated himself to serving their needs. To many he was known as Saint Philip, though he wore shabby robes and denounced the acquisition of wealth for the church that many of the Josephites had insisted upon. His main concern was tending "his flock," which included anyone who came to him in want of food, clothes, or peace for their souls. The afflictions of the poor were often decreased to a more tolerable level by his compassion or by those who came to assist him in his selfless struggle.

Arriving early that morning, Synnovea, together with Ali and Natasha, had addressed themselves to the task of preparing a meal in the kitchen located in a lean-to behind the chapel. They had deliberately chosen to wear garments that were plain and made from a common cloth, even though the richness of their coach clearly attested to their wealth. Soon after the food was cooked, Synnovea busied herself handing out loaves of bread and ladling a hearty stew into the wooden bowls held forth by the ragged and hungry who shuffled past. Natasha distributed apparel from several bundles she had collected from friends, while Ali entertained the children with mimes and craggy-voiced songs, allowing their mothers to search out clothing with which they could warmly outfit their families for the approaching winter.

Into this gathering of obviously destitute humanity, Aleksei came swaggering, bearing himself in the guise of the rich and mighty prince he envisioned himself to be. When he espied the countesses, he strode purposefully forward, forcing the more unsightly ones to scurry out of his way. With flamboyant mockery, he bowed before the two *boyarinas* and chortled scoffingly as he paused to take stock of their surroundings.

"How generous both of you are to devote your time to these paltry beings. I'm sure Ivan Voronsky would be impressed."

Synnovea did not feel in the least bit disposed toward offering him an affirmative answer. Indeed, had he said only one sun existed in the sky, she would have hastened to find some argument with which to refute his claim. As it was, she welcomed the opportunity to disagree with his comment with unswerving conviction. "And I'm just as sure that Ivan has no real comprehension of charity other than what goes into his own pockets."

Glancing around, Synnovea realized that those who had been waiting in line for food were now hanging back, afraid and reluctant to move past the richly garbed prince. As she considered their diffidence and trepidation, which was so apparent on their faces, she realized Aleksei's presence had kindled a burgeoning fear among the many who had come seeking sustenance.

"Begone with you, Aleksei!" she commanded and swept her hand to indicate those ones who were beginning to shuffle away. "Can't you see what you're doing? They're afraid of you!"

"Afraid of me? Why so?" His astonishment was badly feigned. "I've just come to witness your compassion toward these foul-smelling oafs. Anna will also be amazed when I tell her what you're doing. She didn't think you cared one whit about anyone but yourself. But then, she's not one who is so compassionate that she can adequately judge others." His red lips curved with a patronizing smile. "What has set you on this path of benevolence, anyway? Are you seeking to pay penance for your sins?"

Synnovea settled her hands petulantly upon her slender waist and faced him squarely. "My greatest sin hasn't been committed yet, Aleksei. That's when I hire some henchman to string you up. If it's no great secret you care to hide, may I ask why you're here?"

"Why, I've come as you have, as a benevolent lord to give ease to the poor." He turned and addressed the humble priest. "See here, Philip, or whatever your name is! I've come to give my dues to your cause." He drew forth a few coins of meager worth and scattered them at the monk's sandled feet.

"I will thank God for your kindness, my son," the white-haired monk murmured graciously in reply, kneeling to pick them up. Though he sensed the *boyar* wanted to see him groveling at his feet, he was not so proud that he could ignore the insufficiencies that plagued his small ministry.

"You'd do better to thank me, old man," Aleksei jeered over him. "I have power here on earth to see you imprisoned for consorting with thieves." He swept his hand to indicate the tattered folk who shuffled back or huddled in growing apprehension of the *boyar*'s intentions. Pompously Aleksei questioned, "Have I not seen the likes of these rogues stealing bread?"

"Oh, but surely, if they did, 'twas only a morsel or two, and you would forgive them for such a meager offense!" the monk hurried to entreat as he struggled to his feet. "Many would starve without the small bit of food they are given or manage to find!"

"Have I not also seen you feeding those foul miscreants who are locked in stocks in Kitaigorod? Mayhap you're also in league with those rogues who come to stealthily seek their release. I heard it said that those felons flee the city and then take up with bands of raiders. Perhaps they even stop here for sustenance to see them on their way."

The holy man spread his hands as he begged for understanding. " 'Tis true that you may have seen me helping them, but the law of the city makes no provision to feed the prisoners who are kept in fetters. And who is to say what crimes they have committed? Whether pitiful deeds or those declared unworthy of reprieve among worldly judges, they grow equally famished for a piece of bread or a cup of water. I do not ask them their crimes when I distribute food. I only try to assure them that there is love and forgiveness, whatever their iniquities. But your pardon, my son, are you so perfect and pure that you can cast the first stone at these poor wretches?"

Aleksei's swarthy skin took on a dark reddish hue as he hastened to inform the priest, "I'm a prince! An aristocrat from birth!"

A kindly smile curved the wrinkled lips of the elder. "Do you seek to impress God with your aristocracy when all are equal in his sight, my son? None are perfect, whether prince or pauper."

Tossing his head in contempt, Aleksei confronted the holy man. "Is God blind to thieves and murderers?"

"God sees all, my son, but he also forgives if we make the effort to ask him."

Aleksei scoffed. "If there even is a God!"

"Each man has to decide whether he wants to believe or not. No one can force him to. 'Tis a matter of the heart."

The prince's brows lowered darkly. "I prefer not to. 'Tis foolishness to believe in something you cannot see!"

"God has chosen the foolishness of this world to confound the wisdom of the wise." The monk returned a somber smile to the prince's glower. "Whether you believe or not, my son, you cannot nullify God. He still exists."

"Only in minds more susceptible to such foolishness!"

The kindly priest spoke gently. "I'm sorry, but I do not understand why you have come here if that is your belief. Do you seek counsel from a fool?"

"Oh, I've heard of your kind," Aleksei derided. "You can be certain of that! *Bozhie liudi!* Men of God! Holy fools! That's what they call you! *Skitalets!* Holy wanderers! You set up your *skity* in areas like this in compliance with that so-called order of Nilus Sorsky, that most foolish of fools! But you know as well as I do that Nilus died after his arguments against the wealth of the church were overridden by Joseph Sanin, and thereinafter his followers have been persecuted by the Josephites and the grand dukes of Muscovy . . . ˜s you will be!"

"Your knoˇvledge of history seems well intact, my son, but you havᴇ not yet answered my question. Do you seek counsel from me?"

Aleksei laughed caustically. "You could not possibly instruct me with your fool's wisdom, holy man. I came only to guarantee the safety of my ward while she is among these filthy peasants."

The monk shifted his gaze toward the young countess who, earlier that morning, had arrived with her maid and the Countess Andreyevna. In recent years the latter had proven herself a most gracious and generous benefactress. Though he tended a garden and a small flock of sheep to enable him to serve the needs of the poor, he was grateful when such kindly and charitable workers as these offerᴇ ᴅ theˑ assistance. They had even sent their coachman ⸴ way t ⸴ purchase more food when there had not been enouɡn victuals to feed all those who came. Now, because of them, many more were being fed.

"None here would harm her," the priest declared. "These people are appreciative of what the countess has done for them."

Aleksei objected with a snort of derision. " 'Tis well beneath the countess's station in life to consort with these vile vermin."

"What kind do you suggest she consort with?" the holy man asked with dawning discernment. "Do you mean to persuade her to go back with you, perhaps?"

Synnovea came forward and cast a pointed glare toward the intruder, then without a word, she turned and strode toward the door, luring Aleksei away from the white-haired monk. As she paused at the portal, she voiced her objections to his presence. " 'Tis obvious what your real concerns are, Aleksei. Even Saint Philip is able to see through your motives. If you are capable of any decency, I pray you leave here and let us be."

"You must heed my words, Synnovea," Aleksei insisted.

"I warn you now, Aleksei, that you'd better heed mine! I've had enough of your lies and your filthy attempts to bed me! Now get out of here ere I take a lash to you! And don't ever come back here!"

Overhearing the girl's threat, Natasha approached the prince with an amused smile. "Beware, Aleksei. I do believe the girl means it."

Aleksei's sharply penetrating scowl bore into the younger countess. "I've hired men to follow you wherever you go, Synnovea. You'll not escape me! They'll hound you until you beg me to set you free of them."

"Shall I complain to Prince Vladimir about your close attention?" Synnovea needled. "He has wealth enough to send other guards to protect me from your spite."

"Aye! Send for him!" Aleksei challenged. "He'll insist upon speaking the vows posthaste just to save you from the ruffians I've hired, then I'll have my revenge that much quicker."

Giving her a shallow bow, he bade her farewell and stalked through the door. Synnovea glared after him as he strode to an area across from the chapel where a large party of mounted riders awaited him. From a distance, the men appeared to be nothing more than a large band of unruly rabble dressed in a variety of outlandish garb. It was later that afternoon when Synnovea realized her first assessment was true. They were a wild bunch, proficient at provoking her to outrage as they set up their surveillance in front of the church. After several strumpets joined them, they liberally indulged in large quantities of kvass and vodka and involved themselves in lewd cavorting and riotous dancing. Abashed by their unrestrained revelry, Synnovea could do naught but beg forgiveness of Friar Philip as she took her leave.

"I had no idea I would be causing you this difficulty by coming here."

"No need for you to feel that you're at fault by what these men do, my child," he murmured as his eyes briefly flitted toward the rapscallions who hooted and taunted those who took shelter within the church. "I know you're not of their ilk. The Countess Natasha is kindhearted and generous, and you are very much like her. Do not let these ruffians dissuade you from coming here again. Today you have done a great service for those who are less fortunate. And the coins you have given will go a long way in buying more food."

"I will send my servant with a regular stipend to help you feed the poor."

"Be assured, Countess, that I will use it only to help them."

"I know you will." Synnovea smiled and took a rough, work-hardened hand to press a kiss to it. "I'll come back when I'm free of these men, good father, but for now, it seems that I must contend with their proximity wherever I go."

"Take care, my child, and may God go with you."

Kneeling before him, Synnovea accepted his blessings, then took her leave with Natasha and Ali and climbed into the waiting coach. In response, the pack of rowdies swung up on their mounts and followed the conveyance down the road, deserting the harlots who screamed profanities after them in angry disappointment.

Seeing the need for haste, Natasha's coachman laid the whip to the team, urging the horses to their swiftest gait, but as the thickening shadows of night surrounded them, the rabble grew bolder and came alongside, hooting and chortling as the men displayed their horsemanship with reckless antics and great fanfare. While some showed off their skills by sitting on their mounts backwards or sidesaddle, others performed dangerous capers in and out of their saddles. Had the three women not been so fearful of what lay in store for them along the way, they might have admired the proficiency with which the riders performed. As it was, great sighs of relief were expelled by the occupants of the coach when they arrived home safely. As the rascals gathered in front of the house and loudly chortled, the servants hurried to bolt the doors and set guards to watch.

A short time later the butler heralded the approach of Prince Vladimir and his sons, setting the household into an immediate quandary. Natasha quickly instructed her servants to arm themselves with whatever tool, weapon, or implement they could find to lend their support to the princes in what would likely be a dangerous altercation between the family and the ruffians, but when a maid called her mistress's attention to the fact that the riffraff were now nowhere to be seen, both Natasha and Synnovea flew to the window to see if it could possibly be true. Overwhelming relief rallied their spirits, and almost cheerily they welcomed Vladimir and his sons into the manse, thankfully making no mention of the boisterous bunch who had followed them home.

In the next several days, however, the gang of rowdies made their presence known to Synnovea wherever she went, but it was the smug smirk that she noticed on Aleksei's face, when he stood outside the mansion, that finally settled the matter in her mind. She'd be hanged and quartered before allowing him the ultimate triumph! Thus, quite resolutely, she came to the conclusion that it was far less of a sacrifice to be bedded and besmirched!

Even so tenuous a solution to her problem was enough to calm the brooding consternation that had assailed Synnovea since Anna's decree. She resigned herself to the controversial means of escape, lending her attention wholeheartedly to the task of devising

the tactics by which she could entice the worldly
Colonel Rycroft to serve as her seducer. Though that
feat seemed to present no great challenge, it was the
withholding payment of her virtue that appeared the
formidable part, for the man would have his mind
on claiming that very thing she wanted to preserve.
If his cavalier actions in the bathhouse presented any
evidence of his manly disposition, she was inclined to
think he was quite self-assured and adept at a game
she knew little about, and if she could not control his
ardor to her liking, where would she be left but in
his bed?

"I shall need your help," she begged of Natasha after
carefully explaining her proposal, "but if you've no heart
for it, I'll surely understand. It could mean danger for us
both if my plans go awry. As you've already witnessed
for yourself, Prince Aleksei is adamant about halting any
intervention that would see me rejected as a fit bride by
Prince Vladimir. He is extremely suspicious of you helping me."

"I'm not afraid of that pompous crow, but I have a
concern for what might actually happen to you in this
scheme of yours." Natasha chose her words carefully,
not wanting to dishearten her young friend, yet sensing a
need for extreme caution. "I must advise you to be wary,
Synnovea. I'd not be a true friend if I only encouraged
you to continue and not warned you of the danger you'll
be courting. Frankly, I think you have much more to fear
from the Englishman than you do from Aleksei, at least
for the moment. 'Tis obvious to us both that Aleksei is
acting out of character, trying to preserve your virtue
for Prince Vladimir. Colonel Rycroft has no cause to
play such waiting games. I fear once you encourage him,
you'll be hard-pressed to dissuade him from carrying out
your ravishment forthwith. You're but a girl, innocent of
the passions which can goad a man, and I know if you
tempt him overmuch, you'll likely see how hard he is
driven."

"Surely he is beset with strumpets at the place where he lives. I've heard it rumored that the harlots zealously seek out the foreigners who come here without kith and kin. He's probably exhausted from all their attention."

"Who spills such gossip about the man?" Natasha asked indignantly.

Synnovea gave quick answer, confused by the feelings within her. It was almost as if in the hidden recesses of her womanly spirit, she wanted to lose this argument. "Princess Anna was positive that Colonel Rycroft liberally availed himself of their services."

Natasha threw up a hand as she scoffed in derision, then she leaned forward as if revealing a dark secret. "Well, my girl, I've heard it rumored that Colonel Rycroft has dumbfounded many of his fellow officers by turning down several invitations put forth by a certain number of young *boyarinas* who have recently been widowed and yearn to have him as their lover. In view of the fact that he has refused to accept what has been freely offered by women who are attractive as well as wealthy, do you think he would pay out coins for comfort from women of the streets? He seems intent upon his work and winning you, so if 'tis your plan to trick him, you must take care. He'll not likely consider it kindly if you tempt him unduly and then torment him with a refusal."

Strangely placated by Natasha's reasoning, Synnovea continued to set forth the requirements for the success of her plan. "It is necessary that Aleksei and his rabble are notified at exactly the precise moment so they will carry out my rescue before payment is made. You're the only one I can trust to accomplish that mission," she said. "There will be no help for me if the timing goes awry. Once I leave with Colonel Rycroft, he'll be bent on taking me to his quarters and getting me into his bed. Somehow I must hold him off until Aleksei comes to stop the event. Hopefully, by the time he arrives, things will have progressed to such a state that Aleksei will think he has little choice but to tell my betrothed of my indiscretion.

Vladimir's rejection of me will accomplish the rest."

Natasha sought again to offer wise counsel to her young friend. "What do you expect will happen when Colonel Rycroft and Prince Aleksei confront each other? Do you think the colonel will give you up without a fight?"

"Colonel Rycroft is hopefully wise enough to know that quarreling with Aleksei will do him little good."

" 'Tis doubtful that the colonel will be in any logical frame of mind after being interrupted on the very threshold of consummating his desires."

"Then I'll encourage him to flee ere he is taken. If he refuses, he's capable of defending himself. As for Aleksei, he's far less competent, but will no doubt bring his hired henchmen with him to secure his protection."

"Dear child, I cannot help but fear that this whole idea of yours is dangerous," Natasha fretted. "In time you may be sorry for having scandalized your reputation, but after the deed is done, there will be little you can say or do to make it all right again. Don't think it will go as smoothly as you hope it will either. Even in the best of plans, something will usually go awry. And if you're not the one who'll pay, then have a care for Colonel Rycroft. He's a foreigner in this country. Who will go to his aid if he is taken? Tsar Mikhail may consider the divestment of your virginity an affront to your father's memory and seek retribution from the colonel."

"I will speak in Colonel Rycroft's defense," Synnovea stated stubbornly and, at the elder's incredulous stare, lifted her shoulders in a dismal shrug. "If need be, I'll plead my cause to Tsar Mikhail and admit 'twas I who deliberately enticed him into seducing me for the purpose of escaping marriage to Prince Vladimir."

"Now that should be a tale to raise a few brows," Natasha remarked, conveying her skepticism.

Synnovea went to kneel beside the woman and gazed up at her pleadingly. "Oh, Natasha, if I don't try this, there may be no escape for me. Aleksei will have his revenge, and I'll be forever bound to Prince Vladimir until that time one of us is taken and buried in the grave."

The elder heaved a gloomy sigh. "I think your plan is dangerous, my child, yet I can understand your reluctance in being wed to an ancient. When I was much younger, I, too, loathed the idea of submitting myself to my first husband. Though he was kind, he was great in years, and I found no joy in our bed."

Synnovea laid her cheek upon the woman's knee. "I do not hate Vladimir, Natasha. He is a far better man than Aleksei might have chosen had he been given more time. 'Tis just that . . ."

"I know, Synnovea. There's no need for you to explain. Your head has been filled with glorious visions of love and marriage similar to what your parents shared together. If anyone is to blame for the hopes you cling to, then 'tis Aleksandr and Eleanora. They wanted you to know the same joy and devotion that was theirs."

"Perhaps Anna was right," Synnovea murmured grimly. "Perhaps I've been pampered far too much all my life."

"If that be true, my dear, then I would see all children coddled in the same manner, for you have all the qualities I would desire to see in a daughter." Natasha stroked the dark head affectionately. "Do not concern yourself about Anna and the insults she would lay upon you. She lives in her own private hell, and she seeks to share her fate with others. We must forget her and set our minds now to more important matters, such as refining this ingenious plan of yours. The less left to chance, the better it will be for you . . . and perhaps Colonel Rycroft. Of course, you know there will be a definite chance he will hate you after this. A man's pride is most tender when his affections and emotions are carelessly used by a woman."

"Colonel Rycroft will live through this blow to his confidence far better than Vladimir would if I were to reveal my aversion to him. Should I tell the truth and lay the old man low, even so much as in the grave?"

Natasha wagged her head in woeful denial. "No, no, child! I would not see you harm the old prince in such a way. I only wish there was some way to soften the blow to the colonel. 'Tis a shame to waste the affections of such a man."

Synnovea raised her head and searched the saddened eyes of the elder. "Would you have me give myself to him so his pride may be spared?"

A glum frown puckered Natasha's brows. "If only there was another way to accomplish what you have in mind. I had such high hopes for Colonel Rycroft. I was sure that of all the men who have admired you, he would be the one to win you."

"You saw in him far more than I could see, Natasha," Synnovea replied softly, but she averted her face, not willing to admit that she may have seen more in him herself than she would ever dare divulge to anyone.

"I suppose." The wistful answer waned in the stillness of the room, and it was some moments before Synnovea tore her mind free from her own apprehensions and glanced up to see that the dark eyes had grown misty with tears. Though the woman's doleful mood brought home to her the gravity of her plot, Synnovea could not find it in herself to halt the plummeting grains of time that would see her own ends accomplished in this affair.

Chapter 13

THE PENDULUM SWAYED THROUGH THE LONG HOURS until night followed day and day followed night and the evening of the planned seduction finally arrived. Synnovea was as jittery as a young bride on her wedding night with the realization that Colonel Rycroft would be in attendance and she would actually be trying to beguile him by whatever means proved effective, whether with coy looks, winsome smiles, or sultry stares. Lacking the finesse and skill of a more experienced temptress, she had no way of knowing how to prepare herself for what was to come. In matters of feminine persuasions, she would have to rely on her own instincts, but in selecting a gown, she yielded herself to Natasha's guidance. A rich, deep blue gown of European design was chosen to compliment her fair skin and to reveal just enough of her bosom to be subtly alluring without being overtly vulgar.

"If Colonel Rycroft was greatly affected by a brazen display of bosom, my dear, I'm sure he would have been content with strumpets. Instead, he has settled his eye on you, Synnovea, and certainly with good cause, but I rather doubt that you've given him more than a glimpse or two of a dainty little ear or nape. Therefore, I'm inclined to say the colonel's tastes are more refined in the area of women's attire."

Synnovea lifted a hand in the guise of brushing aside a tumbling curl from off her brow as she sought to hide the

vibrant color that bloomed in her cheeks. She would have
been the last person alive to verbally dispute the woman's theory, but she was wont to wonder if Tyrone Rycroft
would have paid much heed to her at all if he had not seen
as much of her as there was to see.

"Have you told Ali what you're planning this evening?" Natasha asked, settling herself on a chaise as
Synnovea rose from the tub and slipped into the bathing pool that was fed by an underground spring. Ali had
just left, having forgotten the violet balm to rub into her
mistress's skin, and since the bathing room was located
at the far and lower end of the Andreyevna manse, it
was unlikely the maid would return for at least several
moments, which allowed Natasha the time she needed to
further question her young friend. She found herself wor-
rying more and more over what might actually happen as
the time for the intended deception rapidly approached.
"Ali's simply beside herself with the thought of Colonel
Rycroft coming here. Does she have any hint of what
you're going to do to him?"

"What? And have her lay me low with her scolding,
too?!" Synnovea shook her head in denial, but continued
on, voicing an objection to the woman's choice of words.
" 'Tis not what I'm going to do *to* Colonel Rycroft,
Natasha, but what I'll be allowing him to do to me! I'll not
be binding his hands and forcing myself upon his flanks,
as you seem to think I'll be doing. There would surely be
less chance of something scandalous happening if I were
to be so bold! Believe me, if Colonel Rycroft's hands move
as fast and as freely as his eyes are wont to do, then I can
well perceive the hazards of being alone with the man."

Natasha held up a hand to halt the other's testy tirade.
"I'll say no more of it, then, for 'tis plain you are easily
riled by my lament."

"Aye!" Synnovea agreed with a pert nod. "You'd sooner take Colonel Rycroft's side than mine!"

Natasha leaned forward on the chaise and braced her
small, pointed chin upon a slender knuckle as she peered

intently into the brooding eyes of the other. "You may pout and dispute my charity toward him, Synnovea, but you must consider this. I've seen the weapons at your disposal and do tremble in fear at the havoc you can cause in that man's life."

Synnovea reddened profusely as she felt the meaningful flick of the other's perusal and, with an indignant groan, she sank below the surface of the water until she was sufficiently submerged to her chin. "You're not being at all fair to take his side over mine."

"On the contrary, my dear. When you deliberately set out to entice a man with the intention of using him as a pawn for your own gain, I have no difficulty comparing your actions to the deeds of a harlot, but I fear that your ruse is far more damaging. At least a harlot would stay and pay her due, but what of you? The moment he seeks to take you, you flit out the door."

"Natasha! Have pity on my poor hide!" Synnovea complained. "You wound me to the quick!"

"Good! For that's exactly what you intend to do with him!" the elder accused.

The tiny furrows of a sullen frown marked Synnovea's brow as she peered up at Natasha. "Do you like the man so much?!"

"Aye! That I do!"

The straight, delicate nose lifted ever so slightly to indicate an injury ill-met. "And do you loathe me so much for this thing I plan?"

Helplessly Natasha raised her arms in a lame gesture of appeal. "My dearest Synnovea, I understand why you do this thing." She shook her graying head, overwhelmed by her own frustration. "I just have an aversion to seeing you waste what might have been a cherished love."

"I'll never know what I might have had with Colonel Rycroft," Synnovea answered dismally. "I only know what lies ahead for me if I do not gain my freedom. Will you not give me your blessing?"

Again the frosted dark head moved in a negative motion. "Nay, Synnovea, I cannot do that, but I will give you my prayers, for I think you'll be needing them desperately . . . you *and* Colonel Rycroft. Aleksei just might be tempted to kill you both."

"Do you have to be so morose about it all?" Synnovea grumbled.

Natasha stared at the radiant beauty a long moment before voicing a conjecture. "Synnovea, my child, I don't think you have any idea what you're letting yourself in for."

The door opened behind them, and the two women glanced around as Ali hastened in with her skittering little walk. "Here I be at last." She barely paused to take a breath before she rushed on. "An' me hurryin' all the time. Why, if'n this house be any big'er, a body could set the Taraslov manse right square dab in the midst o' it an' still have room for a banquet! Poor Danika's never seen such a large pantry, not ter mention the rooms she an' lit'le Sophia been given. Ye can be sure they're a happy pair."

"Danika is a very talented addition to the staff. An excellent cook," Natasha declared with a chuckle. "I'm sure our guests will soon agree her capabilities are positively unmatched."

"Elisaveta is no less astute, but she fears her labors are mainly wasted at the Taraslovs'," Synnovea interjected as she tried to set her mind to something less disquieting than her planned gambit with Tyrone Rycroft. She glanced up as the old servant came to the edge of the pool. "Why don't you go visit with Elisaveta this evening, Ali? I'm sure she would enjoy hearing about Danika's good fortune. Stenka can drive you over there and then return later to fetch you."

"Aye, mistress, that I'll be doin' for sure, but first I'd like ter snatch a peek or two at Colonel Rycroft. He's nearly the most handsome man I've ever seen."

Synnovea was inclined to demur the farfetched boast, having already suffered much admonition because of the man. "I fear you're exaggerating beyond your usual bent, Ali. The man has a nice enough form, I'll grant you, but hardly the face to turn a lady's head."

Natasha's brows raised in wonder as she contemplated her young friend, but she refrained from giving comment when a few hours could better serve an end to the argument.

The moment rapidly approached until it was nearly time for the guests to arrive. Natasha gave a nod of approval when Synnovea extended the voluminous skirts of her gown and danced around in a slow circle before her.

"Do I pass your inspection, Countess?" the maiden plied with a charming smile.

"Most admirably!" Natasha fervently avouched. "Your necklace of sapphires and pearl teardrops makes your skin look so wondrously fair . . . and the gown . . . well, it's magnificent!"

Smoothing her skirts, Synnovea went to where she could see some hint of her reflection in a pane of glass near the entrance. The stiff ivory collar fanned outward, like the wide petals of an ornate flower, and seemed to frame her face and bosom with its costly scalloped lace. A similar piece of lace, which had been lightly seeded with tiny pearls in the same fashion as the collar, provided a translucent covering across her bosom that seemed at first demure and then, upon closer inspection, most provocative as it tantalized the prudent observer with glimpses of a deep crevice plunging downward between pale, swelling breasts.

The stomacher was made of a rich, heavy velvet stitched with silken threads in an elaborate scroll design. The long trailing sleeves hung open to reveal tightly fitting inner sleeves adorned with ivory lace cuffs lightly sprinkled with seed pearls. The lustrous black hair had been swept high in an intricate weaving of thick strands. At her ears, pearl teardrops hung from sapphires wreathed with tiny pearls and diamonds, while the extravagant necklace finished it all sublimely.

" 'Tis evident you're no pauper's daughter," Natasha observed with a smile. "I fear the poor colonel will have difficulty recovering his wits after he sees you. From then on, he'll be as vulnerable as a bleating lamb being led to slaughter."

"Natasha, please! Have done with your nagging ere I'm rent asunder!" Synnovea implored and, with an injured pout, peered askance at the woman. "The way you harp at me, a body would think you're my mother."

Natasha flung her head back and laughed heartily as she settled her arms akimbo. When her amusement finally dwindled to a smile, she met the solemn green eyes with warm lights shining in her own. "If it's so obvious that I have a mother's concern for you, Synnovea, can you not understand that I value your happiness above all else? Thus I beg you to have a care for the pride of the man you lead into your trap."

From outside the house came the tinkling of tiny bells as a carriage pulled into the lane and, a moment later, the sound of mingled voices as several men approached the mansion. Meeting the woman's stare again, Synnovea managed a tremulous smile as she avowed, "I shall do whatever I can to soften the blow to the colonel."

Natasha inclined her regal head ever so slightly in acknowledgment of the other's promise and moved to greet her first guests. The pledge would be enough to assuage her apprehensions, at least for the time being.

It was nearly a quarter turn of the minute hand when Colonel Rycroft entered the foyer of the Andreyevna manse with his second-in-command, Captain Grigori Tverskoy. The Russian was dressed in a royal blue silk *kaftan* and looked quite dashing, but the Englishman had garbed himself according to the fashions of his homeland and was groomed entirely in black, except for the lace-edge cuffs and a falling collar of the same crisp white lace. Ali waited on the stairs above the entry, and when Tyrone entered, it was to her utter delight that he caught sight of her and swept into a courtly bow.

"You've made my day brighter by your cheery smile, Ali McCabe," he called to her. "So far I've seen none to bless my heart more."

Ali's giggles wafted back over her shoulder as she scampered off to her mistress's chambers. Having seen the Englishman handsomely outfitted in his best, she was content now to make her way by coach to the Taraslov kitchen, where she would seek out the companionship of Elisaveta.

"No wonder Ali is fond of you, Colonel," Natasha commented as he addressed his attention to her. "With a name like Tyrone and enough charm to crumble Lord Blarney's castle, you've managed to endear yourself to her. She is sure you came from the same stock."

"Actually, my grandmother did," Tyrone confided, "but then, she all but raised me, for my own mother often sailed the seas with my father."

"And your father, what is he?"

"A shipbuilder, Countess, and when it meets his mood, a merchant seaman."

"Not a soldier?" Natasha chuckled and swept a slender hand in a graceful flourish as she added, "I would have thought him to be a proud cavalier like yourself, Colonel. Wherever did you gain such skill on a horse if your father specialized in shipbuilding?"

"My Grandmother Meghan is fond of horses." A flash of white teeth accompanied his answer. "Shortly after I was weaned, she had me in a saddle. Even at threescore, ten and three years of age, she still rides for an hour or so every morning."

"Does your grandmother not object to you being here in a foreign land? I'm sure she would prefer to see you now and then."

"She does, but I fear there is no help for it. At least not yet."

The dark brows raised in curious question. "It sounds most serious, Colonel."

Tyrone shrugged and saw no reason to make the deed seem trivial. "I killed a man in a duel, Countess, and since his family had both rank and power, whereas mine had only wealth, I was adv'sed to leave the country until either their tempers cooled or they could see the light of it."

"The light of it being?" Natasha nearly held her breath in apprehension of his answer.

" 'Twas a quarrel over a woman," he murmured candidly.

"Oh." Natasha paled considerably and managed a shaky smile to hide her concern for the innocent who was about to lead this man into a trap. "Are you prone to quarreling over women, Colonel?"

"Not usually, Countess."

"And the lady? Is she content now to have you gone?"

"It matters no more to her, I fear. She died shortly before I left England."

"How sad for you, Colonel. You must have loved her very much to have fought for her."

"At one time, I was thoroughly convinced that my love for her would endure every trial." His lips twitched briefly in a bleak smile. "I was mistaken."

Natasha dared no further questions, for she sensed by the terseness of his reply that he wished to speak no more of the matter. With a smile she shifted her attention to Captain Tverskoy. "How good of you to join your commander in coming here, Captain. I'm sure you'll be pleasured by the presence of Prince Zherkof and his daughter, Tania. I believe all of you came from the same province."

Drawing on the friendship of her old friend and his beautiful young daughter, Natasha deliberately engaged them in a conversation with Grigori before leading Tyrone across the room to where Synnovea was helping a pair of ancient dowagers to the service of *zakuski* and glasses of Amarodina. As she sought to bolster her own emotions for the moment of their meeting, Natasha could only pray that she was doing the right thing for both of them.

"A moment of your time, Synnovea," Natasha murmured, coming up behind the girl. As the younger countess excused herself from the dowagers, Natasha glanced aside to Tyrone. "I'm sure the two of you have met before, but perhaps not with proper decorum."

Though quaking inwardly all the way down to her toes, Synnovea gripped her wine goblet more securely to hide the fact that her hands were shaking and forced a smile as she turned to face the colonel. Bracing herself for that moment when their gazes would meet, she dragged her eyes from his square-toed shoes tied with neat bows, upward along the well-turned, black-stockinged calves and the knee-breeches of black velvet until her gaze reached the braid-trimmed doublet of the same cloth. Her inspection rose higher as the lips, now devoid of any distortion, widened into a roguish grin that revealed dazzling white teeth. Holding her breath, Synnovea lifted her gaze higher still and finally met the startlingly blue eyes that glowed back at her in amusement, then against her will, she felt her jaw slowly sagging. . . .

Natasha raised a hand graciously to introduce her guest. "Synnovea, this is Colonel Sir Tyrone Rycroft, of His Majesty's Imperial Hussars. . . . "

Tyrone swept an arm before him as he stepped into a chivalrous bow. "It gives me the greatest pleasure to formally make your acquaintance, Countess Zenkovna."

Synnovea closed her mouth abruptly and nervously plied the fan to hide her confusion. "Why, Colonel Rycroft, I would never have recognized you," she avowed breathlessly. He straightened to a dazzling height above her, or so it seemed to her, for she could not remember him being so tall. She continued in an unsteady, disconnected rush. "The last time we met, you were soaking wet. . . . Well, perhaps I really didn't look at

you that closely. You were somewhat bruised before . . .
But I'm happy to see that you've fully recovered."

The twinkle in his eyes seemed to slowly evolve into a
rakish gleam. "The last time we met, Countess, I fear we
were both rather damp from the rain, though perhaps not
quite as wet as I've been pleasured to see you."

"Oh!" Though the word was barely audible, Synnovea
plied the fan with disconcerted haste in an attempt to
hide her distress and cool her burning cheeks, completely disregarding the fact that there was actually a
chill in the air. She chanced a sidelong glance to see
if Natasha might have read anything in his comment,
but even when reassured that nothing untoward had
been noted by the woman, she still could not slow
the fluttering of her heart. "Well, no matter," she hurried on in disarray, filling the empty space of their
exchange with an idle comment. "That seems so long
ago now!"

"Does it?" Tyrone's voice was warmly hushed while
his eyes plumbed the depth of hers. "I was sure it was
only yesterday, but then, I relive the experience daily . . .
nightly . . . every hour of my waking."

Synnovea would have fled in whatever direction
allowed an easy escape, but she was abruptly reminded
of her objective when she looked in frantic appeal to
Natasha and found the woman smiling in smug satisfaction. It required no mean mental feat to comprehend
the fact that the elder was absolutely delighted by the
colonel's ability to scatter her wits and dismantle her
defenses so adroitly.

Gathering her shattered poise by the grit of her teeth,
Synnovea tapped her fan lightly upon Tyrone's forearm,
as much to rebuke him for his impudent reminder of their
meeting in the bathhouse as to declare her doubt of his
claim. "Perhaps you should give your imagination a rest,
Colonel. It seems to be caught in a definite rut."

Tyrone's lips twitched with humor as his eyes lightly
caressed her, conveying the significance of his words. "I

assure you, Countess, my imagination ranges far afield, but usually within the confines of the same subject."

Synnovea struggled to keep her mouth from falling open again and to subdue the burning blush that rushed into her cheeks. She could well imagine the quintessence of his dreams if he allowed his mind to dwell on the event in the bathhouse! No doubt she had been mauled and ravished a score or more times in his fantasies!

Whipping up her flagging determination, Synnovea won a battle with her composure and deliberately stroked the fan back and forth along his arm. Had she given vent to her true feelings, she would have used the delicate apparatus in such a vengeful way she would have immediately wiped the smirk from his smiling lips. "You've come to my rescue so many times now, Colonel, I fear I've lost count. I can only hope you're as kind to me in your musings. I would not want to admonish you for being vulgar."

Tyrone chuckled softly at her reproof, allowing that she had just cause to blush, for his imaginings were most sensual and not meant for sharing with a young innocent. "I sometimes find myself a victim of my dreams, Countess, but may I assuage your worries with a pledge of my devotion?"

"A pledge will not suffice," Synnovea responded, slyly taunting him with a bewitchingly winsome pout. She hardly felt vindicated by his feeble excuse and was tempted to extract some further revenge. "I'll need proof of your claim, Colonel, and since I've not seen you for a fortnight or two, you can probably understand how I might be persuaded to think you're only toying with my affections."

Natasha restrained the urge to roll her eyes in disbelief as she witnessed the sassy flirtation. She was now reasonably confident that the colonel could take care of himself, but when the cannons of Synnovea's warfare were fully loaded to the hilt and primed to blow the man's heart right out of his chest, she found it difficult to remain silently detached. Doubting her ability to resist further reaction or remarks, she graciously begged leave of them, hoping against hope that this scheme of Synnovea's would not result in another deadly duel.

"You will watch after the Countess Synnovea, won't you, Colonel?" she cajoled. "I promised the Princess Anna I would keep her well guarded." She chuckled and gave a little shrug as she explained, "I just never committed myself to doing so entirely alone."

The colonel's lopsided grin made an appearance, nearly bedazzling the elder. " 'Twill be my greatest enjoyment to devote myself to the task, Countess Andreyevna."

"Call me Natasha," the woman bade. "All my friends do."

"I would be honored, Natasha, if you will reciprocate with a similar favor. My name is Tyrone."

The woman patted his arm almost in sympathy. "Take care of yourself, Tyrone."

The colonel showed a leg in a courtly bow. "I assure you, Natasha, that I've always tried to do my best in that area."

"Please continue," she encouraged, tossing a meaningful glance toward Synnovea before leaving the couple and joining the pair of elderly women who were giggling as they eagerly sampled the wine.

Except for the roomful of people standing all around them and yet seeming to exist far beyond their private circle, Tyrone felt as if he had been granted a gift he had long coveted. Having been restricted from seeking out Synnovea's company, he did not let the moment go to waste, but filled his starving gaze with the very essence of her beauty. He met her stare as he softly breathed, " 'Tis true enough that you've held my thoughts and dreams entangled, Synnovea. Any man would be hard-pressed to forget what I have seen."

Synnovea groaned inwardly at his audacious reminder. "I'm not accustomed to flaunting myself in front of men, Colonel, and I would take it much amiss if you were to speak to anyone about the incident in the bathhouse or anything else which would cause me shame."

"No need to fear, Synnovea," Tyrone assured her with a grin. "I would not share our secrets with anyone."

Synnovea's qualms were greatly eased by his pledge, and she was able to relax as she sipped her wine. "I fear I've been much reproached by worry, Colonel," she admitted. "My mother was English, you see, and she instilled within me an aversion to bathing in public. You were my first encounter to the converse."

His eyes kindled brighter. "I'm glad no other has seen the treasures I've beheld."

Synnovea hardly heard his words, for she found herself preoccupied with his unyielding gaze. In all of her trips abroad and those taken within the borders of Russia, she could not remember a time when she had ever beheld bluer or even more beautiful eyes. They were definitely not the gray she had first supposed they were when she had seen them shadowed in the forest and then later in the bathhouse, for they were a bright azure hue ringed by a deeper sapphire. His warmly bronzed face made them seem all the more vivid, but the same sun that had darkened his skin had also lightened his hair. Pale strands now swept almost entirely across the top of his head, blending into the darker tawny brown that was more in evidence at his temples and the closely clipped nape. It was not in vogue for a man to wear his hair so short, but Synnovea could understand the merit of the fashion when she took into consideration the constant wearing of a helmet. Whatever his reasons, she was impressed with the result, for it was uniquely his style and worthy of admiration. Indeed, in all aspects she had to admit that Ali was right. Tyrone Rycroft was about as handsome a man as she had ever seen! It seemed rather doubtful now that the events of the evening would prove as difficult to bear as she had first supposed.

Synnovea teased him with a beguiling smile and a coy glance. "I was certain the Princess Anna had been successful in frightening you off, Colonel."

Tyrone laughed softly. "She only made me more adamant in my quest to impress His Majesty."

Synnovea bent forward slightly to set her half-filled goblet on a nearby table. A candelabra, sitting atop its gleaming wood surface, bloomed with a dozen lighted tapers that cast their warm glow upon her soft skin. A tingling excitement swept Synnovea as she utilized the illumination to her advantage and deliberately positioned her battery of arms for a foray against the colonel's manly appetite. "Pray tell me, sir, how have you faired in that endeavor?"

"I'm . . . not exactly sure," Tyrone answered haltingly as his eyes dipped to where the tiny flickering flames illumined the shadows beneath the scalloped lace. "His Majesty has not yet granted my request."

"And what request was that, Colonel?" Her breasts warmed pleasurably as she became aware of his gaze penetrating the fragile fabric. She lingered overlong at the task, rubbing a slender finger around the rim of the glass as she tasted the full draught of his perusal. Though she had been ogled and visually admired before, this was like some potent, heady nectar she had never sipped.

"The very same I declared to you when the Princess Anna turned me away from her door . . . to pay court to you." Tyrone leaned forward to claim the goblet as his own and to replenish his memory with a more rewarding view of her creamy pale breasts. Lifting the glass to his lips, he sampled a sip as his warmly glowing eyes delved into hers. "In truth, my lady, you've become my heart's desire."

Synnovea reached out a hand to smooth the lace on his cuff, diligently avoiding his gaze as it caressed her. "Do I dare ask how many other maids you've sworn the same to, Colonel?"

"Ask on," Tyrone whispered, advancing a stealthy step closer, "and I will answer none."

"How is it that you've escaped the banns of marriage so long in life then? I would guess you to be . . . "

"A score, ten, and four, my lady."

"Old enough to be properly wed then . . . if you've paid as much heed to other maids as you've done to me." Synnovea was aware of his eyes flitting downward to her décolletage, but she made no attempt to deny access to his gaze, though her skin burned beneath the heat of those flaming blue brands. It was somewhat surprising to realize that her breathing was affected by his close inspection, for it was difficult to inhale a steady draft when she felt so completely devoured.

"Are there other maids as worthy of a man's attention as you are?" Tyrone queried. "I've not noticed them if they exist."

"Are you so intent upon courting me?" she murmured, finally lifting her gaze to his.

"Most intent," he whispered without hesitation, moving forward until only the boundaries of her skirts held him at bay. The smoldering blue embers touched her lips, and unwittingly Synnovea yielded their softness to the lanquid caress, parting them as she dragged in a trembling breath. She did not know what sorcerer's enchantment he performed upon her mind that she could almost feel the stirring excitement of his mouth playing upon hers while his eyes embraced her lips. She stared as if enraptured as he lifted the goblet and lightly tasted the edge where she had sipped.

"Sweet," he sighed just above its rim. "Just as I imagined you would taste."

Synnovea mentally shook herself free from the fascination of his unswerving gaze and, drawing in a long breath to steady herself, flicked a glance about the room as she tried to calm her quickening pulse with the reality of the world beyond their private realm. All around them, the guests were involved in their own conversations and gave them no notice. Absent were the gossip mongers, hungry for any little tidbit they happened upon. Instead, each guest seemed imbued with a zeal and passion for life, whether they were in age only a score or four times those years. It was what made Natasha's friends so entertaining and alive with spirit and wit. They had no need to seek succor from the accomplishments of others, for they had made the most of their own lives and fortunes.

Catching her breath in surprise, Synnovea stumbled back a step, feeling the light brush of Tyrone's arm against her breast as he reached across her to return the goblet to the table. The contact sent a sudden surge of excitement crashing against the bulwark of her composure to snatch her senses aloft and fling them adrift into a swirling sea of fermenting pleasures. Heretofore it seemed she had only skirted along the outer fringes of a sensual awareness, and it was rather startling to discover how quickly her woman's body could respond to the touch of a man.

Even as her breath remained snared in her throat, Synnovea's widened eyes chased up to meet Tyrone's closely attentive regard. Her face flushed with color as a tawny brow rose in challenging amusement, as if he dared her to accuse him of a crime when they both knew she had tantalized him unmercifully with her womanly softness. She found herself abruptly confronted by the fact that this was no untried youth whom she could blithely lead along with engaging words and flirtatious smiles. On the contrary, it was now clearly evident to her that Tyrone Rycroft knew the game far better than she. The realization struck that she would not be leading him, but rather the converse. He would be leading her to a fate she fervently wished to avoid.

Of a sudden her strategy seemed greatly flawed in contrast to his boldness and ardor, for he was progressing with greater dispatch than she had ever considered possible, posing an insurmountable hindrance to her aspirations. The alacrity with which he moved would see her tossed upon her back and divested of her virginity before she ever had a chance to reach his quarters.

"I must beg to be excused a moment," she breathed unsteadily, knowing she had to have some time alone to bolster her courage.

"May I be of some assistance, my lady?" Tyrone asked in exaggerated politeness. She seemed so distraught by his touch, he wondered if he might have actually mistaken her feigned detachment while his eyes had lingered on the curves enticingly revealed beneath the lace. "You seem greatly disturbed."

Synnovea gulped back a retort, recognizing the esprit in his wayward smile. She had to keep her wits in good order and not accost him for his forward pranks or all would be lost. Lifting a hand to halt his advance, she shook her head and tried to step past him. "I must go."

"Perhaps a glass of wine will help soothe you," Tyrone suggested, deftly catching her fingers within his and bestowing a soft kiss upon them. He was genuinely reluctant to see her leave, for he was not at all sure she would come back. After all, she had fled like a frightened rabbit once before when he had tried to press her for an answer to his question of courtship.

"I must go!" Synnovea gasped again, beginning to panic as she felt her fingers trembling against his lips. Disentangling her hand from his, she pressed her palm flatly against his broad chest, as if wary of being further detained. "Please move aside, Colonel."

"Will you come back?" The tawny brow jutted upward again as he queried, "Or should I forget we've ever met?"

Though quietly spoken, the inquiry pierced through her with the keenness of a sharply pointed spike. It was the tone of vulnerable disappointment that stabbed at her heart and made her pause and stare up at him in amazement. As she searched those blue orbs which observed her closely in return, she realized of a sudden that this was no casual game for Colonel Rycroft; he was serious about courting her and having her for his own.

Synnovea's panic ebbed, and she was able to quell her trepidations as she recognized his concern. How could a man force a woman to yield to his ardent bent when he sincerely cared for her feelings? A tentative smile was wrenched from her as she traced a slender finger along the cording that trimmed the front of his doublet. "I'll be back," she promised in a hushed voice. "Will you wait for me?"

"As long as it takes," Tyrone vowed, taking her slender fingers within his again and bringing them again to his lips to lightly brush a kiss upon them.

This time Synnovea responded with a warmer smile as she accepted the gentle touch of his lips as a peace offering. Though she had reluctantly endured nearly a dozen such kisses from Vladimir on the night of their betrothal, she realized by the excitement that now raced recklessly through her senses that even having her hand kissed by Tyrone Rycroft was an altogether totally different experience from anything she had heretofore encountered.

Leaving him to stare after her, Synnovea hurried across the great hall and made her way upstairs to her chambers. Ali had gone to visit Elisaveta some time earlier, which now allowed Synnovea the solitude she desperately needed to sort out all the strange new emotions and sensations she had so recently become aware of. She paced like a caged cat through the spacious suite of rooms, finding no source of clarity with which to deal with her confusion. What became evident to her, however, was the stark contrast between her jaded reaction to Vladimir's ardent wooing and the stimulation she had previously and more currently experienced with the colonel. Even tonight, before he had even touched her, she had been all aflutter at the idea of being with him, as if by his mere presence he could set her senses to reeling like those of some silly, hopelessly giddy maid. Apparently there existed a great gulf between her feelings for him and the apathy she felt toward her betrothed.

Pushing open a window, Synnovea leaned back against the frame and gazed up at the starlit sky as her thoughts flitted over the moments she had just spent with the Englishman. She wanted to feel the bracing coolness of the night air against her skin and to inhale long draughts to chase away those strange, unfamiliar yearnings which had been evoked by his touch. In retrospect, the softly grazing caress of his arm against her breast was even more arousing when she contemplated the forwardness of the man to fondle her, albeit surreptitiously, but nevertheless in public.

The moon came out from behind a cloud, and Synnovea cast her gaze downward as a movement across the thoroughfare caught her attention. Shading her eyes against the glow of the candlelight in her room, she peered intently through the lantern-lit darkness until she was finally able to distinguish the shadowed figures of two men standing side by side. It was a moment more before she recognized the shorter one as Prince Aleksei. His companion was obviously one of the guards he had hired to watch her, but she found that one's appearance greatly troubling to her. Though the man's head was covered with a *karakul* similar to those preferred by Mongolians in bygone years, his powerful frame was strangely familiar to her.

Commanding her full attention, Aleksei swaggered forward and settled his hands on his slender hips as he stared up at her. His soft chuckle broke the silence of the night, and as she watched, he laid his head back upon his shoulders and roared his mirth to the night sky. Synnovea stiffened as the sound mocked her and grated on her good temper. She knew without a doubt that he was laughing at her, scorning whatever hopes she had of escaping him, but his derision only served to solidify her resolve to lead Tyrone Rycroft into her trap.

Chapter 14

Sᴛɴɴᴏᴠᴇᴀ REGAINED HER FORTITUDE WITH AN INTENSITY
that would have shocked Aleksei had he known he'd
been instrumental in perfecting it. Her pride had been
stung, and she felt a craving desire to see his mockery
set awry. Like a full-blown temptress, she addressed
her attention to her appearance, preparing it for the
broadside she was now determined to launch. Resolved
to show no clemency lest she find herself wedded and
bedded forthwith, she readjusted her laces, cinching her
slender waist more tightly while loosening the gown ever
so slightly above her bosom, which not only allowed for
better breathing, but better viewing as well. She was
committed to setting Tyrone back on his heels with a
more impassioned courtship, and if Natasha's warnings
about the hazards of pushing a man beyond his limits
were correct, then she would make the colonel fairly
quake with frustration until he would be compelled to
fly with her to his apartments.

In completing her revamping, Synnovea fluffed the
scalloped lace outward so the rounded curves of her
bosom could be more readily appreciated, and then
slackened the catches of her necklace until the largest
pearl pendant dangled enticingly into the silken crevice.
Lastly, she dabbed violet water upon her throat and
earlobes and softened a few wispy curls about her face,
all for the benefit of the man she meant to entrap.

Synnovea examined both fore and aft in the tall look-ing glass provided within her dressing chamber and pronounced herself fit and trim. Surely no seaworthy galleon had ever been outfitted for battle with quite the same equipment and weapons as she possessed within her cache, but this fine vessel of womanly softness was rigged for the fiercest contest yet, the allurement of no pompous youth, but a man of considerable knowledge and experience.

Like a fresh breath of spring air, Synnovea descended the flight of stairs to the hallway adjoining the great room and paused near the entrance to search out her quarry. She found the colonel standing with several men a short distance away, and by the swiftness with which his eyes reached her above their heads she could almost believe he had been waiting impatiently for her return. His perusal was slow and meticulous as it swept her, measuring every detail of her beauty as one admires and assesses a treasured art piece. Synnovea had no difficulty in supposing that he saw and understood things about her that no one else did and in a way few others ever would. When his eyes touched her hair, she knew he had seen the glory of it tumbling down her naked back. When his gaze lingered on her breast, it was as if he had, for his enjoyment, memorized every detail of that moment when those pale orbs had glistened wetly beneath the warm glow of the lanterns. Even when the blue eyes swept the length of her skirts, it seemed as if he scanned their fullness for some hint of the sleek thigh and calf he had once viewed.

Synnovea trembled at the sensations he aroused, feeling as if he had just caressed her from head to foot. The heat crept into her cheeks as she snatched her mind free from the slavery of the moment's thoughts, yet the impressions still remained, blend-ing with the memories of their first encounter, when he had lifted her from the murky depths of the dark waters and she had clung to him in desperation, hardly aware of what effect her naked body had on him.

Having become only slightly more acquainted with him, she was made even more cognizant of his manliness now than she had been then. Her breasts almost ached with the nearly tangible remembrance of that moment when she had been caught tightly against his hardened chest. She could even visualize in vivid detail the fascinating play of muscles across his shoulders, the rippling sinews along his narrow ribs, and the taut, flat belly, so briefly glimpsed and yet well defined in her mind, with its tracing of hair that mentally led her eye downward to the pure manly heat of him. Now when she stood pliant beneath his smoldering gaze, all her senses combined to remind her of what she had already experienced, yet she could not totally catch the import of what lay beyond. Her virgin mind, mired in the depth of her innocence, knew nothing beyond the vale wherein she had hitherto roamed and the careful but vague tutoring her mother had imparted on the duties of a wife. It was the ragged slope which rose like a barrier beyond her limited knowledge that baffled her and yet beckoned with promises far more provocative and lurid than anything her mother had ever painted.

Synnovea slowly inhaled a deep breath and then with a long shuddering sigh, released it. Seizing her composure with a stubborn will, she dragged its limp and sagging form up the full length of her spine in an effort to bolster her wit and cool her fevered imagination and the cravings that had evolved perplexingly into a pulsating excitement. She could not allow herself to get caught up in appeasing her curiosity or becoming enamored with carrying out her seduction. It would be difficult enough to maintain her poise when her pulses raced and her body warmed to the stirring memory of that moment when she had found herself clasped naked in his arms.

Slowly Synnovea released another trembling breath and became convinced that she had calmed herself enough to meet Tyrone's smilingly direct gaze without quaking. She was at ease and confident as he came toward her with measured gait. Lifting her head, she met his unwavering stare and, despite her preparations, felt the heat of a blush suffuse her as his glowing eyes burrowed down into hers. He stepped close beside her, and her breath faltered in her throat as his hand stroked along her back, evoking strangely pleasurable shivers up her spine, and then settled on her waist where none could see.

"You're even more beautiful now than when you left a century ago," Tyrone whispered softly as he bent to sample the fragrance of her. "Or is it that I've forgotten the details in so long a time?"

The green eyes chased upward to meet his as Synnovea realized just how perceptive the man really was. She was aware of those smiling blue spheres delving into hers as if he were intent upon searching out and reading every secret of her mind, but she was sure he had no need to read her thoughts. It seemed not even the smallest feature of her changed appearance had escaped his awareness.

In truth, Synnovea had no way of discerning just how thoroughly she had managed to confuse Tyrone, nor could she have clearly perceived how heartened he was by her heightened sensuality, when he had been expecting her to return wrapped up in a shawl like some aging spinster, fiercely adamant about guarding her virtue.

"I've ventured far and wide as a soldier," he continued in a husky tone. The keenness of his insight was made even more apparent to her when his gaze slid downward into the loosened bodice. "But no maid has ever held my eye and mind so firmly entrapped by her beauty as you do, Synnovea. 'Tis hard for me not to touch you as I want to do."

"You flatter me with your exaggeration, Colonel." She was acutely aware of his fingers tracing along the laces of her gown and was just as certain that had they been alone, he would have tested the security of the knot

which held the silken strings in place. "I've never met
a man more astute in the mores of a woman that he can so
easily detect when she has repaired her appearance." She
lowered her lashes, then coquettishly flicked a sidelong
glance upward from beneath their silken length as she
asked demurely, "Am I to be faulted for wanting to look
my best for you?"

"Can any man fault perfection?" Tyrone countered
glibly. His smile was hypnotic, commanding her stare.
"You've gained my complete and undivided attention,
Synnovea. I only wish we were alone so I could prove
how genuinely I covet your companionship."

Sensing the effectiveness of her ploy, yet cautious of
claiming the prize too quickly, Synnovea smiled engag-
ingly as she tried to slow her own quickening pulse.
There was something completely sensual about the way
he made her feel, and it was by no means an unpleasant
experience. "Should I dare imagine you wish to take me
to your quarters, Colonel?"

" 'Tis my most fervent desire, Synnovea. Indeed, the
merest thought of being alone with you takes my breath
away. I'm prone to remember the bliss of our first
encounter in the bathhouse and do fervently wish such
a meeting might be repeated."

"I think I should be cautious of such an event," she murmured coyly. "You allowed me to escape unscathed then,
but would you permit it a second time?"

" 'Tis extremely doubtful that I'd be able to display
such restraint again," Tyrone admitted and grinned with
a charm that was becoming familiar to her. "Still, if such
an occasion were gifted to me again, I would hope you'd
feel inclined to call me by name. After all, we've been
through enough together that it would seem appropriate. Is Tyrone so difficult for you to say? Or Tyre,
if you would have it so. 'Tis what my grandmother
calls me."

Synnovea tested the names as if sampling a luscious
fruit. "Tyrone. Tyre. Tyrone." She smiled as she made

her decision. "Until I know you better, I think Tyrone will have to suffice."

"Your lips make the name sound sweeter than honeyed mead," Tyrone assured her while his eyes tarried almost hungrily on her mouth. "But then, I would enjoy tasting the sweet nectar of your lips far more. No doubt teaching you to kiss would be a scrumptious feast."

Synnovea's surprise displayed itself in a disconcerted blush. Though it was not considered proper for a young maid to be well versed in the art of kissing, she was reluctant to have him think her an ignorant chit. "What makes you think I'm in need of instruction?"

Tyrone's lips curved with amusement. "I thought you an innocent from the very first, certainly one bereft of a well-seasoned knowledge." He lifted her fingers to his lips as he warmly avouched, "Indeed, my sweet, I'd be jealous if you were otherwise."

Placated by his endearment and the persuasively gentle kiss he bestowed on the tips of her fingers, Synnovea met his smiling regard. "Should I be jealous of all the women who have taught you?"

Tyrone chuckled at her impudent rejoinder. "You needn't be, my lady. Since our first meeting, I've been your absolute slave."

Synnovea arched a winged brow to convey her doubt and challenged him in light repartee. "I wonder whose slave you truly are, Tyrone. If mine as you claim, then I've not seen much of you of late."

Tyrone pressed a hand to his chest as he struck a pose of honest regret. "A complaint you must surely take up with the tsar since it has been his pleasure I've been serving, but even while gratifying his desires, you've been on my mind."

"A viable excuse, I suppose . . . Still, I've heard rumors and I've no real assurance of your claims."

Sensing her desire to discuss the women in his past, Tyrone gave her no opportunity to make further inquiries. "Though 'tis my wont to keep your beauty well hidden from every eye but mine, Synnovea, I must share your delightful acquaintance with a friend."

As the colonel raised his hand to silently beckon across the room, Synnovea allowed her gaze to range slowly over the faces of the guests in search of the one he motioned to. A few of the candles had been snuffed to lend emphasis to an old and plainly garbed blind man who sang a ballad of a princely warrior and a beautiful maid. In general, the guests appeared enthralled by the poetic lilt of the story, for they gave little heed to others as they sat and listened with close attention to the storyteller.

The one who responded to the summons was a Russian who stood with a young maiden and her father near the far wall. After noticing the colonel's gesture, the handsome gentleman excused himself from the pair and wended his way through the guests as Tyrone took Synnovea's arm and drew her farther away from the door. Taking care not to let his voice intrude upon the song, he introduced the one who halted before them.

"May I present my second-in-command, Captain Grigori Tverskoy . . . The Countess Synnovea Zenkovna."

Giving her a decorous bow, Grigori replied graciously in English. " 'Tis indeed an honor to finally make your acquaintance, Countess." As he straightened, the captain gave her a jaunty grin. "I'm sure you don't remember me since you were rather occupied with Ladislaus at the time, but I was fortunate enough to be among those who came to your assistance after your coach was attacked by the band of outlaws. Of course, the tribute belongs solely to Colonel Rycroft, who ordered our detachment to turn about and search out the cause for the gunshots we heard."

Synnovea laughed lightheartedly. "I'm sure I need not tell you how grateful I am for your participation, Captain, and to your commander for his attention to duty."

"I sincerely believe, Countess, that Colonel Rycroft has derived great delight in having been the one to accomplish your rescue. Although he performed nearly the same service for several *boyarinas* who had been accosted by ruffians at a coach station several days prior to the attack on your carriage, it seemed his most fervent desire to deny such a possibility when they invited him to meet their father upon our expected return to Moscow."

Tyrone lifted a challenging brow as he grinned back at the man and, glancing askance at Synnovea, applied some good-natured needling in reverse. "There was one of them who, above all of her sisters, found it particularly hard to get through a doorway. Nevertheless, she was bent on winning Grigori for her spouse, and to save himself, he hid in the smokehouse until she gave up her search and finally departed with her kin." Tyrone raised his head and, noticing that the young maiden who stood at Prince Zherkof's side was timidly eyeing the captain, he inclined his head ever so slightly in her direction. "I do perceive there's yet another wistful one awaiting your attention, my friend. You do seem to have a flair for enchanting sweet young damsels."

Grigori's smile broadened as his eyes found the one who longingly stared at him. He faced his commander again and, with a crisp click of his heels, begged leave of them. "Since we are at liberty tomorrow, Colonel, I'll not be going back with you in the hired livery. I've accepted Prince Zherkof's invitation to spend the evening at his home and reminisce about the village where we both grew up."

With a wry grin Tyrone watched the captain hasten back to the girl and her father. "I do believe the princess has endeared herself to Grigori far better than most," he observed. "Otherwise, he would be running to the stable to hide."

"Perhaps I should take heart that you're here with me and not hiding out somewhere," Synnovea remarked, smiling at him as she arched a winged brow.

Tyrone chuckled at the foolish notion that he should flee from her presence. "Were I you, my lady, I would consider myself the one being pursued. If it must be made any clearer to you, I'm quite ravenous for your companionship."

Synnovea laughed softly in response to his declaration and was aware of his lean fingers entwining hers. He led her across the great room to where they could view the storyteller better and chose a place to stand near an arched alcove that led to the garden. The doors were opened, allowing the fragrance of its blossoms to sweep inward on a gentle breeze, and as the two of them were totally involved and completely sensitive to the presence of the other and wanting yet daring not to touch, Synnovea realized it was not the chill in the air that made her shiver. The stimulation of Tyrone's nearness and the clean, illusive scent that wafted from him made her aware of her own vulnerability. She could not ignore his close attention yet strangely felt no inclination to shy away from his eyes when they brazenly ventured where his hands could not. Though he studied every detail of her, he made no attempt to hide his fascination, prompting her to openly confront him with a smiling glance.

"Are you so starved for companionship, Colonel, that you must devour me for your sup?"

"Were we alone, Synnovea," Tyrone murmured huskily, "I would show you just how hungry I am for you. Until then, I must feast upon your comeliness the only way I can."

The song advanced, and while the soft voice weaved its wondrous magic, Synnovea continued to be breathlessly aware of the lingering regard of her companion and her own heightened excitement. Her hope had been to weave her seductive web so tightly around Tyrone Rycroft that he would be completely vulnerable to her wiles, yet she was now of a mind to think such an achievement would not necessarily be of her own making, but of his. Still, fearing failure and its consequence, she continued with her game, teasing him with a more intimate view of her bosom as she raised on her toes and leaned toward him to whisper near his ear.

"Have you seen the garden? 'Tis a rare sight even at night."

Stepping away, Synnovea smiled up at him in secret invitation and then slipped from his side like a gracefully floating wraith. Gliding through the alcove, she entered the enclosed garden and, moving far from the doorway, positioned herself beneath a tree where the bright moon, filtering through the wavering leaves, cast fluttering flashes of light on the ground around her and over her gown. She waited in the hushed still of the night, seeming as cool and serene as a high priestess of Roman hierarchy, but the tranquility she exhibited was well feigned, for she trembled with the uncertainty of what was to come and from emotions too nebulous to clearly comprehend. She now understood the importance of Natasha's warnings, for she really had no true concept of what lay beyond the door she had opened, though she was sure that before the evening was done her womanly wiles would be tested far beyond measure.

It was a few discreet moments later when Tyrone entered the garden. At first his step was cautious as his eyes flitted along the moonlit paths and probed the shadows, then he discovered what he sought half-hidden within the mottled light. In a moment he was standing before Synnovea, and for one split second, he searched her uplifted face and the translucent eyes that seemed to mirror his own yearnings, then his mouth descended, seizing hers in a wildly amorous kiss that went through her with the same effect as a well-aimed broadside. Their sighs melded into one as his mouth played eagerly upon hers, softly caressing, his tongue gently probing, testing her response until she lifted herself and slipped her arms about his neck. His kiss was indisputably more effective

than the volley of womanly enticements she had hoped
to launch against him. It was a sweetly thrilling heady
mead, more intoxicating than any brew she had ever
tasted.

They came apart with a breathless gasp, panting as
if they had raced with abandon across the steppes,
but Tyrone was hardly content with merely a sip. He
was famished for the full draft. His hands slid slowly
down her back, molding her soft form closely against
his hardened frame as his open mouth returned to
devour hers with a hungering greed, twisting, turning,
crushing, penetrating deeply into the warm sweetness
until Synnovea nearly swooned at the intensity of his
passion. There was now no need for her to pretend a
beguiled trance. Her world spun in a wildly whirling
dervish, and she lost what feeble grasp she had hitherto
managed to retain on reality. All thoughts of artfully
devised tactics were sundered beneath the onslaught of
his flaming kiss.

Turning her face aside to catch a trembling breath,
Synnovea sought to set aright the careening flight of
the earthbound sphere wherein she was caught. She
was dizzy from the intensity of his ardor, yet he was
the only stabling core in her reeling world to which
she could cling. A warm shiver went through her as
his parted lips traced to her ear and lightly nibbled a
delicate fold. His open mouth traveled downward along
the pale column of her throat, branding her skin with
feverish kisses and soft flicks of his tongue. Synnovea
closed her eyes, overwhelmed by the pleasure of his
wandering kisses and equally enraptured by this first
sampling of sensual delights. Completely yielding the
ivory column of her throat to his fancy, she tilted her
elegantly coiffured head back until it brushed the high,
stiff collar, leaving naught but the rich, weighty necklace
to impede the fiery descent of his lips. The temptation
was too great for Tyrone. He paused but a mere fraction
of a moment before he bridged the expanse and pressed

his lips upon the swelling ripeness above her gown.

Synnovea caught her breath at his daring advance. His boldness was most expressive of his manly passions, yet her trembling disquiet was not entirely due to the abashed modesty of an innocent maid. Instead, it was sparked by the flaring flash of ecstasy that catapulted through her senses. Indeed! Allowing his lips freedom to roam her breasts was far more exhilarating than teasing him with a brief glimpse or two of her bosom and a deeply plunging crevice.

Steeling herself against some strong, urgent inner prompting to abscond with her virtue intact, Synnovea held fast to her resolve and persevered through the deliciously titillating moment, reasoning that it was, after all, only a soft brushing caress, hardly harmful to anything but her reserve. Still, she laid a cautious hand to his chest, availing herself of an opportunity for escape, should the need arise.

Tyrone's tactics had been forged through long years of experience as a soldier and an adequate number as a lover and a husband. He had traversed the road of conquest long enough to know by heart the rules of the game, whether it was in bed with a woman or on the field of battle with the enemy. When no evidence of resistance was clearly presented, he was wont to consider that his opponent was acceptable to the idea of surrender, and thus he was inclined to regard Synnovea's reticence as acquiescence. Yet he was one to move with caution until reasonably assured of his position, and lifting his head, he sought her lips again with a fervor she seemed unable to resist. As a soldier, he clearly understood the wisdom of applying the strategy of retreat to confound the opponent. His maneuver was a skillful diversion to mollify whatever fears the maid might be harboring and to surreptitiously arouse her senses until he could abet his cause and encourage her compliance, although one sampling of her soft, sweet flesh only made him impatient to reclaim the ground he had already plundered.

Tyrone realized he had seized a small victory when the hand resting on his chest slid upward behind his neck. He mentally smiled as the slender fingers slipped through the short hair at his nape, but he gauged himself carefully and allowed a moment to pass before his mouth moved on, leaving hers throbbing from the fiery zeal of his kisses. He savored again the fragrant dew of the throat and dared to venture farther over softer, more tantalizing ground.

Synnovea held her breath as his kisses progressed with feathery lightness across her breasts, but she was hardly prepared for the devastating salvo he was about to launch. Before she could pull away and coyly reprove him for his daring, his hand slipped inside her bodice. This time a gasp was snatched from her throat as her breast was cupped within his warm, eager palm and then bared to the cooling night air and to the molten heat of his open mouth.

"Nay, sir! You must not!" Her shocked gasp was a desperate whisper in the night as her daunted propriety rallied in full strength. " 'Tis not proper!" She sought to push herself free, but he held her secure with an arm, forbidding her escape.

"Sweet Synnovea, do you not ken how much I want you?" he breathed warmly against her flesh. "I am a man harshly beset by my desire to have you. Yield to me, sweet love."

In her whole entire life Synnovea had never experienced such wildly wanton sensations as when his warm tongue stroked slowly over her nipple, flicking sparks across the very tips of her senses. She felt consumed by the liquid fire that spread through her body. The rapturous delights aroused by the sultry heat of his mouth blunted her will to resist as she relished each blissful, strumming caress across the gutstrings of her senses.

Tyrone craved much more than only a teasing taste of such sweetness. Raising his head, he searched the limpid pools of green for any evidence of fear or hesitation and found none to dissuade him from his purpose.

Lifting her into his arms, he cast a glance about in search of some private place where he could lend her his most intense and ardent attention. Though he had been reluctant to take his ease of her without first securing some private haven for the patient nurturing of her pleasure, his passions were soaring well beyond the point of caution. It did not matter so much now that he could not hold her naked in his arms. A shadowed spot would serve his mounting desire to make her his own, and if it had to be done while they were both fully clothed, then it would not be the first time he had fought the voluminous skirts of some rich creation to appease the fierce ardor of love.

Synnovea was overwhelmed by her own willingness to comply, but some shred of sanity remained in the nether regions of her brain, allowing her to recognize the folly of being taken in a moment of recklessly spent passion. She struggled to keep the scattered fragments of her wits together as she looped her arms about his neck and nestled her face close to the side of his. "Please not here, Tyrone, I beg you. If you would have it so, I'll go with you to your quarters."

Afraid to break the impassioned trance and trust her when her ardor cooled, Tyrone stared down at her through the shadows, painfully aware of the hungering ache in his loins that had manifested itself into a throbbing density. He needed to assuage his cravings within the womanly heat of her ere the tormenting agony rent him asunder. When he considered the delay and the chances of her abandoning him again, he knew he could not endure another lengthy wait.

"I need you now, Synnovea. 'Twill be hard for me to wait." His softly rasped appeal could hardly convey the torment that roiled within him. His passions assailed him as he lowered his mouth to taste again the sweet ambrosia of her skin, nearly splintering her reserve.

Synnovea's senses reeled, and for a brief moment, she forgot everything but the ecstasy of being devoured by the hot waves of bliss that pulsated through her. It was only by dint of will that she cleared her mind and fortified her determination.

"Would you instruct a virgin in so open a place?" she breathed close to his ear. "Where we could be discovered by anyone who might happen upon us?"

Reluctant though he was to delay the moment, Tyrone straightened and leaned his head back upon his shoulders as he struggled with his hard-pressing desires. She was right, of course. This garden was no treasured place where lovers could leisurely feast on their passion. She deserved much more, he thought, if only because he desired her more than any woman he had ever known, including Angelina. He had displayed care and patience with his virgin bride a thrice or so years ago. The very least he could do with this maid was to pamper her with the same consideration.

"Waiting will test me sorely, Synnovea, but if that is your desire, then I'll gratify your wish." He kissed her again passionately and let her feet slide to the ground between his, then watched in pained forbearance as she steadied herself and straightened her clothing. "Will you come with me now?" he urged. "The coach I've hired is waiting in front."

"A moment more I would beg of you," Synnovea whispered, regaining her breath. She was still a-tremble and could in no wise ignore the burning craving he had aroused within her woman's body. "If you'll wait here for me, I'll return to you as soon as I've changed my gown and fetched a cloak."

"Surely there's no need for that," Tyrone reasoned, anxious to accomplish the union and ease his lusts. "I'll keep you warm, and your gown will be of little consequence once we reach my quarters."

Synnovea blushed at his insinuation. The idea of being stripped of her clothes filled her mind with wanton visions of the two of them coming together totally devoid of clothing. The threat of being nakedly confronted by his maleness again almost made her demur the occasion, but she could not thrust aside her only chance to be free of Prince Vladimir and thwart Aleksei's plans. Her whisper wavered in strength as she gave an excuse. "I would prefer to prepare myself for you."

Tyrone relented to her request, understanding her womanly petition. It was her right to claim some time of preparation and come to him when she was ready to receive him. "Another kiss before you go." He slipped his arms about her and clasped her close to him. "It must last me."

Synnovea met his parting lips with her own and, gleaning from her meager knowledge, slid her tongue provocatively into his mouth. Somewhat abashed by her own forwardness, she sought to leave quickly, but the gentle enticement was enough to awaken a desire within Tyrone to prolong the kiss. A long moment passed before he released her, and this time Synnovea was the one reluctant to leave his embrace.

"Another," she pleaded. Wrapping her arms about his neck as he lifted her hard against him, she could feel the thunderous pounding of his heart.

"We must go ere I take you here and now," Tyrone whispered raggedly as his hand wandered down to clasp her buttock and press her to him. " 'Tis painful to wait so long."

Though the layers of her skirts prevented any intimate contact, his plea made her aware of his urgency. Grateful for the shadows that hid her dismay, Synnovea set herself from him and peered up at him through the moonlight. The intense frown that creased his brow clearly betrayed his needs, if nothing else did. "I'll go now and change my gown and fetch my cloak. Will you wait for me here?"

"Aye, love, but hurry!"

Tyrone almost groaned aloud in frustration as he observed her flight. He paced to and fro, seeking to turn his thoughts elsewhere and thereby ease his plight, but he knew if she did not come back, it would be difficult for him to endure the long ride home alone. He had never forced himself upon a woman before, but the way Synnovea held his mind entrapped, he'd be strongly tempted to seek her out in her chambers upstairs.

Chapter 15

BREATHLESS AND SHAKEN, SYNNOVEA PAUSED JUST OUT-side the garden doors to take herself firmly in hand. It would have been a mild assessment of her overwhelmed sensibilities to say that she felt strangely akin to a dis-mantled frigate listing back into port. Her womanly weapons had been spiked and plundered, while the sails of her self-assurance, which only a short time ago had billowed wide with the winds of her own arrogant presumption, now hung slack, deflated by the full import of her naïveté.

Still trembling from the lustful intensity of Tyrone's advances, Synnovea did what she could to smooth her hair and repair her appearance, but she had no hint of how she might subdue the gnawing disturbance within her woman's body. She had never imagined how intense-ly she could be affected by the kisses of a man, for no suitor had ever stirred her to the degree Tyrone Rycroft had. Indeed, except for Vladimir, she had never tolerated more than a slight brush of a kiss against her lips, least of all the ardent exploration of her mouth and bosom. Even now she found it impossible to quench the hungering fires that burned within her, and when the moment rapidly approached wherein she would have to subject herself to the perusal of others, she was confronted by the need to present a calm exterior even though inwardly she still trembled from the ecstasy of his caresses.

In a few brief moments, she would have to trade gowns with Natasha, and to pass that one's critical and keenly perceptive inspection, she knew she would have to summon some semblance of her lost composure. Her greatest worry was having to undress in the presence of the woman, for she feared her breasts were still rosy after Tyrone's passionate kisses. There was no question in her mind that if Natasha gleaned some idea that his advances had progressed as far as they had, the game would be over before it even had a chance to begin.

Feebly Synnovea gathered the reins of her determination and fortified herself for the moments ahead. Even if Natasha became suspicious, Synnovea knew she would have to find some way to placate the woman's questions or face the threat of the elder reneging on her commitment to help.

Lifting her chin with a hard-won air of serenity, Synnovea entered the great room and cast a glance about in search of Natasha. She met the dark, radiant eyes across the length of the room and slowly inclined her head in a singular nod, then in stilted grace, she made her way across the dimly lit room to the hall. Her pace quickened as she ascended the stairs, and almost in a frantic rush, she burst into her chambers and gained the safety which was afforded her there. For a moment she leaned weakly against the door, panting as if she had just won a difficult race, and by slow degrees, her trembling eased to a more tolerable level. Collecting her nerve, she strode to the front windows and, opening the draperies, stood before them. Aleksei came forward out of the shadows to make his presence known to her. At his mocking salute, she withdrew and indulged herself in a languid smile of victory as she pulled the silken hangings carefully closed behind her again.

By the time Natasha joined her, Synnovea had managed to doff her gown and clothe herself within the rich, velvet folds of another creation, this one of a deep green hue which by its simple elegance complimented her beauty. Not being of the same convictions as Natasha, she had chosen the gown especially for the occasion, and this time the décolletage was purposefully tempting to insure that the coals of Tyrone's interests were kept alive until the two of them reached his place of residence. It was one thing to cope with his ardor, but quite another to satisfy his questions if he became suspicious of her motives for accompanying him.

Preserving a reasonable facade of decorum, Synnovea wrapped a shawl around her shoulders to hide from view any telltale blush that might have remained on her bosom. As jealously as she had guarded the secret of her first encounter with Tyrone, so she would likewise keep hidden everything that had transpired between the two of them this night. Not even Ali would be aware of the present events, for the idea of the maid's visit with Elisaveta had been conceived for the express purpose of sending her well out of sight and hearing.

Presenting her back to Natasha, Synnovea let the woman tighten the laces of her bodice and then turned to help the elder out of her *sarafan*. As she did so, she heard the soft tinkling of tiny bells that heralded the approach of her own coach.

"I hear Stenka coming back from the Taraslovs' now," she announced. "He's been given instructions to wait in front until I come down."

"Do you think he can really be fooled into thinking that I am you?" Natasha asked apprehensively. To say that she was nervous about this ruse was clearly an understatement, especially after hearing from the colonel's own lips that he had been involved in a deadly duel over a woman. He had not explained how the woman had died and that plainly worried her for Synnovea's sake. Still, she knew the girl had committed herself to seeing this travesty accomplished, and it might do more harm than good to frighten her now with such revelations.

"Try not to say anything to Stenka to make him suspect that you've come in my stead," Synnovea cautioned.

"The game might be hindered if he realizes his mistake, for he'll want to stop and question you before he leaves. With Aleksei close by to watch, that would be risky. If Stenka isn't able to get a good look at you, he'll just assume he's taking me out for a ride. I've already told him where he's to go, and though he's clearly confused by my desire to leave the festivities, he'll obey without question."

"I've allowed Prince Zherkof to think that you've taken ill and are temporarily indisposed, so he won't be surprised at the length of time I'm gone while he's under the assumption that I'm tending your needs. He's promised to serve as host in my absence, so as long as none of the other guests see us leave, we should be reasonably safe. Where did you leave Colonel Rycroft?"

"He's waiting for me in the garden. He hired a coach for this evening, so there's no need to use yours."

Natasha spoke through the deep blue gown as it was lowered carefully over her head. "Naturally he was terribly agreeable to all of this, taking you to his quarters and all the rest, I mean."

"Reasonably so." Synnovea refused to elaborate as she tightened the bodice for the woman.

Natasha studied her newly revised appearance in the tall looking glass. Sweeping a hand admiringly across the elaborate collar, she mused aloud. "From a distance Aleksei might not be able to tell us apart." She turned her head to consider her reflection from different angles, then frowned testily as she plucked at her hair. "But I fear this grayed thatch will give me away. Have you a veil to cover my head?"

"This one will do." Having already considered the matter, Synnovea lifted a white lace mantle which she had worn in Aleksei's presence and draped it loosely over the woman's head to cover the silver-streaked tresses.

Turning with a smile, Natasha submitted herself to Synnovea's inspection. "How do I look?"

"Beautiful, as always," Synnovea assured her with an eager nod. "Now stand in front of the window, as if you're looking for the coach, and let Aleksei see you. Once you're outside, don't let him get close enough to recognize you. As long as he thinks I'm the one climbing into the coach, he'll be curious enough about my destination to follow along with his men until Stenka stops the coach. By that time, I should be at Colonel Rycroft's quarters."

"Does Aleksei know where the colonel lives?"

"If he doesn't, he'll make a point of finding out ere long," Synnovea replied dryly.

Natasha heaved a pensive sigh and reached out to pat the younger's cheek. "The way Colonel Rycroft doted on you this evening, he'll not likely want to delay claiming his pleasure too long. You might have some difficulty holding him off until Aleksei arrives."

"If I cannot put him off, then I'll have no one else to blame but myself," Synnovea murmured, averting her face from Natasha's gaze. She was rather amazed by her own dwindling commitment to achieve that precise end and knew that somehow she would have to renew her waning determination to produce the result she had earlier aspired to attain.

"I must go." Natasha sighed and consoled herself as she mused on her lonely excursion through the city. Her mouth lifted in a puckish smile as she proposed a more attractive arrangement than Synnovea had planned for her. "Perhaps I could trade places with you and go with Colonel Rycroft, while you leave in my stead and tour the city alone."

Synnovea laughed at the impossible suggestion. "I doubt that such a change of plans would secure the same results."

Feigning a pout of disappointment, Natasha protested her lonely task. "But 'twill be so dreadfully boring riding through the city alone, and the colonel is *so* handsome."

No reprieve came, and with a dramatically heaved sigh of resignation Natasha straightened her demeanor and readjusted the mantle over her head to better hide her hair. She braced herself for carrying out the deception and, lifting her chin in an elegant manner, stepped before the window to look out, pretending a casual search for the coach as she held back the draperies. As she did so, Synnovea pressed close against the wall, keeping herself carefully óut of sight until the silken panels were again closed to the outside world. After brushing a kiss on her friend's cheek, Natasha bade farewell and left Synnovea waiting in the silence of the room until the sounds of the departing conveyance were heard. Several more moments were allowed to pass before the younger countess deemed it safe to peer through an opening in the draperies. Her heart leapt with a rush of triumphant jubilation as she spied Aleksei and his hirelings following the coach down the thoroughfare.

"No doubt he thinks to catch me unawares and unattended," Synnovea vented the conjecture smugly. " 'Twill serve his pride well to be made the fool."

Sweeping a black velvet cloak around her own shoulders and lifting the hood carefully over her head, Synnovea left the chambers and hurriedly made her descent by way of the private stairs near Natasha's rooms. In another moment she was in the garden flying into Tyrone's arms.

"I was beginning to wonder if you would return," he murmured as he snatched her hard against him.

Synnovea tilted her head back and, meeting his searching lips, savored his passionate kiss for a long moment until she could feel her limbs weaken apace with the hasty thudding of his heart. Breathless now with anticipation, they parted, and smiling down at her, Tyrone caught her hand and led her around the house to his waiting coach. He lifted her in and spoke briefly to the driver in Russian, having learned enough words to get him to and from his quarters, then he climbed in and took a seat beside her.

"You're progressing very well, Colonel," Synnovea commented with a soft laugh as he closed the door behind him. "It doesn't take so long to understand you now."

"Had I known I'd be coming here to this country, I would have started three years earlier learning the language." Tyrone tossed her a grin over his shoulder as he leaned forward and closed the shades over the windows, securing their privacy. The coach lurched into motion, and with a laugh he fell back into the seat, then leaned over her as his glowing eyes probed the darkness to delve into the shining luster of hers. "Just as long as you can fully understand me whatever language I may speak, fairest Synnovea. That's all that matters to me. Discovering you here has been worth it all."

"I was certain Natasha had told you I'd be at her house tonight."

"You've been well worth my coming to Russia," he explained, clarifying his statement. "As for tonight, I'm very glad you came back, Synnovea. I was just beginning to seriously consider searching you out and taking my pleasure of you wherever I could find you."

Reaching up a hand, Synnovea gently caressed his cheek and traced the lines of laughter near his mouth before brushing her fingers lightly across his lips. "You tease me, sir."

Tyrone gave no definite answer to her supposition as he whispered, "I had no idea how long a century could be until I found myself waiting for you in the garden."

The slender fingers swept down the bridge of his lean, aquiline nose, following its noble descent. "How goes the time now?"

"Much too swift, I fear."

Her thumb smoothed a tawny brow before the tips of her fingers moved admiringly down a lean cheek again. "What must we do to keep it still?"

"Stay with me forever," he answered.

Her hand paused in its flight as she stared into the blue eyes that watched her unrelentingly. "I only have a pair of hours to spend with you. I must go back tonight."

"Then each moment that flies past will be forever lost to me," Tyrone murmured, turning his face into her palm and pressing an ardent kiss into it. He lifted his head and caressed the beautiful visage with his lips in the same way she had traced her fingers over his face. "I must make haste to make you mine."

"I pray you nay." Synnovea sighed against his mouth as it played upon hers. "Rather, I would urge you to relish the time we spend together and make of it a lasting memory which we can both treasure. Is it not better to savor love slowly to glean every measure of pleasure from its offering?"

His lips brushed her brow and descended to feel the quickening pulse in her temple. "Your wisdom astounds me, Synnovea. If not by experience, where do you attribute its source?"

"My mother," she breathed, fingering the silken closures that fastened the front of his doublet.

"A wise woman. She must have loved your father dearly to give up her homeland and all that she had known to come here to live with him."

" 'Twas no great sacrifice, considering what they had together." A plaintive sigh slipped from her lips. "I wish I would have had them with me longer. The Princess Anna was a poor replacement, and Prince Aleksei a ravenous rake. To be sure, any woman is better off fleeing from him ere they're introduced. I lived in constant dread of him catching me unawares. Though I was hampered by his threats, I consider it a miracle that I have thus far escaped intact."

"His threats?" Tyrone queried, raising his head to peer down at her.

Beneath his searching gaze Synnovea could not hold back a blush. "Prince Aleksei made it obvious that he wanted me in his bed, and he threatened dire consequences if I resisted him."

"Though I can't blame him much for wanting you, I abhor his methods of persuasion."

"How well you express my sentiments, Colonel Sir."

His open mouth lowered to hover closely above hers. "I much prefer that you come to me willingly."

Synnovea's lashes trembled downward as she yielded to the fiery heat of his kiss, and it was a long moment later when Tyrone finally raised his head, leaving her sighing with blissful pleasure. In a shaky whisper she acknowledged, "Your kisses make me willing."

"Do you find them satisfying?"

"Nay, not satisfying," she complained, following him with reaching lips until she leaned toward him. "They only make me want more."

Chuckling softly, Tyrone swept her hood from off her head and gratified her questing lips with soft, lingering kisses as his lean fingers plucked at the ties of her cloak. When the silken cords fell free, he pushed the velvet from her shoulders, letting the garment fall unheeded to the seat behind her. Like hard flint when flashing sparks are struck from its surface, the sometimes blue-gray eyes glinted with desire as Tyrone slowly perused the tantalizing feast before him. Synnovea watched him in the meager light, wondering if she had erred by revealing so much. She held her breath in anticipation as he lifted a finger and traced it languidly across her shoulder, caressing the delicate collarbone, weaving a path ever downward until it reached the top of her gown. For a time he seemed content to follow the plunging neckline until Synnovea, shivering in expectant suspense of that moment when he would actually venture beneath, pressed toward him with lips eagerly parting as she sought his mouth again. It was the only way she knew to halt the exploration of her bosom, but it was much like fighting fire with fire. His kiss delved deeply, touching to the very marrow of her womanly being, flicking awake all of her senses as his open mouth slanted across hers and greedily plumbed the dewy sweetness.

Even as his lips played upon hers, Tyrone reached to her far hip and, slipping a hand beneath her buttock,

pulled her across his lap, turning as he did so until he
could lean back in the seat. Synnovea was hardly aware
of anything beyond his kiss, and it was not until she drew
back for a trembling breath that she realized her skirts
were no longer underneath her. Beneath her buttocks
she could feel the manly boldness of his loins and the
muscular hardness of his velvet-clad thighs. The shock
jolted through her with the reality of his unswerving
quest to see his end accomplished. Indeed, given a little
more time, he might have made use of the carriage ride
to appease his lustful bent.

Realizing her vulnerability, Synnovea sought to leave
his lap, but Tyrone gently detained her within an
encircling embrace. He was most anxious that she stay,
for it was much more gratifying to his senses when she
was not fettered by countless layers of skirts and petticoats. He was certain that nothing could have aroused
him more than feeling the weight of her soft, naked thighs
on his except having his own bare beneath hers.

"Don't leave me, Synnovea," he whispered cajolingly
against her ear. "I like to feel you close against me."

Seeking to distract her, Tyrone kissed her again, this
time without reserve, holding nothing back as he fully
explored the mettle of her resistance. His open mouth
crushed hers in frenzied greed, ravishing the intoxicating
sweetness and demanding that she answer him in kind
until by slow degrees Synnovea dismissed her objections
as immaterial and gave him what he sought, tentatively
at first as she allowed her tongue to be drawn into his
mouth and then with passion as she met his daring
thrusts with equal fervor.

When he lifted his head, the blue eyes glowed smilingly
into hers while his hand moved across her bosom, roaming the hills and vales until it came to gently rest upon her
shoulder. There, his thumb casually slipped beneath the
seam that joined the top of the bodice with her sleeve.

Synnovea was eager for yet another sampling and
pressed closer as her parted lips caressed his softly

yielding mouth with feather-light strokes. He seemed to hold back, meeting her playful kisses with pondered care. Experiencing some disappointment at his lack of fervent zeal, Synnovea clasped her fingers behind his neck and, resting her forearms upon his chest, peered up at him in the meager light.

"Are you bored with my novice kisses?" she questioned in a tiny whisper, confounded by his lack of avid participation.

Tyrone smiled at the absurd notion. "I'm entranced by every part of you, Synnovea, though at the moment I find your gown especially tempting."

His gaze flicked down to stroke the pale, silken orbs which swelled within the shallow shell of her bodice. Though she seemed oblivious to what she presented him as she braced herself against his chest, Tyrone was most appreciative of the shadowed view.

When his eyes lifted again to meet hers, they glowed with the smoldering heat of brightly burning coals, and just as Synnovea had wanted, his open mouth came upon hers with the same urgency that only moments before had demolished the barriers of her feminine resistance, but this time Tyrone was eager to progress.

With a subtle sweep of his hand, he brushed the sleeve from her shoulder and continued downward, encouraging the plunging descent of the bodice until he had freed the delectable fullness from the meager covering of her gown. His hand eagerly cupped and roamed the soft, warm flesh, appeasing at long last the yearnings of his dreams and ever-goading desires. Encouraged by her lack of resistance, he tugged down her bodice still farther, while the arm behind her back arched her spine to lift her naked breasts higher. The delicately hued fullness gleamed pale and lustrous in the faint light and was as enticing as any rich, lavish feast after a lengthy famine. Tyrone was starved and avariciously relished the fare as his hand captured a breast and his mouth lowered to search out the sensitive peaks and press warm, lingering

kisses upon the vales and hills that his lips traversed.
Synnovea could not draw an even breath as his greed
consumed her. The fires pulsed within her loins and grew
hotter with each passing second, but Tyrone was hardly
content with ground already gained. He desired it all.

Intent upon savoring the stirring ecstasy he evoked
within her, Synnovea was unaware of his free hand slipping beneath her skirts until it swept along her thigh and
settled where no other had ever dared touch her before.
Had he scalded her, the effect would have been the same.
With a shocked gasp, Synnovea struggled to rise and
found his mouth covering hers once again, silencing her
protests. The fiery heat of his kiss bespoke of his lusting
need, but it sent Synnovea into a frenzy to be touched in
so intimate a manner. It was like being shaken by jolts
of fire!

"Please! You mustn't!" she gasped, tearing her mouth
free. Wedging an arm down between them, she caught
his wrist and sought to halt his advancing intrusion. "You
mustn't! Not here!"

Reluctantly Tyrone withdrew his hand, though it took
every measure of restraint he could ransom from his
floundering will to curb his ardor. It was like binding
himself up in a steel cage to crush his rutting instincts
and not take her then and there. Though he had been
convinced by the heat of her response that she had been
willing, he was no fool to think he could force her and
still give her pleasure. The idea was paramount in his
mind that with a little patience Synnovea could become a
mistress whom he could cherish as much as any wife. He
wanted to nurture her carefully through the intimacies
enjoyed by a loving couple and arouse her to such heights
of rapture she would find it hard to withhold herself
from him in the future. With such a goal in mind, he
knew he would have to bide his time, just a little while
longer.

"Come, Synnovea," he coaxed as she clutched an arm
across her naked breasts to shield the rounded curves

from his gaze. He lifted her cloak and spread it protectively around her shoulders, allowing her the covering she so anxiously sought. "Calm yourself, love. I won't hurt you."

Synnovea still quaked from the shock of his invasion and was not entirely willing to yield to him as he encouraged her to relax against him. Slipping a hand into the opening of her cloak, she snatched the gown up over her breasts and refused to look at him, afraid he would glimpse a different kind of fear than he might have expected to find. It seemed extremely doubtful to her now that she would be able to escape his ardor, for his daring exploits appeared to be without barriers or reserve. When his hand had made its claim on her, she had felt as if she had just been flung face-to-face with the stark realization of his single-minded course. For the life of her, she could glimpse no way of avoiding what he intended without retiring herself posthaste from his presence. The proud hawk which she had chosen to carry her through her soaring quest was becoming increasingly more difficult to handle, and unless some unexpected good fortune rescued her from the sharp descent of his plunging flight, she would be carried to his nest and devoured for a succulent morsel ere the night was out.

Tyrone freed a softly curling strand of dark hair that had become entrapped beneath her cloak and laid it within the velvet cowl as he spoke soothingly to her. "The way I touched you, Synnovea, is no different than what every husband and lover does with the one he adores. 'Tis common in marriage."

"We are not married!" Synnovea groaned, suddenly haunted by an image of her mother's deeply distraught visage.

"Would you feel any different if we were?" he queried and continued with disarming candor. "You appear to want this union as badly as I do, and yet you seem to have no idea what you should expect. Dearest Synnovea, were you to return the favor in like fashion, I would surely consider it a delicious sweetmeat ere the feast is entered."

Synnovea's eyes chased upward, and she stared at him in some amazement until Tyrone casually shrugged and smiled.

"Do you think me untouchable, Synnovea? Nay, love, I'm a man and I want you as a husband wants his wife. I want to touch you, love you, and do yearn that you do the same. The giving of pleasure is only natural during a time of intimacy." He laughed as she relented and allowed him to pull her close against him. "I thought you knew what to expect."

"I've never been with a man before," Synnovea murmured and tentatively relaxed against him. "Although my mother told me what to anticipate in marriage, her instructions were rather general and somewhat lacking in detail. No doubt she thought my husband would fill in the particulars. I'm sure she must be turning over in her grave by now. This is hardly the kind of thing she desired for me. An honorable marriage was what she presumed I would someday have."

"I'll be as careful as any husband," Tyrone promised with compelling warmth. "You need not be afraid I'll misuse you. 'Tis much more enjoyable to a man when a woman responds with matching fervor."

Holding her close, Tyrone relaxed back into the seat, listening to the soft tinkling of silver bells in the stillness of the evening. He made no further effort to advance his cause in the carriage, though it was difficult to ignore the tantalizing softness within his arms and to thrust from memory the sweet silkiness of her woman's flesh. Still, his patience appeared to assuage her fears, for it was she who, with a softly mewling sigh, snuggled closer to his chest. He smiled in pleasure, pressing his cheek against her brow, and was satisfied for the present to nourish her affection.

The coach swayed to a halt before the two-story, narrow structure which Tyrone rented within the German district of Moscow. Had there not been a shortage of available housing in the community at the time of his arrival, he would have secured for himself smaller quarters, thereby saving on rents and perhaps even a few coins that went toward the cleaning of the house. The rooms were sparsely furnished yet neat enough for his tastes, thanks to the efforts of a bovine widow who came on a regular basis to keep it so, but having to deal with the city's segregation of foreigners proved to be a tiresome inconvenience most of the time. It was a lengthy jaunt to where his Russian recruits were quartered and an even longer one to where Synnovea was ensconced.

Stepping from the carriage, Tyrone lifted Synnovea to the ground beside him, then paid the coachman and, with her assistance in translation, promised the man a goodly sum for his time if he would wait at the end of the thoroughfare for the space of a pair of hours. The carriage rumbled off down the road as Tyrone faced Synnovea. Taking her up into his arms, he kissed her with all the passion he had so recently held in check, then with a chuckle he drew away and nuzzled her cheek, drawing a giggle from Synnovea as he staggered haphazardly toward the door.

"You make me drunk with delight," he crooned in her ear.

"Then I pray you sober quickly lest you stray too far from the path," she urged, glancing over her shoulder to see what risks lay ahead as he tottered precariously along the edge. Locking her arms firmly about his neck, she sought to brace herself for the fall that seemed forthcoming.

Tyrone's laughter rang out, and Synnovea gasped in surprise as he caught her to him and spun about in a swiftly whirling eddy. It was immediately apparent to Synnovea that he was well in command of his faculties and only teased her for the sheer enjoyment of it. When he came to a halt, she was dazed and breathlessly weak, completely pliant within his arms. Though the world still careened crazily around her, her only lucidity seemed to be his hotly burning lips devouring hers again.

They reached the door, and Tyrone bent slightly askew to unlock the latch as he complained about its temperamental tendency to come apart if not carefully worked. With a sigh of accomplishment, he disengaged the bar and then nudged the stout plank open with a shoulder, then whirled inward into the dark room, sweeping her around with a laugh as he kicked the door closed behind him. Growing serious, he braced his feet wide apart and leaned back against a nearby wall as he kissed her again with the same amorous vigor he had earlier displayed. His arm slipped from under her knees, and her voluminous skirts were snared high on his thigh as her feet came to rest on the floor between his.

"Give me a moment to catch my breath," Synnovea pleaded weakly against his lips, nearly overwhelmed by his fierce ardor. "My world has turned helter-skelter and still reels about my head."

Tyrone loosened his grasp and claimed her hands to bestow on each a zealous kiss, then he straightened and led the way across the room, where he struck tender to several wicks and gave light to the chamber. With a casual gesture, he indicated the room at large, which was furnished with nothing more grand and comfortable than several straight chairs, a small table, a desk and a pair of tall cabinets.

Synnovea stood beside him and glanced around, aware that the time for her reprieve was flitting past on rapid wings. She was in the hawk's nest now; it would only be a matter of moments before she would become his prey. Though the threat of that happening no longer frightened her, it was far from her objective.

" 'Tis clean enough," Tyrone observed casually, "but I fear rather stark for a woman's taste."

"It looks the way I imagined it would," Synnovea responded with a hesitant smile. "You are, after all, a soldier in His Majesty's service, here for only a brief time before you're gone again. You keep it amazingly well, despite that fact."

"I pay a woman to clean and cook for me," Tyrone admitted, lifting the cloak from her shoulders and folding it over the back of a nearby chair. As if bedazzled by the beauty of the flawless ivory skin, he reached out and lightly rubbed a hand over her shoulder, while his gaze roamed downward into her gown. Fascinated by the perfection he saw before him, he added distantly, "She comes for an hour or two each day, but leaves before I return. If not for the fact that she probably outweighs me by several stone, I'd say she's afraid of me."

"Perhaps I, too, should be afraid of you," Synnovea murmured timidly, aware of the warming glow in his eyes and what it could lead to. "I hardly know you, and yet here I am alone with you."

Tyrone kissed her brow as he breathed a question. "Were you afraid of me in the bathhouse?"

Synnovea found no will to resist as his lips caressed hers with quick, light kisses. "I was outraged at your audacity to watch me when you made no effort to inform me of your presence."

Tyrone peered down at her with a grin teasing his handsome lips. "Would you have allowed me to watch if I had made my presence known to you?"

"Of course not!" She smiled, growing warm and pliant in his arms. "How can you ask such a thing?"

"Then perhaps you can understand why I didn't want to enlighten you. The temptation to observe your bath far exceeded my ability to resist. Even now, I would like to see you as you appeared then and hold you as I did in the pool." He continued to caress her lips with brief kisses as he asked, "Has anyone ever told you how absolutely beautiful you are without your clothes?"

Synnovea struggled to free her mind from the enchantment of his kisses. Aware of the trembling disquiet within her, she faced away from those lips and eyes that were capable of rendering her weak with the most captivating and persuasive powers. "Women are not usually inclined to offer comment," she answered faintly over her shoulder, feeling his chest come in contact with her back as he stepped close behind her, "and since you were the only man to catch me unawares, then I must accept your judgment, whatever it may be."

Tyrone was hardly disappointed by her stance, considering it afforded him an irresistible view of her meagerly clad bosom. The soft sheen of her bosom glowed intriguingly in the warm light of the candles, whetting his senses until he was sure there was molten lead flowing through his veins. Gazing down upon such lush fare, he spoke from present observation. "Your breasts are as sweet as the dew upon the honeycomb and so soft and tempting, it staggers my wit to think of making love to you."

Synnovea could not subdue the blush that crept into her cheeks as she allowed her imagination to also conjure such an event. If the moment became as heady to her as his amorous attentions had been thus far, she was wont to wonder if she could endure the ecstasy of it. But then, she reminded herself again, she was not here to be ravenously consumed as his quarry.

Tyrone bent and bestowed a kiss on the tantalizing nape as he quietly inquired, "Are you truly afraid of me, Synnovea?"

"I didn't think so until tonight," she replied honestly and shivered with anticipation as his hands slipped up from her waist and approached her breasts. Her breath stilled in wonder as his fingers teasingly brushed the peaks until they tightened beneath the cloth of her gown. Seizing tentative rein on her weakening resistance, Synnovea laughed shakily and, moving farther away from him, tossed a glance over her shoulder. "Now I'm sure I am."

"Then perhaps a glass of wine might soothe your fears," Tyrone suggested, plucking open his doublet as he went to search through a small cabinet. Doffing the garment, he hung it over the back of a chair and then loosened the front of his shirt down to his waist as he examined several flagons. When he turned with a small cup and the bottle he had selected, Synnovea realized it was not within her power to ignore his altered appearance. Her gaze delved into the opening of his shirt as she admired an abbreviated view of his firmly muscled chest that was lightly covered with crisply curling hair. She was boldly reminded of a time when she had clung to him and been distantly aware of his hardened chest. Now the memory seemed as clear and corrosive to her tranquility as the man himself. In his every action and deed, no matter how great, small, or insignificant the feat or movement, he exhibited an uncompromising masculinity that in her opinion made other men seem somewhat lacking. She had, with a great measure of curiosity, contemplated many of that same gender throughout her lifetime and travels and was sure, when viewed from a physical sense, the colonel was a notch or two above most, certainly far above the white-haired Prince Vladimir. Truly, an image of the elder garbed only in his leggings made her appreciate the memory of the Englishman's unadorned form all the more.

Tyrone paused beside a table to pour the wine and then came to her bearing only the mug. For a long moment he caressed her lips with a soft kiss before yielding her the offering of *chereunikyna*. "We'll share," he said against her mouth. "The taste of you makes it sweeter for me."

With trembling fingers, Synnovea raised the drinking vessel and, beneath his warming attention, sampled a sip from its edge. When she gave back the cup, Tyrone drained the contents, then slowly caressed her soft mouth with his again.

A long moment later he drew back and stared down into the limpid pools of green, then inclined his head toward the narrow flight of stairs that led up a dark passageway. "I'll go upstairs and light some candles for us."

Synnovea lifted a hesitant glance toward the blackened void above the steps. "What's up there?"

"My bedchamber," Tyrone answered and cocked a curious brow as he saw her shiver. " 'Tis more comfortable upstairs than it is down here, Synnovea." He swept a hand about to indicate the furnishings around them. "As you can plainly see for yourself."

"Of course," she said in acceptance of his statement. Now that the moment swiftly approached wherein he would rend her virginity upon his pallet, Synnovea was challenged by the fact that there was little time remaining to make good her escape, and yet here she stood. Even as she sought to quell the sudden qualms that assailed her, she felt as if someone else was standing in her stead, doing everything she would have condemned a fortnight or two ago. It was a bold fact that in a scant few moments, everything that she had encouraged with her flirtations would end in a culmination of his desires, not necessarily her own. When faced by the truth of what she had instigated, she found it impossible to meet his gaze.

Tyrone was too sensitive to the mood of the woman he had become enamored with not to detect an abrupt change in her disposition. Though he was bewildered by her cooling ardor, it was abruptly and clearly evident to him that Synnovea was not totally committed to the idea of letting him make love to her. He had grave doubts that even his kisses could adequately appease whatever fears she now faced, and it seemed prudent to allow her some time alone to consider her choices.

Resigning himself to the bleak and disappointing possibility of being left without the sweet solace of her passion, Tyrone approached the stairs as he commented ruefully over his shoulder, "I'll be back in a moment."

Chapter 16

THE SOUND OF HIS FOOTSTEPS LIGHTLY SCRAPING against the wood planks seemed to resonate in diminishing waves throughout the house as Synnovea faced the last stronghold of opposition to her quest. With the game nearly at its end, her own conscience had rallied in objection to her devious schemes and now sought to beat down her resolve with bludgeoning blows that seemed too painful to resist. Honesty! Honor! Integrity! Modesty! Scruples! Virtue! Kindness! Everything her mother and father had cherished, she was reducing them all to an ashen heap of deceit and scandalous behavior with her mischief, treading brazenly where other milder, more timid and obedient maids would have trembled in fear, all because she wanted a man whom she could love as a husband. The path she had chosen was hardly moral. She had deliberately tempted a man whom she knew had desired her and, by allowing him to become intimate with her, would soon be breaking the hopes of another who had aspired to have her as his wife. Why could she not endure the hardships thrust upon her for the sake of honor like other women had done? her conscience argued. Long years ago Natasha had taken an older man as husband and had later reaped a love she had greatly treasured. Why could she not do the same? What made her so obstinate that she must flaunt the rules of society to gain her own end, while leaving in her wake the shattered spirits of the ones she had hurt?

Synnovea almost cringed as she thought of Tyrone being at the forefront of those injured by her deception. For some reason she could no longer blandly dismiss his involvement as being of no consequence. He was a human being! He had feelings! He was susceptible to being wounded by her antics!

What was she to do? How could she escape from all that she had planned?

Just go!

Synnovea winced in pain as the guilt-driven command lashed across her mind, and she took several stumbling steps toward the door as unspent sobs solidified into a painful lump in her chest, then she halted abruptly, sick at heart, knowing what her departure would cost her. There was that element within her that urged her to go, but there was another conflicting voice which bade her to hold fast lest she suffer the consequences.

A sense of panic began to build within Synnovea as she found herself caught in a struggle betwixt the two. Broodingly her eyes wandered back to the black velvet doublet dressing the chair, and inwardly she groaned, realizing she could not go through with her ploy. Colonel Rycroft was everything Natasha had said he was; he didn't deserve to be entrapped by a conniving woman.

Choking back the sobs as she heard him coming down the stairs, Synnovea snatched up her cloak and fled to the door. In a panic, she seized the latch, ready to fly, but in her haste, the handle broke off in her hand, frustrating her efforts to leave before she had to face him.

"Synnovea. . . . "

She whirled at the sound of her name and stared at him with tears blurring her vision. He stood on the bottom step with a hand braced on the low beam above his head, just watching her. She could see the pain in his face, feel it in her heart; she ached for him and for herself, but there was no help for it. She must fly!

"Don't go," he rasped. "Don't leave me."

Synnovea tried to find the strength of a denial within her, but her voice was gone, and she could only open and close her mouth as she struggled in mute agony to deliver the words that would effect her escape.

"Stay with me . . . please. . . . "

His appeal tore through her, and her heart crumpled within her. The cloak slid from her hand as she took several faltering steps toward him. "We must hurry! 'Tis urgent that I leave. . . . "

Suddenly Synnovea found him standing before her, sweeping her in his arms as she wrapped her own about his neck. It seemed in a thrice of steps he was up the stairs, following the beacon of light that came from the open doorway at the far end of a dark, narrow hallway. Upon entering the bedchamber, he stood her beside the large, rough-hewn four-poster. Skimpy draperies were drawn over a pair of windows on the far side of the bed, but they were effective in providing them privacy.

Tyrone's mouth plummeted down to seize hers in a wildly ravaging, fiercely possessive kiss that went through her like a sizzling bolt of lightning. Her emotions were like a blazing arrow, with vanes ignited, coursing swiftly through her senses, setting her whole being aflame. There was no halting its flight now that her passion had been unleashed, for it soared swiftly to its mark, sinking deeply into the heart of the man who desired her.

Tyrone's fingers tore at the lacings at the back of her gown, and in another moment he was sliding the garment and the chemise down her silken body, following their descent with his hands until the two pieces fell in a large, puffy mound around her stockinged calves. He was just as anxious to rid himself of his clothes and quickly completed the task as Synnovea timidly perched on the edge of the bed and slipped her stockings off. Surreptitiously she witnessed his unveiling, allowing her gaze to slide down his tall form as she brushed a hand back and forth across her brow to hide her scrutiny. The wide, muscled shoulders, the trim waist, and flat, taut belly were just as she had remembered them, but it was the proud fullness evidencing his desires that drew forth a heated blush to her cheeks.

Sensing her perusal, Tyrone reached out and pulled her arm away so he could see her face. Though he could detect a darkening bloom of color in her cheeks, he spoke in a cajoling whisper. "No need to feel embarrassed, Synnovea. I give you leave to look at me. You may even touch me if you so desire."

Synnovea stared up at him in painful chagrin, unable to fully understand his cavalier nonchalance. He seemed totally unconcerned by his nakedness.

Tyrone shrugged casually, sensing her protracted discomfiture. "I'm not ashamed of the fact that I'm a man and that I want you, Synnovea. I yield to you everything that I am."

His eyes burned with a brighter flame as his own gaze raked her. Taking her hand, he pulled her up to him until her soft breasts were crushed against his hardened chest. His thumbs replaced the broad expanse in a provocative titillation of the pliant peaks until he snatched her breath with each voluptuous flick. Sweeping the length of her body with one long tantalizing caress, he kissed her with an eagerness that left her breathless.

Synnovea gasped in earnest and laid her hands cautiously on his broad shoulders as he lifted her from her feet and settled her intimately against him. His stance was far more purposeful than the bathhouse had prepared her for, yet he made no attempt to forge through the fragile barrier as he teased her with slow, provocative movements of his hips. The warmth of him deliciously strummed across the fibers of her senses, and her breath came back in halting, panting gasps as the excitement mounted within her, building in stunning leaps and bounds that made her tremble in enraptured bliss against him. He lowered her to her feet as his fiery kisses began to wander downward over her pale breasts. Of a sudden Synnovea knew not where to put her hands, and almost in an anxious frenzy she rubbed them hard against his chest, feeling his firm nipples beneath her palms. Slipping her arms around him, she clasped her hips to his again, seeking to appease the indistinct and totally indescribable void that craved to be sated, but she found no relief despite the pulsating bedlam in her loins. Grinding her teeth in frustration, she slipped a hand between them with a bolder purpose, nearly snatching the breath from Tyrone's lungs.

"Hurry," she urged, drawing him back with her to the bed. Whatever instinct drove her goaded her far beyond the panic of being discovered by Aleksei.

"Have a care, Synnovea," Tyrone rasped. He was being dragged far too close to the brink of expulsion for him to be assured of his own ability to withstand such delicious torment. "The pleasure is too sweet. I cannot contain myself much longer."

Relinquishing her claim on him, Synnovea stretched back upon the bed and writhed in sensual grace as she slid across the fresh, cool sheet to make room for him. Tyrone followed, bracing on a knee beside her as the sharply gleaming eyes swept her with a burning heat, taking in the full bounty of her beauty before he leaned down and covered her parted lips with his open mouth, kissing her with all the ravenous cravings of a man nearly famished for the complete and total fulfillment of his desires. Sliding an arm beneath her waist, Tyrone lifted her across the feather ticking and then stretched his long form against her silken softness, gently parting her thighs as he lowered his narrow hips between them. Synnovea tensed, waiting for the pain to come, but he whispered words of reassurance as the caressing lips brushed her temple. " 'Twill be over soon, love. Try and relax."

Still dreading the moment when he would thrust through the barrier, Synnovea averted her face and tried to subdue her trembling as the unyielding hardness intruded, testing the delicate shield of tightly resisting flesh. A searing pain suddenly ripped through her loins, and with a startled gasp, she pitched upward, causing Tyrone to lose whatever small, minute ground he had gained. Driven by his burgeoning need, he nearly bore her down again to complete his entry, for he was shaking almost to the core of his manly being. Only by a hard-won control did he curb the instincts that besieged him. He pulled back, allowing her a moment to calm herself, and began to kiss and caress her again, though it took every measure of willpower he was capable of to maintain a gentlemanly forbearance.

"I'm sorry," Synnovea whispered tearfully beneath his lingering kisses. "I'm sorry."

"Shhh, love," Tyrone soothed, stroking the soft, womanly warmth of her.

This time Synnovea surrendered herself to him, totally abashed that she could have acted like a cowardly chit when she had desired the consummation as feverishly as he had, but Tyrone was hardly encouraged by what he found, for even with the damage done, she was still for the most part a virgin and far too small to allow him easy access into the warm sheath.

Synnovea's hand came up to rest tentatively upon his chest. "May I touch you again?"

"Not yet, love," Tyrone answered haltingly, shaken by the pain of his mounting excitement. "Just relax and let me pleasure you, then I'll have mine."

It seemed only a passing of a moment before Synnovea found her pain and embarrassment eclipsed by the stirring bliss he awakened within her. Overwhelmed by the pleasure of his persuasive fondling, she began to tremble and sigh beneath his wandering kisses until the strange sensations swept through her in strengthening swells. Tyrone worked his magic until her soft mewling sighs were transformed into astonished gasps, and she began to twist and writhe beneath his caresses. The shuddering rapture broke upon her, and of a sudden she was pulling him down upon her, leading him to the tender breach and eagerly arching her hips against him.

Tyrone felt a surging need for haste himself and was trembling nearly as much as she as his hands clasped her hips firmly for the final thrust, then a distant sound intruded, wrenching his mind clear with a brutal abruptness.

"What is it?" Synnovea whispered as he lifted his head to listen, then her eyes widened as she heard the clatter of horses' hooves thundering to a halt outside the house.

"Someone's coming!" Tyrone replied as if astounded by the untimely intrusion.

Synnovea moaned in despair as he snatched away and rolled to the edge of the bed. Grabbing up his clothes, he thrust his feet through a pair of leggings and, jerking them up over his naked hips, hurriedly fastened them.

"Get your clothes on, Synnovea!" he bade. "Hurry!"

She just stared at him, frozen by the realization of what she had done. Despite her change of heart, everything was occurring just as she had planned. In another moment Aleksei would be ordering his men to break down the door, and Tyrone would be caught in the middle, just where she had deliberately contrived to place him.

Seeing her horrified stare, Tyrone grabbed her by the arms and gave her a shake. "Good lord, woman, what ails you? Do you not ken? There are men outside the house, and in all likelihood they'll be coming in here! I cannot defend the two of us with you stark naked!"

Sweeping her off the bed, he set her to her feet and then gathered her clothes. He dumped them on the bed near at hand and shook out her chemise just as a heavy fist pounded on the front portal and a mumbled voice called through the barrier.

"Colonel Rycroft! I must speak with you."

"Lift your arms!" Tyrone commanded in an anxious whisper, ignoring the summons for the moment. As Synnovea complied, he yanked the chemise down over her head and settled it into place around her slender waist.

"I can dress myself!" she declared, coming to her senses as she felt his lean fingers fastening the tiny buttons between her breasts. "You'd better get your clothes on and then go!"

"What?! And leave you here by yourself to confront these men alone?" Tyrone laughed harshly, denying the possibility. "If I leave at all, Synnovea, I'll be taking you with me."

From down below, the rattle of the broken latch accompanied a garbled question. "Colonel Rycroft, are you there?"

It was obvious from another testing of the lock that the portal could not be easily opened. Heavy fists began to pound on the planks, demanding entry.

"Colonel Rycroft, we know you're in there!"

Tyrone stepped to the door of his bedchamber and yelled down the stairs. "I'll be down in a moment."

"You must come now, Colonel!" came the abrupt reply. "I know the Countess Synnovea is with you. If you do not open this door immediately, my men will break it in."

"Aleksei!" Synnovea whispered. Meeting Tyrone's questioning glance, she blushed and lifted her slender shoulders in a pained shrug. "He hired men to watch Natasha's house."

"Good lord, Synnovea! Why didn't you tell me earlier? We could have gone elsewhere." Tyrone gave her a gentle shove toward the bed. "Get your gown and shoes on. We've got to get out of here!"

His statement was promptly underscored by the sudden contact of several stout shoulders against the front door. Another crashing blow soon followed, testing the sturdiness of the formidable barrier.

Seeing now a chance to escape the consequences of her ploy and therefore a reason for haste, Synnovea instantly obeyed as Tyrone yanked on a pair of hide breeches, boots, and a shirt. Belting on his sword, he seized her hand

and led the way downstairs. He paused briefly to judge the strength of another assault against the front portal and roughly estimated the time they had remaining before the sturdy planks would give way, then he scooped up her cloak from the floor and, wrapping it about her shoulders, pulled her along with him to the back door.

Drawing forth his sword, Tyrone laid a finger across his lips, then motioned for her to stay where she was. Receiving her nod of compliance, he carefully slid the bolt back from the lock and opened the door. His slow, cautious tread was noiseless as he slipped through the portal. Pausing just outside with his sword at the ready, he carefully scanned the shadows, slowly turning until he glanced up toward his right, then like a flash of quicksilver in the night, the blade whipped upward to block the descent of another which came down from the lofty perch of a fellow who had climbed atop a pair of wooden barrels leaning against the house. The man's shout brought the sound of running feet as Tyrone parried his next blow, but any hope for escape with Synnovea dwindled rapidly as a dozen more stalwarts came charging around the corner of the narrow house. Tyrone retreated quickly, slamming and bolting the door behind him.

"Get upstairs!" He jerked his head in the direction of his bedchamber. "I'll try to hold them off down here!"

"You must leave me and escape!" Synnovea cried frantically.

"Woman, do as I say!" Tyrone enjoined. "I'll not leave you alone to your own defense!"

Frustrated by his commanding tone, Synnovea clenched her fists as she tried again, raising her voice to be heard above the jarring jolts against both doors. "Will you please listen to me, Tyrone? I know what I'm saying!"

"What?! And allow Aleksei the chance to rape you before he gets you to safety? Go, I said!"

Groaning in despair, Synnovea whirled toward the stairs just as the front portal crashed inward, bringing several stout hearties stumbling in with it. Their entry hastened Synnovea's flight though she heard Aleksei bellow her name from a safe distance behind the first battery of men. Tyrone leapt to cover her retreat with the long blade boldly in evidence.

"Seize him!" Aleksei railed out the command as he thrust a long finger in the colonel's direction.

Tyrone chortled as he mocked the prince. "Have you no skill to do it yourself?"

A half dozen men plowed forward to accomplish the order and then immediately stumbled back, yelping at the pain of newly inflicted wounds.

"A weighty purse to the one responsible for this rascal's capture," Aleksei promised, incensed by the colonel's tenacity. "You wanted him! Now here he is! Do with him what he did to you and those who rode with you! Seize him!"

Tyrone had no chance to answer as a full dozen of the brawny fellows stormed toward him again, forcing him to retreat up the stairs. Gaining the upper level, he dashed into the bedchamber and slammed the portal behind him. He tossed the sword onto the bed and pulled a tall, weighty cabinet across the doorway to bolster the strength of the heavy planks. Synnovea watched in bewilderment as he grabbed a small chair and leapt across the room to throw it through a window. Whipping the top sheet from the bed and tying a knot in the end, he stepped beside the opening to peruse the small ledge that jutted out from beneath the window, as well as the ground far below. With a beckoning gesture, Tyrone bade her to come near.

"I'll lower you to the ground from the ledge, then I'll climb down behind you." He glanced toward the door as the ponderous blows strengthened against it, and he raised his voice slightly to a louder whisper in order to be heard above the din. "If I don't make it, run to the carriage and have the driver take you back to Natasha's! Do you understand?"

"I understand, Tyrone, but I most desperately plead with you to flee ere you're taken."

Sweeping her into his arms, Tyrone thrust her through the window and clasped her hand tightly as she balanced on the ledge, then as a loud chortle came from down below, Tyrone leaned out to see a man with a long, shaggy mustache and a lock of hair sprouting from a bald pate striding toward the window with arms outstretched.

"Oh-ho! Colonel Rycroft! We meet again, eh? So good of you, my friend, to toss the wench down to me." The huge man chortled in uproarious mirth. "The little pigeon is tasty sweetmeat, eh? Now I take for myself what you have had."

"Petrov!" Synnovea gasped in shock and glanced back at Tyrone, who cursed beneath his breath.

"That means Ladislaus is here, too!" he muttered. "I must question the sort of friends Prince Aleksei associates with!" He helped Synnovea back though the window and swept her to her feet. "I fear the prince has made the place secure against our escape if he's hired those miscreants to seek me out. You can be certain they're hungry for revenge, a fact I'm sure Aleksei was aware of when he went searching for them."

"How would he have known where to find them?" Synnovea asked in confusion.

" 'Tis a question I'll have to ask Aleksei if I'm given the opportunity."

"You'll have a greater chance of making good an escape without me," Synnovea replied, slipping her hand inside his open shirt to lay it upon the muscular chest. "Will you not try? I promise you, Aleksei will not let these men take me, not when there's a chance the tsar will find out. . . . "

Tyrone scoffed at the idea. "Aleksei may not even have a choice if Ladislaus is with them. That brigand wanted you before. He may not stop until he takes you for sure this time."

"Please listen to me, Tyrone! I've no liking for Aleksei or for Ladislaus either, but if you leave me and seek your freedom, then you may be able to arrange an assault to take me back. You snatched me away from Ladislaus before. Can you not do it again?"

Tyrone lifted a museful brow as he considered her suggestion. It was certain that if they were both captured together, he could not accomplish her rescue when there was such an overwhelming force eager to take him. "I might be able to arrange such an event. Some friends of mine are living nearby. English officers. If I can get through, they'll rally to help me."

Beneath the ramming bombardment, the wood facing around the bolt began to splinter away from the door, prompting Tyrone to take up his sword again. As he sheathed the weapon, the tiny splotches of red that marred the whiteness of the sheet caught his attention. He paused a brief second to consider them before he came back to Synnovea.

"I'll finish what I started ere long," he promised in a warm whisper and pressed a hurried kiss upon her lips. "Save yourself for me."

Fighting back a rush of tears, Synnovea braved a smile. "Be careful!"

Tyrone grinned down at her, then strode to the window, throwing back over his shoulder, "You can tell both Aleksei and Ladislaus that I'll be back to kill them if they hurt you."

Synnovea flew to the window to watch as he ducked through the opening and climbed onto the outer ledge. There, Tyrone braced his feet wide to balance himself, then tucked two fingers into his mouth and, much to Synnovea's astonishment, whistled loudly, bringing Petrov racing back to serve as his audience of one. The brawny giant gaped upward as Tyrone grinned down and swept him a jaunty bow.

"So good of you to come when I call, Petrov. Now catch me if you can," he taunted with a chuckle and, springing from the ledge, dove directly toward the burly one, who

staggered backward in stupefied amazement. Synnovea
clapped a hand over her mouth to squelch a frightened
scream, but any sound that might have escaped her was
promptly overshadowed by the loud, wavering warble
that issued forth from Petrov's thick throat. His scream
strengthened to a deafening roar until it was abruptly
squelched into silence beneath the falling weight of the
colonel.

As Tyrone had hoped, his daring dive was sufficiently
broken by the thief's bulk, and no worse for wear, he
drew back a clenched fist to deliver a powerful blow
to the stout jaw of the dazed man, knocking him completely senseless. The large head lolled limply as Tyrone
tested the brigand's response. Satisfied, he jumped to
his feet and dusted off his clothes as if on a casual
errand. Turning with a lopsided grin, he swept into
another debonair bow, this time for the benefit of
his lady love who still stood with a hand clasped
over her mouth as she watched from the window
above.

Laughing in relief, Synnovea applauded his daring
feat and then blew him a kiss before he whirled and
raced toward a nearby house. Though she observed
his flight closely, he soon disappeared into the night,
leaving her strangely disquieted, yet relieved by his
escape.

The cabinet began to slide inward, and a moment
later Synnovea whirled to face the men who burst
through. Ladislaus led them, but he halted just inside
the chamber as his pale eyes quickly scanned the
length and breadth of it for the Englishman. Dragging the large furry cap from his flaxen head, he
strode briefly to the bed, considered it a long moment
before his eyes chased to her, then swept to the
fluttering draperies at the window. Crossing the room
with long strides, he leaned through the opening
and gazed down at the form sprawled upon the
ground.

Synnovea lifted her chin and gave Ladislaus her best attempt at a haughty demeanor as he came back to her with a grin. "You're too late," she announced. "The Englishman has gone."

"I can see that for myself, Countess. I'm also aware of the pretty bauble he left behind." The sky-blue eyes raked her cloaked form before he reached out a hand to thoughtfully rub a soft curl between his fingers. "You've allowed my enemy to feed upon your rich treasures, my beauty. I'll forgive you for that, for there's clearly enough to spare, but I would know where he has gone."

"Do you think I would tell you?" she asked in amazement.

Aleksei pushed his way through the door, safely behind a horde of others. "Don't waste time trying to get any answers from her," he snapped. "She'll never tell you where her lover has fled. You'll have to find him yourself." Turning imperiously, he snapped his fingers to the bandits, sending them running out again. "Remember!" he shouted after them. "A weighty purse to the one who captures him!"

Aleksei waited until they had raced from the room, then he glowered challengingly at Ladislaus. "Well? Will you let your men scour the area for him alone, or will you hunt him down yourself?" He arched a brow at the hulking man as he ridiculed, "Don't tell me you're afraid of him."

Ladislaus scoffed at the man's gibe. "There's only one coward here, and I'm looking at him."

Aleksei's dark eyes flared at the insult. "From what I hear, you ran when the Englishman appeared on the scene."

"Be careful," the giant warned him ominously. "One less *boyar* in this city will not be noticed."

Synnovea glanced between the two, hoping they would get into a violent argument and forget about Tyrone long enough to insure his escape. She smiled tauntingly at the prince as she faced him. "Your hired henchman doesn't display much respect for your position, Aleksei. Has he been in your employ for long?"

The lord-of-thieves snorted loudly at her prodding inquiry. "No man employs Ladislaus. Your precious prince left Moscow to search me out when I let it be known here in the city that I was seeking the whereabouts of a certain Englishman. Otherwise, you would not be seeing us together."

"Is it your intent to kill the Englishman?" she questioned warily.

"I will allow the prince to have his due ere I take mine," Ladislaus replied and smiled mockingly at her. "In any case, Countess, after we're finished with the colonel, there will be little left for you to enjoy."

"*If* you manage to take him!" Aleksei interjected with rancor. "I'm sure this delay will cost you his capture."

Ladislaus smirked at the other man. "I promised you we'd take him, and so we shall."

With that, the thief spun on a booted heel and strode from the room. Several moments later his voice was heard outside the window as he loudly bade Petrov to rouse from his stupor.

Contemptuously Aleksei glanced about the room, disdaining the plain, barren look of it, then his eyes blazed as he spied the tiny smatterings of blood that stained the sheet. Whirling upon Synnovea, he lashed out in fury, laying the back of his hand viciously across her cheek and sending her reeling across the room to the far wall.

"So, you bitch! 'Tis true! You've given yourself to that blackguard!"

Synnovea staggered in a daze and blinked several times as she struggled to focus her gaze, then shakily tested her jaw and a bloody bottom lip, feeling as if the whole side of her head had been slammed against a solid brick wall. She was vaguely aware of the blood trickling from the corner of her mouth, but she ignored it as she glared back at the prince in cold contempt. "Once I would have given myself to Colonel Rycroft for no other purpose than to thwart your plans, Aleksei, but henceforth, I will seek after his companionship with diligence. Without a doubt, he's more of a man than you'll ever hope to be."

"You will watch him pay!" Aleksei railed, incensed by her disparagement. His much inflated pride was sorely tested by the fact that she could take a foreigner to her breast after fiercely denying him that same privilege, but now the added insult of being told she would willingly share her company with the other man only made him more enraged. "I will see that he suffers exceedingly because of you!"

"You'll have to catch him first, Aleksei, and I really don't think you or your hired lackeys are skilled enough for that task," Synnovea derided caustically.

"I'm of a different opinion, my dear." Aleksei smirked in contempt. "You see, Ladislaus and his men have grown to loathe the Englishman almost as much as I do. 'Twill only be a matter of time before the good colonel falls into their hands. They'll lie in wait for him until he appears, then pounce on him as they would a ravenous dog who's gotten free of his cage." The prince crossed the space between them and, stepping close before Synnovea, sneered into her face. "Once I have him within my grasp, I'll make sure he remembers this night forever. Before I'm done with him, I'll see the hide stripped from his back and then assure myself that he'll never bed you or any other woman again as long as he lives."

Some distance away from the house the dense darkness was held secure within a cluster of trees growing close along the narrow dirt lane, and it was here that Tyrone paused to canvass the open, rutted stretch. Peering carefully up and down the thoroughfare, he then scanned the area bordering it. No dark image or specter moved beyond the copse, not even the coachman who snoozed atop his conveyance, which had been halted a short distance away. Tyrone silently unsheathed his sword and crept to the outer edge of the trees, warily pausing there a long moment as he again surveyed the terrain. He was unable to put aside the feeling of uneasiness that had settled down upon him after his entry into the grove, for it seemed that all was not as it should be despite the openness of the place beyond where he stood. Still, he was unable to detect any movement or even an incongruous shadow which might have alerted him to another's presence. He was, however, a man who had learned to take heed when his senses warned him of danger. For the sake of caution, he eased back a step and was about to turn in stealthful retreat when a sudden pain exploded inside his head. He sagged to his knees as a billion piercing lights burst in a sea of radiant color before his eyes and then slowly dimmed to a dull shade of gray. Through the tenebrous gloom he was vaguely aware of a dark shape stepping close and an arm rising high above him, but his hampered faculties were sluggish and slow to react as a stout club came crashing down upon his head again, darkening the murky shadows into the deepest shade of night until all that remained of his world was total oblivion.

Chapter 17

I N THE SILENCE OF THE STILL NIGHT, A GROWING DIN
caught Aleksei's attention, and he raised his head to
listen as the sound of rumbling wheels and thundering
hooves heralded the approach of a coach and a large party
of riders. Shouted orders accompanied the arrival of the
conveyance and its large escort in front of the colonel's
quarters, and a moment later Ladislaus called up the
stairs.

"You can come down now, Your Most Gracious Highness." The contempt in his tone was too conspicuous to go
undetected. "We've caught the Englishman!"

The giant's words shattered Synnovea's confidence
and chilled her heart with fear. She had been so certain
that Tyrone would escape, for his ability had seemed to
extend well beyond most men, but now faced with his
capture and the full import of Aleksei's threats, she could
only tremble in dread of what he and the highwayman
intended.

"Now you'll see!" Aleksei flaunted his triumph with a
chortle.

Catching Synnovea's arm in a cruel vise, he hauled her
along behind him as he hurried down the stairs. The
rented livery had been halted in front, where Ladislaus
now waited with Petrov and several of his men. Another
score or more miscreants were still mounted on their
steeds beyond the coach.

Confronted by their vast number, Synnovea suddenly understood the reason for Tyrone's lack of success in gaining his freedom. There were enough of the rogues present to form a human web around a wide area, greatly reducing the chances for a successful escape. It was just as apparent to her that Aleksei had been willing to promise Ladislaus and his men a large stipend to see his orders carried out, one way or another.

The long fingers gripped Synnovea's arm none too gently and drew a sharp wince of pain from her as Aleksei shoved her roughly against the conveyance. Bracing a hand against the outer wall of the carriage, he leaned toward her and smirked in satisfaction as he squeezed a finely boned wrist, making her writhe in silent agony. "Be warned, my girl. If you try anything, I promise you that it will go worse for the Englishman."

Witnessing the intimidation, Ladislaus stepped beside them and, with a satirical glint in his pale eyes, fixed the *boyar* with a pointed stare until he finally gained the man's attention. Then, as if amused by the prince's baffled regard, the thief grinned broadly and swung open the carriage door. "Your quarry is inside, Great Prince Aleksei," he announced, jerking a thumb inward. "He's all trussed up, like a goose waiting for the roasting, just the way you wanted him. He shouldn't do any harm to you now."

"Excellent!" Aleksei exclaimed buoyantly.

Feeling a roiling mixture of terror and revulsion, Synnovea wrenched free of Aleksei's tenacious grip and, thrusting both hands against his chest, shoved with all of her strength, managing to catch him by surprise. He stumbled back from the driving force of her determination, and Synnovea whirled, wasting no moment as she scrambled up into the dark interior of the carriage. Immediately Aleksei recovered his balance and, barking out a command for the brigands to secure the doors on the far side, flung himself inward and seized her arm to halt her flight, but he soon realized there was no need for force.

The sight of Tyrone's ominously still form cauterized Synnovea's mind with a burgeoning dread. With a moan of despair, she sank to her knees beside the seat upon which he lay as still as death, curled on his side with his wrists and ankles securely bound and joined by a single length of woven leather rope. Such caution was no doubt intended to greatly restrict his mobility against the threat of him launching an attack when he awoke, reassuring her that he was at least alive.

Fearing the seriousness of his injuries, Synnovea searched for an open wound beneath his shirt and along his long torso. Her hopes rallied briefly when she found no evidence of an injury, then her worry intensified into panic as she slipped her fingers through his tousled hair, seeking to cradle his head, and touched a swollen lump, the ridge of which was marred by a bloody gash. A gasp escaped her lips as she lifted her hand before her face and stared at the large, dark splotch that gleamed wetly in the tenebrous gloom.

"That's only the beginning," Aleksei needled, recognizing her rapidly expanding apprehensions. His cocky arrogance was greatly inflated by the power he now held within his grasp. While the Englishman remained his hostage, he could make the girl beg for mercy, and he promised himself that before he finished with the man, he would see her groveling at his feet. Piece by bloody piece, he would exact his revenge upon the colonel and see her reduced to a quivering mass of daunted humanity. "Take comfort, my dear. Your cherished colonel is still alive, but he'll soon wish otherwise."

"You can't blame him for what I did!" Synnovea cried harshly, jerking around to glare at him.

"Oh, but I can, Synnovea," Aleksei assured her almost pleasantly. He lifted his broad shoulders in an indolent shrug as the conveyance lurched into motion. Even in the silver-hued light provided by the moon, he could see tears glistening brightly in her eyes and streaming in shining rivulets down her face. It irritated him beyond measure that she could display so much concern for the colonel when she had not even shown the least bit of remorse for the wounds she had inflicted upon him. Even now his nose was still tender and sensitive to the touch, not to mention the small lump that had formed where the fracture had been, marring its aristocratic lines. "Colonel Rycroft has taken from me a very special pleasure I had reserved entirely for myself, my dear, and for that, I intend to make him pay dearly." Smiling smugly, Aleksei bent toward her as he promised, "And you will watch it all, my beautiful Synnovea, as part of your punishment."

The green eyes grew cold with hatred. "Reserved for yourself, Aleksei? I thought 'twas your intent to deliver me unsullied to Prince Vladimir."

Aleksei swept a finger below his mustache as he sniffed in stilted confidence. "I might have allowed your husband first taste, but then again, I might not have."

Synnovea held her tongue, knowing she would only provoke him the more if she gave vent to several appellations that might do him justice. Loathing the thought of sitting next to him, she lifted Tyrone's head with gentle concern and slid into the seat, not caring if his blood stained her clothes as she nestled his head upon her lap.

"So loving and kind you are to him!" Aleksei ridiculed. "Once I inform the colonel that he was nothing more than a petty pawn in your frivolous little game, I'm sure he'll feel greatly indebted to you. No doubt he'll want to heap accolades of honor upon your winsome head when I strip from his loins the very jewels of his manhood."

Synnovea clutched a shaking hand to her throat and averted her face, tormented by his threat and by the role she had played in bringing Tyrone into his hands. She knew she would not be able to live at peace with herself if Aleksei accomplished all that he vowed to do. For the easing of her own conscience, it would be better if the overflowing draft of his dark vengeance fell upon her head alone.

Curling his handsome lips in a derisive sneer, Aleksei leaned forward to further antagonize her as he sought some additional appeasement for his rage and jealousy. "Do you know what that means to a man, Synnovea?" He became vulgarly explicit in his verbiage and was spurred on in his crudeness by her sharp intake of breath and horrified stare. Perhaps he might have only imagined the deepening stain that came into her cheeks, but it satisfied him nevertheless to think his prurient comments might have been effective in heightening her blush so much it could be easily discerned even in the shadows. "You're no longer an innocent, Synnovea, so you know I speak true. He'll never have that same ability ever again, and you'll have no one to blame but yourself. I warned you, but you just wouldn't listen. He'll be nothing more than a useless eunuch when I get through with him."

If Synnovea had been able to summon some minute hope that Aleksei would listen to her pleas for clemency, she would have gladly gone down on her knees before him and begged him for Tyrone's release, but he was clearly in a vindictive mood and would not be content until his deeds were carried out. She knew he made no idle threat, and despite her frantic search for some way to effect an escape for Tyrone from this predicament she had entangled him in, she was frighteningly aware that with each whirling turn of the wheels, she and her valiant but senseless suitor were being taken ever closer to a moment of reckoning.

When the conveyance turned into the lane that swept before the Taraslov manse and came to a halt, Synnovea realized she was neither mentally nor physically prepared to face the disturbing ordeal Aleksei had planned for them. She was overwhelmed with regret for having devised the diabolical scheme that had led them to this end, and she knew without a doubt that had some reprieve been extended toward them with payment being her marriage to Prince Vladimir, she'd have gladly gone that very hour to see the nuptials performed.

Ladislaus and his men dismounted and crowded around the coach as if expecting the Englishman to be awake and dangerously raging. They probably enjoyed a great measure of relief when they saw him still insensible to his surroundings and incapable of even the smallest struggle.

Aleksei bade four of the burly outlaws to carry their prisoner into the stable and hang him by the wrists from the bare rafters. For good measure, Ladislaus instructed several more to stand guard with pistols held at the ready, just in case the colonel revived before they made him sufficiently secure.

Aleksei barely considered the idea of Synnovea escaping now, for she seemed most intent upon following the procession which he pompously led. His attention was occupied with giving orders to his recruited culprits, and so delighted was he with the task, he failed to take note of a diminutive form quickly scurrying behind a shrub as he and Ladislaus's men passed with their burden. He was equally unobservant when the tiny, shadowy shade reached out to grasp Synnovea's arm and yank her behind the same bush.

"Ali!" Though the cry was no more than a startled whisper, Synnovea could have shouted the servant's name out with joy, so overwhelming was her relief to see someone who could help. "Why are you still here?"

"As ye can prob'ly guess for yerself, mistress, Stenka is takin' his own sweet time comin' back for me." The Irish woman cocked a curious eye after the departing men. "What's 'at thievin' beastie, Ladislaus, doin' here, anyway? An' Prince Aleksei with him?"

"Ali, you must help me!" Synnovea had no time to answer the woman's questions. "Colonel Rycroft is in great danger."

"Well, I fig'ered as much meself, seein's as how he's bein' toted an' guarded by so many," the servant commented dryly. Ali peered around the bush, closely watching the four as they hauled their captive through the door of the stable. "But I haven't a ken what I can do ter save himself from all 'em foul brutes."

"You're my only hope, Ali, so listen carefully!" Synnovea directed. "You must leave here quickly and halt the carriage on the street before any of these men see you. Once you find Stenka, have him take you immediately to the tsar's palace and urge a guard to fetch Major Nekrasov for you. Tell the major that Ladislaus is here in the city and Colonel Rycroft is in imminent danger. It is imperative that a force of men come immediately to his rescue. Do you understand?"

"Aye, 'at I do, lamb," Ali whispered, "but I gotta go now! I hear Stenka comin'!" With a leaping skitter, she raced off down the street as the conveyance rumbled up the thoroughfare toward the manse.

Now with some small hope for Tyrone's rescue flourishing within her breast, Synnovea caught up her skirts and raced after the men who had crowded within the inner perimeters of the stable to watch as their justice upon the Englishman was administered. Tallow lanterns had been lit here and there to lend them light, and anxiously Synnovea slipped through a narrow breach in their broad-shouldered ranks until she reached the open space where Aleksei stood. Winning his haughty consideration, she suffered a moment of panic as she perceived his heightened exhilaration. Facing her, he smirked in obvious glee and raised a hand to beckon her forward.

"You're just in time, Synnovea." He casually indicated the long form that now hung from a rafter. "We were about to awaken your handsome lover with a cold bath. Would you care to admire him for one last moment ere he's forever scarred and impaired?"

The strength ebbed from Synnovea's limbs as her eyes found Tyrone. His head dangled limply between his naked, upstretched arms, while his ankles were spread and chained securely to a pair of weighty anvils positioned a short distance away on either side of him. He wore only the leggings that he had donned beneath his breeches, but now, with his body stretched upward, they drooped around his narrow hips, barely preserving his modesty.

Synnovea stifled an anguished moan as Ladislaus reached up a hand and seized a short thatch of pale-streaked hair, jerking his captive's head upright. With a snort of derision he let it fall again, and in the next instant a whole bucketful of water was flung full into Tyrone's face, bringing him around to a half-muddled state. His head lolled listlessly between his shoulders as the trickling water cascaded down his body, weighing down the leggings until they sagged limply against him. Once more the pail was filled from the watering trough and heaved into his face, this time startling Tyrone, who came fully awake with a gasp of surprise. Tiny droplets of water sprayed outward as he flung up his head and glared about him. His gaze softened briefly as it paused on Synnovea, but his eyes hardened just as quickly when he noted the dark bruise on her cheek and the split and swollen bottom lip.

Aleksei stepped forward almost jauntily and thrust a tallow lantern near the Englishman's face to see him better. "So, Colonel Rycroft, we meet at last."

"Forbear the introductions," Tyrone growled, and squinted against the light to fix the man with a piercing scowl. "I know who you are. You're the toad that tried to force the Countess Synnovea into serving your pleasure. It must gall you considerably to think that she prefers me over you."

Aleksei laughed harshly in loathing disdain. "About as much as it might provoke you to be told she only used you for her own devices. Only a few days ago my ward became formally betrothed to Prince Vladimir Dimitrievich. She swore to see herself degraded by the likes of you rather than submit to the marriage. So you see, my friend, you've been foolishly duped into believing she cared one whit about you. 'Twas but a mere ruse she invented to save herself from an arrangement of marriage she abhorred."

Tyrone shifted his gaze to Synnovea, feeling the pain of her treachery penetrating as deeply as a sharp steel-tipped spike. Though she stepped awkwardly forward and struggled in vain to speak the words that came to her lips, he knew of a sudden that everything that Aleksei had said was true. He had been used! Deceived! Played the fool! And now he would pay for it!

The blue eyes turned coldly from her and swept the leering faces of the men who closely watched him. He had heard their sniggering laughter as someone made the translation into Russian, and now glancing around, he recognized several from his first encounter with Ladislaus's pack. It was obvious to him that they were gloating over their good fortune to have seized him at last.

"So now you have me in your trap." He faced Aleksei with the declaration. "What do you plan to do with me?"

"Oh, I've reserved for you a special punishment, Colonel, one I'm sure you'll forever revile, but 'twill serve to remind you of your folly in sullying a Russian *boyarina*. Indeed, my friend, after tonight you'll never be able to make love to another woman as long as you live. After you're given a proper lashing, you'll be gelded while the girl is forced to watch."

Tyrone gnashed his teeth as he tried to whip his legs outward to catch the man within their vise. A warning shout came from one of Ladislaus's men, but the ponderous iron weights only moved a small degree and refused to be sufficiently propelled forward, even by Tyrone's enormous strength. Just the same, Aleksei stumbled back hastily to a safe distance and looked at the colonel with eyes that momentarily portrayed some evidence of his fear. When he regained his aplomb, Aleksei gave a crisp nod to the tall, brawny fellow who had stripped himself to his waist to bare a massive chest that was covered with a thick thatch of curling black hair. It was the Goliath who had once sent the colonel's helmet sailing off his head. Now it seemed he would have the personal pleasure of dealing out the punishment upon their adversary.

The Goliath hefted a many-tongued whip as he strode to a spot slightly behind and to the right of Tyrone. "Brace yurself, Englishman!" he rumbled deeply. "The weapons I wield are most often spikes and cutlasses, but I can assure yu, yu'll wish for a quick end ere I'm finished."

Aleksei smiled in eager anticipation. Bracing his feet apart, he folded his arms like some dark-skinned sultan as he awaited the first scourging stroke. The titan drew back his arm, shaking out the lash in preparation.

"NOOOooo! Oh, please! You mustn't!" Synnovea threw herself at Aleksei's feet and violently sobbed out a plea. "You have won, Aleksei! I yield to you! Please, I beg you! Don't do this thing! I'll give myself to you! Only, please don't hurt him!"

"Do you think I'd take his leavings?" Aleksei jeered as he glared down at her. "You were merely one of the colonel's fleeting fancies, my dear! Don't you know that? Bedding every wench who strikes his fancy is what a soldier does best when he's not chasing his foes. There's no accounting for how many others your precious colonel has had before he bedded you! But no! You had to give yourself to him! Well, I don't want you now! After this, as far as I'm concerned, you can serve Ladislaus's pleasure and belong to him. 'Twill be a fitting punishment for ignoring my warnings." Lifting his head, Aleksei looked inquiringly at the leader of the thieves. "What say you, Ladislaus? Will she be payment enough for you?"

Synnovea's head snapped around, and she stared in horror at the flaxen-haired hulk whose ice-blue eyes gleamed back at her above a broad grin.

"Oh, Great Exalted Prince," he casually mocked. "With the colonel rendered his just due, she will be more than payment enough for me. My men, however, will have to be paid out in gold, as you have promised."

Whirling back to face Aleksei, Synnovea glared at him. "You wouldn't dare attempt this outrage! The tsar . . . "

Aleksei intruded curtly. "The Countess Andreyevna was responsible for you during the absence of my wife. If she allowed you to wander off with the Englishman, and you and he were never seen again . . . then the fault for your disappearance will lie with Natasha. That's all the tsar will ever know about this matter."

Dismissing her, Aleksei inclined his head to the bare-chested brute. That one hauled back the whip, and an instant later it fell, bringing a pained grimace from Tyrone and a sobbing scream from Synnovea as she threw herself between him and the one who dealt out his punishment. Clasping her slender arms tightly about his lean waist, she settled herself to be his shield and glowered back at the men in defiance, but her protection was rejected by the one she sought to spare.

Tyrone's rage was supreme; he saw the taunting grins of his foes through a reddened haze of towering fury, but he had no need for them to vocally call him a fool for having played into the countess's hands. The throbbing pain at his back was not nearly as unbearable as the one that pulsed within his heart and brain. Gnashing his teeth in a savage snarl, he tossed her away with a sideways heave of his body.

"You conniving little bitch! Get away from me! Even if these louts mean to skin me alive, I'll take nothing from you, least of all your pity and shelter! As far as I'm concerned, Ladislaus can have you! With my most earnest blessings!"

Aleksei chortled in uproarious amusement as he contemplated the beautiful and completely astounded visage of the countess. " 'Twould seem that neither of us want you anymore, Synnovea. That must be a new revelation, to have not one but two men reject your attentions." He picked up the end of a barn rake and, holding it like a sword, nudged her farther away from the colonel, afraid of going near the man. "Now get back and let the fellow be dealt his due. Learn from his example and grit your teeth against the pain of our rejection. Be content that Ladislaus still wants you."

With an imperious nod, Aleksei bade the Goliath to continue, but retreated hastily to a safe distance again before the second stroke fell. Blinded by a deluge of tears, Synnovea stumbled away to a dark corner and cringed in silent, agonizing anguish each time the strips of leather repeated their venging descent. She heard no sound, no mumbled plea for mercy or pardon issue forth from Tyrone's lips though he hung helpless before the master whip, but every blow that was laid to the stalwart back ripped through her with equal savagery.

Covering her head with her arms as the scourging continued, Synnovea could not still her convulsive and violent shivering. Though she had lost count through her own unending torment, she was crushingly aware of the ominous repetition of the punishing whip. Each time the lash fell, she recoiled in horror, then shuddered in agonizing dread as the whip was dragged back for another blow. The strain seemed beyond her measure to endure, and her spirit whimpered beneath the cruel and terrible punishment exacted upon her.

Though Tyrone now sagged limply in his fetters and had no strength to raise his head, his valor and spirit had not yet been daunted. His display of unyielding tenacity captured the reluctant admiration of those who had sought to deliver their own form of justice upon his frame. Ladislaus and his followers were a band of outlaws who had lived and fought with the smell of death all around them for a good many years. They had taken the worst of what the colonel had given them. Some had died by his hand, but it had been an honorable fate, with weapon in hand. It was in their minds that this stalwart enemy deserved the same consideration. A flogging was what they reserved for whimpering, cowardly dogs, and as they all knew, Colonel Rycroft was a warrior of superior skill and courage. Thus, as a whole, the brigands ceased to enjoy the whipping. Instead, they began to mutter among themselves, growing increasingly more agitated as Aleksei pressed for at least a hundred or more lashes. Two score and ten marks crisscrossed Tyrone's back before the flogging finally ceased, but it was only because the Goliath who had laid them on threw down his whip in disgust and refused to pick it up again.

"Are you mad?" Aleksei railed in outraged astonishment. He was unique and suffered no similar convictions of honor and respect. He would insist that his revenge be sated to the utmost. "I give the orders here! And *I say* you must carry out the discipline as I see fit . . . or I swear, you will not be paid!"

"We've done your service!" Ladislaus roared as he strode forward to confront him. "You'll pay us or you'll die!"

Petrov smirked as he drew forth a gleaming blade and twirled the shining tip between his thumb and forefinger. "We take payment out your hide, maybe, just like you mean the Englishman to pay."

"I'll pay you after he's gelded and not one minute sooner!" Aleksei persisted, too incensed by their lack of commitment to consider the threats against him.

"Do it yourself then!" Ladislaus snarled in derision. "We'll not hurt him any more for the likes of you! As far as we're concerned, he's paid his due. We're fighting men and give him honor as a swordsman. If you had wanted us to duel with him, then we'd have seen him killed by our blades, but not your way." Contemptuously the brigand jerked his chin outward to indicate the bloodied, lacerated back. "Your way is the penalty for gutless cowards. Outnumbered by scores, the English colonel was taken and abused by your decree, but I tell you this, *boyar*, he's more of a man than you'll ever hope to be!"

It was the second time that evening Aleksei had heard the likes of that particular insult, which only infuriated him the more. His reddened lips drew back in a white-toothed snarl as he cursed them all for their refusal to help him, then whirling, he snatched up a sharp blade and plowed forward to seize the top of the leggings. Tyrone struggled to protect himself against the mutilation and struck out in defense of himself, but in his much weakened state, his efforts proved far too feeble.

It was Synnovea who threw herself against Aleksei with fierce determination. She was committed to stopping him from doing his evil, even if she had to accept the thrust of the blade at the sacrifice of her own life. Clawing his face and hands with her long nails, she savagely fought him, seeking to turn him aside. When he attempted to yank free of her, she sank her teeth into the hand that held the knife. A pained yowl was wrenched from Aleksei's throat, but she gave the scream no heed as she clenched her teeth tighter, drawing blood and forcing his grip to slacken until the blade finally plummeted from his grasp. Snatching free, Synnovea stooped to retrieve the weapon, but the dark eyes of her antagonist flared with a raging fury. With a curse he caught her by the wide-spreading cloak and whirled her around with all the strength at his command, in a raging temper flinging her deliberately into a sturdy post. Jolted nearly senseless by the sudden, painful impact, Synnovea staggered away in a stunned daze.

Dismissing her with a satisfied smirk, Aleksei caught up the knife again and plunged toward the object of his jealousy, but the stables rang with a loud bellow of rage as Ladislaus leapt to Tyrone's rescue and knocked the blade from the prince's hand, sending it skittering across the rough board planking of the floor.

"No more! I'll not let you do this thing! You've had your time of bloodletting! Now be content, or I'll see you unmanned myself!"

All reason was sundered beneath the unrestrained fury of Aleksei's indignation, and he gave no thought to backing down in the face of the other's challenge. "You filthy barbarian! How dare you threaten me! Why, I've had better men than you slashed and split in twain for daring to oppose me!"

"You frighten me unduly, my friend," Ladislaus taunted with a smirk and gestured casually over his shoulder as his men gathered close around them. "Perhaps you should consider the error of your ways. We've no liking for *boyars* of your ilk."

Suddenly the stable door burst open, and Ladislaus and his men jerked around in surprise as Major Nekrasov charged through, quickly followed by the first thrust of at least a dozen armed soldiers. Ladislaus immediately recognized the man who led them and the rather resplendent uniforms of the new arrivals and promptly decided the time was critical for him and his men to make a swift departure. It was one thing to accost a small detachment of soldiers in the wilds, but quite another matter entirely to set themselves against the tsar's imperial guards inside the limits of Moscow, where any number of troops could be waiting to pounce on him. He had no clear opportunity to seize the wench, for he knew from experience that taking her would involve him in another fray with the major, the likes of which, at the precise moment, he wished to avoid. With great leaping strides, he raced across the stables as he shouted warnings to his compatriots, sending them fleeing in every direction and through any available opening or door. Outside they fought their way to their mounts and, once astride, never looked back in their race to put the gates of the city well behind them.

Aleksei was not so astute. He stepped forward to protest this intrusion into his private affairs, then he stumbled back in stunned awe as he recognized the one who strode through the widening barrier of soldiers. Struck speechless, he fell to his knees before his sovereign lord.

"Your Majesty!" His voice squeaked as it reached a high octave. "What brings you here to my house at this late hour?"

"Mischief!" Tsar Mikhail thundered as his dark eyes ranged about the interior. He acknowledged Synnovea's quickly executed curtsy and briefly noted her bruised face and disheveled appearance before he stepped to the colonel. Tyrone had lost his tenuous grip on reality and dangled pendulously from the ropes that secured him to the rafters. He was completely oblivious to the tsar, who visibly winced as he considered the striped and bloody back.

"Cut Colonel Rycroft down from here at once!" Mikhail commanded, gesturing to Major Nekrasov, who ran forward with several other men to lift and loosen the Englishman from his bonds. "Take him to my carriage. He'll be tended by my own physicians tonight."

Nikolai glanced yearningly toward Synnovea as his men took up their burden, but she paid him no mind as she gathered the colonel's clothing within her arms and wept over the bundle a moment before handing it over to a guard.

"Please be careful with him," she pleaded through her tears as they carried Tyrone to the door.

Mikhail raised a brow as he contemplated her concern, then faced Aleksei with a sharp question. "Did you have some reason for whipping this man?"

"Your pardon, Your Most Sovereign Lord and Majesty," Aleksei mumbled as he bowed again contritely. He spoke discreetly so as not to win the disfavor of the tsar. "Colonel Rycroft was caught at his quarters with our ward, the Countess Zenkovna, and he did indeed defile her in his bed. We could hardly allow his affront to a Russian *boyarina* to go unpunished and were in the process of administering a just punishment."

"And so you consorted with thieves to see it done?"

"Thieves, Your Majesty? How so?" Aleksei seemed greatly perplexed.

"Did you not know whom you were dealing with?"

Aleksei sought to play the innocent. " 'Twas the first time I laid eyes on the men. They said they were for hire, and I engaged them to instruct the colonel on the folly of insulting a Russian maid."

Mikhail frowned as he turned to peer across the room at Synnovea, who had managed to regain some of her composure. "Do you have anything to say in this matter, Countess?"

"Your Majesty . . ." She spoke pleadingly from a distance, as if wary of tarnishing his presence with her guilt. "May I be allowed to come forward and speak in the colonel's defense?"

Mikhail beckoned her near. "Come, Synnovea. I'm interested in hearing what you have to say."

Going before him, she humbly knelt and refused to lift her eyes as she felt the shame and dreadful burden of what she had contrived to do and what she had actually brought about. "I beg your most humble pardon, Your Majesty. I am the one at fault for what has happened here. I could not find it within me to accept the circumstances of my betrothal to Prince Vladimir Dimitrievich and did intentionally entice Colonel Rycroft to take me into his bed. I preferred to forfeit my virtue rather than be bound to the contract of marriage that had been arranged for me. Do with me as you may, Your Majesty, for I am guilty of this havoc that has befallen the colonel."

"I'm sure Colonel Rycroft would have found it hard to resist you, considering your beauty and his great desire to court you, Synnovea." As he voiced his observations, Mikhail lifted his consideration to the prince. That one offered no explanation for the betrothal, though Mikhail was sure everyone within his court knew he had been seriously pondering the colonel's request to court the Countess Synnovea. Either his cousin and her husband had ignored that particular possibility or they had been totally deaf to the winds of gossip.

Mikhail looked down upon the bowed head of his subject and laid his hand gently upon the disarrayed curls. "I would talk more of this with you and the colonel, Synnovea. You may arrange a time to see me two days hence, but for now I would have you find safety beyond this house. Is there someone you can go to?"

"The Countess Andreyevna is a good friend of mine, Your Majesty. My coach should be waiting even now to take me back to her home."

"Good! Then go! And mind you, speak no word of this matter to anyone. I would not have any anger aroused against the colonel, nor would I see you harmed by wagging tongues. Do you understand?"

"Your kindness is beyond measure, Your Majesty."

When Synnovea had gone, Mikhail faced Aleksei again with a stiff smile. "Where is my cousin anyway? I would have a word with her."

"The Princess Anna is not here, Most Sovereign Lord. Her father was ailing and asked her to come and stay with him for a time."

"Should I believe this matter falls solely upon your shoulders?"

Aleksei gulped and tried to recoup his scattered wits as he carefully asked, "What matter do you mean, Your Worship?"

"Did you not make arrangements for the betrothal between the Countess Synnovea and Prince Vladimir Dimitrievich while you had full knowledge of the colonel's interest in courting her, or should the blame be solely laid to Anna?"

Aleksei spread his hands in a helpless quandary. "Of course we heard of the colonel's interest, but we were not aware that we had to give him heed. At the time, it seemed prudent to arrange a marriage between the girl and Prince Vladimir Dimitrievich, considering the old man's wealth and the fact that he would treat Synnovea kindly. At least Anna thought so."

"I see." Musefully Mikhail pursed his lips as he pondered the prince's answer. "And did Anna not hear of my considerations toward the colonel?"

"What considerations are those, Your Majesty?" The dark brows came together as Aleksei feigned bemusement. "Have we erred in some way and offended Our Supreme Highness?"

"It could be," Mikhail retorted sharply, growing angry. He sensed the other man was attempting to persuade him with a guise of complete innocence, which he was not necessarily disposed to believe. "Perhaps I might have erred in sending the Countess Synnovea here to be your ward. I should have taken into serious consideration the fact that the girl was raised without the usual strictures most *boyarinas* grow up with. In view of her upbringing, 'tis understandable that she might have rebelled against your authority when you arranged such a betrothal for her. Nevertheless, that matter is of no consequence now. You will discreetly inform Prince Dimitrievich that the Countess Synnovea is unable to marry him, since I have decreed otherwise. I must warn you if you spread one word of this beyond Vladimir, who hopefully is wise enough to keep silent, I will personally be in attendance when your tongue is detached from the place where it now resides. Have you any questions?"

"None, Your Most Gracious Worship. I will be completely reticent concerning this matter." Extremely anxious to placate the tsar, Aleksei bowed several times to lend emphasis to his ingratiating show of respect.

"Good! Then we understand each other."

"Most affirmatively, Your Majesty."

"Then I shall say goodnight and farewell, Prince Taraslov. I hope you will never be so foolish again to address your venom toward someone I have given favor to, nor hire thieves to see such mischief done. I have yet to judge you on the truth of this affair, but I'm patient enough to see justice carefully preserved until I am otherwise persuaded. For your sake, I hope you are innocent of deliberately consorting with thieves."

Chapter 18

SYNNOVEA ARRIVED EARLY AT THE PALACE OF FACETS to keep her appointment with His Majesty Mikhail, the Tsar of all the Russias. It was exactly two score hours after His Royal Highness had first bade her to come see him, and though her apprehensions had not been alleviated, she was waiting outside his private offices, seemingly composed and sweetly demure in a mauve *sarafan*. It was here in this alcove that she became a most compassionate witness to the carefully executed entrance of Colonel Rycroft. She was seated in a place where he could not miss noticing her, but with rigidly set jaw and stern features, Tyrone stubbornly refused to acknowledge her presence in the antechamber as Major Nekrasov escorted him to the room where the tsar awaited him.

In the solitude following Tyrone's passage, Synnovea found herself painfully haunted once again by the memory of the angry sneer she had detected in his voice shortly after the first stroke of the whip had fallen. He had thrust her from him in distaste and given Ladislaus leave to take her, strengthening Natasha's warnings that he would come to hate her for her planned entrapment. At the time the elder had spoken those words, his feelings for her hadn't really seemed to matter that much, yet the knowledge of Tyrone's rejection now filled her with a gloomy regret that she could find no relief from. Though her disquieted mind formed a volume of excuses to convince him with, she realized that even if the explanations had been worthy of offering, her efforts to placate him would be for naught. It was apparent that Colonel Rycroft was unwilling to even recognize her existence and would refuse to hear her pleas. Indeed, so bleak were her hopes to reconcile herself to him that it would not have surprised her at all to hear the objections he presently presented to the tsar's suggestions.

"I plead your pardon, Your Majesty." Tyrone tried to maintain control over his darkly brooding disposition, but it was difficult to even think of contemplating the tsar's proposals. "I must respectfully decline. I could never take the Countess Zenkovna to wife now, knowing how she used me for her own end. If in months and years to come my life's blood is required on the field of battle, then I hope that it will be spilled honorably as a soldier in your service, but your recommendation is too much to ask of me."

"I fear you have mistaken my words, Colonel Rycroft." Mikhail smiled benignly. "I do not request your compliance with my proposition. While you are here in this country, you will obey my every directive, and it is my pleasure that you take the Countess Zenkovna to wife with all possible haste. I promised her father before his death I would give my attention to the welfare of his daughter, and I would be lax in the performance of that pledge if I allowed you to escape your personal involvement in this affair without seeking some retribution."

"Was not the scarring of my back enough payment for my involvement?" Tyrone asked bluntly.

"The whipping was indeed dreadful, but it hardly corrects the problem. The Countess Zenkovna has confessed her guilt in deliberately enticing you and in seeking you out to be her champion of sorts. . . . " He glanced up briefly as a faintly audible snort came from the colonel. After musing on the man's disdaining visage, he continued with even more determination. "Nevertheless, you were the one who accomplished the deed and are the only one who can properly amend the situation. After all, you're no young whelp who can plead foul play. You're old enough to accept the consequences of your actions and, may I presume, far more knowledgeable about this matter than the maid? 'Tis obvious to me that she had good reason to believe you were willing to have her, or she would never have considered her defilement by you as a viable option."

"Your Majesty, will you not kindly ponder my position?"

Mikhail was losing patience with the persistence of the man and demanded, "Was she not a virgin in your bed ere you took her?"

Tyrone's lean cheeks flexed with the tension of keeping his own temper from exploding. "She was a virgin, but—"

"Then there is no more to be said! I would not have another man mend your wrongs because you were duped by a young chit! Would you roar deception on a field of battle if you were tricked by a general still wet behind the ears?"

"No, of course not, but—"

Mikhail slammed his open hand down flat upon the arm of his chair. "You will either marry the Countess Zenkovna, or by heavens, I will see you discharged without honor from your service here."

In the face of such a threat, Tyrone could only concede to the man's authority. He abruptly clicked his heels as he gave the tsar a crisp salute to signify his acceptance of the other's command. "As you so deign, Your Majesty."

Mikhail reached up and jerked on a silken cord, bringing Major Nekrasov back into the chamber. "You may escort the Countess Zenkovna into my presence now."

Tyrone dared to interrupt, halting the major with his plea. "I beg a moment more of your time, Your Majesty."

"Yes? What is it?" Mikhail was immediately skeptical of what the colonel would request.

"I will abide by your order as long as I am here, but once I leave, I will no longer be under your authority." Tyrone paused as the tsar inclined his head in cautious agreement with his statement, then he continued in a respectful tone. "If you find at that time that I have pleased you in the performance of my duties and have held myself from the Countess Zenkovna, which may be certified by her inability to produce an heir of mine, will you then grant me an annulment of this marriage ere I return to England?"

Major Nekrasov's head snapped around, and he glanced between the two men, feeling horrendously distraught by the prospect of Synnovea's marriage to the colonel. He could not even begin to understand the man's request, for he would have gladly endangered his own life in his quest to have the countess as his wife.

Mikhail was abruptly taken aback by the petition, but he could find no excuse to deny it. After all, if the dissolution was not granted here within the boundaries of Russia, the colonel would probably seek it in England, and Mikhail was not willing to subject the countess to that particular humiliation. "If all will be as you say, Colonel, and you still wish such a separation near the time of your departure, then you may have your petition granted, but I must remind you that you still have three years here to serve."

"Three years, three months, and two days, sire."

" 'Tis a long time to withhold yourself from so enchanting a woman, Colonel. Can you even consider being successful in that endeavor?"

Tyrone faced the question frankly in his own mind. He had no real or firm assurance that he would be capable of ignoring Synnovea as his wife or that he could curb his desires to such an extent, but he wanted to leave himself an opening wherein he could dissolve the marriage should he find no further reason to continue with her. At the present moment, he was hell-bent to go his own way without her because of her deception, but there was always the possibility that in the future his mood would soften to the idea. He could not foresee such an event happening within the next several days, certainly not with the anger roiling inside of him now, but in the coming months and years, who could say where his passion would lead him? As the tsar had unerringly pointed out, Synnovea was as enchanting as she was beautiful, and when it had obviously been his foolish desire to trust her, he could not guarantee that he would never fall victim to her siren's song again. Then again, his heart might never be completely healed of its wounds. "My failure or success will be revealed prior to the time of my departure, Your Majesty. You may take full account of the condition of our marriage then."

"I will hope that by that time your heart will be softened by forgiveness, Colonel." Mikhail sighed. "So beautiful a woman to ignore. I once considered taking her for a bride myself, but I didn't think she would be able to stand the stricture of the *terem*. I would be appalled to see her hurt by your rejection of her."

"You may save her the pain in years to come by allowing us to go our separate ways now," Tyrone suggested, peering at the tsar from under his brows.

"Never!" Mikhail flung himself from his chair in a fitful rage. "By heavens, you will not maneuver your way out of this marriage! Indeed, I will see you wed before the week is fully out!"

Tyrone was wise enough to realize when he had been defeated and when immediate obeisance was prudent. Placing his hand to his chest, he bowed stiffly before the Russian tsar, though the agony of his movement nearly splintered his control. "As you deem fit, sire."

Mikhail gave a crisp nod to Major Nekrasov, who turned abruptly to carry out his order. As he entered the antechamber, Nikolai managed a wan smile as he approached the woman he both admired and cherished.

"Tsar Mikhail would like you to come in now, Synnovea."

A hesitant smile touched her lips as she rose to her feet. "I thought I heard shouts. Is His Majesty very angry?"

"Surely not with you, dearest Synnovea," Nikolai assured her.

"Did he say why he wanted me to come?" she asked uneasily.

"I was not permitted to stay in the room while he spoke with Colonel Rycroft. You'll have to ask him that yourself."

"I never thought I would anger so many people by what I did. . . . " Her words trailed off as she realized that Nikolai was regarding her quizzically.

"And what may that have been, Synnovea?"

She lowered her eyes hurriedly to avoid meeting his gaze any longer than she had to. " 'Twas nothing I am proud of, Nikolai, and I would rather not speak of the matter if I can help it." Then she suddenly recalled that she had not thanked him for what he had accomplished in coming to the colonel's rescue. Lifting her head, she laid a trembling hand upon his. "I shall be eternally grateful to you for helping us, Nikolai. I never dreamt you would be bringing His Majesty with you. However did you manage to accomplish such a feat?"

"I did nothing more than tell him that Colonel Rycroft was in danger, then His Majesty could not be stopped. 'Twould seem the Englishman had already won the tsar's favor and respect by his own merits, Synnovea. Quite clearly, that truth is worthy of great importance, for 'twas that fact alone which prompted His Royal Highness to fly to the Englishman's side and which no doubt saved his life." Nikolai glanced toward the chamber where the tsar held unofficial court and hastened to announce, "I must take you in now, Synnovea. Tsar Mikhail is waiting for you."

Synnovea drew a deep breath in an effort to settle her restive nerves. Giving Nikolai a nod, she allowed him to escort her in. As she entered on his arm, her gaze flitted quickly about the large room and immediately found Tyrone standing ramrod straight, slightly to the left of the tsar's chair. He made no attempt to glance around in her direction but rigidly held his stance as Mikhail beckoned her forward. She obeyed and sank into a deep curtsy before the monarch, then waited in trembling silence as Major Nekrasov took his leave through a nearby door.

"Synnovea, I have made several decisions concerning your future this afternoon," Mikhail announced. "I hope you will not find them too burdensome."

"Your will is my command, Your Majesty," she answered quietly, though she noted her voice declined in strength as she spoke. She had no idea what lay in store for her, but she was resolved to find no fault with what was commanded her.

"I have decreed that you and the colonel will marry. . . ."

Astounded by his revelation, Synnovea jerked her head up and looked around to see Tyrone's response. Though he still refused to meet her inquiring gaze, the muscles in his sun-darkened cheeks tensed and flexed as he sought to check his vexation.

"Before the week is out," Mikhail continued, giving her hardly enough time to catch her breath. "You will be married in my presence day after the morrow. That should give you enough time to decide several matters between the two of you. 'Tis unthinkable that a Russian *boyarina* should live within the German district. Therefore, Synnovea, you may ask the Countess Andreyevna if she can accommodate your presence as a personal favor to me, and knowing that she will, I'll consider the matter already settled. Once the ceremony has been completed, the two of you may celebrate as you see fit. I'm sure Natasha would enjoy making much of the occasion, and though the colonel is somewhat indisposed yet with his back, I would urge you both to participate in such a way as to make it seem a festive occasion. It is not oft that the Tsar of all the Russias personally initiates the union of two of his favored subjects. You may consider my attention in this affair as a personal compliment to you both. Now, are there any other concerns you wish discussed?" He waited as each made comment in the negative, then smiled as he bade them. "Then you may go."

Together they paid homage, Synnovea with a sweeping curtsy and Tyrone with a painfully accomplished bow. When he straightened and turned crisply on a heel to make his exit from the room, Mikhail halted him promptly.

"Colonel Rycroft, I would hope you will consider how fortunate you are to be gaining such a beautiful bride and treat her accordingly. Is it not proper for a gentleman of your country to graciously escort his intended upon his arm and make a show of cherishing her, especially while there is an audience in attendance? If there is no such requirement in your country, then I shall deem that here in this land, the circumstances warrant such care. Do I make myself clear, Colonel?"

"Absolutely, Your Majesty," Tyrone replied succinctly and, stepping beside Synnovea, stiffly presented his arm as he faced the door. She was aware of his roiling displeasure in having to offer any chivalrous gesture to her, but she had also been mindful of his gaze briefly sweeping her from head to foot before he faced the portal. She had already stored in her memory an image of his appearance and had no need to return the perusal to see how aloofly proud and handsome he looked. Indeed, he was much too pleasing in face and form to allow her racing pulses to slow to a normal pace. She was surprised by the fact that her hand trembled as she laid it lightly upon his sleeve and was just as amazed to realize how deeply she was affected by his proximity. She had been distantly detached and nonchalant before the evening of her gambit, but now, much to her surprise, her insides were aflutter with emotions too ambiguous to clearly evaluate. The question that plagued her dealt with the recent change that had taken place within herself. How could she, the haughty Synnovea, have grown infatuated with a man in so short a time?

"Is your coach outside?" Tyrone inquired as they entered the antechamber.

"Yes," she answered timidly, aware of his displeasure in having to accompany her even for these few brief moments. "But you needn't escort me out if you find the task too burdensome."

"I've been ordered by His Majesty to show you favor," he replied curtly, "at least while we have an audience. Until we find ourselves alone, I will try to comply with the directive given me."

As the Field Marshall came strolling through the front portals, Tyrone came to an abrupt halt and greeted the man with a crisp salute, but after the man passed on by, Synnovea looked up at Tyrone in sudden concern, taking note of the ashen hue that had invaded his face and the muscles that had tightened to a taut rigidity in his lean cheeks. He seemed to endure a moment of sharp discomfort, then with a careful twitch of his shoulders he finally reclaimed control of his bearing. Stoically he continued his advancing stride until they had put the interior of the edifice behind them, albeit at a more deliberate pace.

Managing the steps with only a wince or two, Tyrone handed her into the waiting carriage and, closing the door, stepped back with an abbreviated salute to Stenka. As the conveyance pulled away from the palace, Synnovea leaned back against the seat, biting a quavering lip and squeezing her eyelids tightly shut against the tears that welled up within her soul. Despite her effort to stem the flow, they fell in widening channels from her dark lashes. One could say she had made her bed and now would lie in it, but it gave her no pleasure to think there was so much resentment bound up within the man who would soon become her husband.

When the carriage arrived at the Andreyevna mansion a short time later, Natasha was at the front portal, anxiously awaiting her return, but now with an unchecked torrent of tears cascading down her cheeks, Synnovea choked out a lame excuse and rushed past her. She fled to her chambers, where she found herself confronted by Ali and a barrage of dismayed questions.

"Oh, me lamb! Me lamb! What has broken yer heart so?"

Mumbling a plea for the maid to leave her, Synnovea fell facedown across the canopied bed and sobbed in bleak misery until she felt totally drained of emotion. The once delicate eyelids grew swollen and seemed to scratch her eyes as she tried to contemplate sleep as a respite for her anguish, but such relief failed to come and give her ease. Thus for a time she stared listlessly across the room, taking distant note of the brightly colored leaves fluttering to earth beyond the panes of glass. Some time later a light rap came upon the door, and in mute dejection Synnovea rose and let Natasha into the room.

"I could not wait a moment longer." The woman made the excuse for the interruption as she searched the reddened eyes with grave concern. "Dear child, what evil has happened to bring you to this end? Have you been banished from the Court?" A lame shake of the beautiful dark head gave tacit answer. "Denounced by the tsar?" A disquieted, slashing gesture of a slender hand was the negative response. "Sentenced to a nunnery?"

"Not anything so trivial," Synnovea whispered miserably.

Natasha lost her aplomb and, catching the girl by the shoulders, shook her as she demanded in desperation, "Good heavens, child! What has His Majesty decreed your sentence to be?"

Synnovea gulped back another gush of tears and carefully pronounced each word as she gathered them together in a strained reply. "His Majesty, Tsar Mikhail, has ordained that Colonel Rycroft should marry me ere the week is out."

"What?" Natasha almost shrieked the word out in jubilation. "Oh, great sainted mother! How could he have been so clever?"

Synnovea frowned glumly at her friend. "You don't understand, Natasha. Colonel Rycroft hates me, just as you warned me he would. He wants nothing to do with me, and he is especially loath to take me to wife."

"Oh, my dear child, lay aside your grief and dismay," the older woman cajoled. "Don't you see the way of it? The colonel's anger will surely soften in time. A man can hardly ignore a woman who is his wife."

"He detests me! He loathes me! He did not even want to escort me from the palace!"

"Nevertheless, he will change," Natasha reassured her. "What are the arrangements to be?"

"His Majesty asked if you would take the two of us in. . . ."

Natasha chortled as she stroked a finger thoughtfully across her chin. "Never let it be said that Tsar Mikhail is not shrewd and wise enough to handle Russia's affairs on his own. Why, just by this mandate he has shown his ability to manage matters wisely." She smiled into Synnovea's teary eyes and tried to encourage her. "For a time your rage and aversion to each other will punish you both, Synnovea, but when your anger is spent . . ." She lifted her shoulders in a lighthearted shrug. "Only God knows the end of all things. We can only wait and see, hoping for the best."

Natasha went to open the door and smiled down at Ali, who stood just outside, fretting anxiously. The elder's sad eyes and deeply wrinkled countenance clearly denoted the great distress she was suffering. Taking the frail hand into hers, Natasha drew the servant in.

"You'll never guess, Ali," she said through a bright smile. "Colonel Rycroft has been commanded by the tsar to take your mistress to wife."

The wispy brows jutted upward in surprise. "Ye don't say!"

"Ah, but I do," Natasha assured her. "In fact, they're to be wed ere the week is out, which undoubtedly must mean day after the morrow."

"So soon?" Ali squinted up at her in surprise. "Are ye sure?"

"Your mistress has said it herself."

"Then why is she so put out?" Ali asked warily. She was genuinely perplexed, for she was unable to understand why any woman would grieve over the idea of being wed to such a fine specimen.

"A mystery, to be sure, but her lamentations are bound to turn to joy, do you not agree, Ali?" She paused briefly to receive the tiny woman's eager nod. "Aye, Ali! 'Twill only be a matter of time. But we must plan a feast for them! A celebration to mark the event! We must bid the colonel to encourage his friends to come, while we invite our own." Natasha laughed with the sheer excitement of it. "I'd almost be tempted to invite Aleksei just for the pleasure of seeing him suffer, but I fear his presence would only provoke the colonel, and we cannot have that. Of course, Princess Anna will be shocked when she returns to find the couple already wed. When last I saw her, she was absolutely in a snit over the colonel petitioning the tsar for Synnovea's hand." Natasha leaned near the Irish maid as she continued to voice an avalanche of conjectures. "If you ask me, Ali, I'd say the Princess Anna was just jealous because of the attention the colonel bestowed upon your mistress. After all, our fair-haired princess isn't getting any younger, and she's not the beauty she used to be. Instead of making the most of her advancing age, she's probably more inclined to dream of her vanquished youth." Natasha threw back her dark head and laughed with amusement. "I hope she is utterly devastated when she hears about Synnovea's marriage. 'Twill clearly be what she deserves after denying the colonel the right to see your mistress.

Indeed! They might have been married sooner, if not for that witch."

"Go away, the two of you!" Synnovea moaned in wretched misery. "You're making light of all of this, while you obviously feel no concern for me. I tell you I'm suffering such grievous woes, I fear I'll not sleep for a year!"

"Then we'll leave you to mourn in solitude," Natasha replied without sympathy. "Ali and I will happily do the planning since you find yourself completely indisposed." She made her way toward the portal and paused there to glance back at the younger woman. "Where are the vows to be spoken anyway? Did you think about that?"

"His Majesty made the decision for us. They're to be said in his presence at the palace."

"Then we'll have to find you a rich gown to wear. You must look your very best for both the tsar and the colonel."

"I don't think either of them will care what I look like," Synnovea retorted gloomily.

"Nevertheless, you must be outfitted in a grand manner if you're to bestir some warm response from the colonel."

Ali was quick to report. "Me mistress had already settled on a *sarafan* for her wedding to Prince Dimitrievich. 'Tis 'bout as pretty as anything you'd ever be able ter make or find in so short a time. I think 'twill do her justice, a pink one nearly as comely as she."

"The day will be fair," Natasha proclaimed, "and the bride shall be absolutely breathtaking . . . "

"Absolutely breathtaking!" Major Nekrasov whispered to himself a pair of days later as he witnessed the entrance of the Countess Synnovea into the palace. She was garbed in a pale pink satin *sarafan*, the wide sleeves and lower skirt of which were liberally embellished with delicate gold stitchery and masses of large pinkish pearls. More pearls of varying sizes were spaciously interspersed over the rest of the costume and encrusted an elaborate *kokoshniki* which had been placed upon her dark head. A delicate fringe of stringed pearls, nearly as tiny as small seeds, hung down from the head-piece and formed a covering for her brow, accentuating the stirring beauty of her face. Truly, she looked so regal and yet so winsomely fragile, Nikolai was sure his heart would break at his loss.

Tyrone was speaking with Grigori and had his back to the door when Synnovea came in, but when Natasha moved from her side and hurried across the room to speak with Nikolai, the colonel turned his head slightly to surreptitiously observe his intended. None but Grigori and Nikolai were aware of his careful inspection, but it was apparent to each that his perusal was far more exacting than his mood of angry reticence appeared to support.

Synnovea finished straightening her gown and glanced around, but when her eyes paused on the one who stared and the blue orbs moved slowly upward along her lithe form to finally meet hers, Tyrone turned away with only a brief nod of his head, as if to deny his close perusal. His coldly forbidding detachment drained the warmth from Synnovea's heart, and as she searched his aloofly handsome profile, she could find no reason to hope that his anger had abated.

A directive soon came to them from the chapel where Mikhail was waiting with a priest, and Synnovea's heart lurched within her breast as Tyrone came to reservedly present his arm to her in immediate compliance with the summons borne by a servant. Laying a trembling hand lightly upon the sleeve of his dark blue doublet, she gathered her aplomb and moved beside him as the others fell in behind them.

Synnovea felt strangely detached from the ceremony, as if she wandered aimlessly through a shadowy gloom somewhere beyond the room wherein they had been led. All she was aware of was Tyrone sometimes standing or at other times kneeling beside her, of his brown hand taking her pale, thin fingers in his grasp to slide a large signet ring upon her first finger, and of his lips lowering dutifully upon her own to seal the bonds. Feeling rather overwhelmed by his tall, manly presence and then by his abrupt departure, Synnovea closed her mouth, realizing it had opened quiveringly beneath his. Her cheeks flamed at what seemed to be a blunt rejection of her response, and as he stepped away, she kept her eyes lowered, afraid she would see some mockery or repugnance evident within his gaze.

It seemed only a few brief moments after the vows were exchanged that they were receiving the good wishes of the tsar and being escorted to her carriage. They rode in taciturn silence to the Andreyevna estate, which seemed to drag out interminably since Natasha had taken the initiative to advise Stenka to take the long way back so the guests could arrive before the bride and her groom. Tyrone sat on the far side of the seat from her, as if she were something tainted he wished to avoid contact with. A tentative glance in his direction convinced Synnovea that his handsome features had not softened. His lean jaw still flexed with angry tension, and the blue eyes were partially masked by lowered lids as he braced his chin on a knuckle and glowered out the window.

Carriages were still being unloaded before the house when Stenka pulled the team to a halt at the approach to the drive and there awaited a chance to deliver his mistress and her new husband directly before the front stoop. The weather had turned crisp after a hard rain the night before, and not enough time had elapsed to allow the mud to completely dry to a solid footing under the wheels of the coach. The rear two became so firmly mired in the stiff sludge they could not be pulled free by the team, much to the consternation of Stenka and Jozef.

Leaning his head out the window, Tyrone apprised himself of the situation, but he was hardly in the mood to wait until another pair of horses were brought around to lend their strength to the four. Stepping down, he crisply gestured for Synnovea to slide forward to the door and, when she cautiously complied, took her up in his arms. Considering his apparent aversion to her, Synnovea was painfully flustered by his assistance and could not determine whether to wrap her arms around his neck or to settle a hand warily on his chest or his shoulder. When a moment later she felt his booted feet slip in the sludge, she gasped in sudden alarm, afraid that she would be dropped in the muck, and flung both arms tightly about his neck.

Natasha was at the front portal when they arrived, and while she escorted Synnovea to their guests, Tyrone doffed his muddy boots and made his way in stocking feet to the kitchen, where a manservant promptly took the boots away to have them cleaned. While Tyrone waited for the man's return, a young girl of an age about three years peeked at him from behind her mother's apron, gaining his attention. Tyrone could not accurately decipher the reason, but when he looked at her, he caught a glimpse of something within her manner or appearance that immediately reminded him of his young bride. Though he might have laid the cause to the wide, beautiful green eyes and softly curling dark hair, he was more of a mind to wonder if the association stemmed from the apprehension and faltering timidity which was so apparent in her small face and which he had recently perceived in his wife's manner and visage. In recent days he had seen little evidence of that haughty maid he had once met in the bathhouse and could well imagine that Synnovea was as much afraid of him as this tiny elfin creature who shied away from him now.

Giving the girl a grin, Tyrone knelt down on one knee beside several wooden blocks that were scattered over a small area on the floor and began to build a structure. The child watched him in growing fascination. Degree by small, cautious degree she approached to admire his handiwork and giggled in sudden glee when a difficult addition to the edifice caused his creation to tumble into a disorganized heap. Danika observed the making of their friendship with a warm smile even though she found it impossible to understand the man as he spoke with her daughter.

Synnovea came to fetch Tyrone for the wedding guests who awaited his presence, and having been told of his whereabouts, hesitated just outside the open doorway as she tried to gather her nerve before interrupting the pair. He laughed and chatted with the young child, but the girl could only shrug her shoulders in confusion, unable to catch the drift of his sentences. Still, the slowly blossoming smile that touched the tiny lips evidenced the compelling allurement and effectiveness of his charm. Synnovea found her own heart strangely warmed by his gentle manner with the girl, and a soft, poignant smile curved her own lips as she remembered his careful nurturing of her person even while he had been in the heat of passion. Were it not for his animosity toward her now, she might have been pleased to have such a man as her husband. Even as he was, with his mood dark and foreboding, he was decidedly more satisfying to her senses than Prince Vladimir could ever have been.

Finally the manservant brought Tyrone's boots back and presented them clean and neatly polished. After slipping them on, Tyrone rose and took the girl's small hand into his. "I must leave you," he informed her, "but now that I'll be staying here, I'd like to come here in the kitchen again and visit with you now and then. Will that be all right with you?"

The child looked at him, bewildered by his apparent question, then as Synnovea entered the kitchen, her face brightened and she ran quickly and took the countess's hand, having become immensely fond of the woman in the short space of time they had lived together in the same house. Tyrone straightened to his full, stoic height and reticently observed his bride as she spoke to the girl in Russian. The child's face grew radiant, and turning to the colonel, she dipped into a deep curtsy and eagerly babbled an answer.

Synnovea translated, finally lifting her gaze to his. "Sofia says she would be delighted if you would come and visit with her as often as you would like."

Tyrone noticed his bride's heightened blush as he continued to stare at her. It became apparent to him as she hurriedly dropped her gaze that she misread his close attention as some fierce displeasure over her presence and interference. He did not feel generously inclined to explain that, despite his anger and hostility toward her, he could hardly disregard her beauty and her beguiling manner.

"I didn't mean to intrude," Synnovea apologized shyly, laying a gentle hand upon the girl's head as the child lightly fingered the pearls that adorned the *sarafan*. "I just thought you might have wanted your words translated, that's all."

"You'll have to teach me the language now that we'll be living under the same roof," Tyrone said with cool reserve. "We'll have to pass the time together somehow."

Synnovea's head snapped up at his quip, but she had no time to analyze his meaning before she caught the sound of hurrying footsteps. A brief moment later Natasha burst into the kitchen.

"Synnovea!" the woman gasped breathlessly. She clutched a hand to her heaving bosom as she tried to compose herself enough to speak. "Prince Vladimir and his sons are here! They've come to look Colonel Rycroft over as your new husband, and from the mood they're in, he'll likely be needing reinforcements."

Tyrone mockingly questioned his young wife. "Your rejected betrothed, I presume?"

"What are we to do?" The question was no more than a frantic whisper as Synnovea fretted over what conflict might arise. She could not bear another attack on Tyrone.

"Calm yourself, madam," her new husband advised. " 'Tis not the first time I've met one of your suitors. I just hope this particular prince doesn't prove as irascible as the last."

"You'd best be careful," Natasha warned him. "Prince Vladimir's sons have a strong penchant for brawling, and they like nothing better than settling arguments with their fists. In other words, Colonel, they might make Aleksei seem like a saint in comparison."

"Then the next moments may very well see the end of our celebration," Tyrone remarked ruefully. Raising a brow as he bent his gaze upon Synnovea, he offered his hand. "Shall we face them together, my dear? After all, 'tis not everyday a rejected swain meets the husband of his promised betrothed."

Synnovea felt the sting of his sarcasm and responded in stilted reproof. "You have no ken what this brood is capable of doing when riled. Besides, you're in no fit condition to make light of the matter."

"Perhaps not, my dear, but the introductions should prove interesting."

"If you survive them!" Synnovea rejoined and finally deigned to give her hand over into his as they stepped into the hall.

Tyrone responded with a brief twitch of a sardonic grin. "I suppose I should brace myself to face not only these but a whole legion of discarded suitors you've left in your wake. It just might prove more challenging than fighting all the enemies of the tsar. Had I been more astute, I might have taken a warning from our very first encounter when I sought to save you from Ladislaus."

Synnovea dared to voice what his statement seemed to insinuate. "Perhaps you might have even reconsidered my rescue had you known what would happen in the future."

"Mayhap," Tyrone replied, feeling in no mood to reassure her otherwise. Still, when Synnovea tried in sudden vexation to withdraw her hand, he held the slender fingers firmly within his grasp. "Tut, tut, my dear. We must obey His Majesty and keep up appearances for our guests."

At his chiding Synnovea bestowed a heated glower on him. Despite her struggle to draw her hand away, she could not win her freedom without creating a scene, which she was certain he would be wont to do if she vexed him unduly. Thus, in an overtly chivalrous manner, Tyrone escorted her into the great hall as any cherished bride of yore might have been.

"Gentlemen and ladies, my bride and I welcome you to this fine house," he announced, pausing just inside the crowded room. At the applause and burbling compliments of their guests, the couple managed to convey their appreciation with a stiff bow and a graceful curtsy.

Prince Vladimir was not so gracious. He was feeling as ill-tempered and surly as an old, wounded bear. He had swung around with a loud snort of derision when his eldest son had nudged him and warned him that Synnovea and her groom were approaching the room. Now as the couple passed through their guests, his faded blue eyes fixed piercingly on the tall man at her side, while his offsprings gathered close around the pair, as if to flaunt their willingness to fight to the last man.

Now clasping Tyrone's arm closely against her, Synnovea glanced about in growing trepidation, wondering what would come of it all. It greatly disturbed her to think that her husband would again be called upon to pay the penalty for her outrageous scheme.

A short distance behind the bellicose clan, Grigori and several English officers lowered their goblets and cautiously observed the proceedings, for it seemed the princes' most fervent intent to entrap the groom in a brawl. Considering the colonel's avid quest to have the girl, they had not been surprised when they had heard he had gotten into a fray with her guardian, who had hired men to punish him for his audacity, nor were they astonished by the repercussions they were now witnessing, no doubt caused by the tsar's quickly executed directive that the couple should marry posthaste to negate further intervention. It was no secret that trouble usually followed one who coveted a forbidden treasure.

"So! You're the rascally devil who stole the maid from me," Vladimir rumbled. "What are you Englishmen anyway? Savages that you must steal our brides from beneath our noses and make off with them to do your evil, lecherous deeds? You intruding rake, you should be horsewhipped!"

The threat seemed imminent as his sons muttered pugnaciously and pressed forward. Tyrone cocked a challenging brow at the white-haired *boyar* as the elder's hand settled on the hilt of his sword. The intimidation was too obvious to ignore.

Synnovea started to step forward to make her plea, in hopes of placating her former betrothed, but she was halted from accomplishing her objective when Tyrone caught her arm and pulled her behind him. He was no more inclined now to hide behind a woman's skirts than he had been when he had hung from the wooden beams in the Taraslov stable.

"Stay out of this, Synnovea," he ordered. "I am quite capable of handling this matter on my own."

"But Prince Vladimir might listen to me," Synnovea whispered imploringly, glancing over Tyrone's shoulder at the towering ancient. Daring much, she reached up a trembling hand to lay it against her husband's chest. "Please let me try."

Prince Vladimir loudly harrumphed at her marked concern for the foreigner and, taking a step forward, caught hold of the colonel's sleeve to pull him around. "Would you take counsel from a woman?!"

"Aye! If there is wisdom in it!" Tyrone retorted, jerking free of the man's grasp. "No man instructs me as to whom I shall pay heed!"

An angry growl began down deep in the old man's chest and came forth as a contemptuous snarl. "The tsar may have asked you to come here and give our armies instructions, but you'll find most *boyars* are offended by the presence of foreigners here in this country. You not only intrude into our ways of doing warfare, English knave, but you tamper with our women, as well!"

"Who bleats about intrusion?!" Tyrone questioned sharply. "I knew the girl before you did and did beg His Majesty to give me leave to court her. You came after and did connive with Prince Taraslov ere you considered the tsar's behest. Would you argue with a royal decree when the vows were spoken in Tsar Mikhail's presence?"

A low snarl tore free of Vladimir's throat as his temper flared. "I served the gentleman's due and followed the formal rite of behavior in seeking the Countess Synnovea out as my betrothed. Where were you when the contracts were being signed and sealed?"

Tyrone sneered at the ancient's feeble declaration. "I was forbidden to enter the Taraslov house or to see the maid by those same devious folk who sealed the documents with you. By deed and favor, I had more claim to her than you or those other sniveling cowards did. Were it not for me, she would never have reached Moscow, but would have appeased the lusting appetites of some bastard thief who seized her for his own!"

"You think because you saved her once from a band of thieves that you own her now?" Vladimir bellowed incredulously.

"Nay!" Tyrone flung back. "She is mine because we did speak the vows together, as witnessed by the tsar! So I pray you vex me no longer with your trifling arguments, for I am not gently disposed to any who would seek to take her from me." He moved back a step, cautiously scrutinizing the sons who moved aggressively closer. Retreating another step to insure that none would be at his back, he glanced briefly toward his young bride and received from her an expression of teary gratitude, apparently for his outspoken claim to her. It totally astounded him that she had failed to gain any insight into his character. What did she think he would do? Discard her as some foul vermin to the swine?

"The tsar's commands take precedence over everything else, do they not, my lady?" he softly mocked, then instantly lamented the gibe when he saw evidence of the hurt and bewilderment he had inflicted. There was an obscure part of his character that made him want to reassure her, but quite another side of him that craved reparation for having been carelessly used. His pride held him back from showing her compassion, while his sense of honor refused to wound her further in front of one who had dared challenge his claim to her. It was truly a war of emotions that held him prisoner, and he had no idea which would succumb before the other.

Tyrone faced Vladimir and his sons again, and for their benefit, he sought to play the cordial host and managed a casual shrug without being unfavorably reminded of the discomfort he still suffered from in his back. "If you and your sons would stay and join us in the feasting, good fellows, then you are welcome to enjoy the festivities. Willy-nilly, go or stay, you are invited to do as you wish."

"So good of you, English colonel!" Sergei derided in disdain and clapped Tyrone on the back, making him suck in his breath sharply. At very close range, Synnovea saw her husband's wide shoulders tense with the agony of the other's touch, and she winced in sympathy for him, wanting to help him in some way, but she knew Tyrone was not one to stand and accept a woman's mewling attentions when he was faced with opponents of an angry bent. The blue eyes blazed in sudden fury as he swung around to face the youth, while his breath slashed through clenched teeth. Sergei's feigned friendship was completely fragmented beneath the awe-inspiring dimensions of Tyrone's rage. Seizing the young man by the front of his *kaftan*, the colonel yanked him forward until Sergei could see firsthand the seething wrath that fairly flamed in the bright eyes. It frightened him mightily, and he reacted instinctively, winning his freedom with a frantic jerk, but in the very next instant, as he was trying to scramble away, he was seized again by the scruff of the neck and his left arm was caught and twisted painfully behind his back. At his loud yelp, his brothers leapt forward to intervene, but another agonizing wrench brought a desperate appeal from Sergei that they should hold fast to their places.

"Have a care where you touch me, whelp," Tyrone gritted close behind the youth's ear. "Or I swear you will leave here with only one arm. Do I make myself clear?"

Vladimir and all of his sons had full command of the English language and each clearly understood the warning. It was the father who stepped forward with a booming voice and demanded Sergei's release. "Let him go, or I'll set the dogs to your foul carcass ere this night is over."

Tyrone scoffed at the huge man, not even remotely affected by the threat. "Then call off these baying hounds you have around you now or you'll have good reason to hunt me down."

Vladimir raised his bushy white brows in wide surprise. It was a rare man indeed who stood up to him and his sons with such unswerving fortitude. Lifting a wrinkled hand, he gestured for his family to retreat, and in response Tyrone sent Sergei sprawling forward into his brothers.

Claiming their attention with a sudden chuckle, Tyrone magnanimously laid a hand to his breast and inclined his head and shoulders in an abbreviated bow of apology. "I must humbly beg your forgiveness for my brief display of ill temper, gentlemen. I was involved in a confrontation with a band of ruffians a day or two ago, and they did their best to lay open my back. 'Tis tender yet, so as long as you keep your hands from me, then perhaps I can respond to your visit with as much grace as a favorable host might."

Sergei rubbed his bruised arm and sullenly mumbled a conjecture. "You rile easily, Englishman."

"A fault I struggle with when pain is inflicted upon me." Tyrone looked around at the members of the family and saw that their gazes were now directed toward Synnovea. Stepping aside, he deliberately took her arm and drew her forward, clearly establishing his claim upon her for the benefit of the sons and, in particular, the elder, who directed a longing glance toward her. "Have you come to congratulate me on my good fortune in taking so sweet and fair a bride?"

His question was a farfetched travesty of the truth, but Tyrone was not above exacting a small measure of revenge for their attempt to bully him. He laid an arm about his wife's slender shoulders as he raised a goblet from a servant's tray and held it aloft.

"Gentlemen, may I toast the Lady Synnovea Rycroft, wife of my beknighted self and good woman of my future house?" He sipped the wine and, dipping his head nearer his bride's ear, murmured encouragement as he handed the goblet to her. "Drink up, my sweet. Remember we are to make merry for our guests."

Major Nekrasov had entered the great hall in time to hear Tyrone's toast and was none too pleased by it. It seemed insidiously deceptive, considering what guarantee the man had coerced from the tsar. If he had not been at odds with the Englishman before now, then Nikolai was instantly of such a mind. He promised himself that he would warn Synnovea of her husband's plan and beg her to hold herself aloof from him until that time the colonel would leave for England.

Incredibly eager for such an opportunity to present itself, Nikolai closely watched the couple for the rest of the afternoon, but as the day aged into late evening, his disposition grew decidedly more morose. The couple mingled with their guests as if they were totally taken with each other. Hand in hand, they stood together and decorously bade farewell to Vladimir and his sons. Later,

when they were called to a lavish banquet which had
been laid out before them, the two shared a place of honor
at the head of the table, which Natasha had taken special
delight in directing them to, and sat so close together it
seemed to Nikolai they could have been joined by flesh
to one another. He was greatly disturbed by their display
of compatibility and even more afraid of what Synnovea
would soon be yielding to the man. Throughout the festive celebration she seemed so shy and sweet in her new
husband's presence, as if she really doted on the man,
and it nearly broke his composure to watch the colonel
handling her with such bold familiarity, as if he had a
right to touch her after the pledge he had gained from
the tsar! The possessive fondling was almost too much
for Nikolai to bear! Long fingers stroking along her lean
ribs or up her arm, pausing casually near her breast or on
her hip or gently laying hold of her slender waist to draw
her closer against his side . . . it all bordered closely on
the fantasies which Nikolai had held so dear, of one day
claiming Synnovea as his own.

The worst of his worries was yet to come, Nikolai
realized, for the couple would soon retire to their bridal
chamber, and he could glean no hope of abstinence from
what he had witnessed throughout the afternoon. When
confronted with the Englishman's tendency to touch and
handle his wife so freely, Nikolai refused to trust the man
to hold fast to the letter of his bargain with the tsar. He
desperately wanted to caution Synnovea about her husband's duplicity in hopes of preventing their union, but
he was repeatedly frustrated in that quest, for he found
no clear chance to catch her alone or anywhere away from
the colonel's proximity. His hazel eyes followed gloomily
when she finally left the hall, escorted by Natasha and
the handful of women who had been invited and whom
Synnovea cherished as her closest friends.

In the moments following her departure some of the
men began to chide Tyrone for stealing the most beautiful maid from beneath their noses. Though there were

also questions concerning the haste of the marriage, he refused to elaborate on the reasons and brushed the inquiries off with a suggestive grin.

"You have all heard rumors of my impatience to court the Countess. Can you not imagine my eagerness to bed her?" Tyrone took another sip of the fruit-flavored vodka and braced himself against the molding of a door as he swept his arm about and declared, "The tsar took pity on my pain and cast down all other plans for her betrothal by arranging the marriage between us himself. 'Tis all!"

Nikolai smiled dismally at the subtle twisting of the tale. The colonel spoke no lie, but depicted a completely different view for the guests than what had actually taken place. It pained him that Synnovea had not been around to hear her husband's guileful misstatement.

A short time later Natasha returned to the great room to announce that the bride was awaiting her groom. The men chortled in glee as they crowded close in around Tyrone, who drained his cup in what appeared eager anticipation. Only he was cognizant of his ongoing attempt to deaden more than the wounds in his back, for the idea of being privately ensconced with Synnovea in a bedchamber for a whole night had already stirred memories that sorely vexed his intractable objective.

As his friends crowded near, Tyrone grimaced and immediately retreated as they made to pound him on the back. "Have a care or you will make me useless to my bride," he hastily cautioned. "The condition of my back has a way at times of dismissing everything else from my mind. Therefore, I beg you to proceed with care in your attempt to cheer me on, lest I be deterred from my purpose."

"Lift him on your shoulders, lads!" an English officer named Edward Walsworth encouraged. "He needs be carried to save his strength for better things. Besides, he's sampled the wine so well, he may be unable to find his way upstairs to savor other things."

Amid their guffawing laughter, Tyrone was hoisted onto their shoulders and then carted upstairs as their booming, outrageously ribald chants accompanied their ascent. In the anteroom of Synnovea's apartments, they lowered Tyrone to his feet before the entrance of the adjoining bedchamber and crowded in close behind him to get a rare glimpse of the bride, who had been outfitted for her husband's pleasure.

Tyrone would never have seen a need to deny the fact that he had liberally indulged in the libations throughout the celebration. Even so, he could not believe his heavy imbibing could have caused his heart to lurch so ponderously within his chest as he beheld a sight that he had both feared and yearned to see. From the very first moment of their meeting, he had been aware of Synnovea's unrivaled beauty, but now when he faced the fact that she was his by right of wedlock and he could exercise the many prerogatives which that particular union allowed him, he felt a sharp pang of regret that he, in the heat of outraged pride, had foolishly allowed himself to set such extreme limits on his manly lusts.

Standing within the circle of her attendants, Synnovea looked as enticing and breathtaking as any bride had a right to look. Her dark hair had been separated into a pair of braids to signify her newly married state and then interwoven with gleaming gold ribbon. An exquisite robe of shimmering gold silk flowed loosely to the floor from her slender shoulders, and though the meager glow of the candles did not allow his gaze access through the lustrous cloth, he knew that beneath its translucent length and the gossamer gown she wore underneath, she was just as soft and beautiful as she had been in his arms only a brief few days ago. The sight of her was enough to set his body battling with his brain, and with the subtly demoralizing and relaxing effects of the strong drink he had consumed, Tyrone was not at all sure if his staunch objectives would long withstand her stirring beauty. It seemed rather absurd to punish her by his abstinence when it would mean a far greater torment for him.

Bah! Tyrone's mind rebelled at his lack of stern discipline. He was allowing himself to be led to his doom like some bleating ram to slaughter, just as she had lured him before with her soft eyes and sweetly cajoling ways. If he wasn't careful, ere long he'd be standing red-faced before the tsar, trying to explain how he had been enticed from his purpose on their wedding night and had gotten her straightaway with child.

The manly guests loudly hooted their approval of his bride's comeliness, and glancing their way, Synnovea graced them with a timid smile. The Princess Zelda leaned near to whisper in her ear, and immediately the green eyes chased to her husband as a sudden blush stained her cheeks.

Tyrone raised an arm and braced it against the framework of the doorway, well aware that he had become the topic of the two women's discussion. From the way their flitting perusals swept the length of him, he could believe their dialogue had something to do with his physical attributes, which Synnovea possessed firsthand knowledge of. The fact that she refrained from offering comment seemed to deter the other woman from voicing further assumptions, though it hardly kept his bride from meeting his gaze with more candor than she had hitherto displayed, at least since their marriage vows were spoken.

His entry into the chamber had brought to mind a similar event a thrice or so years ago when he had glimpsed his first wife, Angelina, bedecked in her bridal finery. His mood had been different then, buoyant and cheerful as was common among bridegrooms anticipating the taking of first fruit. It could be like that again, he told himself, if only he would relent. . . .

Or it might be even better, the thought intruded as he pondered the difference in his courtship of the two. In comparison to his sudden attraction to Synnovea, his final capitulation to Angelina's pleas now seemed quite lengthy in retrospect. Angelina had been the offspring of his parents' neighbors, but he had, for the most part, ignored her during her younger years. She had finally attracted his attention only a pair of years before their wedding, but it had been more like the wearing down of his manly resistance by a sweet young thing which had finally brought their marriage into being.

Other courtships had waned for different reasons, some because of the brevity of time allowed by his profession, many by his dwindling interest or a realization that a deeper union with a particular woman was not in his best interest. He could hardly commend his coolheaded logic this time. Indeed, considering his zeal to have Synnovea, it seemed incredibly farfetched to even suppose that he could be successful in ignoring her presence in the same room, much less the same bed.

He had asked Natasha with all the discretion he had been capable of mustering to provide him with separate quarters no matter how tiny or cramped, but the woman had smiled graciously and given the excuse that she usually had so many guests that it seemed unlikely she would be able to grant his request without restricting her gregarious penchant for hospitality. Thus, as he contemplated the tempting view within the bridal chamber, Tyrone had to face the realization that he would either repent of his resolve very soon or he would find himself spending a great deal of time away from the house.

Glancing back over his shoulder at his cavorting and frolicking guests, Tyrone shushed their loud bantering until the murmuring comments of the women could be heard above the din. He ambled forward to the circle of ladies, and his eyes gleamed as he carefully regarded the radiance of his bride. While her attendants observed every glance, every movement the pair of them made, Synnovea gave him a hesitant smile, but her eyes watched him carefully in wary distrust. With a stiff bow to the ladies, Tyrone sent them scurrying and sniggering from the chambers, then he stepped close to his bride.

"For the benefit of our guests, madam," he whispered as his justification for imposing his attention upon her, then he lifted her delicate chin to kiss her full upon the mouth, much more for his own sake than for the benefit of his companions.

Synnovea wanted to lean against him and yield her lips completely to his inquiring kiss. The scent of some strong intoxicant pervaded her senses as his open mouth moved upon hers with leisured deliberation, but she kept reminding herself of her earlier chagrin when she had willingly allowed her lips to part beneath his and then been made to feel the fool. She was not amenable to being shamed again by his rejection.

Tyrone raised his head slightly and gazed down into her upturned face, having suffered some disappointment at her cautious restraint. He was no fool to think that this night or any other would even be remotely gratifying as long as he kept himself from taking his pleasure of her. The thought struck harshly against his pride that no matter the goals he had aspired to achieve through total abstinence, when he was this close to her, he was clearly aware of the absurdity of such a notion.

Wending his way back to the anteroom, Tyrone drank a last toast with the men, but he was not so much into his cups that he was oblivious to Nikolai covertly regarding Synnovea through the doorway. It came as no surprise that he resented the man's effrontery to ogle his wife, and tonight perhaps more than any. After being confronted by so many of her suitors, he was not of the temperament to share even the merest glimpse of Synnovea's unconfined beauty with yet another man, especially one who had followed closely on his heels to copy his manner and plead with the tsar for permission to court her.

Deliberately Tyrone reached back a hand and pushed the door closed behind him, then lifted his eyes challengingly to the major, letting it be known that Synnovea was his until he saw fit to leave her. He stared until Nikolai, flushing to a dark angry red, abruptly turned on a heel and made his exit.

Chapter 19

THE GUESTS FINALLY TOOK THEIR LEAVE OF THE BRID-
al chambers, and the stout wooden portal was closed
behind them, allowing the groom to secure the bolt
against the possibility of any prankish deed befalling
him or his bride. When a few of his fellow officers had
lingered to offer advice on the proper schooling of a virgin, Tyrone had nodded with museful care, and though
he had appeared to listen to every word, his thoughts
had wandered, as if beguiled, to enticing memories of
Synnovea sliding naked across his bed, eagerly making
room for him. Even after he had consumed enough vodka
to dull the lacerated rawness of his back, he was still
unable to cast that image and similar haunting visions
from mind. His judgment was not so sluggish that he
couldn't discount most of his companions' suggestions
as irrelevant. If he held true to his own resolve, then
surely their counsel was for naught, even if he were of
a bent to use it, which was far from the case. It was not
that he considered his own skills significantly better than
theirs; indeed some who had provided instruction were
touted to be daring roués and masterful lovers of several
or more women at any given month or year, whereas he,
as pragmatic about his personal life as he was with his
career, had limited himself to only one serious romantic
commitment at a time throughout his mature life, the last
and, until recently, the most pronounced being his late

wife, Angelina. He just simply preferred his own way of doing things, at least when it came to nurturing a woman's pleasurable participation in the intimate games of love and passion. The temptress he had just married had proven herself excitingly responsive to his lovemaking, if indeed he could believe her fervor genuine and not part of her ploy, and if Angelina's dying confessions could be measured as trustworthy, then by her own vow, she had fallen more in love with him after their marriage. It had only been during that long period of time he had been away in service to his country that she had grown lonely enough to be otherwise beguiled. Or so she had sworn to him on her deathbed when she had, with her last breath, begged him to forgive her.

Tyrone made his way into the bedchamber and, with careful diligence, approached the great, canopied bed where his second wife awaited him. She had doffed the golden robe, and at present her womanly form was discreetly shrouded by a sheet which she had dragged over her bosom to hide everything the filmy gown would have readily flaunted. As he loosened his doublet, his smoldering gaze raked over the hills and valleys that formed a provocative terrain under the covering.

"Tsar Mikhail was right," Tyrone remarked with languor, then cursed his tongue for having lost its subtle eloquence. Even with his faculties somewhat encumbered with the strong drafts he had consumed, he could not lightly dismiss the turmoil he was about to suffer by keeping himself from her. "You are very beautiful, madam. Perhaps beyond the measure of any woman I've ever known."

All signs of Synnovea's feigned gaiety had fled shortly after the departure of the ladies, and she now watched her husband guardedly, wondering what to expect from him in his present mood and condition. Would he vent his wrath upon her slender frame and insult her for having used and tricked him? Was she about to rue the day she had ever conceived of the idea of using him in her gambit?

"We've had no moments alone in which we could talk, Tyrone. . . . "

"So, you wish to talk." He painstakingly executed a bow and then stumbled back a step before he managed to straighten himself again. He grinned as if amused at himself. "You must excuse my condition, madam. I've progressed somewhat out of character tonight, for I've amply partaken of the fruit of the vine . . . or rather, that deadly libation you Russians quaff so copiously. Wicked stuff, that vodka, but it eases my pain. . . . " He laid a hand over his heart as if mutely declaring the area where serious injury had been done. "What matter did you wish to discuss, wife o' mine? My aversion to being used?" He rubbed his breast as if sorely chafed at the idea. "Aye, that has caused me severe wounding by your lovely hand. None else could have cut me to the quick so deftly. While I pledged you all I could offer, paltry though it be, you played me for a fool. Now this poor buffoon is caught, bound by chains of wedlock, and he spies such delectable sweetmeat in his bed, his mind is befuddled with his lusts, but there is no escape for him." Clasping a bedpost with one hand, Tyrone leered at her and leaned outward, twirling his free hand through the air, as if urging an audience to respond. "What think you, madam, of my folly? And of yours, pray tell? In ridding yourself of one proposed husband, you have caught yourself quite another entirely. Are you satisfied with what your mischief has brought to bear?"

Synnovea lifted herself cautiously from the pillows, carefully holding the sheet clutched over her bosom. "I was not willing to marry Prince Vladimir. . . . "

"You've made that abundantly clear ere now, madam." The invective came back in sharp retort as Tyrone doffed his velvet doublet and tossed it into a nearby chair. His effort to attain a stupefied state had not been successful, for he was not so inebriated that he could be casually insensitive to the sight he was presented. Slender tapers burned in a candelabra that stood on the table behind her, and through the filmy tissue of the pale yellow gown, the tiny flames eagerly cast their radiance, temptingly detailing her shoulders, arms, and enough of her bosom to whet his hungering imagination and to arouse within him a lusting desire to again peruse everything the sheet held from view.

Tyrone felt more than a bit harried by circumstances as he contemplated his young bride, for it dawned on him as his eyes leisurely assessed her beauty that he wanted her even more now than he had before their aborted union, if such a thing were possible. No woman had ever provoked his imagination to the same degree Synnovea had. Even from the very beginning she had held such a tenacious grip on his mind that he had found his life disrupted by a zealous desire to have her. Now it seemed he was destined to be punished even more. His obsession was fused with a yearning for revenge and a need to assuage his pain, pride, and frustration by the only means by which he could gain relief. If she had deliberately played the harlot to entice him into her game, he argued with himself, would he not be justified in using her for just that purpose?

"What I'm asking, madam, is whether or nay you're pleased with what your game has reaped?"

Synnovea's cheeks warmed to a vivid hue as she struggled to find an answer that would adequately mollify his resentment and rage. If she told him she was exceedingly satisfied to have him as her husband, then he might think she had intentionally set out to achieve that end. On the other hand, it would be a deliberate lie to say that she had not become enamored with him. Or had she blindly ignored her feelings for him all along and was just now beginning to realize the existence of her growing attachment?

"You cannot answer me?" Tyrone demanded caustically.

Synnovea started slightly at the animosity in his tone, and nervously offered a softly spoken supplication. "Can you not see the truth of the matter yourself?" She lowered her gaze from his steely-eyed stare, doubting that any answer she offered would suffice. So why in heaven's name did she have to try and explain her contentment to him, she wondered, when she could do naught but tremble beneath that fierce, unrelentingly hawkish gaze? "Would not any maid prefer you for a husband above some ancient patriarch, my lord? But I had not planned to entrap you. . . . "

"Nay!" His tone was snide. "You only wanted to use me like some worthless plaything and cast me aside when you had finished with me! I was nothing more to you than a rutting coxcomb, madam! An eager gallant who would serve your temporary needs, and the price you were willing to extend for my services was evidently your virtue!"

Turning from her in a manner of angry dismissal, Tyrone careened across the room and entered the dressing chamber, where he found himself confronted by masses of shoes neatly arranged in little silk bags upon the shelves, tapestry-covered hat boxes and lacquered jewel coffers set in order, as well as ornate chests and armoires filled with gowns, petticoats, and lace-trimmed chemises. Amazed by the abundance of clothes, Tyrone bemusedly tested the rich cloth of several and lifted the delicate batiste of a chemise against the light to admire its gossamer cloth.

His own clothes and possessions had been prudently unpacked and placed carefully in order beside hers, but surprisingly more conveniently at hand. He was rather amazed by the consideration shown toward him. True, Ali might have wanted to favor him with such an arrangement, but the tiny servant would never have taken the initiative to do so unless her mistress had first directed her.

Wincingly stripping the shirt from his back, Tyrone laid it aside and, selecting one of the two available pitchers that felt the coldest to his hand, splashed the chilly water into the basin. He revived somewhat after washing, at least enough to allow him to entertain some hope of remaining levelheaded once he slipped into bed beside his bewitchingly comely wife. Past that point, he was relying on his slightly blunted state to lead him quickly into a deep slumber, from whence he hoped he would be hard-pressed to awake until morning.

For his return to the bedchamber, Tyrone donned a pair of leggings to conceal his nakedness, which at the present moment seemed of crucial necessity. The side of the bed closest to the antechamber appeared to be designated as his own since it had been left vacant by his bride and the top sheet had been folded down invitingly. As he negotiated his way there, he avoided meeting his bride's cautious gaze and, in want of another diversion, perused the bedchamber, noting its wealth of space, rich appointments, and softly feminine elegance. It was most apparent that Natasha had treasured the girl enough to see her comfortably ensconced in what had to be one of the best chambers in her mansion. He had not indulged in such luxuries since leaving England, and only then in a much less splendid fashion. The Tudor house his father had bequeathed to him at the event of his marriage to Angelina was large and comfortable, but it was furnished in the same style as its design, which was definitely less than soft and ornate when compared to this womanly nirvana.

Pausing beside the candelabra, Tyrone pinched out the tiny flames and then turned his back upon his bride, prudently trying to avoid the visual stimulations that were there just waiting to be relished. If he had ever wondered what pleasurable torture would be like, then he was catching a clear sense of it now. When the silken sheets and delicate gown hugged her curves so provocatively, it was pure agony to think that, by his own decree, he could not taste, touch, or titillate the bountiful treasure of her feminine form. Just the simple awareness of her proximity and the memory of her responsiveness to his passion sent the hot blood rushing into his loins, making him immensely grateful for the shadows that allowed him some shelter as he released the leggings and lowered them past his hips. Seating himself on the edge of the bed, he doffed the garment and reached for the sheet, not wanting to lend her any feelings of triumph over his lack of rigid discipline.

The candles burning behind Synnovea provided the only light for the chamber, but it was enough to show her the ugly weals that slashed and crisscrossed her husband's back. The marks extended far to his right side, where the ends of the lash had fallen, and though most were healing, a swollen area along a wider gash indicated a corruption of flesh beneath a dark scab, prompting her to spring from bed.

Tyrone was not a man of such sturdy control that he could resist taking note of her thinly veiled nakedness when it was presented. Looking over his shoulder, he watched her snatch the golden robe over her head and flit toward the dressing room as the garment slid down her gown. When she came back a moment later, she was carefully carrying a large basin filled with water, a small towel draped over her arm, and a squat jar containing a putrid-smelling balm.

"There's a place on your back that has become tainted," Synnovea informed him, placing the large bowl on the bedside table. "You'll need it cleaned and a poultice applied to draw out the poison."

Tyrone had pulled the leggings into his lap, perhaps for the first time in his life self-conscious about what his manly nakedness might reveal. " 'Tis of little bother to me now, madam."

" 'Twill be if you let it go," Synnovea argued, striking flint against tinder as she paused to relight the candles. "I'll need your dagger to open the wound. . . . "

"I said let it go!" Tyrone stated adamantly, foreseeing the disaster that he would invite if he allowed her hands to touch him. He could have easily borne the agony had it been only his back he was thinking of, but it was that roiling, seething cauldron of pent-up passions he was now battling to hold in check that he worried about the most. One soft touch of her hand would likely see all his restraints and resolves totally sundered.

Synnovea challenged his authoritative tone. "Why won't you let me tend it?"

"I can do it myself," he growled stubbornly.

"Not hardly," she gently scoffed and inclined her head toward the small bench that sat near the bed. "Now will you please sit there and let me tend to your back?" A long moment passed as she watched the creases between his brows deepen into an ominous scowl. Tyrone would not look at her, but stared toward the flickering flames of the candles until she leaned toward him with a prodding question. "Colonel Rycroft, are you afraid of me touching you?"

Tyrone's temper exploded. "Yes, dammit! I told you before! I want nothing from you, least of all your pity. . . ."

At his thunderous blast, Synnovea stumbled back a step to stare in painful confusion at his rigid, uncompromisingly handsome visage, but he was being obstinate and refused to meet her gaze. With tears of distress springing up in her spirit as well as her eyes, Synnovea caught up the bowl and, with a choked sob, whirled around, flinging a wide-reaching spray of water across his chest in her haste to flee.

Tyrone started up in surprise, losing his prideful modesty as his protective shield tumbled from his lap. Even in the brief instant it took for him to recover his wits and snatch for the falling leggings, Synnovea's tear-filled eyes flicked toward him and then widened in amazement.

Tyrone ground his teeth as her questioning stare flew up to meet his. With a low growl, he flung away the fickle garment, seeing no further reason to conceal himself from her. What more was there to hide when a mere glance had stripped him of his pride? "What did you expect?" he snapped. "I'm not made of stone! Good lord, woman, leave me alone!"

With that, he jerked the sheet up to his waist and, rolling onto his left side away from her, claimed his place in bed. Refusing to look at her, he punched the pillow beneath his head and glowered angrily across the bed.

Synnovea was no less miffed by his display of temper. She carried the basin back to the dressing room and there gave vent to her spite by donning another nightgown, one which covered her better from toe to wrist to neck. The streaming rivulets that coursed down her cheeks could not be checked even as she returned to the bedchamber. Bestowing a teary glare upon his ignoring back, she blew out the candles on his bedside table and stalked around to her side, where she did the same. She slid into bed and settled herself on her left side far away from him, then after briefly considering the discomfort of her tenuous perch, bounced twice on the bed as she scooted back a cautious degree from the edge. Yanking the sheet and quilt high over her, she tossed him a withering glare over her shoulder, and then huddled beneath the covering where she continued to weep in silent misery.

Tyrone was enraged, without a doubt more at himself than he was with his bride. All she had been trying to do was tend his wounds, but his thoughts had not been so innocent. He had become increasingly distraught over the strong urgings of his body while she stood so temptingly close, and the reality of his inconsistency had only heaped coals upon his kindling temper, which had sprung to fiery life. No matter how he or his pride had been damaged by her scheme, it did not negate the fact that he still yearned to pull her down upon the mattress and relieve his ever-mounting lusts in the sweet warmth of her. Even now, seeing her dark head and slender form close beside him in the bed, he had to fight an overwhelming desire to take her in his arms and kiss away her tears and soothe her sobbing with gentle words of reassurance.

The temptation was too threatening, and squeezing his eyes tightly shut even while the muscles continued to twitch angrily in his cheeks, Tyrone beat down his fierce cravings with white-knuckled determination. His dedication was hard won, but he finally took firm rein on his thoughts and deliberately began to devise plans for a foray outside the city limits of Moscow. It was paramount in his mind that he should send his scout, Avar, to search out Ladislaus's camp before he ventured forth with his men on such an exercise, for it was much easier for one to go unnoticed than a whole regiment.

In the silence of the room, the bride and her groom lay together less than an arm's length apart, totally aware of the other, but stubbornly refusing to speak or to move. They might as well have been statues as taut and rigid as they were. It was Synnovea who first relented to an exhausted sleep, and hearing her soft, shallow breathing, Tyrone was finally lured along the same path. For a thrice of hours or more they dozed, albeit fitfully, but the brief slumber allowed them some respite from the tensions of being together and yet painfully separated.

It was well past two in the morning when Tyrone awakened abruptly, aware that Synnovea was leaving the bed. In some bemusement, he watched her creep stealthily toward the corner of the chamber where a bright shaft of silvery moonlight streamed in through the windows to reveal her cautious movements. His eyes closely followed her actions as her hand reached out and carefully slid his dagger from its sheath, which hung with his sword from the belt he had left draped over the back of a chair. She tiptoed back to her side of the bed, and Tyrone, unable to clearly perceive her intent, tentatively braced for attack, well assured that he could easily overpower her should she make the attempt to attack him. He promised himself that if she tried, he would see their marriage nullified forthwith and let the tsar's threats be hanged. To be sure, his own lucidity would have to be questioned if he remained with a woman who was utterly mad!

Tyrone frowned sharply as he saw her drag up the sleeve of her own gown and lay the edge of the knife along the inside of her forearm. Her objective seemed clear enough for him now. With a low growl, he threw himself across the narrow space, startling a gasp from Synnovea, whose head snapped up at the first intrusion of sound. A pained yelp was wrenched from her as he seized her slim wrist in a forceful vise and easily plucked the sharp blade from her grasp.

"What is it that you intend?" Tyrone demanded harshly. "Would you take your life because you've been forced to wed me?"

"Nay, my lord! 'Twas never my purpose," Synnovea assured him in a voice that quavered almost as much as she was shaking. The shock of his swift assault had left every nerve a-tremble in her body. Indeed, she could well understand how Ladislaus's men had felt when Tyrone had crashed into their midst. The fact that he was now stark naked on the bed beside her did little to ease her dismay. Though the only illumination came from the moonlight, it was enough to clearly define his manly form.

Tossing aside the dagger, Tyrone swung his long legs over the side of the bed and rose to his feet. The chamber brightened considerably after he set spark to several tapers, then he faced her again. Clasping her chin in his hand, he lifted her face to the light and held it thus as his eyes probed hers, seeking some evidence of the truth. His tone was sharply suspicious as he questioned her. "What other reason could you possibly have for slicing your arm open with my dagger?"

"Please, Tyrone, you must believe me. It was never my intent to end my life." Her own voice faltered as she tried to reassure him, and she explained in painful chagrin. " 'Tis only that we are here . . . in this room together . . . and yet you do not seem inclined to lend me your attention. On the morrow, the ladies will come and help me dress. If there's no blood on the sheet as proof of my virginity, I will be shamed before my friends."

A slow dawning settled down upon Tyrone, and he arched a tawny brow as he considered his beautiful young wife. It was apparent to him that she was embarrassed by having to plead her cause with him and was just as troubled by her inability to escape the disgrace she would suffer because of their lack of intimacy.

Arriving at an abrupt decision, Tyrone picked up the blade again, startling a flinch from Synnovea as he quickly whisked the point across the inside of his own arm, opening a small gash. Several red droplets welled forth immediately, and sitting beside her again, Tyrone reached to the middle of the bed and blotted his arm on the sheet, then looked around in search of something with which to wipe away the rest of the blood.

"Does that serve your purpose, madam?" he asked as he glanced up to find Synnovea staring at him in wide-eyed amazement.

"Yes, most certainly," she hastened to reply, somewhat astounded by his gallantry. She would never have expected him to make such a sacrifice for her when his manly pride was obviously still stinging from her careless use of his passions. Another man might have liberally indulged himself in revenge by allowing her to be shamed before her friends. Why had he not done the same? Despite her trepidation in his presence, Synnovea could not still a hesitant inquiry. "I never expected such understanding or kindness. Why did you do it?"

Tyrone casually dismissed his actions with an abortive laugh, unwilling to let her think that he could be easily maneuvered by her feminine wiles again. "Lend no claims of noble chivalry to this daunted fool, madam. 'Twas not as much for your reputation as it was for mine. Forsooth! Without evidence of our union, my cohorts would naturally think me incapable of performing the deed, so I yield to yet another of your ploys, madam, this time to save face before my own friends, for 'tis clear you have all the assets to lure the most reluctant husband."

Synnovea lifted her chin as her own pride felt the prick of his needling. "If that be so, my lord, then how is it that you're able to refrain from the coupling expected of us and ignore me as your bride?"

Tyrone made a concerted effort to appear cavalier about a matter which concerned him more than any other, and although he spoke from the heart, he deliberately made light of the injury inflicted upon him. "Oh, madam, were it not for this wounded dignity that flogs me as severely as those brigand's whips have done, I'd not be able to bear the temptation, but with every twitch of pain, I am ever reminded of my folly, and I am laid low by the thought of my own inanity."

"I do not think you inane or a fool, my lord," Synnovea replied, hoping to ease the friction between them. "You are far more knowledgeable than any man I've ever known."

Tyrone raised a brow and, with unmeasured skepticism, taunted her. "Have you known so many men that you can be considered a judge of unquestionable merit?"

Synnovea's cheeks warmed to a vibrant hue as she reluctantly confessed, "Nay, my lord, I've not known so many."

"Then henceforth, madam, I shall consider your lack of experience when you are wont to make such declarations."

"Experience I might not have, sir, but I've a good head on my shoulders and the ability to think for myself," she protested.

"A fine head, my lady," he agreed, intentionally misinterpreting her point. "None better, to be sure. Indeed, 'twas your fair looks that caused me to fall prey to your whims."

Petulantly Synnovea glanced away, struggling to maintain her poise. She was beginning to think that this particular Englishman could be just as infuriating as he could be aggressive.

Having temporarily won the battle of words, Tyrone lent his attention to his latest wound. Dragging the tail of her gown out from under her, he began to wipe away the ever-freshening droplets of blood, but under this casual guise, he surreptitiously admired the slender thigh and the curve of her hip which had been brought into view. While his eyes hungrily skimmed her gown, recent memories were brought to mind, and against his will, he recalled several nights ago when he had eagerly caressed all the womanly curves the garment now closely hugged. Greatly distracted, he continued to dab the gown to his arm until she faced him with a querying look and he found a need to turn his attention elsewhere. Becoming cognizant of the liberal offering he had provoked with the deft blade, he used that as a plausible excuse for having lingered over his task.

"With all this blood, our friends will be influenced to believe the worst. They'll be more inclined to lend you sympathy for having endured my savagery."

In spite of the tension, Synnovea dared to challenge him by lifting a quizzical brow as he glanced up at her. "If you were so worried about your reputation, sir, why is it that you allowed me to think of the matter first before you provided the remedy? Despite your protests, I think I should thank you for not letting them think me a . . . " she paused before she finished, wondering if she put words to his thoughts " . . . a trollop."

Old memories came flooding back to haunt Tyrone, and he looked away with a pensive sigh. "I suppose preserving his wife's honor is the very least a husband can do, so think what you will."

Synnovea's eyes gleamed with sudden moisture as she struggled to convey her thoughts. "I have trouble believing you're of such a mind to consider me worthy of your protection, especially when it's a matter regarding my virtue."

Tyrone stared at her in some surprise. Whatever anger he had felt toward her, it had never been his desire to see her buffeted about by slurs or slights from others. Though tempted to offer assurances, he could not totally relent and dismissed her statement with a languid shrug of his shoulders and a noncommittal reply. " 'Tis a fact you know little about me, Synnovea."

"Aye," she agreed gloomily. "I know nothing at all about you, Tyrone."

"Some men are most compassionate," he rejoined. "Others are completely insensitive to a woman's need to be protected from vicious slander. I once knew a man who, after hearing the gossip another had spread abroad about his wife, called her lover out in a duel. The swain made light of her affection and let it be known that he had used her merely for a whim and had tossed her aside when she began to bore him. He was one of those casual gallants who plucked fruit from every lifted skirt. Had the husband been as vindictive as Aleksei, he might have gelded the man and left him to pine in remorse for all the women he had once bedded."

"What happened?" Synnovea asked hesitantly. "Did the lover apologize or did they settle the matter in a duel?"

"The husband killed him," Tyrone answered with rueful bluntness. "The woman was in her fifth month and thought to make amends to her husband when he returned after a lengthy absence. Obviously the babe was not his, but he pledged to take his wife to the country and stay with her until the child was born. For some strange reason, she imagined that she would be able to make everything right again if she rid herself of the other man's child. In her quest to dismiss the babe from her life, she threw herself down the stairs while her husband was away, thinking to kill the child she was carrying. She accomplished her goal, but she took a fever and, a week later, died in her husband's arms."

Synnovea lifted her eyes to his and asked carefully, "Was this woman someone you were fond of, Tyrone? You seem greatly troubled by this tale." A long silence followed in which her husband stared off into space, and she tried again, wondering what connection he had had with the woman and what she had meant to him. "Your sister perhaps?"

Looking away, Tyrone finally breathed a sigh. "No matter now, madam. She's gone, buried in the grave."

Another long moment passed between them as Synnovea watched his aimless attempts to stem the small flow of blood, then she took hold of her courage and dared to intrude into the painful silence. "Will you not let me tend your arm?"

Tyrone was set to brush aside her offer, but he realized with some surprise that he was unwilling to injure her again with another brusque refusal. Grudgingly it seemed, he relented. "If you must."

Suddenly a-smile, Synnovea leapt from the bed, amazing her husband, who was gifted with a most provocative view of long, shapely limbs and a winsomely rounded derriere as her gown swirled outward from her body. When she returned with a fresh basin of water, Tyrone was seated on the bench which she had earlier directed him to. Knowing it would be difficult to remain distantly detached from her, he had engaged the use of a small towel to drape his loins and was grateful for its presence when she moved close against his thigh to dress his arm.

Synnovea brushed aside the hand he held clasped to the cut and made quick work of bandaging it as Tyrone closely studied her. Her skin seemed almost translucent in the candlelight and as delicate as the fragile features. Her lashes were lowered as she attended his arm, hiding those pools of dark green that seemed at times capable of delving into his very being, even at times when he was the most reluctant. With all the fiery urgings roiling within him, he could not ignore the gown's soft fabric that permitted the light to silhouette her curving form and to detail her full-blown womanliness. His blood warmed no small degree.

"May I tend your back now?" Synnovea questioned diffidently when she finished dressing his arm. Bracing herself for another tirade, she refused to look up at him, though she was not unaware of his close perusal.

"Do what you will with me, madam. I'm too tired to argue with you." It was a lame excuse for giving in to her beguiling manner, but it served him well enough for the moment. He was tired and had no desire to continue his tirade throughout the night. Much to his relief, Synnovea went to fetch the dagger and the jar of ointment, allowing him to release the breath that he had held tightly confined while she stood so closely against him.

Upon her return, Synnovea gently washed his back with mild soap before she carefully applied the tip of the blade to the pus-filled lesion. Tyrone stiffened slightly as she slit it open, but he found himself amazed by her gentleness. During his years as a soldier, he had become well acquainted with the hurried roughness of military surgeons, and the touch of her hands seemed more like a lover's soft caress.

Working quickly, Synnovea flushed the wound clean until fresh blood oozed from the newly opened gash, then with tender compassion she smoothed the balm over it. Tearing a large, clean towel into long strips, she wrapped them around his back and chest, leaning close as she wound the length completely around him.

"Hold the ends for me," she instructed behind his ear as she slipped her arms around him and brought the two pieces together in front of his chest. As she felt his fingers accept the ends, her eyes lightly caressed his temple where stray wisps of the tousled tawny hair had fallen. Of their own accord, her eyes swept down his lean cheek to the crisp, chiseled lines of his jaw. Though she had enlivened many a deficient daydream with images of her Englishman, she had never been provided the opportunity to examine his features from that particular angle before. She found it no less fascinating than any of the other views she had been allowed to peruse. She could only wonder what his reaction would be if she slowly stroked her tongue along his ear, if he would reject her advance again, just as he had when he had pulled away from their nuptial kiss, or if he would turn and meet her eager lips with his.

Resisting the urge, Synnovea moved around in front of him to secure the ends of the bandage with a double knot over his chest. "I never meant for this to happen, Tyrone," she stated in a cautious tone, wary of bringing up the subject again, but needing to speak her mind. "I never wanted to see you hurt."

Tyrone laughed with caustic disbelief. "I could almost be convinced of your charity toward me, madam, except that I've been painfully instructed not to trust your treacherous ways. That particular lesson has been seared into my memory as deeply as the scars on my back."

"I was desperate," Synnovea pleaded in a strained whisper, dearly hoping he would understand. "I could not bear the thought of being married to Prince Dimitrievich. I favored the loss of my good name rather than his attentions as a husband. And you were so willing . . . so overwhelming in your ambition to have me. . . . "

"Aye! I was willing!" Tyrone readily acknowledged. "How could I not be? Your beauty tempted me from the beginning, and in your resolve, you deliberately lured me with a sweet promise. I saw it in your eyes and on your lips. How could I have known you were purposefully leading me into a trap, one that very nearly cost me my life! I'm much relieved to find my head still attached, madam, and my manhood in good working order!"

A hot blush warmed Synnovea's face as her eyes were drawn to the towel which scantily concealed his loins. It rather amazed her that she could be so curiously forward about looking at him now, as if she had a right to do so. "I didn't know Aleksei would be so enraged . . . I never dreamed he would become so violent. . . . "

"The hell you say!" Tyrone growled. Coming to his feet, he made no further attempt to hide his nakedness as he strode past her to the far end of the room, then as she turned to watch him in some bewilderment, he came back to stand close in front of her. At least his anger helped to cool some of the heat in his loins, if not the roiling resentment burning within him. Settling his hands on his narrow hips, he leaned toward her slightly as he gave voice to his rage. "I know not what moment you singled me out as your victim, madam, but no well-tried harlot could have accomplished the task with such winsome appeal. You were as alluring as any earthbound goddess ever craved to be. Aye, madam, that you were. Though I've wandered here and yon time and again, I've seen no finer wench, no fairer form to tempt me more. 'Tis the cunning way you employed your charms that saw me duped like some foolishly rutting apprentice. Madam, you were so sweet and beguiling, I never had a chance against your powers of persuasion. Your eyes were so warm and inviting, your lips so soft and yielding, your breast so eager to be touched, and like some blind, weanling fool, I did think your silken thighs anxious to receive me. Even now, I yearn to appease my desire. There's an ache in the pit of my belly, and although I am much gratified to be able to feel this lusting need, I am nevertheless distraught because of this damnable yearning that goads me. I know well enough, should this continue, you will rend my manhood more thoroughly than Aleksei's blade ever hoped to."

Synnovea stared up into the eyes that fairly blazed into her own, not knowing what to say to ease his indignation. He was so offended by her ploy to save herself that she could see no hope of placating him. He was incensed because he had let himself be deceived by a woman, and yet she had been carried away as much by his passion as he had been by her wiles. Her enticement, at best, had been totally unskilled and naive, whereas his manly persuasions had been more firmly bolstered by experience and a most fervent intent to have her. 'Twas true that she had set out to accomplish her will,

but somewhere in the midst of it all, she had surrendered
to him not only her body, but her heart as well. She would
never have been so eager to yield him her virginity had he
not worked his enchantment on her. Yet, if she tried now
to convince him of that simple fact, she would no doubt
be ridiculed for having fabricated a farfetched fantasy.

Still, he had not ceased to amaze her since the vows
were spoken. He had played the part of bridegroom so
well before all their guests, she had been caught up in
his spell, but once behind closed doors, he had held
her at arm's length, totally confusing her. None could
dispute his greater strength and capability to take what
he wanted from her by force, and yet, when both of them
knew that making love to her was what he wanted to
do, he had elected to endure the raging turmoil within
him rather than treat her as a wife. How could she ever
understand him? How could she make him understand
her? What great feat would it take to reconcile his feelings
toward her and make him again the lover she could not
deny?

"Tyre." Synnovea's voice was soft, like a silken caress
stroking across the nettles of his pride. "Could we not go
to bed and talk for a while . . . I mean, about each other?
I don't know you at all . . . and I would like to . . . very
much."

A terse laugh escaped Tyrone as he dropped his head
back upon his shoulders and stared for a long moment at
the shadowed ceiling. He tried to collect his thoughts, but
he was like a caged beast distracted by his lusts, an animal
smelling the bloody scent of a bitch, driven to a raging
hunger by her nearness and yet, because of some hidden
barrier that harkened back to his injured pride, he refused
to salve the rutting instincts which goaded him. And all
she wanted to do was go to bed with him . . . and *talk!*

"Synnovea, Synnovea," he groaned and rolled his head
upon his shoulders as if sorely beset by a great pain. "You
turn my being inside out, my night into an excruciating
anguish, my day into a living hell . . . and then cajole so

sweetly in my ear. What am I to do, say you nay when you pluck the strings of my heart with your silken pleas? I have no heart for diatribes when you ply your fetching ways upon me."

Synnovea waited in silence until he lifted his head and fixed her with those penetrating blue orbs. Her voice was a soft whisper in the stillness of the chambers. "Truly, Tyrone, I did not foresee such hurt to come to you. You were the one I chose to perform the deed with, but 'twas never my intent to bind you to me against your will."

Tyrone sighed heavily, giving in to her gentle manner, at least for the moment. He gestured lamely to the bed, knowing what distress it would mean for him to lie close beside her and not touch her, and yet for the time being, he was willing to let the arguments lie dormant. "We can talk, if you wish, Synnovea, or go to sleep if you're of a mind."

Purposefully he took a deep, steadying breath, as if he were about to be plunged beneath a gigantic wave, and followed her to the edge of the bed, where he watched her crawl to her side. His eyes longingly observed the molding of her gown to her buttocks before she crawled beneath the covers and drew them up beneath her chin. She was careful to keep her eyes averted as he slipped in beside her, and then she rolled over on her side to face him, as if expecting a whole flood of revelations to rush forth from his lips.

Tyrone mentally groaned at the idea and, rolling onto his stomach, reached back for the candelabra and blew the tapers out. He was appreciative of the darkness that soon shadowed their faces, for it was a fact that he could lose himself in those beautiful green depths and would thereby be willing to yield her anything and everything he was capable of giving.

"Can we not just go to sleep?" he murmured cajolingly. "Of late, I've been unable to get much rest, and I must confess I'm in desperate need of it now."

"Whatever your pleasure may be, Tyrone," Synnovea

answered softly, grateful for his cordial manner. Her eyes followed his movements as he reached down to the foot of the bed and pulled the down-filled comforter over her, then with a smile she wiggled down into the warmth he had provided, content to have him near.

Chapter 20

T HE SUN HAD CLIMBED ABOVE THE TREETOPS AND WAS
just spreading its radiance over the city when Tyrone
struggled up from the depths of his rapturous dreams
and slowly roused to a vague awareness that this was
not just another lustful fantasy he was basking in. It was
warm, real, and alive! As full reality finally penetrated
his stupor, he flicked his eyes open, half-expecting
Synnovea to be awake and deliberately teasing him.
She was there, all right, snuggled closely against him
with her head on the same pillow that gave him comfort.
Against his shoulder, he could feel the delicate pressure
of her cheek and the faint, tickling brush of her warm
breath.

She had thrown an arm across his chest, and beneath it,
her meagerly clad bosom assailed him with its delectable
softness, bestirring to vivid life the very dreams he had
been reveling in. A slender thigh rested intimately over
his loins, and if that alone was not enough to completely
undermine his self-enforced restraints, he could feel her
womanly warmth nestled temptingly against his own
thigh.

Confined to the mattress by her shapely limbs, Tyrone
felt as if he had been lashed with silken bonds upon a
rack of torture, upon which he was being presently and
ruthlessly scourged by his growing desires. Her naked
softness enhanced his plight to an excruciating level, but

what was even more disturbing to his sense of justice was his inability to foresee any abatement of his travail until he finally surrendered to a strengthening urge to forge through the last remaining shreds of her virginity and claim his husbandly rights.

By His Majesty's decree and his own sacred oath spoken before a priest, he was committed to her now as her spouse, and despite his foolish assurances to the tsar, he was eager to roam where he had said he would not. Indeed, the present moment seemed incredibly ripe for the reaping of marital bliss. Simply by amending their postures a scant degree here or there, he could penetrate the vulnerable flask of her womanhood and satiate his yearning for the sweet nectar of requited passion.

Indulging in an occasion he had never before been granted, Tyrone studied his bride at his leisure. He saw no evidence of the wily vixen he had imagined would be boldly vexing him. Instead, he beheld an innocently slumbering maid not even a stoic heart could resist. Studying her in a light which afforded finite detail for his inspection, he found himself marveling at his wife's uncommon beauty. She had a fresh, natural radiance about her, with features delicately defined. Black, softly curling wisps framed the perfection of her oval face, leading his eye briefly to where a stray lustrous strand spiraled loosely over a dainty ear. Below elegantly winged brows, the thick spikes of her long lashes lay in stygian stillness upon her cheeks, where, in reassuring contrast, a rosy bloom blossomed, giving ready evidence of a vibrant life. Her soft lips were beguilingly parted in slumber, temptingly ripe for a lover's passionate kiss. Had he not been holding himself rigidly in check, Tyrone knew he would have been persuaded to test them with his own.

The fragrance that clung to her brought back to mind the heady taste of her skin and the sweet dew of her soft breasts. There was no need to strain his imagination to muse on the ecstasy which he knew would await him if he allowed his body to merge with hers. The problem he was presently contending with was in trying to ignore such lush promises of delight when they were well within his grasp.

It was apparent from the way Synnovea had attached herself to him that she had been drawn in her sleep to his warmth, for the sheet and coverlet had fallen to the floor, leaving only the lace-trimmed nightgown to provide her comfort from the chill now evident in the room, but the garment had ridden up, leaving the curve of her hip and the length of a slender thigh naked to his gaze. Such a provocative sight was immensely unnerving to a man who had chosen to endure the rigors of abstinence rather than expend his lusts indiscriminately upon the women of the streets, or with certain wives whose husbands had ventured to Russia just as he had done. One coquette in particular had repeatedly sought to break his continence, and though the two-score-eight-year-old General Vanderhout was probably not aware of his young wife's prurient proclivities, nearly every officer under his command knew that Aleta Vanderhout had a wandering eye and an insatiable appetite for handsome young lovers. Tyrone had discouraged a number of her impetuous advances with excuses that he had been otherwise engaged, which had not been altogether untrue even when he had been off duty, for most of that time he remembered being incredibly absorbed in trying to think of ways that would prove successful in getting Synnovea into his bed. Now, when she was here as his wife, literally in his arms, he was being forced to consider whether his plight as defrauded suitor was reasonable and justifiable. Perhaps with a clearer insight into his real reasons for feeling resentment toward her, he would come to realize his outrage was nothing more than a thin facade for a wounded heart and pride, and that both were incredibly susceptible to being consoled by that very same one who had caused the injury. When his eyes caressed such fairness, it was difficult for him to remember that she had duped him at all.

It was much in his thoughts that Synnovea was the treasure he had worked so diligently to gain, and without her ploy he might never have won her at all. Instead of resenting her deception, perhaps he should appreciate the fact that she had possessed enough intelligence and fortitude to successfully thwart her guardians' attempts to marry her off to Vladimir. Had she been forced to wed the ancient, he knew he would not have accepted his loss lightly. In view of that fact, could he not suspend the continuance of his portrayal as offended bridegroom long enough to consider his good fortune in being able to call her his wife?

He knew only too well that beneath a regal exterior Synnovea was everything a man could dare hope a woman to be. She was beautiful, passionate, witty, and charming. Indeed, it was difficult to even imagine a man growing bored with such a wife even if he were to grow as ancient as Vladimir and gain as many sons from her loins. Thus, it seemed rather foolish to continue to deny himself the bountiful harvest of his windfall and ignore their association while he tried to debate the severity of her crimes. It was obvious that whatever punishment he devised for her, he would get the worst of it himself.

Reluctant though he was to leave such sweet torment, Tyrone realized he would be hard-pressed to hold himself in check while his thoughts probed the extent of repercussions that might befall him for predicting his failure and henceforth acknowledging his unwillingness to comply with his own limitations. Carefully easing himself free of the entanglement of her satiny limbs, he slid across the bed, and, without pause, came to his feet, but immediately he found cause to repent his lack of caution. A sudden, splintering pain exploded in his head which made him wonder if he had been caught in the clutches of something abhorrently evil. Clasping both hands to his throbbing temples, he held his head carefully in place until the anguish finally eased to a more tolerable level, then he stumbled to the dressing room and, there, splashed cold water over his head and shoulders. He thrust his long legs into a pair of breeches, and having been granted leave for the day, he grabbed casual clothing, then went back to the bed, where he allowed himself another long admiring perusal before he lifted the sheet and coverlet from the floor and tucked them carefully over his sleeping wife.

Leaving the chambers behind him, Tyrone made his way downstairs, where he asked directions from a passing servant. It was his good fortune to encounter one who had been taught English by the Countess Eleanora Zenkovna while she lived. As he led the way to the bathing chamber, the manservant seemed amiably disposed toward exercising his command of the language.

"Yor bride come here vhen she vas young child. Beautiful she vas! And her mother, too! Zhough zhe boys alvays chase zhe Countess Synnovea, she give zhem no mind. She vas more interested in her studies and traveling vith her family. She had zhe mind of her own."

"Nothing has changed," Tyrone commented dryly, drawing a chuckle from the servant.

"She is much like zhe Countess Andreyevna, I zhink. Both can make a man's head svim. At least, my lord, yu vill not grow bored as long as yu live."

"That's my greatest worry! Just how long I will manage to live married to the lady!"

Rumors of the colonel's confrontation with Prince Vladimir and his sons had spread through the manse shortly after the initial reception, so the old man was not too surprised by the younger's comment. "Even a few scant years vill seem like heaven, sir," he assured the Englishman with a twinkle in his eyes, then he swung open a door for him. "Here ve are, Colonel Sir. Enjoy yur bath."

Tyrone slipped through the portal and found that many of his friends were already there, having stayed through the night. They had gained the march on him by at least an hour and now welcomed him with hearty bantering, chiding him for rising so late, as if he had discovered worthier diversions with which to wile away his time. Tyrone cringed in pain at their gleeful laughter, but seeing his grimace, they only crowed the louder.

Grigori came forward with a towel wrapped around his hips and handed a small vial of vodka to his commander. "This should ease your plight to some degree."

"Or put me in the grave," Tyrone quipped. He tossed the drink down with a shiver of revulsion, promising himself henceforth that he would carefully limit his consumption of the libation in the future. To say the brew was deadly was, in his estimation, a definite understatement of the truth.

"What happened?" Lieutenant Colonel Walsworth gestured to the bandages that still bedecked Tyrone's torso and arm. "What has your lady done to you? Did she claw at your back, or try to hold you off?"

Tyrone waved away the officer's raucous speculations. "Spare me your humor, Edward, until I'm better able to handle the abuse, or I'll be wont to seek revenge."

"There's another day of celebration planned," Grigori informed his commander with a chuckle of his own as he spoke through Walsworth's hearty laughter. He casually shrugged when he won Tyrone's dubious regard. " 'Tis common here in Russia to make the most of every occasion. It saves us from the tedium of our long winters. And, of course, our fruited vodka seems to lighten the spirits even before we're into any festivity."

"Try to keep your wits clear, my friend," Tyrone cautioned him. "On the morrow we must return to duty."

Grigori followed him to a more secluded corner of the bathing chamber where a large bathtub was being filled by a manservant. "You sound as if you have something dire on your mind."

Tyrone flicked a glance toward the servant and, for the sake of caution, delayed his answer until that one had left.

"As soon as it's practical, I intend to confront Ladislaus in his lair and hopefully capture him and the leaders of his band. On the morrow I plan to introduce some new tactics to the men in anticipation of that event."

"Do you plan to leave your bride so soon after the vows were spoken?" Grigori asked in amazement. More than anyone, he knew how ardently his commander had sought to win the maid and was surprised that he would consider leaving her within the near future.

"You know I cannot allow my personal life to interfere with my responsibilities," Tyrone rejoined phlegmatically. "His Majesty would be the first to reprimand me for allowing my own comfort to divert me from duty. Still, 'twill take some time for my back to properly heal, and the tsar has already informed me that he would like us to put on a parade for some foreign diplomats in the near future. Between the task of readying ourselves for that and the campaign, we should be kept enormously busy."

"Your bride is very beautiful, and you've not taken any time off for yourself since you've arrived here. I thought under the circumstances you would be staying in the city and training the troops here."

"Winter is approaching, and if I delay 'til the spring, we may never be able to find Ladislaus. We'll have to plan our strategy and condition the men for the exercise. I want all of us to be thoroughly confident of our ability to take Ladislaus and his men. We can't leave anything to chance."

"If you're so adamant about going, we should send out a scout to search for Ladislaus's camp."

"I've already thought of that. Avar will be the likely choice to go. He has no love of Ladislaus after the brigand stole away his sister last year."

"How did Prince Taraslov find them, anyway?"

"Ladislaus was intent upon spreading the word around the city and countryside that he was looking for me. 'Tis not too hard to guess that Prince Taraslov responded to the call when he found the need to get me out of the way.

Whatever their connection, it was my impression that the two were not the best of friends."

"Considering the thrashing they gave you, 'twas your good fortune that the Lady Synnovea sent her maid to the castle to bid Major Nekrasov to come to your rescue."

Tyrone was clearly bemused. He could not remember when Synnovea might have had any opportunity to send Ali on such an errand, at least not while he was in full command of his senses. "When was this?"

"Major Nekrasov told me Ali was the one who brought him the message that you were in trouble. It seems the old woman was there at the Taraslovs' when your captors carried you into the stable."

Tyrone chuckled and shook his head, still somewhat confused by the captain's revelation. "Then I must express my sincerest gratitude to Ali. Until now, I never really knew how I was actually delivered from their schemes, except that Major Nekrasov and Tsar Mikhail were there when I needed them the most."

"Ali told the major that her mistress had sent her to fetch him and that you were in grave danger." Grigori scrubbed a hand over the bristly stubble that covered his chin as he cocked a querying brow at his commander. "But how could the Lady Synnovea have been at the Taraslovs' when she was supposed to be sick in bed here? At least, that was what Prince Zherkof had been led to believe." Grigori waited for the colonel to reply, though that one seemed suddenly intent upon loosening the knot that held the bandages together over his chest.

Tyrone's eyebrows flicked upward noncommittally. "Perhaps she wasn't upstairs as Prince Zherkof had supposed. Perhaps she was with Ali at the Taraslovs'."

Grigori cautiously lowered his voice as he sought to glean some understanding of the affair. "The Countess was with you, wasn't she?"

Tyrone frowned sharply as he grasped the bandages with both hands and ripped the strips in twain. "Even if true, Grigori, do you think I would actually tell you?"

"Whether or nay you do, my friend, your answer will go no further than the two of us. You know that."

Tyrone was not willing to cause Synnovea any shame, despite her flagrant disregard for his emotions. "Would I boast of such an event? The lady is my wife."

"Tsar Mikhail was most anxious to have the vows spoken in haste," Grigori gently prodded with a smile. "What really happened?"

Tyrone feigned an exasperated scowl. " 'Tis doubtful you'll ever be promoted to major if you don't learn to keep your questions to yourself."

Grigori chuckled at the other's wit and voiced a few of his own conjectures. "Now, my friend, I know you're no liar, so I rather suppose Prince Taraslov and Ladislaus caught you unawares and ordered the whip laid to your back. And if Ali was sent to fetch Major Nekrasov, then I'm inclined to believe the Lady Synnovea was taken to the Taraslovs' with you. If you were forced to marry her, then I can better understand why you were so out of sorts with her yestermorn."

"Who said I was out of sorts with her?" Tyrone was surprised at the captain's accurate assessment of his feelings.

"It all falls into place," Grigori mused aloud, ignoring the colonel's question. He thoughtfully stroked a hand across his bristly chin again and grinned up at his friend. "You were obviously caught with the girl and forced to pay penance by her guardian, Prince Aleksei. . . . "

"The devil you say! He wanted her for himself!"

"Then you were whipped for taking the lady from him." Grigori's eyes danced with humor as he heckled his commander. "All this time, you've been hot and eager to take her into your bed. You just couldn't wait for the tsar to give her to you. Now you've had to pay for your error and are angry with her. . . . "

"What the blazes!" Tyrone barked, feeling the prick of truth in the man's conclusions. "Do you imagine that you can read my mind now? What makes you think I'm angry with her?"

"I know you, my friend." Grigori briefly lifted his wide shoulders in an indolent shrug. "If you weren't upset with her, then you'd stop this feeble pretense. . . . "

"Ho now! So I'm pretending, am I?"

"If things were as they should be between the two of you, you wouldn't care if the whole Russian army came marching into this house to seek you out. You'd still be making love to her upstairs, and you wouldn't come down until you had thoroughly exhausted your cravings."

Tyrone stared at the younger man who seemed to know him better than he knew himself. He could not argue the point, for he had very nearly done just that.

"And what's more, you're not going to be satisfied until you make peace with her and settle this riff which has risen between the two of you. If you love her, as I think you do, you'd hasten to make amends."

In a show of irritation the colonel tossed the bandages aside. " 'Tis not that simple, Grigori. I mean nothing to her!"

"I challenge the truth of that statement," the younger man argued. "The Lady Synnovea seems quite taken with you."

Tyrone scoffed in blatant skepticism. "An actress of great merit. I applaud her skill."

"Spare her such slander, my friend! 'Tis absurd to think she doesn't care for you!"

"How can you claim to know the mind of the maid when she bemuses me at every turn?" Tyrone angrily questioned. "I have no idea what she's thinking, though recently I foolishly imagined I did!"

"Colonel! Does our friendship mean naught to you? Do you consider me a loyal compatriot? A *tovarish*? Have I not proven my worth as such? Did I not warn you that Major Nekrasov had followed your lead and, nearly stepping on your heels, had rushed to the tsar to plead for his own cause? You wanted to challenge the man outright for the right of claiming her hand, and I cautioned you to wait. Can you not perchance perceive that someone else might be more adept at seeing the truth of this matter than you are? You're too close to the heart of it to view it clearly. You're anxious for answers and entertain hasty judgments. Let your wife have some chance to prove her love."

Tyrone heaved a weary sigh. "She'll have plenty enough time to demonstrate her feelings toward me while we're here. I can't very well have the marriage annulled while Tsar Mikhail is breathing down my neck to see that I comply with his edict."

"Your work here in Russia would not be very effective if you were allowed to do such a thing," Grigori pointed out, feeling somewhat piqued with his friend for having even contemplated such a thing. "We Russians have a way of taking offense when one of our *boyarinas* is cast off or embarrassed by a foreigner. Aleksandr Zenkov was a diplomat who was well respected in this country. I would urge you as a friend to tender favorable treatment of his daughter."

"Great Caesar's ghost! What do you think I would do? Beat her?" Tyrone was incredulous. "Synnovea is my wife! If for no other reason than that, she is deserving of my protection and care!" A bit outraged at Grigori's warnings, he doffed his breeches and stepped into the tub. As he settled his long frame into the steaming bath, he sucked in his breath as the hot water reminded him of the mangled condition of his back and the area Synnovea had recently tended. Still feeling the weight of the captain's perplexed stare, he raised a challenging brow at the man. "Was there something else you wished to discuss with me?"

Thoughtfully Grigori perched on a nearby stool. "You've managed to bemuse me more than any man I've ever known, my friend. You speak of distancing yourself from your wife, and yet in the next breath vehemently declare that she's yours to care for. When you first came here, you seemed loathe to involve yourself with any woman, as if you hated them all. During that space of time I never saw a soldier fight as fiercely as you did. Although you held true to the codes of honor, once you were instructed to serve vengeance upon the enemy, you did so with a determination that no foe could long withstand. You seemed to take no account of the danger your valor provoked, as if you really didn't care if you were killed—"

"Of course I cared!"

Grigori was not easily put off by the interruption. "In a way, I suppose you did, but 'twas my worry that you gave no serious heed to the risks. Indeed, if you felt a task was too dangerous for any of us, you were the one who took the chance. . . . "

"There's something to be said for experience, or have you not realized that yet?" Tyrone countered tersely. "I have more expertise in the skills of fighting than anyone in our regiment and have faced death many times over. If my ability had not been well seasoned by actual clashes of arms, I wouldn't be here now doing what I'm being paid to do . . . instructing the rest of you."

"I just wonder if you'd think about the perils of warfare more carefully if you were content with your life. . . . "

"You probe too deeply, *tovarish*," Tyrone mumbled through his hands as he vigorously soaped his face, "and though I understand that you're trying to find some logic in it all, I can give you no guarantee that I'll be doing anything differently from now on. God willing, I'll serve out my due and live to tell of it."

"That is a prayer I'll say for both of us, my friend, that we will have long life and good fortune. I will also make an earnest plea that you take into account the brevity of our lives even without the threat of conflict and hasten to restore goodwill between you and your bride."

Tyrone rinsed the soap from his face and peered up at the man who grinned and casually saluted him before leisurely sauntering away. In his absence Tyrone leaned back in the tub as he ruminated over Grigori's words.

Though they had vexed him, he could not discount the fact that they had been spoken with as much truth as good intent. His brows came together in a museful frown as he recalled some of his rather expeditious advances into the roiling core of several frays, including his attack on Ladislaus's band. In retrospect he had to admit his actions might have seemed somewhat daring, maybe even reckless, and perhaps it might have been possible that he hadn't shown as much concern for his life as he should have, but in each event he recalled having determined the necessity for a strong show of force. Had he acted otherwise, innocents might have suffered, and Synnovea would have belonged to Ladislaus rather than to him, a situation he would have detested, despite the discord that presently existed between them.

Properly groomed and handsomely attired, Tyrone was accompanied a short time later to the bridal chamber by those same men who had carried him upstairs the night before. When his companions called out for entry at the door, the sounds which abruptly emanated from the suite of rooms were somewhat reminiscent of the gabble of geese clustering closely together on a pond. After a brief space of time, the portal creaked open a narrow space to allow a young maid to peek through.

"A moment please . . . my lords." The plea was punctuated with giggles and breathless halts. "The Lady Synnovea . . . has not yet finished . . . dressing. . . . "

"Bid her to come forth so we might see," Walsworth bade with a chortle.

"Come now, maid," Tyrone cajoled as he plied his best grin on the girl. "Would you also hold the groom at bay when he comes forth to see his bride? Stand aside, I say, and let me enter."

Synnovea's muffled voice came from within the bedchamber, bidding the young *boyarina* to step aside. In prompt response the doors were flung wide to permit the men passage. They entered to the vivacious laughter of elegantly garbed ladies and a pair of chambermaids who skittered about in an energetic attempt to remove a tub from the dressing room. While the men had made use of the bathing chamber downstairs, the wide-lipped copper vessel had served Synnovea's needs upstairs, allowing her the opportunity to bathe and perfume herself in privacy before she and Ali were joined by giggling maids and curious matrons who craned their necks in an effort to assess the condition of the bed and its sheets. Ali was still smoothing down the hem of her mistress's *sarafan* when the men came striding through the portal, intruding too quickly. Synnovea whirled away from their searching eyes as she tried to fasten the last silken frogs that closed her gown, frustrating Zelda's efforts to cover the loosely flowing black hair with a veil. In the next moment the young *boyarina* stumbled back in surprise as Tyrone halted beside them and lifted the shimmering cloth from his wife's head.

"If it matters naught at all, Princess, I'd rather see my wife's hair unfettered by braids and veils," he declared with a dashing grin, but Zelda's horrified stare immediately warned him that his preference was probably not in line with tradition. His smile turned somewhat dubious. "Apparently it does make a difference."

With green eyes dancing with delight, Synnovea glanced over her shoulder at him, pleased that he should lend his manly consideration to her when her friends observed them so attentively. As he leaned near, she fleetingly caught a whiff of a spiced, manly fragrance and, underneath it, the clean scent of soap. Her eyes admiringly swept his features as she explained the necessity for the veil. " 'Tis unheard of for a married woman to reveal her hair to anyone but her husband, my lord. 'Tis a Russian custom. If you would like me to leave it unbound when we're alone, you need but tell me."

Tyrone reached out and slowly stroked a hand down the softly waving length, recalling the first time he had fed his gaze upon the long tresses, though at the time he had been reluctant to waste the opportunity to peruse her sleek, naked form by savoring the beauty of her hair. When gifted with so much more of her to look at, he had been anxious to take in every curve and vale that would later be hidden from him. "I would prefer it," he said simply and, with a gracious nod of apology to Zelda, returned the veil to her. The princess accepted the filmy cloth with a demure smile and hurried to attach it, leaving Tyrone to meet the broad grin of his second-in-command as he approached with a chilled glass of watered wine. Tyrone accepted Grigori's offering as the younger man gave comment.

"Perhaps the Lady Synnovea would enjoy teaching you the language along with some of the customs of our country. I'm sure you would both glean some benefit from the lessons."

"Since Synnovea and I have already spoken the vows, I see no need for your matchmaking talents, my friend," Tyrone commented with chiding humor.

The captain's grin expanded as he gave ready retort. "A good *svakhi* would not rest until she has made sure you are both content with each other. And if you're not happy, Colonel, then how will I ever get my promotion?"

"What fickle friendship you portray!" Tyrone admonished with a chuckle. "And here I was sure you were entirely sincere. Instead, you seek only to advance yourself!"

Grigori shrugged good-naturedly. "I have to do it somehow."

His rejoinder drew a hearty round of laughter from the men, while it brought appreciative smiles from the women. Natasha swept into the room a moment later to invite her guests to come and partake of the feast Danika had prepared for them. After first bidding the colonel to escort his bride downstairs on his arm and to lead the procession, she encouraged the other men to choose their spouse or an unwed maid to whom they could lend assistance, then with a smile she accepted Grigori's gallant invitation for the same service.

"What do you think of your commander's choice for a bride?" Natasha questioned, turning a smile upon the young Russian.

"I perceive it to be an excellent match, my lady. I admire your taste in friends."

"And I yours," she replied with a gracious nod. "But tell me, what does the colonel have to say about it all?"

"I'm sure that nothing but good will come from this union, Countess," the captain offered magnanimously. "In time I think the two will be very happy."

Sensing the astuteness of the officer, Natasha nodded in contentment, quite willing to accept his conjecture, for it was exactly what she had wanted to hear from him.

The revelry was launched with much feasting and tippling as the couple sat together at the morning feast. Exhorted by the guests to follow the customs of the land, they kissed to sweeten the meal after each crescendoing cry of "*Gorko! Gorko!* Bitter! Bitter!"

A short time later, a small band of hired *skomorokhi* entertained them and performed colorful mimes in which the guests bedecked themselves in outlandish costumes and, for the amusement of all, eagerly participated in the games and dances. Even Tyrone found himself laughing as the wine eased the pain of his lacerated back, and he cavorted about the house and grounds with his bride, chasing others and being chased, hiding and then seeking.

The jester played his part with enthusiasm, growling and howling, sniffing and snarling as he laid the pelt of a gray wolf across his shoulders and prowled in search of any likely damsel who would be the firebird. He was still roaming far afield when Tyrone quickly whisked Synnovea outside and chose a hiding place where the trunks of two trees grew closely together behind a large shrub. Deliberately matched together in the pairing off of couples, they waited in silence for the approach of the wolf, but it was difficult for each to ignore the presence of the other while they were tightly wedged in the narrow space. Even through the heavy satin of her *sarafan*, Synnovea became aware of the increasing pressure of his loins and the heavy thudding of his heart. Small tremors of pleasure awakened her own slumbering passions, and hopeful of his response, she leaned closely against her husband and lifted her eyes to find his smoldering with an unmistakable warmth.

Intent upon each other, neither of them noticed the advance of the jester until that one spied the copious hem of Synnovea's gown jutting out from behind the tree. The "gray wolf" howled in victorious glee, startling the couple apart, and promptly seized his captive's wrist. Dragging her off toward the manse, the jester chortled in glee as he glanced back and found Tyrone scowling after them in great annoyance. It was no more than what the jester had expected from such a newly wedded groom. Still, he gave the husband no reprieve, but hid the bride in a place not easily accessible to discovery. Tyrone appeared a few short moments later, making an effort to present a guise of good humor. At his entry, the "gray wolf" skipped about him and tauntingly bade him to seek out the "captured firebird" in the gilded cage ere the "evil brothers" kill him and claim her as their prize. The laughter-laden foray saw Tyrone dodging the mock ploys and attacks of his friends and sprinting through the house in his quest to find Synnovea first. It was the tiny Sofia who beckoned to Tyrone from the kitchen door and surreptitiously pointed toward the pantry. There, with a triumphant shout, he swept his young wife up in his arms and dashed ahead of his "diabolical kin" to deliver "the firebird" before the "Tsarina" Natasha, who laughingly crowned him with a flower-bedecked garland of green. It was this prize that Tyrone took back to the kitchen. Kneeling before the tiny Sofia, he placed it upon the girl's head, winning a radiant smile from her and a quick, timid brush of her lips upon his cheek. When Tyrone returned to the portal where he had left Synnovea, he found a strange warmth glowing in his wife's eyes which had naught to do with passion.

"You seem to have a special flair with children, Colonel Sir Tyrone Rycroft. Have you ever considered siring any?"

"Several times," he responded, remembering the disappointment he had suffered after each of the three times Angelina had miscarried in the first two years of their marriage. Her fluxes had not come with any regularity, and the physician who had treated her had given her a variety of herbs to strengthen her childbearing ability. Tyrone still found it rather ironic whenever he considered the success of her healing, for she had deemed it necessary to endanger her own life to rid herself of the other man's child.

"Then you are not against having children?" Synnovea queried forthrightly.

"That, madam, is not my difficulty," Tyrone responded with equal candor. He took hold of her elbow as he escorted her down the hall from the kitchen. " 'Tis the deceit I can't abide. How can I know the truth of your heart when you've proven yourself capable of chicanery?"

"How can I know your heart when you look at me with desire one moment and then seemingly disdain me in the next?" she countered in frustration. "Are you fickle, Colonel? Your lips speak of diatribes, but when I look in your eyes, I see something else entirely."

"Aye, madam, there's a certain duplicity I've recently discovered in myself which tears me completely apart inside," Tyrone readily admitted. "With your coquettish smiles and winsome looks, you have the power to reach down inside a man and turn him inside out with but a mere tweak or two. Though he may stand valiant and resolute against the challenges of a thousand other entities and fierce foes, he is helpless to protect himself against your wiles." Tyrone halted and faced her squarely as he hoarsely avowed, "I cannot deny, Synnovea, that you're able to tempt me beyond my ability to resist, but I fear I would be a fool if I did not try to build a fortress to shield myself from the pain I fear you will inflict."

Synnovea was not inclined to yield him ground in this sensitive argument. "Prithee, sir, do not lend such harsh judgment to my cause. I intend you no hurt. I only seek some mutual ground upon which we can meld together and be content in this marriage of ours. I see you struggling to keep your distance from me and wonder if you will always be reluctant to nurture me with your attentions, as well as with your child?"

A tawny brow jutted sharply upward in surprise at her blunt question. "Always, madam? Who knows what the morrow will bring, but you should know well enough by now that making a child will require further involvement. . . . "

"Do you object to further involvement?" Synnovea asked without guile.

"At the present time, madam, I must confess that I fear indulging in the intimacy which would be required in making a child. 'Tis much like a siren's song that a man hears and then is forever held captive in its silken chains. Once fed, 'tis doubtful that I would be able to resist you whatever your ploys."

" 'Tis no siren's song I weave, my lord, but a wifely hope that you will not leave me bereft of your attentions. If not for you, I would have no knowledge of what is beyond the mere joining of our bodies. 'Tis you, sir, who tease and then deny, and like a helpless sparrow, I must wait for the hawk to seize his prey ere I'm also fed."

Tyrone stared down at her in some surprise. He knew he had taken her to that lofty pinnacle of pleasure he had aspired to reach himself, but he was rather amazed that she could voice her own yearnings with such openness and ease. He found her frankness most intriguing, inspiring him to make confessions of his own.

"Aye, madam, I'm most anxious to relieve this gnawing hunger that drives me like some rutting stag in the wilds. You've grown no less beautiful and alluring since you went with me to my quarters. You would tempt any man, and I'm probably more susceptible than most."

" 'Twould only be a physical thing for you to make love to me. Men are like that, I've been told," Synnovea prodded, frustrated by the lack of consistency between his words and actions. If he were as vulnerable to her womanly wiles as he maintained, then why did he remain so aloof to the idea of making love to her? "Why not me? You said yourself you've been without feminine companionship for some time now, so I would assume any woman could serve your needs."

"Not necessarily, madam."

A lovely brow raised in wonder. "I've heard there are harlots aplenty who roam the German district. Have you never considered them in your quest for a companion?"

"Never," he stated brusquely. "You'll learn in time that I'm rather particular about the woman I bed down with."

"Which really doesn't include me anymore." Synnovea's voice broke slightly as she valiantly fought the tears that welled up in her eyes.

Unaware of her distress, Tyrone gave quick retort. "I didn't say that, Synnovea, so don't put words into my mouth."

Keeping her face carefully averted to hide the wetness on her cheeks, she questioned him. "Have you been so wronged that you are loath to make love to me and give me your child?"

Tyrone glanced away, reluctant to give an answer that would commit him to serving her desires, no matter how much he might have welcomed both the sowing of the seed and the reaping of the harvest. Well aware that he trod on unstable ground because of his own fermenting passions, he feigned an impatience to join their friends, leaving Synnovea discouraged and dismayed as he deftly avoided her pointed queries.

It was late in the afternoon when General Vanderhout and his beautiful young wife, Aleta, came to the house. Although neither seemed overly enthusiastic about wishing the newly wedded couple well, they extended a few superficial congratulations while the other guests were there as witnesses, but Vincent Vanderhout was eager to display the power of his authority, and soon called Tyrone aside, leading him into the garden where they could talk privately.

"Must I remind you, Colonel Rycroft, that it's the right of a commander to be directly informed of an officer's intention to marry. 'Tis obvious your clandestine affair with this woman has cost you your bachelorhood, if not a bad report from me. I must verbally take you to task for your negligence in showing proper respect to a high-ranking officer—"

"Your pardon, General," Tyrone interrupted, growing annoyed with the pompous man. When he had made his decision to come to Russia, he never committed himself to asking permission from any foreigner to deal with matters involving his own personal life. It had been difficult enough to accept the tsar's interference, and though he was tempted to tell the general that his marriage was none of his affair, he checked the impulse to argue with the man. Instead, he used the truth as an effective means by which to silence the elder. "It was the expressed wishes of His Majesty, Tsar Mikhail, that I marry the Countess Synnovea."

"*What in the hell have you done, Rycoft? Get the maid with child ere you spoke the vows?*" the Dutchman railed. "Damnation! Have you no regard for the fact that you're on foreign soil?"

The muscles tensed in Tyrone's lean cheeks as his eyes grew icy cold. Fearing that his own explosive temper would be ignited, he dared not meet the man's glowering gaze, but came abruptly to attention as he looked stoically over the shorter man's head and snapped out a reply. "Nay, *General!* The Countess Synnovea was a virgin when I married her, *sir!* If it's any of your business, *sir!*"

General Vanderhout's eyes narrowed as he fixed the colonel with a sharply piercing glare. "Be careful,

Colonel Rycroft. I can arrange for your swift dispatch to England."

"I would not advise it, *General*, without first taking the matter up with the tsar, *sir*!"

The general's mouth twisted in ill-restrained fury as he sought to find a threat that would be immensely effective in reducing the colonel down to the size of a squealing piglet. Failing, he harrumphed angrily and stalked back into the house, leaving Tyrone to contend with his own wrath. He was sure that everyone in the house had heard their shouts, and though he could take a measure of comfort in the fact that his own friends would show discretion and maintain a respectful silence, he was not so sure about all the others.

With a snarled curse, Tyrone turned crisply and made his own departure from the garden, purposefully avoiding that area of the house where the general had gone. At present, he wanted to throttle the man for daring to chide him for his marriage to Synnovea and for being so audacious about matters that were far too personal and intimate to be discussed at the top of one's lungs. The mood he was in, he'd lay the fellow low if he saw him again before his ire cooled. Therefore, he thought it best to seek the privacy of the rooms he shared with Synnovea rather than come to blows with the man.

His flight up the stairs was swift and uneventful, and Tyrone heaved a sigh of relief when he gained the safety of his chambers. There, the vexing tide of anger began to slowly recede as he paced about the room. He doffed his doublet and flung it into a chair, then tugged the tail of his shirt free of his breeches before drawing the garment over his head. It, too, was tossed aside and came to rest on the discarded coat before he entered the dressing room, there to splash cold water over his head and chest, which helped to some extent to ease his raging resentment of the general.

He had draped a towel over his wet head and was in

the process of drying his face when he stepped through the doorway leading into the adjoining bedchamber. Pausing there to finish the task, he was taken sharply aback by surprise when he felt a small hand slowly slide down his flat, taut belly. Unaware that Synnovea had entered, he almost pulled away in a halfhearted attempt to continue his self-restraint, then he remembered his disappointment when she had pulled timidly away from his inquiring kiss the night before. Despite his earlier intentions to delve more thoroughly into the consequences of his actions before proceeding, he smiled behind the towel as the hand leisurely fondled him.

Intent upon savoring the delicious excitement of her touch, he made no more than a casual effort to dry his hair, but with a sigh of pleasure, yielded himself totally to the overwhelming feelings that assailed him. He heard her soft cooing sigh of admiration, and his breath was momentarily halted as her caresses grew more purposeful, amazing him with the instinctive knowledge she had but recently gleaned. He sucked air into his lungs with breathless gasps, aware that his pridebound tether was being tested severely by her seduction. Her fingers began to search for the opening to his breeches, and intending to help her, he pushed the towel back from his head, letting it fall around his neck. His reaction when he recognized the woman who stood before him was tantamount to taking a sudden plunge in an icy stream.

"Aleta!"

"Yu naughty man, yu," the fair-haired woman chided with a coyly affected accent. Smiling up at him, she slipped her arms around his neck. "Gettin' married in such haste! Tsk! Tsk! Yu havef had the vomen in a fretful dither since it vas announced yu marry the Countess. Vincent said yu havef intruded upon the tsar's good humor by gettin' his late ambassador's daughter in trouble, and now yu havef tu pay yur due. Aren't yu sorry now yu never come and let Aleta take care o' yur needs?"

Tyrone's disappointment was supreme. It took all of

his control not to vent his resentment upon the woman for not being the one he had thought her to be and for causing such havoc in his body. Reaching up, he dragged her arms from around his neck and set her from him. "Your pardon, Aleta, but I've always been reluctant to bed the wife of my superior officer. You ought to know that such adventures are dangerous and pose too much of a threat to an officer's career."

"Oh, Tyrone, yu know yu're not afraid of anything, let alone a voman like me." Snuggling closely against him once more, she smiled up at him with eyes that were warm and limpid with desire. "Yu should come see me vhen yu vant some real entertainment, Tyrone. I'll do anything tu please yu. I can make yu forget that little twit yu married. She doesn't know the first thing about pleasing a man, especially one as lusty as yu."

"Aye, she has much to learn, but I rather enjoy the prospect of teaching her how to please me." Again Tyrone set the woman at arm's length and somehow refrained from showing a sneer as he stalked through the antechamber and snatched open the door leading into the hall. "I think you'd better leave now, Aleta. Neither my wife nor your husband will appreciate you being here."

"Come now, Tyrone, yu'll never be satisfied vith such an ignoramus as yu havef married. Yu need a more experienced woman tu take care o' yur needs." Smiling at him with sultry eyes, she came to him again and pressed her body full-length against his as she searched for the opening to his breeches.

Catching her by the shoulders, Tyrone pushed the woman away angrily. "Aleta! I'm not in the mood! Can't you understand that?"

"I know better, Tyrone!" she argued, coming back as if on the rebound and rubbing herself eagerly against him. She slipped her hands behind him and tightly clutched his buttocks. "Yu vere in the mood just now!"

"I thought you were my wife!" he snapped.

"Oh, Tyrone, it's not goin' tu hurt her tu share yu a little.

Don't be so damn noble! Yu havef enough for both of us."

Tyrone seized the woman's chin and forced her to meet his heated stare. "I see it must be made plain to you, Aleta, so I'll no longer mince words. I'm not interested in anything you have to offer me, so please . . . just go away!"

"Yu *are* afraid of my husband!" Aleta accused, finding it hard to accept that he did not want her.

"I want no trouble from him, that's true!" Tyrone agreed tersely. "But I want nothing from you either. Make an effort to understand me! There will never be anything between us, so please, just leave me alone. And from now on, stay far, far away from me!"

Aleta's lips twisted in a grimace of disdain, and with a brief dip of his head, Tyrone accepted her scorn as her compliance to his plea. Straightening her clothes with a jerk, Aleta faced the doorway, intending to stalk out in an overt display of rage, but she gaped in sharp surprise when she finally saw the woman who had halted near the open doorway several moments earlier. Aleta's startled gasp claimed Tyrone's immediate attention, and he faced his wife, who stared back at him with a curious quirk elevating her brow.

"I hope I'm not interrupting anything." Her meager smile indicated her lack of concern in that area.

"Synnovea . . . I . . . " Tyrone hoped he did not look as guilty as he felt at the present moment. "I . . . just came up here to get away. . . . "

"No explanations needed," she assured him with a noticeable rigidity. "I heard you arguing with the general downstairs and could not endure the stares that turned my way when everybody else heard them too." Her gaze turned to Aleta, who seemed momentarily frozen by the chilling stare of the green eyes. "Had I known this woman would be here, trying to get into your breeches, I would have come better prepared to interfere. Indeed, she might have had better success getting at what she so obviously wanted if you had told her you have buttons fastening your breeches instead of laces."

Tyrone had to cough behind his hand to squelch a sudden desire to chuckle. It was apparent Synnovea felt a great measure of annoyance with the other woman and desired to assert her rights as his wife. He was not unappreciative of her scowling glare which followed Aleta as that one stalked away from them.

"An anxious admirer, perchance?" Synnovea needled with a perplexed smile. "Tell me, Colonel, is she the reason you're not interested in me?"

"Don't be absurd, Synnovea! That woman means nothing to me! I don't even know how she got into our room, except that she must have followed me and barged in when I wasn't aware. I was drying my hair and mistakenly thought you had come in when the woman accosted me."

Synnovea folded her arms petulantly and, glancing upward, derided his answer. "Well, if you mistook her for me, then I suppose I shouldn't be too worried about you getting too amorous with her, should I?" She bestowed another sharp glower toward the rapidly departing figure and added crisply, "However, she did seem to enjoy handling you . . . as if she had been encouraged by a response."

Tyrone responded with a lopsided grin. "All women are not paragons of virtue like you are, my dear. She didn't need any encouragement."

Taking exception to his comment, Synnovea snubbed him with a well-articulated toss of her veiled head and left him to watch the angry twitch of her skirts. It came to him as he observed her flight that for all of her touted beauty, Aleta Vanderhout held no candle to his wife, whether in grace, charm, or feminine pulchritude.

It was relatively early when Tyrone begged compassion from their friends and shushed their protestations with an explanation that the duties of the morrow required him to be fully alert. Laying his arm around his bride's shoulders, he waved them off, then followed behind her as she led the way up the stairs.

Ali was waiting in the upper chambers to help her

mistress get ready for bed and while the two women retired to the dressing room to carry out the toilet in privacy, Tyrone set out his uniform and equipment for the next day. When he went in search of his military trappings and weapons, he felt no hesitancy about intruding upon the pair of women until he caught sight of Synnovea in a complete state of undress. Her arms were stretched upward to receive the nightgown the servant held, and as Ali faltered in some confusion, all the conflicts he had battled throughout the day and the prior night came back to assail him unmercifully. Mumbling an inquiry about the location of his gear, he hardly noticed when Ali quickly pointed toward an upper shelf, for he was too occupied admiring the nakedness of his wife. Finally stepping beyond her, he collected what he had gone to fetch, and on his return, gained a frontal view before the gown descended to hide those wanton breasts, creamy smooth belly, and provocative hips from view.

In the bedchamber Tyrone let his breath out in slow, shallow drafts as he stripped to his breeches. In an attempt to cool his brain and body from all the heated conflicts he had endured throughout the day, he sat down on a bench at the foot of the bed and busied himself with the task of organizing the accoutrements of a soldier. It took a stern effort of iron-bolstered will to redirect his thoughts to something less frustrating than the vision he had just left in the adjoining room, but when Ali made her departure and his wife entered the chambers wearing a gown that molded itself with endearing delight to her shapely form and with her long hair flowing in shimmering waves around her shoulders and down her back, the tenuous grip he had held on his desires began to weaken.

Synnovea was in a singular mood herself after being unduly punished by a goading reminder of Aleta's visit to their bedchamber and Tyrone's brief venture into the dressing room. After feeling the heat of his gaze, she had struggled to quell the growing hunger in her own body, but having failed, she was now famished for his attentions and not at all willing to accept another night of taciturn reticence from him.

"How early will you be leaving in the morning?" she asked, pausing close beside him as he polished his sword.

"Shortly after dawn, but there's no need for you to get up, Synnovea. I'm used to fending for myself. Besides, Ali said that Danika would have some food ready in the kitchen and a basket packed for me to take. 'Tis doubtful I'll be back until late, so you need not wait up."

"I don't mind waiting up for you," Synnovea murmured softly, wondering if getting him to respond to her nearness was a foolish idea. He was deliberately concentrating on his labors, trying not to look at her. Still, Synnovea was not incapable of winning his regard when she wanted it, and she was most anxious to have it now.

With feigned casualness, she slipped her slender fingers through the short strands at his nape, bringing his head around with stunning abruptness. "Your hair is getting longer." She breathed the words almost in a sighing caress. "Would you like me to clip it for you?"

"Not tonight," he answered, only vaguely aware that he had even spoken as he found himself staring into her soft green eyes.

"It wouldn't take long," Synnovea coaxed, lifting the tawny strands on the sides and top of his head with her fingers. "Only a snip here or there to neaten the edges."

"It's getting late, and I need my rest." Tyrone made the excuse even as his gaze slowly descended to the wealth of beauty barely concealed by the thin lawn gown. Against the candlelight glowing behind her, the fabric was more like a vaporish veil covering her body, and his gaze seemed compelled to probe the gossamer mists, wandering from the tempting fullness of her delicately hued breasts, along her narrow ribs, down to where her long, sleek limbs were enticingly joined.

A sudden sharp pain shattered the interlude, drawing a surprised start from Tyrone. In search of the cause, he glanced down and realized that he had sliced open his thumb with the well-honed blade while he was distracted.

"Hell and damnation!" he growled. "I can't even polish my sword without suffering some damage when you come near me!" Tossing her a glare, he paid no heed to her look of wounded dismay as he commanded curtly, "Get into bed before I slice off something vital and serve Aleksei's end doing so."

Fighting against a strengthening urge to dissolve into tears, Synnovea retired hastily to her side of the bed and sat on its edge. There she launched glowers aplenty against the sturdy back of her husband as she petulantly braided her hair. Sniffing often, she finally drove Tyrone to seek refuge in the dressing room ere he apologize for his rudeness and coddle her with his zealous regard.

When he finally returned to the bedchamber after washing himself and donning a robe, he found Synnovea had taken shelter beneath the covers, having pulled them up high under her chin. By her offended silence, she clearly demonstrated her resentment for having been boorishly reproached by him. Even when he slipped into bed beside her, Tyrone knew by her efforts to hug the edge again that he would not have to worry about being unduly tempted by her flirtatious ploys tonight. It was apparent she wanted nothing more to do with him, at least not for the present time, and though he should have been relieved that his willpower would not be strained overmuch, he was not at all pleased with himself for letting Synnovea believe he didn't want her near. On the contrary, he enjoyed her company so much, he wanted to savor much more of it, and the only way such aspirations could be appeased would be to make her his wife in every way.

Chapter 21

I F TYRONE RYCROFT HAD ONCE IMAGINED HE WAS USING every ounce of energy he was capable of expending toward impressing the tsar, he soon realized that trying to keep his mind from dwelling on Synnovea while he was away from her demanded much more of his concentration and determination than he had ever thought of devoting to the accomplishment of his first objective. His preoccupation with Synnovea seemed far more intense now that they were married and ensconced, not only in the same chamber at night, but, lending much to his disquietude, in the very same bed. While he remained within such close proximity to her, he felt constantly assailed by opportunities he had once eagerly taken advantage of. When he had every chance to observe his young wife in varying degrees of dishabille, he was forced to turn his lusting gaze away in order to curb his growing excitement and the plain, unadulterated enjoyment he derived from just watching her. So great was his struggle to maintain a taciturn mien and to deflect the heavy bombardment of temptations that besieged him, he even contemplated returning to his old quarters just to get some much needed rest, for he was nearly at the end of his wits trying to find an effective escape from the provocative titillations he had to endure in their bedchamber. Had his back been properly healed and his agility restored to the degree that he would have felt confident of his prowess in a deadly combat of arms, he would have ridden out in search of Ladislaus immediately upon his return to duty just to keep himself from suffering the chagrin of defeat in his own bed, especially so soon after he had foolishly begged the tsar to grant his request.

Disinclined to cast any disparagement against his wife by publicly distancing himself from her, he elected to push himself and his regiment relentlessly through long hours of difficult training, seeking to deplete his own strength and vitality until he traversed the threshold of pure exhaustion. Only by draining himself of the energy to function normally at night could he hold out any hope of resisting the sweet enticements of Synnovea's presence and deter the ever-mounting possibility that he would yield to his desires. It caused him some chagrin to remember how quickly he had responded to Aleta's caresses while thinking she was Synnovea, and it took no mean feat of logic for him to realize that he would not be able to withstand a similar seduction if it came from his wife.

It became part of the daily rote that he shared the breaking of the morning fast with Natasha, whose habit it was to rise at dawn. He would then leave the house and be gone until well after the evening repast had been concluded, at which time he would come dragging back home, thoroughly spent. He would then spend an hour or so in the stable, where he fed and groomed the tall black that Ladislaus had left behind and the fine, liver-chestnut steed that he reserved primarily for the purpose of demonstrating the quality of horsemanship he aspired to encourage in his men and for the parades they performed for the tsar. The stallion was one of a pair he had brought from England and would be returning with, if he or the animal lived that long.

Finally, upon leaving the stable, he would enter the house, and though much in need of a bath, he would eat his victuals at the table in the kitchen where both

Danika and Synnovea waited on him. He was sure he would have paid less heed to the server and given more consideration to the fare had Danika been the only one laying out his meal, for even bone-tired, he could not ignore the delicious sight and fragrance of his wife as she bent over him or passed near.

After the meal, he soaked his aching body in a steaming bath before finally climbing the stairs to their bedchamber. Once there, he collapsed upon the bed, thankfully too tired to even talk. His one concession to Synnovea's wifely bent was to allow her to rub a soothing balm over his back for the purpose of keeping the scabs and skin pliable and the scarring to a minimum. For this, he doffed his robe and reclined facedown upon the mattress after Synnovea had neatly folded down the top sheet and coverlet. It did not take long before her gentle massaging relaxed him, and even while she continued to knead his work-strained muscles, his breathing gradually deepened until her quiet, gentle ministering lulled him to sleep.

It was during these moments that Synnovea began to experience feelings pleasantly associated with being a wife. No harsh words of rebuke disturbed the unspoken harmony between them while she served her husband's needs, and if she had not yet become his wife in actuality, at least by yielding himself into her care Tyrone was granting her the privileges and familiarity reserved for a wife. It seemed rather doubtful to her, after witnessing his rejection of Aleta, that he would have allowed the woman to enjoy the intimacy involved in handling his naked form, and thus, Synnovea was warmly comforted by the unconstrained way in which he gave himself over into her care, even if she wasn't exactly grateful for his continued reticence.

It was toward the end of the following week when Tyrone surprised her by coming home relatively early for a change. She was in their rooms when she caught sight of him riding down the road toward the manse and, after quickly checking her appearance in the silvered glass, she hurried downstairs until she reached the back door. Pausing there, she smoothed the kerchief, apron, and peasant skirts she had donned that morning to help Natasha sort through some stored items, and then, assuming an unruffled guise, she strolled leisurely along the path leading from the house and through the open doors of the stable.

Tyrone did not notice her entrance straightaway, for he was absorbed in the task of shampooing the long tail of the chestnut. He had his back turned to her, and it was not until Synnovea came around the end of the grooming stall where he was working that he finally noticed a movement out of the corner of his eye and glanced around. As they were wont to do whenever she came near, the cerulean-blue eyes slid over her in a lingering assessment of her appearance. For a long, distracted moment, Tyrone continued squeezing the suds through the stallion's tail as he took pleasure in watching his wife. Although her smile was hesitant, it seemed eager to stay even as a deepening blush was stirred forth by his meticulous regard.

"You're home early," Synnovea commented, unable to think of anything better to say. Her own gaze dipped to the shirt that hung away from his torso and admiringly swept the view it afforded her.

Tyrone inclined his head toward the end of the stall where he had left a wooden bucket he had earlier filled to the brim. "Can you bring that pail over here and slowly dribble the water over the tail so I can rinse it?"

Eager to have an excuse to be near him, Synnovea lifted the ponderous pail and, chewing on a bottom lip as she concentrated on the burdensome task, hauled it forward. She braced her slender feet wide apart as she lifted the bucket higher and obeyed her husband's directive. Intent upon perusing the man rather than the flow of the water once it ran from the tail, she did not notice her shoes getting splashed until she felt the wetness soaking through her dark stockings, then she looked down with a grimace and considered the black, water-speckled slippers.

"Here, let me have the bucket," Tyrone bade, lifting a hand to accept it from her. "You're getting wet."

"No, wait! Just let me take my shoes off," Synnovea urged, setting the bucket aside. She hurried to the far end of the stall where she slipped out of the soaked slippers and, lifting her skirts high, doffed her stockings, then pulled the back hem of her gown and petticoats between her thighs and tucked them within her waistband, displaying a tempting length of silken limbs.

Now it was Tyrone's turn to be preoccupied with what his wife exhibited. "You'll catch your death," he cautioned, watching her small, bare feet pad through the water as she returned to her task. "Then I'll be blamed for asking you to help me."

"Oh, but I want to," Synnovea readily replied, then wrinkled her slender nose as she cast a cautious glance about the stone floor of the grooming stall. "Besides, I'm more worried about stepping in something."

A soft chuckle came from Tyrone as he spread out the horse's tail beneath the fresh flow of water she supplied. "I didn't realize you were so squeamish, madam."

"There are a number of things I try to delicately avoid," Synnovea acknowledged. "Stepping in horses' dung is one of them."

Tyrone laughed at her wit, never having realized before that washing a horse's tail could be so enjoyable. She seemed favorably disposed to lending him whatever assistance she could as he cleaned and groomed both horses, and during that space of time they were able to relax with each other and warmly savor the congenial harmony that existed between them.

As he snuffed out the last lantern that hung near the horses' stalls, Tyrone saw his wife cast a repugnant glance toward the straw-strewn path leading to the door. Grinning with amusement, he took pity on her plight and bade her to tuck her stockings and shoes in her apron pocket and then climb up on a low stool, from whence he lifted her onto his back, much to her delight.

"I haven't ridden like this since I was a child," Synnovea informed him through her giggly laughter. As enchanting as a young girl romping with her father, she slid her arms around his neck and whispered close to his ear, "But don't let anyone see us, Tyrone. They might not understand my lack of modesty."

" 'Twill be our secret, madam," he rejoined, tossing a slanted grin over his shoulder.

"Good!" She smiled with delight at the intimacy of the moment and, taking great care not to hurt his back as she leaned closely against him, folded her arms around his neck. Her right hand slipped inside the front of his shirt where her fingers teased and stroked his left breast with casual familiarity as she softly sang a child's song in Russian, almost cooing in his ear.

Then her mood changed as she laughed and, swinging her bare calves out on either side of him, wiggled her slender toes as she enjoyed the moment to the utmost. Leaning close to his ear again, she teasingly whispered, "Is it as much fun for a man to ride astride a horse as I'm having riding you?"

Somewhere along the line, Tyrone had shed his prudent inhibitions and now pinched her buttock, eliciting a giggly squeal from the puckish little sprite who rode his back. "Calm yourself, madam," he implored with a chuckle. "We're nearing the house, and with your giggling, we'll be having everyone watching from the windows."

"Too bad it's so cool in the gardens," she murmured in his ear as she remembered their first adventure there. "I'd like to see where you would have taken me had we stayed and made love together."

The coy invitation did not go unnoticed and though Tyrone was suddenly of a mind to turn aside and find a spot to accomplish the copulation, he saw Natasha smiling at them from the open doorway. The brief surge of resentment he felt toward the woman at that particular moment made him realize just how closely he had actually been to forgetting his resolve and satisfying himself with his wife. He knew it had only been Natasha's untimely intrusion that had sparked his ire, not the woman herself. Curbing any feelings of irritation that were wont to linger, he drew his wife's attention to the one who awaited them. "We've been found out, madam."

"A pity," Synnovea sighed in disappointment. "We were once so close to completing the union . . . and now I fear you will never finish what you started."

Tyrone let her remark pass without comment as Natasha came out to meet them, but in his mind he had often questioned what the end results might have been, had he been given time to breach her virginity completely and consummate their passion.

Later that evening, when they were getting ready for bed, he casually informed her that on the morrow there would be a parade and demonstration of military arms taking place in the Kremlin and that several companies of Hussars would be performing for the tsar and his foreign guests. Since he had been instrumental in setting the stage for the exhibitions, which were becoming almost a regular event, he and his men would be at the forefront of the presentation. She would be expected to attend, along with the other officers' wives, and in view of the fact that it would be an open affair, she could invite Natasha or anyone else she had a mind to.

"Even Ali can come," Tyrone added as he tossed a grin toward the tiny maid who had hurriedly scurried to the doorway of the dressing room to listen. "Many of the other wives will be bringing nannies and nursemaids to tend their children. I rather think Ali will enjoy the outing."

Seeing the maid's bright and buoyant smile, Synnovea responded with chiding amusement. "Now that you've done your best to enlighten her, my lord, 'tis rather doubtful that I'd be able to keep her away from the event."

"Would ye be wantin' somethin' afore ye bed down, my lord?" Ali eagerly inquired, bestowing her usual favor on him.

"Thank you, Ali, but I have everything I need for the time being."

"Then I'll be wishin' ye good night, sir . . . an' the same ter ye, mistress." She took her leave with her little skittering scamper and then, with a last wink over her shoulder at Tyrone, closed the door behind her.

"You must realize by now how much Ali has come to adore you," Synnovea stated as she doffed her dressing gown and tossed it aside. Crawling to the middle of the bed, she sat back on her heels and watched him as he readied his best military attire for the next day's presentation. "Your constant coddling has made her nearly impossible to live with."

Tyrone paused as he hung his doublet over the back of the chair and, looking around at his wife, raised a dubious brow. "What is she doing now that annoys you so?"

"She thinks nothing of leaving me in dire straits while she scurries off to meet your needs. Indeed! She can't even talk about anyone else but you!"

"I see." His lips turned with a curiously amused quirk. "I can understand how that might annoy you, madam."

It was actually the maid's prodding encouragements that were meant to inspire her into being more attentive to her husband's every need that Synnovea found most frustrating. How could she be the kind of wife Ali urged her to be when Tyrone all but ignored her? "I'm beginning to believe the two of you are in league together. And now Natasha has started pleading your cause, having likewise become one of your admirers. In fact, Danika tells me that you've taken to breaking the morning fast with her. I can only wonder what mischief that will brew. No good for me, I'd wager."

"Your situation is surely not as grave as you make it seem, madam. Ali and Natasha will always be your fast and loyal friends."

In expectation of her continued service in kneading his back, Synnovea had gathered the salves and several small, clean towels on a tray that was now on the bed beside her. She only waited for him to stretch his long form out beside her, but Tyrone was inclined to linger overlong as he paused near the bedside table to partake of the mulled wine she had poured him and to savor the fetching sight she presented. The dark tresses had been freed from the braids and, now waving softly, flowed around her shoulders and over her breasts to hide from view that to which the lace-trimmed gown would have eagerly adhered. With the brightly glowing tapers burning behind her, penetrating the delicate batiste and defining the rest of her body, it was all Tyrone could do to suppress a growing urge to sweep her down upon the bed and have his way with her.

This afternoon had proven to be the last straw in Tyrone's tolerance for his own stupidity. He was completely fed up with this foolish game of abstinence he had set himself to and was determined to seek a way to put it to a proper end. Perhaps the more honorable thing to do prior to making love to his wife would be to face the tsar and confess that he had suffered a change of heart and wanted to retract his petition, then in years to come he would not be so prone to view himself as merely a man whose will had been ultimately enslaved by the irresistible powers of feminine seduction. Still, it seemed rather doubtful he would be able to gain an audience with the monarch before the bonds of his restraint actually snapped, for that possibility seemed impending after this afternoon.

"Perhaps I should worry about these sunrise tête-à-têtes you and Natasha engage in." Despite her close friendship with the countess, Synnovea was pricked by the knowledge that Tyrone had rejected her own offer to join him at the morning meal but was now enjoying the older woman's company.

"Why so?" Tyrone stared at her in some bewilderment.

Synnovea shrugged aloofly. "When a woman is as beautiful as Natasha, age really isn't a factor. Besides, nine years isn't much to speak of. 'Tis obvious you like her company more than mine."

"Such a notion is mightily farfetched, Synnovea," Tyrone admonished with an incredulous chuckle. How could she even think such a thing was true when he had never in his lifetime experienced the emotional upheaval she was presently putting him through? In all the days and months he had spent with Angelina, even in their best and worst times together, she had never held his mind so imprisoned that he had been forced to consider barricading his wits against the persuasive influence of her enchantment. Even from their first encounter, the opposite had been true with Synnovea. When she had forgotten him after he had secured her escape and he had found himself without a horse in the middle of the forest, he had cursed her for her lack of compassion and ingratitude. Since their marriage, frustration, animosity, resentment, and sometimes outright anger had constantly vied with the deceptively potent forces of passion, love, compassion, gentleness, as well as a strengthening desire to nourish and protect her as any adoring husband might. He was ever reminded that she was his wife and that all the aspirations he had once sought to bring to fruition could now be his for the simple taking . . . that very moment he chose to relent.

"Even if you were of a mind to be worried about what Natasha and I discuss, Synnovea, you need have no fear. We seem just as prone as Ali to limit our choice of topics to a singular subject. All we ever talk about is you." Holding the goblet in his hand, he gestured toward her as he made a point. "Between Ali and Natasha, I probably know more about you than either one of them separately. From what Natasha has told me, 'twould seem you've been able to completely frustrate more than a few suitors, not to mention several haughty French diplomats who made the blunder of thinking you were some untutored chit from the steppes of Russia."

Synnovea lifted her delicate chin in sudden annoyance. "You must understand me quite well by now," she observed petulantly, offended by Natasha's apparent willingness to discuss past confrontations which still rankled her. She had not been gently disposed toward those supercilious oafs who had lewdly ogled her and tried to converse with her in badly enunciated Russian while bantering in French with their companions about the scandalous behavior of *boyarinas* who were wont to bathe naked with strange men in public bathhouses. It was obvious they had desired such an experience with her, but in well-articulated French, she had denied being able to understand their broken attempts at Russian, while in fluent English she had derisively commented to Natasha that in her estimation they were nothing more than country bumpkins who had probably never ventured beyond their French ports except on that one particular occasion. The fact that she had known several of them could understand English had allowed her to deliver the final coup de grace to their much inflated arrogance.

"The workings of your mind are much too complicated for any simple fellow to clearly comprehend, madam," Tyrone replied to her conjecture. "But then, perhaps I'm not the only one you're able to bemuse. I think there are times when you totally confuse Natasha and, I venture to guess, yourself as well."

Synnovea paused a long moment in museful reflection before she was willing to admit she had such a weakness. " 'Tis true I cannot always discern a real sense of my emotions. At times, my respect for a person has been cloaked by feelings of affection until that one who has won my esteem seeks to kiss or bestir some tender response from me, then I feel my hackles rise and I have to hide my revulsion lest I shatter the confidence and hopes of the one I once honored. A few have been able to discern my dwindling enthusiasm and have derisively dubbed me the icemaiden." She lifted her slender hands in a dramatic portrayal of one who protested an injury. " 'No tenderhearted snow maiden is this!' they complained, seeking to mollify their badly wounded pride. 'She is far too cold and reserved!' "

Tyrone had never been wont to voice such complaints, for he had always found the converse to be true. Synnovea was too warm, alive, and alluring for him to even contemplate reprimanding her for those specific faults. "Tell me, madam. This revulsion you make mention of . . . " He eyed her closely as he cautiously presented his question. "Did you not experience it with me, too?"

Synnovea's face softened sublimely as a smile of gentle amusement teased her lips. "Nay, my lord, and that is truth. I was sure you were a cad after our first encounter in the bathhouse, but much to my chagrin, I could not cast you from my mind. Though I would have preferred otherwise, you became the champion with which I liberally enhanced my fantasies. Even now, I find myself comparing other men with you, but I fear all of them are found wanting."

Tyrone was surprised by the strange effect her answer had on his heart. Springing forth from its core, a growing warmth radiated through his whole being, softening his mood and reshaping his opinions. Still, he was cautious, wary of being duped. " 'Tis a handsome compliment you give me, Synnovea. Considering the many suitors who have tried to woo you, I could take encouragement to heart, but 'tis apparent you cared not a whit about the wounds you inflicted upon me by your deception."

Synnovea lifted her eyes to his in silent appeal, reluctant to end the evening with another argument. Tyrone had no need of verbal pleas when those silken-lashed orbs conveyed far more warmth and softness than mere words could ever do. With a sigh of compliance, he abstained from further comment and set the goblet aside. Doffing his robe, he half-turned to toss it into a nearby chair, failing to note the appreciative stare of his young wife.

In the past days Synnovea had been allowed freedom to knead his back to whatever degree and limit she had felt disposed to and, in so doing, had become enamored with the idea of gaining full liberty to touch and look at the complete man. After all, he was her husband and he had allowed her that particular privilege even before they had spoken the vows together. She most ardently desired such rights now.

When Tyrone faced the bed again, he became immediately aware of just where his wife's stare was directed. Aleta's attack on his person had not been any more intriguing than those curious green eyes that now boldly stared at him. Making a concerted effort to breathe normally, he teased, "If the sight of my nakedness disturbs you, Synnovea, perhaps I should take up the habit of wearing a nightshirt."

Synnovea lifted her chin to a lofty level and met the eyes that carefully observed her reaction. "If you care to remember the event, my lord, you once gave me permission to look at you whenever I wanted to. Does it bother you if I stare?" Her eyes chased downward briefly, and with a feeling of satisfaction, she answered her own query. "Aye, I see that it does. Indeed, my lord, you seem most susceptible. Perhaps you *should* wear a gown to bed if you're so easily aroused by my perusal."

With a lopsided grin Tyrone returned a gentle scoff to her suggestion. Her daring only whet his appetite the more, increasing the strain of holding himself detached from her for even a little while longer. "I'll wear no woman's garb to hide this conspicuous plight of unfulfilled passion, madam. Let it serve to remind you of your wily schemes to unman me."

Miffed that he should goad her again about her ploy to seduce him, Synnovea chided, "You undoubtedly have your wits tucked beneath your tail, sir, to rouse so easily. . . . "

"This is no tail we speak of," Tyrone informed her with a chuckle. "Nor do I carry my wits beneath it." Had he not derived much enjoyment from their conversation and her obvious interest in the subject, he would have ended the ogling and bawdy discourse anon, but he was wonderfully stimulated by her interest and felt no inclination to hide himself from her regard as he settled on the bed beside her. "Although, of late, madam, I tend to agree with you. 'Tis where my thoughts have centered of late."

Synnovea closed her eyes briefly, trying in vain to regain her aplomb. When she opened them again, she tossed her chin to indicate the area they discussed and replied in a satirical vein. "I've seen enough to know, my lord husband, that you're led about by your lusts as surely as if some sweet maid had hooked a large ring in your nose. 'Twas so from the very beginning, when you held me captive in the bathing pool."

"Held you captive?" A tawny brow jutted sharply upward in challenge to her claim. "I was merely trying to save you from a drowning."

"Had you not been spying on me, that threat would never have existed," Synnovea argued pertly.

"But the sights were so irresistible, I could not think of denying myself the opportunity to admire you."

"You plagued me from the first to gain permission to court me. Now you hold yourself from this marriage as if you've been terribly wronged, but from what I've been able to perceive, Colonel Sir, 'tis only your pride that has been badly mauled. You're highly offended because you imagine that you've been duped, but tell me, dear mate o' mine, what is the difference between us? You had intended to have me for your pleasure, while I had an earnest need and was willing to give you what you wanted most to see my own desire fulfilled."

"A harlot does the same," Tyrone stated tersely, losing all signs of humor at her logic. His eyes took on a smoldering darkness as he met her astonished stare. "Did you not play your game for your own profit?"

Synnovea caught her breath at his insult. "I'm no harlot, sir!"

His angry reply snapped back with quick dispatch. "Nay, madam, only a virgin with the heart of a harlot!"

"You wound me to the quick!" Synnovea complained, drawing threateningly close to tears. "And you have no cause! You know I've been with no one else but you!"

Tyrone once again agreed. "Aye, but I must beat off your suitors with a savage zeal or see my own life taken! They're akin to a pack of wild hounds, smelling a bitch in heat. Should I believe you never gave any of them encouragement?"

For a brief moment Synnovea gaped back at him, speechless with outrage, then she regained her voice with vigor and hotly denied his allegations. "I never!"

"You encouraged me!"

"You sought to have me!"

"Aye! That I did! But tell me true, madam, since I am bereft of the ability to read your mind. Why did you single me out from all the other men who wanted you? Any of them would have gladly done the service, but you sought me out to perform the deed for you! Can you explain your reasons?" He jerked his head jeeringly as he argued. "Major Nekrasov would have made love to you and willingly married you in haste. . . . "

"Whereas you were more inclined to take your pleasure and flee ere you paid the dues," Synnovea retorted with a comparable show of disdain.

"You know me not at all, woman!"

"That's true!"

"And you change the subject! Can you not tell me why you chose me?"

Synnovea shook her head in angry frustration until the long, curling tresses swayed softly about her shoulders. Again she sought to argue her case. "From the very beginning you displayed no hesitancy in your desire to take your pleasure of me, whereas Major Nekrasov never once made an advance toward me." Her reply was clearly the truth, but only in part. Tyrone's attentions had excited her from the very beginning, incredibly more so than the man they made mention of. Why could he not understand that her fondness for him had been much at fault in this matter of choosing him above all others?

Tyrone scowled at her, far from satisfied with her answer. "I never made any improper advances toward you either until I was deliberately deceived into believing you wanted my attentions."

"Nay, but you clearly conveyed to me what was on your mind. You told me repeatedly you wanted to court me."

"Was I the first man to tell you that?"

"You were the most persistent!"

"So! You chose me only because I was the most persistent, and yet I seem to remember your complaints against Prince Aleksei and the actions of Ladislaus. If they were hot to have you, madam, then I'm inclined to believe there were others just as zealous."

"What do you want from me? Blood?" Synnovea cried in exasperation and threw herself down upon her pillow, refusing to say another word.

Tyrone had knowingly harassed her, hoping to hear something quite different than what she had actually given him, but her replies had left him tersely unappeased. Angrily he grabbed the tray that bore the ointment and shoved it onto his bedside table, then reached to the foot of the bed to snatch the covers up over them.

Synnovea could not readily dismiss his irritation when his harsh breathing reminded her of his rage. With the same care one takes when a savage beast has settled its long, powerful form nearby to await the right moment to pounce, she drew away from him until the edge of the bed once again became her haven. The hour aged and still there was no respite for either of them. As his tossing and turning gave evidence of his continued restlessness, she finally braced up on an elbow to look at him. "Neither one of us can go to sleep while we're still angry with each other, and with everything that you must do on the morrow, you'll need your rest. Would it help if I rubbed the balm over your back?"

"No!" Tyrone's reply was sullen and curt, for he was genuinely provoked with her for having once again awakened all the emotions he had been trying to squelch.

Feeling painfully alienated from him, Synnovea rolled onto her back and folded an arm across her face, making no effort to halt the tears that flowed down her cheeks. If she had not feared being scoffed at, she would have given him a reply that might have astounded him, but there seemed no mending of the rift that presently separated them.

Realizing his denial of her offer had been spoken in a tone of sharp irritation, Tyrone raised above her to offer an apology for his ill humor, but when he saw the tears streaming profusely down her cheeks, he realized he had behaved no better than a hoary ogre. It caused him pain to see her crying, and with a heavy sigh he repented of his dark mood, knowing she was right. He would never be able to sleep until their quarrel was mended.

Sliding closer, Tyrone lifted her arm away from her face despite her struggle to keep it there and then laid his own close around her as his eyes traced her averted profile. "Synnovea, I'm sorry. 'Twas not my intent to be so harsh with you." He reached up and, with a thumb, gently wiped away the tiny rivulets that flowed down her face, feeling a keen sense of remorse for having treated her so unfairly. His breath brushed her face as he watched her intently, but the delicate eyelids trembled with Synnovea's efforts to avoid meeting his gaze. "Can you not understand, Synnovea, that after desiring you so desperately and wanting you for my very own, my temper was goaded by the thought that you only wanted to use me for a time before you cast me away? I have no way of knowing if I should trust my feelings whenever I'm with you.

Angelina pledged her troth to me in marriage, too, and then . . . "

The green eyes flew wide in horror, and Synnovea rolled away from him as if she had been stung. From the edge of the bed where she balanced precariously, she stared at him in roweling apprehension, her tears forgotten. "Are you telling me, sir, that you're married to someone else?" She flailed the air with a clenched fist, warning him to keep his distance as he reached out a hand to draw her back. A cry of outrage tore itself from her throat. "You deceived me! You let me believe you were without a wife! And all this time, while you played the injured one, you told your lies and duped me!"

"Synnovea! It's not what you think!" Recognizing her panic, Tyrone rose up close beside her and would have taken her by the arms, but she snatched away and glared at him in loathing disdain.

"Don't touch me, you *lying lout!*"

"Dammit, Synnovea, listen!" he barked and grabbed her by the arms, giving her a little shake as he commanded her to give an ear to his words. "I was married in England several years ago, but my wife died before I came here! You are quite properly the *only* wife I now have!"

The sharp, piercing ache that had catapulted through her, which had been mingled with a disturbing sense of having been cruelly betrayed, now slowly dwindled into a feeling of reprieve. It was as if her life had been given back to her, as if he had been absolutely lost to her and was hers once again.

Another thought dawned, and again Synnovea carefully examined the lean, handsome visage so close above her own. "You're the man you spoke of a short time ago, aren't you? The husband whose wife betrayed him with another. . . . "

A pained frown creased Tyrone's bronzed brow as he acknowledged that fact. "I'm the one."

"How could any woman have betrayed you?" Synnovea questioned in amazement. She could not even imagine the vilest harlot seeking after another if she had such a man for a husband.

Moving away to his side of the bed, Tyrone folded an arm beneath his head as he braced back on a pillow. For a long moment, he stared at the canopy above their heads until Synnovea came and perched beside him. Feeling her close regard, he finally deigned to meet her gently inquiring gaze and, with a halfhearted smile, began to speak. "Angelina was younger than you when we first married. Had she lived, she would have been your age now. Even before suitors were allowed to call upon her, she had men swarming about, waiting in droves to bid for her hand. It did not hurt that her father had wealth and made provisions for a rich dowry. Once she reached a proper age, she spent much time at court and was entertained by the best of roués. Our parents were neighbors, you see, and I watched all of this from afar as she was growing up, thinking her naught but a child. She saw me out hunting one day and rode out to talk with me, perhaps to show me that she had grown up since last we talked. She was witty, charming, beautiful, everything a man could want in a wife. She told me that even as a child she had dreamed of one day becoming my wife and had set her cap to win me after being a distant witness to several of my courtships over the years. She was dedicated to the idea of wearing down my resistance until I finally proposed. I married her without taking into full account that she might grow bored with my frequent absences from home after being so avidly courted by other swains. You know the rest. While I was away in the third year of our marriage, she betrayed me with another man who made light of the affair after she told him of the babe they had made together. He ridiculed her for having taken him seriously and boasted to others of his deed and his bastard whelp that was growing. I came home and found Angelina trying to hide her condition from the world, even though she was already well along by then."

"You say nothing of love, and yet I sense that you cared for her," Synnovea subtly prompted.

"I cared for her in a way any husband might care for his wife," Tyrone conceded, but checked himself before he added, But I care for you more.

"I'm your wife," Synnovea reminded him timidly. "Does that make any difference?"

"Aye." Tyrone allowed one slow nod and the single word to suffice as his answer, not daring any further explanation. If she really knew how his heart was wont to treasure even her merest smile, he feared she might seize upon his fondness and use the knowledge to his own painful chagrin.

Synnovea was not overwhelmingly reassured by his meager offering, but she was eager to encourage his affection. As winsomely as any loving wife, she snuggled close against his side, laying an arm across his chest and her head upon his shoulder. "I'm glad, Tyrone," she sighed softly. "I like being your wife. Only, I wish it could be better between us."

Tyrone felt very much like a man whose wits had just been staggered by shock. This was not the declaration of an uncaring and self-minded maid, which he had once been thoroughly convinced she was. Yet even with his rallying hope and determination to set aside his abstinence, he dared not air his feelings just yet, for fear she might use her wiles to try and tempt him beyond his ability to resist.

"I'll be going after Ladislaus in the very near future," he informed her. "I have every intention of bringing him and other members of his band back to justice. I don't know just how long I'll be gone."

"I'll miss you," Synnovea said quietly as she sought to blink back the tears that came quickly to blur her vision.

"Natasha will keep you company in my absence and make the days seem shorter."

Somewhat afraid to trust her voice, Synnovea managed a noncommittal shrug. She loved Natasha, but she much preferred having him near.

"I'm free the day after the morrow," Tyrone murmured as he turned his face into the softly curling tresses. "If you've nothing better to do, would you be willing to teach me the language?"

Eager for the opportunity to spend some time with him, Synnovea nodded against his shoulder. Then as he spread the sheet and comforter over them again and pulled her closer with an arm, she wiggled deeper under the covers, not caring how her gown slid up over her thighs. She laid her cheek upon his chest and then, with her fingers, lightly traced his nipple before raking them through the crisply curling hair growing close around it. Nuzzling her face there, she lightly brushed her lips against the pink crest before tilting her head downward to hide her smile. Once again she settled her cheek upon his chest, aware of his arousal, but quite content to let him battle his emotions within his own brain and body. At least she could take heart that she still had the ability to kindle his passions.

Tyrone mentally groaned and, seeking some defense from her coquettishness, lifted his arm from around her and rolled over onto his side, setting the barrier of his back between them. Synnovea's purposes were only temporarily deflected. Once again she snuggled to him, this time tucking her thighs beneath his naked buttocks and pressing her unbound breasts against his back.

With only the thin cloth of her gown between them and every swelling curve remarkably designed for the purpose of tormenting him, Tyrone was completely deprived of every sane thought except one, and that was the realization that he had been utterly foolish to ever imagine that he could have long denied himself the very treasure he had craved so fervently.

Chapter 22

Ⓢ⌒Ⓢ

ALI WAS CLEARLY ECSTATIC OVER THE IDEA OF SEEING
the colonel perform in a parade which she had heretofore
only heard rumors about. She was perhaps the driving force behind their early arrival at the Kremlin,
but definitely not the only one eager to witness the
events. Synnovea was both excited and nervous over
the prospect of seeing Tyrone and his men performing on the field for the tsar. She was most anxious
for him to attain all of his goals for a flawless exhibition, especially now that there were other troops
of Hussars eager to win from his unit the distinction of
being the best and most impressive.

For her husband's pleasure, Synnovea had donned a
dark iridescent green taffeta of European design. She had
followed the limitations laid out for a married woman
in her country and had fashioned an enveloping cap of
elaborately rich velvet for a covering for her head. The
effect was similar to a large sultan's turban adorned with
sweeping black feathers and the bejeweled clasp Tyrone
had once brought back. Synnovea had no way of knowing
that in a few short weeks she would see her creation
become the craze among European wives who had been
there to view the headpiece.

Natasha had been caught up in the enthusiasm
of their outing and was vivacious in both mood

and spirit as she left the carriage and hurried past friends and acquaintances, waving greetings to all. Prince Zherkof hailed her from afar and hastened to catch up with them as she, in turn, tried to keep pace with Synnovea. Arriving at the pavilion where the other wives and families were gathering, Synnovea paused to take a deep breath, much to the relief of the two women who had lagged behind in her wake. Rosy cheeks on all attested to their precipitous flight across the grounds in the crisp morning air.

"You should be grateful that Tyrone wasn't here to witness your arrival, my dear," Natasha exclaimed breathlessly as she dabbed a lacy handkerchief to her cheeks. Even on such a chilly day, her face was flushed with a rosy hue that had been stirred forth by their dispatch. "Otherwise, you might have given your husband the impression that you were anxious to see him all spiffed and polished."

"How you do run on, Natasha," Synnovea chided with a lighthearted laugh. "I suppose you just came along to needle me and have no real interest in watching the proceedings. If that's all you've come for, perhaps Prince Zherkof can entertain you while I watch the parade." She inclined her head imperceptibly to indicate the gray-haired man who was rushing toward them. "He's coming now to save you from this dreadful boredom we've addressed ourselves to. . . . "

Natasha chuckled at the girl's spirited banter. "A team of Prince Zherkof's finest horses couldn't drag me away from this event, my dear. You know that as well as I do."

"Of course," Synnovea answered with a smug smile. "I just wanted to hear it from your lips."

Both women swept into a deep curtsy as Prince Zherkof joined them. The man's dark eyes twinkled admiringly as he complimented Synnovea on her apparel, but when he settled his gaze on Natasha, they glowed with a different light, one of avid adoration. Even after several gentle rejections, he had not lost hope that Natasha would some-day relent and accept his proposal of marriage. After all, it was what everyone had been expecting for some years now.

"Perhaps such fine feminine pulchritude should adorn the tsar's pavilion where it can be better viewed," Prince Zherkof magnanimously suggested, "and where I can better serve you both."

Synnovea gently declined the favor. "I fear I must forgo your gracious invitation, Prince Zherkof. My husband is expecting to see me here, and I would not have him think I had refused to come. Of course, there is no reason why Natasha cannot join you."

The prince was eager to convince the older woman. "So many of our friends are there, Natasha." The cor-ners of his mouth twitched with amusement as he confided, "Even the Princess Taraslovna has made it a point to be there. I think she's trying to get back in the tsar's good graces. And you'd be amused to see that sober little cleric whom she dotes on try-ing to attach himself to the Patriarch Filaret. I've no doubt his holiness can see through Voronsky's compliments and will eventually grow bored with the man. Whatever happens, the events should prove interesting."

"I'll come later, Vasilii," Natasha pledged with a warm smile. "Perhaps after the parade, when you're not so busy introducing diplomats and foreign emissaries to His Maj-esty. Will you be able to join us this evening for dinner, or must you attend the banquet for the dignitaries?"

"Alas, my services will be needed at the banquet." He looked at her in eager hope. "Another time, perhaps?"

"Of course, Vasilii, but we'll talk of it later."

His dark eyes gleamed back at her. "After the parade?" At her nod, he lifted her hand and bestowed a kiss upon her slender fingers. "I will return to fetch you."

The pair of women smiled as they observed his depar-ture through the gathering throng of people. Synnovea slanted a curious glance toward her companion, who continued to stare after him.

"Do you suppose you'll ever marry him?"

Natasha heaved a sigh of contentment. "In time perhaps. I just want to make sure the memories of my late husband will not come between us. After having the best, 'tis hard to be satisfied with anything less."

"From what I've been able to determine about the man, I rather doubt that you'll be disappointed with Prince Zherkof or his love for you."

Natasha's dark eyes danced with humor as she met the other's gaze. "What will the gossip mongers say about me then? That awful Natasha Catharina Andreyevna! Married again for the fourth time! Disgraceful!"

"There's not a woman your age who isn't jealous of you."

" 'Twill certainly give Anna Taraslovna something to talk about. After all these years, she's never forgiven me for being Aleksei's first choice as a wife."

Synnovea stared at her friend in astonishment. "I didn't know."

Natasha lifted her shoulders briefly in a casual shrug. " 'Twas nothing of any consequence to speak of, my dear. Aleksei and I barely knew each other, but after a brief meeting, he vowed to have me. He offered my parents a contract of marriage, but they had already promised me to my first husband. It was as simple as that. Nothing more came of it, and a pair of years later he and Anna were wed."

"I always sensed there was some intrinsic reason for Anna's hatred of you. Now I understand more clearly."

"Goodt morn'n!" The salutation came from behind them, and both women turned to find Aleta Vanderhout smirking at them. Immediately the woman's gaze descended as she considered the well-dressed elegance of the two, especially the stylish flair of Synnovea's gown and cap. Then she simpered in a voice dripping with derision. "My! My! Yu two certainly try and steal all the men's attention away from the rest of us, don't yu? Why, itz a wonder yu're not out there on the field with them."

As graciously as she could manage, Synnovea turned to her friend as she swept a hand to indicate the fair-haired woman. "You remember Madame Vanderhout, don't you, Natasha? She came to your house after the wedding."

Natasha inclined her head briefly in answer as she recalled the shouts of General Vanderhout filling the manse. "Of course! How could I forget? Your husband had me searching the whole house for you so he could expedite his departure. I nearly collapsed from exhaustion doing so and was most thankful when you made an appearance."

Aleta declined comment as she faced Synnovea with a brittle smile. "How goodt o' yu tu come out tu see yur husband's parade, Synnovea. Or havef yu really come tu view all the other men?"

"Why should I, when my husband is the most handsome among them?" Synnovea managed an equally stiff smile as she silently vowed to let herself be hanged and quartered before allowing Aleta the privilege of seeing her upset by her presence. "Though I can well understand why your eyes might roam elsewhere, there's absolutely no reason for me to follow your lead."

Natasha delicately coughed behind a handkerchief as she made a gallant effort to keep her composure. It was only through an act of incredible perseverance that she was able to maintain her dignity, especially when she was confronted with the sight of Aleta's jaw slowly dropping. That one literally stared agog at Synnovea.

An uncomfortable moment of silence elapsed before Aleta looked beyond the two women and suddenly smiled. Quickly excusing herself, she stepped past them, now intent upon leaving the pavilion.

Synnovea stared after her as Natasha leaned close to whisper, "I sense Aleta has given you just cause to dislike her."

Synnovea tossed her head at the very idea of what the woman had done. "That shameless little trollop had the nerve to accost *my* husband right in *our* chambers!"

"What unmitigated gall!" Natasha's lips twitched with a threatening smile. "And how, might I ask, did Tyrone meet this brazen overture?"

Detecting the esprit in the older woman's response, Synnovea relaxed considerably until her eyes fairly danced with delight. "Thankfully he answered in a manner any wife can approve of, and since neither of them knew of my presence, the rebuff seemed genuine."

"I'm glad Tyrone didn't disappoint you, my dear, but I never thought he would. He's quite enamored with you, you know."

Synnovea replied with a small shrug. "I can't be sure of that with the way things still are between us, but then, the same could be said of me." She met the elder's look of smiling amazement. "You were right about him, Natasha. Everything you ever said about him is true."

Natasha laughed softly. "I'm glad you're finally beginning to believe me."

Again they turned to watch Aleta make her way through the growing crowd of people. Her primary goal appeared to be a Russian *boyar* who seemed intent upon carefully perusing the young ladies who passed in front of him. When Aleta reached him and laid a hand on the man's shoulder, he turned to face her.

"Aleksei!" Synnovea clutched a trembling hand to her throat as she remembered her last confrontation with him. A vision of Tyrone hanging by his wrists from the rafters came back to haunt her, and for a moment she was shaken by a memory of the fear that had ruthlessly assailed her that night.

Natasha raised her own worried gaze to Synnovea's pale visage and watched as her young friend struggled to control a violent shivering. "Synnovea, my child, what's wrong? You look as if you've just seen a ghost."

Shaking uncontrollably, as if she stood unprotected in

a crisp, freezing wind, Synnovea continued to stare at the swarthy prince, seemingly transfixed by a stunned stupor. "Aleksei would have killed Tyrone for what I did, Natasha. In my zealous quest to gain my freedom from Prince Vladimir, I nearly saw Tyrone's life forfeited . . . all because of my own selfish desires."

"Hush, dear," Natasha soothed. "It's all in the past now. Things have turned out well. You should forget what Aleksei tried to do to you both."

Synnovea's fears were not so easily set aside. "I see no reason for Aleksei to be here, except to cause trouble for Tyrone."

"But how can he, my dear, when Tsar Mikhail is here to witness his malicious pranks?" Natasha reasoned. "Aleksei would not be so foolish."

"The man is abhorrently evil, Natasha. He's vicious and spiteful, and one of these days, he'll seek his revenge on us when we're least expecting it. I don't trust him."

"Neither do I, but that doesn't mean I'm going to let him steal my joy." Natasha affectionately laid an arm around the slender waist of the younger woman and turned her about until they faced in the opposite direction. "I wouldn't worry in the least about what Aleksei might do here, when he'd be clearly overwhelmed by all of Tyrone's friends. He wouldn't dare offend your husband when there's a chance he would arouse so large a number against him, and the tsar, to boot."

Synnovea calmed her concerns, realizing there was much logic to be garnered from Natasha's encouragements. Aleksei was too much of a coward to start trouble in a place where he would quickly suffer defeat.

"Me lamb, look!" Ali nearly jumped up and down in exhilaration as she pointed toward a mounted troop of men approaching the field. At the forefront rode Tyrone, resplendently bedecked in a short red coat trimmed with cuffs and collar of dark green and liberally embellished with braid and looped cords of shining gold. Dark green

breeches were worn beneath black, thigh-high boots polished to a glossy sheen. A silver helmet, with a short
brim that was worn low over his brow, sported a red
plume, signifying him as the officer in command of this
particular troop. The feather dipped and fluttered in the
light buffeting breezes and was readily visible, allowing
Synnovea to locate him quickly as they rode across the
field to give homage to the tsar.

Synnovea's heart thumped in her breast as the trum-
pets sounded a fanfare. In the next moment the horns
fell silent, and then a low rumble of drums began almost
softly, then the volume grew by ever-strengthening
degrees until the drumbeats became pulsing vibrations
that matched the sudden, smooth, sweeping advance of
the first cavalry unit onto the field. The mounted Hussars rode not as separate individuals, but in unison, as
if they were all of the same body and completely in
harmony with their steeds. Seeming securely attached
to their saddles, they performed a maze of maneuvers
that held Synnovea completely entranced. She watched
in rapt attention as the troop split apart to circle the
grounds in opposite directions, then rode across the field,
crisscrossing the paths of others from the opposing line
before coming together again in a dazzling, intertwining
display of horsemanship. A moment later the riders
divided again, this time in squared-off columns. After
another circling sweep around the field, they merged like
slender blocks melding together. On and on they rode to
the fascination of everyone who was there to witness the
sight, drawing applause and sighs of admiration from
even the most stoic.

The thrills intensified for Synnovea soon after the
troop began to perform their maneuvers closer around
the pavilion where the wives stood. Ali skittered
about like an excited hen, pointing at the colonel
and boasting to other servants that he was her master. Even a warning twitch or two on her skirts by

her mistress was not enough to remind the woman to pay attention to proper decorum and not to boast.

"Magnificent!" Natasha commented, seeming to put the younger woman's thoughts into words.

"Yes, he is, isn't he," Synnovea murmured, completely distracted by the sight of her handsome husband leading the procession. With a sudden certainty, she knew that none of the other regiments would be able to bestir the heart of the tsar more than Tyrone's troop had, for if her own reaction proved to be an indication, then His Majesty's heart would be nearly thumping out of his chest.

The corners of Natasha's lips twitched upward as she glanced around at her companion. "I was talking about the performance in general, my dear, but yes, your husband is, too."

A deepening blush stained Synnovea's cheeks as she glanced in some embarrassment at her friend, but Natasha's laughter was warm and inviting, completely infectious. The gaiety of the younger woman could not be long contained, and both women relented to their mirth, enjoying it at its richest.

Princess Zelda hurried to join them as Tyrone's unit left the field and another cavalry troop rode out to perform for the tsar. "What did I tell you, Synnovea? Isn't your husband magnificent?"

Natasha and Synnovea dissolved into laughter again, lending to Zelda's complete bemusement until Synnovea took a moment to explain to her that they had just been elaborating on that very fact.

"There are many women here who hold that same opinion," Zelda confided. "You'll likely see a fair sampling when this is over. They simply adore the colonel!"

Synnovea was somewhat troubled by the princess's prediction. "More of Aleta's ilk?"

Zelda placed a pair of fingers across her smiling lips as she glanced around obliquely, then she leaned near her friend to whisper, "More subtle, I hope!"

"What do you prescribe that I do to stake my claim?" Synnovea questioned, responding with humor to the animated gaiety of her friend.

"Oh, didn't your husband tell you?" Zelda asked with amiable enthusiasm. "You'll be presenting your colors to him. It's become a private tradition among the wives, so you'll be able to disappoint all the other women who want your husband for their own. Many are well aware of the fact that in the past he's gone without a lady's colors. They may have no ken of his marriage and might try to offer their colors as consolation."

Synnovea's eyes clouded with sudden worry. "But Tyrone didn't tell me, and I've no colors to give him."

Thoughtfully Zelda scanned her friend's apparel and took note of the elegantly embroidered green scarf that was tucked beneath the high collar. "If you've nothing better, I'm sure that will suffice. 'Tis beautiful."

A smile brightened Synnovea's face as she doffed the silk and modestly closed her collar to hide her throat. Zelda nodded her approval and was there some time later when Tyrone rode up to the pavilion with the other men. Several young women crowded about him as he dismounted and complimented him profusely on his horsemanship. Their adoration extended to congratulatory pats on his back or caressing strokes along his sleeves as they sought to delay him, and as Zelda had foretold, some had scarves in hand and were anxious to make the offer, but Tyrone was most eager to extricate himself from their attention and, politely thanking the women, stepped past them. Sweeping off his helm, he strode purposefully to where Synnovea awaited his approach with a brilliant smile.

"I've been told 'tis the custom among the wives here to present their husbands with colors," she murmured warmly. "Would you honor me by accepting my colors?"

Tyrone presented his arm for her to tie on the scarf as he gave a ready answer. " 'Tis to my honor you give them, madam."

"It was thrilling to watch you today."

Her eyes conveyed such warm admiration as she attached the silk that Tyrone had to remind himself to breathe. " 'Twas thrilling to have you here watching me."

Natasha touched Synnovea's arm and whispered a warning. "Anna is coming with that goat, Ivan. She looks terribly put out."

Annoyed by the interruption, Synnovea turned just as the woman marched up the steps to the pavilion. The princess's thin jaw was rigidly set, and as she halted before Synnovea, the gray eyes bestowed a glare that was meant to penetrate with the same efficiency as two piercing slivers of frozen steel.

"The minute my back was turned, you started playing your foul little games to embarrass me before my cousin. I would never have left Moscow had I known what mischief you would connive to brew in my absence."

Zelda interrupted cautiously. "This really doesn't concern me, so I'd better leave now and find my husband." She squeezed Synnovea's hand in gentle encouragement as she pressed a cheek against the other's and whispered, "Anna is just irate because you escaped her little ploy to see you married off to Prince Dimitrievich."

Stepping away, Zelda almost stumbled over Ivan Voronsky, who had halted close behind her, apparently in an attempt to overhear what was being said. He sneered in obvious distaste as Zelda stared at him in surprise, then with a hurried excuse, the young princess made her departure.

"Another little witless friend of yours, I presume," Ivan observed derisively, glancing over his shoulder at the fleeing girl. Turning back, he fixed Synnovea with a glare as she made protest.

"Princess Zelda can hardly be considered witless, sir! Nor are you the one to judge the wisdom of another when you have no idea what that word means!"

"Have you room to boast on any account?" Ivan challenged. "I know what you are! I've known it all along! You're naught but a filthy little slut!"

The cleric's thin arm was seized in a steely vise, eliciting a sudden yelp from the man who looked up to meet the glaring blue eyes of the Englishman.

"Be careful, toad," Tyrone rumbled. "Someone might be tempted to break that thin, scrawny neck of yours and do the world a great favor. In other words, little man, if you can't keep a civil tongue in your head when you're talking to my wife, I might be obliged to do it myself."

Releasing the smaller, wide-eyed man, Tyrone took his wife's hand in his. "His Majesty has requested that I bring you to his pavilion ere we involve ourselves in the celebrations to be held afterwards." He glanced briefly to Anna and gave the woman a curt nod. "If you will excuse us, Princess. The tsar will be wondering where we are."

Tyrone settled his helmet on his head and pulled Synnovea's arm through the crook of his. "Come, madam. We must not keep His Majesty waiting."

"I'll tag along with you," Natasha announced. "Prince Zherkof wanted me to join him and since the air has grown quite offensive here, I've decided to seek a more fragrant location." Natasha smiled smugly as she met Anna's glower, then with a soft, smug chuckle and an elegant toss of her head, she joined her friends as they made their way toward the royal pavilion.

Tsar Mikhail was standing with the Field Marshall when the three arrived, but he eagerly left the man to focus his attention on Tyrone and Synnovea. "Well! I'm happy to see the pair of you looking fit! Indeed! Marriage seems to agree with you both." His dark eyes gleamed as he paused briefly to contemplate Synnovea. "You appear to be quite happy, my dear. Is all well with you?"

"Very well, Your Majesty," she affirmed with a timid smile.

Mikhail turned slightly to face the man at her side. "I must say I've never seen a better performance from your outfit, Colonel Rycroft. In fact, you seemed in remarkably good spirits while you were out there on the field." A threatening smile twitched at the corners of his lips. "Actually, even though I've been much awed by the display of your troop before, I was wondering what had motivated you so wondrously today above all your past performances, then I chanced to see your gaze turn toward the other pavilion, and then I gleaned some understanding of the reason. . . . "

Tyrone's bronzed features darkened even more as he struggled to subdue a deepening blush. "My most humble apology, Your Majesty, if I seemed distracted. . . . "

Mikhail quickly held up a hand to halt the polite plea. "I welcome with great appreciation whatever it was that encouraged the unparalleled perfection of your performance, Colonel. You completely delighted me and my guests far beyond the measure I was expecting, which was great." Thoughtfully he tapped his forefinger to his lips as he continued to curb his amusement. "It would not grieve me in the future if you allow that particular inspiration to encourage you. When you are so animated, it's to my benefit."

Tyrone responded with a crisp bow. "I am grateful for your kind indulgence, Your Majesty."

"Perhaps at a later date we should discuss your last petition. I'm sure you'll want to consider withdrawing it."

Tyrone's eyes dropped briefly as he suffered through a moment of painful chagrin, then taking a deep breath, he squared his shoulders and confessed, "You see through me very well, Your Majesty. I would be most kindly pleasured if you would forgive my impertinence and allow me to retract the petition."

"Of course!" Mikhail grinned broadly. "I was sure in time you would want to reconsider."

Chapter 23

THE NEXT MORNING SYNNOVEA LET HER HUSBAND SLUMBER on while she and Ali made use of the bathing chamber downstairs for her morning toilet. It was evident to her that Tyrone was in great need of rest, considering the long hours he had been devoting toward the training of his men and preparing for the foray they would take outside the city. The manse had been filled to overflowing with good wishers the night before, and amid all the feasting and imbibing, Synnovea had not been able to find a moment alone with her husband, for the guests had refused to let him leave their presence until the wee morning hours had come and gone, and for a change, it was she who had fallen asleep while waiting for him to come upstairs.

Tyrone roused from his slumber a pair of hours later and, realizing the place beside him was empty, launched himself from the bed before he noticed Synnovea sitting in a chair beside the windows. For a moment he stared, savoring the vision. She was clothed in a softly hued dressing gown and was busy mending a pair of his breeches that had been snagged during one of the practiced assaults he had been recently engaged in.

"Good morning," he murmured.

Synnovea admired his long, naked torso as her gaze swept upward to meet his inquiring smile. Her own was bright and cheery. "Good morning."

Tyrone raked his fingers through his hair, somewhat abashed by his tardy rising. "I didn't know I would sleep so long."

Setting aside the mended breeches, Synnovea rose and, brushing past him with a smiling glance upward, went to the door. "I told Ali I would let her know when you were awake, so Danika could send up some victuals for you."

She opened the door and called to the maid, who came quickly to receive her instructions. While she was so engaged, Tyrone entered the dressing room, where he wrapped a towel about his hips and lathered his face in preparation for a shave.

"I think it's about time I devoted some attention to teaching you Russian," Synnovea called to him from the bedchamber. "Are you agreeable?"

Tyrone stepped to the portal and braced his hand against the doorjamb as his lips stretched in a lopsided smile. "I was wondering when you would get around to it. I've been waiting."

Synnovea reached up a hand and tossed her loose tresses with an air of playful indifference as she reproved him for his extended absences. "You haven't been around long enough for us to even speak, much less allow time to instruct you."

"I'm here now, madam," he avouched, taking careful note of her scantily covered form as she moved about the room. "And I sincerely pledge my troth that I will be your most willing student."

Synnovea wondered if there was, at last, cause for her to be suspicious of the grin that twitched at his lips. She came to him and took the razor from his hand.

"*YA khaCHU paBRItsa,*" she said, then carefully pronounced the syllables, urging him to repeat them as she pressed him down into a chair. She plied the sharply honed edge slowly along his cheek, whisking away the stubble and the lather he had applied as he warily eyed her askance, trying to follow her movements. She said the phrase again as she leaned over him and scraped the soap from his jaw. *"YA khaCHU paBRItsa.* I want a shave. Now repeat it."

"YA khaCHA paBRItsa."

"CHU!" She took his chin firmly in hand and, lifting it up, forced him to look full into her face. *"YA khaCHU paBRItsa.* Say it right this time."

"YA khaCHU paBRItsa."

Synnovea smiled, wiping the rest of the lather from his face. "Excellent!"

Tyrone watched her lay aside the razor and then raised a dubious brow as she picked up a pair of scissors, which she brought threateningly near. Her eyes gleamed impishly as she snipped the air, prompting him to lean his head far back in obvious distrust of her intentions.

"YA khaCHU paSTRICHsa. I want a haircut."

"How do you say I *don't* want a haircut?" he queried dryly.

A giggle punctuated her answer. *"NYE NAda paSTRICHsa."*

"NYE NAda paSTRICHsa," he repeated with a wry grin.

"Coward!" she accused through more giggles as she slipped her fingers through his short locks and briskly ruffled them. With a playful growl, he moved forward out of the chair, dipping his shoulder downward and sweeping her onto the broad expanse as he came to his feet.

Synnovea squealed in glee and braced her hands upon his back as she tried to right herself, but Tyrone whirled her about the room until it seemed to sway and dip all around her. Coming to a halt, he lifted her high above him before letting her slide slowly down the length of his body. The towel came loose, and before her toes touched the floor, the ties of her dressing gown slipped free, allowing the garment to fall open. Her hips came to rest against his with stunning results, and of a sudden Synnovea found herself staring up at her husband's chiseled features as he carefully perused her bare breasts. She waited in breathless anticipation, wanting him to touch her, yearning to feel his warm mouth upon her skin. She could not read his thoughts, and wondered if he was again frozen by the war that raged within him. Hoping to urge him beyond that conflict, she shrugged out of the robe in silken languor and moved her body in a mesmerizing, leisurely undulation as she stretched against him. Feeling his pulsing excitement, she curled her arms around his neck and teasingly rubbed her breasts against his bare chest as she reached up to touch her parted lips lightly to his.

"When will you make love to me?" she breathed softly against his mouth. "When will you touch me . . . let me touch you? We can't go on like this . . . I'm a woman, and you're my husband. . . . "

A light rap on the door intruded into the moment, and with almost a start of surprise, Tyrone raised his gaze and scowled at the offending portal.

"Who is it?" he barked tersely.

"It's me, milord," Ali replied. "I've come with your victuals, but there's a messenger waiting downstairs for ye. He says your scout has returned wit' word that he's found Ladislaus's camp an' wants ter talk wit' ye 'bout it. He wants ter know if'n yer scout should come here, or if ye'll be returnin' ter camp any time today?"

Tyrone briefly debated his choices, hating to leave now when the moment was ripe for him to consummate their marriage, but knowing that Avar would be exhausted after his return to Moscow, he delayed their nuptial joining for what he perceived would only be a little while longer. "Tell the messenger I'll ride over myself and speak with the scout."

Catching Synnovea and whirling her around in a circle again, Tyrone hooted in glee and then gave her an exuberant hug, before he set her to her feet again. Grinning down at her, he leaned down to caress her mouth with an ardent kiss and then rushed into the dressing room, there to properly outfit himself in clothes. When he returned to the bedchamber, he took up his sword and began belting it on as he stepped behind her. He was almost sorry to see that she, in roiling disappointment, had donned her dressing gown again. This time, without hesitation, he pulled her back against him and slipped a hand inside the robe to cup a round breast, halting her breath with the ecstasy of his touch.

"I'll return this afternoon as soon as I can," he whispered against her ear, sending warm shivers down along her quickening senses. "Will you wait for me?"

Eagerly Synnovea nodded, laying a hand upon his as she leaned back against him. "Please hurry."

Turning her about, Tyrone pulled her into his arms and kissed her passionately, holding nothing back. He left her nearly swooning from the fervid intensity of his kiss, but with a hope now blooming near her heart, Synnovea smiled and, a few brief moments later, waved to him from a window where she watched his departure.

Synnovea's joy seemed far too immense to keep it to herself, and until early afternoon she spent her time lifting the spirits of nearly everyone in the manse. Humming to herself and skipping along the halls, now and then pausing to perform the intricate steps of a folk dance, she became an enjoyment both to watch and to hear. Natasha smiled smugly to herself and, exchanging a knowing nod with Ali, came to the decision that everything was mending well in the Rycroft family.

Into this time of lighthearted gaiety, the darkening brumes of gloom soon descended to strip away Synnovea's exhilaration and her aspirations for the future. The dreaded harbinger came in the form of Major Nekrasov, who after passing Colonel Rycroft on the square and then pondering for several hours on the matter, finally deemed the time was ripe to inform the lady of her husband's intentions. Thus, Nikolai presented himself at the Andreyevna manse and politely requested a moment of privacy in which he could speak with the Lady Synnovea. He was allowed entrance and then bidden by a servant to wait in the open area of the great hall until the lady could be summoned from his mistress's chambers. A moment later Synnovea entered the room and came forward to graciously extend her hand in welcome to the major, who eagerly clasped it and bestowed a kiss upon its pale, flawless skin.

"How good of you to come see me, Nikolai," she murmured with a smile, then, indicating an oriel where they could be observed but not heard, led the way there. "I trust you've been well."

"Fairly so," Nikolai replied, savoring her beauty in the delicately hued shards of light that streamed in through the pale, translucent mica panes. "Of late, I've been much distressed by your marriage and have not had the heart to seek solace in the company of another woman."

"Oh, but you must try, Nikolai!" Synnovea encouraged. "There can never be anything between us, and I would grieve to see you so saddened by my marriage to the colonel."

"How can you be happy with him?"

The question caught Synnovea off guard. Though something within her warned her not to ask him to explain, she stared at him in some confusion, goading Nikolai to continue.

"Does he treat you as a husband should?"

She carefully gathered her words to feign a casual reply. "And why should he not? I am his wife."

Nikolai rushed on, fearing that the colonel had yielded to the strong temptation of her beauty. "Your husband told the tsar that he would hold himself from you until that time he was scheduled to leave, and then he had the effrontery to ask His Imperial Majesty to grant him an annulment from the marriage ere his return to England."

"You must be mistaken . . . " Synnovea began, feeling a coldness settling down deep within her.

"I heard him myself!" Nikolai insisted.

"Why have you come to tell me this thing now?" Synnovea queried suspiciously as her heart constricted in pain. "What is your purpose?"

The major detected a note of irritation in her voice and rushed to allay her distrust. "I came here to pledge my loyalty should such an occurrence happen. If you will accept me, I would be honored to exchange the vows with you once your present marriage is dissolved. I want to cherish you as a wife should be cherished."

Synnovea whirled to face the window where she struggled to hold back a violent eruption of tears. The reasons for Tyrone's restraints now seemed painfully, horrendously clear. He had intended to rid himself of her and their marriage before he went home to England. She was to be carelessly discarded as a wife and, if used at all, would soon be forgotten once he made his way back to the isles of his homeland.

"How long does he plan to remain here?" she questioned bitterly over her shoulder.

"A little over three years . . . until his tour of duty is fulfilled."

"Thank you for warning me, Nikolai," Synnovea said in a tiny voice, "but when there is so much time betwixt now and then, I cannot promise my hand to you, not knowing what will happen. We both must wait and see what the years will bear. Perhaps you will fall in love with another and regret any troth you pledge to me."

"Never!" the major cried emphatically.

"Nevertheless, 'tis best to bide our time 'til that day Colonel Rycroft leaves. I would not have him think me unfaithful to the vows we exchanged until they are truly severed."

"You would hold true to such oaths when you know they mean nothing to him?" Nikolai inquired in amazement.

Synnovea faced him with all the dignity she could muster. "There's a lot of time for him to change his mind. I would not want to jeopardize that possibility."

"But why?" Nikolai insisted, unable to understand. "Surely any other maid, upon hearing what I have just revealed, would be sorely offended."

Synnovea replied with a restrained shrug. "Perhaps the colonel spoke in haste and in resentment of the hurt which I caused him." Her lips curved into a sad smile as she added, "Perhaps because I love him too much to give up the battle ere it's barely begun."

Nikolai's shoulders slumped with defeat, and unable to find an effective argument to negate her hopes, he sadly took his leave of her, having sensed no encouragement from her to allow his return once he left the house.

Nikolai went outside and was in the process of making his departure when he realized he had delayed far too long in making the initial decision to come, for he now espied Colonel Rycroft riding down the lane toward the manse. Though he hurried to mount and be on his way before the man reached him, his haste lent incentive to the other to close the space between them with rapid dispatch.

"Major Nekrasov!" Tyrone nearly gnashed his teeth as he greeted the man with a forced smile. "What brings you here? Should I assume you've come on some errand from the tsar, or have you taken leave to visit my wife in my absence? I was sure I saw you earlier on the square, and it comes to me now that you did stop and watch me pass. What should I think? Have you come on my heels again to claim some of my wife's time for yourself?"

Nikolai grew red-faced with ill-suppressed ire, and after his disappointment with Synnovea, he was not in the mood to feel kindly disposed toward the colonel. "I came here to see your wife, but what does that matter to you? Would you not be relieved to have her taken off your hands?"

Tyrone swung down from his horse and tied the reins to the hitching post, then stepped around the stallion to peer up at the man. "We might as well settle the issue right here and now, Major, if 'tis your intent to try and take her off my hands." He scoffed in angry derision. "You've seemed eager enough in the past and have proclaimed your objective every time my back is turned. This time we'll settle the issue face-to-face."

"The matter is already settled," Nikolai stated sharply. "The lady obviously prefers to believe you will not leave her behind upon your return to England."

Tyrone's brows shot up in surprise until he recalled that Major Nekrasov had been there at the palace when he had foolishly uttered his statement to the tsar, and now it was obvious that Synnovea knew about his pact as well. "Perhaps I don't intend to leave my wife behind at all," he retorted, incensed by the man's haste to inform her. "Perhaps I intend to make love to her every chance I get and keep her so fat with babes in her belly that you'll have no chance to interfere again. Now begone from here before I thrash you to a bloody pulp."

Nikolai was not so easily threatened. "Just be warned, Colonel, if you don't want her, there are others who do, and if I hear one whisper of your mistreatment of her, you'll rue the day you ever came to Russia. Do I make myself clear?"

" 'Twill be a bloody cold day in hell, my friend, ere you'll hear such rumors," Tyrone growled.

"Good!" Nikolai nodded crisply. "Then perhaps you will live long enough to return to England."

With that, Nikolai reined his mount around and kicked the animal into a thundering canter. Tyrone watched him go, then with a muttered curse, whirled on a heel and raced into the manse. Finding no evidence of his wife's presence in the lower rooms of the house, he leapt up the stairs to seek her out in their chambers. The door rebounded against the wall as he charged through the portal, and with a start of surprise, Synnovea turned from the windows, quickly brushing away the tears that streamed down her cheeks as she faced him.

"Major Nekrasov was here," Tyrone spoke the obvious as he peered at her questioningly.

"He came to see how I was faring," Synnovea replied, somewhat warily. Sensing his intention to discuss the ins and outs of the man's visit, she moved past him to the open doorway. "Natasha has delayed the meal until your return and is awaiting our presence down below."

Tyrone tried to curb his impatience, knowing this issue would have to be discussed at length in the privacy of their chambers and not aired before others. Facing the door, he lifted his arm to Synnovea in invitation, and she, in turn, laid her hand upon his sleeve.

"You look beautiful tonight, Synnovea," he murmured in an effort to break the stilted silence.

"Do I?"

"Almost as beautiful as the day you came to the palace to speak the vows with me."

Synnovea spoke distantly. "I was not even aware that you had noticed me then. You seemed quite disturbed by the whole affair, so much so I was half expecting you to call a halt to the ceremony ere it was done."

"I was greatly troubled."

"I suppose any man hates to be coerced into a marriage he abhors."

"I do not abhor the marriage, only the circumstances that brought it about."

"Did you resent me encouraging your lusts, Colonel? I seem to remember they were already brewing."

Her aloofness did not dissipate during the meal, and not knowing how to repair the damage without having his words seem trite, Tyrone found himself descending into a dark, brooding mood as he watched his wife. He held his cup out often to be refilled, while he found no desire to take solid nourishment. For the most part, he ignored Natasha's attempts to draw him into conversation while his gaze hardly strayed from Synnovea.

Though other men might have shown some sign of being affected, Tyrone seemed coldly sober when he finally made his excuses to Natasha for an early retirement and escorted his wife upstairs. While Ali helped Synnovea dress for bed before the stove in the bedchamber, he doffed his clothes in the dressing room and returned to the larger room, garbed in a heavy robe. He lounged in a chair, watching Ali brush out her long hair and knew that Synnovea's hostility had not wavered in the least when she bade the servant to braid her hair.

"I prefer it loose," he stated curtly, waving the old woman away.

Reluctantly Synnovea answered Ali's questioning glance with a nod, and the old servant took her leave, closing the door behind her. Now having gained the privacy he had been waiting for, Tyrone went to his wife and tried to take her in his arms, but she eluded his grasp and went to stand beside the small writing desk that stood near the windows. From a drawer she took a small, leatherbound book of sonnets, which she intended to read until she fell asleep.

"Major Nekrasov was here." Tyrone took up the conversation where he had left off, finding no encouragement in her forbidding manner. "Is it your custom to entertain men while I'm away?"

"We were never really alone," Synnovea explained stiffly without glancing around. "We were in sight of everyone who happened past the door. . . . "

"Obviously the major fancies himself in love with you," Tyrone interjected. "Given the opportunity, he would no doubt take you to bed. He seems most willing."

Synnovea felt the sharp edge of his sarcasm and, in hopes of avoiding another confrontation with him, raised on her tiptoes to blow out the slender taper that burned atop the desk. She had been wounded and needed some time to adjust her thinking before coming to any firm decision. "Major Nekrasov has been a good friend to me in the short space of time I've known him, Colonel. If not for him warning Tsar Mikhail of Aleksei's intent, you'd not be here today, at least not as a whole man."

"He seems most willing," Tyrone restated with emphasis, needling her as he stepped close behind her. "The same as I was." He laughed sharply. "I proved so willing, you thought nothing of using me for your little gambit.

You had no qualms about letting me touch your soft breasts. Would you use him for your purposes . . . and let him fondle what you now withhold from me?"

Synnovea whirled to face him, and for the first time Tyrone caught a glimpse of a fury he had not known her capable of. As he stared into those thoroughly enraged green eyes, he realized in some awe that she had either been very adept at controlling her emotions until now or had found no reason to display her temper. She had always been so pleasing in manner even when he had deliberately provoked her that he had never expected her to reach such heights of rage.

"I have withheld nothing from you, sir!" she snarled. "You've drawn the boundaries yourself so you can demand your freedom once you return to England! After setting such limits between us, would you *now* have me welcome you with open arms? 'Tis your intent to leave here unshackled, so how can you cast the blame upon me for withholding myself from you tonight? How can you expect anything more? You neither want me *nor* the burden of this marriage. Though you spoke the vows, you made no honest commitment to me, at least not in your heart or in your head! Thus, you have no right to question me. You have no right to play the jealous husband! And as for that, I see nothing wrong in accepting the company of Major Nekrasov when you've shown no interest in having me as your wife. He overheard your gallant request for freedom from this marriage when you stood before the tsar, and he came here to ask me to marry him once you leave."

"Did he now?!" Tyrone displayed a range of temper she had never seen before, and this time it was Synnovea's turn to feel astonished. He advanced on her with rage distorting his handsome face, and before that towering wrath, she could do naught but stumble back in sudden fear. "Would he also sample your wares ere he speaks the vows with you and cuckold me while I lay lusting for you in our bed?" he growled. "Be damned! 'Twill not happen

to me again! I'll have no other man spilling his seed in my wife behind my back!"

Synnovea gasped in outrage, and her hand came forward with an angry sweep, cracking loudly against his cheek. Tyrone's head jerked aside with the impact of her blow, and when he looked at her again, his eyes blazed with a new fire beneath ominously lowered brows. His lean nostrils flared, and the muscles in his cheeks flexed tensely.

"The major will claim no virgin's blood upon your thighs," Tyrone rumbled. His hand reached out, seizing the top of her gown and, with one forceful swipe, ripped it completely open down the front. Synnovea gasped and stumbled back in surprise. For one brief moment she gaped down at her pale breasts gleaming in the candlelight, then whirled to flee, but Tyrone caught an arm about her waist to prevent her escape and, snatching her around to face him, took her hard against him. His eyes burned into hers for a split second of time, then his mouth plummeted down to seize hers in a demanding kiss that seared her to the very core of her being. Though she tried to push herself free, Synnovea could not move in his fierce embrace. Neither could she turn aside from the unrelenting invasion of her mouth as his tongue probed for an answer. His kiss deepened, slanting crushingly across hers in a savage assault that heralded his unswerving purpose. No protest could be made against his all-consuming passion, but as his head lowered and his kisses traveled downward, the fires began to leap and spread out of control. Her world turned topsy-turvy as his open mouth came upon her breast. He snatched the breath from her lungs with each stroke of his tongue until she twisted in his embrace, not knowing whether to seek her freedom or to pull his face closer.

Tyrone straightened and, tugging open his robe with one hand, discarded it with a shrug. He pushed the gown from off her shoulders and let it fall unheeded to the floor, then his eyes followed the lead of his hands as they boldly ranged down her body, claiming each curve, each hill and crevice, the highest peak, the deepest valley, igniting her senses even as she struggled to deny the possibility.

His lean nostrils flared as he bent and swept her into his arms, and in two long strides he was to the bed, lowering her amid the pillows and covering her sleek form with fervent kisses. A trembling beset Synnovea, blending with a shiver evoked from the cool sheets and the draft of air that swept over them. Sensing the chill, Tyrone rose and braced a knee on the edge of the mattress and, stretching upward, reached out to draw the heavy hangings closed around the bed to keep the cool air from drifting over their naked bodies. The long sinews in his arms and thighs flexed with his every movement, betraying his strength. He seemed to Synnovea in that moment as magnificent as any fabled lover that had ever been created in the imagination of a woman. No casual admirer could have denied his handsome features or the way his tall, broad-shouldered form complimented his uniform, yet only a woman who was intimately involved with him could fully appreciate the way his wide chest tapered to a lean, muscular waist and his narrow hips flaunted the boldness of his maleness. Even as she stared up at him in some awe, Synnovea realized she felt an anxious dread of what was to come and yet a strange excitement that made her tremble at the thought of becoming his wife in deed as well as by decree.

In the next moment he was bearing his weight down upon her, and this time Tyrone had no patience to wait. A broad hand slipped beneath her and lifted her hips against the fullness he displayed, scorching her thighs with the branding heat of his arousal. His hard, gleaming eyes delved into hers as if they would look into her very soul as he thrust the stalwart blade homeward. Suddenly a fiery pain exploded in Synnovea's loins, drawing a small cry from her as he pressed deep into the warmth of her. It seemed to Tyrone as if eons had passed since he had known the sated relief that he now sought. He forged well past the apex of clearheaded logic, sundering all of his plans for a nurturing initiation as he took his pleasure of her with bold, rapid strokes, vaguely aware that he was being rough, yet unable to stop the intensifying exhilaration that threatened to erupt. His hardened hips were relentless, attesting to the urgency of his quest, and as his muscular body moved with strengthening vigor against hers, his hoarsely rasping breath filled her ears, conveying to Synnovea's heretofore virginal mind a clear awareness of his ravaging need.

Finally the storm began to settle as the zeal of passion ebbed from Tyrone's body. In that small space of time Synnovea fully understood all the frustration he had endured during their most intimate moments together. At first, any feelings of pleasure had quickly diminished with the pain of his intrusion, but all the sensations he had aroused with his caresses had been revived, despite his urgency. Now when he had obviously no initiative left in reserve to bring her to that height of ecstasy he had deliberately introduced her to once before, she craved relief from the gnawing hunger that now roiled in her loins. She had no way of knowing that she would spend the better part of the next hour trying to cool the flaming fires he had lit within her, yet had not taken time to quench.

Embarrassed to tell him that she only wanted what he had given her before, Synnovea averted her face, refusing to look at him as he tried to kiss and talk with her.

"I'm not an ogre, Synnovea," he whispered as his lips paused against her temple. "And we are married, no matter what Major Nekrasov might have said."

After an incredibly long silence, Tyrone finally gave up trying to get her to look at him, and with a sigh of resignation, lifted himself from her. Relieved of his weight, Synnovea once again took refuge at the edge of the bed, where she curled into a tight knot and refused to look his way.

Any apologies now would have seemed insincere, Tyrone thought morosely as he rose and roamed restlessly about the room. Pausing beside the bed, he considered the tiny smattering of bloodstains on the sheet and what the presentation of her slender, curving back signified. Though she was obviously outraged at having been so callously used, he could not deny, despite the ponderous burden around his heart, that the vexing pain he had battled for so long was gone now, vanquished, and for the first time since their encounter in the bathhouse, he felt as if he could sleep through a whole night without awakening from the lustful dreams that had so often beset him. Indeed, he found it rather amazing that he had held himself back as long as he had.

Chapter 24

TYRONE COULD NOT EVEN THINK OF MAKING ANY PREParations to leave Synnovea the next morning when he knew she would not be in a mood to forgive him. As the first morning light streamed through the windows, bathing the chambers with a soft pinkish cast, he stood beside the bed, watching his wife sleep, unable to recall any moment he had ever spent alone with her that he had not considered totally pleasurable. Though he might have been averse to admitting it to anyone but himself after his whipping, her planned seduction had been the most provocative moment in his memory until last night, when they had finally been joined as one. Now it was difficult to imagine that he had ever experienced the equal of such bliss. Without a doubt, she had completely ensnared his mind and, perhaps now, even his heart.

He had dreamed of her again and then been snatched to full awareness by the soft, tantalizing pressure of her womanly form close against his bare back. She had been seeking his warmth again in her slumber, but his plight had only been intensified, for those soft curves had been utterly devoid of clothing and completely vulnerable to his slightest whim. Faced again with such overwhelming temptations, he had resolved to give her time to adjust to the change in their conjugal relationship and to settle her mind on accepting his husbandly attentions. Otherwise, his long-suffering abstinence had come to an end. She was his wife, and he wanted to treat her as if his whole world revolved around making her happy.

When he looked back over the time he had known Synnovea, Tyrone realized now that there had been something profoundly lacking in his relationship with Angelina. Though he had been fond of his first wife, he had never really treasured her with all of his heart, mind, and body as he had Synnovea from the very first. Perhaps down deep in his mind, he had never thought of Angelina as a mature woman, for she had been more like a child, ever vying for his affection and demanding to be shown affirmation of his devotion in great and ardent displays, hanging on to him at times when he had just wanted to sit quietly for a few moments and converse with her or visit with his grandmother or his parents without having to restrain her physically from distracting or embarrassing him by her constant attempts to kiss and fondle him.

In retrospect, Tyrone was wont to think that Angelina had grown up believing she could command anyone's love, just as she had demanded her parents' attention, being the only child upon whom they had bestowed their devotion. When Angelina had been forced to share his time or affection because of visits from his family or friends, she had later pouted and complained that he didn't love her and that he cherished everyone else far more. Once, she had even urged him to prove his love by lending his attention solely to her, at which time he had countered her suggestion and had promised to comply if she would give up her friends and family for him. Vehemently refusing such an agreement, she had then been compelled to allow him the same privilege of visiting those whom he had cherished or regarded as close companions.

It was bold in Tyrone's mind that in strong contrast, Synnovea was very much a woman in every sense of the word and not at all afraid of anyone usurping her rights and privileges as his wife. She had suffered a brief uncertainty because of the morning meals he usually spent with Natasha, but by her gentle encouragement of tiny Sofia's growing affection for him, she had proven her willingness to share him with others. There had only been one real instance where her jealousy and disdain had been clearly manifested, and that had been after Aleta had sought to seize his attention, along with other things, in the doorway of their chambers. No one could dispute her right to be outraged by a woman who tried to get from him everything he had been withholding from her.

Now here he was, struggling with an overwhelming desire to wake Synnovea. Still, he held himself in check, knowing she would be in no frame of mind to listen to him after he had forced her to serve his pleasure. Even so, when he dressed and went downstairs to join Natasha in the dining hall, he was no less disturbed by his inability to hide his disquietude.

"You seem preoccupied this morning, Colonel," the woman commented, having affectionately settled on the form of address that, in her mind, most aptly suited him. He was a man who was accustomed to giving orders and having authority, though she suspected at times he was totally at a loss as to know how to deal with his young bride. "Is something troubling you?"

Tyrone leaned back in his chair as a long sigh slipped from him. "As the day approaches for my departure, Natasha, I find myself reluctant to leave Synnovea. It makes me wonder if it will get any easier in the future."

Natasha studied him a long moment before she gave answer. "If I didn't know better, Colonel, I'd be tempted to think that you have fallen in love with the girl."

Her conjecture failed to surprise Tyrone. "What am I going to do?" He made no attempt to hide his concern as he confessed, "Major Nekrasov came here yesterday to inform Synnovea that I, in a moment of foolish inanity, had wheedled an agreement from the tsar which would have granted me an annulment upon the fulfillment of my military contract . . . if I, at that future date, could lend viable evidence of my celibacy while married to Synnovea."

The woman's brows lifted in mild surprise. "Do you have any hope of accomplishing that feat, Colonel?"

"Had I been in full possession of my faculties at the time, madam, and not been so seethingly outraged by Synnovea's ploy, I would have realized ere I made the attempt that I would quickly fail in that particular endeavor . . . and so I have. Only now, Synnovea wants nothing to do with me."

"I wouldn't worry about her reticence, Colonel, as long as you intend to make it right with her in the near future."

"That's the problem. I don't have much time to persuade her before I leave. I'll be here perhaps a week longer, maybe even a few days more, then I'll be gone for I don't know how long."

"Perhaps Synnovea will consider what is wise and let you speak your peace ere you leave. 'Tis true she can be obstinate at times, but she usually comes around when she can see the truth of the matter." Natasha leaned forward in her chair and laid her hand consolingly upon his as she offered him the only advice that seemed appropriate. "Go about your business as usual, Colonel, but watch for the opportunity to talk with her. Speak the truth, and don't be reluctant to tell her that you really want her to be your wife, even after you go home to England." Relaxing back in her chair again, Natasha contemplated his troubled features for a moment before she quietly asked, "Do you know what you'll be doing when you go home, Colonel? Have you made any advances in settling your problem there?"

Tyrone mulled over her question for a moment as he lent his distracted attention to straightening the napkin in his lap. "I have a house in London where I lived with my first wife. It's there waiting for us when the time comes for me to leave here. The other matter remains to be seen. My father has not said as much in his letters, but I fear the parents of the man I dueled with have not yet forgiven me for killing their only son. Still, I'm resolved to establishing my home there, once I leave here." He glanced up to meet the dark eyes that rested on him. "Do you think that Synnovea will be happy there . . . with me?"

A gentle smile touched her lips. "I think Synnovea will be happy anywhere, as long as she's with the man she loves. Actually, she has an aunt in London . . . her mother's sister, who is now her only living relative. It will be good for Victoria to have her close at hand. Of course, I will miss her dreadfully. . . . "

It was Tyrone's time to lay his hand reassuringly upon the woman's. "You'll be welcome at our home any time, Natasha. Your visit would give Synnovea and me a chance to return the favor you've extended toward us while we've been living with you."

"Oh, posh!" Natasha laughed and dismissed the idea of repayment with a wave of her hand. "I've enjoyed every moment you've been here and will continue to enjoy your presence until you must leave. Without both of you here, I'd be naught but a lonely old woman!"

"What?!" Tyrone chuckled, doubting the possibility. "With all your friends? I find that hard to believe, Natasha."

"Synnovea is as near to my heart as any daughter I might have had," Natasha avouched as her dark eyes grew misty with tears. "You both are like family, and although I have many good friends, there is that strong tie which binds my heart to Synnovea that none other will ever replace. Her mother was my very best friend; Eleanora was the sister I never had, and so, my dear colonel, you will always have to indulge the times I'm wont to act the mother hen."

Tyrone grinned as he teased, "A mother-by-marriage, so to speak."

"I pray you, Colonel! Show some respect for your elders!" Natasha insisted, then allowed her laughter to merge with his.

When the meal was concluded, Tyrone heeded Natasha's advice as much as he was able and rode off to work without going back upstairs. Much to the relief of his men, he was in a much more tolerant mood than he had been in of late. In the ensuing days he talked over the difficulties of the raid with Grigori and the scout, Avar, as he carefully devised the strategy they would use. While they worked with maps, drafts, and diagrams of the area where Ladislaus's camp was located, the lower grade soldiers took an accounting of supplies, weapons, and equipment, then stocked, repaired, or replaced what was needed and discarded what was not.

In anticipation of their departure, Tyrone allowed his men a pair of days off. Since they would be gone for at least a fortnight, he took his own time off along with the rest, but avoided forewarning Synnovea, sensing her pensive mood and unrelenting reserve. It had initially been his plan to talk with her about his forthcoming leave the night before he was sched-uled to take it, but after putting in such long hours with his men during the day, by the time Synnovea came from the dressing room and joined him in bed, he was already fast asleep. Of late, it had become her custom to dally overlong and out of sight until he finally reached that particular state, negating any possibility that would allow them to talk or do any-thing else.

Settling down beside him this late evening, Synnovea took care not to awaken her husband, well aware that he had earned the right to rest after pushing himself with great mental and physical feats throughout the day. Despite her aloofness whenever he was in atten-dance, she enjoyed the idle time to closely observe him while he slept. By now, his hair was longer than she had ever seen it. Heavy, straggly wisps fell across his brow and onto his temples, leaving him looking like some legendary Greek god from tales of yore.

He had recently taken a long slash across his cheek from a lance thrown by the youngest and most inexperienced soldier in his outfit, whom he had been trying to teach the art of throwing the weapon. The youth's clumsiness had nearly cost him an eye, and although her husband had tried to wave away her concern, saying it was no more than a light scratch which was not serious enough to merit her attention, Synnovea had insisted until finally, with a deep sigh of resignation, Tyrone had thrown up his hands and relented, acquiescing to her demand that he settle himself in a chair and allow her to cleanse and tend the wound. His lack of concern had been justified, for eventually no trace would remain as evidence of the injury, but Synnovea had not been reassured of that until he had allowed her to examine the abrasion more closely.

Such wounds were not anything new to Colonel Sir Tyrone Rycroft, Synnovea mused, leaning over him. There were small nicks and scars all over his body. She mentally counted two or so on his chest, another several along his arms, and a long one just above his groin where long ago a lance had glanced off his thigh and sliced across his lower abdomen, doing no serious damage, but nevertheless leaving proof of its passage. She was immensely grateful the weapon had struck no lower, for it might have rendered him incapable of provoking her with his manly passions.

Noticing the chill in the room, Synnovea carefully tugged the covers up over his shoulder as he lay on his side facing her. His eyes slowly opened to stare at her with only a vague awareness. Even so, a faint, lopsided smile traced his lips, warming her heart more effectively than any clever argument could. Some strange, loving feeling stirred within her, making her almost catch her breath as an indescribable joy encompassed her heart. Sliding as close to him as she dared, she laid her head on the same pillow as her eyes caressed his face. A moment later his arm came around her, pulling her against his

long form, and with a contented smile, she closed her
eyes, totally gratified to be in his embrace.

Synnovea woke late the next morning and was surprised to find that Tyrone had not yet made his
usual early departure. She heard him in the dressing room shaving, and while he was thus occupied,
she quickly slipped from bed and, donning a robe,
flew from the chambers. Calling for Ali, she hurried downstairs to claim the bathing chamber for her
morning toilet and was there several moments later
when Tyrone intruded into her bath. She glanced up
in alarm as the door swung open and, seeing him
amble boldly in, she hurriedly bade Ali to fetch her a
towel.

"No need to rush, my dear. I'm taking a couple of days
off before I'm scheduled to leave, so I'm really in no great
hurry."

"I was wondering about that," Synnovea answered
from the other side of the large towel as Ali held it up
to hide her exit from the tub. "You're usually gone by the
time I even wake."

"The men needed a couple of days off to relax before we
started out, and I was much in need of a good rest myself."

"You should have told me." After briskly toweling herself off with a smaller towel behind the makeshift screen,
Synnovea quickly smoothed a lotion over her skin before
donning a robe. "We could have been better prepared."

Tyrone smiled slyly, having successfully caught her in
the kind of disarray he had hoped to find her. Better
planning would have seen her up and garbed ere he
had a chance to rise. "I saw no reason to disturb the rote
of your day, madam. I just thought I'd come down and
share your bath."

Tyrone grinned as the tiny servant glanced around in
some wonder. "Ali, will you be kind enough to fetch
a bucket of hot water to warm your mistress's bath?"
he cajoled pleasantly. " 'Twill suffice for my needs this
morning."

A bright sparkle in the woman's eyes accompanied her giggle as she curtsied sprightly and flew across the room to do his bidding, leaving Synnovea to face her husband alone. The silken robe had molded itself to her damp skin and presented such delights to his closely attentive gaze that he felt his wits lagging somewhat. Ali sharpened them again when she came back and, urging her mistress aside, emptied the full pail into the bathtub.

"I'd best get in while it's hot," Tyrone mused aloud, plucking at the ties of his robe.

"Ali, leave us!" Synnovea bade instantly, seeing no hesitancy on his part about disrobing in front of the maid. The small woman scurried out as the garment dropped to the floor behind her, and with a grin, Tyrone settled into the warm, scented bath and idly scrubbed his chest as he closely eyed his wife.

Synnovea flounced about, angrily berating him. "Have you grown so accustomed to the mores of this country, my lord husband, that you now think naught of stripping before my maid? Why, you would shock poor Ali to the core! I doubt if she's ever seen a naked man in her whole entire life!"

"Perhaps 'tis time for her to gain some knowledge of men," Tyrone responded, admiring the robe's cloying eagerness to reveal his wife's curves, while hiding her actual nakedness to a degree that she mistakenly thought adequate. In her casual acceptance of its function, she gave no mind to its plunging décolletage and the undulating skirt that now and then swept open to reveal her long, sleek limbs.

"Ali has come three score and two years through a lifetime, and you now say she ought to gain some knowledge about men?" Synnovea was incredulous. "What do you think she should do? Go out and snare herself a lover at this late date? I have no doubt that Ali has settled on spinsterhood out of preference and has no need for such enlightenment. In fact, I've never heard of anything so ridiculous!"

Tyrone casually shrugged his broad shoulders. "You never know when she might get trapped in a bathhouse with a strange man. Without proper instruction, she could drown from the shock."

"Oh, you!" At his taunting grin, Synnovea looked around for a weapon and, choosing a bucket of icy water, christened him as no kindly priest would ever dream of doing.

Tyrone caught the full contents of the bucket in his face and, with a shocked and strangling gasp, came up out of the tub, stark naked and intent upon catching the winsome culprit. He swung one long leg over the rim and, blinking to clear his blurry vision, searched the chamber for his wife. Synnovea was already running toward the door, having decided it was high time for her to make a swift departure.

Throwing the portal open, Synnovea raced out, hearing Tyrone's padding footfalls coming after her. Casting an anxious glance over her shoulder, she gasped in alarm as she found him in full pursuit and hard on her heels. Bent on escape, she turned back and then came to a sudden tottering halt as she nearly collided with Natasha. Her startled gasp was immediately followed by another as she stumbled back several awkward steps into the solid bulk of her dripping wet husband. Knowing full well that he was as bare as the day he was born, Synnovea made a concerted effort to keep well in front of him as she tried to smile at the countess.

"Good morning, Natasha. A fair day, isn't it?"

"I came down to visit with you," the older woman commented with droll humor as she cocked her head to the side in an effort to catch a better glimpse of the muscular flanks Synnovea tried so hard to conceal. "But I see that you already have more than adequate company."

Synnovea stepped cautiously around in front of the woman's line of vision as she gallantly sought to preserve her husband's modesty, which she was sure he was seriously lacking. Lamely she stated, "You're probably wondering why Tyrone is here."

"Is that who it is?" the countess teased. " 'Tis difficult to recognize him without his uniform." She spoke past the girl as she addressed the man. "I missed you at breakfast this morning, Colonel, but I can see you had better things to do."

"I have the day off, Natasha, so I thought I'd take your advice. It might be the last chance I have before I leave."

"I wish you luck," she bade, then crinkled her brows as she contemplated the way his hair hung wetly over his ears. "Did someone try to drown you, Colonel? You look a bit bedraggled."

As Synnovea closed her eyes in painful chagrin, Tyrone settled his arms akimbo and gave the older woman a brief nod before he bent a purposeful stare upon his wife's head.

"Perhaps you will reconsider your departure, madam, and return with me so we may discuss matters more thoroughly," he suggested, quite willing to stand there and argue the point with his comely wife. There was already a puddle around his feet, but if she didn't soon relent, the possibility of it growing larger did exist, for he was not nearly as sensitive about his nakedness as she appeared to be.

Synnovea responded with a stiff nod, refusing to glance around. "If you wish, my lord."

"Good!" Tyrone replied and grinned in satisfaction. "I'll be waiting for you, madam, so I beg you not to be long. I may completely shatter Ali's innocence if I have to come searching for you." With a dip of his head to Natasha, he pivoted on a bare foot and stalked back into the bathing chamber as Synnovea hurriedly retreated in an effort to hide his departing form.

Natasha's brows twitched upward in amusement as she caught a glimpse of Tyrone's bare backside beyond his wife's slender frame. She could not resist a museful comment. "You know, Synnovea, the more I see of the colonel, the more he reminds me of my late husband."

Dipping into a quick, shallow curtsy, Synnovea made an excuse for her haste and, with a mortified groan, whirled and fled back through the doorway.

Natasha waved her hand in dismissal, trying to maintain her poise, which seemed to be infused with brief lapses into laughter. "Of course, my dear," she called after the younger woman. "Anytime."

Slamming the door closed behind her, Synnovea flung herself after Tyrone and ground her teeth as she demanded, "Have you no propriety?"

Tyrone faced her, settling his hands low on his hips. "I'm not going to wrap myself up in a monk's habit just to suit your delicate nature, madam, if that's what you're prattling about. Nor can you make me believe that Natasha hasn't ever seen a naked man. As for that, I'm certainly not ashamed of the fact that I am one."

"No, indeed! You strut about like a proud peacock and display your possessions before every woman who happens to be near!"

"What does it matter to you? I could lay my treasures on a block and you would not care! You'd rather keep that soft sheath reserved for some other gallant's blade than give me comfort and solace."

Synnovea gasped at his accusation. "That's not true!"

"Oh?!" Tyrone waved an arm eloquently in the air as he derided her denial. "Then if not for me and not for others, madam, then pray tell the name of the one you reserve it for? Yourself? As a trophy of your departed purity?"

"Of course not!" Synnovea flounced past him in a huff and then whirling, verbally accosted him. "At least I don't flaunt myself around like some knavish hawk, always eager for a peck or two!"

"If I appear *eager*," he stressed the word she had used, " 'tis only because I'm starved for want of that sweet succor you barricade behind that fine belt of chastity.

Though I waste away, you would keep the key well hidden in the coffer of your mind."

"What? Would you have me serve you as a common doxie?" Synnovea came toward him, deliberate and provocative, with a small shrug encouraging the fall of her robe from a smooth shoulder. "That's how you wanted me in the first place, wasn't it? Unwed, but in your bed? Your paramour? My dear Colonel, does it not prick you sore that you've been made to speak the vows with me? Indeed, it does! I've heard it so rumored that in a thrice of years you do intend to deny that you ever spoke them and would no doubt name whatever scion you beget to be your bastard whelp."

"I intend no such thing, madam!" Tyrone declared, wrapping a towel around his hips. "If you refuse to take solace in my simple assurance, then I'll lay in your hands documents to guarantee my name to all my heirs. Would such a deed suffice to appease your anger?"

Synnovea pondered his question aloofly. "In part, it might."

"What else would you have from me?"

"Only time will see the way of things," she answered. "Nothing can bind you more than the vows we spoke, and it remains to be seen whether or nay you will hold true to them."

"Would you, then, consider going with me before the tsar to hear me plead for a retraction of my request? It has already been done, but if you insist, I'll go before him again."

Synnovea raised her gaze to his in curious question. "Would you be willing to do such a thing?"

"I would not have offered had I not been willing."

"Seeing is believing, sir!" She tossed her head like a child playing at a game. "Perhaps I might be reassured when the event takes place."

"Then can we not be at peace until I leave to search out Ladislaus? Perhaps you will find yourself free of me ere the month is out, and this argument will be for naught."

Synnovea searched his face in sudden worry. "I would have you come back unscathed, Colonel Sir."

"I will try my best." Taking up his robe, Tyrone tossed it over his shoulder as he bade her, "Give me leave to spend some time with you before I depart. After this week I may not see you for a while."

Her eyes skimmed his long form worriedly. "Would you go upstairs like that?"

"Aye!" Tyrone said bluntly, squelching any possibility of her persuading him otherwise.

Rather than vex him further, Synnovea acceded to his disregard for propriety and, leading the way up the flight of stairs, crossed the antechamber to their rooms as he closed the door behind them. He stepped briefly into the dressing room, then came back to her with a pair of scissors in his hand.

"*YA khaCHU paSTRICHsa.*" He said the syllables carefully as he handed her the implement. "*MOZHna pakaROche ZAdi.*"

Synnovea pushed the curling tresses back from her cheek and smiled up at him. "Just in back? Don't you need it cut on the sides, too?"

"*MOZHna pakaROche pa baKAM . . . paZHAlusta.*"

"You're progressing very well, Colonel."

"*Bal'SHOye spaSIba.*"

Synnovea laughed and tightened the belt of her robe. "You're welcome." Pointing with the scissors to a straight-backed chair near the window, she directed, "Sit over there where I'll have better light."

Tyrone complied and once again took account of the clinging robe as she came toward him. It was hard to think of sitting still for a haircut when he would have preferred taking her to bed.

Synnovea embarked upon her task by running a comb through the tawny thatch. "Your hair is so thick you need a proper shearing."

"Have you ever done this before?"

"Once or twice for my father, but he always preferred his manservant to trim his hair."

Tyrone arched a brow in some doubt as he met her gaze. "Was there a reason for his preference?"

Synnovea's lips twitched as she tried to suppress a smile. "None that he cared to mention, but I rather suspect it was the loss of an ear or two that might have prompted him to get someone else to do it."

Tyrone grimaced in feigned fear and ducked his head, drawing her laughter as she eagerly worked the scissors close to his ear. "Be careful, madam, I'll need my ears to hear that scoundrel Ladislaus."

"Of course, my lord." Synnovea moved between his thighs and, slipping her fingers through his hair, lifted a lock to clip and continued on in the same manner, trying to cut as evenly as she could.

"I'll need another bath after this," Tyrone observed, brushing the hair from his naked shoulders.

Tucking the tip of her tongue between her teeth, Synnovea leaned forward and carefully snipped along his brow, then finally straightened and brushed the loose wisps away from his face. "That's what you get for intruding into mine, Colonel."

"The bathing chamber is spacious enough for the two of us," Tyrone argued.

"I know your propensities and don't intend to be caught sporting with you in the bathing chamber."

"Will you sport with me here?" he asked, reaching a hand around her hip to clasp her buttock and draw her closer within the spread of his legs.

Synnovea thrust off his hand with a sideways jerk of her hip, a motion that raised the elevation of Tyrone's brows by a high degree as her unbound breasts bounced almost out of her robe, close in front of his face.

"Be warned!" Synnovea cautioned. "You're at my mercy, and I have no qualms about shaving your head to forestall the likelihood of any young maid lusting after you."

"Can you do that little motion again?" Tyrone coaxed, tugging at the tie of her robe. His attempt was immediately discouraged by a stinging slap on his knuckles.

"Behave, or you'll regret it," Synnovea warned and, catching a lock of hair on his chest, twisted it with a vicious jerk, wrenching a wince of pain from him.

"Lay off, vixen!" Tyrone flinched again as she snatched her hand away, carrying with it several stray wisps. Rubbing his still-stinging chest, he complained, "You have a way of twisting the very heart right out of a man."

An elegant eyebrow rose challengingly as Synnovea returned his words on him. "And you, My Lord Colonel Sir, have a way of wrenching the very heart right out of me. You leave me caught between a rock and a hard place, not knowing if we have a marriage that will last 'til we die or only a few months, 'til you grow tired of me."

"Dammit, Synnovea!" Tyrone swore, starting to rise. "Don't start that again! I've already offered you assurances."

"Sit down!" she commanded, shoving him back into the chair. "I'm not through cutting your hair!"

"Why don't you just cut it off and be done with it!" he muttered.

She looked pointedly toward his lap, where the towel had ridden up. "I don't think you'd sit still for it."

"Hell and damnation!" Tyrone threw up his hands. "Would you geld me, too!"

"Don't curse at me!" Synnovea scolded. "I'm not one of the men in your regiment! I'm your wife!"

"That I know quite well, madam!"

"I wonder." She tossed her head with a flippant air.

"If this is the way we're going to spend the day, I'm going back to the camp!" Tyrone tried again to rise, but with a hand widespread upon his chest, Synnovea pressed him back into the chair.

"I said I wasn't finished! Now sit there until I am!"

Grinding his teeth, Tyrone forced himself to endure the clipping, which had turned a bit sour with her chiding, but Synnovea worked the scissors closely around his ear, ignoring his scowl. His irritation soon ebbed and was quickly replaced by a most ardent interest in the sights so irresistibly near at hand. She twisted slightly to judge the results of her work, oblivious to her robe falling aside to reveal a goodly portion of a round breast and then, unsatisfied, she straddled his leg as she painstakingly trimmed around the curve above his ear. She moved behind him to cut the back, then returned to face him again and stepped astride his other thigh as she neatened his sideburns.

"There!" she said at last, tucking her robe between her legs and perching on his thigh to consider the finished task. The fact that her bare knee rested lightly against his loins did not seem to affect her, though Tyrone was of a different bent. He could not imagine how she could be otherwise distracted when he was nearly beside himself trying to maintain rigid control. If it was her intent to punish him, then she had chosen a most effective way to accomplish that feat.

Smoothing the shortened hair beneath her hand, Synnovea commended her own efforts. "It looks good!"

"Am I allowed to move now?" Tyrone queried, running his hand up her thigh.

Synnovea looked directly at him, as if awakening from a daze. She recognized the passion smoldering in his eyes and felt her own pulse leap in eager response. With startling clarity, the thought came to her that she wanted him to make love to her.

Sensing no reluctance in her softening visage, Tyrone tugged the ties loose and, spreading her robe, encouraged its fall from her shoulders to the floor. His hands rose in a slow, ascending voyage from her hips, lightly skimming her ribs and fondling her soft, eager breasts as he watched her lips part and her eyes grow limpid with desire.

Beyond the framework of the windows on the eastern side, the sun hovered behind a thin layer of clouds, and in the muted light, her pale bosom gleamed with a soft, lustrous sheen, tempting him to savor the intoxicating view. She laid her hands upon his wide shoulders, arching her back as his mouth and tongue bestirred her senses, and when finally he raised his head, she met his searching lips with a fierce ardor that matched his own. With a daring that amazed even herself, she swept a hand downward over his chest, past the flat, hard belly to make her claim upon him. His surprise was what she had expected, a sharp intake of breath dragging through tightly clenched teeth, but the shock was not his alone. His passion seemed to flare out of control, growing hotter, harder, bolder until she snatched away in some awe. Abashed by her own temerity, she would have torn herself away completely, but his arm was already there, curving about her waist, bringing her back against him.

"Nay, love, don't go. 'Tis your right."

Synnovea's mouth parted in surprise as she found herself staring into the flaming orbs of blue. Her own eyes were wide with wonder, staring into his, while her soft lips moved with mindless words that neither of them heard. His gaze probed hers as his hand moved down to stroke along her thigh, and Synnovea made a valiant effort to turn away from the hypnotic power that held her transfixed, half afraid she would lose herself in them, but as his open mouth covered hers, his searing kiss went through her, dulling her awareness to everything but the two of them. She lost all thought of holding herself detached from him as he lifted her and then settled her astride his naked loins. Small, bursting shards of scintillating excitement washed through her at the warmth of his intrusion, and for a long moment, they savored the coupling, embracing and kissing passionately, touching and being touched as only lovers in love are wont to do, then her hips began to respond to his, languidly at first, then with an ever-strengthening rhythm as she answered him with a zeal that matched his own. The liquid fire surged through her, sweeping her along on a towering wave of molten passion until the brilliance of their ardor burst upon them with a blinding radiance.

Breathless in their quest, they clung to each other as their lips merged in an impatient, frenzied kiss that attested to the soaring delight of their union.

It was mid-afternoon when they went downstairs to visit with Natasha in the great room. The older woman could hardly mistake the change in their attitude, for each seemed reluctant to be apart from the other for even a short distance or a brief space of time. They held hands like lovers entranced and were wont to exchange warm, unswerving glances that communicated things beyond the discernment of others, except that Natasha knew and understood, having once experienced a great love herself. Synnovea's soft gazes clearly revealed her preoccupation with her husband, which encouraged Natasha to believe that the girl's devotion ran far deeper than mere infatuation. As for Tyrone, he was clearly involved with his young wife. He devoured her every movement, her every smile, her every questioning glance. He answered her, asked her opinions, listened to her with interest as he entwined his long, lean fingers with her slender ones or laid an arm around her shoulders to bring her close against his side. Neither of them appeared the least bit abashed by their ardent display of affection, but laughed when they found Natasha smilingly observing them.

When they retired at an early hour that evening, Natasha was far from surprised. She cautioned Ali to stay away from their chambers until she was summoned, and it was not until mid-morning of the next day that the servant was bidden to join her mistress downstairs in the bathing chamber. For the first time in her life, Synnovea felt strangely embarrassed by her own nakedness in front of the woman, but when Tyrone entered a few moments later, no protecting towel was called for. Instead Ali found herself banished upstairs, where she contented herself, humming happily as she laid out her mistress's clothes for the day.

Natasha declined Tyrone's invitation to join them on an outing, having accepted Prince Zherkof's plea to spend the day with him and his daughter. Finding himself in the carriage alone with his young wife, Tyrone was hardly disappointed. While Stenka took them on a tour of the city, they discussed a myriad of matters, sometimes sensually explicit and titillating as Synnovea probed his manly knowledge and experience, other times as innocent as the story of her childhood or what gifts they should buy for Sofia, Ali, and Natasha, just in case he would be gone for an extended period of time and not be able to share with them the joy of *Svyatki*, or the Christmas season.

Tyrone had recently found himself mulling over his affairs like one whose days were severely numbered, and as the days passed, bringing his scheduled departure ever nearer, his thoughts turned increasingly inward. He had always had to cope with the threat that he might never come back from an expedition, but he now found himself actually brooding because of his great reluctance to leave Synnovea. There had arisen within him a growing desire to make her understand that if anything happened to him, she would always be welcomed at his home in England, should she ever have a desire or a need to visit his family. There was now a chance that she would be left with his heir, and in such a case, it was not right that his parents and grandmother only receive word of his death and never learn about his wife and the child they had made together. And so, while they were alone together in the carriage, he took the opportunity to reassure Synnovea about his family's desire to know about her should he not come back, but the idea that something ominous might happen to him filled her with fearful dread.

"I could not bear your loss," she wept, flinging herself against his chest. "You must take care of yourself and come back to me."

"I will do my best, madam," Tyrone murmured against her brow. "Now that I have found you, I desperately want to come back."

"You must! You must!"

"Dry your tears, Synnovea," he coaxed gently. "We'll be leaving the carriage soon, and people will wonder why you've been crying."

Synnovea reluctantly sat up and dabbed at her reddened eyes and nose, then sniffed and lifted her gaze to her husband's softly querying smile. "Is that better?"

Tyrone impulsively clasped her to him again and seized her lips in an ardent kiss as he was suddenly struck by the full import of how miserable he would be away from her. "I pray the time may go swiftly. I cannot bear to think of leaving you and not being able to see you, touch you, love you."

Clinging to him, Synnovea made an attempt to be brave. "A month or two from now, the anguish will be over, and I'll be welcoming you back into my arms. We must take courage now and pray that no harm will come to you."

Tyrone glanced around as Stenka halted the carriage on Red Square, then he turned to face Synnovea again with a plea. "We have so little time together. Let us not waste it all here where I cannot hold you and kiss you as I yearn to do. I'd like to return home as soon as possible."

Synnovea smiled and slipped her hand into his. "We'll hurry."

Stenka was left waiting at the coach while the couple hastened off toward the marketplaces of Kitaigorod. After making their selections, they soon returned with their gifts, a golden necklace for Natasha, a lace-trimmed nightgown and woolen shawl for Ali, a dress for Danika, and a doll and a brightly decorated wooden dollhouse for Sofia.

Tyrone lifted Synnovea into the conveyance and was about to climb in behind her when he noticed his second-in-command waving to him from afar, trying to catch his attention through the milling crowd. Pledging to promptly return, Tyrone left his wife and hastened to where Grigori was waiting.

"You seem happier than I've seen you look for some time, my friend," Grigori remarked with a smile. "Marriage finally seems to agree with you."

"Why didn't you come over to the carriage to speak with me there?" Tyrone inquired, sensing something dire was troubling the man.

The captain's face clouded. "I didn't think Synnovea should hear the news I bear, which you, my friend, need to be made aware of. Aleta is pregnant, and General Vanderhout is boiling mad. He swears it's not his."

"How can he be so sure of that unless they're not sleeping together?"

"Which seems to be the way of it. I heard it whispered that he's suffering some infectious malady of late that prevents him from indulging his wife's appetites."

"Infectious malady?" Tyrone frowned in confusion. "You mean . . . "

Grigori held up a hand to halt the flood of questions that seemed to be on the very tip of the colonel's tongue. "Again I've heard it whispered that he's been forced to consider what wench gave it to him, for he's not been exactly faithful to Aleta either."

"Two of a kind," Tyrone mused aloud.

"Anyway," Grigori continued. "Aleta has spread the rumor that you are the cause of her condition. . . . "

"The bitch!" Tyrone cried, and then almost groaned as he thought of Synnovea hearing such gossip. "It's not true, of course!"

"I know that, but General Vanderhout doesn't! It seems he's looking for you. You'd better hope that we manage to leave before he finds you."

"Aye! But what can I tell Synnovea? She's bound to hear all this filth while I'm gone if I don't tell her now."

"I agree! 'Tis better you tell her yourself rather than allow anyone else to wound her. Will she believe you?"

"She must!"

Seated inside the coach, Synnovea was content to inspect the gifts they had purchased. When she became aware of a shadowed form filling the open doorway, she glanced up with a smile, expecting to find Tyrone beside the coach, making ready to join her, but the greeting froze on her lips as she met the smoldering dark eyes of Prince Aleksei.

"Synnovea, my little icemaiden," he greeted huskily. "I didn't know it was possible for you to grow more beautiful in so brief a time. Can it be, my dear, that you've become enamored with your husband? Perhaps you can even be grateful for my lenience in allowing your husband to keep what he no doubt treasures most."

Synnovea's icy glare conveyed her contempt, nearly chilling him to the bone. "I'm extremely grateful that Ladislaus and His Majesty kept you from doing your foul deed, Aleksei. But tell me, why do you brave my company when my husband is so close at hand?"

Aleksei arched a brow at her, displaying his rampant distrust of her little ploys, and then glanced cautiously around, trying to search the colonel out in the crowd of people. "You tease, of course, Synnovea. What man would foolishly leave his beautiful wife alone where some dastardly villain could approach her?"

"I'm not alone," Synnovea reminded him, sweeping her hand around to indicate both the driver's and footman's seats. "Stenka and Jozef are with me, and should I scream, I'm sure they'll both be here a mere step or two before my husband arrives."

"Tsk! Tsk!" Aleksei admonished. "You ought to know by now that I can have their hands lopped off should they dare touch me. . . . "

Synnovea countered with a disdaining sneer. "I don't think so, Aleksei, not when His Majesty warned you about your manners. But tell me, do you intend to remain until my husband returns? Or will you flee like the coward you are?"

"I doubt that your husband is here at all, madam, so cease your feeble ruse." Aleksei smirked and, swinging up into the coach, settled himself across from her as he considered her heightened beauty. "You know, Synnovea, I might be persuaded to share my attentions with you after all. You're clearly worth the effort it will take to forgive you."

"Please! Forbear the struggle!" Synnovea enjoined. "Lend me your hatred instead! I'm better able to cope with your disfavor."

"I've heard rumors that your husband will leave the city soon. You'll need a man to comfort you while he's gone."

"Why should I settle for your attentions when I've had the best there is?"

"You're still such an innocent, my dear." The swarthy prince leered at her in unswerving arrogance. "After you've been with me for a while, you'll learn how to recognize a real man."

"A real man!" Synnovea scoffed. "Why, you pompously braying ass! You haven't even a simple notion what the word really means! Do you honestly think you can judge a man by the number of trollops he claims to have bedded? Real men are much more admirable in the eyes of a woman, and from my point of view, you're no better than a boorish swine who mounts the closest haunch to serve his own rutting lusts. My husband is much more of a man than you'll ever hope to be, Aleksei, let me assure you!"

Aleksei's pride was again pricked by a comparison he had heard much too often. "I see that you've not yet learned to curb your tongue, Synnovea! But you err if you think I can do naught to wound you!"

He leaned forward with narrowed eyes to continue voicing his threat, then somewhat reminiscent of a dog that had just been scalded, he leapt aside with a start of surprise as he glanced toward the doorway and found the tall, broad-shouldered form of Colonel Rycroft filling the open space. Before Aleksei could scramble out the other side, Tyrone seized the hem of his ruby-red *kaftan* and dragged the man steadily across the seat as the prince frantically searched for a leverage against the relentless vise. Stumbling to his knees onto the floor in front of Synnovea, Aleksei clasped his arms tightly around her legs, pressing his face into her lap as he tried to resist. He was sure the colonel meant to thrash him severely in retaliation for the savage whipping he had been forced to endure. He grimaced with the strain and raised his head to glare up at her as she tried to shove him away.

"Be warned, Synnovea! I'll do more than see your husband gelded! The next time I'll set the dogs to eating his foul carcass! Synnoveaaa. . . . Help meee!!"

Snatching Aleksei by the scruff of the neck, Tyrone growled in his ear as he hauled the man away from Synnovea. "You sniveling coward! Where is your courage when Ladislaus is not at your beck and call?"

The prince's arms and legs thrashed wildly about as he was dragged swiftly through the door and launched through the air. He came to earth a short distance away and skidded through the muck of slimy vegetables a vendor had tossed from his cart. The prince scrambled to his feet, and without so much as a downward glance at the clinging bits of offal that adorned his gold-trimmed *kaftan*, he clasped its hem and made his departure with great, leaping strides.

"Colonel Rycroft!" The name was barked from a different vicinity, and as Tyrone spun around, General Vanderhout stalked forward, displaying an outraged indignation over what he had just seen. "What is the meaning of this offense? Have you gone mad?"

"The man insulted my wife!"

General Vanderhout blustered angrily. "How dare you attack another man for a fault you're guilty of!"

Tyrone faced his superior directly. "A fault I'm guilty of?" A tawny brow arched sharply in question. "I've just heard rumors of your wife's condition, General, but whether you believe me or not, I'm not at fault."

"Aleta says you are, and for that offense, Colonel, I will see you stripped of your rank and sent home in disgrace."

Tyrone muttered a curse as he felt the sting of Aleta's conniving revenge. It seemed that she was finally seeking retribution for his rejection of her, but he was not about to accept her accusations without defending himself. "I suggest, General, that you learn the truth of this matter before you proceed further with your claims. You'll save both yourself and your wife a great deal of embarrassment."

General Vincent Vanderhout reddened to the neck of his shirt as he struggled to find an appropriate rejoinder to refute the colonel's claim of innocence. With equal fervor he searched for a threat to adequately frighten the man, but when he met the steely stare of those blue eyes, he could do naught but sputter and spew in frustration.

"I must be leaving now, General," Tyrone continued tersely, "but if you wish to address this matter further, be assured that I have witnesses to testify in my behalf, several high-ranking officers who can verify the number of times I've turned aside your wife's invitations. Her indiscretions are none of my affair, but I'll not let her damage my life by the lies she has spilled about me." Inclining his head with a crisp nod of farewell, Tyrone ended the conversation abruptly. "Good day, General."

"This is not the end of it, Colonel Rycroft!" Vincent Vanderhout railed as Tyrone climbed into the carriage. "You'll hear about this again!"

Tyrone cursed through grinding teeth as he leaned back in the carriage seat. " 'Twould seem a woman scorned truly has the sting of a venomous viper."

"What has happened?" Synnovea searched the angry visage for some clue as to what had ignited his temper.

"Aleta is pregnant," Tyrone stated bluntly, "and General Vanderhout claims he is not the father, therefore she has taken the initiative to lie and say that I am." He looked around and shook his head. "I'm not, Synnovea. I swear to you I've never touched that woman except to thrust her from my sight."

Synnovea leaned forward and gently pressed her brow against the side of his neck, dissolving most of his anger as she whispered, "I believe you, Tyre."

Tyrone did not know which had vexed him more, Aleksei intruding upon Synnovea's presence or his confrontation with Vanderhout. His wife settled his brief debate.

"Aleksei has heard rumors that you'll be leaving soon," she informed him. "He has now decided that he would like to resume his efforts to have me in his bed."

Tyrone leaned back to stare at his wife in surprise and recognized the worry in her face. Lifting an arm around her shoulders, he soothed her fears as much as he was able. "I'll set men around the house to watch over you in my absence. Aleksei is not man enough to confront armed guards."

Synnovea searched the eyes above her own. "I'll miss you terribly, Colonel Sir!"

" 'Tis a fact, madam, that I'll be leaving my heart with you," he whispered. "Guard it well for me."

"I'll never betray you," she promised softly, bracing herself upon his chest. Lightly rubbing a finger over his chin, she smiled up at him as she divulged her feelings. "I think I love you, Colonel Sir."

Tyrone lowered his mouth to hers as he softly murmured, "And I, madam, know without a doubt that I love you."

In the next pause of a heartbeat, their lips came together in a kiss that sealed their vows of love more thoroughly than any spoken word. It was a long time before they pulled apart, and once again that evening they retired early to the upper chambers to spend many wakeful hours sweetening their passion with mutual demonstrations of their devotion.

Chapter 25

THE SUN CONCLUDED ITS LANGUID JOURNEY ACROSS THE welkin blue and seemed to pause above the distant line that marked the end of its passage, as if delighting in its own magnificence, much like an actor posturing grandly before making his nightly departure from the stage. Crimson rays flared out across the western sky, piercing the thin, ragged clouds that mischievously sought to veil the fiery brilliance of that great and notable visage. Replete in its unyielding condescension, the daystar finally bowed its head of its own accord and sank slowly from sight, allowing the heavy curtains of dusk to close behind it. Only a soft, rosy aura remained to evidence its passing, until that too dwindled beneath the trailing hem of an ebon cloak that scattered a myriad, glittering crystal lights in its wake.

Tyrone swung astride the huge black and casually drew the reins through his lean fingers as his men followed his lead and mounted their steeds. The rapidly consuming darkness was what they had been waiting for to mask their advance up the hill, which Avar, Grigori, and a small vanguard of twelve soldiers had ascended only a short time earlier to take captive the pair of guards living there and to secure the area for the larger force of soldiers. On his previous scouting expedition, Avar had clandestinely observed the two lookouts from a protected shelter long enough to become familiar with their normal routine. Whether by use of soft, reassuring whistles which came at regular intervals, or by sharper signals that alerted the camp of approaching danger, Avar had the knowledge to enable the detachment of soldiers to continue a covert surveillance of the canyon below them. In securing the hilltop for his commander, he had already employed a birdlike trill to placate the half dozen or so stalwarts who kept watch over their camp.

Tyrone raised his arm and swept it forward in a silent command for his men to make their advance up the hill. He had already directed the axles of the supply wagons and the gun carriages to be well greased and the wooden wheels to be wrapped with leather strips to muffle the noise of their ascent. The horses' hooves had been similarly padded, for it was of paramount importance that his men gain their position and remain undetected until they were well assured Ladislaus was in the camp, then they would launch their attack. If an alarm sounded ere he was securely caught in their trap, the chance of capturing the thief was less than nil. Tyrone was adamant that nothing go wrong. He had come too far to think of springing his trap before the fox was in the bag.

Tyrone had determined at the very onset that his primary objective for this foray would have to be the capture of Ladislaus and, at the very least, the more important members of his band. By stripping away the major leadership, Tyrone hoped to seriously hamper the remnant's ability to regroup. Without Ladislaus's leadership, he could foresee the remainder being dispersed in a state of chaos or some time thereafter scattered by those prone to struggle for positions of control. If his planned assault proved successful, then the prisoners would be taken back to Moscow, where they would be subsequently judged for their crimes. Whatever happened beyond that point was not within his power to decide, but if found guilty, they could either be held for eons behind sturdy walls or be escorted to a place near the Lobnoe Mesto for public execution.

This was no casually planned raid Tyrone was attempting to carry out, though the main portion of those positioned in places of higher military authority had been led to believe his objective was of no great import. Word had trickled out, appeasing the curiosity of those who made it their business to know the whereabouts of the tsar's forces. Thus, when Tyrone and half of his regiment rode out of Moscow in full view, the townspeople hardly raised a brow, for they were certain they knew every detail of his mission. To insure that such would be the case, Tyrone had deliberately bypassed his immediate superior, that being General Vanderhout, and, with Grigori serving as his interpreter to insure that he would be clearly understood, had taken his petition directly to the Field Marshall who had been completely receptive to the idea of ridding the countryside of Ladislaus's army of bandits. Tyrone's appeal for secrecy had influenced the Field Marshall to casually let the word be spread among the other officers of the division that the English colonel would be leading a large company of his men out on practice maneuvers in an area far afield from where they would really be going.

General Vanderhout had been totally outraged when he learned that he had not been apprised of the colonel's plan well in advance of when the orders were actually issued. He had angrily insisted that another officer be chosen to lead the campaign, but repeatedly was frustrated in his attempts to forestall the scheduled departure. His brows had lifted to heights of unparalleled disbelief when he heard that the colonel had requisitioned a half dozen small cannons affixed on their own ribauldequins and twice that number of artillerymen to man them, but the general could do little but fume and spew in high-flying indignation, for a direct mandate from the Field Marshall negated the possibility of anyone denying the colonel's requests. General Vanderhout had been in no mood to see the Englishman's smallest wish granted, not when Aleta had named the man as the one who had cuckolded him. So great was his resentment, Vanderhout spent a whole three days berating his wife for bedding down with a fool and lambasting the campaign her lover-colonel had devised. By the time he had detailed every flaw he could imagine in Tyrone's strategy, Aleta knew about as much as any officer in the division and took no pains to keep it to herself, thereby helping to secure the secrecy the colonel and his men had desired and needed.

A day's ride beyond the city, Tyrone had sent Avar to scout out the area ahead of them with a detachment of twelve Hussars commanded by Grigori. Four of these had served as vedettes who rode outpost either fore or aft of the remaining eight during the day. In the evening, two of the twelve reported back to Tyrone and were replaced by the same number of men from the main troop who then rode forward to join the advance guard. With orders to capture any spies that would perchance report back to the thieves, they had kept careful surveillance for offshoots of Ladislaus's band, avoiding the possibility of the miscreants' obtaining advance warnings of their coming. Thus, they managed to arrive at the foot of the hill with no member of that outlaw band the wiser.

Tyrone carefully scanned the darkness enveloped by the encroaching trees as he led his men up the hill by way of a longer trail that allowed the larger conveyances easier access. The moonlight provided enough illumination for their climb, but it also threatened to reveal their presence if some wayward sound attracted the curiosity of the thieves. When a sudden rattle of a falling kettle made a horse rear and whinny in fear, Tyrone was quick to react. Whirling his steed about, he came alongside the lumbering wagon from whence the offense had occurred and sternly admonished the young soldier who drove it.

"Dammit, Corporal! Belay that racket ere you wake the dead!" he growled. "I told you to secure every last pot and kettle this cook wagon could hold. Did you need a nursemaid peering over your shoulder to remind you to get it done?!"

"*Izvinitye!*" The young man jerked his shoulders briefly upward in an anxious shrug as he apologized and then struggled to find the English words that would adequately answer his commander. "I did, sir!"

"Obviously not well enough!"

"Something broke, I think."

Tyrone jerked his thumb over his shoulder. "*Gavaritye!* Get up the hill! You can make your excuses later."

Some moments later, Tyrone breathed a deep sigh of relief when the last wagon reached the summit, thankfully without further incident. Grigori and Avar were there to assist him in directing the men in setting up the camp. Though the whole company had been cautioned about the need for secrecy, it was impressed upon them once again as they labored beneath the cover of darkness that all would be lost if they alerted the thieves to their presence.

Whispered orders were given as the supply wagons were unloaded and then pushed into a narrow niche between towering firs. The horses were tied in similar protected sites near the edge of their encampment, while the cannons were very carefully positioned among the firs growing close along the ridge of the hill. Their sights were directed outward toward their targets, and leaden balls were stacked in generous mounds near the ribauldequins. The sod-roofed stone hovel where the guards had lived would be used as a cookhouse while they remained there, but beyond its stone steps, no campfires would be permitted in any area where the glow could be detected by anyone down below.

After the men finally settled themselves to get some sleep, Tyrone wandered about the encampment with Grigori and Avar and acquainted himself with both the advantages and faults of their hilltop position. Below him, the narrow basin was spotted here and there by glowing campfires that illumined the steep crags and rocky hills which closely encompassed Ladislaus's hideout. Protected by this impenetrable fortress of stone, the robber-bastard prince and his followers must have enjoyed total autonomy from the rest of the world for a good many years. The only paths by which a man could either enter or leave were through the passes at each end, both of which were well barricaded and continually patrolled by two armed lookouts. A third sentry climbed to the bluffs buttressing the pass to gain a better vantage spot for viewing anyone coming in or out, making it virtually impossible for a foe to escape detection once he entered the gorge.

Although the summit had been reasonably accessible by the path he and his men had taken, Tyrone had trusted Avar's earlier observations and had made his plans accordingly. He could now see for himself that descending from the mount directly into the ravine where the thieves were housed was no easy feat, for it would involve a nearly perpendicular drop. Thus, in the last weeks of their training, his men had practiced climbing and lowering themselves by ropes down the Kremlin wall. It was by this method they would gain entry into the valley. The ropes had already been attached to the larger trees edging the bluff and would be kept in coiled heaps at the base of each trunk, allowing the lengths to be easily thrown down for a rapid descent into the basin, a strategy the thieves would not be expecting.

"Everything is arranged just the way you had planned, Colonel," Grigori commented, gesturing casually toward the lower camp. "Once we utilize the cannons, Ladislaus and his band will be imprisoned down there. It will take another gun blast or two to open the passes again."

"The plan seems simple enough to forestall the possibility of failure," Tyrone remarked, then in rueful reflection continued. "Still, I've seen the best of schemes come to naught when fate has been set awry by the most asinine reason. We have no guarantee that Ladislaus is down there, or that he will soon return if he is not. We can only wait here until he appears. Pray that it not be in the dead of winter."

"That I will most fervently do, Colonel. I have no liking for the frigid winds that will test us sorely on this hill," Grigori murmured grimly.

As if to lend a sampling taste of what the captain dreaded most, a cold blustery morning followed the regiment's nocturnal arrival to the summit, blowing in plumes of snow that whisked into the cowls of wide-flying cloaks and flapping tent doors, as well as frosting fingers and noses. The crisp chill might not have been so difficult for them to bear, had they spotted their quarry, but no one saw any evidence of the towering, broad-shouldered bulk of Ladislaus, even though Tyrone and his men carefully canvassed every crevice and cranny they could see from their lofty perch. Not even the powerfully built Petrov or the towering Goliath were sighted, leaving the soldiers little choice but to bide their time until the rascals came within their grasp.

A full fortnight came and went, and still they saw no glimpse of their prey. Tyrone began to grow restive with gnawing impatience. He could only wonder where the bandits had taken themselves and what mischief they were presently about, if they were busy attacking unsuspecting travelers again or perhaps raiding a village in some area far afield from their camp. Unable to endure the waiting without knowing what was happening beyond their hilltop perch, Tyrone sent Grigori and Avar out in search of some hint of the man, but as he waited for their return, he chafed in unbridled restlessness, wanting to ride out to scour the countryside himself. He knew the full folly of being discovered by Ladislaus and was forced to abide the passage of time, though he longed desperately to have the waiting behind him so he could return with fervent haste to the one he loved.

* * *

Synnovea felt overwhelmed by a similar desire as the distant moon made its lofty approach toward center stage. The cold and silvery essence of the lunar sphere lent no warmth or cheer to comfort her, but remained aloofly detached in its nocturnal setting as her bedchamber grew still and hushed with an oppressive silence. Through the whole length of this blustery eventide, she could look forward to nothing more exciting than passing the long hours alone in the huge bed which, before her husband's departure, she had eagerly shared with him. Sometimes treasured memories would wash over her like softly cresting waves, bringing mental images vividly to life, and she would stare at the canopy above her head, almost feeling his presence. If she closed her eyes, his face would loom in her imagination, awakening her senses to sweet remembrances until it seemed she could almost hear his huskily whispered words. Such memories only aroused a longing hope that if she opened her eyes again, he would be there, and all would be as it should be.

Synnovea heaved a soft, languishing sign as she turned from the windows and meandered aimlessly about the elegant bedchamber. Were someone to ask, she would avow that Tyrone had been gone for at least an eternity, for it truly seemed as if her whole life had paused in its solitary flight, like the moon when it lends the illusion of being momentarily frozen in its heavenly orbit, tricking the minds of earthbound creatures.

While the days plodded past in halting slowness, Synnovea began to understand more precisely how one could suffer an unbearable loneliness even in the midst of caring friends. Though Ali liberally practiced her Irish wit in hopes of entertaining her, Synnovea could do naught but vaguely smile at the tiny woman's valiant attempts. Even Natasha's companionship did not ease the gloomy feelings that had plummeted down upon her after Tyrone's departure. Hourly she struggled with a longing to have him with her again, loathing the wars and conflicts that necessitated his leaving, and though she sought to keep her fingers and mind actively occupied, she found no abatement for the anxieties that rose out of her fear for him. The threat of Ladislaus was too real, too well marked in her memory to allow her to dismiss her apprehensions with mere menial tasks. When she knew Tyrone would be in serious danger seeking out and confronting the outlaw, it was all she could do to remain behind like any dutiful wife and not go searching after him.

Social outings had not helped, but had set her more on edge when both Prince Aleksei and Major Nekrasov had dared to approach her in public. Though the presence of a pair of hefty guards riding atop her coach or following closely behind when she went about on foot had dissuaded each from extending his visit to anything more than a few moments, they had voiced their causes with equal fervor. Concerned that his earlier visit might have caused her dismay, Nikolai had displayed his merit as an honorable gentleman by offering a quietly spoken apology, whereas Aleksei had proven himself just as adamant about having her for his own as he once had been. If anything, his quest for fleshly appeasement and simple revenge had grown stronger since she had become the wife of a man he now considered an adversary. It seemed that stealing her away from the Englishman, either by captivation or by forcible capture, had become something of a challenge to him, and it annoyed him greatly when he was kept from his purpose by the pair of men Tyrone had hired to protect her.

" 'Twould seem your husband is afraid of being cuckolded during his absence." Aleksei had smirked in haughty arrogance. "A chastity belt might have been less costly than employing those clumsy oafs."

A less than tolerant smile accompanied Synnovea's response. "Why, Aleksei, can it be that you're enraged because he's actually dared to circumvent your lecherous little ploys by engaging men who are completely loyal to him and who refuse to be intimidated by the likes of you?"

Aleksei's dark eyes skimmed her with a strange mixture of angry insolence and hungry fervor. "You seem very self-assured, Synnovea, almost like some well-preened swan gliding over the warm waters of a lake, completely oblivious to the dangers of a hungry wolf lurking in the tall reeds near shore."

Synnovea lifted a lovely brow in chiding admonition. "Be careful, Aleksei, that you don't get snared wallowing in the treacherous bogs of conceit ere you learn your lesson. His Majesty has not yet forgotten your last miserable undertaking to steal me from the colonel. This time your efforts might cost you your head."

Her reminder had not been kindly accepted by the prince, whose eyes had chilled to a piercing darkness that promised dire repercussions. "You should have learned from our last encounter how deadly serious I can be, Synnovea. I so hate to repeat a lesson I've already taught, but 'tis evident that you're not willing to take me at my word."

With a last smug sneer, he had stalked to his waiting conveyance. Now nearly a week later, Synnovea had cause to hope that he had given up on the idea of seizing her for his own lecherous purposes, for she had not seen him around the house or even in the company of Anna or others he had been known to consort with. She could only wonder if perhaps he had left Moscow in search of some new conquest upon which he could expend his prurient lusts.

Synnovea snuffed the candles beside the bed and then slipped between the cool sheets, remembering when Tyrone had been there with her and how his arms would reach out and draw her close against his naked form. There was now only an empty void to greet her as the darkness closed in around her. She rubbed her hands briskly along the sleeves of her nightgown, fighting the chill of the lonely bed. Finding no enveloping, comforting warmth that sufficed as well as her husband's, she drew Tyrone's pillow to her breast and hugged it as fiercely as she desired at that moment to embrace him. Later, when thoughts of him meandered through her drifting dreams, she felt as light and airy as thistledown sailing on a gently wafting breeze.

Though naught but a pair of hours later, it seemed to Synnovea that she had only enjoyed a few moments of sleep before she was being snatched to awareness by a broad hand clapped tightly over her mouth. It masked nearly half her face and was most effective in squelching the scream that was torn from her throat. In the next moment a gag served the same purpose as it was stuffed into her mouth and secured by a narrow strip of cloth. In tying the band behind her head, the man leaned over her, and panic set her heart to hammering even more frantically within her breast as she recognized the pale, scruffy thatch that covered the man's head in the moonlit room.

Ladislaus!

Though she could utter nothing more than a groan of despair, her mind screamed the name out in dread as she struggled against the overpowering strength of his huge hands. He deftly flipped her onto her stomach, and against her will, seized her wrists and lashed them securely behind her back, then he wrapped the bedclothes tightly around her until, to her dismay, her breathing was seriously restricted by the padded coverlet. Thrashing her head back and forth, Synnovea sought to find an opening from whence she could draw breath until Ladislaus finally recognized her dilemma, rolled her over, and tucked the quilt beneath her chin.

"Is that better?" His voice was liberally imbued with levity as his pale eyes gleamed close in front of her own. In the meager light of the room they seemed to sparkle with merriment. "I would be dreadfully put out if you were to pass away from lack of breath ere I made love to you, my beauty."

A thousand insulting epithets came to mind as she struggled valiantly against his greater strength. Indeed! The slurs might have liberally addressed his person had she been able to speak past the gag. The most Synnovea could do was glower at him in outrage, but evidence of her agitation hardly accomplished her release. Chuckling down at her, Ladislaus swept her from the bed and tossed her casually over a shoulder, then paused as he considered the open door of her dressing room.

"I suppose, like all women, you would rather attire yourself in rich trappings than wander about my house naked. I would thoroughly appreciate such a sight, but I rather doubt Alyona would."

Stepping into the room, he stuffed a wide variety of womanly accoutrements into a large satchel, then tossed a heavy winter cloak over his arm before crossing the chambers to the anteroom. In the hall outside her rooms, he paused to listen until reassured that the household had not been awakened, then with long, running strides, he raced along the shadows of the corridor and leapt down the stairs. He left the manse by way of a garden door and ran around to the side of the house where, beyond the gate, a handful of his men stood waiting with their horses.

Synnovea raised her head, frantically searching for her guards. Much to her dismay, she found them tied together at the base of a tree on the garden side of the brick wall. Though they struggled against the cords that bound them, they were unable to do anything more than helplessly observe the progress of her capture, for they had been sufficiently gagged shortly after being overwhelmed by the greater force of men. Despite their loud grunts and straining growls, they could not halt Ladislaus from shouldering her through the ornate gate.

" 'Twill be light soon," Ladislaus observed as he lifted her into the waiting arms of Petrov, who had swung up into the saddle when he saw his leader approach. "We must leave the city ere the sun comes up to mark our departure, or Prince Aleksei will call on the tsar's soldiers and set up a chase to try and halt our flight."

A deep chortle accompanied Petrov's reply. "Prince not like you take his gold an' girl, too, after he warn you to bring her straight to him wit' no tricks."

Through the darkness, the gleam of a wide-toothed grin offered proof of Ladislaus's jovial indifference as he looked up at his friend. "Prince Aleksei never paid us for doing his last bidding, my friend, when he promised you and the rest of the men gold and the girl to me. 'Twas his folly to seek us out a second time. He should have known we'd want to collect what was due us."

"The English colonel not like you take his bride either. He come after you, I think . . . and maybe he even catch you if you take time wit' the girl."

"He'll have to find us first, eh Petrov? And I, for one, don't intend to slow down until we reach the safety of our camp." He caught the dark mane of the stallion Tyrone had once owned and leapt onto the animal's back. Leaning down to pat the steed's neck, he grinned up at the giant. "You will see, Petrov. I will ride his wench just like I ride his stallion. He cannot stop me now."

Tyrone swung around in surprise as Grigori tossed back the flap and swept through the opening of the tent.

"Colonel!"

"What is it?" The question was filled with dread, for Tyrone knew his second-in-command well enough to perceive that whatever was troubling him was of a serious nature. If his tone had not been an indication, then the worried frown he wore was.

"Ladislaus is coming!"

Tyrone almost smiled and relaxed, thinking he had become too easily unnerved with all the waiting. "At last! I had nigh given up hope."

"Colonel! There's more!"

Tyrone halted, once again feeling a coldness creeping through his vitals. "More? What do you mean, more?

Does he bring the whole Cossack clan back with him?" The anxious frown of the younger man did not waver, spurring Tyrone's impatience to know the worst of what the man had to tell him. "What frets you, Grigori? Dammit, man, tell me!"

"It's your wife . . . the Lady Synnovea. . . ."

In one long stride Tyrone was across the tent, clasping the front of Grigori's cloak as his apprehension deepened to a cold, hellish fear. "What about Synnovea?"

"Ladislaus has taken her captive, Colonel! She's with him now, even as they ride toward the camp!"

"Are you sure?" In agonizing anguish Tyrone slowly beat his limp fists against the other's chest as he demanded his statement be affirmed. "Are you sure?"

"Avar and I both saw her, Colonel! She's riding behind Petrov on his horse, and from a distance, it appears as if there's a long tether binding her to the man."

"Damn!" The expletive exploded from Tyrone's lips as he stepped past Grigori and strode out of the tent. Heedless of the cold, brisk wind that quickly penetrated his woolen tunic, he strode to where Avar stood waiting and bluntly questioned, "Are you sure you're not mistaken, Avar? You saw her, too?"

In unwavering response, the scout met the probing stare of the blue eyes directly. "Zere iz no question, Colonel. It iz yur wife. Ve vaited in zhe coverin' of zhe trees vhen Ladislaus rode past, just tu make sure. Ve saw her face. Zere vas no mistakin' her."

"How can this be?" Tyrone clamped a hand to his brow as the horror of their announcement crushed down upon him with merciless gravity. Frantically he searched his mind for a plan of action that would secure her immediate release, but knew that none was totally free of danger. Whirling, he faced his second-in-command as that one joined them. "I've got to free her, Grigori! I've got to go down there and meet Ladislaus face-to-face!"

"Colonel, I urge you to wait here until they ride into camp," Grigori cautioned, understanding his friend's monumental distress. "Otherwise, Ladislaus may escape and take her with them."

"But if it's Synnovea . . . " Tyrone was set to argue with all of his heart.

"Then you must be exceedingly cautious of what you do. If they slip out of our trap with so precious a prize in their grasp, we may never get her back. You must think it through carefully. We have no choice but to wait until we close the trap around them, preventing their escape."

"I've got to go down there before the trap is sprung and get Synnovea out of there!" Tyrone barked impatiently. "Or else they'll use her as a hostage against us."

"If you're set on going down, Colonel, please consider the possibility that you'll be giving them a second hostage, one they'll likely kill! Ladislaus may very well have you cut down just out of spite."

Fretting over the dilemma that now faced him, Tyrone raked his fingers through his wind-tossed hair as he debated his choices, but only briefly. Coming swiftly to a decision, he spoke brusquely. "Even thieves should know what a white flag is for. I'm going down to talk with Ladislaus, and I intend to make him understand how perilous his position is. If he kills Synnovea or me, then he'll have to answer to the cannons. I have to convince him that there will be no escape for any of them once the passes are closed into his camp. When faced with that threat, I rather doubt that even Ladislaus will prove unreasonable."

Avar carefully crept into the trees growing close along the edge and braced his hand on the trunk of a fir as he leaned forward to observe the happenings in the canyon below. Looking back at his commander, he raised a hand and silently beckoned him near. From that vantage point, the two of them watched as Ladislaus led his party through the pass.

"Colonel, I vould advise yu tu proceed vith all possible haste before Ladislaus has time tu relax an' settle his mind on yur vife. My sister iz down zere somevhere. Maybe I find her an' take her back vith me."

Tyrone clapped a hand upon the scout's shoulder in an unspoken farewell and then stepped away from the edge. He gave orders for his horse to be saddled and a white cloth to be tied on a standard, then he donned a weightier leather doublet that would better guard against their weapons, and perhaps even the cold that had settled its frigid breath upon them this morningtide. His second-in-command observed him in grave concern, as if brooding about all the reckless perils he seemed wont to engage in. In view of the fact that he carried no weapon to defend himself, Tyrone felt a great need to reassure his friend and, with unswerving sincerity, avouched, "By God's mercy, Grigori, I'll come out of this alive with my wife at my side. I tell you now that I have a reason to live, but she's down there in my enemy's hands. Without her, I think my very breath would end."

Releasing a laborious sigh, Grigori squared his shoulders and met his commander's searching stare with a rueful smile. "My mother always swore I worried too much, Colonel. Perhaps she was right."

Tyrone managed a lopsided grin in response. "Each of us has a tendency to do that at times, Grigori. I'm not exactly calm and collected myself with Synnovea down there. Above all, we must convince that braggart thief we are deadly serious. You understand what needs to be done in my absence. When I give the signal to fire the cannon, close their back door promptly. You know what the plan has been, so I'll leave the rest to your own discretion as you observe the sequence of events."

"Don't worry, Colonel." Grigori managed another bleak smile. "I'll make Ladislaus sit up and take notice."

"Good! If I have no other option, I'll climb up here by way of a rope with Synnovea on my back. Keep your eyes sharp and be ready to drop one down should I come running."

"Believe me, Colonel, we'll be watching your every movement," Grigori assured him.

Tyrone swung onto his horse and, after taking the reins in one hand, accepted the flag with the other. He gave a crisp nod of farewell to Grigori, then kicked the stallion toward the trail that offered him the fastest descent.

Down in the valley below, Ladislaus reined the stallion to a halt in front of the largest house in the camp and dismounted as his men slowly dispersed and continued on to different areas of their small village. In nothing less than simple and pure exhaustion, Synnovea acquiesced and accepted Ladislaus's assistance as he lifted her from the back of Petrov's mount, but in desperate need of support, she leaned against the horse as the leader-thief unsheathed his knife and cut the leather cord that had bound her to the brawny giant throughout the major part of their journey.

Grinning up at Petrov, Ladislaus boasted in good spirits. "You see, my friend, how tame the wench has become?"

Petrov grunted in unfaltering skepticism. "Wait 'til she get her breath back, then you see. Maybe she even come after Ladislaus again to kill him."

"Ahhh, nooo, Petrov!" Ladislaus argued in good humor. "You don't understand my way with women. I will let this one have a bath and some sleep. She'll be a different woman when she's well rested. I tell you, Petrov, she'll love me when she wakes!"

"Umph!"

Turning toward the source of the small, contemptuous snort, Ladislaus lowered his gaze to the girl who peered up at him with brooding resentment. As he stared down at her, he could find little evidence behind the drooping cowl of her cloak that she was the same richly attired countess whom he had seen alight imperiously from her coach. He beheld instead the face of a small, grubby sprite who had seemingly taken enormous delight in antagonizing nearly every one of them. At least a score of his cohorts had felt the sharp sting of her wit, as well as the pang of a small kick, blow, or bite whenever they had mistakenly ventured too close. Only Petrov had seemed exempt from her abuse, perhaps because the giant had allowed himself to become her protector of sorts. It was that good fellow who had repeatedly stepped between her and those who sought retribution for the grievances she had liberally dispensed, and though those hearties had been further provoked by her smugly challenging smile, none had dared to test her benefactor's brawn in their quest for appeasement.

Making no effort to brush back the snarled tress that hung down across her face now, the recalcitrant countess peered up at him jeeringly through the tangled, weblike veil of hair. Her lean jaw was smudged with a streak of black, while the whole of her face was covered with a heavy grime which had settled there during their flight across a dusty field. Undoubtedly she was too exhausted to consider lifting herself from her slouched position, which seemed mainly supported by the horse's rump.

"You see!" Petrov warned as he glanced down and jerked his thumb at her. "She kill you quick if you crazy enough to trust her! Just like other night, when she try escape and take my knife."

Ladislaus rubbed the healing slash across his palm as he vividly recalled his foolish endeavor to take advantage of the girl's attempted flight. Through slitted eyelids, he had watched her lean carefully over the loudly snoring Petrov and sneak his knife from its sheath, then she had surreptitiously slashed the cords that had fastened them together. Though Ladislaus had fancied the idea of catching her and having his way with her while the rest of his men slept, he had not been prepared for her vicious assault when he had crept into the shadows after her. By the very skin of his teeth, he had jumped back in time to avoid the wicked, death-threatening, downward slash of the knife after she leapt from hiding and tried to attack him. He had grabbed at her, thinking to disarm her, but in the next instant had been made painfully aware of the tip of the blade opening a rent across the flesh of his palm. If not for his men being wrenched from a sound sleep by his loud curse, the little chit might have made good her escape. As it was, she had been dragged back screaming and kicking as she laid every insult she could think of upon their scruffy hides.

"Alyona!" Ladislaus bellowed at the top of his lungs as he faced the house.

The front door was thrown open with sudden force, and in the deafening silence that followed, it rebounded with a loud crack. A young, dark-haired woman, ponderously close to delivering a child, emerged from the house and petulantly came out to stand at the edge of the porch where she scowled down at Ladislaus. The dark eyes lifted briefly to Synnovea, bringing that one to attention, then once more the woman's gaze settled in cold contempt upon the man.

"So! Yu havef brought a voman home tu share yur bed at last, az if I havef not served yur lustin' needs all zese many months. Vhat do yu intend? To throw me aside now zhat I'm fat-bellied vith yur bastard vhelp?"

Ladislaus chuckled and casually waved aside her angry question. "Now, Alyona, you know I've never made any promises to make you believe that you'd be the only one. A man like me enjoys a little variety now and then!"

"A man like yu, ha!" Alyona tossed her head in disgust. "Yu mewl so sweetly beside me in ze bed an' tell me zhat yu love me vhen yu vant my favors, zhen vhen I'm so swollen vith child I can hardly move, yu bring zhis . . . zhis . . . "

"Lady Synnovea Rycroft," Synnovea quickly supplied the information with a ready smile, glimpsing some small chance of escaping everything Ladislaus had planned for her through the presence of this small, tenacious woman. It was all too apparent to her, even if it wasn't to him, that Alyona resented the idea of sharing him with another woman. "Wife of the Englishman, Colonel Sir Tyrone Rycroft, Commander of His Imperial Majesty's Hussars," Synnovea announced, then ended in a quickening rush that completely exhausted her breath as she turned a blazing glare upon her abductor. "Who - will - surely - kill - this - bumbling - oaf - if - he - so - much - as - lays - one - dirty - finger - on - me!"

Sensing the two of them were in immediate accord with one another, Alyona returned the smile as she acknowledged the introduction and swept a hand toward the door in cordial invitation. At least Ladislaus had not yet bedded the woman, which awakened some small hope that she could halt him from serving his own selfish lusts and hurting her in the process. "Come in, my lady. No doubt yu are veary of yur ordeal an' vant a bath. . . . "

Ladislaus grinned, foolishly thinking he would be able to manage both women, now that they were becoming acquainted and apparently were willing to be congenial to each other. Deducing that he could liberally partake of the hospitality they were extending toward each other, he started to climb the stairs after Synnovea, but was brought up sharply by a small hand held up in unfaltering defiance.

"*Nyet! Nyet!* Yu go tu stables tu wash! The house vill be ours alone!"

"Come now, Alyona," Ladislaus cajoled and then bristled in some discomfiture as Petrov vigorously tried to curb the explosion of a chuckle by wiping the back of his hand across his grinning mouth. "You can't do this to me! Not even my own men would dare such a thing!"

"Yu stay away!" Alyona railed, stamping her small foot in outrage. "I forbid yu tu come inside!"

Climbing the stairs anyway, Ladislaus spread his arms wide to encompass the small woman in a great bear hug in hopes of somehow placating her, but Alyona snatched away in vehement determination and glared up at him.

"Yu leave this house zhis instant, Ladislaus, or I vill! I vill not stay here in yur camp an' give birth tu yur child vhile yu make 'nother one vith zhe colonel's vife. Do yu hear?"

"Damnation, woman! I can't let you order me about as if I were some whelp wet behind the ears! What will my men think?"

Alyona raised on tiptoes to glare into his face as she gritted out the question, "An' vhat vill *yu* zhink, Ladislaus, if I leave yu now? Do yu vant me tu go? Does beddin' down vith zhe colonel's vife mean so much tu yu zhat yu do not care if I go or stay?"

"Alyona, you know I'm fond of you. . . . "

In unabated pluck Alyona faced him with small fists clenched tightly at her sides. Despite the initial terror she had suffered when he had snatched her from her parents' home a year or so ago, she had come to love him dearly, but she wanted more from him than just a casual dalliance. His child would soon be born, and she wanted him to treat her with the same regard any man would extend toward a cherished wife. "Ladislaus, yu make choice now! Zhe colonel's vife or me!"

The lord-of-thieves raised his hands lamely in mute appeal. As much as he had wanted to pleasure himself with the countess, down deep inside he knew he could not abide Alyona leaving, for she had come to mean quite a lot to him in the months they had been together. She had been like a fresh, sweet breath of air coming into his stale life. While holding herself from him in stilted reserve, she had played the offended maiden to the hilt until gradually it was his heart that had been melted by her quiet, staid presence in his house. To his amazement he had found himself caring for her in a gentler way, courting her with wildflowers and long walks in the woods, nurturing her with sonnets of love from a book he had found in a trunk which he and his men had purloined from a wealthy rake. He had even taught her to read, and she had in turn placated him by sweetly reciting the verses. How could he bear to let her go when she would be taking his very heart away?

A gunshot snatched Ladislaus's mind abruptly from the matter of choices to the immediate needs of the moment. Of primary concern was the safety of his camp and everyone within it. He turned abruptly away from the two women even as Petrov spun his horse around to face the barricaded entrance where a guard was shouting and waving his arms in an attempt to gain their attention. The nearly bald-pated giant raised a hand and held it to an ear to listen, then promptly conveyed the information to Ladislaus.

"One man ride toward camp with white flag. The guard need know, should he be allowed in?"

Ladislaus leapt from the porch and, setting his powerful arms akimbo, frowned toward the pass a long moment before he squinted up at Petrov. "Can they tell who the man is?"

The single braid of flaxen hair fell over a massive shoulder as Petrov leaned his head back and cupped a hand to his mouth to project his shout. "Who comes? Do you know?"

Again Petrov returned the broad hand to an ear to hear the other's answer, then gaped down at his companion, fully astounded by what he had just heard. "They say English Colonel come! He ride your horse!"

"What?" Synnovea gasped, flinging herself to the porch rail. Tremblingly she shaded her eyes from the glare of the sun reflecting off the snow as she looked toward the entrance.

Ladislaus was of a different bent and hooted in glee at the idea of his adversary coming into their camp. "Let him come, if indeed that rascal comes alone!"

In petrified silence Synnovea waited an eternity before she saw the lone rider emerging from the narrow pass. When a guard pointed toward the house where they stood, her husband raised his head to look and then urged the stallion into a leisurely canter. Even from a distance Synnovea had no need to see the tawny hair before she knew for certain that it was her own beloved, for none rode with the same confident ease he exhibited. Her eyes fed upon his every movement until he faced the lord-of-thieves from only a short distance away.

Synnovea would have scrambled down the steps and flung herself toward him, but Ladislaus held up a hand and barked out a sharp command that she hold fast to the place where she stood. Reluctantly she obeyed, but managed a reassuring smile for her husband when he glanced away from Ladislaus long enough to peruse her and assure himself that she was all right.

"You enter my camp like a witless fool, Colonel, with naught to protect you but your own arrogance!" Ladislaus chided. Musefully he scanned his rival, spying no scabbard or pistol, only an empty sheath where a knife should have been. "You come bearing a white flag and completely unarmed, eh? Do you not fear that my men will drag you down from my horse and strip the flesh from your bones, just as they did the last time we met? I'm sure you have scars to remind you of that event."

"I've come for my wife," Tyrone stated unflinchingly. "I'll not leave without her."

Ladislaus laughed with boisterous mirth and spread his arms wide in outrageously exaggerated amazement as he reminded his foe, "But you said I could have her, my friend. Don't you remember? Pray tell, Colonel, have you changed your mind?"

"If it's a fight you want, Ladislaus, I'll give it to you," Tyrone avouched with a noticeable lack of humor.

"What?! And cheat my good fellows out of the sport of tying you between two horses and wagering which steed will get the better of you in the end? Come now, Colonel, I'm not as selfish as all that."

Tyrone lifted a hand and, glancing briefly toward Synnovea, beckoned her to come near. She obeyed promptly, eliciting a growl from Ladislaus, who leapt forward to catch her, but the thief was halted promptly by the bulk of the black stallion when Tyrone prodded the animal into his path. Grinding his teeth in rage, Ladislaus sprang forward to seize his adversary from the saddle, but Tyrone reined the animal sharply about again, deftly jarring the brigand's senses when that one met the whirling steed head to head, the hard way. An audible *thunk* was followed by an even louder pained howl before Ladislaus stumbled back in a dazed stupor, clasping a hand to his face. A quick swipe of a finger beneath his nose assured him that he was bleeding profusely from the left nostril.

Petrov coughed abruptly to halt another threatening burst of laughter, then straightened his demeanor, taking on a doleful countenance as he swung down from his steed and solicitously helped Ladislaus to the steps of the porch where he urged their leader to sit for a moment until he recouped his lucidity. Alyona flew inside and, a brief moment later, reappeared with a wet cloth which she dabbed gently beneath Ladislaus's nose.

While their attention was diverted elsewhere, Tyrone reached down and, grasping Synnovea's arm, quickly swung her up behind him, just as Petrov's flintlock made an ominous appearance. The cyclopean bore was leveled convincingly toward the middle of the leather doublet as the huge man rumbled out a warning, "Keep very still, Colonel, or you die now!"

Though Synnovea pressed close against her husband's back in anxious fear, Tyrone countered the threat almost casually. "If you kill me, Petrov, these hills will crumble down upon your shining pate. I swear they will."

Petrov hooted loudly in amusement, then leered at the colonel as he scoffed in disbelief. "Are you God to call down mountain upon us?"

"Give an ear, Petrov," Tyrone urged. "Attend my words carefully. If you need evidence of my power, I'll give you a small sampling. But first, I must kindly insist that you divert your aim for the moment, forestalling the possibility of your weapon discharging accidentally."

Petrov's eyes flicked quickly toward the rugged, tree-lined hilltops as he wondered what to make of the man's proposal. He was curious and slowly raised the pistol, but held it firmly in a position where he could swing it around again upon the man. As he closely observed the colonel, that one raised the white flag and then brought it down sharply in a fluttering descent. Instantly a thundering explosion rent the silence, followed, in quick succession, by several more blasts. Petrov started in sudden shock and, swinging around to his left, gaped in utter amazement as the cannon balls repeatedly pummeled the hills around the second entrance, loosening large boulders and rocks that began to tumble into the canyon. The falling debris gave expeditious momentum to the guards who had been on duty there. Spurred on by a churning fear, they sprinted toward the middle of the camp, casting anxious glances over their shoulders as they sought to outrun the falling fragments.

At that precise moment, hardly anyone noticed Tyrone whirling the steed about and racing toward the far side of the canyon. Having been snatched from his daze by a much greater shock than he had earlier experienced, Ladislaus scrambled quickly to his feet and then pointed, bringing Petrov's attention to bear upon the two who were obviously attempting an escape despite the questionable direction they were taking.

"Shoot the horse! Shoot the horse!" Ladislaus barked, nearly jumping up and down as Petrov raised his flintlock and held it carefully steady for a moment before slowly squeezing his finger. The discharge was followed by a mere pause of a heartbeat, then the horse collapsed in a cartwheeling roll that sent its riders flying helter-skelter.

Tyrone swore as he rolled and tumbled to a halt in a large patch of snow, then he gnashed his teeth in fierce determination as he leapt to his feet and raced back to where his wife lay motionless upon the ground. She stared as if in a stunned stupor at the sky above her, but he had no time to shake her from her trance. Instead, he swooped her limp form into his arms and started running desperately toward the hill, from the top of which his men urged him on with encouraging shouts as they tossed the ropes down the incline. The thundering hoofbeats of at least a dozen horses quickly overtook him, immediately forestalling the success of his flight as the highwaymen passed him by and then drew their steeds to a skidding halt in front of him. Briefly facing the leering men as they brandished their swords in the air, Tyrone backed cautiously away as his eyes swept about, keenly searching for an open path. In turn, the men nudged their mounts toward him, grinning like fools lusting for revenge. Clenching his teeth in unrelenting fortitude, Tyrone dashed to the left and then skidded to a halt on the right, ran backwards, then forwards, all the while dodging, twisting, circling around, only to be brought up short at last. Everywhere he turned, the rogues closed ranks, forbidding his penetration of their strength. Finally Tyrone could do naught but accept his entrapment, though death seemed imminent, for they had tightened the snare securely around him, allowing no place for him to run. Slowly he collapsed to his knees and, gasping breath into his lungs, bent over his wife, intending to bestow on her parted lips a kiss of farewell, then he realized her eyes were closed with a stillness that made his heart lurch in fear. While his own breath rasped from his throat, he could detect no slightest sign of breath falling from the lips of his wife. He felt an impending shout of remorse building within him, and he let her sag in his arms as he tilted his head far back upon his shoulders and shrieked at the top of his lungs toward the hill.

"Grigori! Avenge us!"

Chapter 26

THE HILL ABOVE TYRONE SEEMED TO EXPLODE AS ANOTH-
er volley was launched outward from the cannons, this
time in a different direction. The men around him
scattered like a whole flock of frightened, squawking
geese as the lead shots began to pelt the opposite end
of the valley. Only one in their number kept his wits and
demanded aid from another two who were ready to fly
with the rest. Commanding their unswerving attention,
the brigand held them fast at swordpoint.

"Ladislaus wants 'ese 'ere two back!" the thief shouted
as the cannons ceased their firing. "Now get down 'ere, ye
yellow-livered snakes, an' bind 'em ter yer horses, or I'll
run the two o' ye through from gullet ter groin!"

Even threatening the two with such an end did not
suffice in holding them for long. In the next instant it
seemed the crest of the hill was swarming with courageous hearties who, swinging out on ropes, thrust
themselves away from the precipice and descended in
great, leaping bounds. Faced by this greater threat, the
three thieves were promptly unified in the strengthening
premise that retreat was far better than certain death.
Lifting high their heels, they brought them down hard
into the sides of their mounts, sending the animals leaping into an all-out, breakneck race toward the entrance
of the canyon where an open space still remained in the
pass. As they neared it, the three brought their nags to

a sudden jolting halt, and almost as swiftly, whirled the animals about to send them flying in the opposite direction, just as Grigori raced into their lair with nearly a whole company of mounted Hussars following behind him with gleaming swords waving high.

Tyrone gathered his wife's limp form up in his arms and held her close for a moment, feeling such remorse he wanted to die. A building sob was wrenched from him as he buried his face against the side of her throat and began to weep, then, like the delicate flick of a butterfly's wings, he felt it . . . the unmistakable beat of a pulse. He jerked his head back and stared in jubilant amazement as the long, dark lashes fluttered against her cheek. Slowly Synnovea roused to awareness with a muffled groan and then stared up at him somewhat vaguely. When she made a valiant effort to smile, Tyrone broke out in grateful laughter.

"Synnovea, my darling! I thought you were dead!"

"Wasn't I?" She grimaced as she tried moving her aching body, then quipped dryly, "If this is what happens when you take a lady out for a ride, my lord, may I never be so foolish to accept your invitation again."

"Are you all right?" he questioned in anxious concern.

"Nooo!" she moaned. "At least I don't feel all right! The way I hurt, I'm wont to believe I've actually died and gone to hell, cruel place though that be, for this is definitely not heaven! Indeed, sir! I've never suffered so much abuse in all my life! I fear every bone in my body is broken!"

"This is no hellish prank, madam!" Tyrone assured her with an amused grin. "You're alive! And I most fervently thank heaven because you are!"

"Can we go home now?" Synnovea queried hopefully. "I would very much like to crawl into our bed and rest my wearied frame for a week or two."

"I'll take you there, my love, just as soon as my men finish rounding up the thieves." Tyrone glanced around him and was assured that the tide of conflict had been abruptly turned to their benefit. Many of the rogues had been caught by surprise and were unarmed, while others, perceiving their imminent capture, had given up without a fight. It was all over in a matter of moments.

Tyrone lifted himself to his feet again, and taking his wife in his arms, smiled down into the green eyes while his own glistened with warm tears. "My dearest Synnovea, you are the most delightful joy of my life," he softly avowed. "And I love you more than simple words can convey."

"Oh, Tyrone, I love you, too!" Synnovea replied, her voice choked with emotion. Wrapping her arms tightly about his neck, she pressed her brow against his cheek as she murmured in gentle reflection, "I think, Colonel Sir Tyrone Rycroft, that I have loved you ever since that very first moment I saw you, when you came charging through the thieves in your quest to save me. To me, my lord husband, you looked as resplendent as a gallant knight in shining armor."

Content to be with him again, Synnovea snuggled her head upon his shoulder as he carried her back to where his men were rounding up the miscreants in front of Ladislaus's house. The prince of thieves and Petrov were sitting on the steps under the watchful eye of a single lieutenant who had bound his prisoners to a post with a heavy length of chain. Alyona was kneeling close beside Ladislaus, dabbing at the trickle of blood that was still in evidence on his upper lip. It seemed his eyes were only for her, as if he realized there was not much time left for them.

Of a sudden Alyona straightened and then rose slowly to her feet as she stared off toward the narrow canyon entrance where a single mounted rider leisurely directed his steed through the rock and rubble that had fallen there. A moment later Avar dismounted before the house just as Alyona rushed down the steps. Throwing her arms wide with a cry of gladness, she hurled herself into the welcoming embrace of her brother.

"Avar! Avar! It seems so long ago!"

The scout drew back with a querying perusal and laid a gentle hand upon her belly as he softly questioned, "Do yu vant me tu avenge yu, Alyona?"

"*Nyet! Nyet!*" She shook her head passionately in a fierce denial and hurried to state her mind. "Avar, if I could, I vould havef Ladislaus as my husband, but they say he goes now tu Moscow, zere tu be hanged maybe."

"From all accounts, it iz the justice he rightly deserves, Alyona. I cannot stop it."

"Maybe zere iz no help for him, Avar, but I still yearn tu take him as husband an' give his child a name."

Bending his head slightly, Avar pressed his lips briefly to her brow. "I'm sorry, Alyona."

With an imperceptible nod, the young woman stepped away and, mounting the stairs again, went inside the house, closing the door slowly behind her. In the silence that followed they could hear her mournful weeping.

Avar approached his commander, who was pressing a cold compress to Synnovea's bruised brow. "Colonel, I havef just now seen a strange thing an' I vould like permission tu ride out vith a pair of men tu see vhat might be happenin'."

Tyrone peered up at him askance as he continued his tender nurturing. "What do you think it is?"

Avar glanced around, taking casual count of their soldiers, then stroked his chin thoughtfully as he lifted his gaze to meet the curious blue eyes. "I think, Colonel, it iz at least a full regiment or more of soldiers, dressed as commoners, passin' near here. Zhey ride in line, like an organized troop, though each vears the garb of a peasant. Zere iz only the leader who vears a cloak vhich looks familiar, and another who vears the clothes of a *boyar*. Zerefore, I vould venture tu guess zey are, for zhe most part, Polish soldiers on the move."

"This far inland?" The query came from Tyrone's lips as he stepped back and stared at the scout in amazement. "Where do you think they are headed?"

"They ride fast after hearin' cannon, Colonel. Toward Moscow, maybe, or in zhat same general direction."

"We must stop them!"

"Ve should, Colonel, but how? Zey outnumber us two . . . maybe three tu one. Zey havef two battery o' cannons besides."

Tyrone beckoned a young corporal forward and pointed toward the horse Ladislaus had ridden in on, the same which the thief had stolen from him some time back. "Strip that stallion, Corporal, and put my saddle on his back. And be quick about it! I've got to ride out with Avar and have a look around."

Returning to Synnovea, Tyrone lifted her carefully in his arms again and took her into the house, drawing a teary-eyed gaze from Alyona, who had curled up on a corner of the bed to cry. In some embarrassment, the small woman rose to her feet and, sweeping her hand toward the place she had just left, encouraged him to place Synnovea on the bed.

"I vill take care yur vife, Colonel. No need tu fear."

Accepting her offer, Tyrone lowered Synnovea upon the mound of large wolf pelts that were lavishly spread upon the bed. "I've got to ride out for a while with Avar," he murmured softly to his wife as he brushed a snarled tress away from her brow. "If you're able to, rest while I'm gone. I'll be back as soon as I can."

Synnovea and Alyona watched in silence as he crossed to the door. There, with a backward glance at his wife, Tyrone made his departure, and in a few moments the women heard the rattle of hooves as the two men rode out together.

"I'm too filthy to rest," Synnovea complained, wincing as she lifted herself up on an elbow. "I would like to wash if I may."

Alyona indicated a large kettle hanging from a hook in the hearth. It was filled nearly to the brim with simmering water, and the fire burning beneath had been recently supplied with stout wedges of dry wood that crackled eagerly beneath the huge iron vat. "I vas goin' tu vash clothes tuday, but if yu vould like, I vill fill a tub vith vater for a bath. Yu soak in good, varm vater, maybe then yu feel better."

"I don't think I've ever heard a sweeter proposal in all my life." Synnovea braced up on the edge of the bed and slowly pushed herself to her feet, grimacing as she did so. All she could remember from the fall was hitting the ground and feeling as if every part of her had been jolted unmercifully by the impact. Beyond that moment, it had seemed as if she had stared at the world through almost a stunned stupor, with her breath paralyzed in her lungs. Some time after Tyrone had lifted her, she had lost consciousness and knew nothing more until she had heard his muffled weeping.

With considerable care, Synnovea stood upright and, after a moment, was convinced she had accomplished a great feat. In preparation for the bath, Alyona hurried across the room to bolt the door, then returned to lay out a towel and a crude bar of soap. Between the two of them, they readied a deep bath which Synnovea was soon soaking in. She washed her hair and wrapped a towel about her head, and by the time she dried herself, she was beginning to feel confident that she would at least survive. Finding appropriate clothing in the large satchel Ladislaus had hurriedly packed from her dressing room, she dressed herself and was in the process of helping Alyona carry out buckets of dirty water when the woman suddenly halted and, sharply sucking in her breath, clasped a hand to her belly.

"It's time," Alyona announced in a tight voice when the pain began to subside. "The baby is comin' soon." She looked up at Synnovea. "Do yu know vhat tu do?"

Synnovea nearly panicked. "Not even a notion!"

"Zere iz an old voman who lives by zhe creek. She knows vhat tu do. Yu must go fetch her and bring her back here."

It was nearly an hour later when Tyrone returned with Avar and found Ladislaus pacing anxiously about in the small space which the short length of the heavy chain allowed him. Concerned by what he had recently seen, Tyrone hardly had time to consider the man's plight, but was nevertheless informed of the camp's current events by the lieutenant as he strode toward the door.

"I'm sorry, Colonel. Ladislaus's woman is inside having her baby. Your wife told us all to stay outside. I would presume, sir, that her order also includes you."

Tyrone was brought to an immediate understanding by the revelation. Glancing at Ladislaus, he realized the man appeared genuinely distraught over what was happening inside his house. It seemed rather strange for the unruly rogue to be so concerned about the girl, which made Tyrone seriously wonder if he was glimpsing some small redeeming quality in the man's character that made him vulnerable to the same cares and concerns of ordinary men.

Grigori came across the yard and, bracing a foot on the bottom step, waited until his commander turned to face him before he asked, "What did you and Avar see out there?"

"At least a full regiment of spies or Polish-trained mercenaries," Tyrone answered bluntly, descending a pair of steps to speak with him.

Grigori deliberated over the matter for a brief time until he ventured a question. "What are we to do, Colonel, with less than half that number of men?"

"We cannot hope to reach Moscow and regroup with the rest of the regiment in time to return and attack them in the field. When we left, General Vanderhout was demanding the rest of our regiment be given over into his care during my absence. Knowing the man is prone to some wild notions, I'm sure they've probably been dispatched on some urgent mission of his. I regret now not having had the foresight to bring the whole regiment with us."

"Colonel, your premise was to avoid being discovered ere we took our place on the hill. Your goal to capture Ladislaus and his bandits has been concluded successfully." Grigori voiced the logic of a close friend who was loath to see his commander blame himself because he was unable to see clearly into the future. "Not one of us expected this foreign intrusion in our land. Still, I find it hard to think that these mercenaries intend to attack Moscow with less than a full army."

"I'm sure you're cognizant of the last two attempts of the Poles to put their own men on the throne. Therefore, I would venture to guess the mercenaries are hoping to catch Moscow by surprise again, which they may well do if General Vanderhout has been foolish enough to strip away a sizeable portion of its strength and defense."

Ladislaus had paused in his restless strides to listen to the two officers and, after a moment, hunkered down on his haunches on the edge of the top step and peered intently at them until they finally deigned to lend him their attention. His grin seemed almost cocky. "You need more men, eh, Englishman?"

Tyrone arched a brow as he fixed the man with an impassive stare. "If you intend to gloat, Ladislaus, I'm in no mood to hear it."

"I wouldn't dare gloat, Colonel, when I know I'll be executed soon after I'm taken to Moscow." Ladislaus tilted his head to the side and shrugged his broad shoulders contemplatively. "With a babe of mine ready to be born, I can't help but wish things had been different, that I might have done something better with my life."

"It seems a bit late for remorse now, don't you think, Ladislaus?" Tyrone jeeringly responded. "You must be as old as I am, give or take a few years, yet I bet you've never considered doing an honest day's labor in your whole life. Now, obviously because you've been caught, you're feeling put out by it all. Well, go weep on someone else's shoulder, my lawless friend. I don't have time to listen to your laments."

"I only beg a moment of your time, Colonel. That's all I ask," Ladislaus bargained. "You just might be interested in what I have to say."

"I'm running short on patience," Tyrone responded tersely.

"What do you think those mercenaries are up to anyway?" Ladislaus pressed, deliberately ignoring the other's lack of enthusiasm.

"No good! Just like you!"

"Now, Colonel," the leader-thief smilingly cajoled. "Didn't I promise you that you'd be interested in my proposition? But if you're so damned sure you and your men can force that whole foreign regiment to retreat into a corner, then perhaps I'm wasting my breath."

A long sigh denoted Tyrone's growing aggravation. "What do you have to say, Ladislaus? I'm listening."

The leader-rogue was eager to voice his suggestion. "Suppose, Colonel, that I and my men joined forces with you and yours to turn back the foreigners. . . . " He peered up at Tyrone and smiled when he realized he had finally gained the other man's full attention. He shrugged his broad shoulders as he continued. "If they're up to doing no good in Moscow, and my band and I help to send them back to where they came from, perhaps the tsar might consider giving me and my fellows a pardon . . . if we each make a solemn pledge that in the future we will apply ourselves diligently to honest labors."

Tyrone stared at Ladislaus in rampant disbelief, unable to seriously consider the plausibility of such an offer. It seemed rather ludicrous for him to even entertain the notion that the man could alter his whole way of life at this late date. The results of trusting him could be as disastrous as believing a leopard could amend his natural proclivity for devouring its prey.

"What would you do?" Tyrone scoffed. "Milk a herd of goats? I'm sure you understand why I have some difficulty imagining you hard at work at such simple chores."

"Perhaps I could be a soldier like you," Ladislaus suggested. "If His Majesty can hire foreigners to teach his soldiers to fight, why can't he recruit men who can fight already? We don't expect to be outfitted in grand uniforms like the rich *boyars* I've seen, but we can still fight in the tsar's service and keep the Russian borders secure from invaders."

Tyrone cocked an incredulous brow at the thief as he asked, "And once you have your freedom, you would not use it to loot and murder again?"

Ladislaus spread his hands, appealing to the colonel's sense of justice. "I've been a warrior a good many years, Colonel. Men have attacked me and I've defended myself as best I can, but a murderer I am not! I've never killed anyone who hasn't first tried to take my life."

Tyrone needled with a wry grin. "And should I believe that you've never lashed a man between two horses. . . . "

"I did but jest, Colonel!" Ladislaus protested with a chuckle. "I make threats I do not mean. I see no harm in that. Such vivid intimidations have been known to deter some men from violence. Besides, you owe me a favor for saving you from that scoundrel, Prince Aleksei Taraslov. 'Twas his most earnest intent to see you gelded." He tossed a grinning glance toward the interior of the house, then stroked his chin musefully as he reasoned further with his captor. "I think, Colonel, you have much to be grateful to me for. Your wife seems most appreciative of your attentions. She would not let me touch her and swore with great tenacity that she would kill herself before allowing me to have her. If you would consider the whole of it, Colonel, she was probably better off with me than that rat, Aleksei. The good prince hired me to kidnap her, but bade me to deliver her straight to him. Consider further, had I ignored his summons, he would have found someone else, perhaps someone of lower esteem, to steal her away, and that one might have served the prince's intentions far better."

Grigori laid a hand upon his commander's arm, drawing Tyrone's attention, and together the two men walked away a few steps from the house. Ladislaus watched the pair closely, hoping they would see their way clear to allowing him the opportunity he had asked for.

"What are you thinking, Colonel?" Grigori asked. "Do you believe Ladislaus can really be trusted?"

"I don't know that for sure, but under the circumstances, I'm willing to take the chance that he can be," Tyrone replied.

"What if he joins with the other regiment against us?"

Tyrone frowned sharply. "Then I'll make him rue this day for the rest of his brief life."

Grigori accepted the colonel's decision with a nod, then followed at a slower pace as that one strode back to the porch to face Ladislaus.

"I have no idea why I should even consider giving you a chance, considering all the trouble you've personally caused me," Tyrone stated curtly. "Prince Aleksei can attest to the fact that you can't be trusted, but his experience with you only whets my willingness to grant a few concessions to you . . . if you prove yourself worthy of them. Let this be known beforehand. Whatever the outcome today, you will return with me to Moscow to allow His Majesty, Tsar Mikhail, to make the final decision for granting a reprieve to you and your men. If you demonstrate the fact that you are sincere in helping us turn back the enemy forces, I will address my plea for your immediate release to His Majesty, but be warned, I'm in no mood to be tricked. If you make me regret giving you this opportunity, you'll be the first one among your followers I will shoot. Do you understand?"

"Quite clearly, Colonel."

"Now, you are absolutely sure your men will follow you in this endeavor?" Tyrone queried as a last consideration toward caution.

Ladislaus chuckled briefly in amusement. "Since they have a fervent desire to live out the hour, I will venture to say, positively!"

Tyrone responded by bidding the lieutenant to free the prisoners. As Ladislaus and Petrov rose to their feet and stretched, the colonel urged them to hurry. "Get to your mounts and gather yourselves and your men together in front of the house here. We'll have to race ahead of the mercenaries in order to position our cannon and spread our forces on the hills in front of them, so we need to be on our way immediately."

Ladislaus hesitated as he glanced toward the door and dared to ask the Englishman for another request. "Colonel, I'd like to speak to Alyona for a moment. If I don't come back, I want her to know that I'm at least trying my best to make a better way for the two of us and our child."

Tyrone stepped to the portal and, opening it, beckoned for Synnovea and the midwife to come out on the porch for a few moments. Ladislaus dipped his head in a nod of appreciation as he passed the colonel, who then closed the door behind him.

Synnovea readily slipped her hand into Tyrone's and went with him to the far end of the porch, where they shared a few private moments together, oblivious to any who might have chosen to stare. Unable to find the words to delicately announce to her that he would soon be leaving again, but perhaps would not be coming back alive, Tyrone slipped his arms about her and held her close with a growing sense of gloom that immediately conveyed itself to her.

"You are riding out again?" Synnovea queried worriedly as she leaned back in his arms and looked up at him, then she glanced past his sleeve and realized that weapons were being passed around to the highwaymen. "What terrible thing has happened to set you in league with thieves?"

"We've sighted a renegade regiment nearby. 'Twould appear they're riding hard toward Moscow, for what end

I am as yet uncertain, but 'tis my belief they plan to enter by stealth into the Kremlin and either kill the tsar or take him hostage. 'Tis not the first time they've tried to seize control of the country by such a plan."

"But how can such a feat be accomplished?" she questioned in amazement.

"By subterfuge . . . and more than a goodly share of boldness. If they've positioned spies or accomplices inside the Kremlin, they are probably hoping to enter secretly."

"Be careful," Synnovea pleaded, letting him gather her close against him again. "You've not yet given me your baby, my lord husband, and if 'tis ever meant that we should be parted by death, I would like some evidence of our love to remain."

Tyrone plied her soft lips with a kiss, then he smiled down into her eyes that were brimming with tears. "We've had so little time together, my love. I hope we will be allowed several decades to spawn a hearty progeny from our love."

Ladislaus strode from the house, and Tyrone left a fervent kiss upon his wife's lips before he crossed the porch and followed the man down the steps. It caused some confusion for both when they realized they had halted beside the same horse.

"This is my stallion!" Tyrone declared emphatically, gathering the reins. "Your horse was shot! Remember?"

"But we made a trade," Ladislaus tried to argue. "Mine for yours; yours for mine."

"Yours is dead!" Tyrone stepped between the man and the horse and swung up in the saddle, then grinned down at the man as that one protested in feigned outrage. "From now on, Ladislaus, you're going to have to limit yourself to your own possessions. I have a serious aversion to sharing my treasures with anyone, and most especially with the likes of you."

Tyrone reined the high-stepping mount about, close enough in front of the man to allow the animal to flick his high-flying tail across the brigand's face, drawing a snort of displeasure from the giant. Taking his helmet from the grinning Grigori, who urged his own horse alongside, Tyrone settled it on his head before he lifted his arm and swept it forward in a command for all to follow. It was the chortling Petrov who led a rather shaggy-looking horse to Ladislaus as his leader muttered grumblingly after the colonel.

"You forgot, maybe, it was your horse you tell me shoot." Petrov inclined his shining pate toward the animal he had brought and grinned. "Maybe this one not so fine as his or the one shot, but better than walking, I think."

The foreign regiment rode over the hill and was halfway across the valley before a sudden warning shout rent the silence. The men gaped in sharp surprise as a solid line of mounted, uniformed Hussars, appearing as if from out of nowhere, halted their steeds on the next rise ahead of them. Cannons were hastily rolled to positions on the brow of the hill, interspersing the calvary unit, while the officer in command slowly raised his sword.

Ordered shouts sent a swelling tide of confusion rippling through the foreign ranks, turning their haste into a mad scrambling dash as they sought to bring up the artillery and spread it out in a more impressive line than the one they now faced. Having the larger force, they hoped to counter the threatening attack and roll the foolish ones back upon their heels. Several musket shots rang out from their ranks, and a pair of Hussars toppled to the ground, but in the very next instant the Russian cannons began to bark with deafening explosions. Recoiling in large plumes of smoke, they sent leaden balls hurtling through the air to bombard those who had intruded upon their land. The shots landed, eliciting startled shrieks from both man and beast as large geysers of dirt were spewed up in front of them. The carnage was more serious as a second barrage was unleashed, punishing them severely for the dead Hussars. A wealthily garbed nobleman shouted at the commander, who in frustrated rage snarled out orders in rapid succession to his men. Obeying, those hearties bared their swords and spurred their steeds forward in pursuit of vengeance, just as a cannon lobbed a leaden ball down upon the princely one.

The Hussars seemed to wait on the hill in unswerving patience as their opponents raced toward them. The rival force of mercenaries quickly gained the first upward slope of the knoll, but just as they did so, out of the corners of their eyes, they caught rapid movements to their left and right. In sudden alarm, they glanced askance between the two, and their hearts failed them with fear as they saw other men, dressed in all manner of array, swarming down upon them. The Hussars seemed to come alive as their commander swept his sword forward in a signal to charge. He led them at a thundering pace, lifting his saber high and rending the air with a warbling wail that raised goose bumps and hackles on friend and foe alike. The intruders considered their plight forthwith and came to the immediate determination that it was foolish to stand and fight against such odds. Expeditiously they wheeled their steeds about, intending to race back from whence they had come, but they abruptly found themselves caught in a box, from which they would find no successful escape.

A pair of darkly cloaked figures crept stealthily through the trees growing near the Kremlin wall until they saw a wagon, carrying fodder for horses, moving briskly toward the Borovitskaia Tower. The two hurried to reach the path as the cart rumbled past, and then they flitted quickly alongside until the farmer halted the conveyance at the gate, where he greeted the sentry with the warm cheer of a close friend and laughingly conversed with him, allowing the wraithlike pair to slip inward without being seen.

The two continued on, one leading the other as if by rote through the trees until they came to a spot near the edge of the Kremlin hill where they had been told to wait until a quarter stroke of the hour. It was at that appointed time when another cloaked shade, this one noticeably smaller than the other two, moved away from the Blagoveshchenskii Sobor and cautiously approached them.

"What are you two about this eveningtide?" a subdued voice asked from the deep cowl as the slight one neared the pair.

"We've come a-gaming for that fanciful dish tsars are wont to seek," came the reply in a gruff voice.

The shorter one dipped his head in acknowledgment of the statement and made the expected reply. "And what is that but a royal seat upon the throne?" The three came together, and the smaller one promptly lowered his tone to a whisper. "Your men have been given their instructions?"

The one with the harsh voice gave the information while his companion stood stoically mute. "At the appointed hour, they will create a diversion for us and start fires throughout Moscow, to which soldiers will be dispatched. The tsar and the Patriarch Filaret will have gone by then into the Blagoveshchenskii Sobor to pray. We are to join ourselves with the rest of our men and kill the castle guards who come to stand watch and then slay the patriarch and the tsar in the chapel. We will hold the Kremlin until the rightful tsar takes the throne and kill those *boyars* who are wont to reject him."

"Good! I assume your men are waiting inside the Kremlin to help you in this endeavor."

"All is in readiness, my lord."

"The other matter is arranged also?"

"What matter is that?"

"Surely you have addressed yourselves to the safety of the new tsar and have found a place here in the Kremlin where he can hide until he is ready to make an appearance, have you not?" The pointed question was met with a tense silence that seemed to demonstrate the confoundment of the two. The small man became enraged. Completely infuriated at the dimwitted simplicity of the dullards, he threw back his hood in a vivid display of fury and advanced on the pair with a snarl contorting his pockmarked face. The back of his short-fingered hand swiped forcefully across the wide chest of the taller one who stood the closest to him. "You fools! He is the most integral part of this whole plot! Where is he?"

"Where any rightful pretender should be, Ivan Voronsky," the taller one finally answered.

Ivan's mind halted in sudden shock. Though the man had spoken Russian, the words had been accentuated with an English accent, allowing a sharply goading fear to seize his mind. He remembered precisely where and when he had last heard it, and that had been a few weeks ago at the military parade held in the Kremlin.

The tall man approached him, sweeping back the hood of his cloak. "Aye, Ivan Voronsky, 'tis I, Colonel Sir Rycroft, at your service." Tyrone swept a hand toward his companion as he casually introduced him. "And the good man, Captain Grigori Tverskoy, to aid you in all your endeavors. Your Polish friends were found out ere they reached Moscow, and I fear your intended tsar was blown to bits by the careless aim of our artillerymen. A tragedy, to be sure. I'm sure Tsar Mikhail would have preferred to see him beheaded alongside of you."

Ivan snatched forth a dagger, intending to sink it into the chest of that stalwart one who addressed him with scorn, but when he raised the weapon, his wrist was seized in a steely grasp. In the next instant his arm was twisted behind his back and wrenched upward, startling a cry from him as an agonizing jolt of pain seemed to rend its way from wrist to shoulder. Almost casually Tyrone plucked the knife from the cleric's hand, eliciting another highly indignant screech from the grimacing lips. At the sound, there arose a confused burble of voices from the area of the Palace of Facets, which quickly became shouted commands for the guards to seek the source of the cry.

Ivan's heart began to hammer heavily in his chest as he realized he was not going to escape from the trap which the two had laid for him. All the money the invaders had put aside for him suddenly seemed a very paltry sum in view of the price that would be exacted from him for treason against the tsar.

"I've got gold! I'll give you all of it if you just let me go!" Ivan pleaded frantically as he glanced over his shoulder. He had to be gone before the palace guards reached them or it would be too late to make good his escape! "It's more than the both of you will ever make in your lifetime! Please! You must let me go!"

"What portion does the Princess Anna get out of what you promise to us? She is your accomplice, isn't she?" Tyrone queried.

"The Princess Anna? Why! She was only a pawn I used to try and enlist the aid of wealthy *boyars* to the cause."

Grigori clasped his fingers in the man's lank hair and lifted his head to peer leeringly into his face. "Have the *boyars* also promised you gold to make it worth your while?"

"No! No! But I tell you there is enough already to fill your coffers to the brim! Those fools would not hear of another Dmitry claiming the throne. Indeed! They seemed content to let a simple puppet rule the land."

"Twice was enough, Ivan," Tyrone responded chidingly. "What fool would seriously consider a third Dmitry returning from the dead? But I think I can speak for the both of us and give you answer. You see, we are quite content with what we have and most grateful for the fact that our heads will remain firmly attached to our shoulders."

Ivan Voronsky's demeanor began to crumple, and he began to sob bitterly, as if all the woes of the world were crushing down upon him. His loud weeping turned to wails of anguish and frustration, until it seemed as if he had no more strength to stand. Weakly he collapsed against the man who held him in an unrelenting vise. Above his muffled weeping, footfalls could be heard running rapidly toward them.

"What goes on here?" an officer demanded, running from the shadows. Unsheathing his sword, he called for reinforcements over his shoulder before slowing his pace to make a more cautious approach. Closely perusing the three cloaked figures, he came to a halt and questioned sharply, "What are you doing here?"

"Waiting for you, 'twould seem," Tyrone replied solemnly, lifting his head to meet Major Nekrasov's startled stare.

"Colonel Rycroft! I thought you were gone!"

"I was," Tyrone answered simply, then inclined his head to indicate the grieving cleric whom he held firmly ensnared by one hand. "We came across a force of Polish mercenaries who had been hired to help this man assassinate the tsar and the patriarch. We camped on the outskirts of the city so none would know of our presence, just in case there were more spies afoot than we had been led to believe. We came here searching for the one whom the mercenaries said they were to meet. The Poles could not lay a name to the traitor, so we had to find out for ourselves. I believe you've met the man before, when you escorted the Lady Synnovea to Moscow. He is your prisoner now."

Nikolai peered down at the glowering cleric who bared his teeth and hissed like a small, poisonous viper caught by the tail. Breathing in some of the foul fumes of his breath, the major was convinced anon that the man's present behavior was a much truer manifestation of his real character than he had hitherto exhibited. Nikolai gestured for the guards who had answered his summons to come forth and take the prisoner away to the Konstantin Yelena Tower, then in stoic reserve, watched them grapple with the snarling, struggling man who had taken on the ferocity of a rabid wolf. Finally they managed to subdue him with two lengths of chain and hauled the maddened beast away at the end of his fetters.

Delaying a moment as he observed their departure, Nikolai turned back almost reluctantly to face his rival. "Colonel, there is a matter of grave concern which you need to be made aware of immediately. Shortly after you left the city, your wife, the Lady Synnovea, was kidnapped by a band of men who closely matched the description of Ladislaus and his cohorts. The Countess Andreyevna said your wife's disappearance was not discovered until the morning, after the guards you had hired to watch her were found gagged and bound in the garden. By then, it was too late to scour the countryside with any hope of halting their flight. I'm sorry."

"Ease your mind, Major," Tyrone replied. "At present, the Lady Synnovea is safely ensconced in my camp outside the city."

Nikolai was momentarily stunned by surprise, and it was a brief moment before he managed a response. "I was sure none of us would ever see her again, considering how adamant Ladislaus was about having her for himself. How in the world did you manage to get her back?"

" 'Twas my good fortune to be in the right area at the right time." A trace of a smile touched Tyrone's lips. "You may be relieved to hear that Ladislaus has decided to repent of his outlaw ways and has come to ask full pardon from the tsar. At the present moment he is also in my camp, sporting a wound that's more impressive than serious, but nevertheless enjoying himself as he shows off his new son. Without the help that he and his men gave us, we would never have been able to capture the mercenaries."

"Ladislaus here? In your camp? Can that possibly be true?"

The lopsided grin made an appearance. The major only reflected his own skepticism when the thief had made the proposal. "I know it sounds farfetched, Major, but Grigori here can confirm the truth of what I say."

"I was reluctant to believe it myself," the captain offered, "but it's true. It seems that Ladislaus dotes upon the sister of our scout, and now that he's a father, feels he must make a better way for his offspring than he had growing up. The man has been tutored by some of the best, but his father . . . a Polish prince . . . would not legally claim him. He has asked the girl to become his wife and, if he is pardoned, he will then avail himself of the opportunity to seek an honest profession."

Major Nekrasov grinned at the wonder of such miracles, then he cleared his throat politely behind a hand as he prepared to speak on another matter entirely. "Colonel Rycroft, you know that General Vanderhout insisted upon taking the rest of your regiment out, along with troops from other regiments, on the premise of evaluating their performance. . . ."

Tyrone braced himself as he and Grigori exchanged troubled glances. "What is it, Major?"

"Well, as far as I've been able to surmise, General Vanderhout had no idea how fierce Cossacks can be when they're set awry. . . . "

"Go on, Major!" Tyrone prodded impatiently as the major paused to look at him. "What has happened?"

"There was a complete rout, Colonel. Your men wanted to stay and fight, but General Vanderhout didn't want to take the chance that they would upset the Cossacks more than they had already. He ordered your men back to Moscow and followed swiftly, making a valiant attempt to outrun the Cossacks, who had threatened to set fire to his heels if he dallied overlong in their territory. Once the general had passed safely through the outer gates of Moscow, the Cossacks entertained themselves with all the debris your commander left behind in his haste, not only muskets, but also several cannons which had been requested by him. The Cossacks built large campfires, hooted and cavorted while they harassed Muscovites morning and night with their newfound artillery. No real damage was done that I'm aware of, but 'twas nearly three days before they finally ceased their chicanery and took themselves off to seek other diversions. Since then, the general has been in hiding. I believe he is ashamed to show his face."

Grigori burst into laughter and made no effort to curb his amusement as Major Nekrasov peered at him obliquely. It was a full moment before Tyrone was able to speak without the threat of following his second-in-command's example.

"All appears to have gone very well in our absence," he commented drolly.

Nikolai closely contemplated the Englishman, who seemed to have trouble hiding a smile even as the moon went behind a cloud. "You appear to be taking the news exceptionally well, Colonel. I was under the impression that you two might have been good friends, what with the general being a foreigner and your commander and all. . . ."

"I need not look to foreigners or those of my own ilk for friendship, Major." Tyrone laid an arm about Grigori's shoulder and pulled him close against his side. "Here is a true friend, Major. He is one who seeks my good, and as for General Vanderhout . . . well, I value him considerably less than even my most casual friends."

Tyrone swept a hand to his brow in a casual salute of farewell. Occasional spurts of laughter drifted back as the pair made their departure, then with something akin to a perplexed smile flitting across his face, Major Nekrasov turned and made his way toward the Palace of Facets, where he would relate everything that Colonel Rycroft had told him to the tsar, then he would escort him to the Blagoveshchenskii Sobor, where he would meet with the patriarch and priest for an hour of private worship.

Chapter 27

THE CITIZENS OF MOSCOW STOOD BACK AS THE REGIMENT of dusty soldiers rode across the area of Red Square, escorting between their ranks another collection of wildly outfitted warriors. A pair of women, one of them bearing a wee babe wrapped tightly in a bundle, rode in a small cart filled with hay, a preference each had insisted upon for at least two diverse reasons. A battery of cannon followed, and at the rear of the procession came the wagons, a pair of which were filled with men, some of them wounded.

It was this sight that greeted Prince Aleksei as he stepped from his sledge. He was still gaping when he took note of the dark-haired woman in the cart, that same one he had ordered kidnapped from the Countess Andreyevna's house. And if that was not enough, her abductor had been seized and now rode at the fore of his cohorts, like some valiant soul on his way to receive a medal.

Aleksei felt a coldness grip his chest that nearly halted his breathing. Only that morning he had been in his chambers and had heard Anna wailing in fear because she had been summoned to the tsar's palace to discuss what she knew about the matter of Ivan Voronsky's treasonous attempt. She was sure that within a matter of days she would be escorted to the Lobnoe Mesto, where she would pay for the crime of befriending a traitor, except that she fervently contended that she had lacked all knowledge of the man's real intentions.

Now here he was, Aleksei brooded, seeing his own life pass before him as the death knell tolled out the hour for his impending doom. Tsar Mikhail had warned him, but he had given little heed to his words. Instead, he had taken great delight in arranging Synnovea's abduction, like some lecherous fool intent upon getting his head separated from his body. It was fear, unmitigated fear that restricted his chest and made his heart apprehensive about even beating!

A heavy crowd of people was gathering on the square, having heard of the success of the troop they were now viewing. Major Nekrasov had first reported it to the tsar, who called the matter to the attention of the Russian delegates, the *zemskiy sobor*. From the *boyars*, it had spread to every area of their city until the loyal citizenry was in awe at the miracle of it. To totally immobilize an invading force, which was rumored to be at least five times larger, and then subsequently halt the assassination of not only the good patriarch but the tsar himself . . . Why, it was a feat eminently worthy of recognition!

Prince Aleksei ground his teeth, abhorring the assembling throng of humanity around him. To be completely surrounded by those who were intent upon hailing the English colonel and that barbaric Ladislaus as champions of the day was the most outrageous affront he had ever had to endure. For their offense against him, he wanted to see both men fed piece by bloody piece to the ravens, for each had stolen what he had endangered his life to have.

"Excuse me! Excuse me!"

Prince Aleksei looked around with a start as a foreign officer jostled him in his haste to get around him. Tossing a frantic look over his shoulder, the man looked as if he feared all the demonic guardians of the netherworld were after him.

"Excuse me!" he asserted again and was about to forge

resolutely past the prince when a feminine voice called to him from somewhere behind him in the midst of the crowd.

"Yo-hoo, Edvard! I must speak vith yu! Vait!"

Almost frantically the one called Edward pressed forward, nearly shoving Aleksei aside as he sought to hurry on his way through the ever-increasing mass of people, as if by some small chance he had not heard the woman. Muttering to himself, he berated his own wisdom severely for having gotten involved. "Fool! Fool! Weren't you warned? But no, you dullard! You just had to bed down with the general's wife! What a fine kettle of fish you've gotten yourself in! Your whole career will be ruined!"

The one who hailed him from afar became most insistent. "Edvard Valsvorth! Yu vill not escape for long if I sic the general on you!"

Edward growled a curse, prompting Aleksei to sharply raise a brow since the expletive was issued within close proximity to his ear. Nevertheless, the man seemed suddenly convinced of the importance of conversing with the woman. Pivoting on the ball of his foot, he did an abrupt about-face and, spreading his arms wide, approached the woman with a great show of enthusiasm, as if actually delighted to see her. "Aleta! How beautiful you look, my darling little flower!"

Aleksei's brows raised to an even greater altitude when he tossed an oblique glance their way, trying to see the source of the officer's dismay. Except for her wide skirts, the woman remained hidden behind the tall man she had accosted, but her chiding voice was hardly subdued, allowing the prince to hear everything she said.

"Yu naughty man, yu! If I did not know better, I vould think yu vere tryin' tu avoid me. Indeed! I should tell Vincent it vas yu he should be searching for instead of Colonel Rycroft! If yu think I'm goin' tu remain silent about all of this vhen yu've made no further attempt tu see me, I vill call down the very hounds o' hell tu seek yu out and name yu the father of my babe! It's all yur fault anyway. I told yu tu be careful, but no! Yu had tu be as inept as a little schoolboy tumblin' his first chit!"

Lieutenant Colonel Edward Walsworth shrugged his shoulders lamely as he tried to cajole her. "Now, Aleta, how can you be so sure I was the one responsible? You were seeing some Russian at the time, weren't you? I vividly recall having heard you say that you had played a prank on the prince by telling him you were the general's daughter and an innocent little virgin. You mean with all your subtle enticements, the two of you never went to bed together?" Edward's tone sounded more than a bit facetious. "If the Russian is not at fault, then perhaps your husband is. Surely you've not tossed him out of your bed."

"Yu oaf! Yu von't get out of this by blaming someone else! Vincent had become painfully impaired with a malady that has stricken him tu the heart, and vhich prevents him vrom carrying out his husbandly duties. No doubt he caught it vrom all those little doxies he liked to cuddle though he had the audacity to try and put the blame on me!"

Surprised gasps were simultaneously rasped inward as both Aleksei and Edward caught the full import of her statement. Aleksei glanced wildly about, seized by a dreadful panic, while Edward demanded harshly.

"By damned, woman! That takes a lot of spite to entice a man into your bed when there's a chance you've been befouled!"

Aleta screeched in rage. "Vhat?! Do yu think I havef been besmirched, too? I tell yu true, I havef not suffered such. . . ."

Edward was seething and leaned down to snarl in the woman's face. "The way you hunt for lovers, Aleta, there's no telling how many men you've caught in your trap!"

Aleksei choked in revulsion as he felt his gorge rise higher in his throat, and like a man who had imbibed far too much, he reeled in a daze until he reached the outer limits of the crowd and then staggered back through the snow to his sledge. His face was ashen as he threw himself into the seat. He forgot about the pair who were still viciously arguing the point; he only realized his folly in believing the woman's ploy.

Somehow Aleksei managed to get home, and stumbling into the house, he called for vodka and scalding hot water to be brought up to his chambers. Servants scurried to obey, and soon a steaming hot bath was prepared, closely conforming with his instructions. Glaring at the valet who waited to attend the lavation, Aleksei sent the servant out with a snarled command and undressed himself.

He sucked his breath in as he settled himself into the steaming bath, but undaunted, he scrubbed himself with vigor until he was nearly bleeding from the abuse, then he leaned back against the tub and quaffed nearly a third of the decanter of the wickedly intoxicating brew. Finally he stumbled to his feet, feeling as if he had been sufficiently blistered inside and out. He was extremely hot, weak, and totally inebriated. Seeking some relief from the agony of his emotions, he flung the bottle away and staggered unsteadily to the bed, where he collapsed facedown upon it. In a dazed stupor he stared across the room and began to mumble incoherently about the awful gore he remembered having seen in his childhood when his father had taken a knife and ended his own life.

Princess Anna did not return home that night, nor did the servants dare to venture up to the master's chambers. By late the next day they were almost relieved to hear riders halting before the manse and, a moment later, an insistent pounding of a heavy fist on the front portal. Boris hurried to open the door, and then stumbled back in some awe as the English colonel and three of his officers barged into the hall without so much as an apology. This time the Englishman spoke in Russian and demanded to see the master of the house forthwith.

"He's upstairs, my lord!" The servant's voice quavered as he tremblingly gestured toward the higher level where the prince's chambers were. "He hasn't been down since yesterday when he ordered us to prepare him a bath. He was in a foul mood, sir, and we were afraid to disturb him."

"I'll disturb him!" Tyrone growled over his shoulder as he leapt up the stairs, leading his men, who followed closely behind.

Boris trailed them, struggling to keep up as he pleaded with the officers to take care lest they endanger all their lives. "Prince Aleksei may be indisposed . . . with a woman . . . and will resent being intruded upon. It's not the first time he's locked us out, but usually he bids us to bring up food for him and his companions to feast upon."

Tyrone's lip curled in a snarl as he tossed a disgusted glance over his shoulder. " 'Twould appear you have coddled that bastard far too long, my friend. Today he will reap another kind of reward, his just due! The tsar has granted me and my men permission to escort your master to prison, and I've come to do so with relish."

The colonel paused briefly before the door that the servant nodded to, then grasped the knob and, turning it, flung the door wide with a solid thrust of his shoulder. His high-flying anger propelled him inward, and he was nearly halfway across the room before he suddenly halted and stared for a moment in rampant revulsion at the sight on the bed. He had been a fighting man for a good many years of his life, but in all that time he had never seen the likes of which now wrenched his stomach. It was an awful thing when a man became so demented that he had to lacerate his own body so cruelly before finally gaining enough courage to end his own life.

Tyrone turned abruptly on a heel and stalked back toward the door where his men had halted. The slight, somewhat repulsive grimace that twisted his lips gave a strong indication that what he had just seen had not been at all pleasing. Boris searched his face and would have stumbled past to see what the colonel had viewed, but Tyrone held up a hand and shook his head, halting the servant.

"My men and I will wrap the prince up in the bed-clothes and take him downstairs for you. He should be kept where it's cold, at least until he's buried."

A short distance down the road Synnovea stood watching from the front windows of the Andreyevna manse as she waited to see if Tyrone and his men would pass with their prisoner, just to make sure that her husband was all right and hadn't been harmed in some way by the devious prince. She almost smiled in relief when she saw Tyrone riding back alone, then doubt and the uncertainty of what might have actually happened assailed her. The idea that Aleksei was still unconfined and uncontrolled left her completely stricken with fear, as if she had just awakened from a horrible nightmare and had not yet been assured that what she had just dreamed was not real and thus could not hurt her. She fervently hoped she would not be thrown back into that dark cavernous pit of the hellish horror by the realization that Aleksei could continue to persecute them even while he searched for a safe abode.

"He's far away by now," Synnovea whispered to herself in an effort to ease her qualms. "He wouldn't dare come back. Why, he's probably trying to find a place to hide from the tsar and all of his men."

Synnovea heaved a sigh to quiet her rambling thoughts as Tyrone turned his horse into the narrow lane that led toward the stables in the back. It was foolish to get herself in such a state of panic, she chided herself, when she had absolutely no idea what had really happened. She was happy to be home, and that was a fact that Aleksei could not take away from her. After a whole blissful night spent grati-fying lustful fantasies with her husband, she had felt as if she had been lifted on a cloud somewhere in the firmament.

Synnovea frowned and canted her head worriedly, trying to listen as she wondered what was keeping Tyrone in the stable. Natasha had escorted Ali, Danika, and Sofia to a fair, leaving the major portion of the house completely to them, except for the servants, who been instructed to appease their every wish but to pleasantly refrain from being seen.

"Synnovea . . . ?"

The voice drifted to her from the very depths of the house, seeming far, far away, as if from the distant end of a long tunnel. Where was it coming from? she wondered.

"Yes . . . ?" she called in answer.

"Come, my love, I have need of you."

"Tyrone? Is that you?" she queried as her feet carried her from the room and to the stairs that led ever downward. The summons had been spoken in English, but the voice was strangely muffled and subdued. "How did you get in the house?"

"Are you coming, my love?"

"Yes, yes, I'm coming! Where are you? I can barely hear you. Please tell me, is anything wrong? You sound so strange."

"Hurry!"

Her heart leapt in burgeoning trepidation. What was wrong? What had happened? Where was he?

"I'm hurrying, my darling! Wait for me!"

"I'm waiting, but you must hurry. . . . "

Her feet were flying now, merely a vague blur on the stairs, going down deeper, deeper, in the very bowels of the manse. With her breath snared in her throat, she burst through the portal, not knowing what she expected to find, then she came to a stumbling halt . . . and stared agape.

From the middle of the pool Tyrone grinned back at her and, throwing aside a long flared instrument that

Natasha sometimes used in calling her servants, he lifted his hand to beckon to her. "Come join me, madam. I'm feeling in rare good form tonight and think we ought to consider appeasing your petition."

"What petition is that, my lord husband?" Synnovea questioned eagerly as she lifted her hands to the silken closures of the *sarafan* she wore.

"I've decided, madam, that we should seriously consider the possibility of further involvement. . . . "

"Indeed, sir?" Her lips lifted in a tantalizing smile as she pushed the silken *sarafan* from her shoulders and aided its descent to the floor. She paused to doff the undergown and then asked in guileful innocence. "How can we be further involved than we are already?"

Tyrone debated her question only briefly. "I was struck by Ladislaus's infatuation with his son and was of the mind that we should prove our love by a similar offering to the world."

"I barely know you, sir," she teased, loosening her hair.

"Then come, madam, and get to know me better. You have a lot to learn, and I am most eager to instruct you in the bliss of our connubial relationship."

"That sounds strangely like a lecherous invitation to me, sir."

" 'Tis a most honest invitation, madam, I assure you, for I've never been more earnest in all my life."

"Earnest about instructing me? Or earnest about making a baby together?"

"Both, madam, both! Just come into my arms and let me show you how sincere I am."

Draping her stockings over a bench, Synnovea descended the steps of the pool and swam across to where he awaited her with open arms. Lifting her up and enfolding her within his embrace, Tyrone gazed down at her with warmly glowing blue eyes.

" 'Tis much better now than it was at the beginning, my love," he whispered with a smile. "Because now, I need not be concerned about losing you to another. Our fears have been set aside by the prudence of one to change his life and by another's decision to end his." He kissed her lips as a startled gasp parted them, then continued on in a softly hushed voice, enjoying the feel of her wet body against his. "Aye, madam, we need not fear Prince Aleksei ever again or be afraid that Ladislaus will lose sight of his love for Alyona and his son. Now that he has been granted a pardon and a promise of a yearly stipend from the tsar to patrol our borders and keep them safe, 'tis doubtful we'll ever see him again. Even Anna has been stripped of any possessions or esteem she might have benefited from in the future, being the tsar's cousin. She has been ordered to return to the house of her parents, where she will be placed under their authority and supervision. It will be left totally to their discretion what becomes of her, for any disturbance she causes in their house will be subject to review by the tsar, who then might be tempted to seek recourse. 'Tis her punishment for not having had the wisdom to discern what Ivan was about, since so many *boyars* said it should have been obvious to her more than anybody, considering how devoted she was to the man."

"Amazing how things have worked out," Synnovea breathed beneath his lips. "The only uncertainty it seems we'll have to contend with is whether or nay Ladislaus will remain true to his word. I hate to think of you going out after him again. Indeed, my lord husband, I am loath to think of you leaving me at all."

"There may be less chance of that possibility from now on, madam. The tsar has requested the immediate departure of General Vanderhout and his wife from Russian soil and has asked me to be the commander of the foreign-led division in Vanderhout's stead, which means, my love, a promotion to brigadier general."

Tyrone laughed as Synnovea gave a gleeful cry and flung her arms tightly around his neck. Holding her close, he sighed, already regretting the fact that in years to come they would not be able to enjoy the luxury of such baths in England. He would just have to do something about that.

Epilogue

THE SHIP FURLED THE LAST OF ITS SAILS AS IT NUDGED against the London quay just as a large coach arrived on the cobbled wharf down below. From the smaller conveyance, an older man alighted and turned to give assistance to a tall, slender woman, perhaps a few years younger than he. Her hair, once a tawny hue, had paled with the passage of years until it shone with the luster of creamy satin. The tresses had been carefully arranged in an elegant coiffure that complimented her fair features and graceful bearing. Another woman, dapperly dressed and at least a score or so years older, was handed down, then debonairly escorted with the other woman to the planking which was being lowered to the dock.

On the ship, a tall man carrying a young, towheaded toddler of an age at least two years emerged from the companionway, and then stood aside as he held the door for his wife, who carefully folded a blanket over the face of their small infant before stepping out into the damp mists that drifted over the ship's decking and the River Thames. Behind her came a tiny servant who wore a sizeable valise over her shoulder, which she had packed for the children. Smiling in response to the younger woman's murmured question, the man reassured her and, slipping his free arm behind her back, accompanied her to the gangplank, where they paused before beginning their descent.

"Tyre! Tyre!" the elderly woman cried through her tears of joy as she lifted an arm to draw his attention.

Eagerly waving back to her, Tyrone called down to her. "Grandmere! I see that you got the letter I sent! I wasn't sure anyone would be here to greet us."

"We wouldn't have missed this for the world, my son," the older man called back. "We've been counting the days! Hurry! We want to see our grandchildren!"

Tyrone leaned his head close to the boy's as he pointed toward the people who awaited them on the quay. "Look, Alexander! Grandpapa!"

The youngster's blue eyes moved warily from his father to take in the three who vied for his attention.

"Alexander . . . Alexander . . . it's Grandmere!" the pale-haired woman coaxingly called. "Where is your sister, Catharina?"

With one small, slightly crooked finger, the young lad pointed toward the baby his mother carried. "Catha?"

His father laughed and caressed his tiny arm. "That's right. Catharina."

Sticking the tip of the digit into his mouth, the little boy eyed his parents, who seemed to meld together for a moment, then Tyrone pulled away to lift the corner of the blanket a careful degree and looked down at the tiny face of his daughter. "She's still sleeping."

"Catharina will be wanting to be fed soon," Ali reminded them from behind.

Synnovea smoothed the dark, fine hair of the newborn whose eyelids flicked briefly in response to the touch. "The little darling appears quite content right now, Ali. Perhaps she'll sleep for a while longer."

"She's a good little girl, just like you were," Ali eagerly lauded.

"Come, my love," Tyrone urged his wife. "Come meet my parents and grandmother, then we'll go home. They're eager to begin loving you and our children."

Synnovea dropped her head upon his shoulder for a moment as he wrapped a comforting arm about her, then with great care he escorted her down the plank.

"My son! My son!" the woman of middling age wept as she hurried forward to greet them with arms held wide. "It's so good to have you back! We missed you so much!"

The Rycrofts clasped their arms around each other with great displays of affection before Tyrone pulled away and eagerly made the introductions. Bringing Synnovea close to his side, he said with an ebullient smile, "Father, Mother, Grandmere, I would like you to meet my wife, Synnovea. This is our maid, Ali McCabe, and our two children, Alexander and baby Catharina, named after Synnovea's father and our close friend, the Princess Natasha Catharina Zherkofa, who will be coming this summer with her husband for a visit, along with another close friend, Major Grigori Tverskoy and his bride, Tania."

Meghan drew the youngster from his father's arms and whispered a secret in the tiny ear, drawing a giggly chuckle from the boy, who pointed to his father.

"Horse! Papa!"

Tyrone grinned down at his grandmother. "Aye, Grandmere, I've already taught him to sit a horse in front of me, so your desire to see him ride with the best will eventually come to fruition."

Through grateful tears, Tyrone's mother smiled with brimming joy as she embraced Synnovea and welcomed her into the family. "Thank you, my dear, for making my son so happy, and for giving us these small treasures of delight upon whom we can lavish our love. I feared I would never see an end to the years that kept us apart, and now that the king has given Tyrone the task of establishing the techniques for drilling cavalry units, we know he'll not have to leave England ever again to fight in some foreign campaign. Perhaps his father can eventually entice him into learning the business of building ships."

Tyrone dared to broach the subject which had caused him to leave England behind him more than a thrice of years ago. "What has happened in my absence?"

"Everything has been settled with the family of the man you dueled with," the elder Rycroft assured his son, clapping him on the back. "In fact, when Lord Gurr heard you were returning, he came to offer apologies for what his son had done to Angelina and for what they had done to you after the duel. He said a man has a right to defend his wife's honor and good name from those who would besmirch them. He was sorry that his arrogance and anger had forced you to flee to Russia."

"As you can see for yourself, Father," Tyrone replied, "it was good that I went away, for I found there a far richer treasure than I ever had here."

"I must say, my son," his mother commented fondly as she admired his undiminished good looks. "You've come back far happier than when you left . . . and obviously richer by far with your family and friends."

"Aye, Mother," Tyrone agreed, glancing aside to his adoring wife. "I am indeed a rich man."